THE GRAPHIC NOVEL

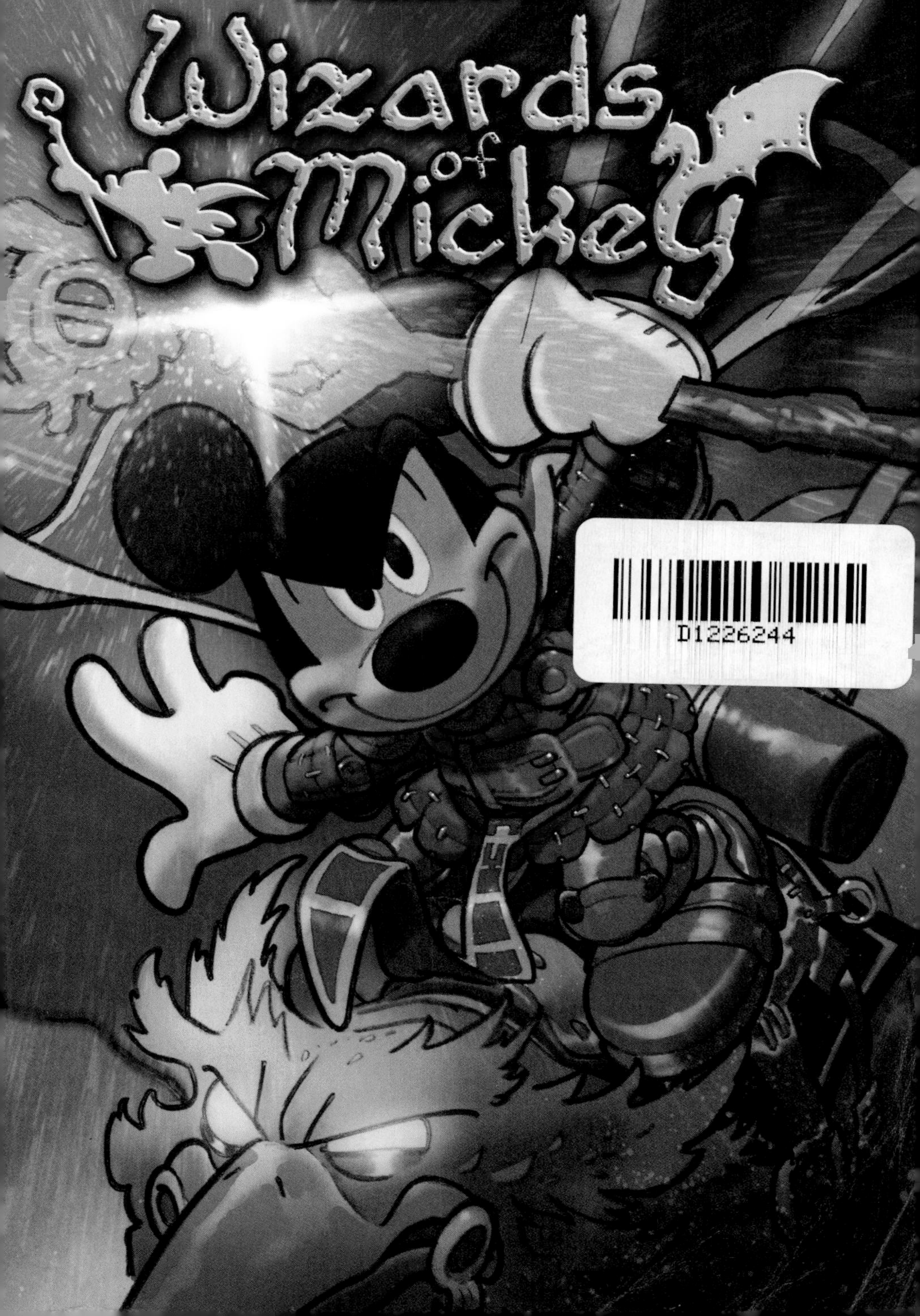
Wizards of Mickey

3

Contents

The Ancient Evil

The New World

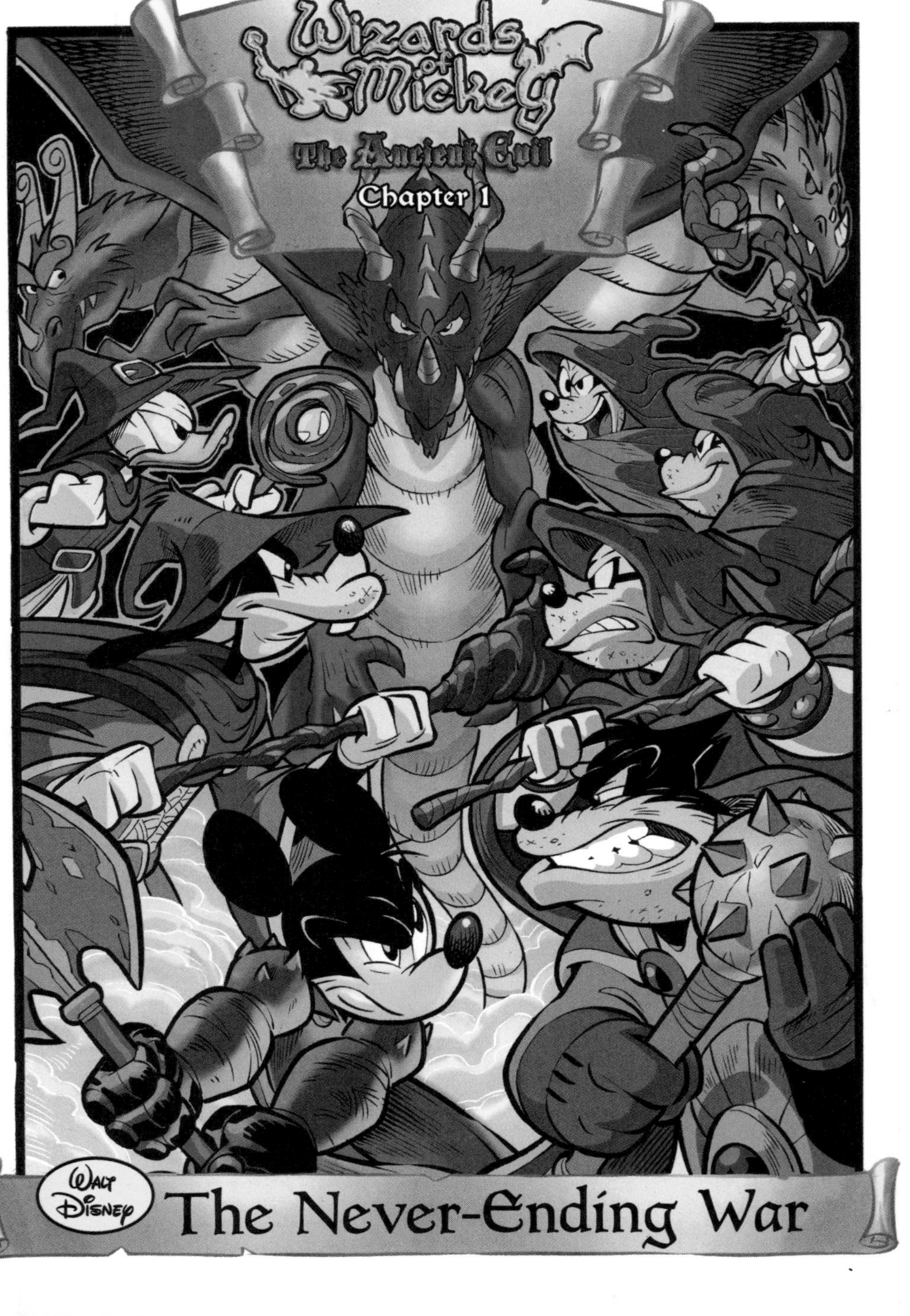
Wizards of Mickey
The Ancient Evil
Chapter 1
Walt Disney
The Never-Ending War

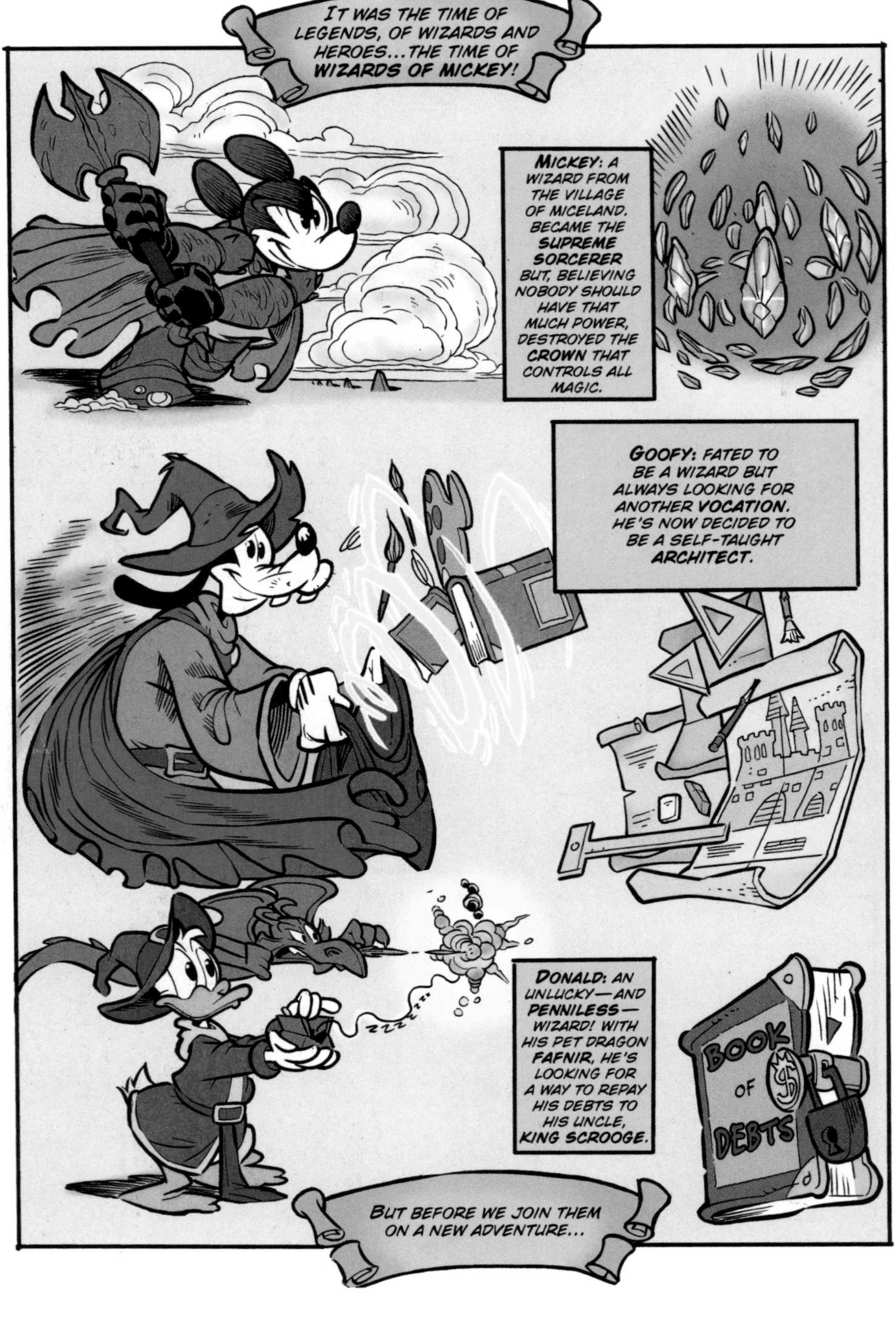
IT WAS THE TIME OF LEGENDS, OF WIZARDS AND HEROES... THE TIME OF WIZARDS OF MICKEY!
MICKEY: A WIZARD FROM THE VILLAGE OF MICELAND. BECAME THE SUPREME SORCERER BUT, BELIEVING NOBODY SHOULD HAVE THAT MUCH POWER, DESTROYED THE CROWN THAT CONTROLS ALL MAGIC.
GOOFY: FATED TO BE A WIZARD BUT ALWAYS LOOKING FOR ANOTHER VOCATION. HE'S NOW DECIDED TO BE A SELF-TAUGHT ARCHITECT.
DONALD: AN UNLUCKY—AND PENNILESS—WIZARD! WITH HIS PET DRAGON FAFNIR, HE'S LOOKING FOR A WAY TO REPAY HIS DEBTS TO HIS UNCLE, KING SCROOGE.
ZZZZZZ
BOOK OF DEBTS
BUT BEFORE WE JOIN THEM ON A NEW ADVENTURE...

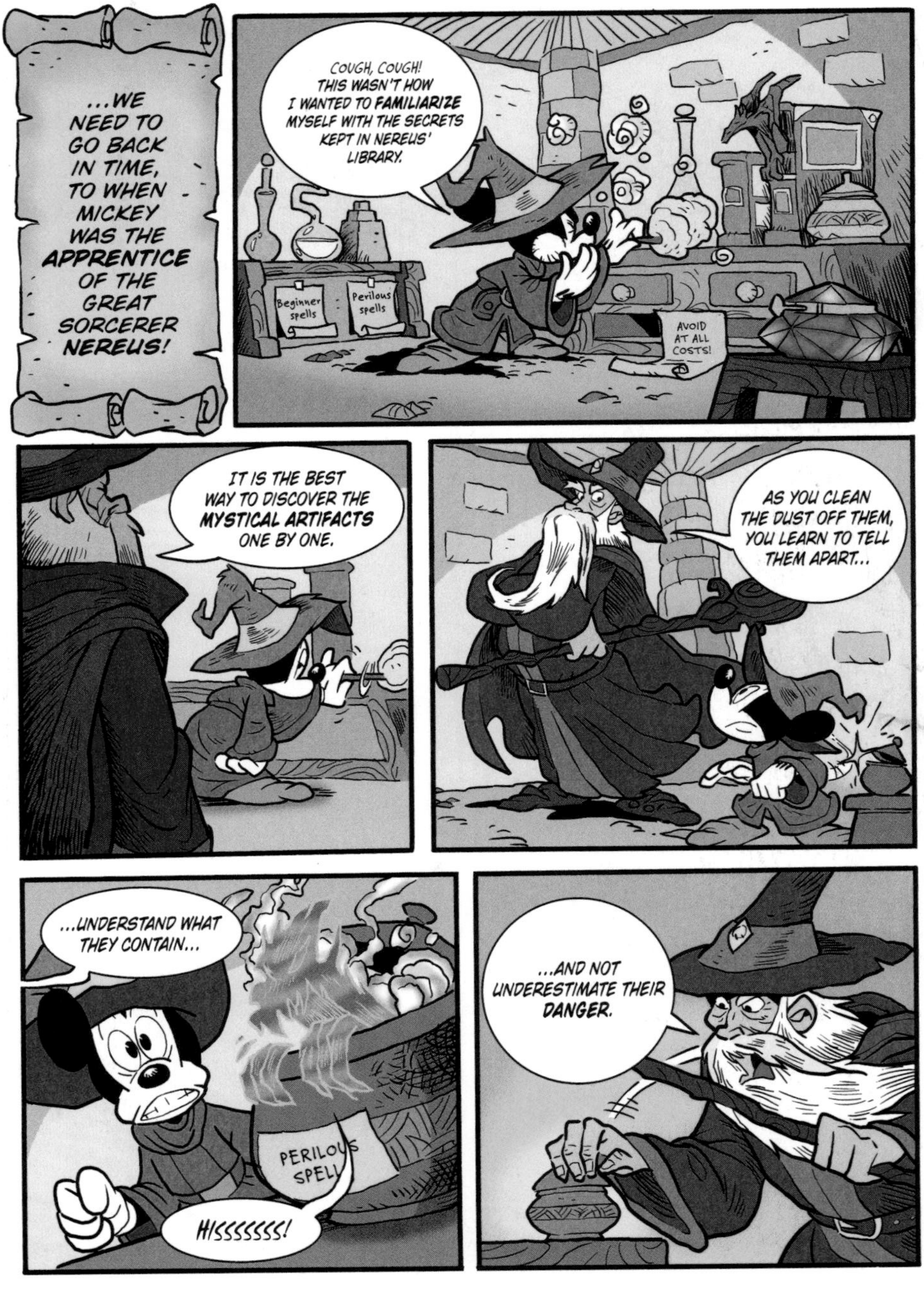
...WE NEED TO GO BACK IN TIME, TO WHEN MICKEY WAS THE APPRENTICE OF THE GREAT SORCERER NEREUS!
COUGH, COUGH! THIS WASN'T HOW I WANTED TO FAMILIARIZE MYSELF WITH THE SECRETS KEPT IN NEREUS' LIBRARY.
Beginner spells
Perilous spells
AVOID AT ALL COSTS!
IT IS THE BEST WAY TO DISCOVER THE MYSTICAL ARTIFACTS ONE BY ONE.
AS YOU CLEAN THE DUST OFF THEM, YOU LEARN TO TELL THEM APART...
...UNDERSTAND WHAT THEY CONTAIN...
PERILOUS SPELL
HISSSSSSS!
...AND NOT UNDERESTIMATE THEIR DANGER.

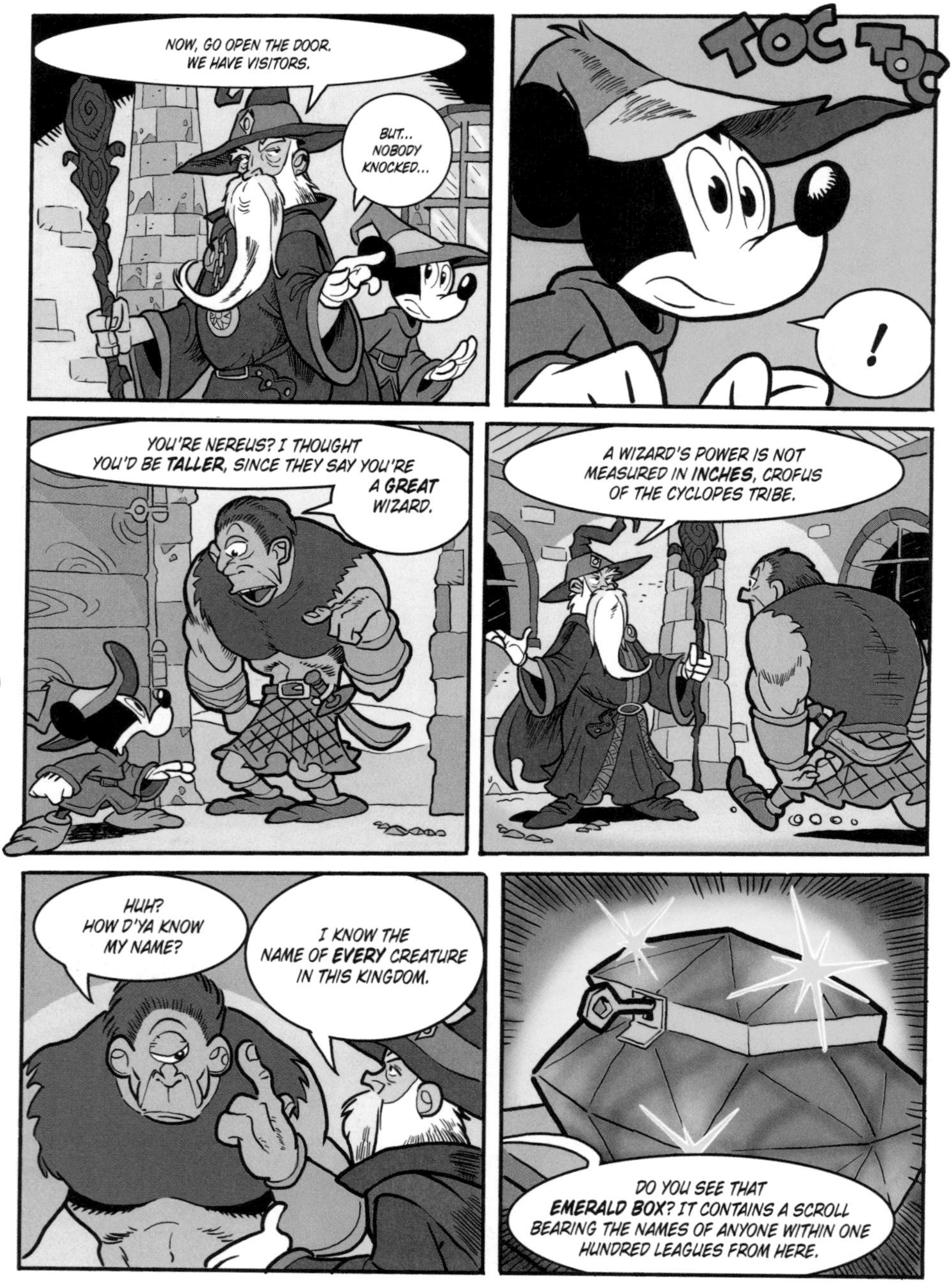
NOW, GO OPEN THE DOOR. WE HAVE VISITORS.
BUT... NOBODY KNOCKED...
TOC TOC
!
YOU'RE NEREUS? I THOUGHT YOU'D BE **TALLER**, SINCE THEY SAY YOU'RE A **GREAT** WIZARD.
A WIZARD'S POWER IS NOT MEASURED IN **INCHES**, CROFUS OF THE CYCLOPES TRIBE.
HUH? HOW D'YA KNOW MY NAME?
I KNOW THE NAME OF **EVERY** CREATURE IN THIS KINGDOM.
DO YOU SEE THAT **EMERALD BOX**? IT CONTAINS A SCROLL BEARING THE NAMES OF ANYONE WITHIN ONE HUNDRED LEAGUES FROM HERE.

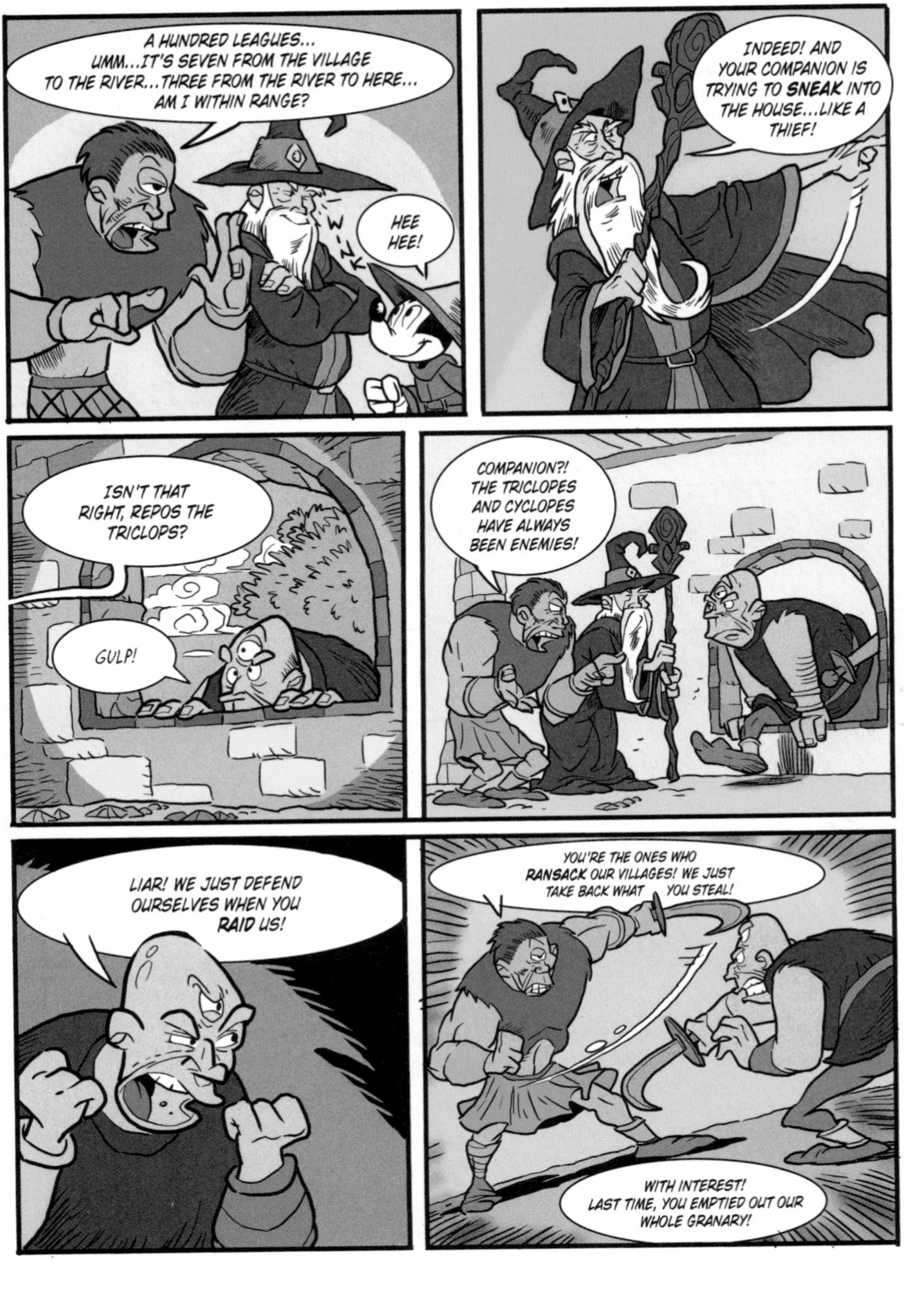
A HUNDRED LEAGUES... UMM...IT'S SEVEN FROM THE VILLAGE TO THE RIVER...THREE FROM THE RIVER TO HERE... AM I WITHIN RANGE?
W-I-N-K
HEE HEE!
INDEED! AND YOUR COMPANION IS TRYING TO SNEAK INTO THE HOUSE...LIKE A THIEF!
ISN'T THAT RIGHT, REPOS THE TRICLOPS?
GULP!
COMPANION?! THE TRICLOPES AND CYCLOPES HAVE ALWAYS BEEN ENEMIES!
LIAR! WE JUST DEFEND OURSELVES WHEN YOU RAID US!
YOU'RE THE ONES WHO RANSACK OUR VILLAGES! WE JUST TAKE BACK WHAT YOU STEAL!
WITH INTEREST! LAST TIME, YOU EMPTIED OUT OUR WHOLE GRANARY!

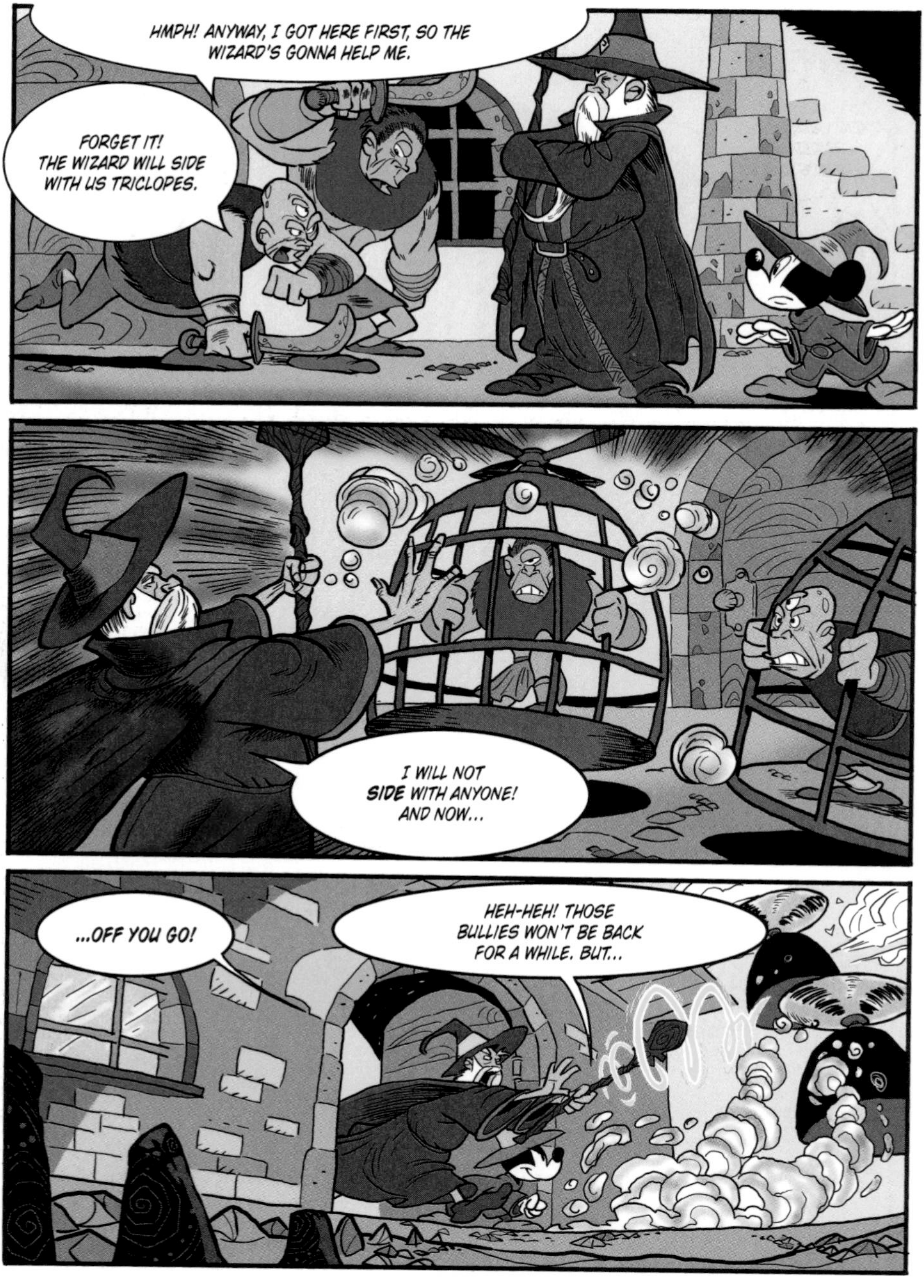
HMPH! ANYWAY, I GOT HERE FIRST, SO THE WIZARD'S GONNA HELP ME.
FORGET IT! THE WIZARD WILL SIDE WITH US TRICLOPES.
I WILL NOT **SIDE** WITH ANYONE! AND NOW...
...OFF YOU GO!
HEH-HEH! THOSE BULLIES WON'T BE BACK FOR A WHILE. BUT...

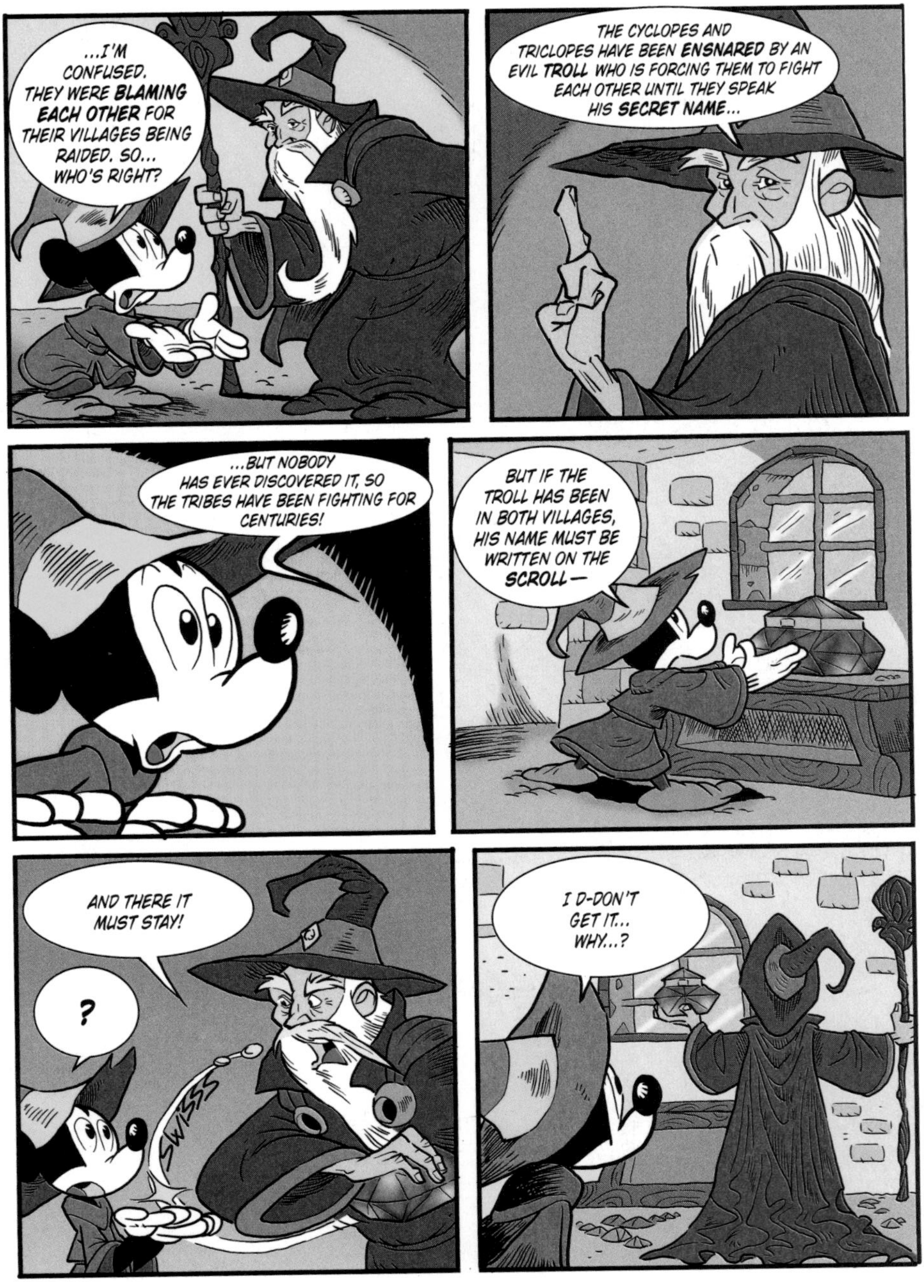
...I'M CONFUSED. THEY WERE BLAMING EACH OTHER FOR THEIR VILLAGES BEING RAIDED. SO... WHO'S RIGHT?
THE CYCLOPES AND TRICLOPES HAVE BEEN ENSNARED BY AN EVIL TROLL WHO IS FORCING THEM TO FIGHT EACH OTHER UNTIL THEY SPEAK HIS SECRET NAME...
...BUT NOBODY HAS EVER DISCOVERED IT, SO THE TRIBES HAVE BEEN FIGHTING FOR CENTURIES!
BUT IF THE TROLL HAS BEEN IN BOTH VILLAGES, HIS NAME MUST BE WRITTEN ON THE SCROLL—
AND THERE IT MUST STAY!
?
SWISSS
I D-DON'T GET IT... WHY...?

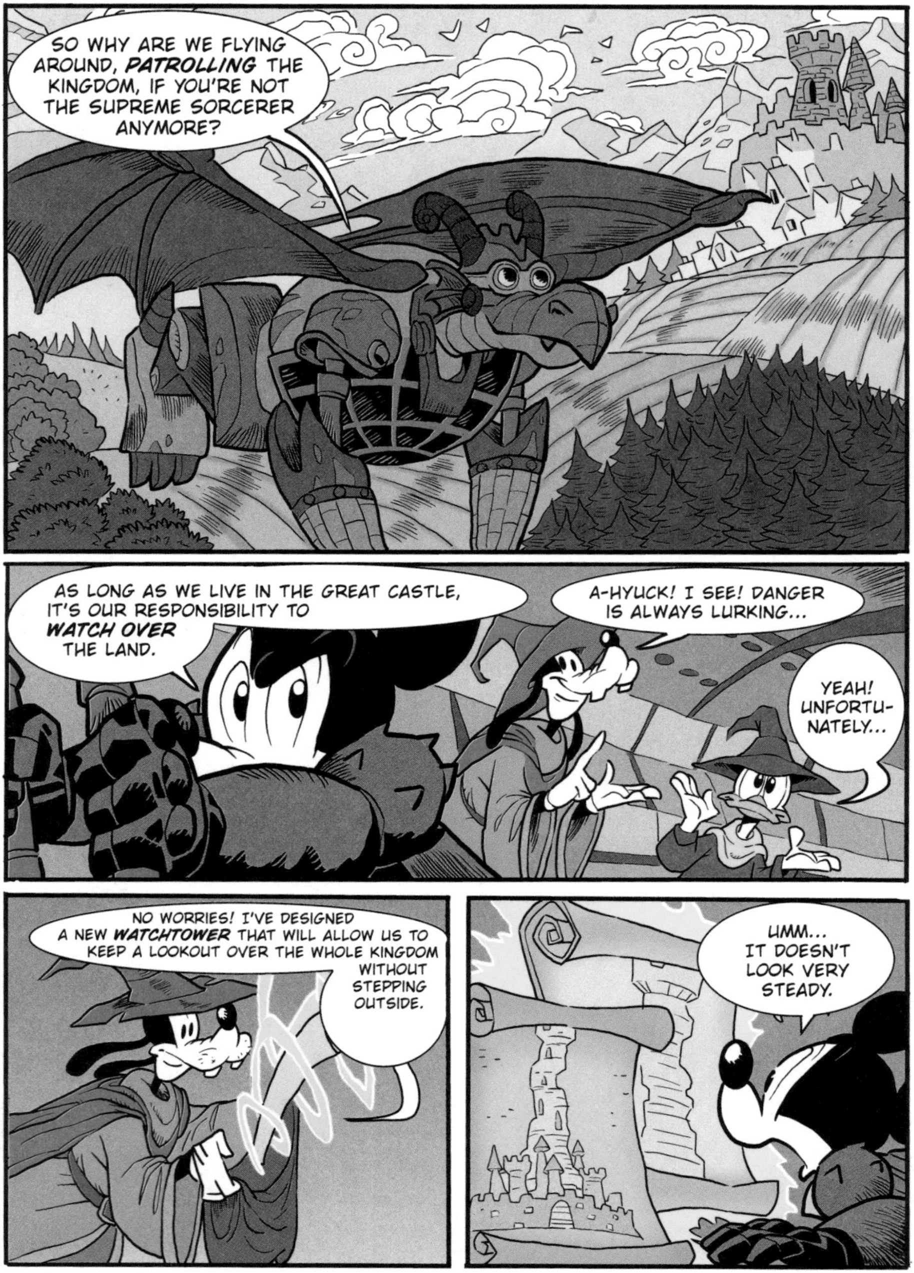
SO WHY ARE WE FLYING AROUND, PATROLLING THE KINGDOM, IF YOU'RE NOT THE SUPREME SORCERER ANYMORE?
AS LONG AS WE LIVE IN THE GREAT CASTLE, IT'S OUR RESPONSIBILITY TO WATCH OVER THE LAND.
A-HYUCK! I SEE! DANGER IS ALWAYS LURKING...
YEAH! UNFORTU-NATELY...
NO WORRIES! I'VE DESIGNED A NEW WATCHTOWER THAT WILL ALLOW US TO KEEP A LOOKOUT OVER THE WHOLE KINGDOM WITHOUT STEPPING OUTSIDE.
UMM... IT DOESN'T LOOK VERY STEADY.

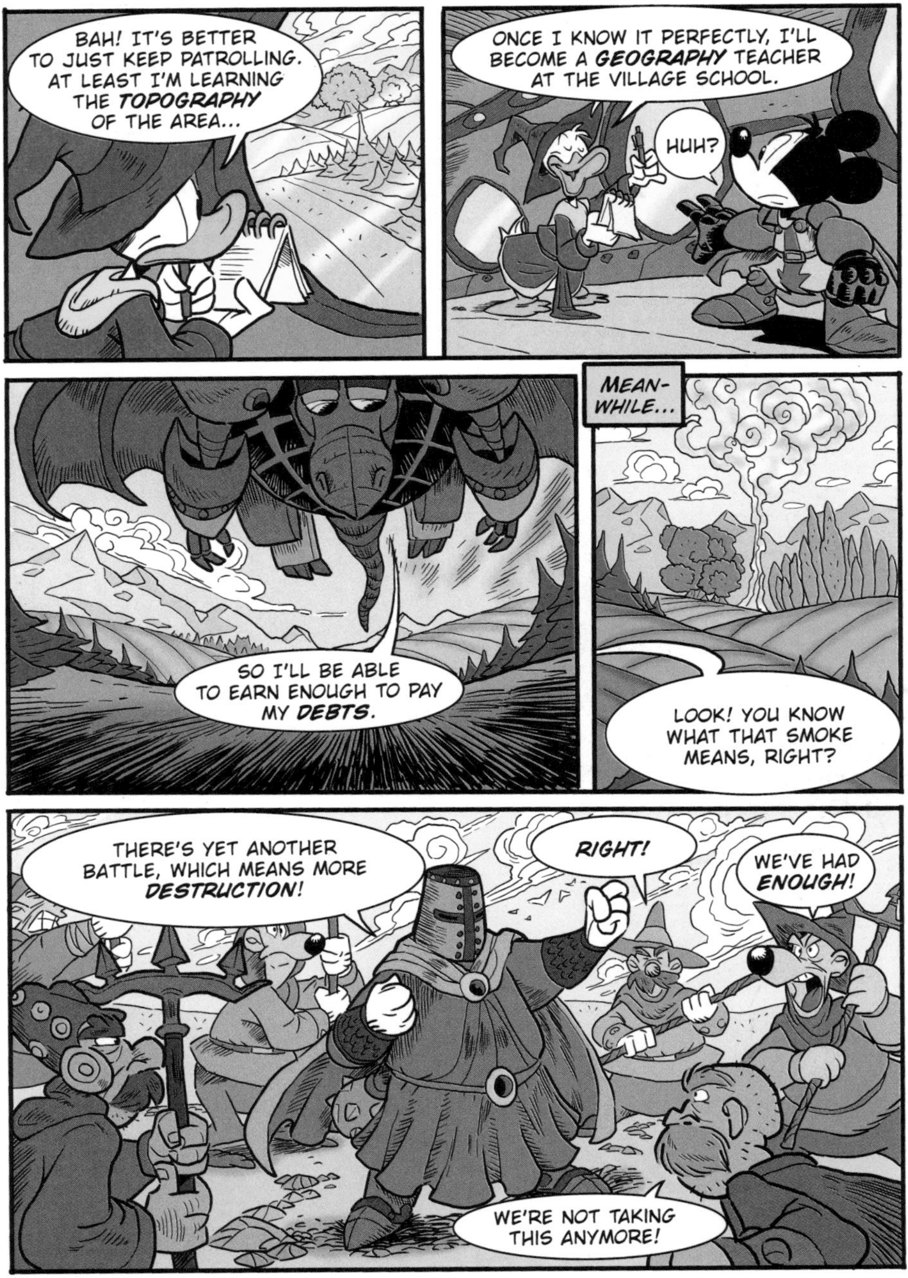
BAH! IT'S BETTER TO JUST KEEP PATROLLING. AT LEAST I'M LEARNING THE *TOPOGRAPHY* OF THE AREA...
ONCE I KNOW IT PERFECTLY, I'LL BECOME A *GEOGRAPHY* TEACHER AT THE VILLAGE SCHOOL.
HUH?
SO I'LL BE ABLE TO EARN ENOUGH TO PAY MY *DEBTS*.
MEAN-WHILE...
LOOK! YOU KNOW WHAT THAT SMOKE MEANS, RIGHT?
THERE'S YET ANOTHER BATTLE, WHICH MEANS MORE *DESTRUCTION*!
RIGHT!
WE'VE HAD *ENOUGH*!
WE'RE NOT TAKING THIS ANYMORE!

LAST TIME, THE FLAMES WERE SO *HOT* MY HENS LAID *HARD-BOILED EGGS.*

A BOLT OF MAGIC LIGHTNING TURNED ALL MY FRUIT INTO *AGGRESSIVE MONSTERS.*

FED UP SEEING YOUR CROPS DEVASTATED? YOU WANNA END UP TRYING TO GROW WHEAT ON BARE ROCKS?

NOOO!

DOWN WITH WIZARDS!

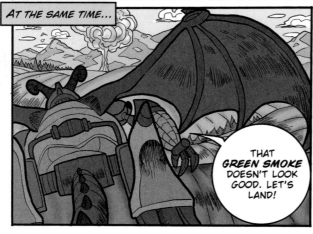

AT THE SAME TIME...

THAT *GREEN SMOKE* DOESN'T LOOK GOOD. LET'S LAND!

WELCOME, WIZARDS OF MICKEY! ARE YOU AFTER SOME *SOUP*?

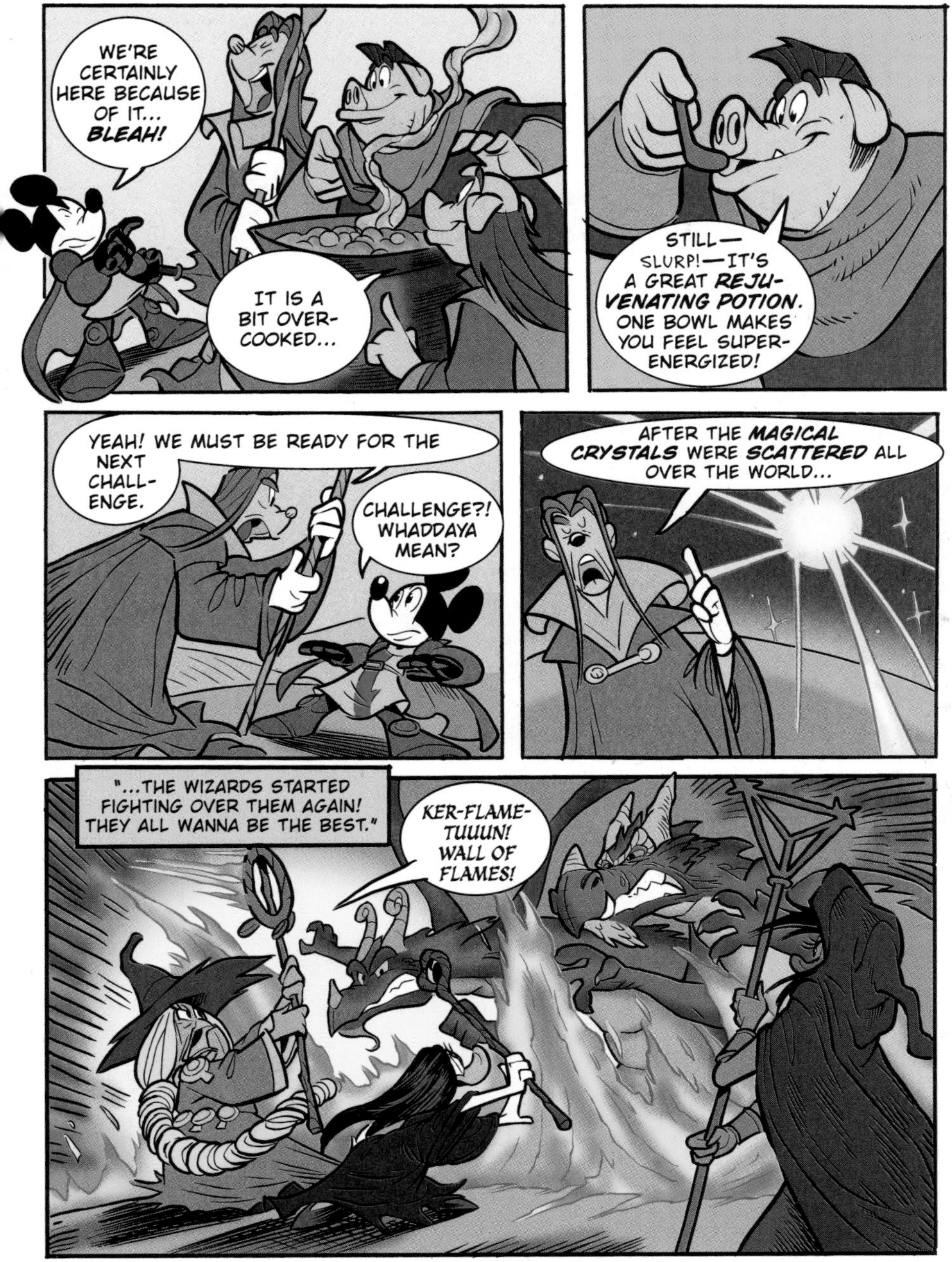
WE'RE CERTAINLY HERE BECAUSE OF IT... BLEAH!
IT IS A BIT OVER-COOKED...
STILL— SLURP!—IT'S A GREAT REJU-VENATING POTION. ONE BOWL MAKES YOU FEEL SUPER-ENERGIZED!
YEAH! WE MUST BE READY FOR THE NEXT CHALL-ENGE.
CHALLENGE?! WHADDAYA MEAN?
AFTER THE MAGICAL CRYSTALS WERE SCATTERED ALL OVER THE WORLD...
"...THE WIZARDS STARTED FIGHTING OVER THEM AGAIN! THEY ALL WANNA BE THE BEST."
KER-FLAME-TUUUN! WALL OF FLAMES!

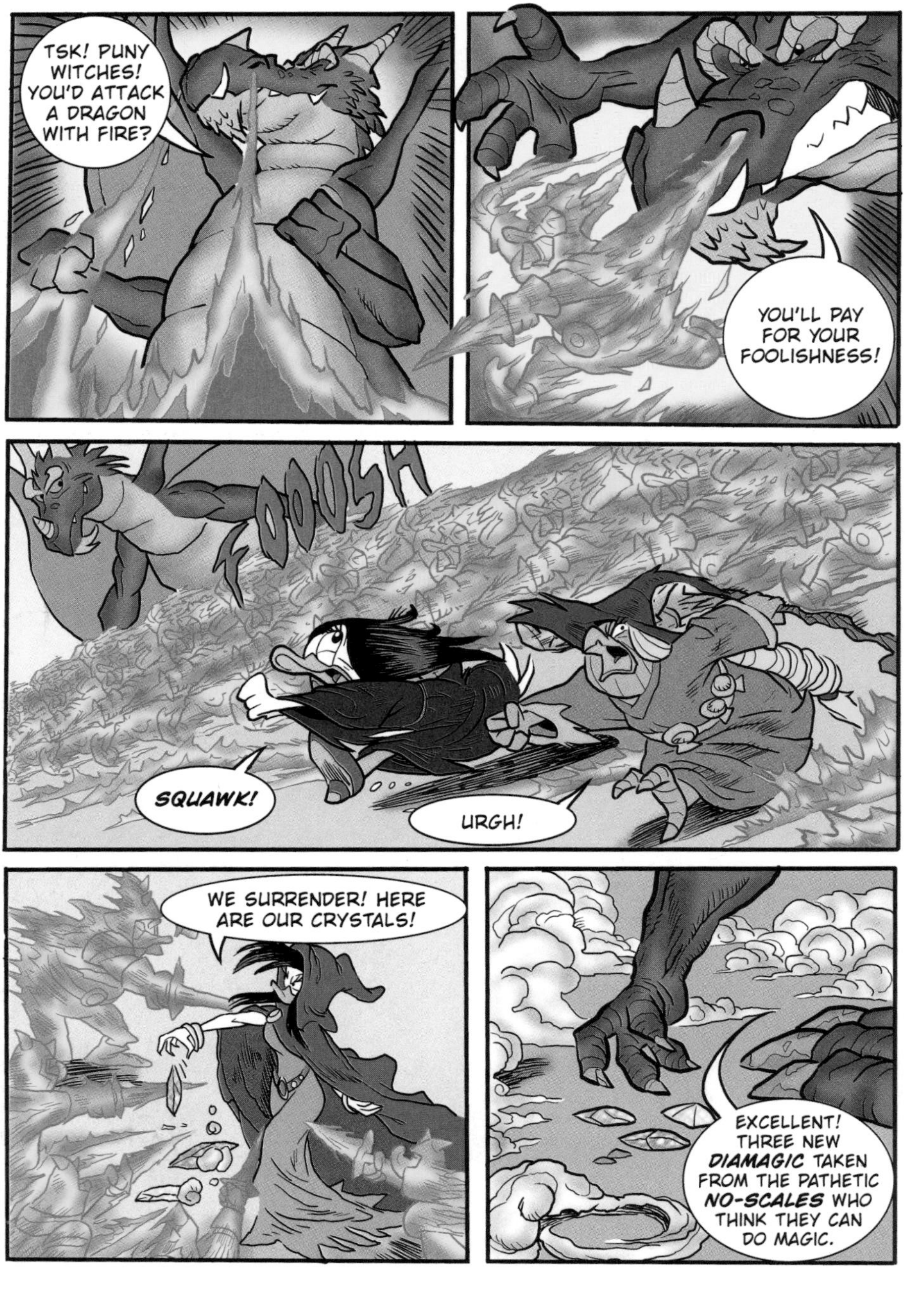
TSK! PUNY WITCHES! YOU'D ATTACK A DRAGON WITH FIRE?
YOU'LL PAY FOR YOUR FOOLISHNESS!
FOOOSH
SQUAWK!
URGH!
WE SURRENDER! HERE ARE OUR CRYSTALS!
EXCELLENT! THREE NEW DIAMAGIC TAKEN FROM THE PATHETIC NO-SCALES WHO THINK THEY CAN DO MAGIC.

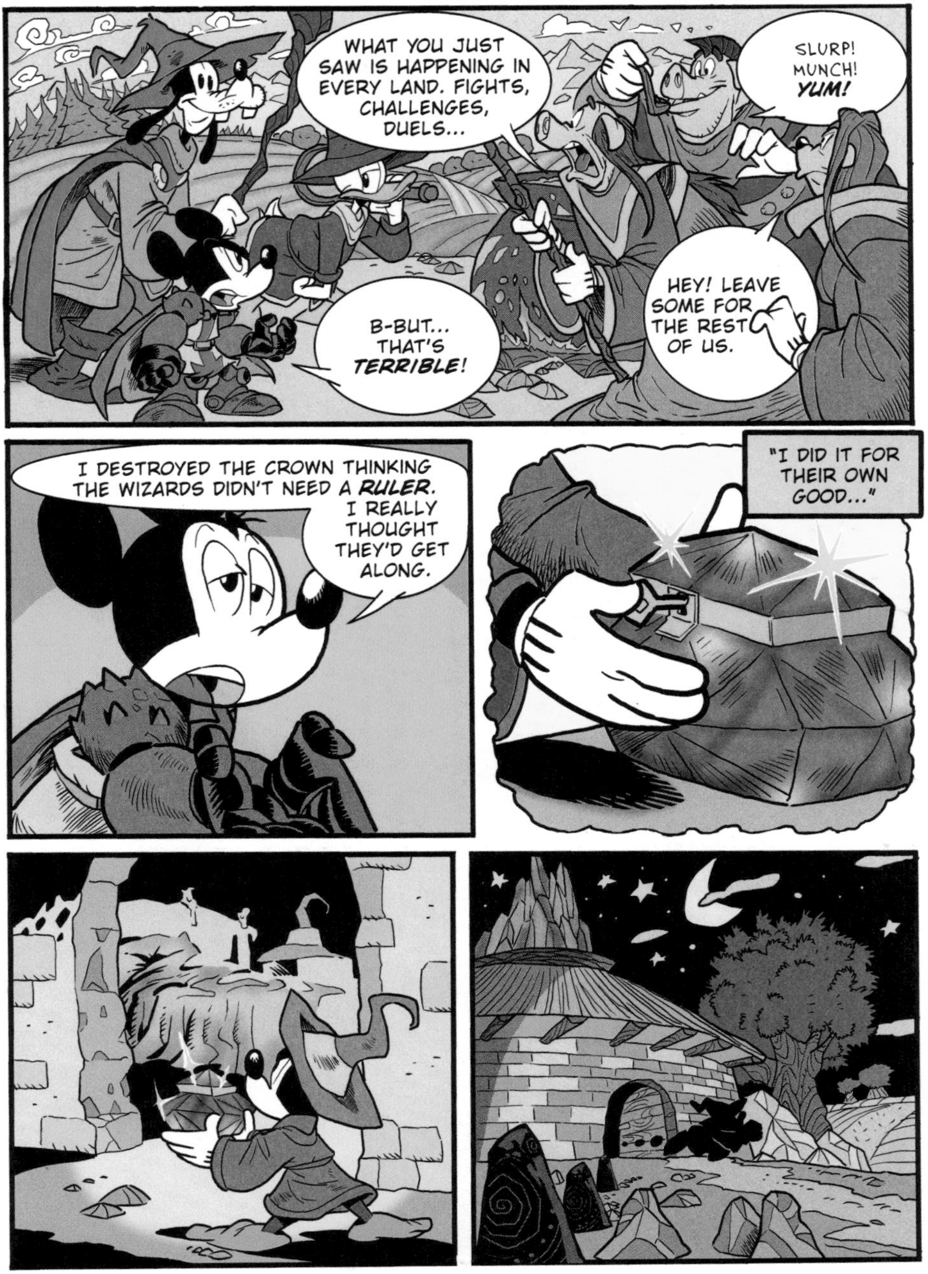

WHAT YOU JUST SAW IS HAPPENING IN EVERY LAND. FIGHTS, CHALLENGES, DUELS...
SLURP! MUNCH! ***YUM!***
B-BUT... THAT'S ***TERRIBLE***!
HEY! LEAVE SOME FOR THE REST OF US.
I DESTROYED THE CROWN THINKING THE WIZARDS DIDN'T NEED A ***RULER***. I REALLY THOUGHT THEY'D GET ALONG.
"I DID IT FOR THEIR OWN GOOD..."

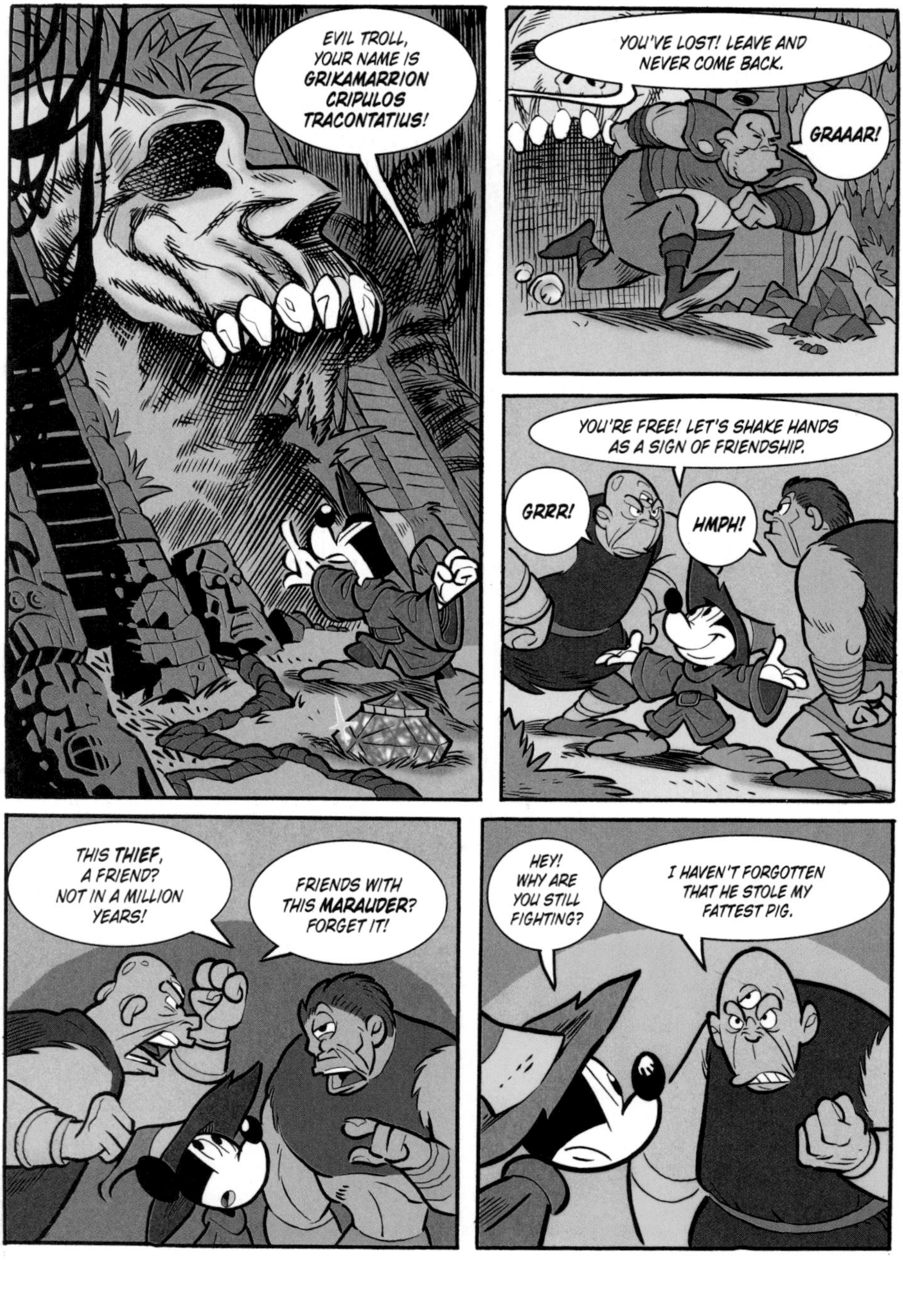
EVIL TROLL, YOUR NAME IS **GRIKAMARRION CRIPULOS TRACONTATIUS**!
YOU'VE LOST! LEAVE AND NEVER COME BACK.
GRAAAR!
YOU'RE FREE! LET'S SHAKE HANDS AS A SIGN OF FRIENDSHIP.
GRRR!
HMPH!
THIS **THIEF**, A FRIEND? NOT IN A MILLION YEARS!
FRIENDS WITH THIS **MARAUDER**? FORGET IT!
HEY! WHY ARE YOU STILL FIGHTING?
I HAVEN'T FORGOTTEN THAT HE STOLE MY FATTEST PIG.

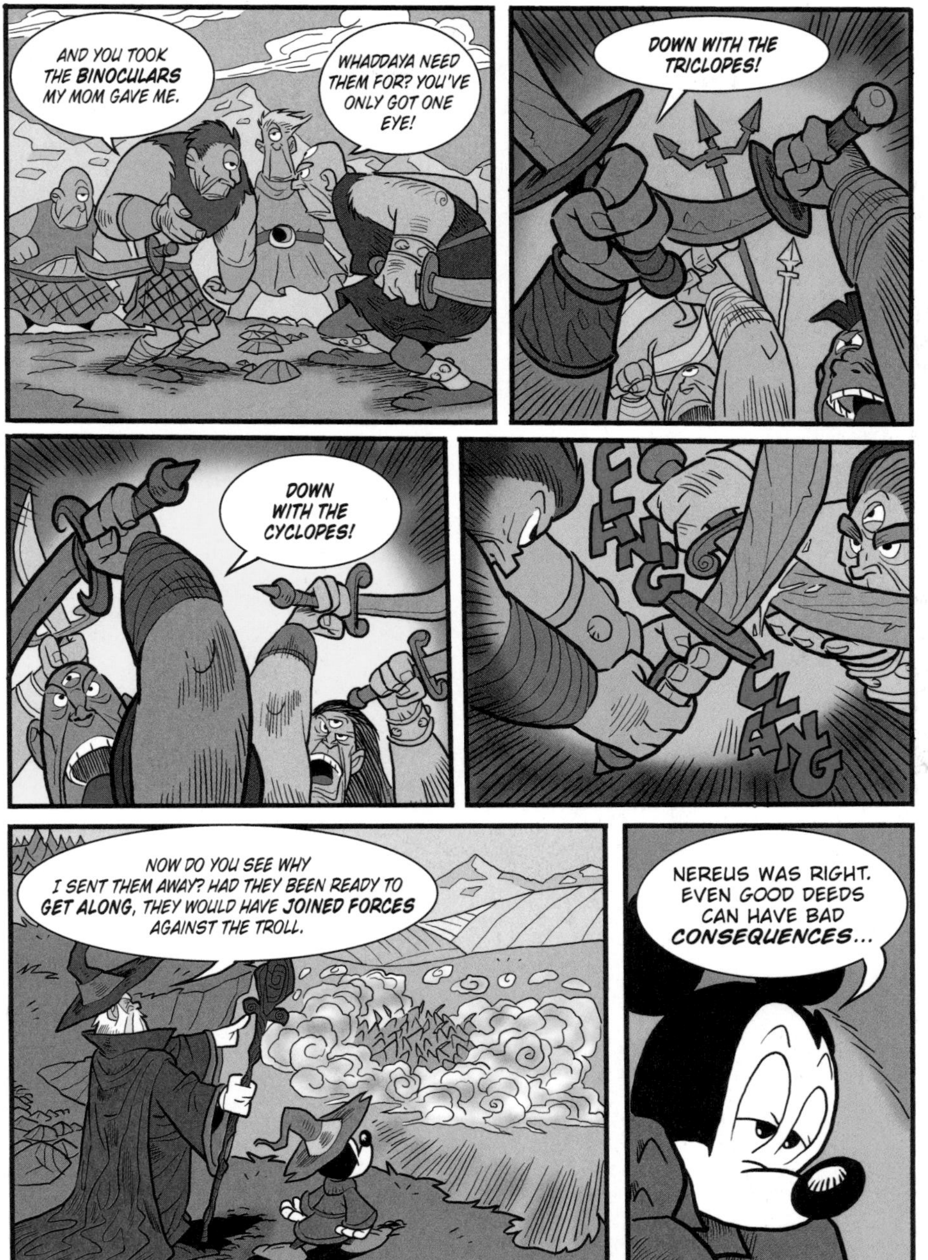
AND YOU TOOK THE BINOCULARS MY MOM GAVE ME.
WHADDAYA NEED THEM FOR? YOU'VE ONLY GOT ONE EYE!
DOWN WITH THE TRICLOPES!
DOWN WITH THE CYCLOPES!
CLANG
CLANG
NOW DO YOU SEE WHY I SENT THEM AWAY? HAD THEY BEEN READY TO GET ALONG, THEY WOULD HAVE JOINED FORCES AGAINST THE TROLL.
NEREUS WAS RIGHT. EVEN GOOD DEEDS CAN HAVE BAD CONSEQUENCES...

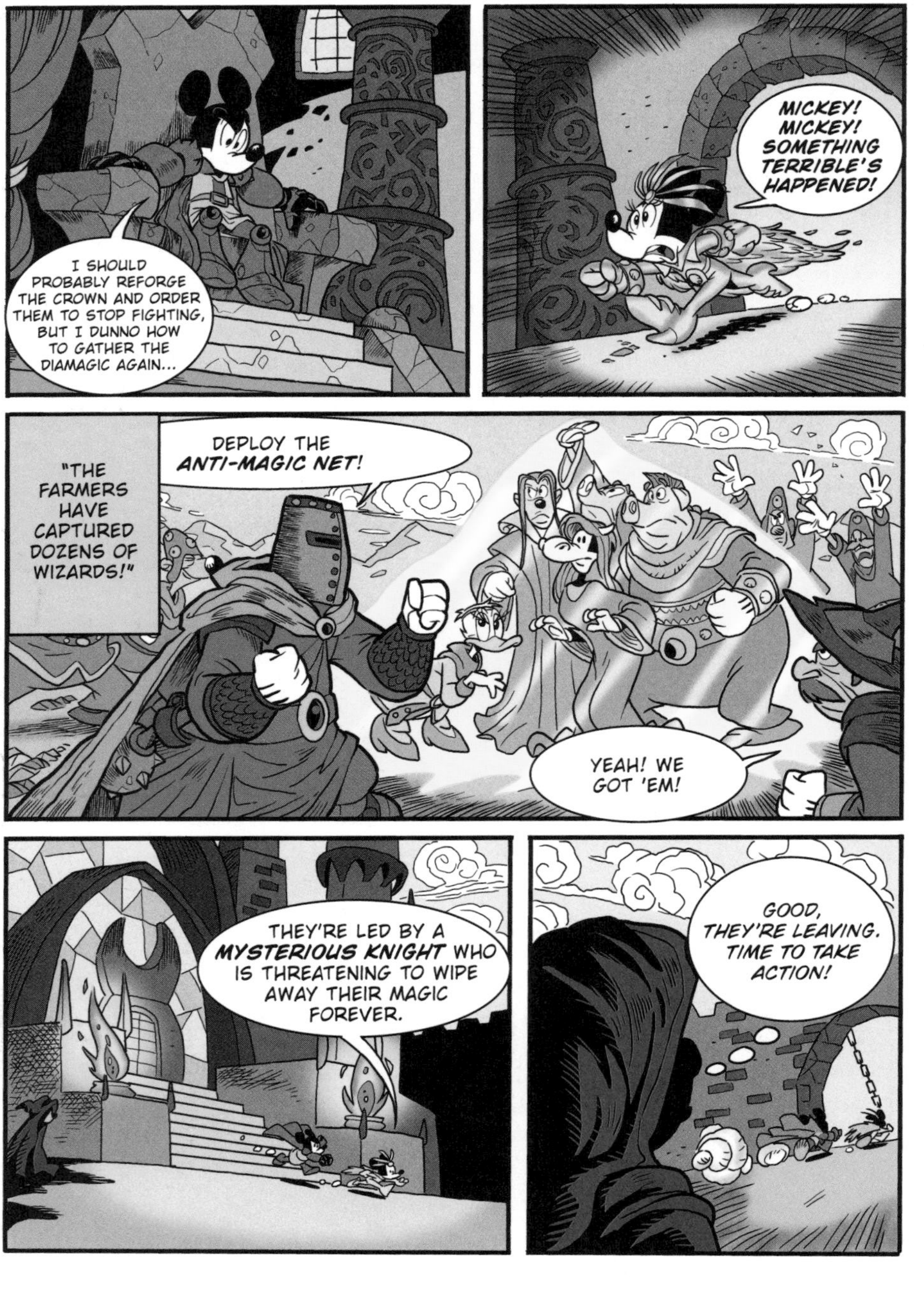
I SHOULD PROBABLY REFORGE THE CROWN AND ORDER THEM TO STOP FIGHTING, BUT I DUNNO HOW TO GATHER THE DIAMAGIC AGAIN...
MICKEY! MICKEY! SOMETHING TERRIBLE'S HAPPENED!
"THE FARMERS HAVE CAPTURED DOZENS OF WIZARDS!"
DEPLOY THE *ANTI-MAGIC NET*!
YEAH! WE GOT 'EM!
THEY'RE LED BY A *MYSTERIOUS KNIGHT* WHO IS THREATENING TO WIPE AWAY THEIR MAGIC FOREVER.
GOOD, THEY'RE LEAVING. TIME TO TAKE ACTION!

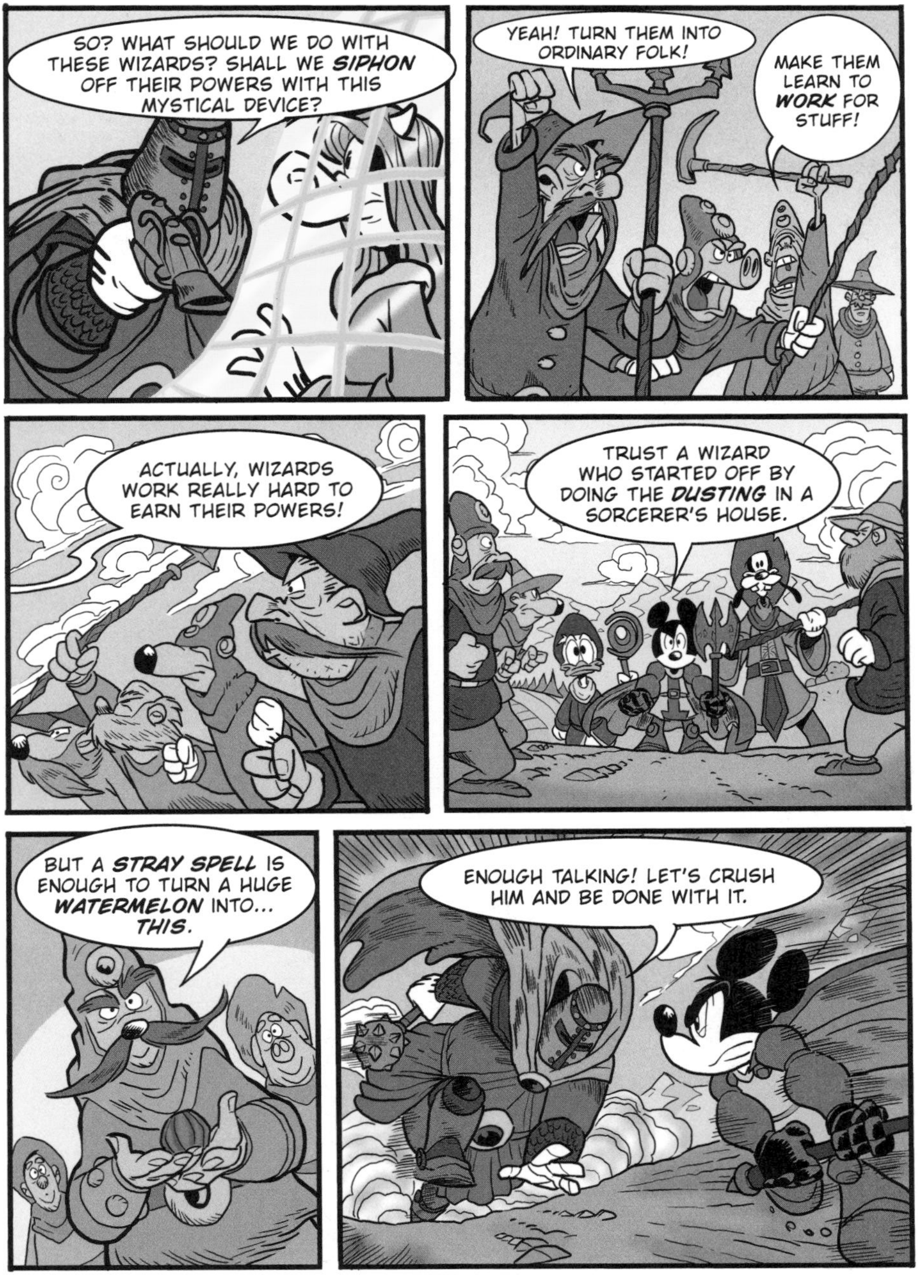
SO? WHAT SHOULD WE DO WITH THESE WIZARDS? SHALL WE SIPHON OFF THEIR POWERS WITH THIS MYSTICAL DEVICE?
YEAH! TURN THEM INTO ORDINARY FOLK!
MAKE THEM LEARN TO WORK FOR STUFF!
ACTUALLY, WIZARDS WORK REALLY HARD TO EARN THEIR POWERS!
TRUST A WIZARD WHO STARTED OFF BY DOING THE DUSTING IN A SORCERER'S HOUSE.
BUT A STRAY SPELL IS ENOUGH TO TURN A HUGE WATERMELON INTO... THIS.
ENOUGH TALKING! LET'S CRUSH HIM AND BE DONE WITH IT.

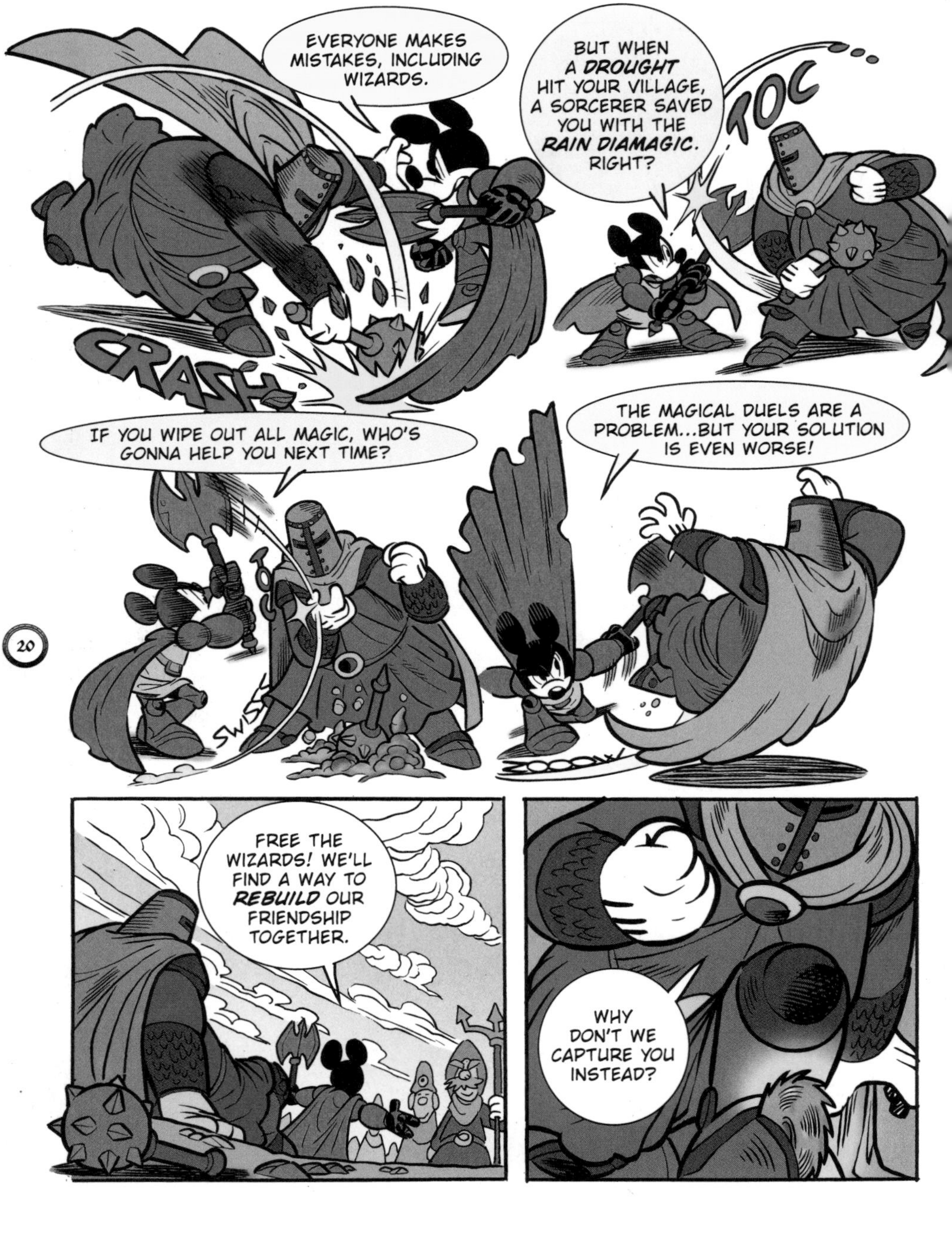
EVERYONE MAKES MISTAKES, INCLUDING WIZARDS.
CRASH
BUT WHEN A DROUGHT HIT YOUR VILLAGE, A SORCERER SAVED YOU WITH THE RAIN DIAMAGIC. RIGHT?
TOC
IF YOU WIPE OUT ALL MAGIC, WHO'S GONNA HELP YOU NEXT TIME?
THE MAGICAL DUELS ARE A PROBLEM...BUT YOUR SOLUTION IS EVEN WORSE!
FREE THE WIZARDS! WE'LL FIND A WAY TO REBUILD OUR FRIENDSHIP TOGETHER.
WHY DON'T WE CAPTURE YOU INSTEAD?

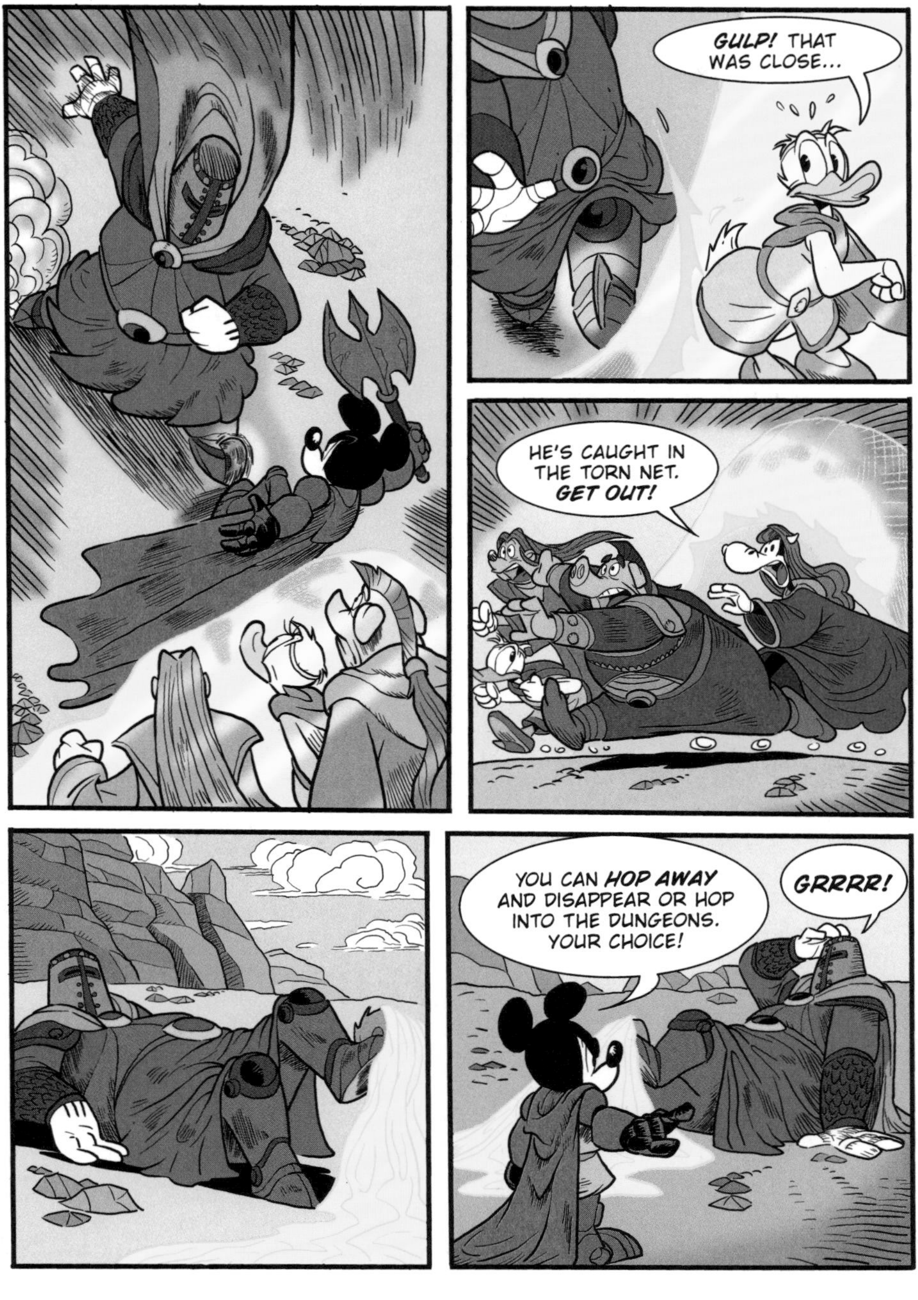
GULP! THAT WAS CLOSE...
HE'S CAUGHT IN THE TORN NET. GET OUT!
YOU CAN HOP AWAY AND DISAPPEAR OR HOP INTO THE DUNGEONS. YOUR CHOICE!
GRRRR!

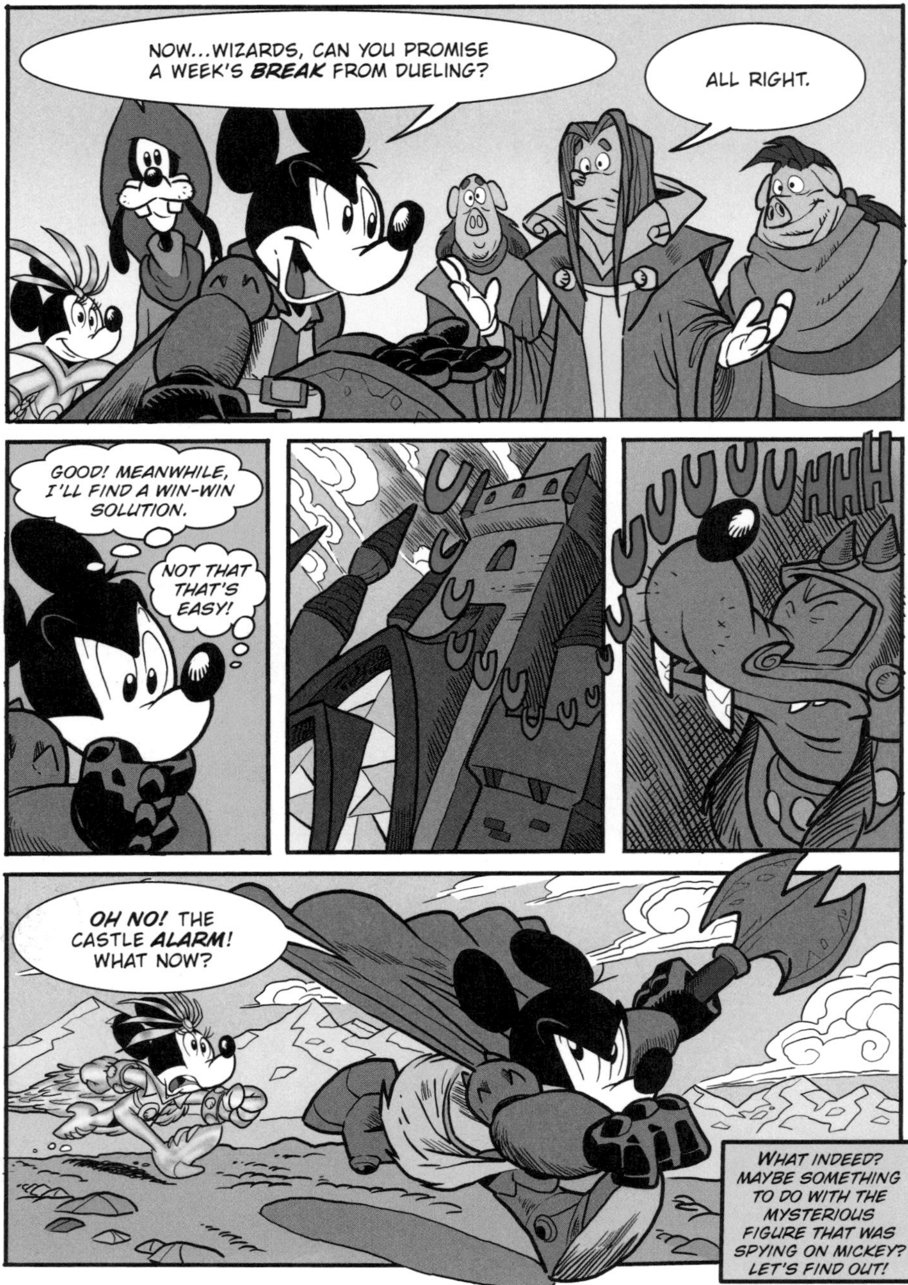
NOW...WIZARDS, CAN YOU PROMISE A WEEK'S BREAK FROM DUELING?
ALL RIGHT.
GOOD! MEANWHILE, I'LL FIND A WIN-WIN SOLUTION.
NOT THAT THAT'S EASY!
UUUUUUUUUUUUUUUUUUUUUUUHHH
OH NO! THE CASTLE ALARM! WHAT NOW?
WHAT INDEED? MAYBE SOMETHING TO DO WITH THE MYSTERIOUS FIGURE THAT WAS SPYING ON MICKEY? LET'S FIND OUT!

THE END

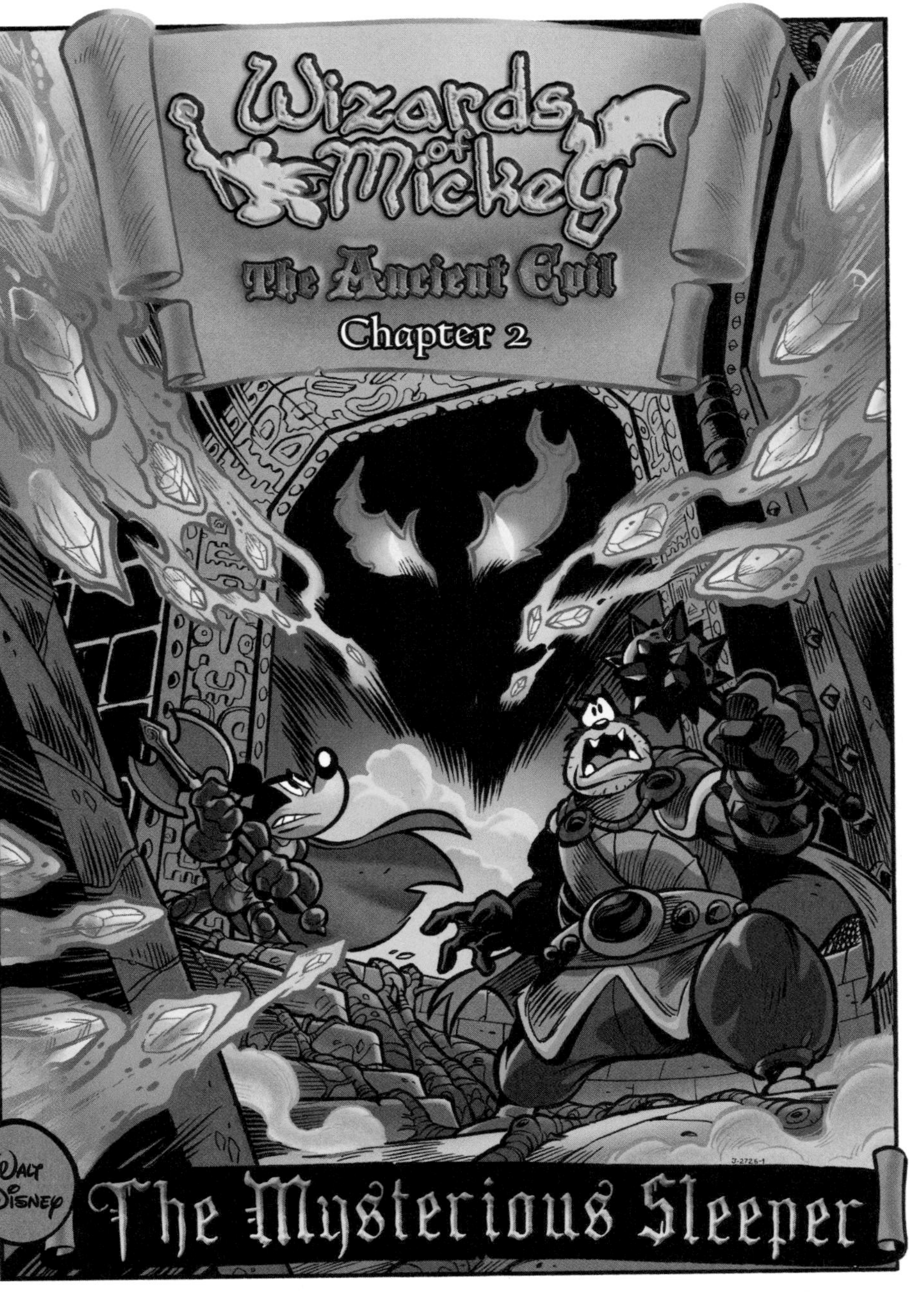
Wizards of Mickey
The Ancient Evil
Chapter 2
Walt Disney
The Mysterious Sleeper

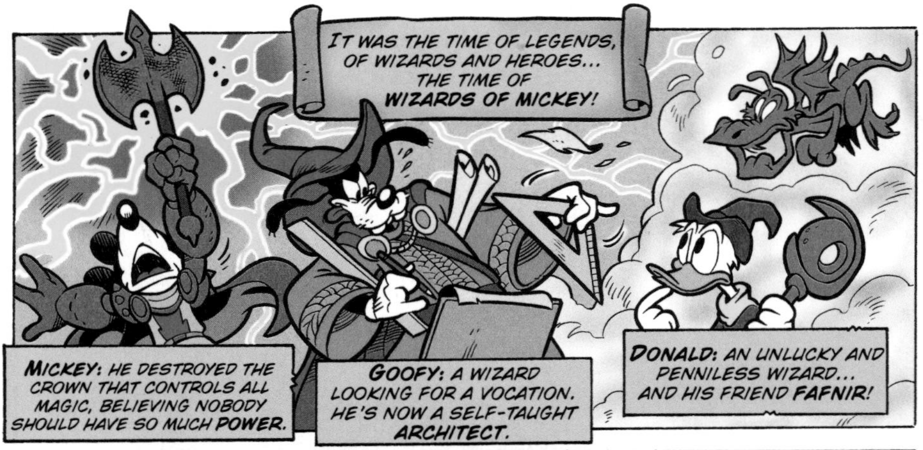
IT WAS THE TIME OF LEGENDS, OF WIZARDS AND HEROES... THE TIME OF WIZARDS OF MICKEY!
MICKEY: HE DESTROYED THE CROWN THAT CONTROLS ALL MAGIC, BELIEVING NOBODY SHOULD HAVE SO MUCH POWER.
GOOFY: A WIZARD LOOKING FOR A VOCATION. HE'S NOW A SELF-TAUGHT ARCHITECT.
DONALD: AN UNLUCKY AND PENNILESS WIZARD... AND HIS FRIEND FAFNIR!

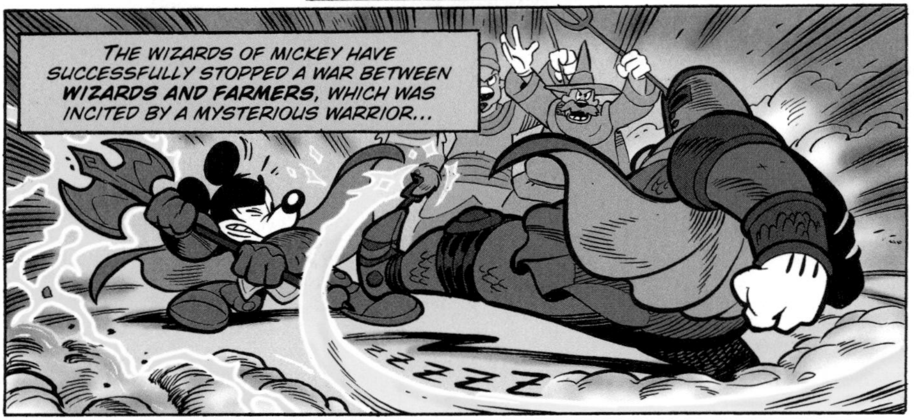
THE WIZARDS OF MICKEY HAVE SUCCESSFULLY STOPPED A WAR BETWEEN WIZARDS AND FARMERS, WHICH WAS INCITED BY A MYSTERIOUS WARRIOR...
ZZZZZZ

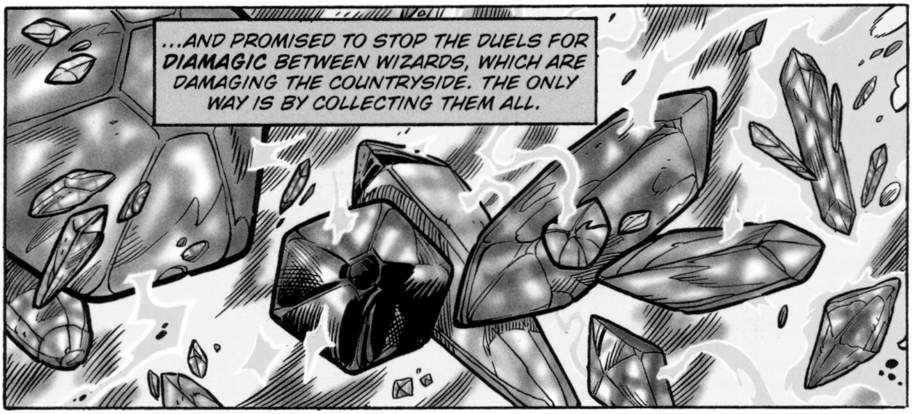
...AND PROMISED TO STOP THE DUELS FOR DIAMAGIC BETWEEN WIZARDS, WHICH ARE DAMAGING THE COUNTRYSIDE. THE ONLY WAY IS BY COLLECTING THEM ALL.

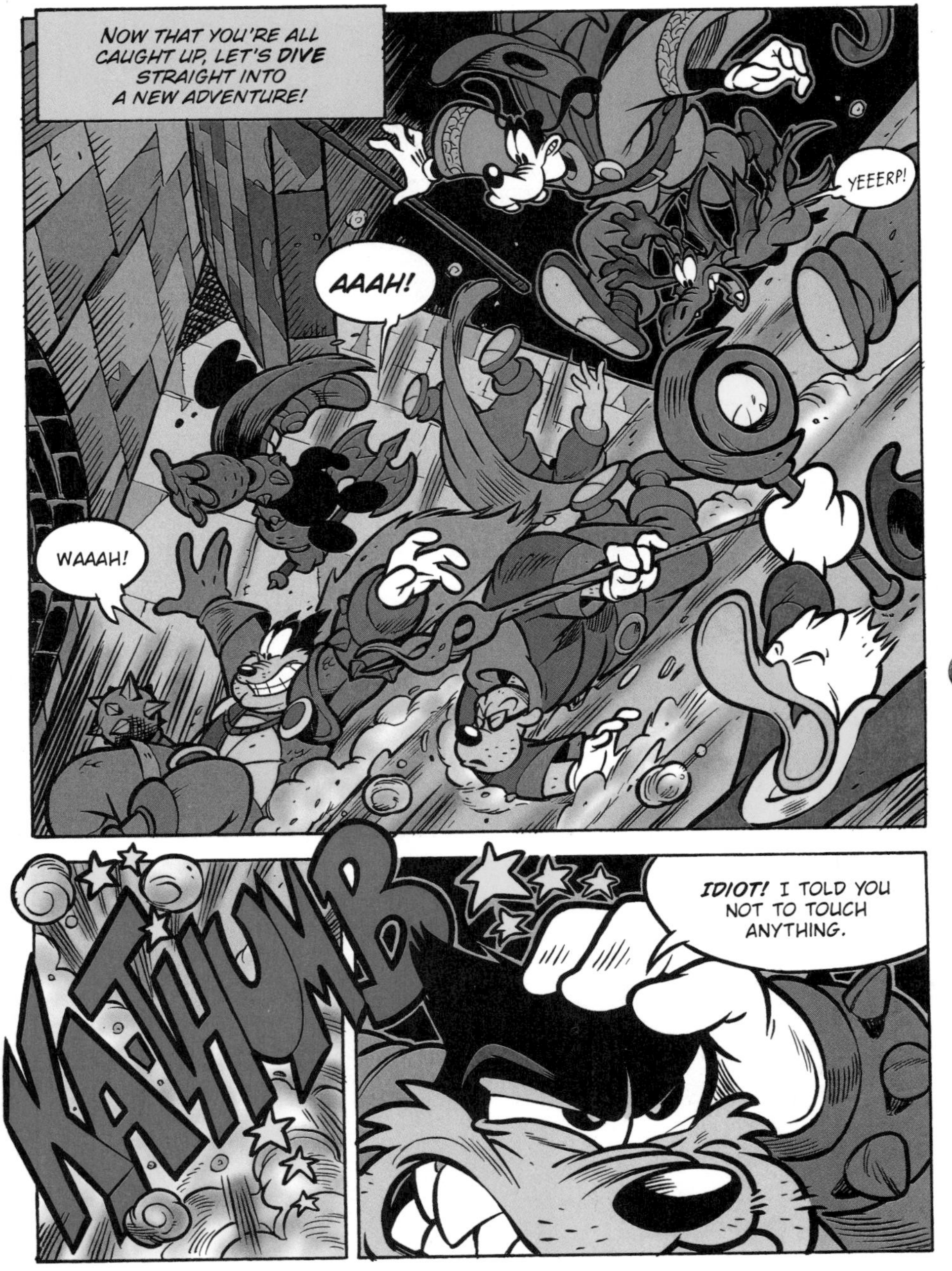
NOW THAT YOU'RE ALL CAUGHT UP, LET'S DIVE STRAIGHT INTO A NEW ADVENTURE!
YEEERP!
AAAH!
WAAAH!
KA-THUMB
IDIOT! I TOLD YOU NOT TO TOUCH ANYTHING.

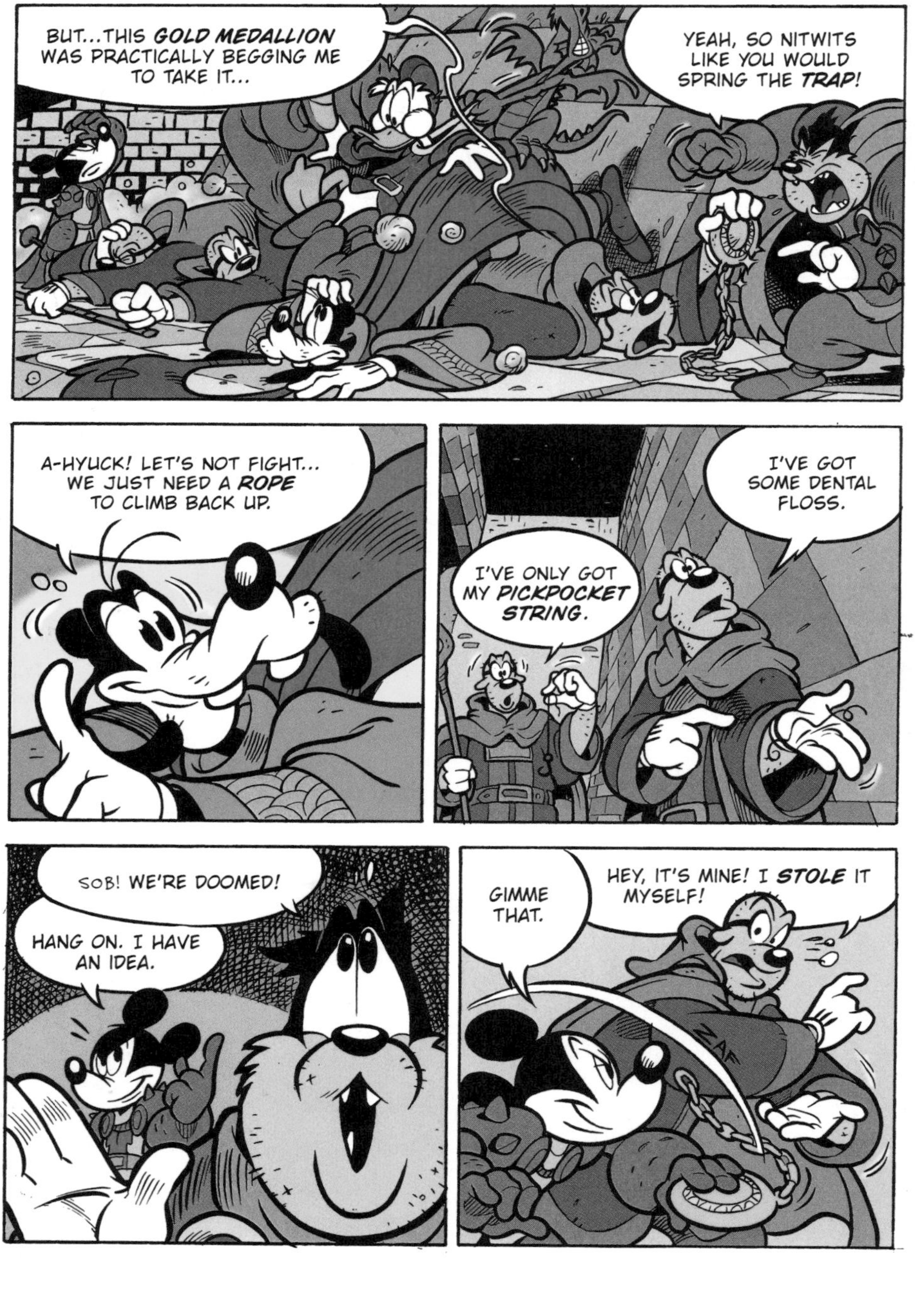
BUT...THIS GOLD MEDALLION WAS PRACTICALLY BEGGING ME TO TAKE IT...
YEAH, SO NITWITS LIKE YOU WOULD SPRING THE TRAP!
A-HYUCK! LET'S NOT FIGHT... WE JUST NEED A ROPE TO CLIMB BACK UP.
I'VE GOT SOME DENTAL FLOSS.
I'VE ONLY GOT MY PICKPOCKET STRING.
SOB! WE'RE DOOMED!
HANG ON. I HAVE AN IDEA.
GIMME THAT.
HEY, IT'S MINE! I STOLE IT MYSELF!
ZAP

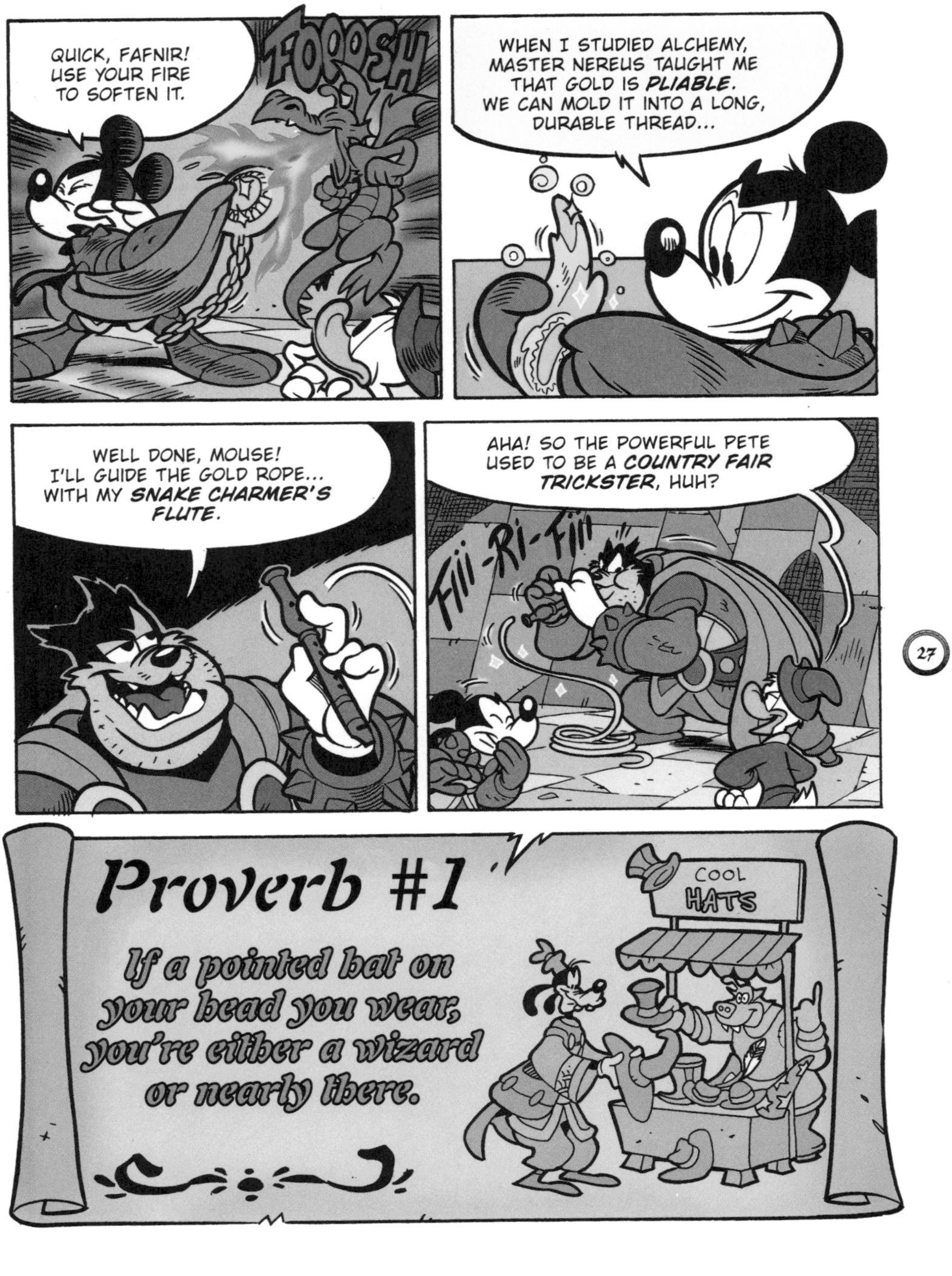
QUICK, FAFNIR! USE YOUR FIRE TO SOFTEN IT.
FOOOSH
WHEN I STUDIED ALCHEMY, MASTER NEREUS TAUGHT ME THAT GOLD IS PLIABLE. WE CAN MOLD IT INTO A LONG, DURABLE THREAD...
WELL DONE, MOUSE! I'LL GUIDE THE GOLD ROPE... WITH MY SNAKE CHARMER'S FLUTE.
AHA! SO THE POWERFUL PETE USED TO BE A COUNTRY FAIR TRICKSTER, HUH?
Fiii-Ri-Fiii
Proverb #1
If a pointed hat on your head you wear, you're either a wizard or nearly there.
COOL HATS

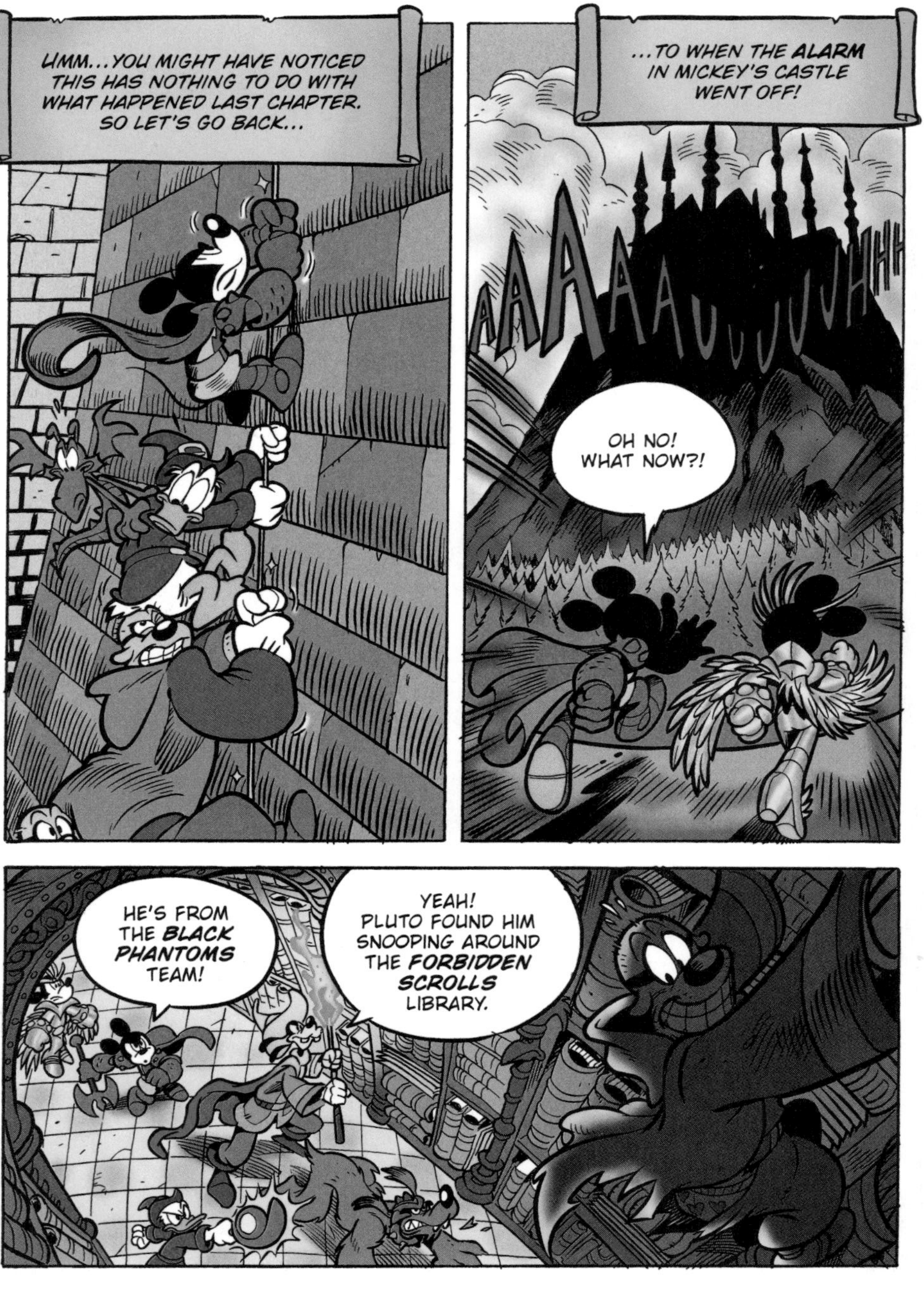
UMM...YOU MIGHT HAVE NOTICED THIS HAS NOTHING TO DO WITH WHAT HAPPENED LAST CHAPTER. SO LET'S GO BACK...
...TO WHEN THE ALARM IN MICKEY'S CASTLE WENT OFF!
AAAAAUUUUUHHHH
OH NO! WHAT NOW?!
HE'S FROM THE BLACK PHANTOMS TEAM!
YEAH! PLUTO FOUND HIM SNOOPING AROUND THE FORBIDDEN SCROLLS LIBRARY.

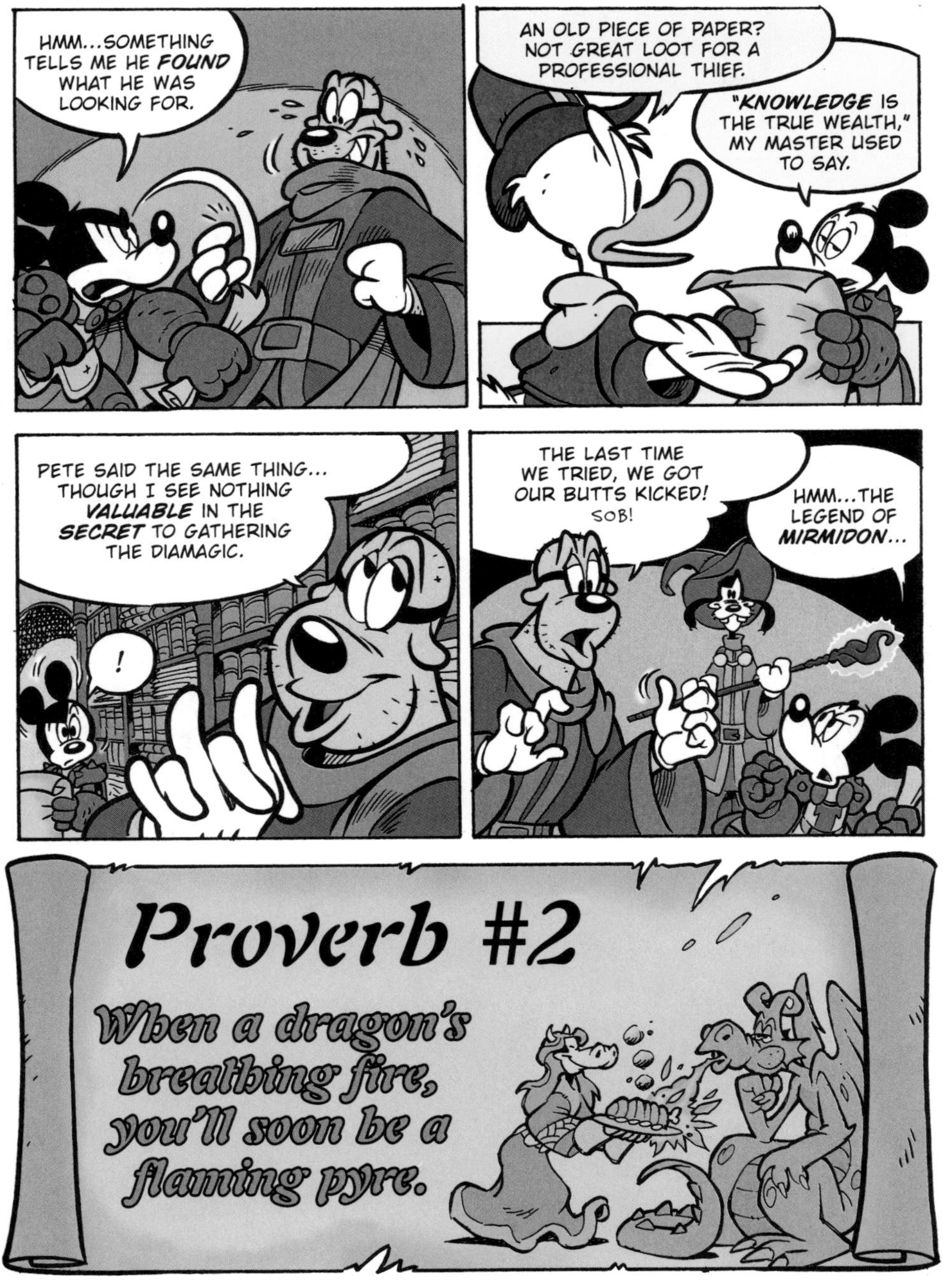
HMM...SOMETHING TELLS ME HE FOUND WHAT HE WAS LOOKING FOR.
AN OLD PIECE OF PAPER? NOT GREAT LOOT FOR A PROFESSIONAL THIEF.
"KNOWLEDGE IS THE TRUE WEALTH," MY MASTER USED TO SAY.
PETE SAID THE SAME THING... THOUGH I SEE NOTHING VALUABLE IN THE SECRET TO GATHERING THE DIAMAGIC.
!
THE LAST TIME WE TRIED, WE GOT OUR BUTTS KICKED! SOB!
HMM...THE LEGEND OF MIRMIDON...
Proverb #2
When a dragon's breathing fire, you'll soon be a flaming pyre.

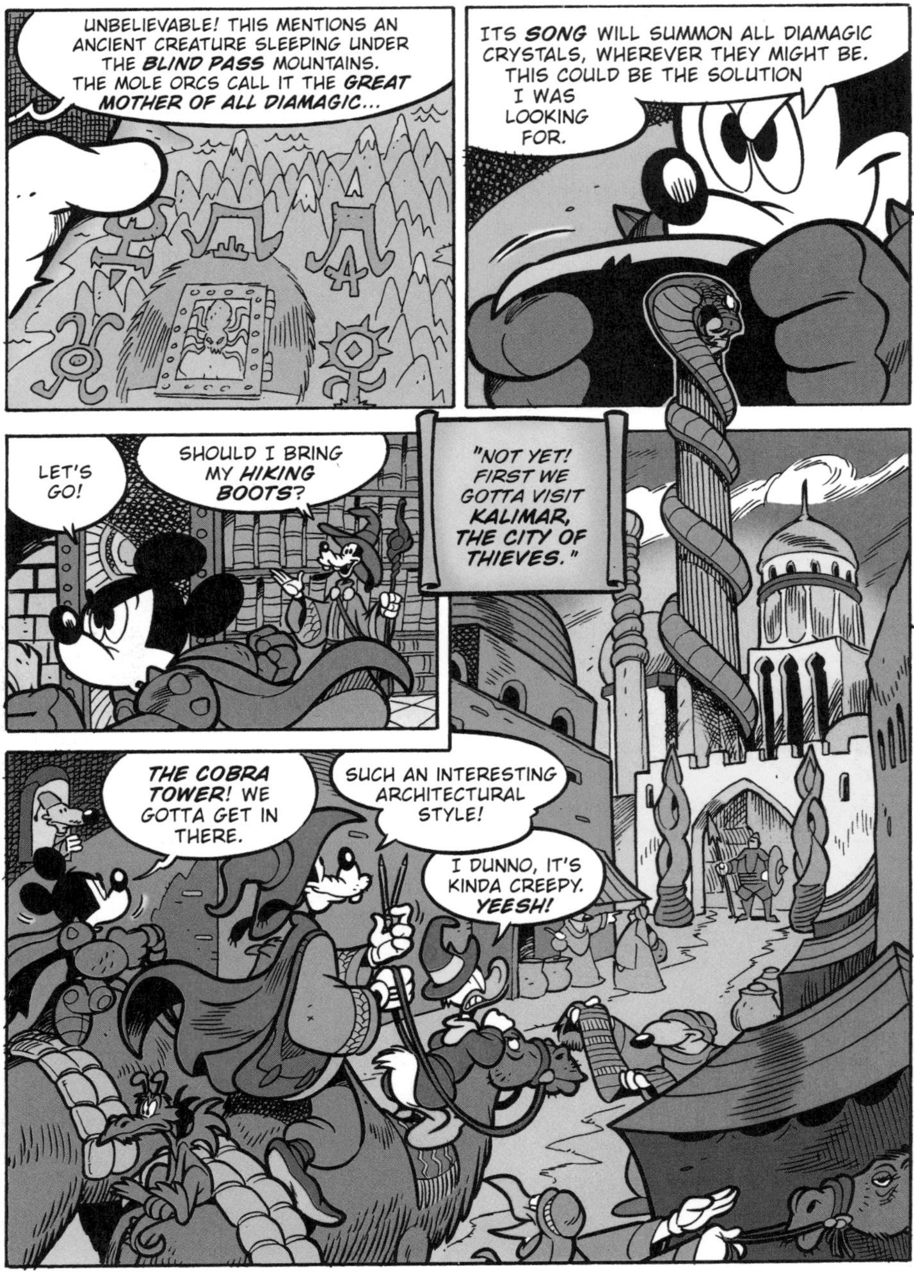
UNBELIEVABLE! THIS MENTIONS AN ANCIENT CREATURE SLEEPING UNDER THE **BLIND PASS** MOUNTAINS. THE MOLE ORCS CALL IT THE **GREAT MOTHER OF ALL DIAMAGIC**...
ITS **SONG** WILL SUMMON ALL DIAMAGIC CRYSTALS, WHEREVER THEY MIGHT BE. THIS COULD BE THE SOLUTION I WAS LOOKING FOR.
LET'S GO!
SHOULD I BRING MY **HIKING BOOTS**?
"NOT YET! FIRST WE GOTTA VISIT **KALIMAR, THE CITY OF THIEVES.**"
THE COBRA TOWER! WE GOTTA GET IN THERE.
SUCH AN INTERESTING ARCHITECTURAL STYLE!
I DUNNO, IT'S KINDA CREEPY. **YEESH!**

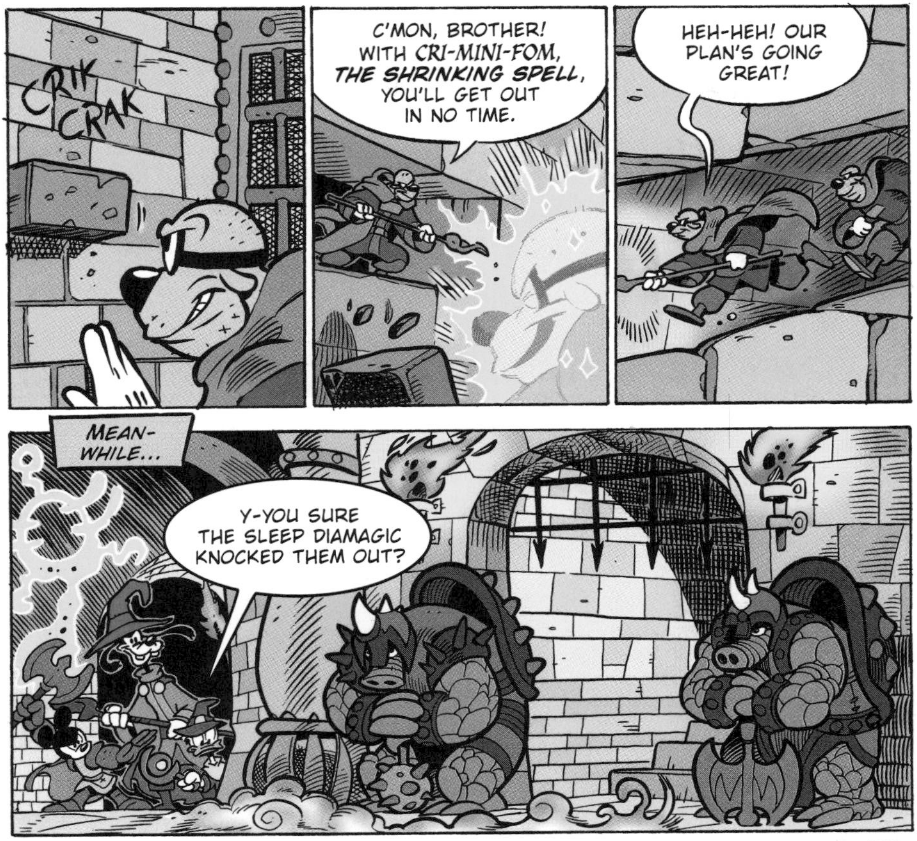
CRIK CRAK
C'MON, BROTHER! WITH CRI-MINI-FOM, THE SHRINKING SPELL, YOU'LL GET OUT IN NO TIME.
HEH-HEH! OUR PLAN'S GOING GREAT!
MEAN-WHILE...
Y-YOU SURE THE SLEEP DIAMAGIC KNOCKED THEM OUT?

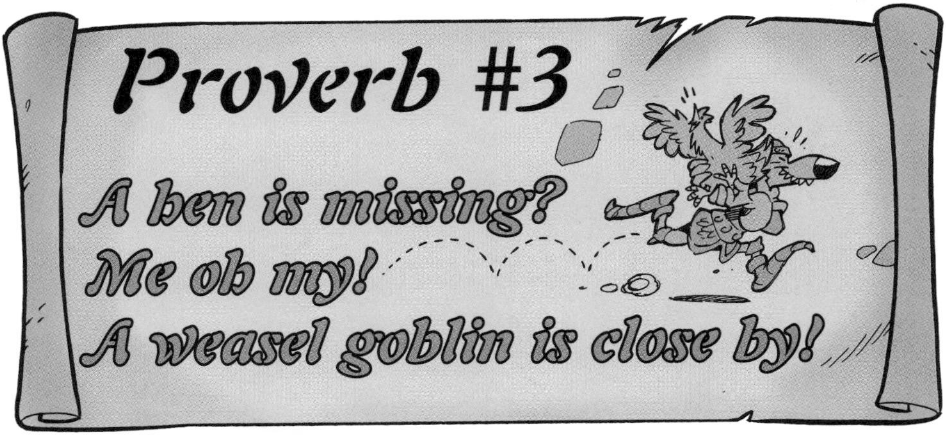
Proverb #3
A hen is missing?
Me oh my!
A weasel goblin is close by!

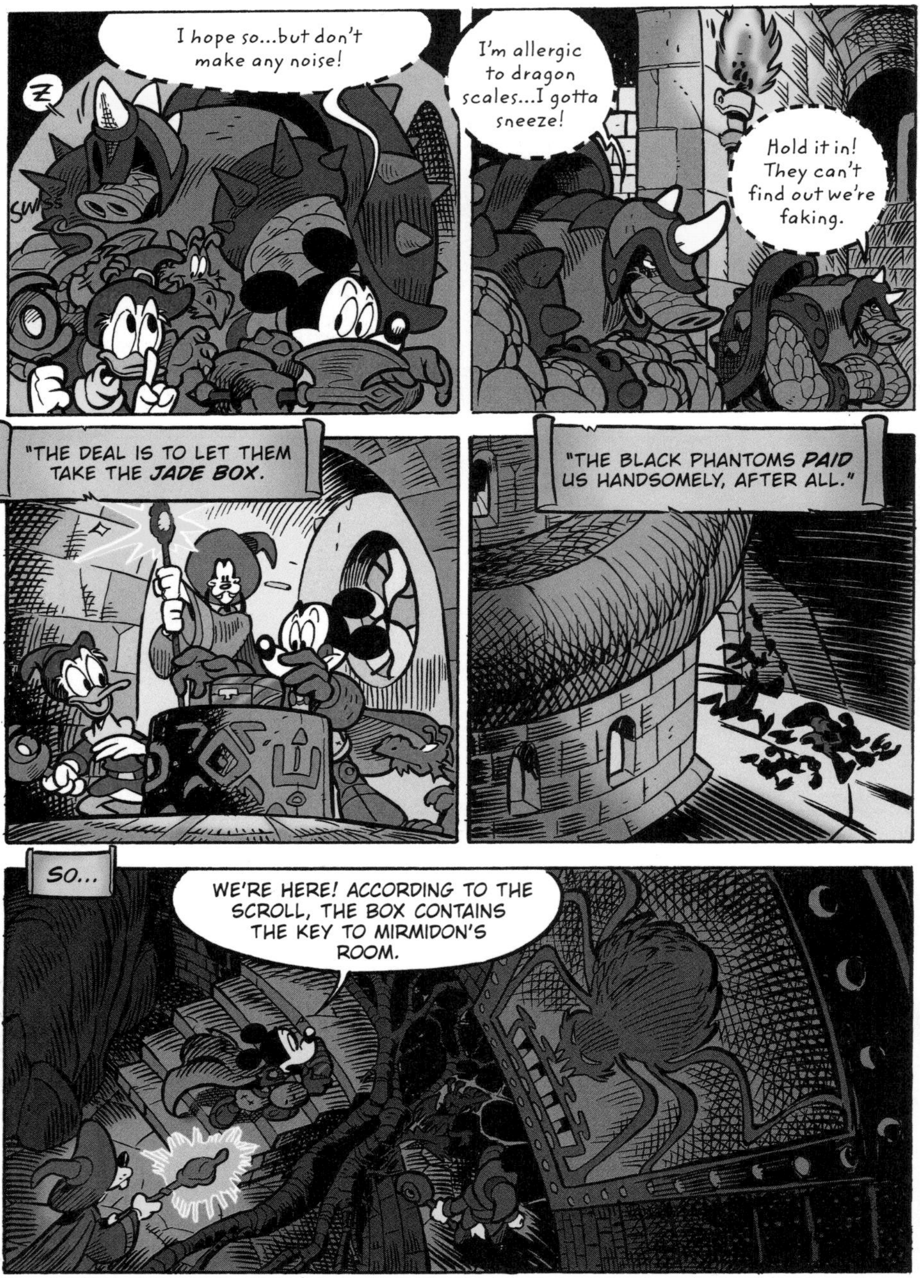

Z
SWISS
I hope so...but don't make any noise!
I'm allergic to dragon scales...I gotta sneeze!
Hold it in! They can't find out we're faking.
"THE DEAL IS TO LET THEM TAKE THE ***JADE BOX***.
"THE BLACK PHANTOMS ***PAID*** US HANDSOMELY, AFTER ALL."
SO...
WE'RE HERE! ACCORDING TO THE SCROLL, THE BOX CONTAINS THE KEY TO MIRMIDON'S ROOM.

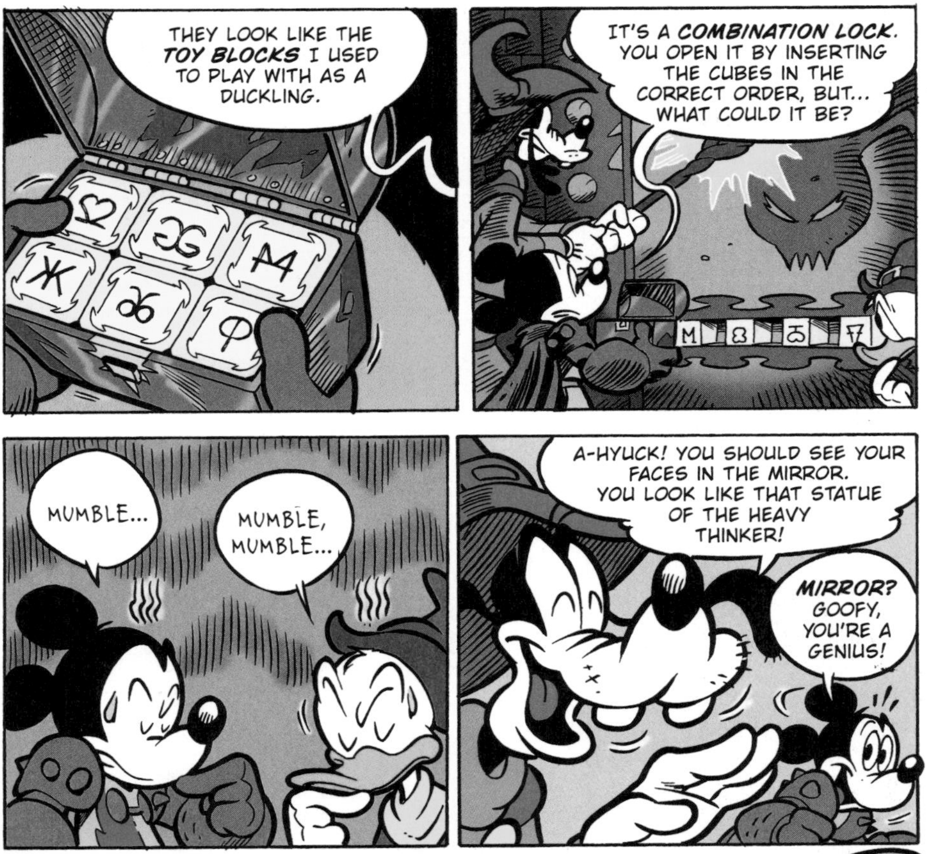
THEY LOOK LIKE THE **TOY BLOCKS** I USED TO PLAY WITH AS A DUCKLING.
IT'S A **COMBINATION LOCK**. YOU OPEN IT BY INSERTING THE CUBES IN THE CORRECT ORDER, BUT... WHAT COULD IT BE?
MUMBLE...
MUMBLE, MUMBLE...
A-HYUCK! YOU SHOULD SEE YOUR FACES IN THE MIRROR. YOU LOOK LIKE THAT STATUE OF THE HEAVY THINKER!
MIRROR? GOOFY, YOU'RE A GENIUS!

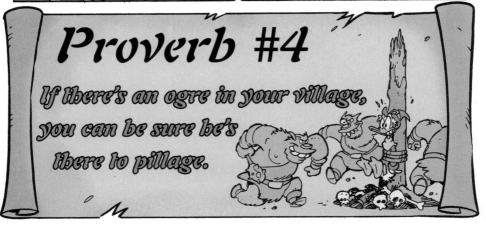

Proverb #4

If there's an ogre in your village, you can be sure he's there to pillage.

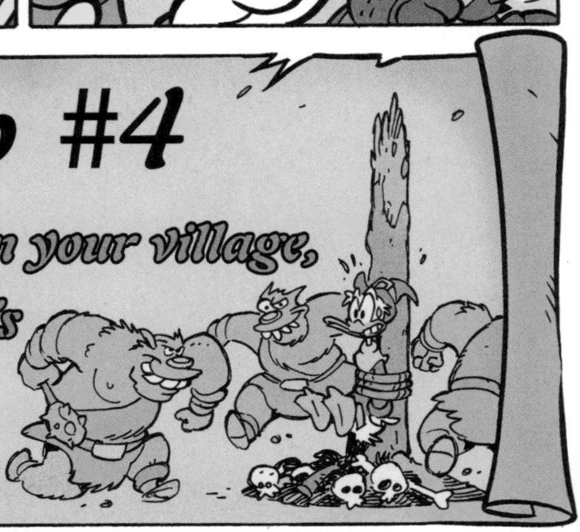

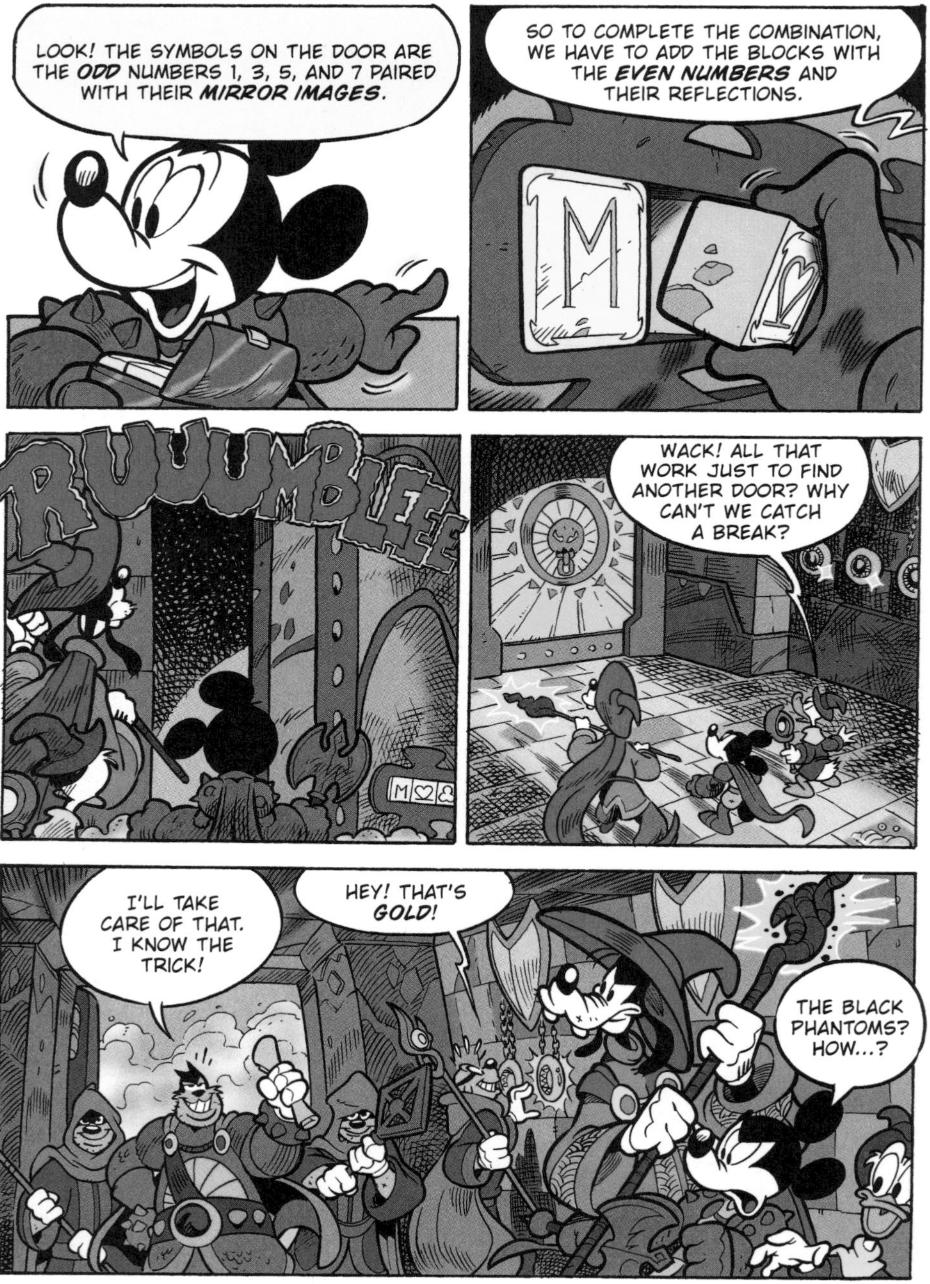
LOOK! THE SYMBOLS ON THE DOOR ARE THE ODD NUMBERS 1, 3, 5, AND 7 PAIRED WITH THEIR MIRROR IMAGES.
SO TO COMPLETE THE COMBINATION, WE HAVE TO ADD THE BLOCKS WITH THE EVEN NUMBERS AND THEIR REFLECTIONS.
RUUUMBLEEE
WACK! ALL THAT WORK JUST TO FIND ANOTHER DOOR? WHY CAN'T WE CATCH A BREAK?
I'LL TAKE CARE OF THAT. I KNOW THE TRICK!
HEY! THAT'S GOLD!
THE BLACK PHANTOMS? HOW...?

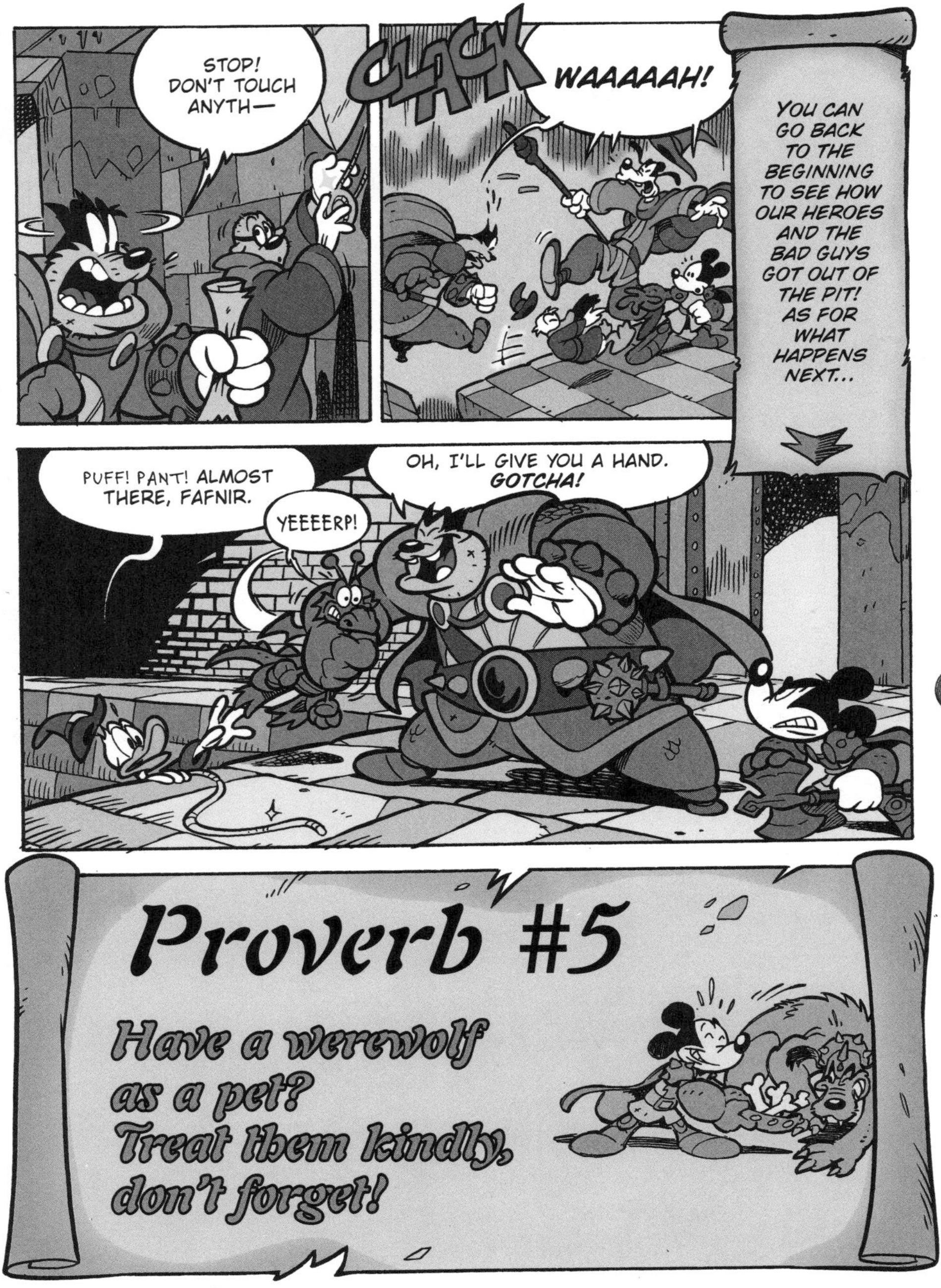
STOP! DON'T TOUCH ANYTH—
CLACK
WAAAAAH!
YOU CAN GO BACK TO THE BEGINNING TO SEE HOW OUR HEROES AND THE BAD GUYS GOT OUT OF THE PIT! AS FOR WHAT HAPPENS NEXT...
PUFF! PANT! ALMOST THERE, FAFNIR.
YEEEERP!
OH, I'LL GIVE YOU A HAND. GOTCHA!
Proverb #5
Have a werewolf as a pet? Treat them kindly, don't forget!

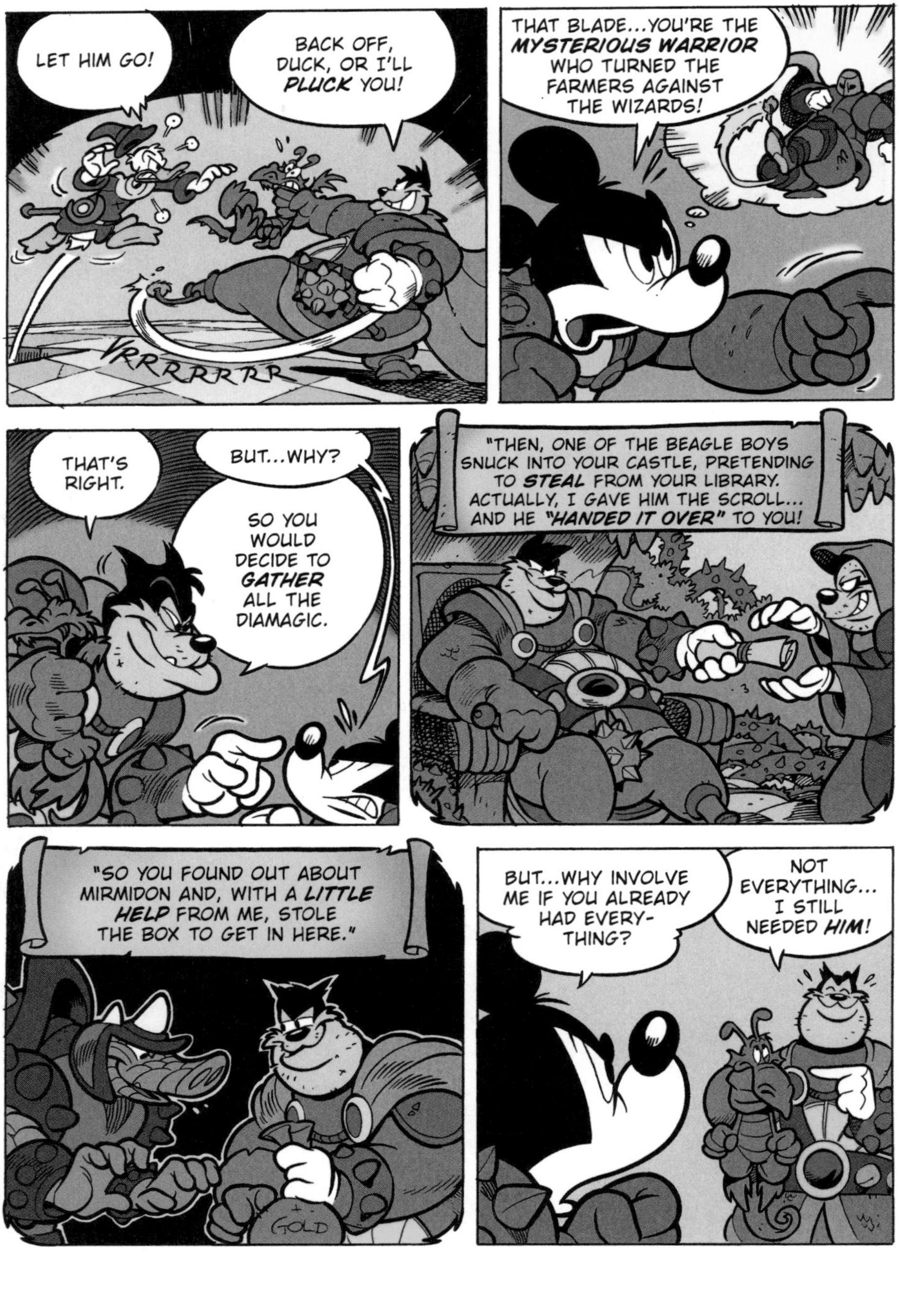

LET HIM GO!
BACK OFF, DUCK, OR I'LL PLUCK YOU!
VRRRRRRRRR
THAT BLADE...YOU'RE THE MYSTERIOUS WARRIOR WHO TURNED THE FARMERS AGAINST THE WIZARDS!
THAT'S RIGHT.
BUT...WHY?
SO YOU WOULD DECIDE TO GATHER ALL THE DIAMAGIC.
"THEN, ONE OF THE BEAGLE BOYS SNUCK INTO YOUR CASTLE, PRETENDING TO STEAL FROM YOUR LIBRARY. ACTUALLY, I GAVE HIM THE SCROLL... AND HE "HANDED IT OVER" TO YOU!
"SO YOU FOUND OUT ABOUT MIRMIDON AND, WITH A LITTLE HELP FROM ME, STOLE THE BOX TO GET IN HERE."
GOLD
BUT...WHY INVOLVE ME IF YOU ALREADY HAD EVERY-THING?
NOT EVERYTHING... I STILL NEEDED HIM!

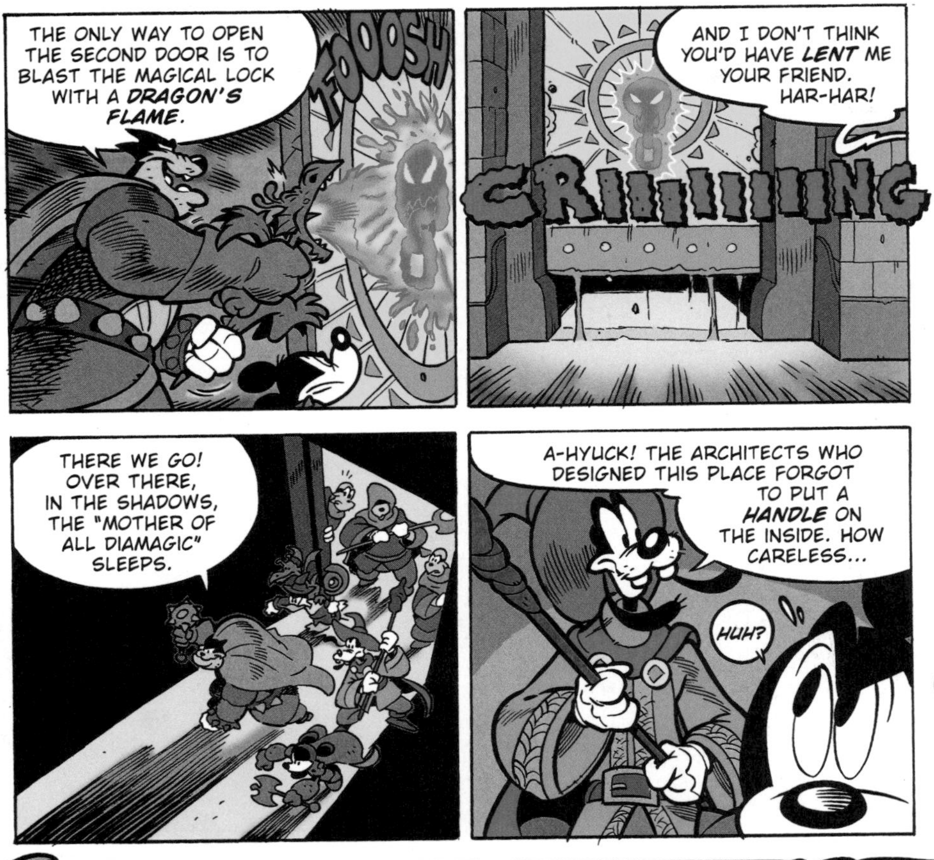
THE ONLY WAY TO OPEN THE SECOND DOOR IS TO BLAST THE MAGICAL LOCK WITH A ***DRAGON'S FLAME***.
FOOOSH
AND I DON'T THINK YOU'D HAVE ***LENT*** ME YOUR FRIEND. HAR-HAR!
CRIIIIIIIING
THERE WE GO! OVER THERE, IN THE SHADOWS, THE "MOTHER OF ALL DIAMAGIC" SLEEPS.
A-HYUCK! THE ARCHITECTS WHO DESIGNED THIS PLACE FORGOT TO PUT A ***HANDLE*** ON THE INSIDE. HOW CARELESS...
HUH?

Proverb #6

A witch who's vain is a mirror's bane.

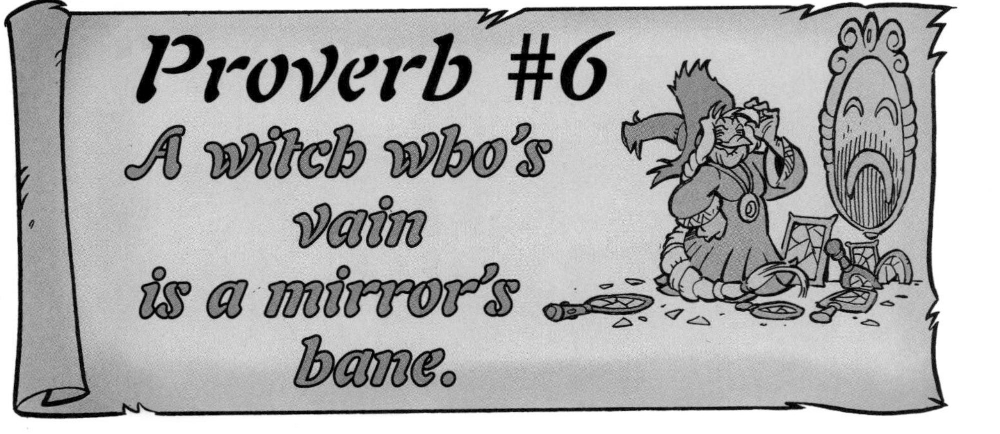

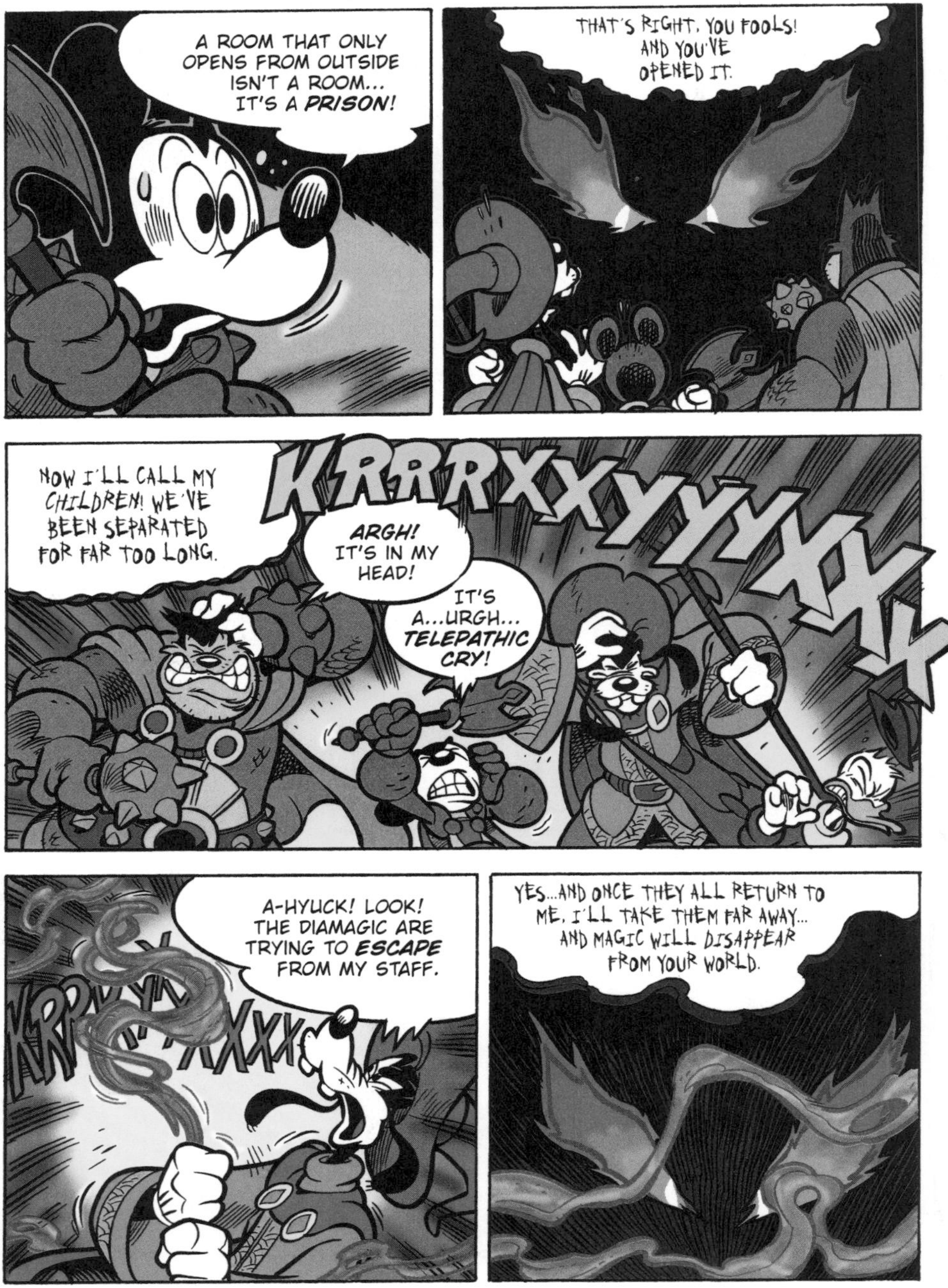
A ROOM THAT ONLY OPENS FROM OUTSIDE ISN'T A ROOM... IT'S A *PRISON*!
THAT'S RIGHT, YOU FOOLS! AND YOU'VE OPENED IT.
NOW I'LL CALL MY CHILDREN! WE'VE BEEN SEPARATED FOR FAR TOO LONG.
KRRRRXXYYYXXX
ARGH! IT'S IN MY HEAD!
IT'S A...URGH... *TELEPATHIC CRY!*
A-HYUCK! LOOK! THE DIAMAGIC ARE TRYING TO *ESCAPE* FROM MY STAFF.
YES...AND ONCE THEY ALL RETURN TO ME, I'LL TAKE THEM FAR AWAY... AND MAGIC WILL *DISAPPEAR* FROM YOUR WORLD.

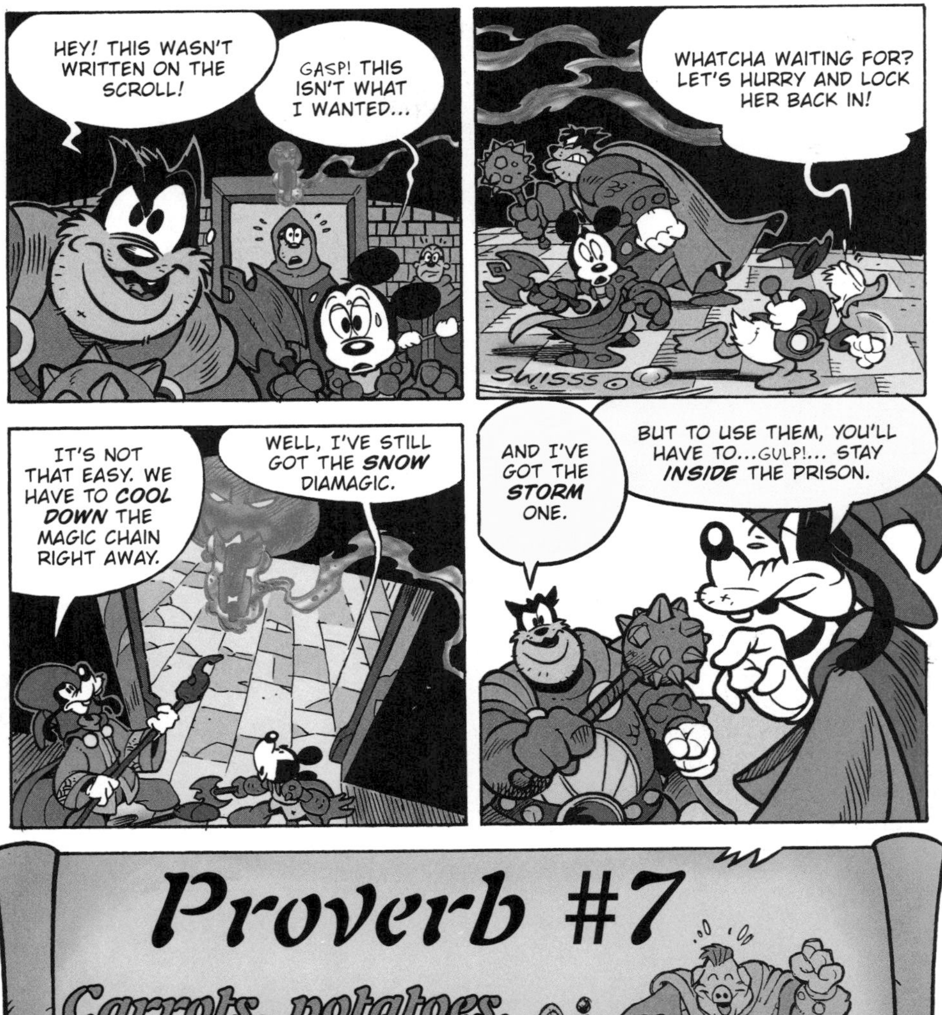
HEY! THIS WASN'T WRITTEN ON THE SCROLL!
GASP! THIS ISN'T WHAT I WANTED...
WHATCHA WAITING FOR? LET'S HURRY AND LOCK HER BACK IN!
SWISSS
IT'S NOT THAT EASY. WE HAVE TO **COOL DOWN** THE MAGIC CHAIN RIGHT AWAY.
WELL, I'VE STILL GOT THE **SNOW** DIAMAGIC.
AND I'VE GOT THE **STORM** ONE.
BUT TO USE THEM, YOU'LL HAVE TO...GULP!... STAY **INSIDE** THE PRISON.

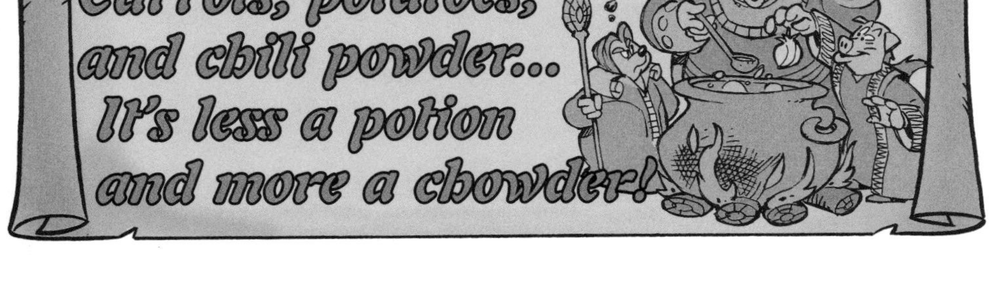
Proverb #7
Carrots, potatoes, and chili powder... It's less a potion and more a chowder!

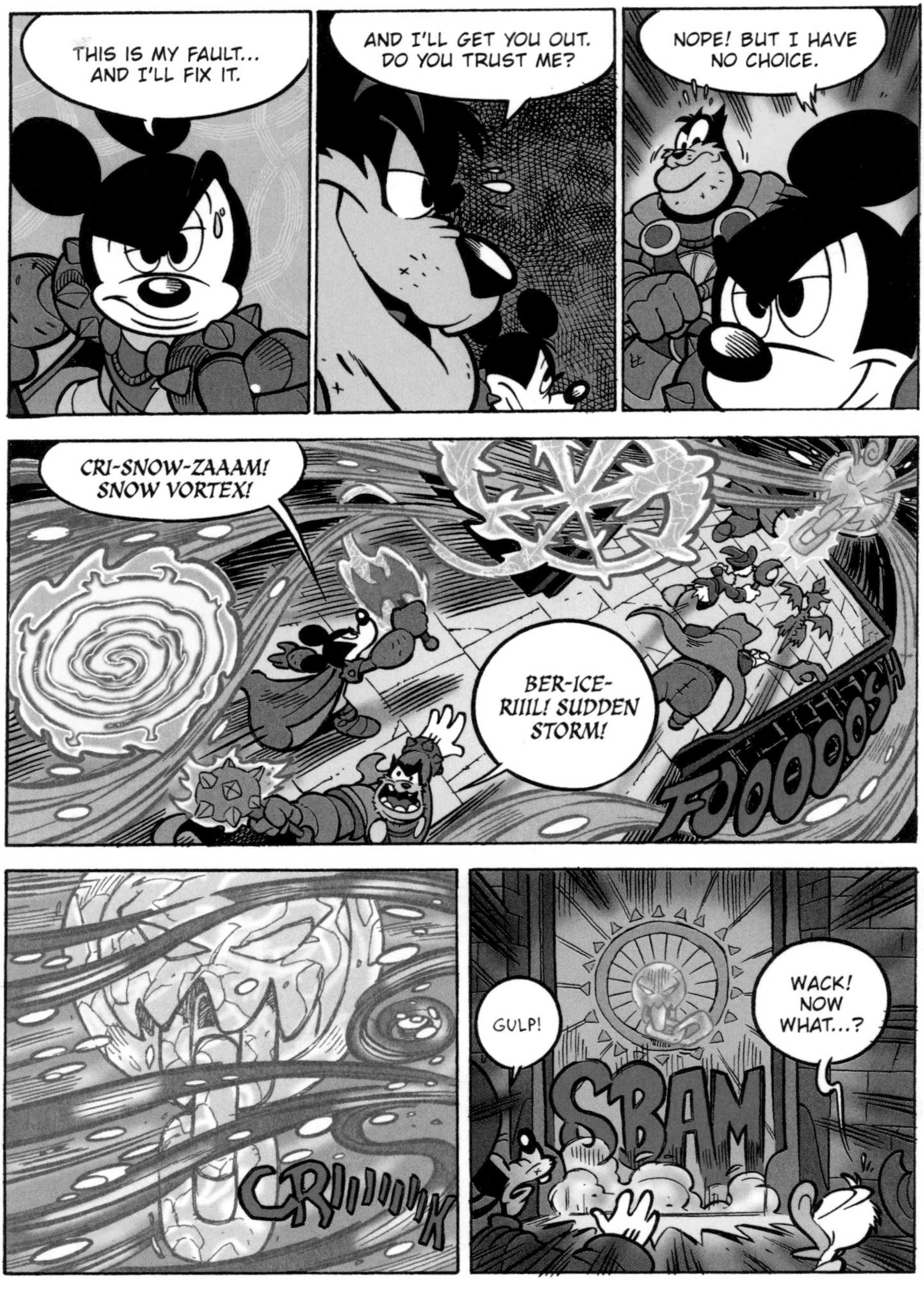
THIS IS MY FAULT... AND I'LL FIX IT.
AND I'LL GET YOU OUT. DO YOU TRUST ME?
NOPE! BUT I HAVE NO CHOICE.
CRI-SNOW-ZAAAM! SNOW VORTEX!
BER-ICE-RIIIL! SUDDEN STORM!
FOOOOOOSH
CRIIIIIIIK
GULP!
WACK! NOW WHAT...?
SBAM

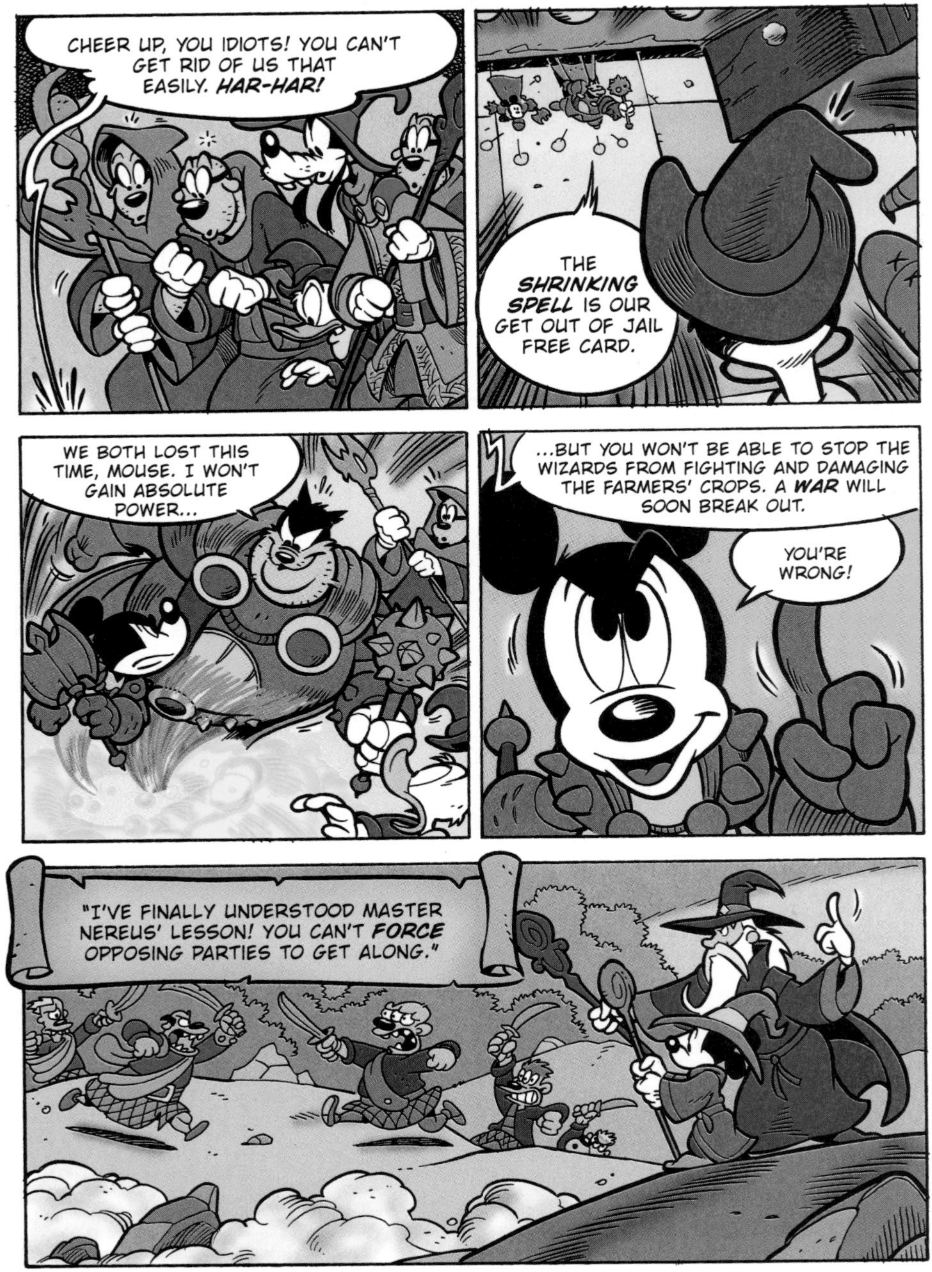
CHEER UP, YOU IDIOTS! YOU CAN'T GET RID OF US THAT EASILY. HAR-HAR!
THE SHRINKING SPELL IS OUR GET OUT OF JAIL FREE CARD.
WE BOTH LOST THIS TIME, MOUSE. I WON'T GAIN ABSOLUTE POWER...
...BUT YOU WON'T BE ABLE TO STOP THE WIZARDS FROM FIGHTING AND DAMAGING THE FARMERS' CROPS. A WAR WILL SOON BREAK OUT.
YOU'RE WRONG!
"I'VE FINALLY UNDERSTOOD MASTER NEREUS' LESSON! YOU CAN'T FORCE OPPOSING PARTIES TO GET ALONG."

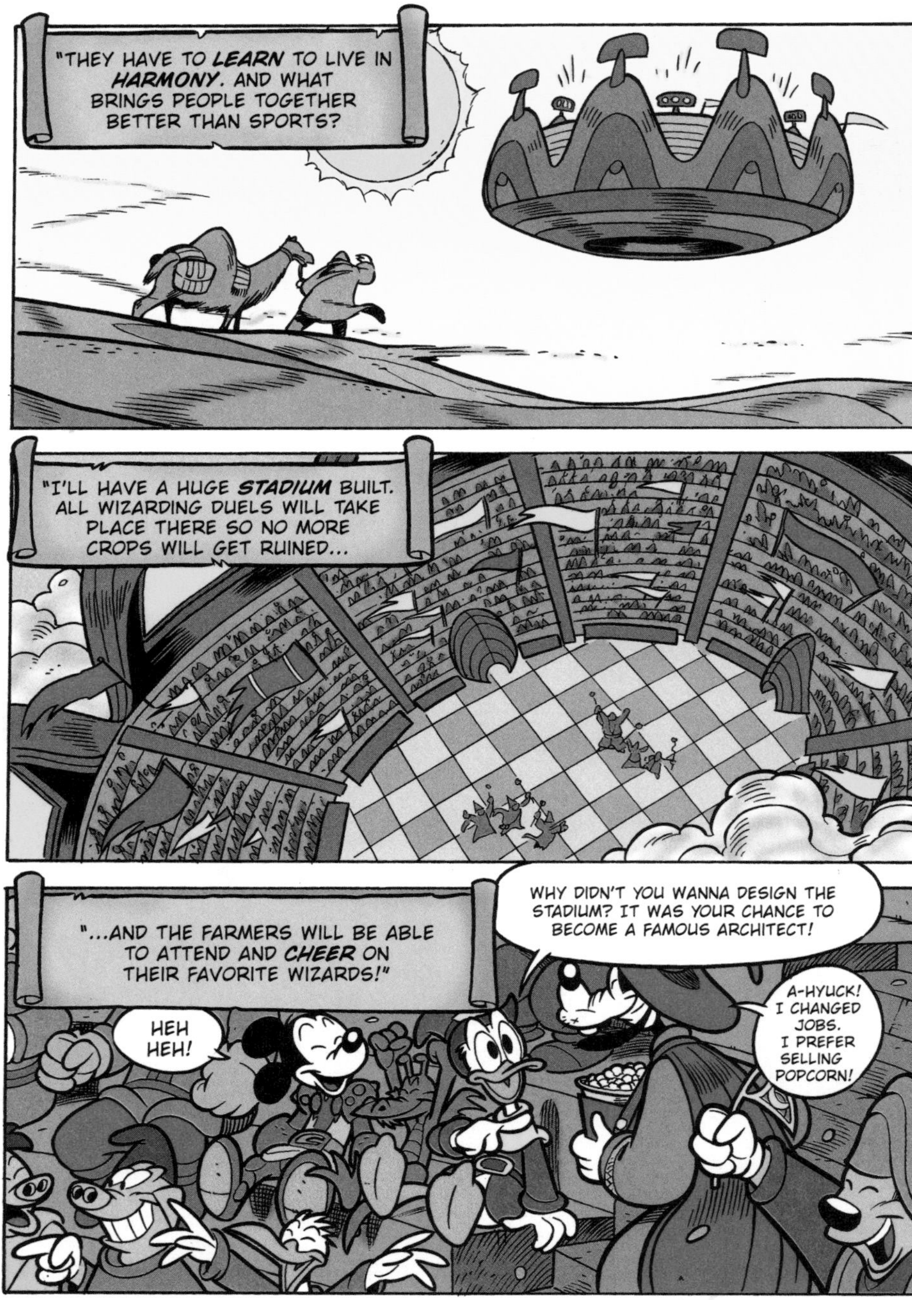
"THEY HAVE TO LEARN TO LIVE IN HARMONY. AND WHAT BRINGS PEOPLE TOGETHER BETTER THAN SPORTS?
"I'LL HAVE A HUGE STADIUM BUILT. ALL WIZARDING DUELS WILL TAKE PLACE THERE SO NO MORE CROPS WILL GET RUINED...
"...AND THE FARMERS WILL BE ABLE TO ATTEND AND CHEER ON THEIR FAVORITE WIZARDS!"
WHY DIDN'T YOU WANNA DESIGN THE STADIUM? IT WAS YOUR CHANCE TO BECOME A FAMOUS ARCHITECT!
HEH HEH!
A-HYUCK! I CHANGED JOBS. I PREFER SELLING POPCORN!

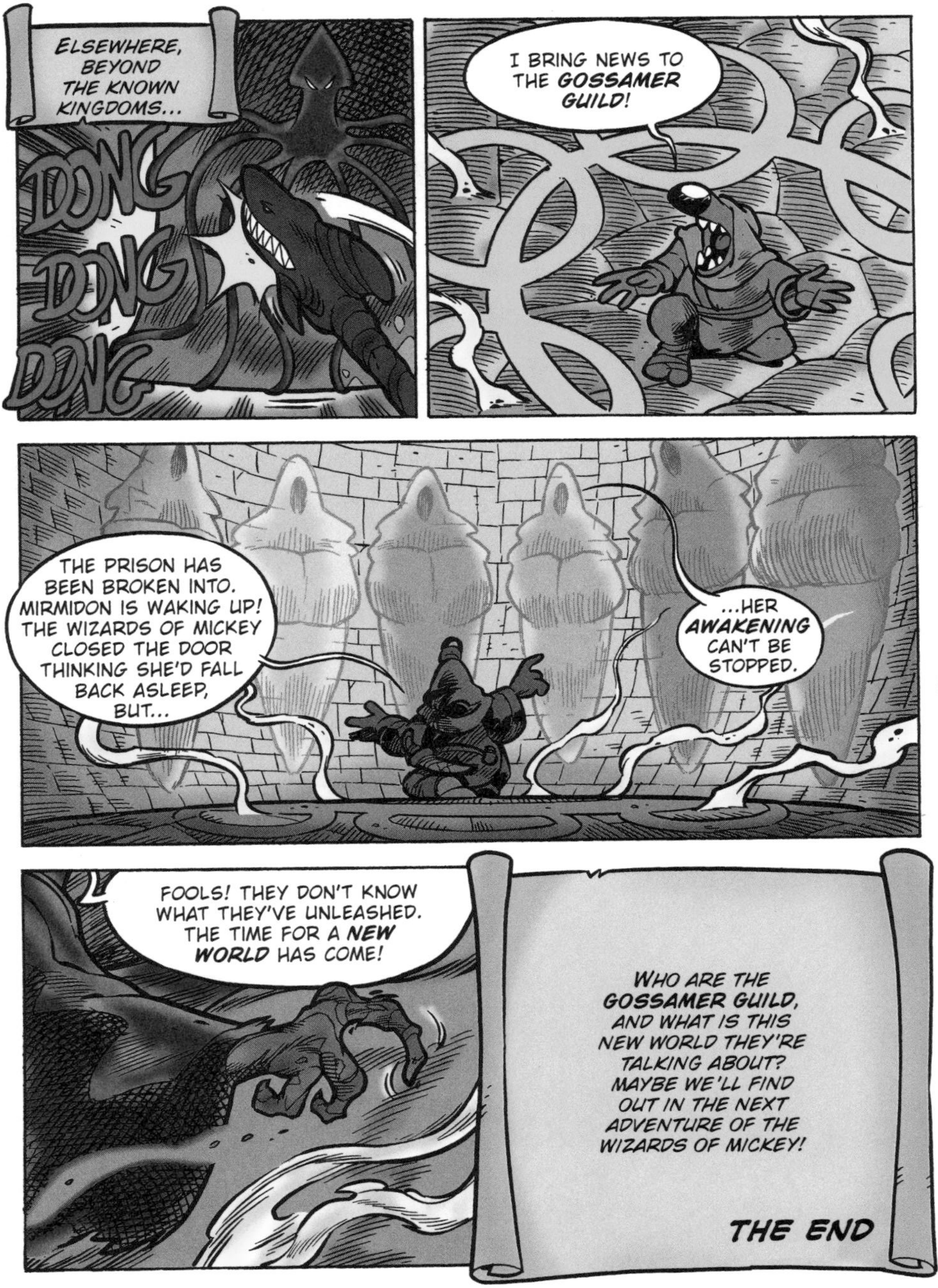
ELSEWHERE, BEYOND THE KNOWN KINGDOMS...
DONG DONG DONG
I BRING NEWS TO THE GOSSAMER GUILD!
THE PRISON HAS BEEN BROKEN INTO. MIRMIDON IS WAKING UP! THE WIZARDS OF MICKEY CLOSED THE DOOR THINKING SHE'D FALL BACK ASLEEP, BUT...
...HER AWAKENING CAN'T BE STOPPED.
FOOLS! THEY DON'T KNOW WHAT THEY'VE UNLEASHED. THE TIME FOR A NEW WORLD HAS COME!
WHO ARE THE GOSSAMER GUILD, AND WHAT IS THIS NEW WORLD THEY'RE TALKING ABOUT? MAYBE WE'LL FIND OUT IN THE NEXT ADVENTURE OF THE WIZARDS OF MICKEY!
THE END

Wizards of Mickey

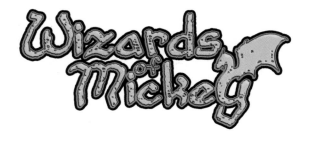

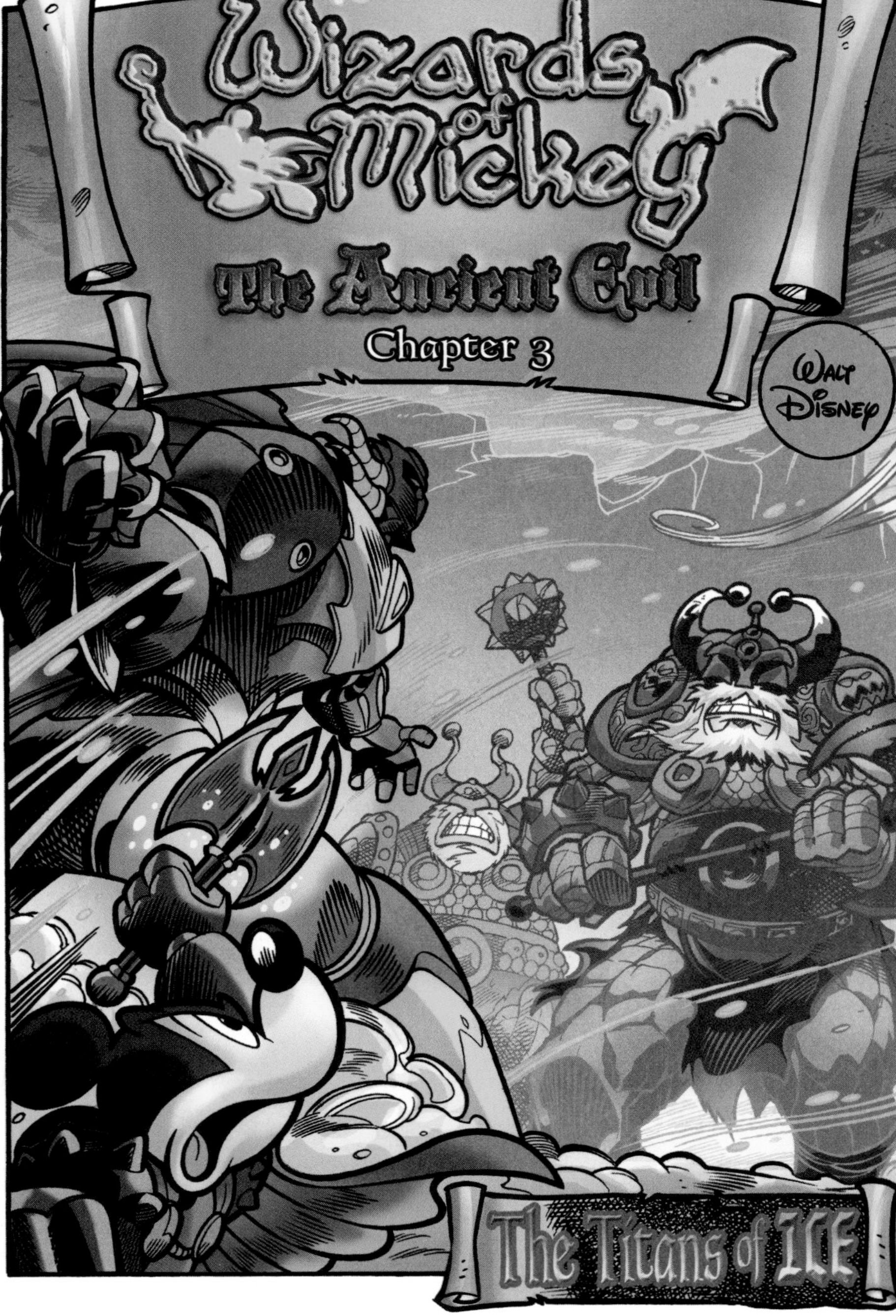
Wizards of Mickey
The Ancient Evil
Chapter 3
Walt Disney
The Titans of ICE

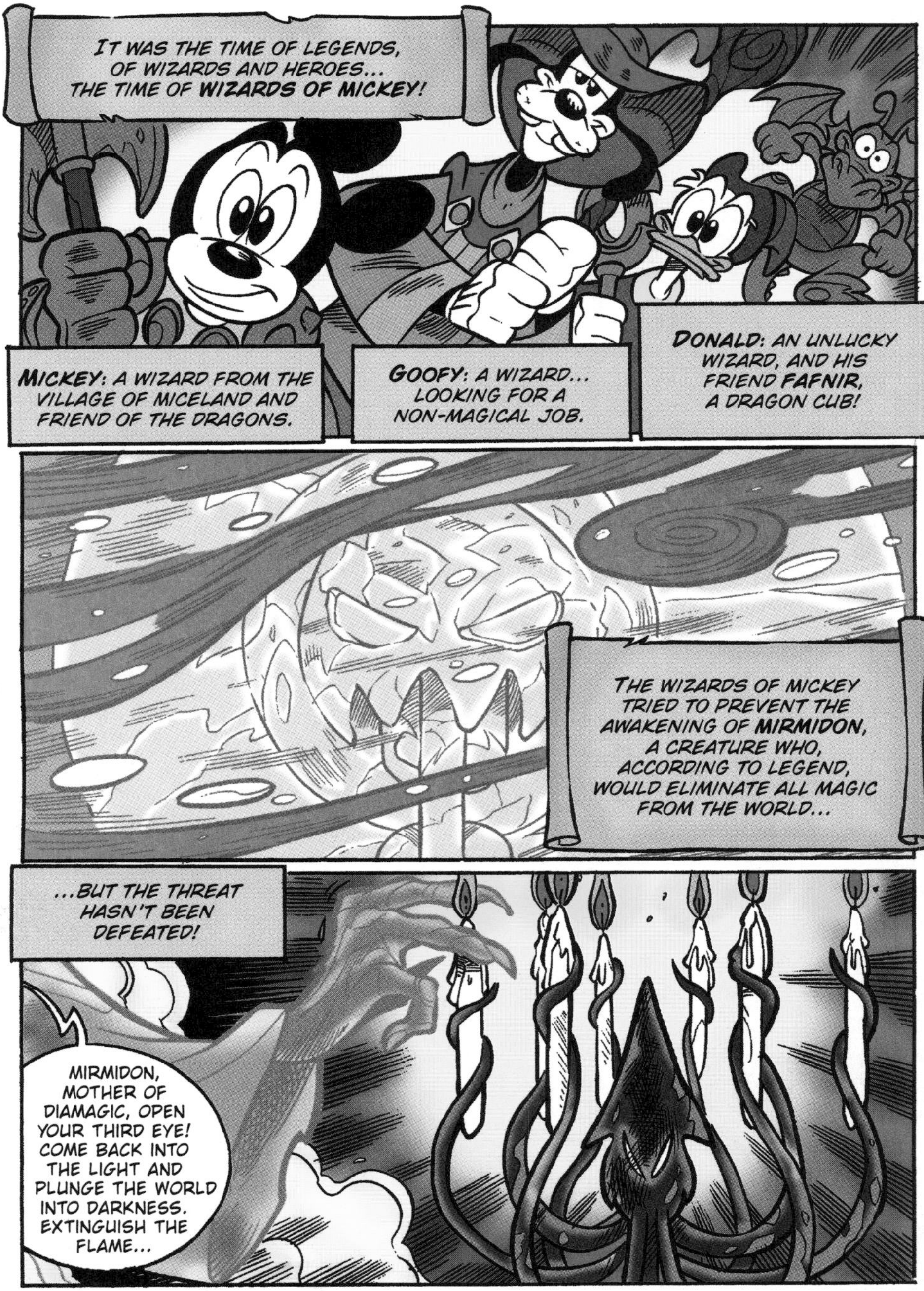

IT WAS THE TIME OF LEGENDS, OF WIZARDS AND HEROES... THE TIME OF WIZARDS OF MICKEY!
MICKEY: A WIZARD FROM THE VILLAGE OF MICELAND AND FRIEND OF THE DRAGONS.
GOOFY: A WIZARD... LOOKING FOR A NON-MAGICAL JOB.
DONALD: AN UNLUCKY WIZARD, AND HIS FRIEND FAFNIR, A DRAGON CUB!
THE WIZARDS OF MICKEY TRIED TO PREVENT THE AWAKENING OF MIRMIDON, A CREATURE WHO, ACCORDING TO LEGEND, WOULD ELIMINATE ALL MAGIC FROM THE WORLD...
...BUT THE THREAT HASN'T BEEN DEFEATED!
MIRMIDON, MOTHER OF DIAMAGIC, OPEN YOUR THIRD EYE! COME BACK INTO THE LIGHT AND PLUNGE THE WORLD INTO DARKNESS. EXTINGUISH THE FLAME...

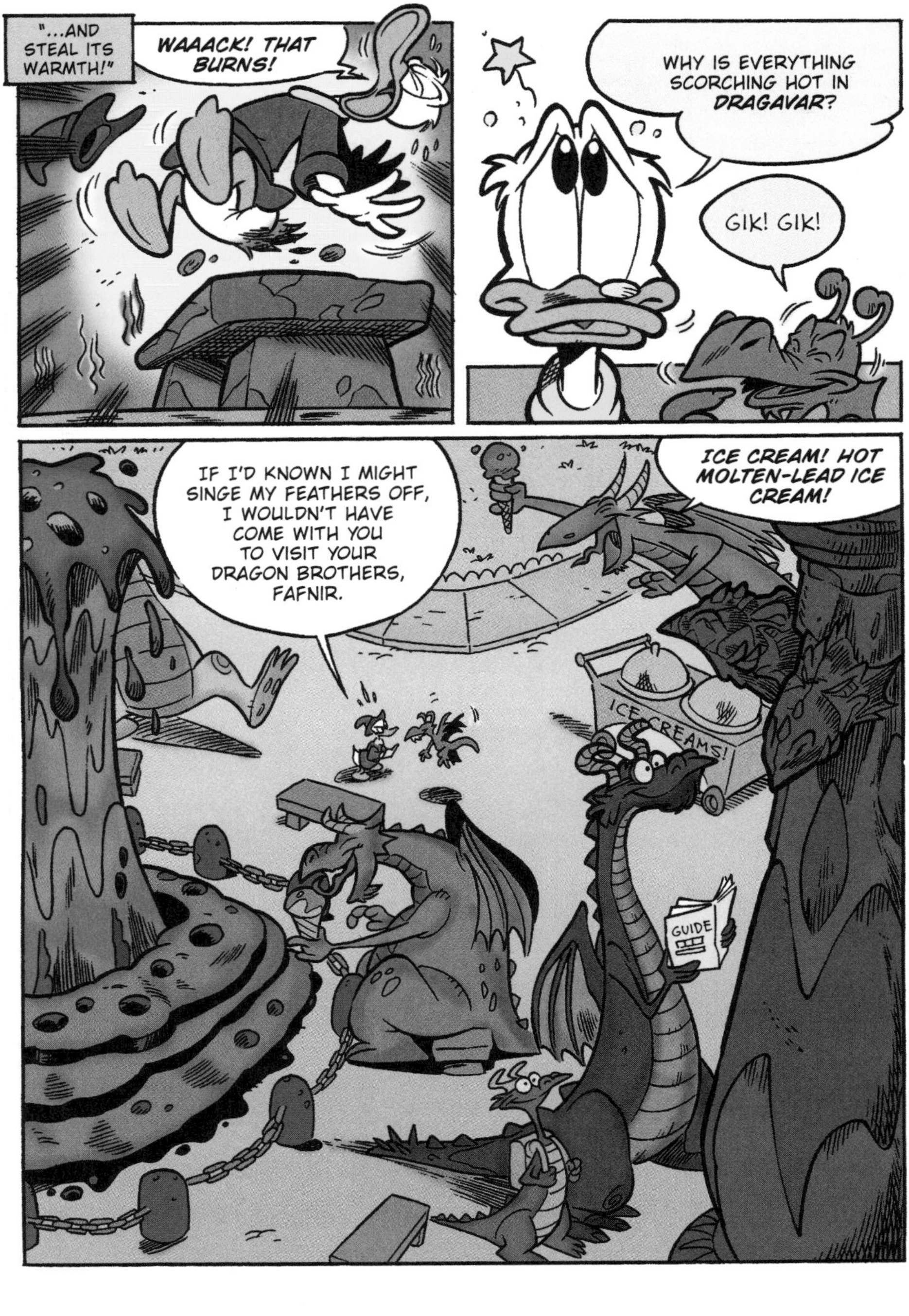
"...AND STEAL ITS WARMTH!"
WAAACK! THAT BURNS!
WHY IS EVERYTHING SCORCHING HOT IN DRAGAVAR?
GIK! GIK!
IF I'D KNOWN I MIGHT SINGE MY FEATHERS OFF, I WOULDN'T HAVE COME WITH YOU TO VISIT YOUR DRAGON BROTHERS, FAFNIR.
ICE CREAM! HOT MOLTEN-LEAD ICE CREAM!
ICE CREAMS!
GUIDE

C'MON, DONALD! TRY THIS. IT'S A DELICACY, A SORT OF CURE-ALL.

YUM!

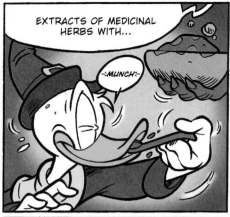

EXTRACTS OF MEDICINAL HERBS WITH...

~MUNCH~

...EXTRA-SPICY *CHILIES!*

THIS IS THE FIRST TIME I'VE SEEN A NO-SCALES SPITTING FIRE! YOUR FRIEND COULD BE AN *HONORARY DRAGON.*

YERP! YERP!

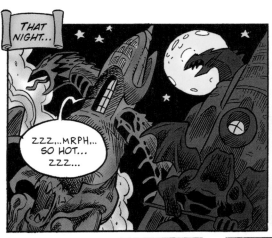

THAT NIGHT...

ZZZ...MRPH... SO HOT... ZZZ...

MMPH... COOL... ICE... ZZZ...

ZZZ...OOF...NOW IT'S TOO MUCH...MRFH...

MMPH...COLD... BRRR, BRRR...

PUT OUT THE FLAME, COOL DOWN THE FURNACE...

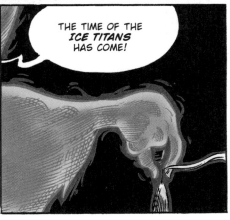

THE TIME OF THE *ICE TITANS* HAS COME!

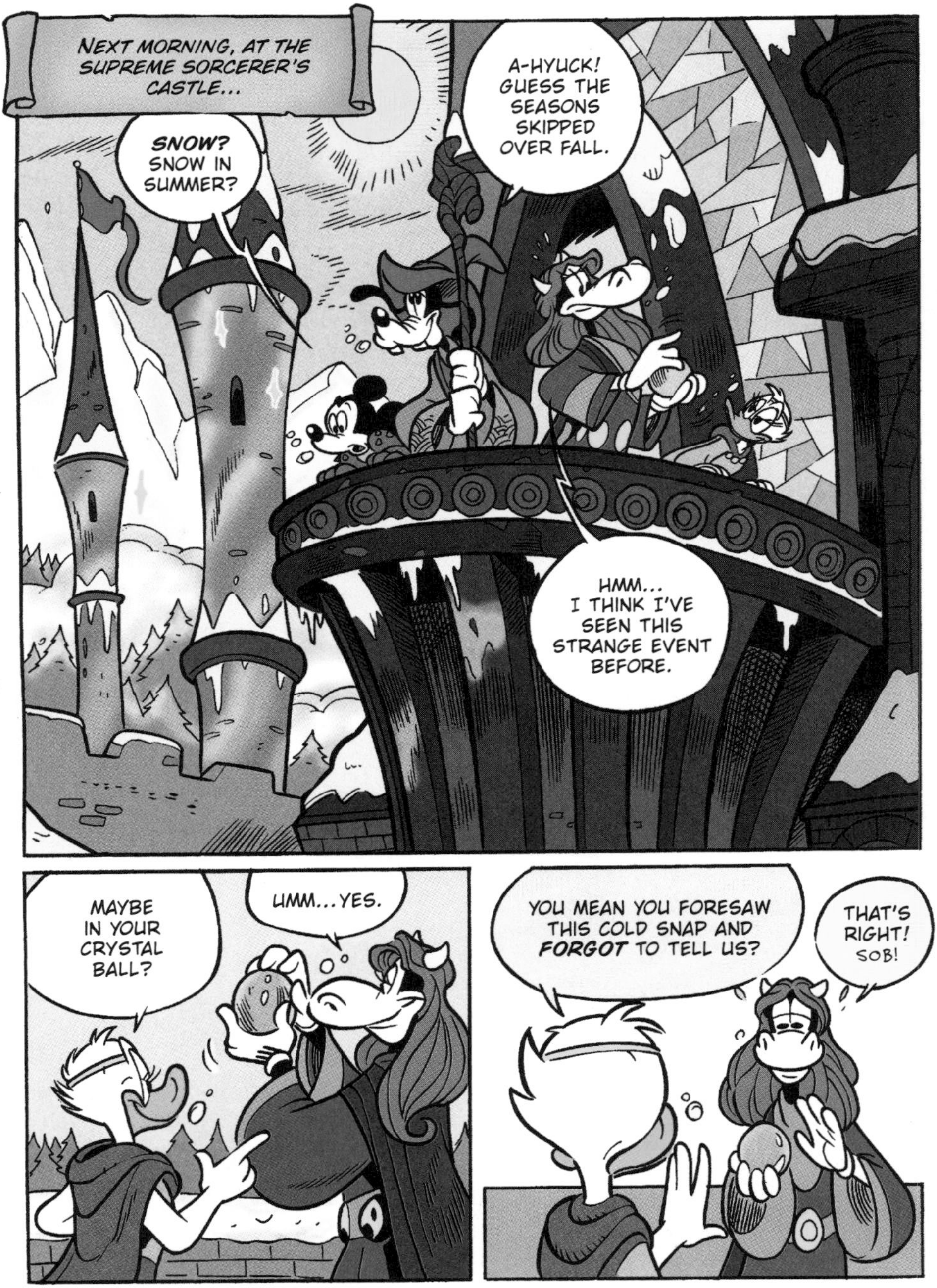
NEXT MORNING, AT THE SUPREME SORCERER'S CASTLE...
SNOW? SNOW IN SUMMER?
A-HYUCK! GUESS THE SEASONS SKIPPED OVER FALL.
HMM... I THINK I'VE SEEN THIS STRANGE EVENT BEFORE.
MAYBE IN YOUR CRYSTAL BALL?
UMM...YES.
YOU MEAN YOU FORESAW THIS COLD SNAP AND FORGOT TO TELL US?
THAT'S RIGHT! SOB!

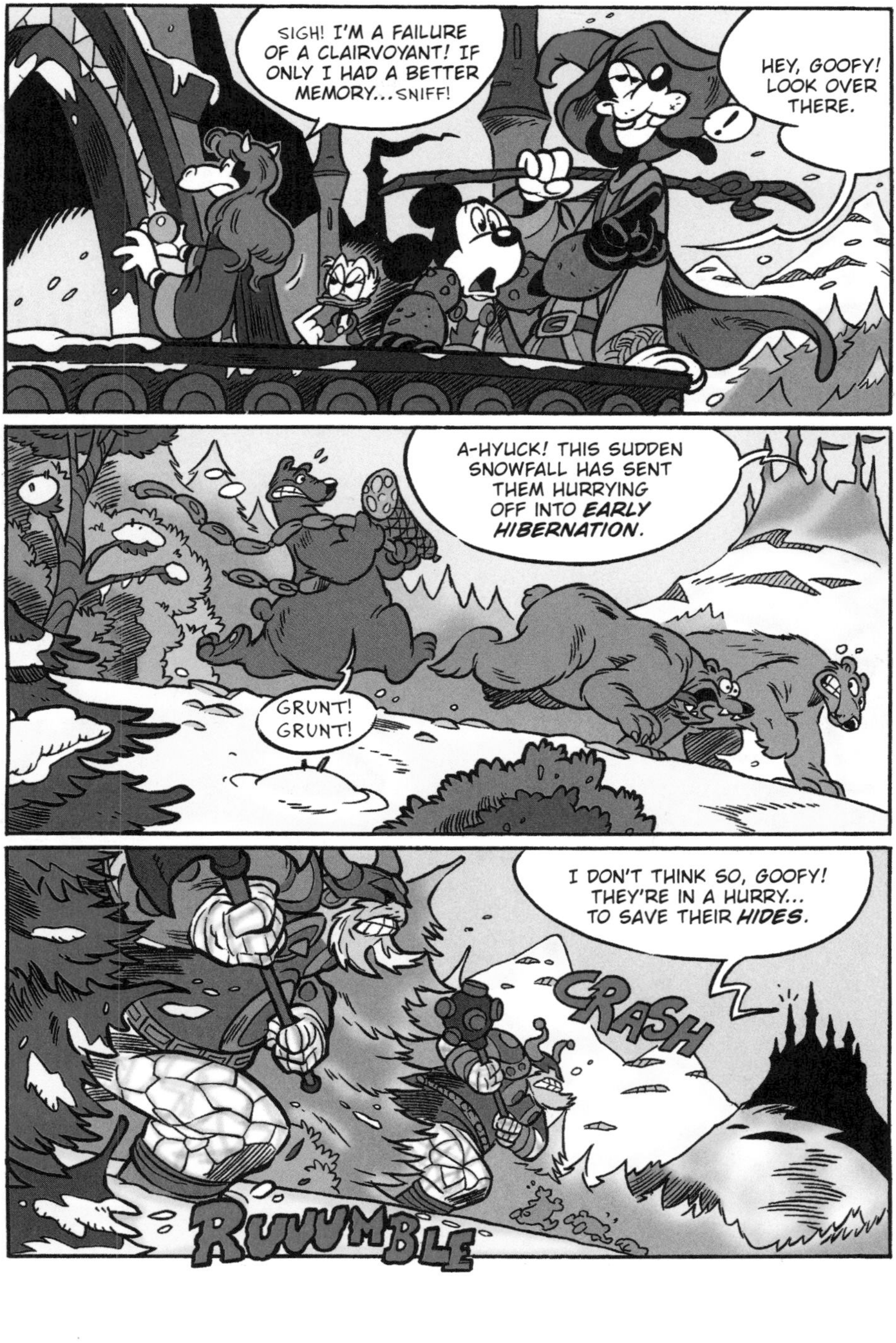

SIGH! I'M A FAILURE OF A CLAIRVOYANT! IF ONLY I HAD A BETTER MEMORY... SNIFF!
HEY, GOOFY! LOOK OVER THERE.
!
A-HYUCK! THIS SUDDEN SNOWFALL HAS SENT THEM HURRYING OFF INTO *EARLY HIBERNATION*.
GRUNT! GRUNT!
I DON'T THINK SO, GOOFY! THEY'RE IN A HURRY... TO SAVE THEIR *HIDES*.
CRASH
RUUUMBLE

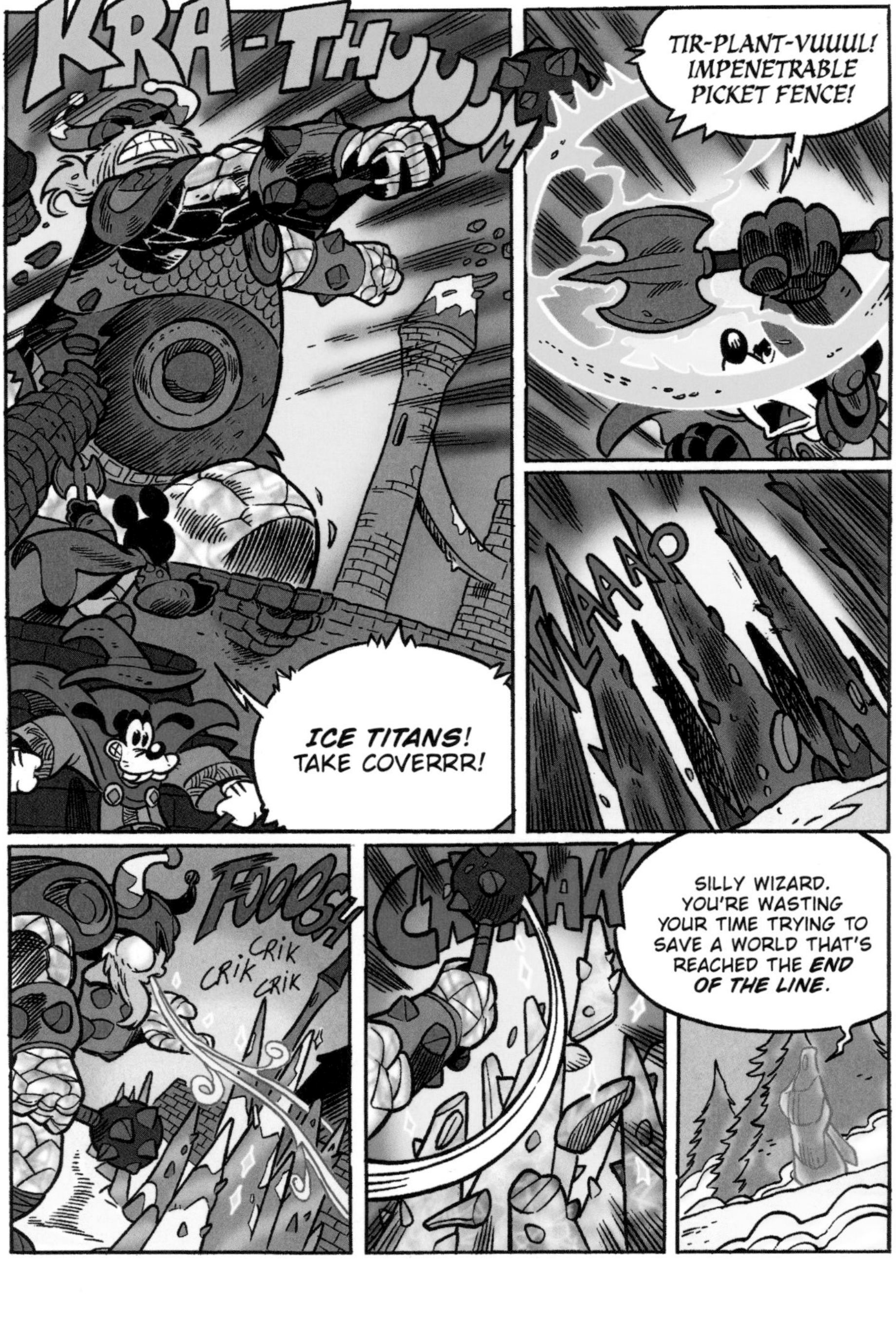
KRA-
TIR-PLANT-VUUUL! IMPENETRABLE PICKET FENCE!
ICE TITANS! TAKE COVERRR!
FOOOSH
CRIK CRIK CRIK
SILLY WIZARD. YOU'RE WASTING YOUR TIME TRYING TO SAVE A WORLD THAT'S REACHED THE END OF THE LINE.

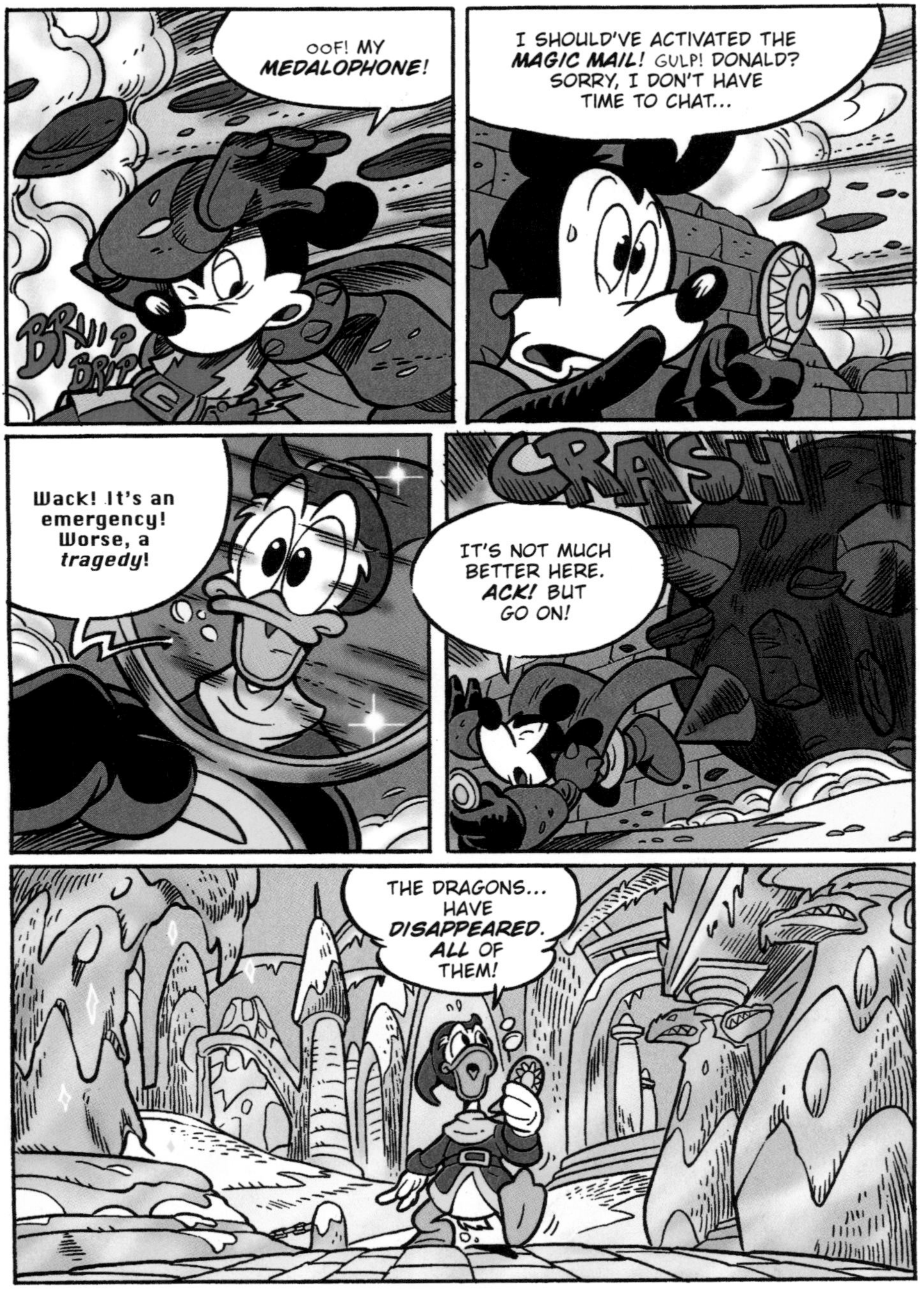

OOF! MY *MEDALOPHONE!*
BRRIP BRIP
I SHOULD'VE ACTIVATED THE *MAGIC MAIL!* GULP! DONALD? SORRY, I DON'T HAVE TIME TO CHAT...
Wack! It's an emergency! Worse, a *tragedy*!
CRASH
IT'S NOT MUCH BETTER HERE. *ACK!* BUT GO ON!
THE DRAGONS... HAVE *DISAPPEARED. ALL* OF THEM!

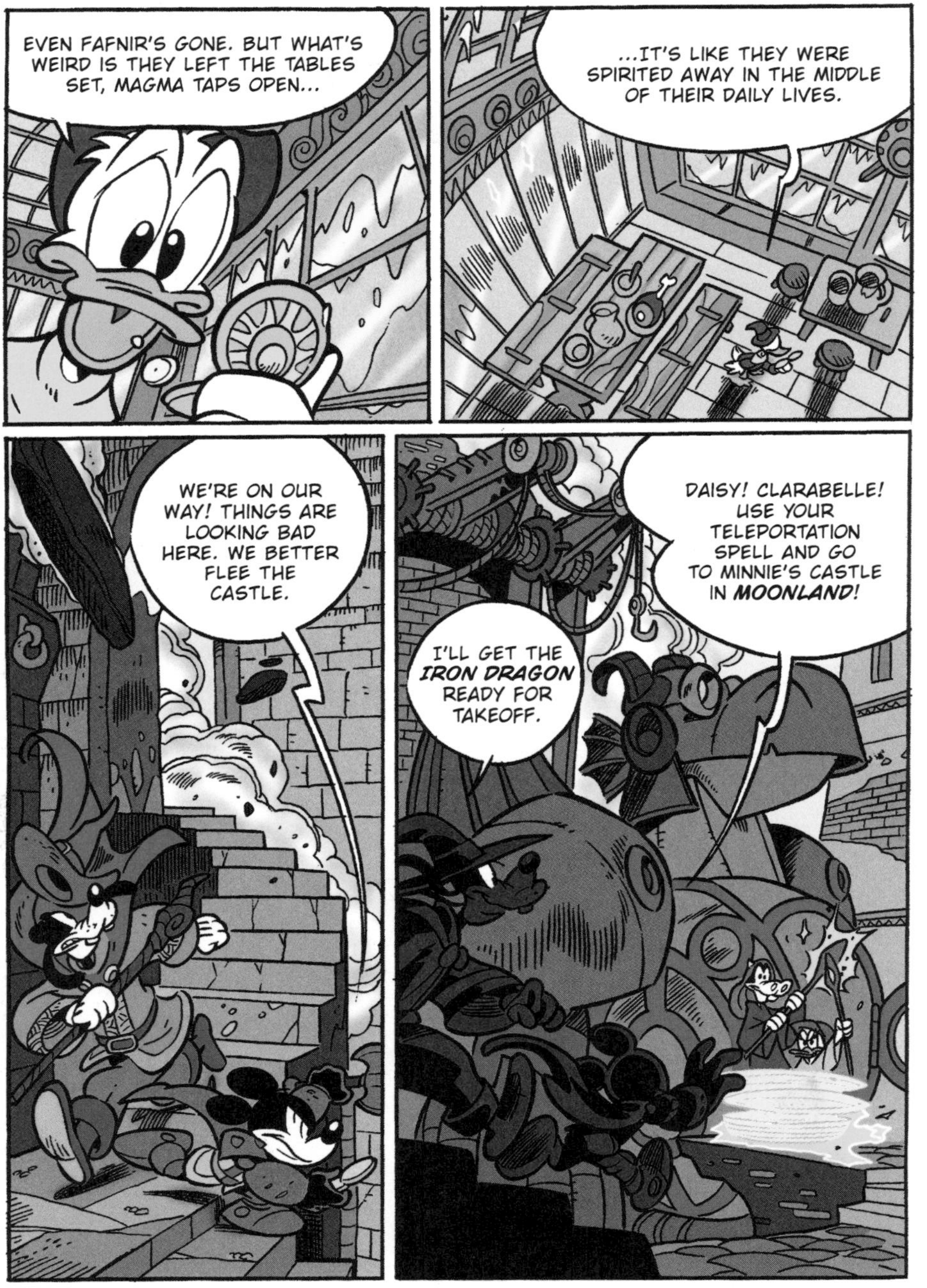
EVEN FAFNIR'S GONE. BUT WHAT'S WEIRD IS THEY LEFT THE TABLES SET, MAGMA TAPS OPEN...
...IT'S LIKE THEY WERE SPIRITED AWAY IN THE MIDDLE OF THEIR DAILY LIVES.
WE'RE ON OUR WAY! THINGS ARE LOOKING BAD HERE. WE BETTER FLEE THE CASTLE.
DAISY! CLARABELLE! USE YOUR TELEPORTATION SPELL AND GO TO MINNIE'S CASTLE IN MOONLAND!
I'LL GET THE IRON DRAGON READY FOR TAKEOFF.

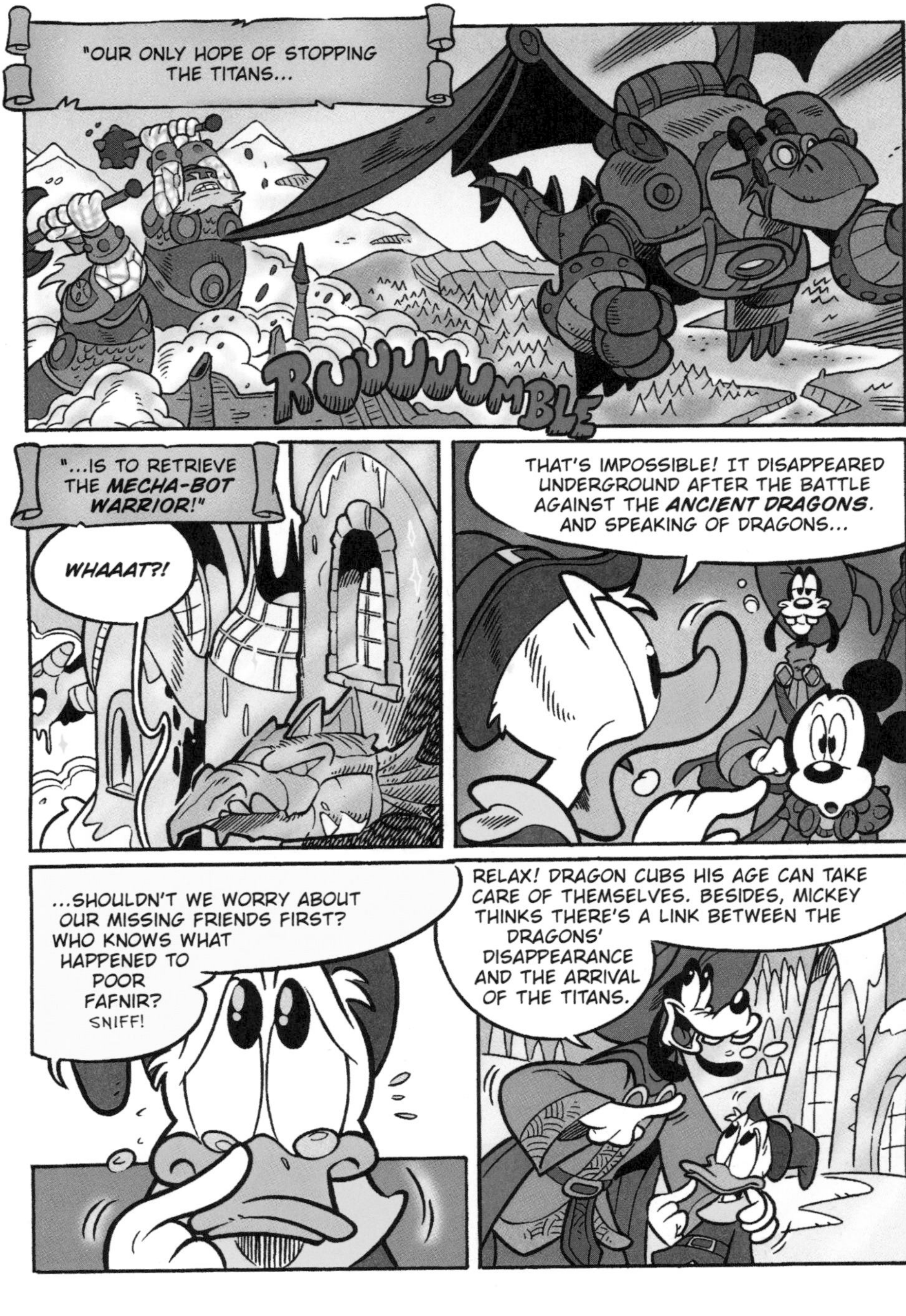
"OUR ONLY HOPE OF STOPPING THE TITANS...
RUUUUUUMBLE
"...IS TO RETRIEVE THE MECHA-BOT WARRIOR!"
WHAAAT?!
THAT'S IMPOSSIBLE! IT DISAPPEARED UNDERGROUND AFTER THE BATTLE AGAINST THE ANCIENT DRAGONS. AND SPEAKING OF DRAGONS...
...SHOULDN'T WE WORRY ABOUT OUR MISSING FRIENDS FIRST? WHO KNOWS WHAT HAPPENED TO POOR FAFNIR? SNIFF!
RELAX! DRAGON CUBS HIS AGE CAN TAKE CARE OF THEMSELVES. BESIDES, MICKEY THINKS THERE'S A LINK BETWEEN THE DRAGONS' DISAPPEARANCE AND THE ARRIVAL OF THE TITANS.

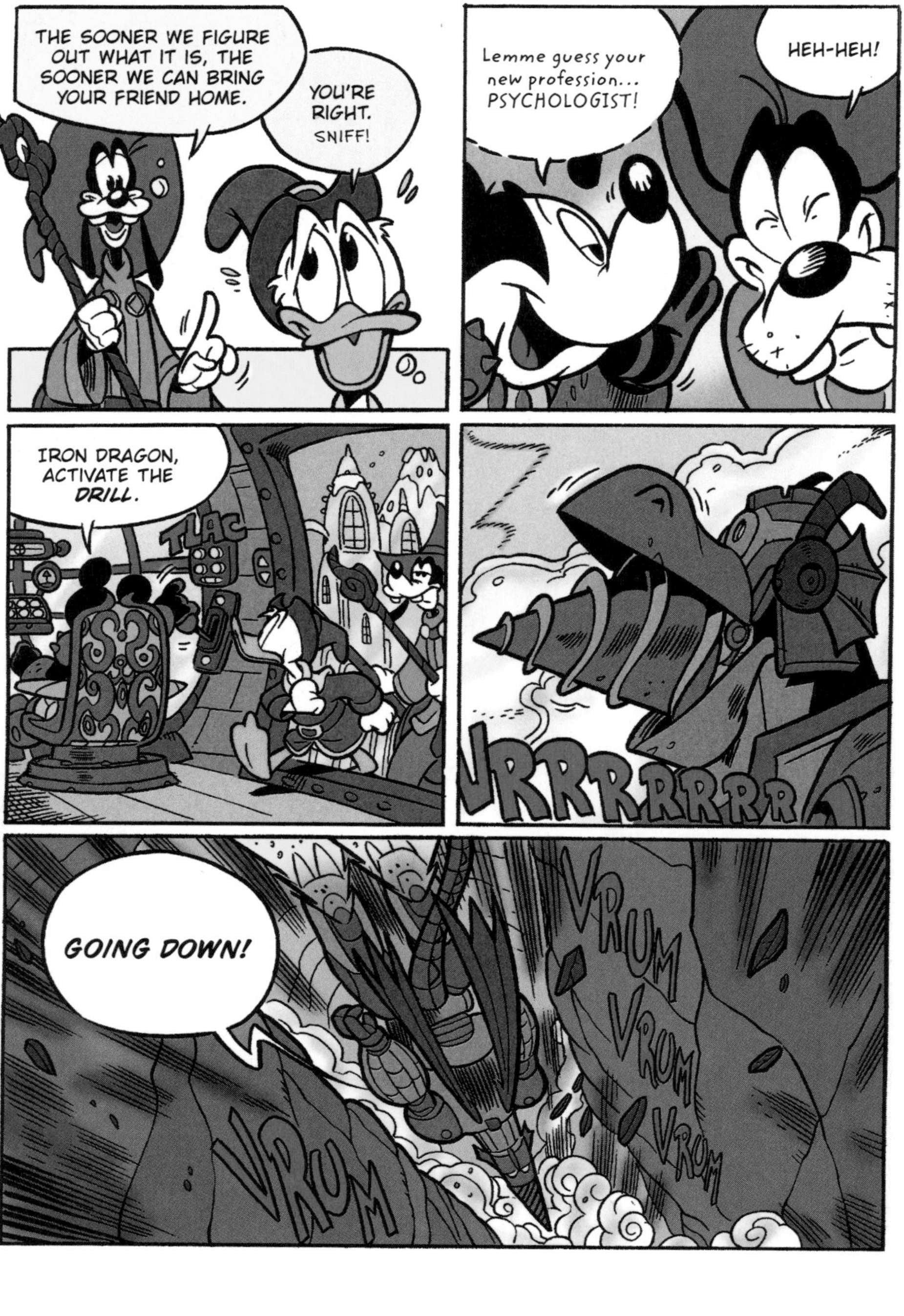
THE SOONER WE FIGURE OUT WHAT IT IS, THE SOONER WE CAN BRING YOUR FRIEND HOME.
YOU'RE RIGHT. SNIFF!
Lemme guess your new profession... PSYCHOLOGIST!
HEH-HEH!
IRON DRAGON, ACTIVATE THE DRILL.
TLAC
VRRRRRRRR
GOING DOWN!
VRUM
VRUM
VRUM
VRUM
VRUM

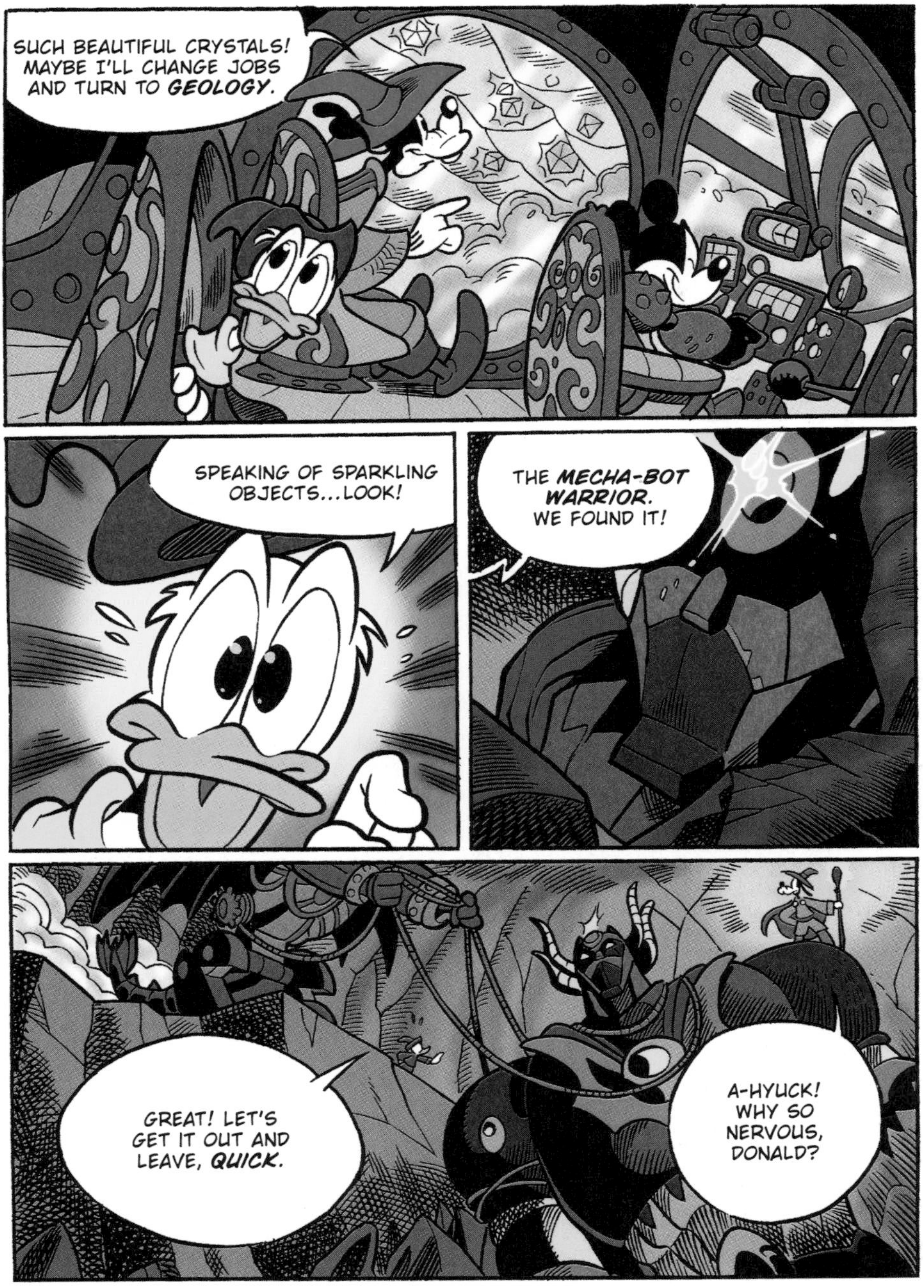
SUCH BEAUTIFUL CRYSTALS! MAYBE I'LL CHANGE JOBS AND TURN TO GEOLOGY.
SPEAKING OF SPARKLING OBJECTS...LOOK!
THE MECHA-BOT WARRIOR. WE FOUND IT!
GREAT! LET'S GET IT OUT AND LEAVE, QUICK.
A-HYUCK! WHY SO NERVOUS, DONALD?

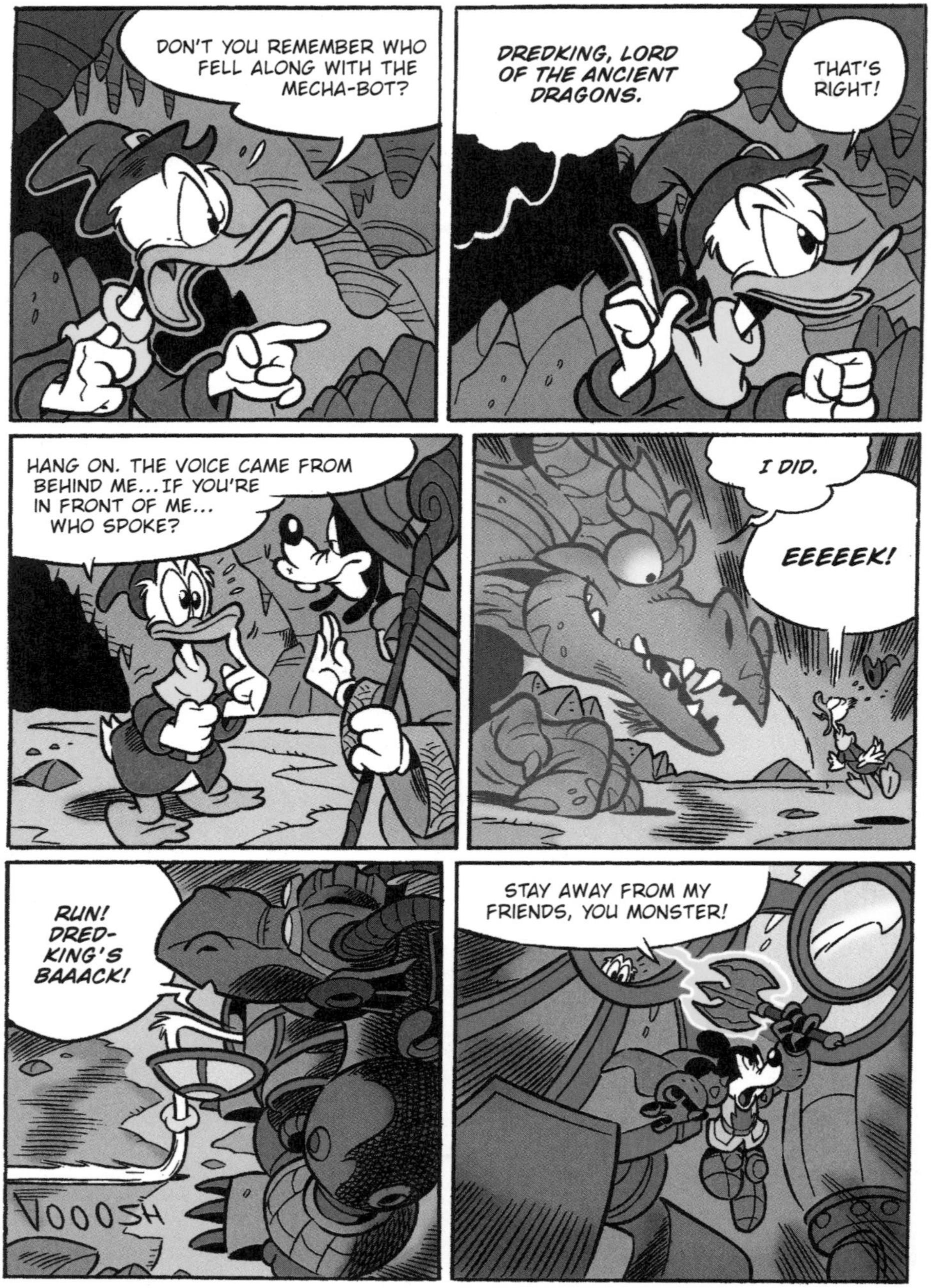
DON'T YOU REMEMBER WHO FELL ALONG WITH THE MECHA-BOT?
DREDKING, LORD OF THE ANCIENT DRAGONS.
THAT'S RIGHT!
HANG ON. THE VOICE CAME FROM BEHIND ME...IF YOU'RE IN FRONT OF ME... WHO SPOKE?
I DID.
EEEEEK!
RUN! DRED-KING'S BAAACK!
VOOOSH
STAY AWAY FROM MY FRIENDS, YOU MONSTER!

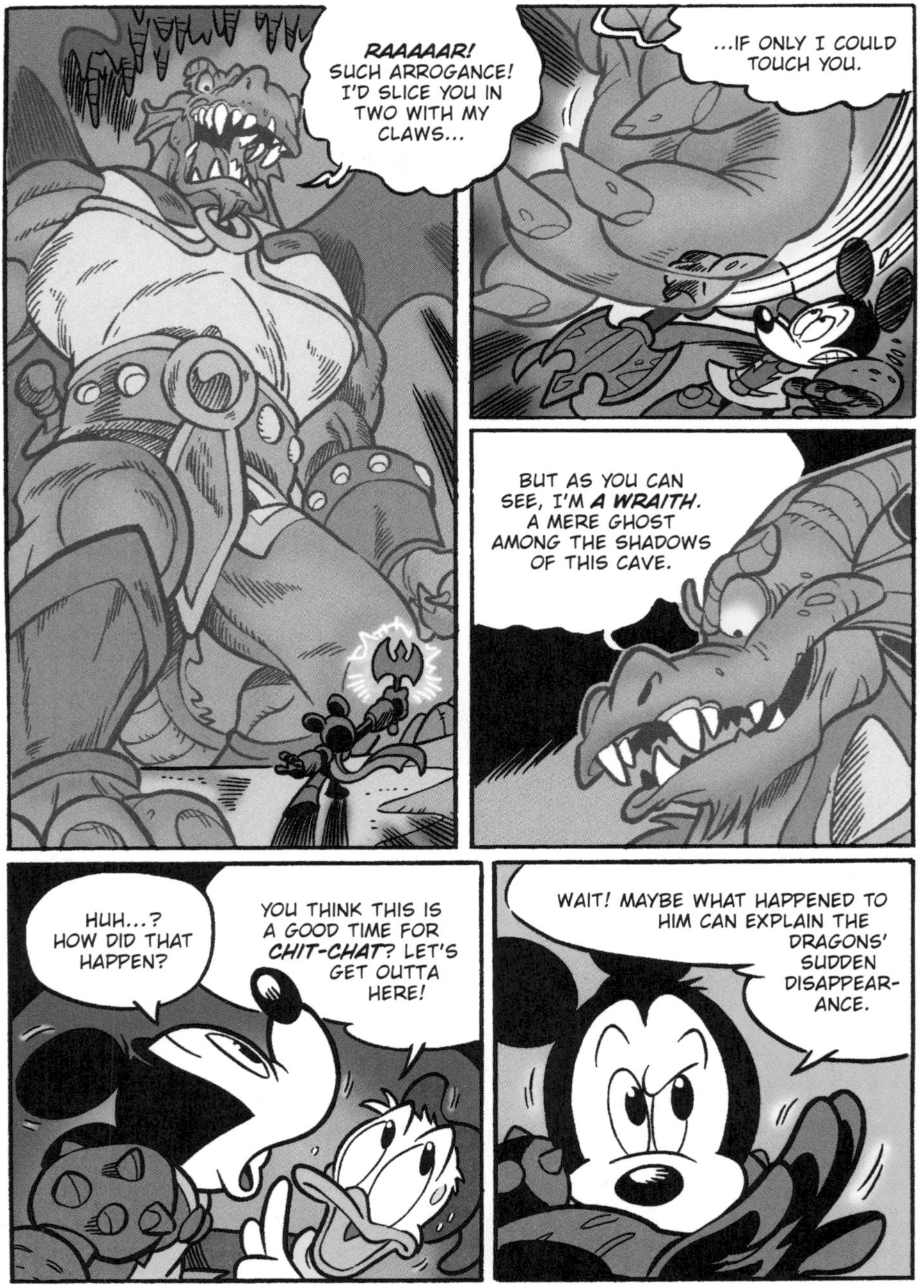
RAAAAAR! SUCH ARROGANCE! I'D SLICE YOU IN TWO WITH MY CLAWS...
...IF ONLY I COULD TOUCH YOU.
BUT AS YOU CAN SEE, I'M A WRAITH. A MERE GHOST AMONG THE SHADOWS OF THIS CAVE.
HUH...? HOW DID THAT HAPPEN?
YOU THINK THIS IS A GOOD TIME FOR CHIT-CHAT? LET'S GET OUTTA HERE!
WAIT! MAYBE WHAT HAPPENED TO HIM CAN EXPLAIN THE DRAGONS' SUDDEN DISAPPEAR-ANCE.

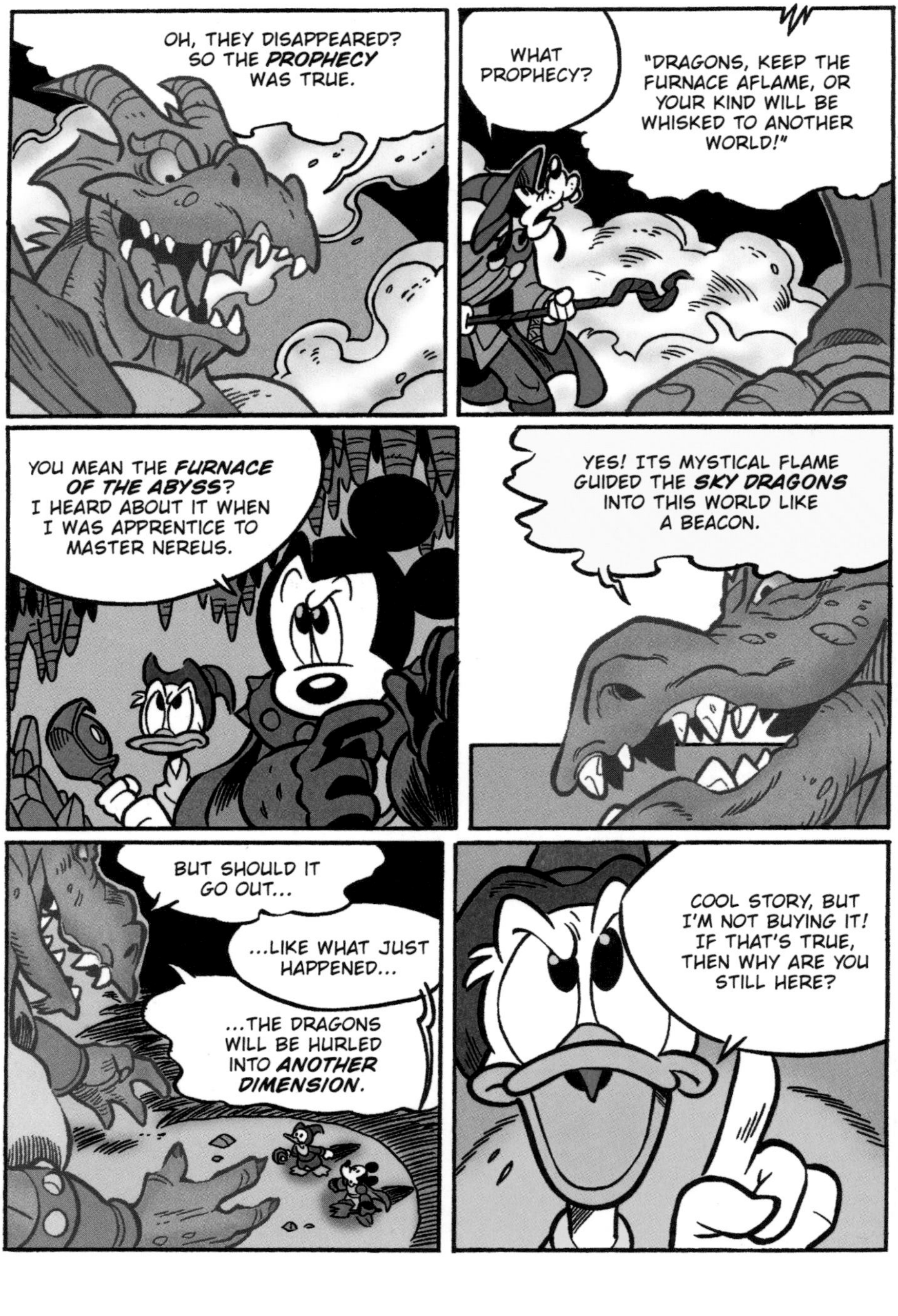
OH, THEY DISAPPEARED? SO THE *PROPHECY* WAS TRUE.
WHAT PROPHECY?
"DRAGONS, KEEP THE FURNACE AFLAME, OR YOUR KIND WILL BE WHISKED TO ANOTHER WORLD!"
YOU MEAN THE *FURNACE OF THE ABYSS*? I HEARD ABOUT IT WHEN I WAS APPRENTICE TO MASTER NEREUS.
YES! ITS MYSTICAL FLAME GUIDED THE *SKY DRAGONS* INTO THIS WORLD LIKE A BEACON.
BUT SHOULD IT GO OUT...
...LIKE WHAT JUST HAPPENED...
...THE DRAGONS WILL BE HURLED INTO *ANOTHER DIMENSION*.
COOL STORY, BUT I'M NOT BUYING IT! IF THAT'S TRUE, THEN WHY ARE YOU STILL HERE?

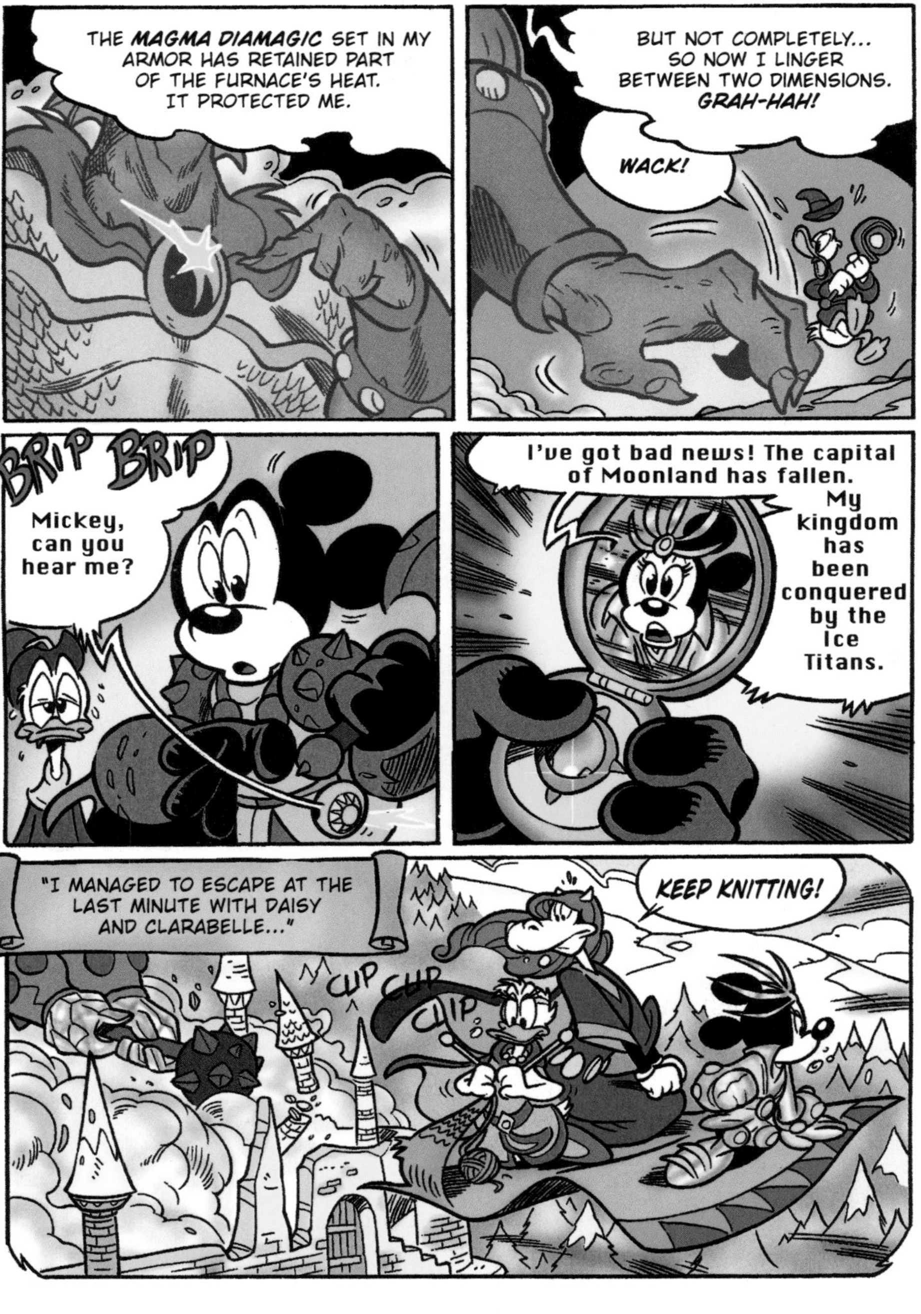
THE MAGMA DIAMAGIC SET IN MY ARMOR HAS RETAINED PART OF THE FURNACE'S HEAT. IT PROTECTED ME.
BUT NOT COMPLETELY... SO NOW I LINGER BETWEEN TWO DIMENSIONS. GRAH-HAH!
WACK!
BRIP BRIP
Mickey, can you hear me?
I've got bad news! The capital of Moonland has fallen.
My kingdom has been conquered by the Ice Titans.
"I MANAGED TO ESCAPE AT THE LAST MINUTE WITH DAISY AND CLARABELLE..."
KEEP KNITTING!
CLIP CLIP CLIP

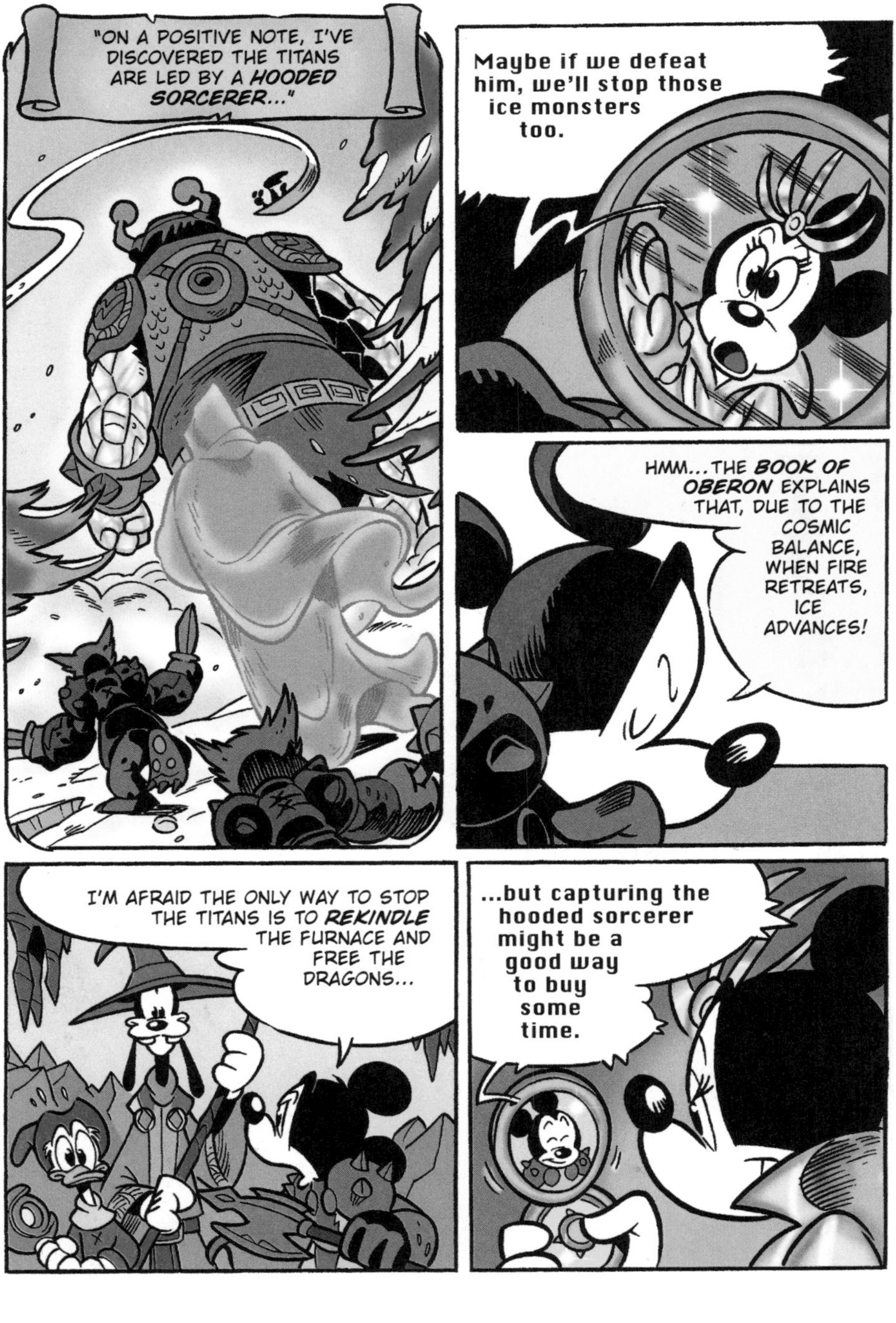
"ON A POSITIVE NOTE, I'VE DISCOVERED THE TITANS ARE LED BY A HOODED SORCERER..."
Maybe if we defeat him, we'll stop those ice monsters too.
HMM...THE BOOK OF OBERON EXPLAINS THAT, DUE TO THE COSMIC BALANCE, WHEN FIRE RETREATS, ICE ADVANCES!
I'M AFRAID THE ONLY WAY TO STOP THE TITANS IS TO REKINDLE THE FURNACE AND FREE THE DRAGONS...
...but capturing the hooded sorcerer might be a good way to buy some time.

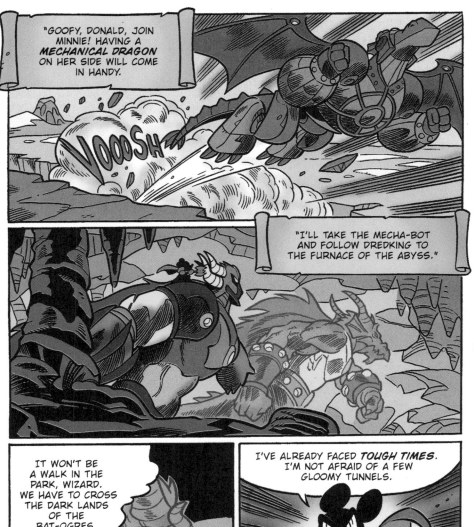

"GOOFY, DONALD, JOIN MINNIE! HAVING A **MECHANICAL DRAGON** ON HER SIDE WILL COME IN HANDY.

VOOOSH

"I'LL TAKE THE MECHA-BOT AND FOLLOW DREDKING TO THE FURNACE OF THE ABYSS."

IT WON'T BE A WALK IN THE PARK, WIZARD. WE HAVE TO CROSS THE DARK LANDS OF THE BAT-OGRES.

I'VE ALREADY FACED **TOUGH TIMES**. I'M NOT AFRAID OF A FEW GLOOMY TUNNELS.

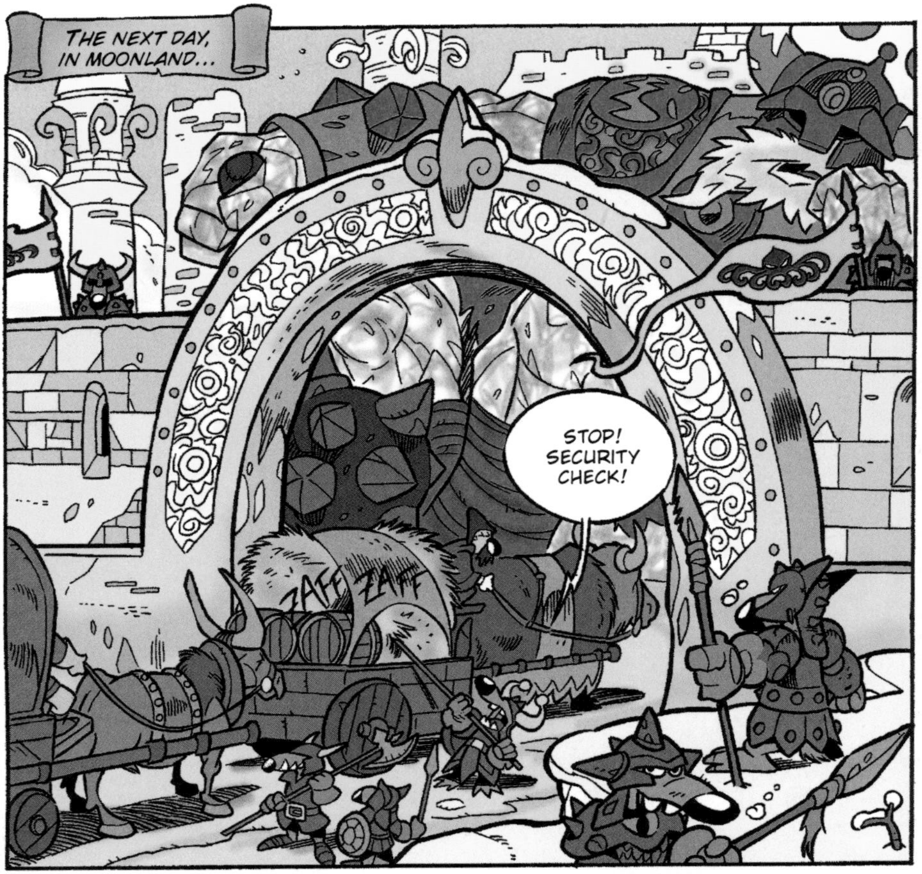
THE NEXT DAY, IN MOONLAND...
STOP! SECURITY CHECK!
ZAFF ZAFF

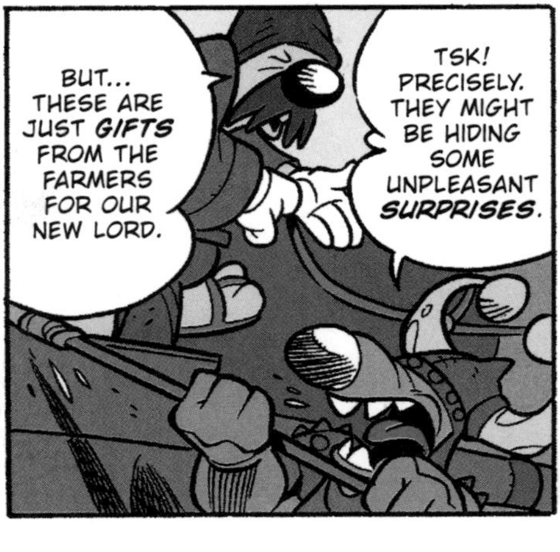
BUT... THESE ARE JUST GIFTS FROM THE FARMERS FOR OUR NEW LORD.
TSK! PRECISELY. THEY MIGHT BE HIDING SOME UNPLEASANT SURPRISES.

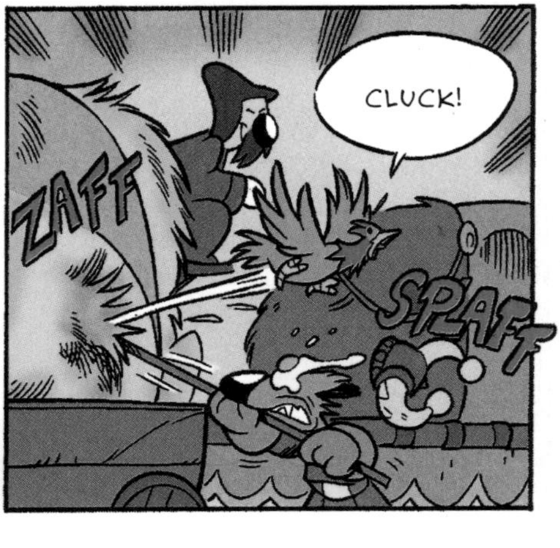
CLUCK!
ZAFF
SPLAFF

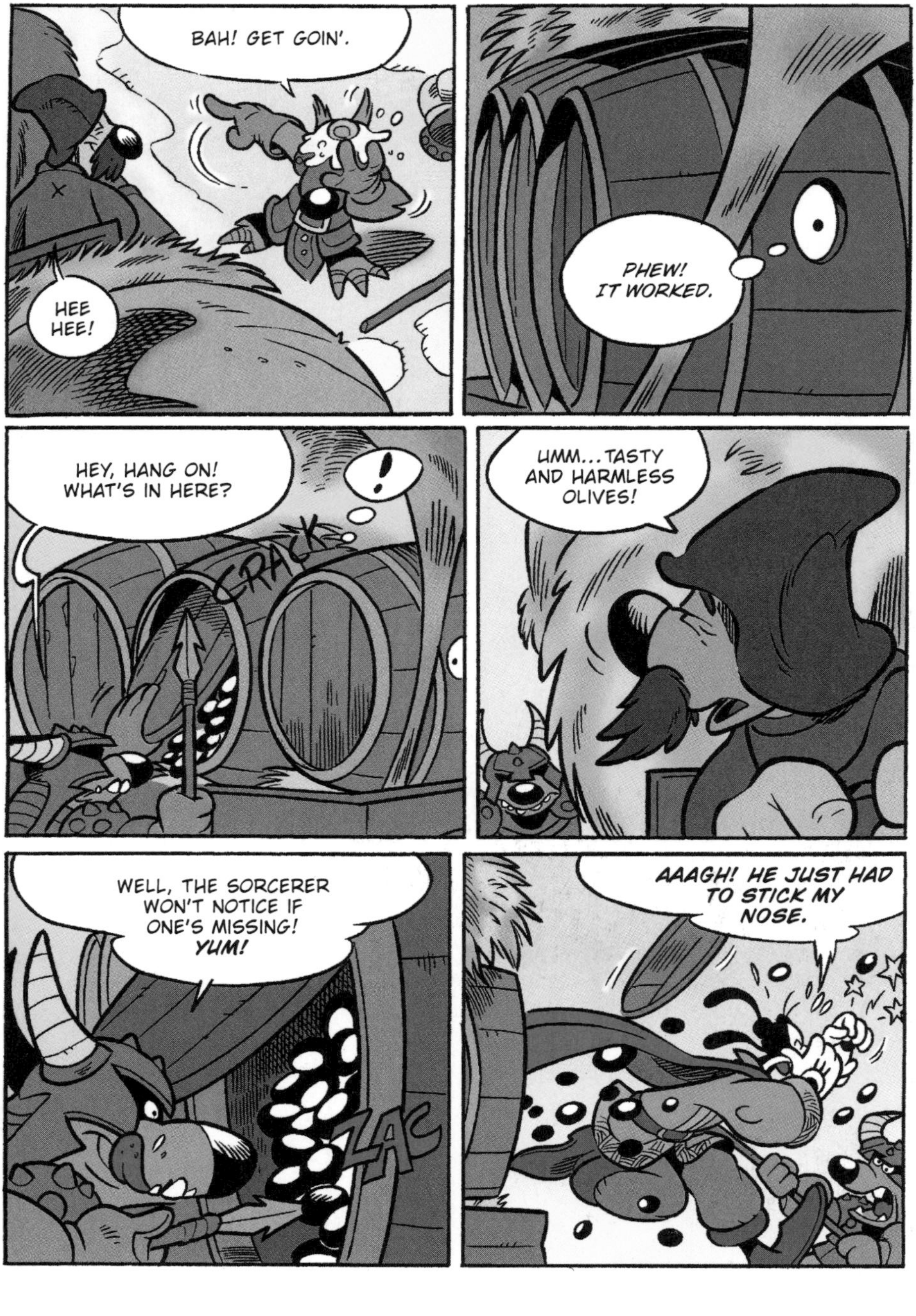

BAH! GET GOIN'.
HEE HEE!
PHEW! IT WORKED.
HEY, HANG ON! WHAT'S IN HERE?
!
CRACK
UMM... TASTY AND HARMLESS OLIVES!
WELL, THE SORCERER WON'T NOTICE IF ONE'S MISSING! YUM!
ZAC
AAAGH! HE JUST HAD TO STICK MY NOSE.

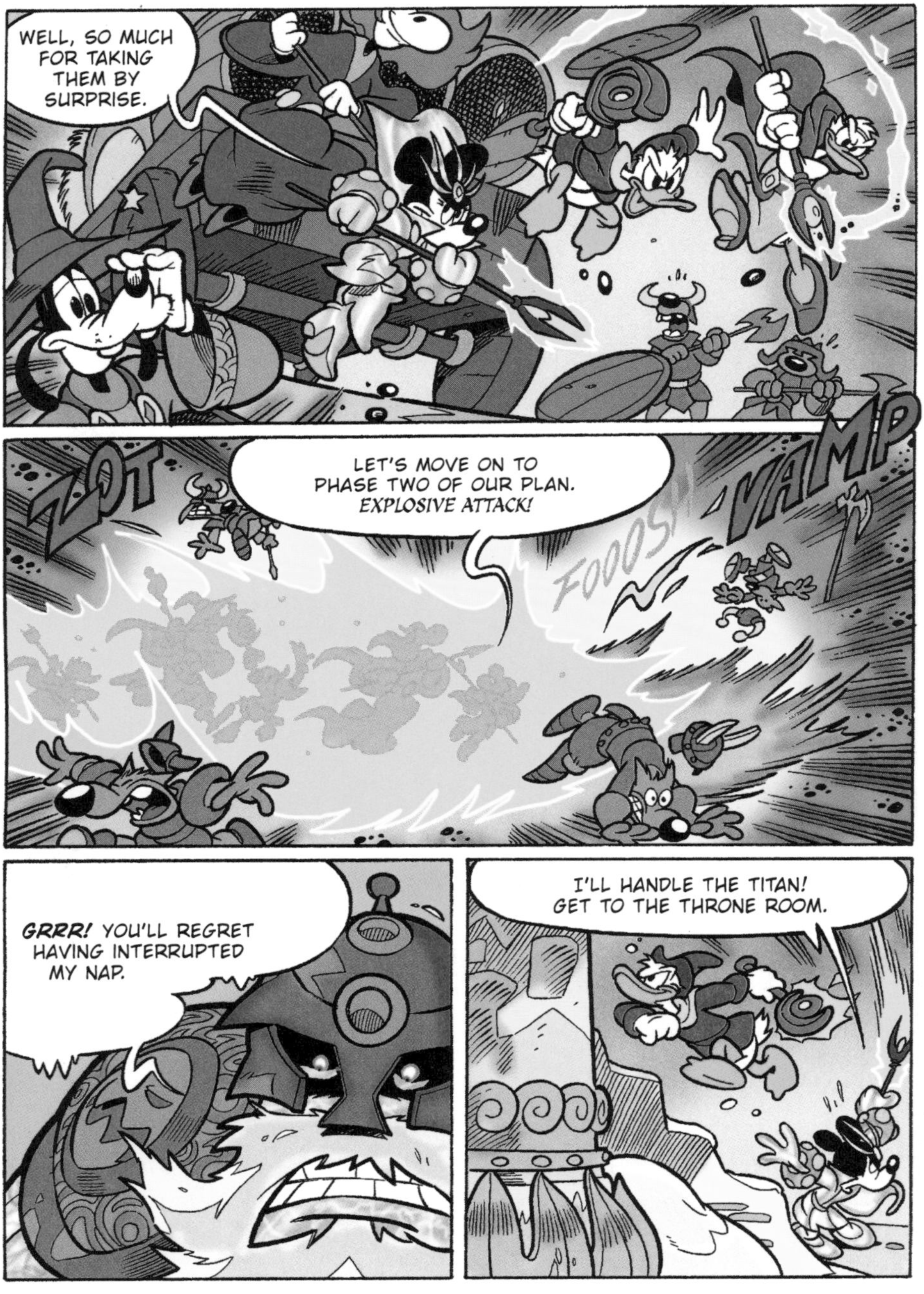

WELL, SO MUCH FOR TAKING THEM BY SURPRISE.
ZOT
LET'S MOVE ON TO PHASE TWO OF OUR PLAN. *EXPLOSIVE ATTACK!*
FOOOSH
VAMP
GRRR! YOU'LL REGRET HAVING INTERRUPTED MY NAP.
I'LL HANDLE THE TITAN! GET TO THE THRONE ROOM.

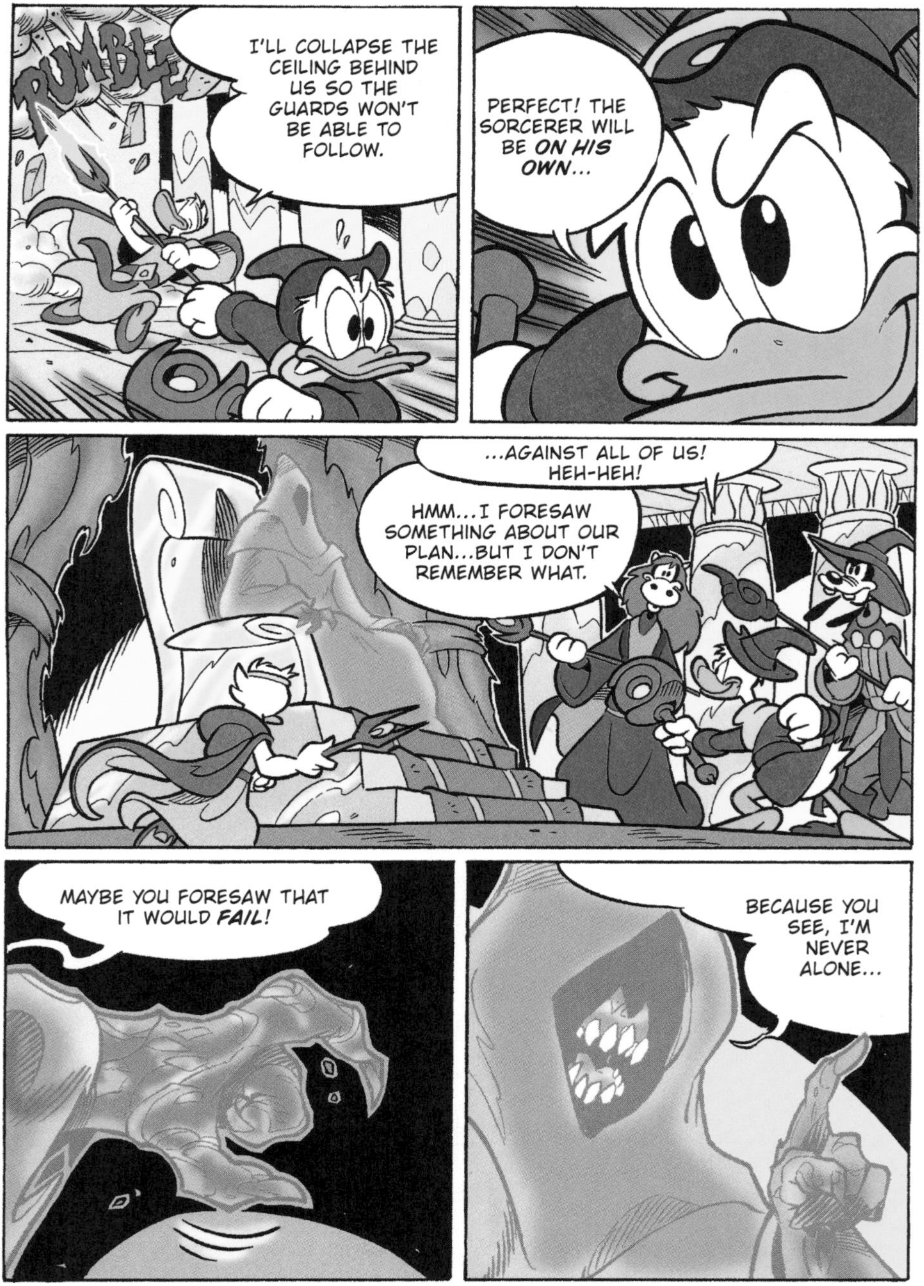

RUMBLE
I'LL COLLAPSE THE CEILING BEHIND US SO THE GUARDS WON'T BE ABLE TO FOLLOW.
PERFECT! THE SORCERER WILL BE *ON HIS OWN*...
...AGAINST ALL OF US! HEH-HEH!
HMM...I FORESAW SOMETHING ABOUT OUR PLAN...BUT I DON'T REMEMBER WHAT.
MAYBE YOU FORESAW THAT IT WOULD *FAIL*!
BECAUSE YOU SEE, I'M NEVER ALONE...

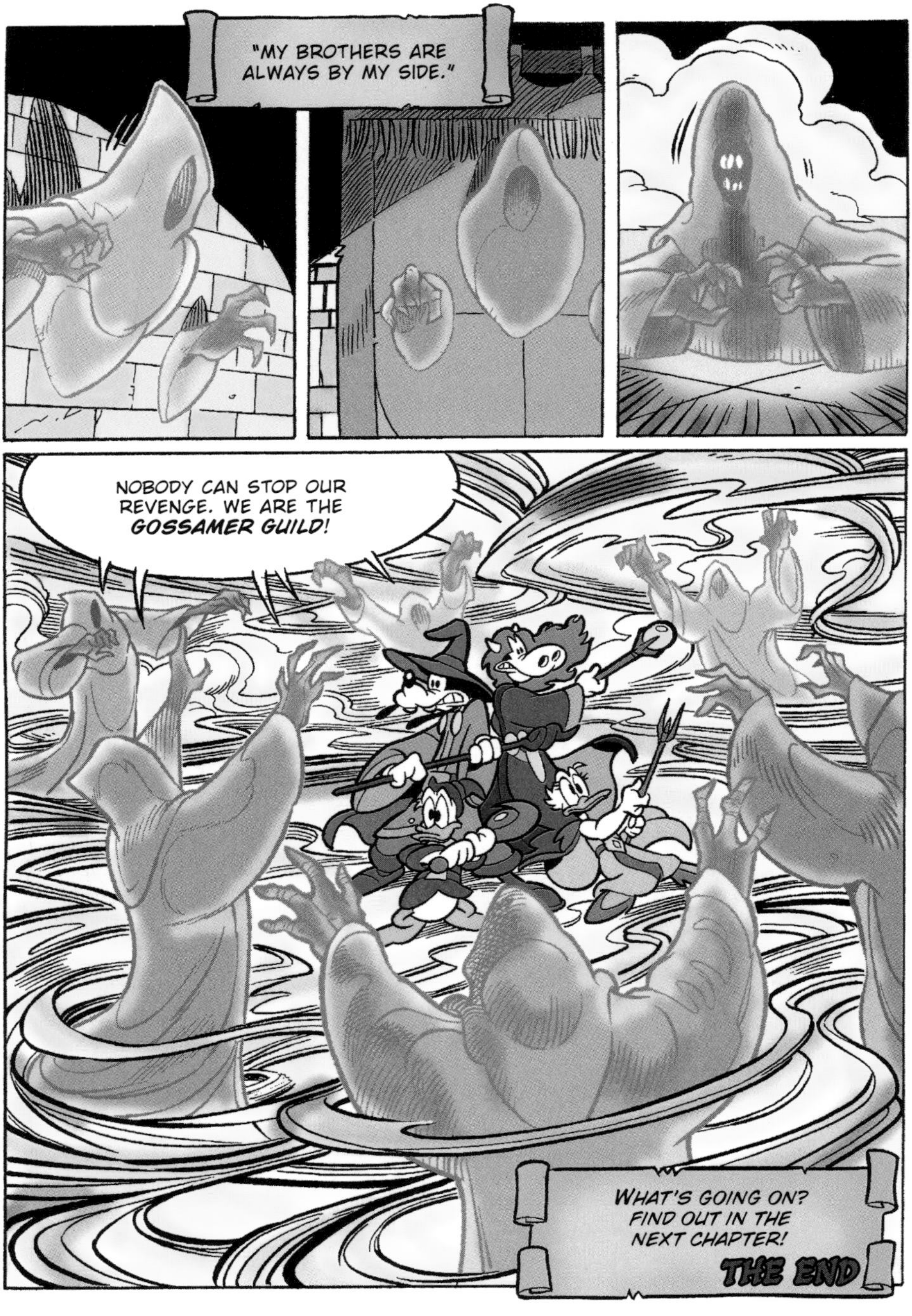

"MY BROTHERS ARE ALWAYS BY MY SIDE."
NOBODY CAN STOP OUR REVENGE. WE ARE THE GOSSAMER GUILD!
WHAT'S GOING ON? FIND OUT IN THE NEXT CHAPTER!
THE END

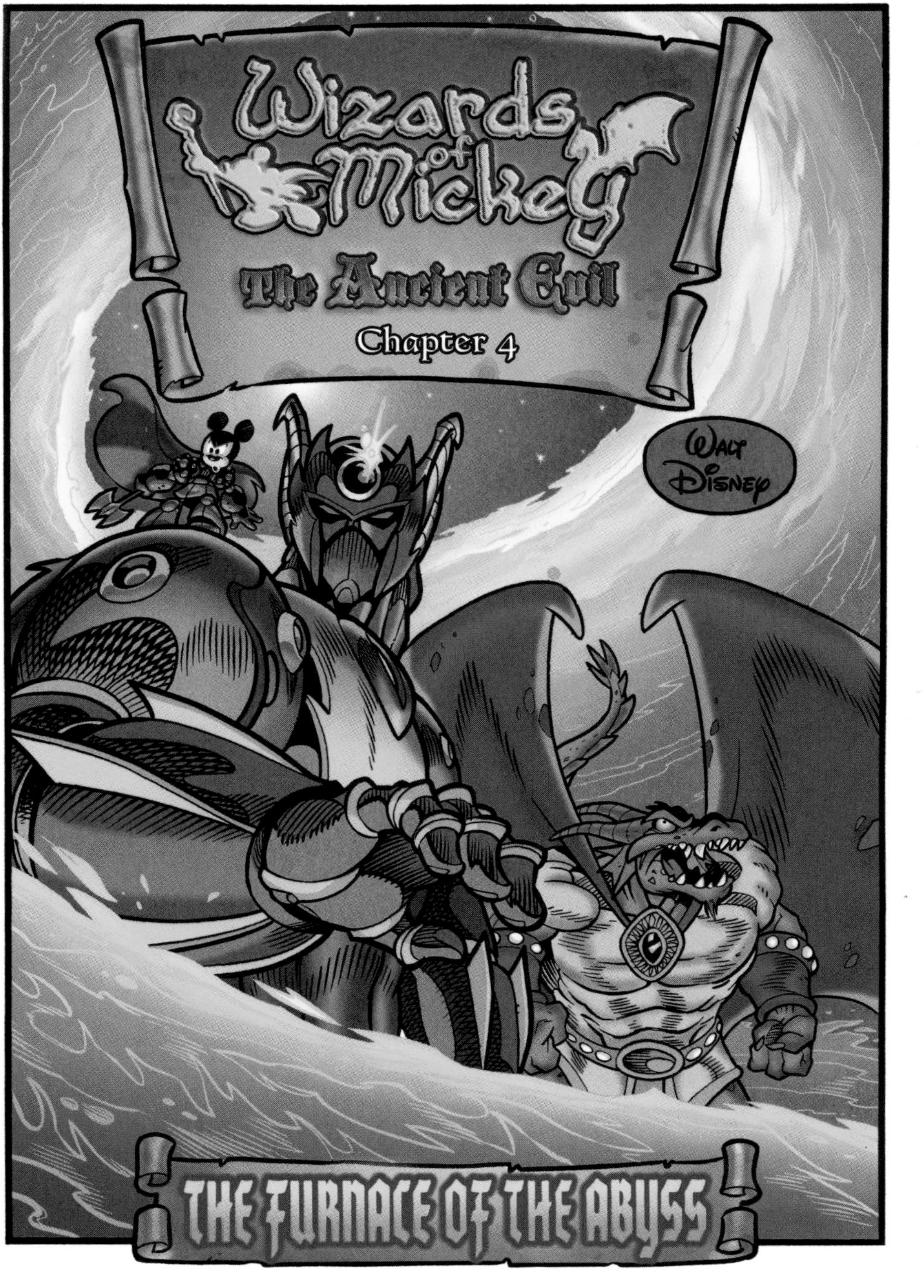
Wizards of Mickey
The Ancient Evil
Chapter 4
Walt Disney
THE FURNACE OF THE ABYSS

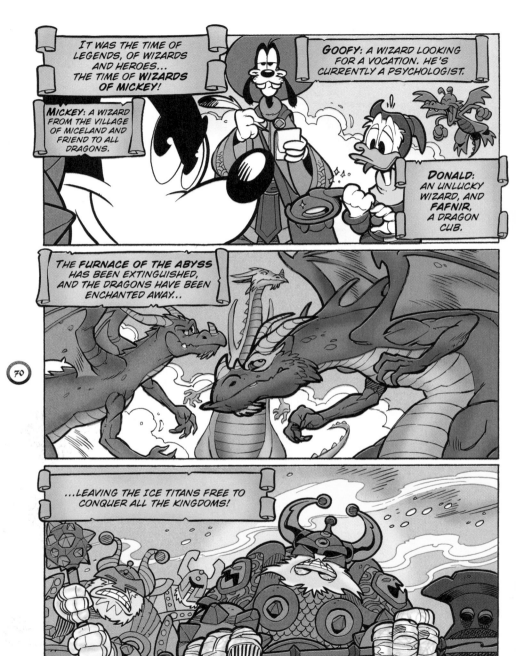

IT WAS THE TIME OF LEGENDS, OF WIZARDS AND HEROES... THE TIME OF **WIZARDS OF MICKEY!**

MICKEY: A WIZARD FROM THE VILLAGE OF MICELAND AND FRIEND TO ALL DRAGONS.

GOOFY: A WIZARD LOOKING FOR A VOCATION. HE'S CURRENTLY A PSYCHOLOGIST.

DONALD: AN UNLUCKY WIZARD, AND **FAFNIR,** A DRAGON CUB.

THE FURNACE OF THE ABYSS HAS BEEN EXTINGUISHED, AND THE DRAGONS HAVE BEEN ENCHANTED AWAY...

...LEAVING THE ICE TITANS FREE TO CONQUER ALL THE KINGDOMS!

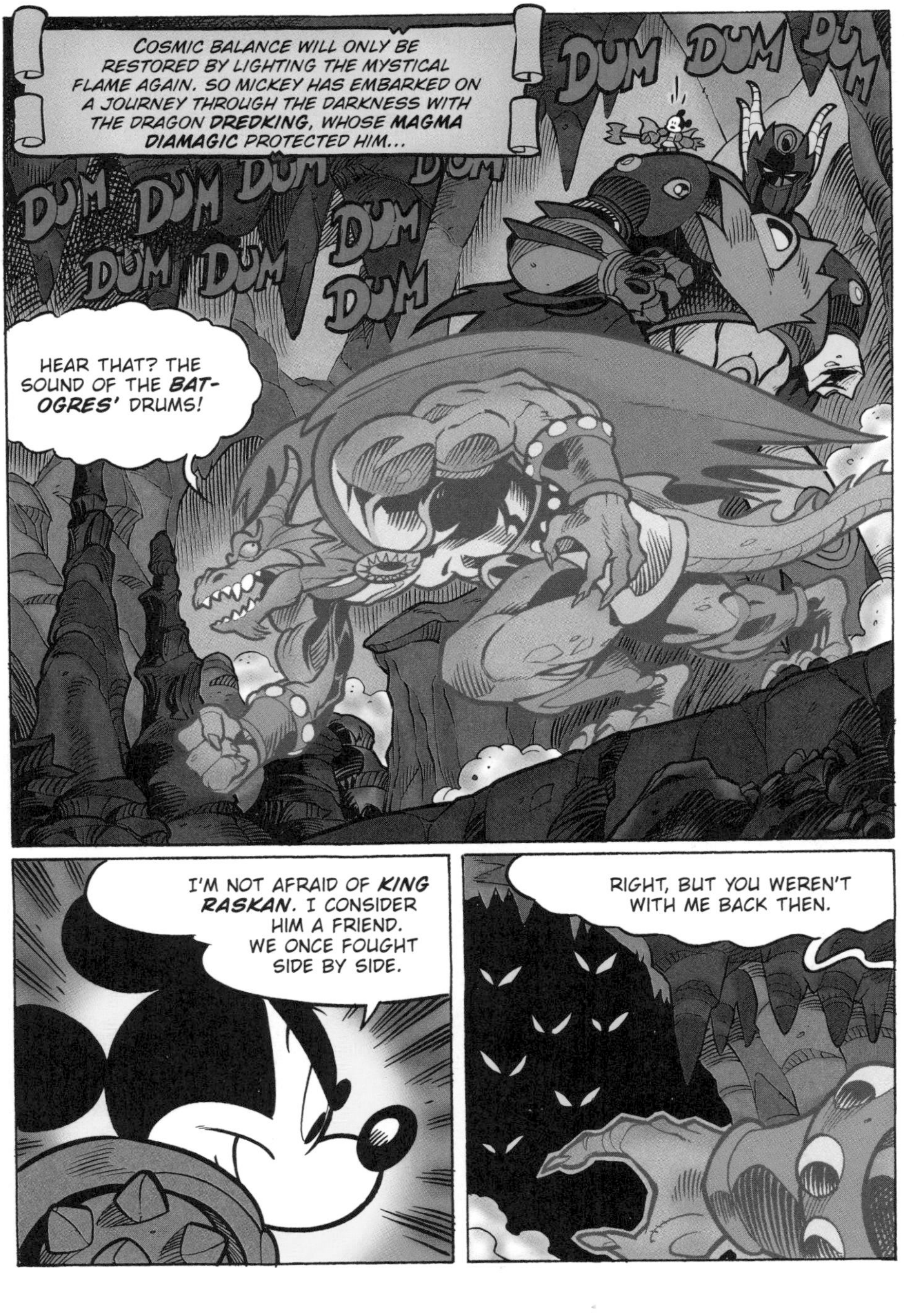
COSMIC BALANCE WILL ONLY BE RESTORED BY LIGHTING THE MYSTICAL FLAME AGAIN. SO MICKEY HAS EMBARKED ON A JOURNEY THROUGH THE DARKNESS WITH THE DRAGON DREDKING, WHOSE MAGMA DIAMAGIC PROTECTED HIM...
DUM DUM DUM
DUM DUM DUM DUM
DUM DUM DUM DUM
HEAR THAT? THE SOUND OF THE BAT-OGRES' DRUMS!
I'M NOT AFRAID OF KING RASKAN. I CONSIDER HIM A FRIEND. WE ONCE FOUGHT SIDE BY SIDE.
RIGHT, BUT YOU WEREN'T WITH ME BACK THEN.

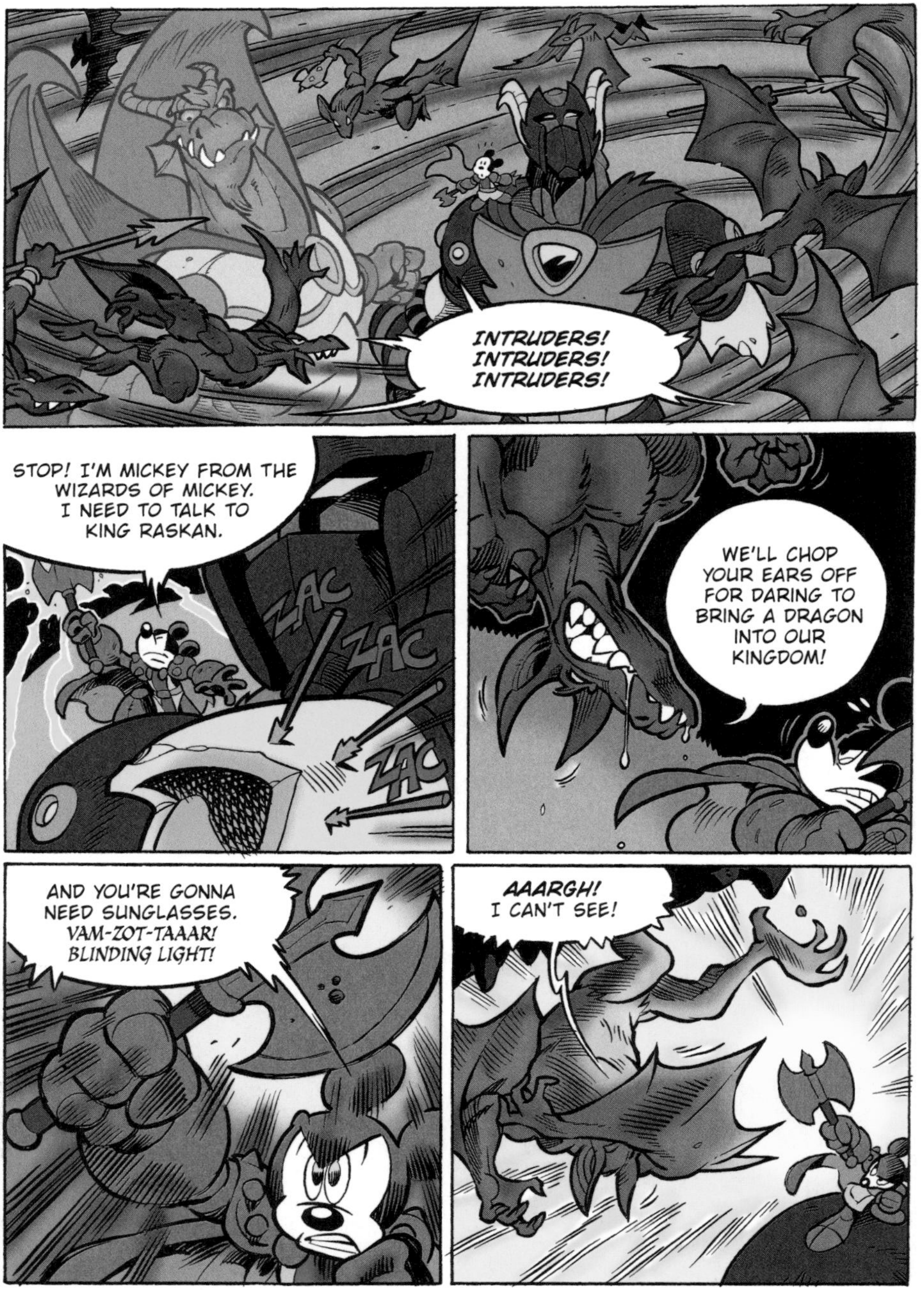
INTRUDERS! INTRUDERS! INTRUDERS!
STOP! I'M MICKEY FROM THE WIZARDS OF MICKEY. I NEED TO TALK TO KING RASKAN.
ZAC
ZAC
ZAC
WE'LL CHOP YOUR EARS OFF FOR DARING TO BRING A DRAGON INTO OUR KINGDOM!
AND YOU'RE GONNA NEED SUNGLASSES. *VAM-ZOT-TAAAR! BLINDING LIGHT!*
AAARGH! I CAN'T SEE!

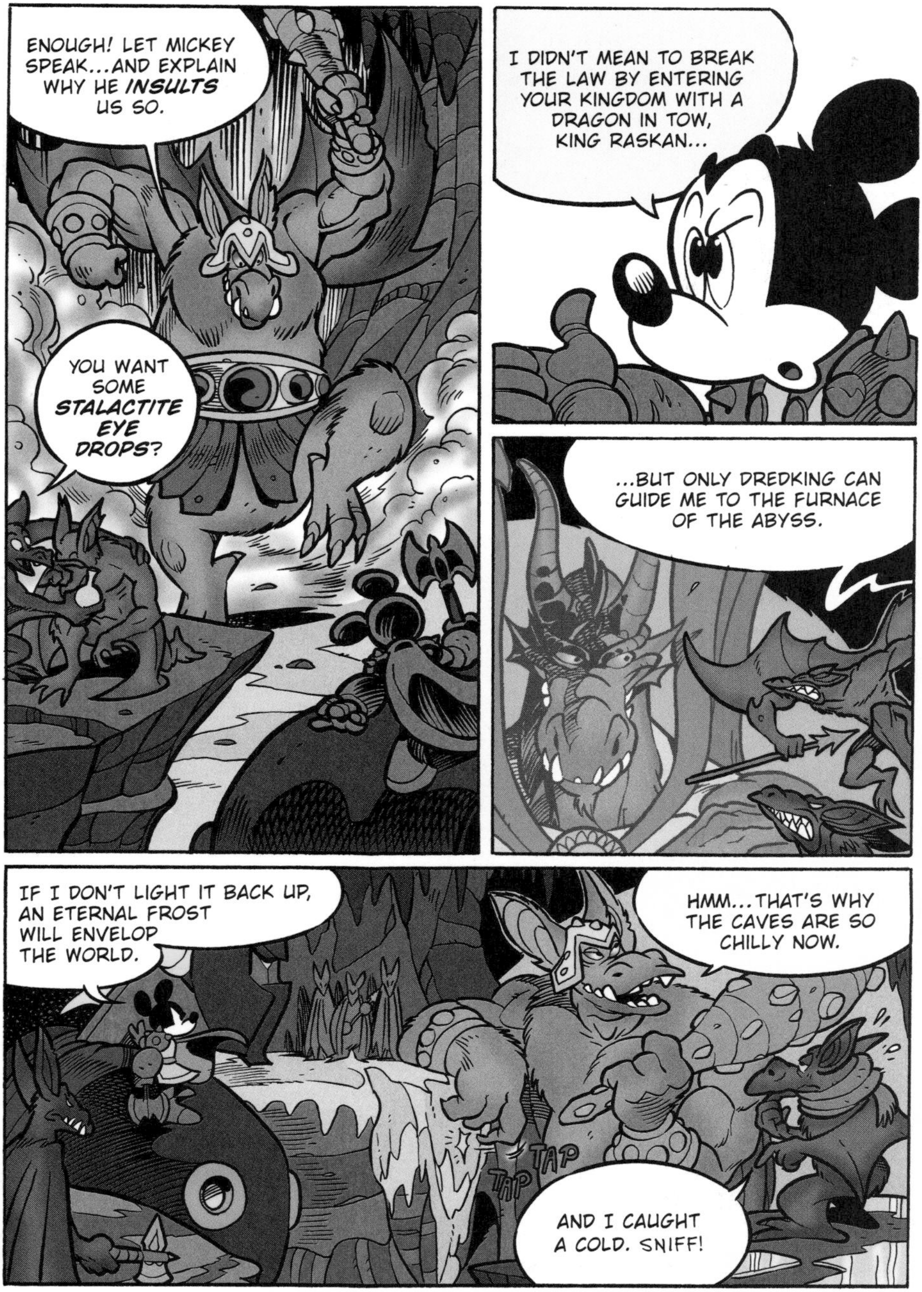
ENOUGH! LET MICKEY SPEAK...AND EXPLAIN WHY HE INSULTS US SO.
YOU WANT SOME STALACTITE EYE DROPS?
I DIDN'T MEAN TO BREAK THE LAW BY ENTERING YOUR KINGDOM WITH A DRAGON IN TOW, KING RASKAN...
...BUT ONLY DREDKING CAN GUIDE ME TO THE FURNACE OF THE ABYSS.
IF I DON'T LIGHT IT BACK UP, AN ETERNAL FROST WILL ENVELOP THE WORLD.
HMM...THAT'S WHY THE CAVES ARE SO CHILLY NOW.
TAP
TAP
AND I CAUGHT A COLD. SNIFF!

MY FRIENDS ARE TRYING TO SLOW THE ICE TITANS DOWN BY CAPTURING THE *SORCERER* WHO COMMANDS THEM, BUT I HAVEN'T GOTTEN NEWS IN TWO DAYS.

TLAC

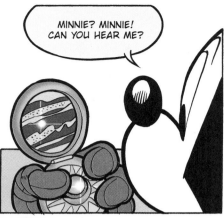

MINNIE? MINNIE! CAN YOU HEAR ME?

Shhh! Quiet, or they'll find me!

OUR MISSION FAILED! DONALD AND THE OTHERS WERE CAUGHT...

"...AND I'M TRYING TO GET BACK TO THE IRON DRAGON."

THREE SKULLS. I WIN!

OOF! SO LUCKY!

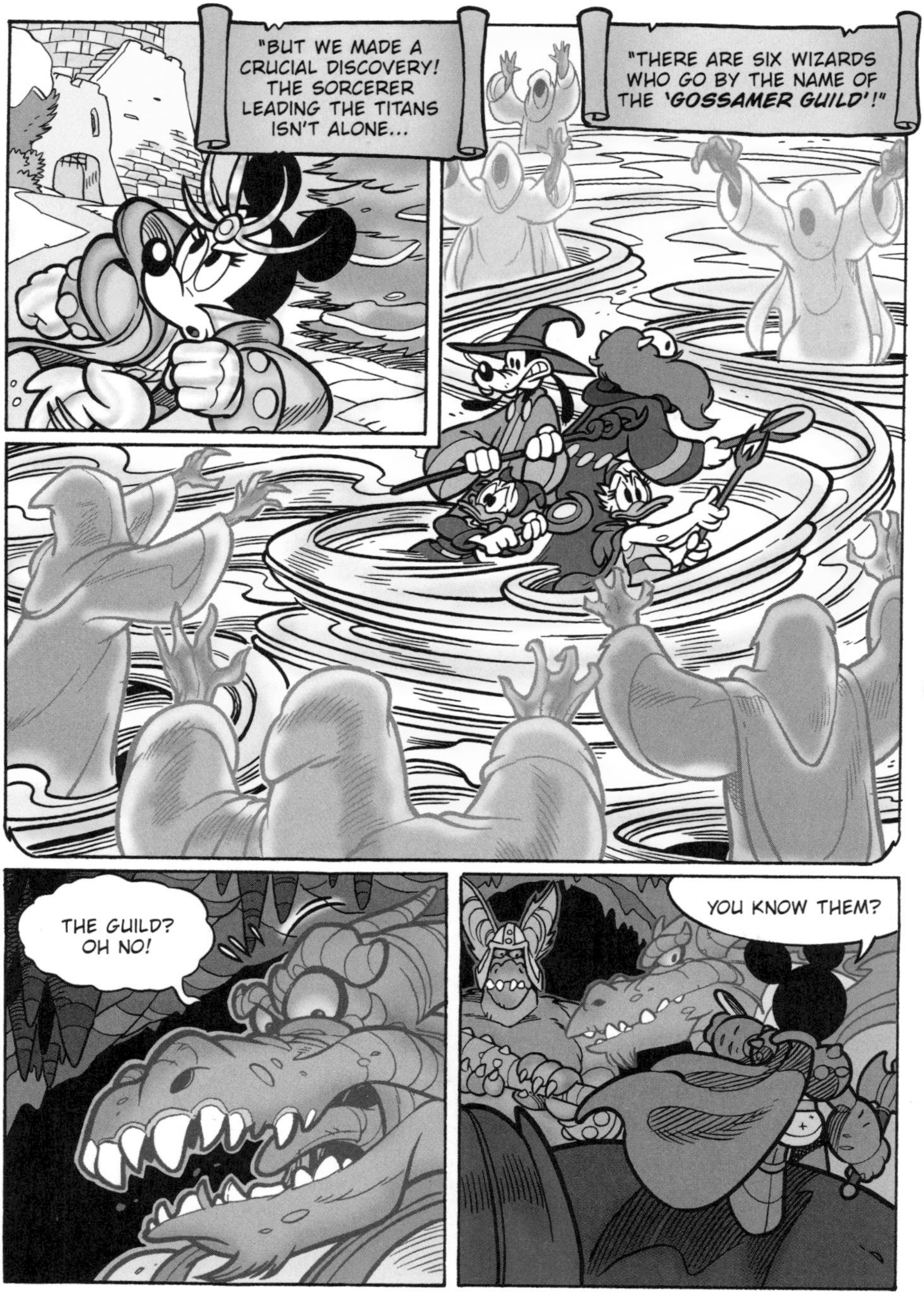
"BUT WE MADE A CRUCIAL DISCOVERY! THE SORCERER LEADING THE TITANS ISN'T ALONE...
"THERE ARE SIX WIZARDS WHO GO BY THE NAME OF THE '**GOSSAMER GUILD**'!"
THE GUILD? OH NO!
YOU KNOW THEM?

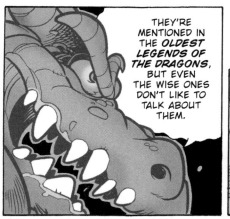

THEY'RE MENTIONED IN THE *OLDEST LEGENDS OF THE DRAGONS*, BUT EVEN THE WISE ONES DON'T LIKE TO TALK ABOUT THEM.

ALL I KNOW IS THAT THEIR EXISTENCE IS LINKED TO THE DISAPPEARANCE OF THE *FIRST SUPREME SORCERER.*

Well, then I'll go to the dragons' city to dig out some info...

...WHILE YOU CONTINUE ON TO THE FURNACE!

"LET'S KEEP IN TOUCH. AND LET'S HURRY..."

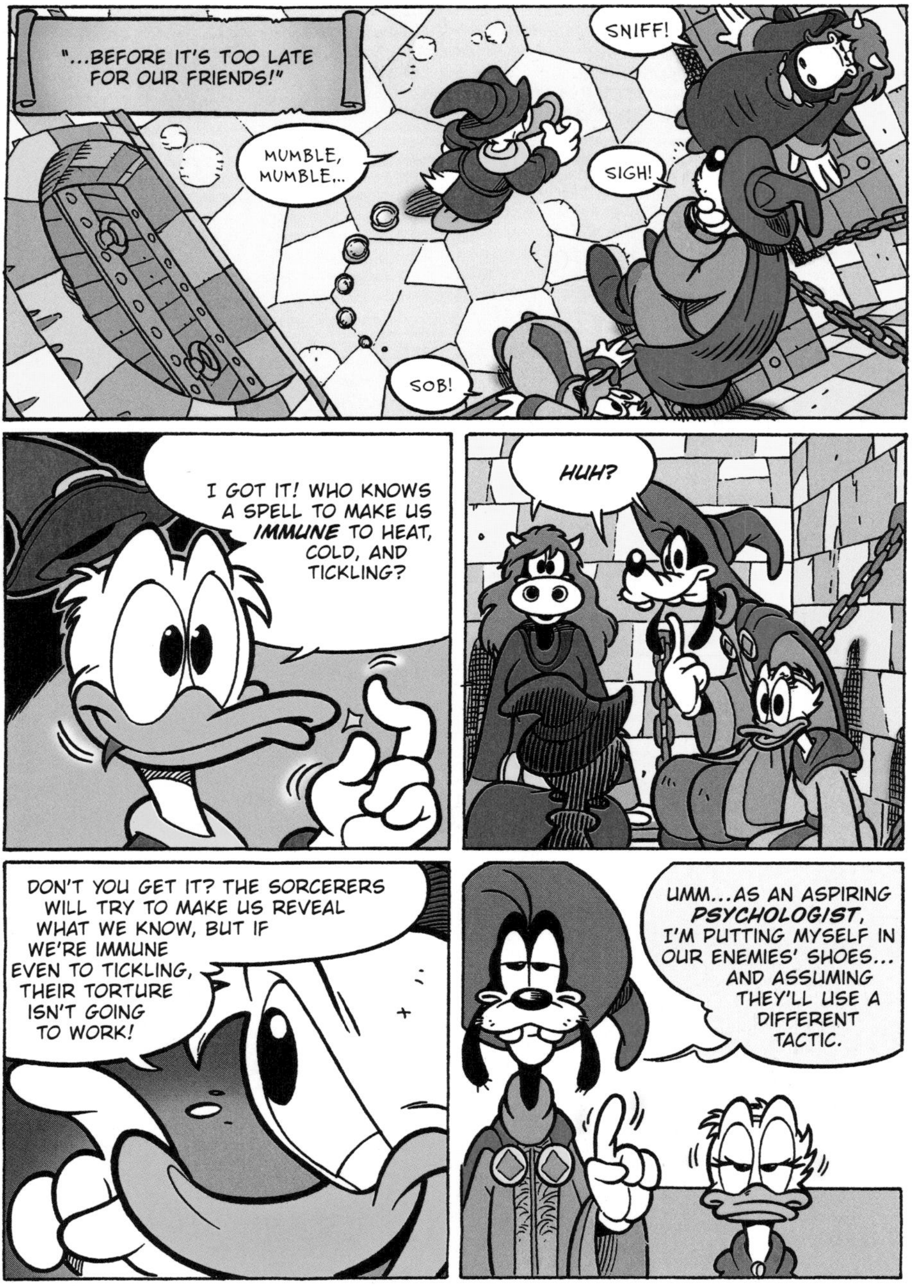
"...BEFORE IT'S TOO LATE FOR OUR FRIENDS!"
SNIFF!
MUMBLE, MUMBLE...
SIGH!
SOB!
I GOT IT! WHO KNOWS A SPELL TO MAKE US IMMUNE TO HEAT, COLD, AND TICKLING?
HUH?
DON'T YOU GET IT? THE SORCERERS WILL TRY TO MAKE US REVEAL WHAT WE KNOW, BUT IF WE'RE IMMUNE EVEN TO TICKLING, THEIR TORTURE ISN'T GOING TO WORK!
UMM...AS AN ASPIRING PSYCHOLOGIST, I'M PUTTING MYSELF IN OUR ENEMIES' SHOES... AND ASSUMING THEY'LL USE A DIFFERENT TACTIC.

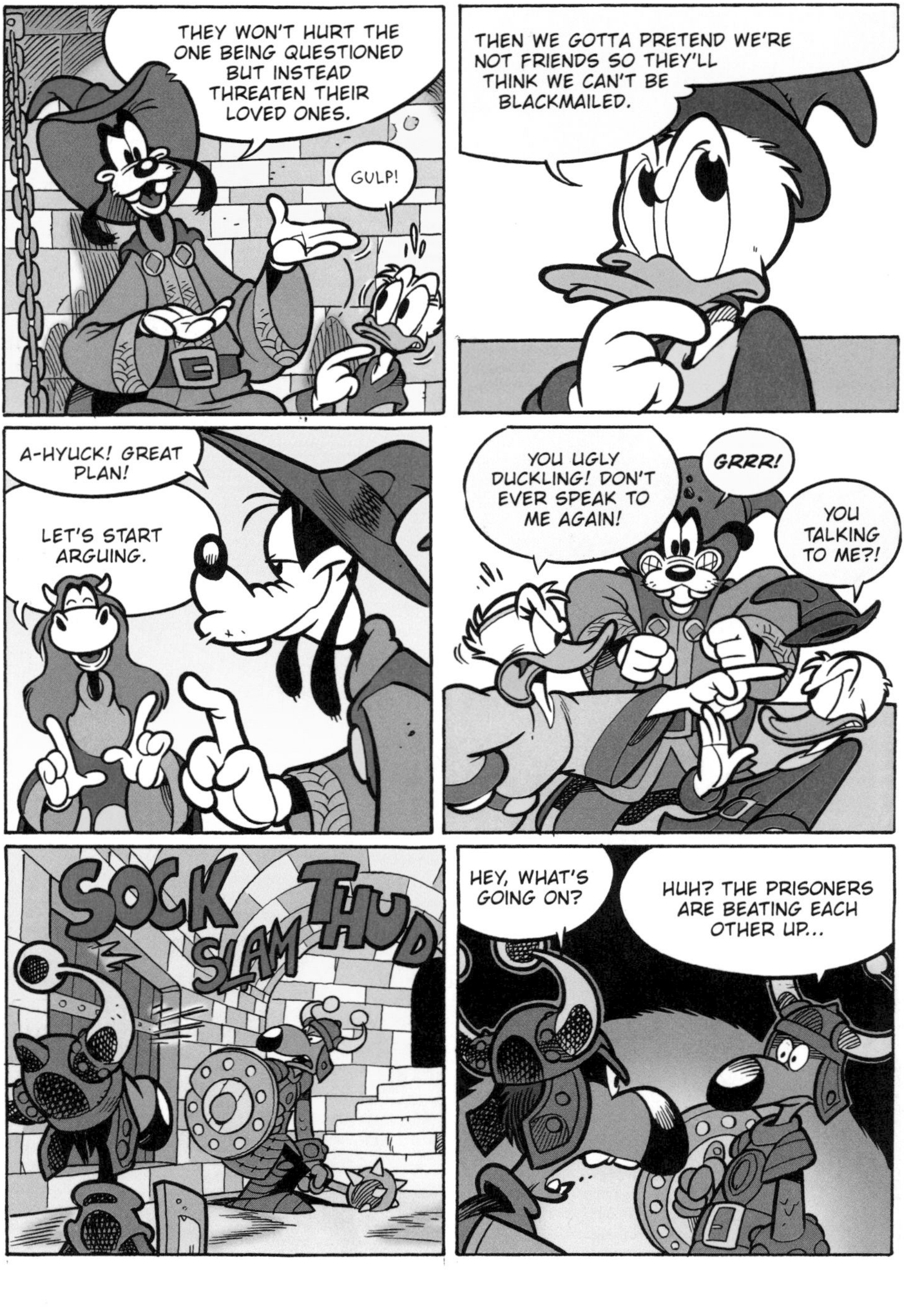
THEY WON'T HURT THE ONE BEING QUESTIONED BUT INSTEAD THREATEN THEIR LOVED ONES.
GULP!
THEN WE GOTTA PRETEND WE'RE NOT FRIENDS SO THEY'LL THINK WE CAN'T BE BLACKMAILED.
A-HYUCK! GREAT PLAN!
LET'S START ARGUING.
YOU UGLY DUCKLING! DON'T EVER SPEAK TO ME AGAIN!
GRRR!
YOU TALKING TO ME?!
SOCK
SLAM
THUD
HEY, WHAT'S GOING ON?
HUH? THE PRISONERS ARE BEATING EACH OTHER UP...

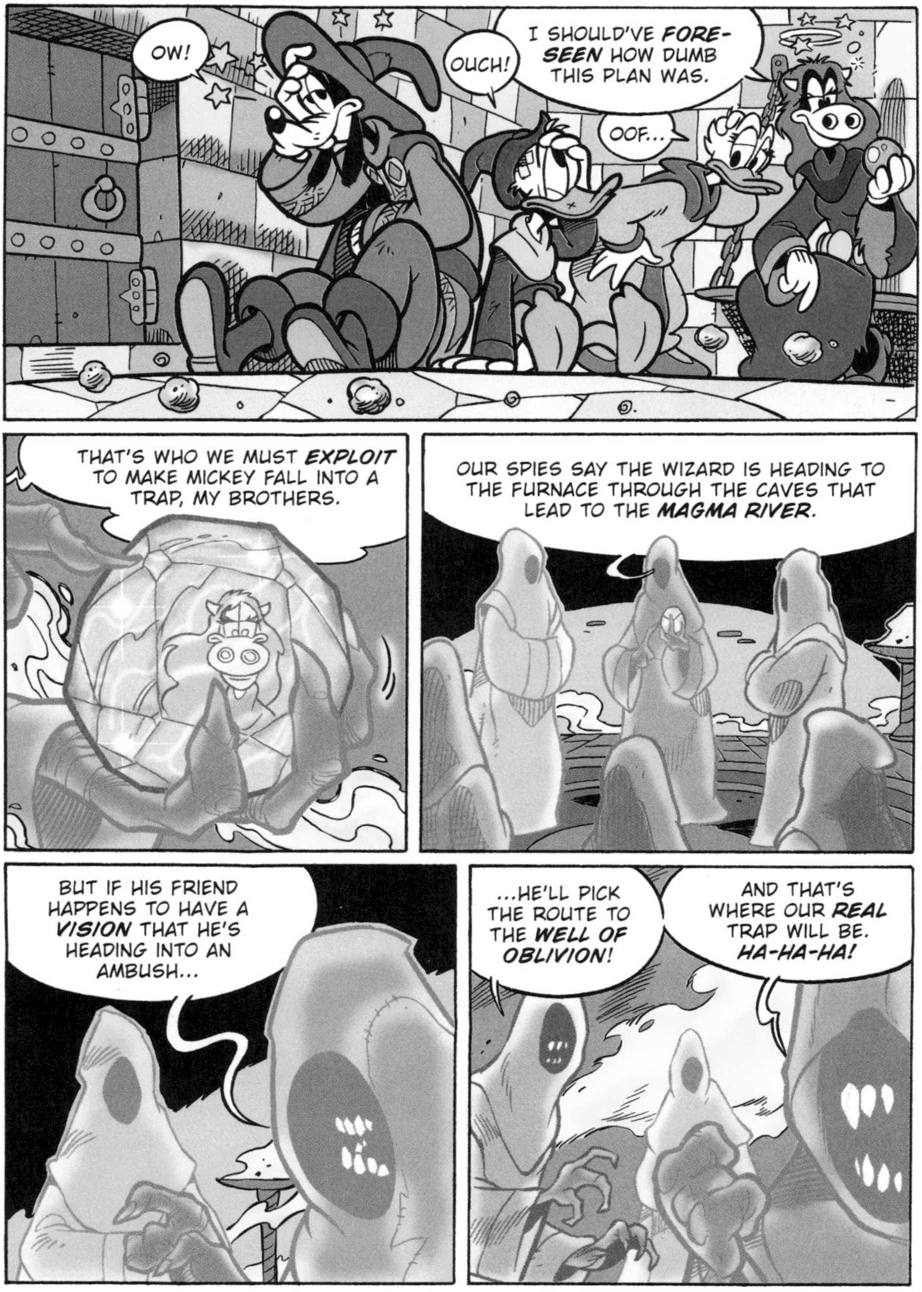

OW!
OUCH!
I SHOULD'VE FORESEEN HOW DUMB THIS PLAN WAS.
OOF...
THAT'S WHO WE MUST EXPLOIT TO MAKE MICKEY FALL INTO A TRAP, MY BROTHERS.
OUR SPIES SAY THE WIZARD IS HEADING TO THE FURNACE THROUGH THE CAVES THAT LEAD TO THE MAGMA RIVER.
BUT IF HIS FRIEND HAPPENS TO HAVE A VISION THAT HE'S HEADING INTO AN AMBUSH...
...HE'LL PICK THE ROUTE TO THE WELL OF OBLIVION!
AND THAT'S WHERE OUR REAL TRAP WILL BE. HA-HA-HA!

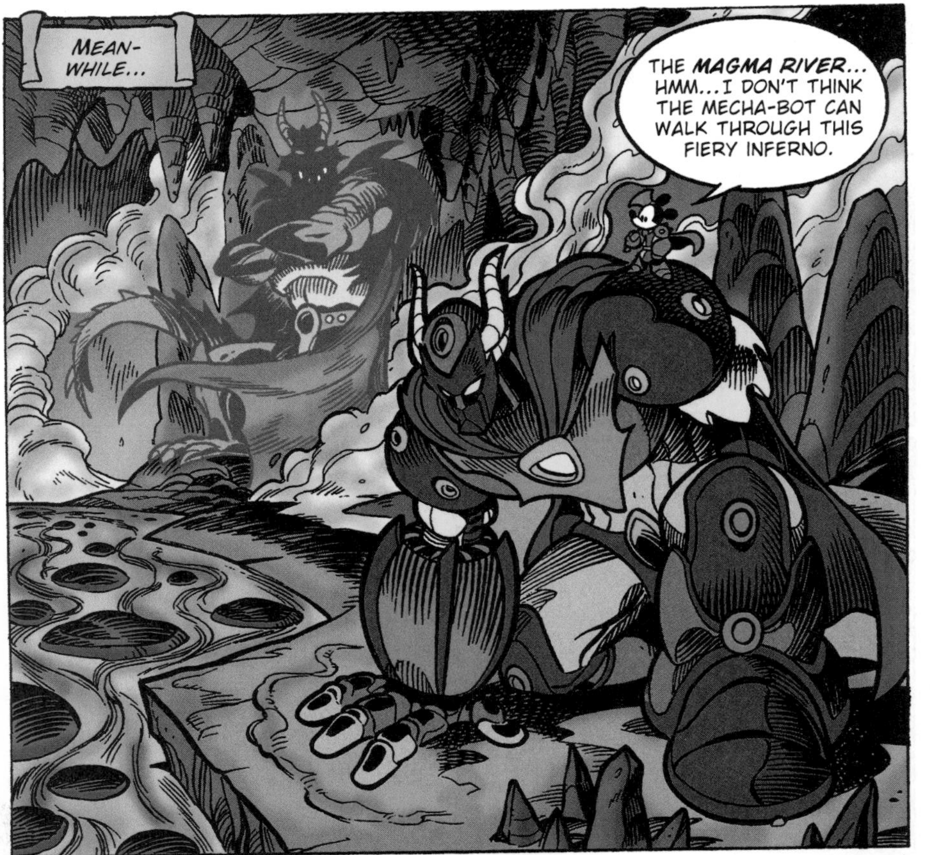
MEAN-WHILE...
THE **MAGMA RIVER**... HMM...I DON'T THINK THE MECHA-BOT CAN WALK THROUGH THIS FIERY INFERNO.

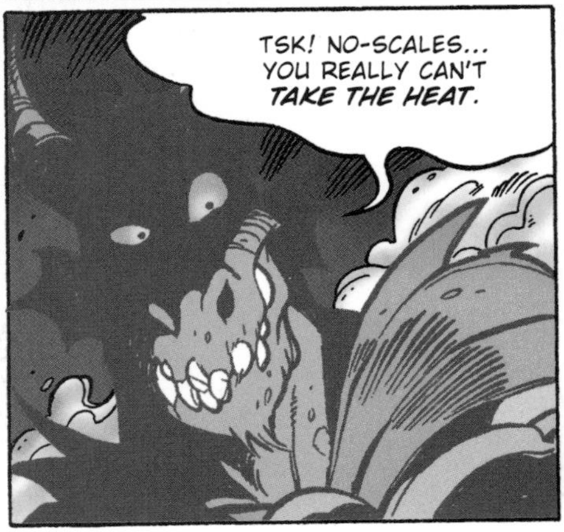
TSK! NO-SCALES... YOU REALLY CAN'T ***TAKE THE HEAT***.

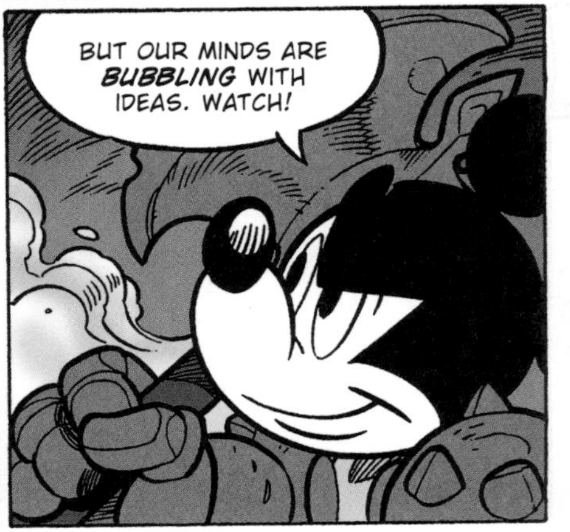
BUT OUR MINDS ARE ***BUBBLING*** WITH IDEAS. WATCH!

CRASH

BRANG

THUD

YOU WANNA TEST PILOT OUR NEW RAFT?

HMPH!

SPLASH

MEANWHILE, IN DRAGAVAR...

OOF! SOMETHING'S NOT RIGHT.

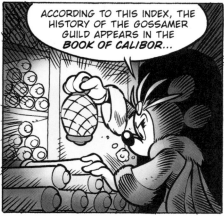

ACCORDING TO THIS INDEX, THE HISTORY OF THE GOSSAMER GUILD APPEARS IN THE *BOOK OF CALIBOR*...

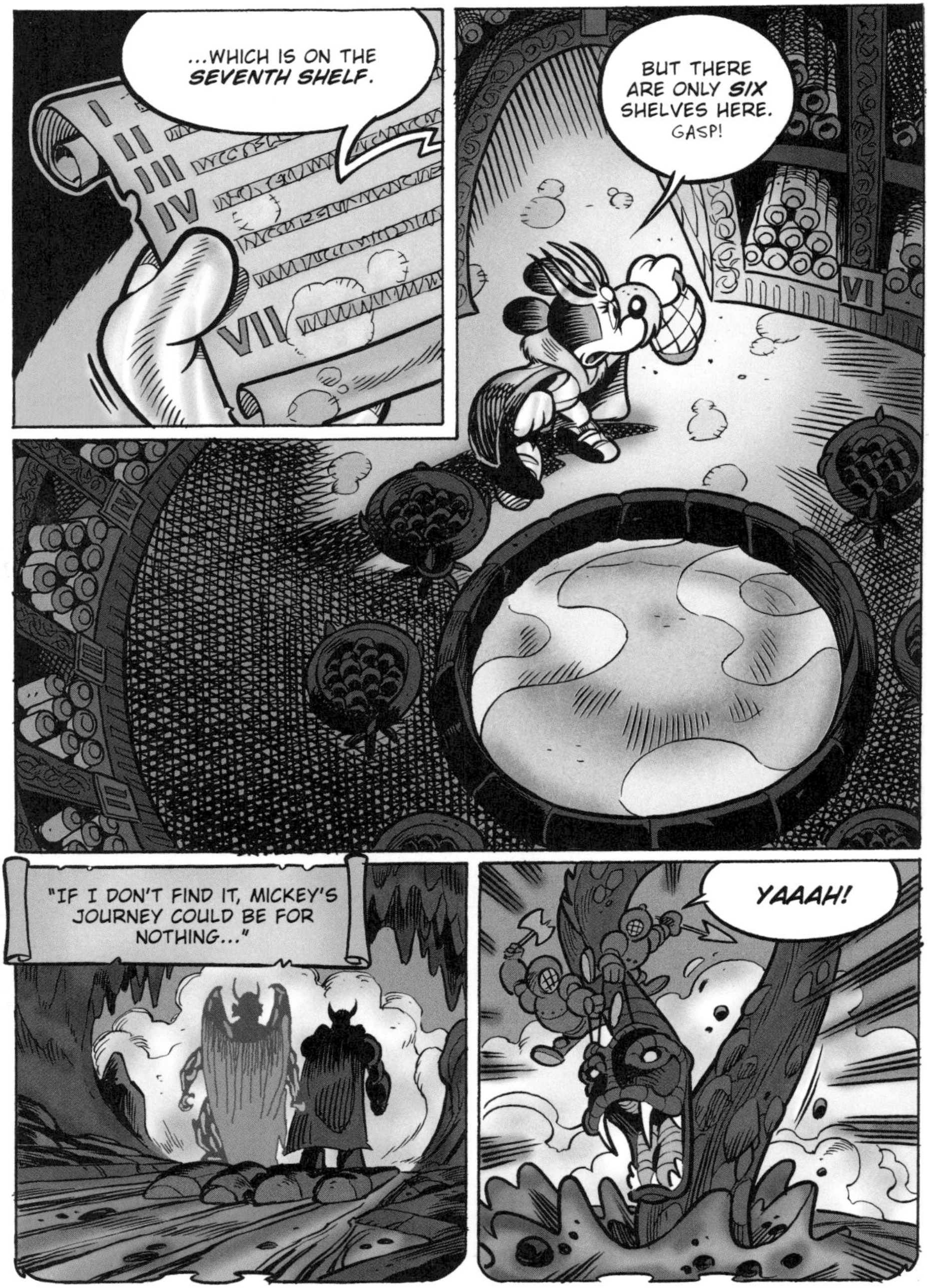
...WHICH IS ON THE SEVENTH SHELF.
BUT THERE ARE ONLY SIX SHELVES HERE.
GASP!
"IF I DON'T FIND IT, MICKEY'S JOURNEY COULD BE FOR NOTHING..."
YAAAH!

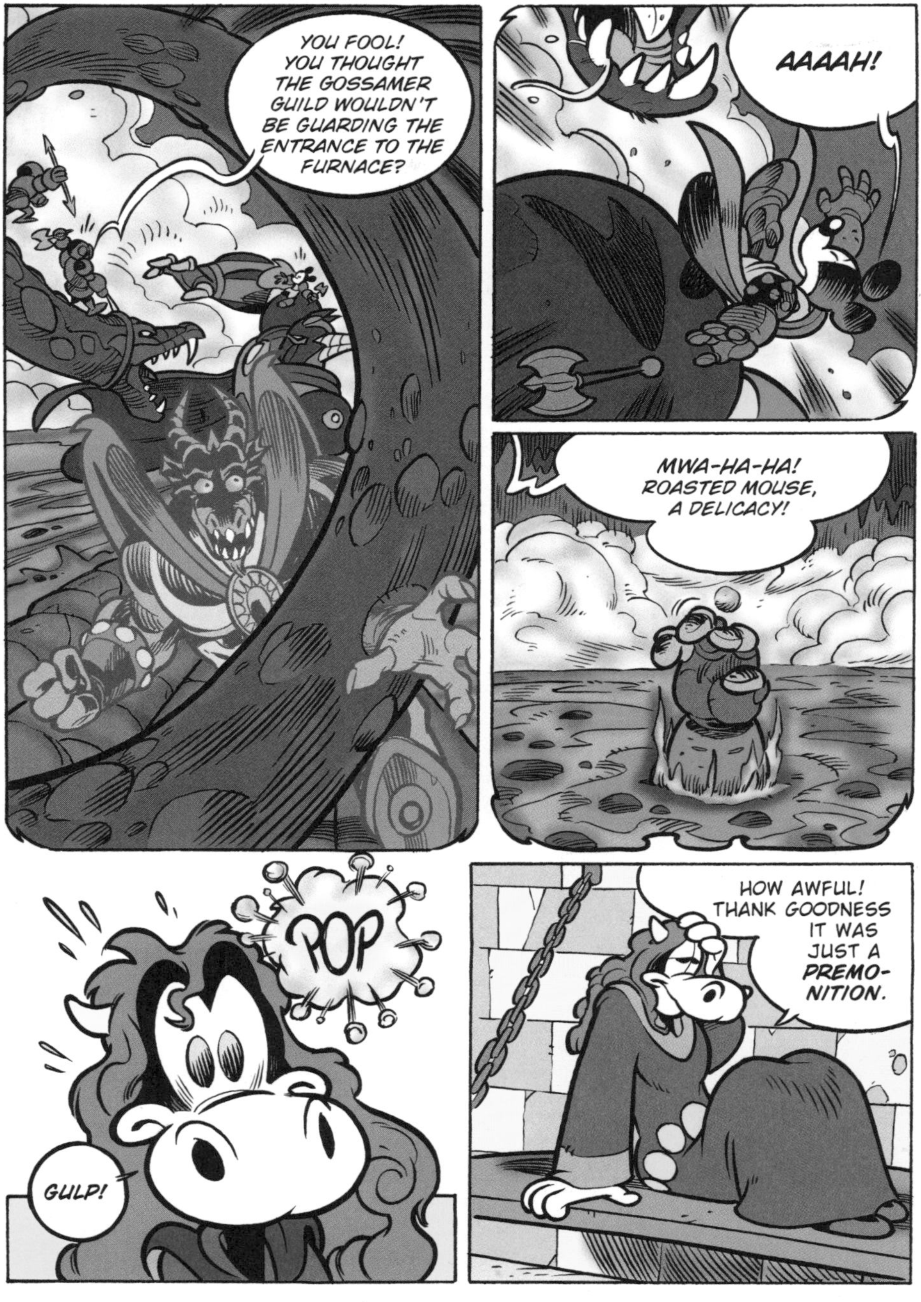
YOU FOOL! YOU THOUGHT THE GOSSAMER GUILD WOULDN'T BE GUARDING THE ENTRANCE TO THE FURNACE?
AAAAH!
MWA-HA-HA! ROASTED MOUSE, A DELICACY!
POP
GULP!
HOW AWFUL! THANK GOODNESS IT WAS JUST A PREMO-NITION.

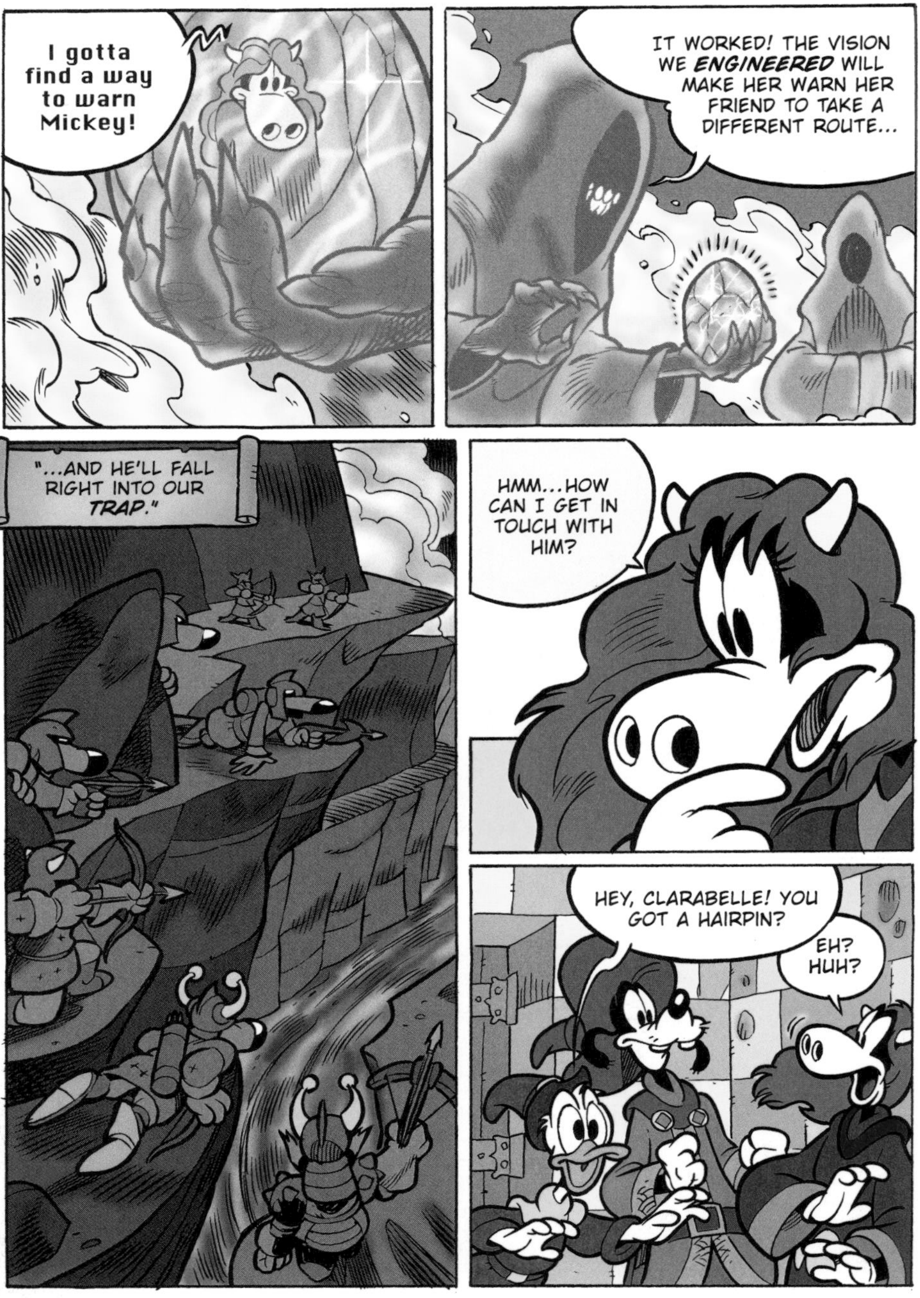
I gotta find a way to warn Mickey!
IT WORKED! THE VISION WE ENGINEERED WILL MAKE HER WARN HER FRIEND TO TAKE A DIFFERENT ROUTE...
"...AND HE'LL FALL RIGHT INTO OUR TRAP."
HMM...HOW CAN I GET IN TOUCH WITH HIM?
HEY, CLARABELLE! YOU GOT A HAIRPIN?
EH? HUH?

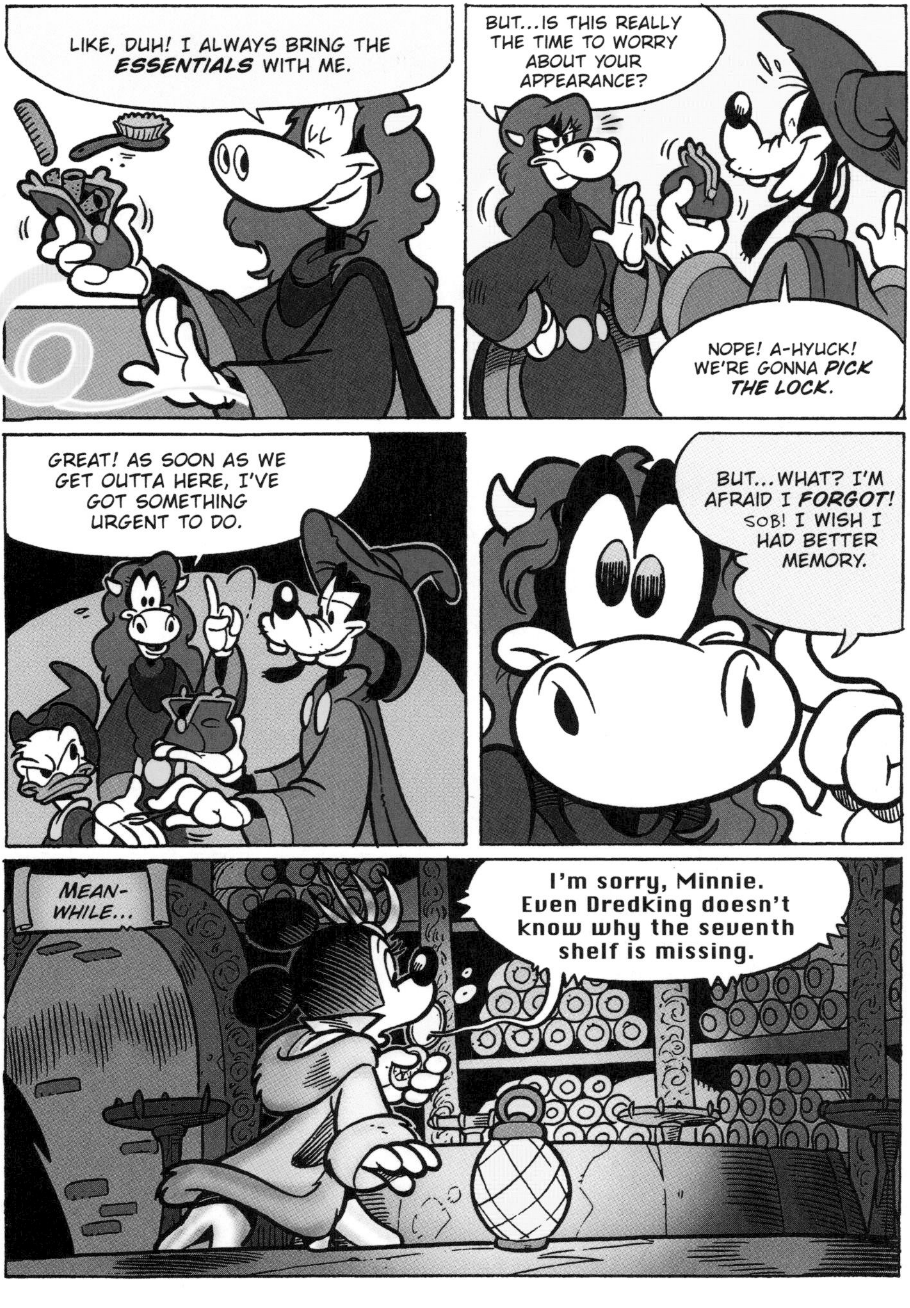
LIKE, DUH! I ALWAYS BRING THE ESSENTIALS WITH ME.
BUT...IS THIS REALLY THE TIME TO WORRY ABOUT YOUR APPEARANCE?
NOPE! A-HYUCK! WE'RE GONNA PICK THE LOCK.
GREAT! AS SOON AS WE GET OUTTA HERE, I'VE GOT SOMETHING URGENT TO DO.
BUT...WHAT? I'M AFRAID I FORGOT! SOB! I WISH I HAD BETTER MEMORY.
MEAN-WHILE...
I'm sorry, Minnie. Even Dredking doesn't know why the seventh shelf is missing.

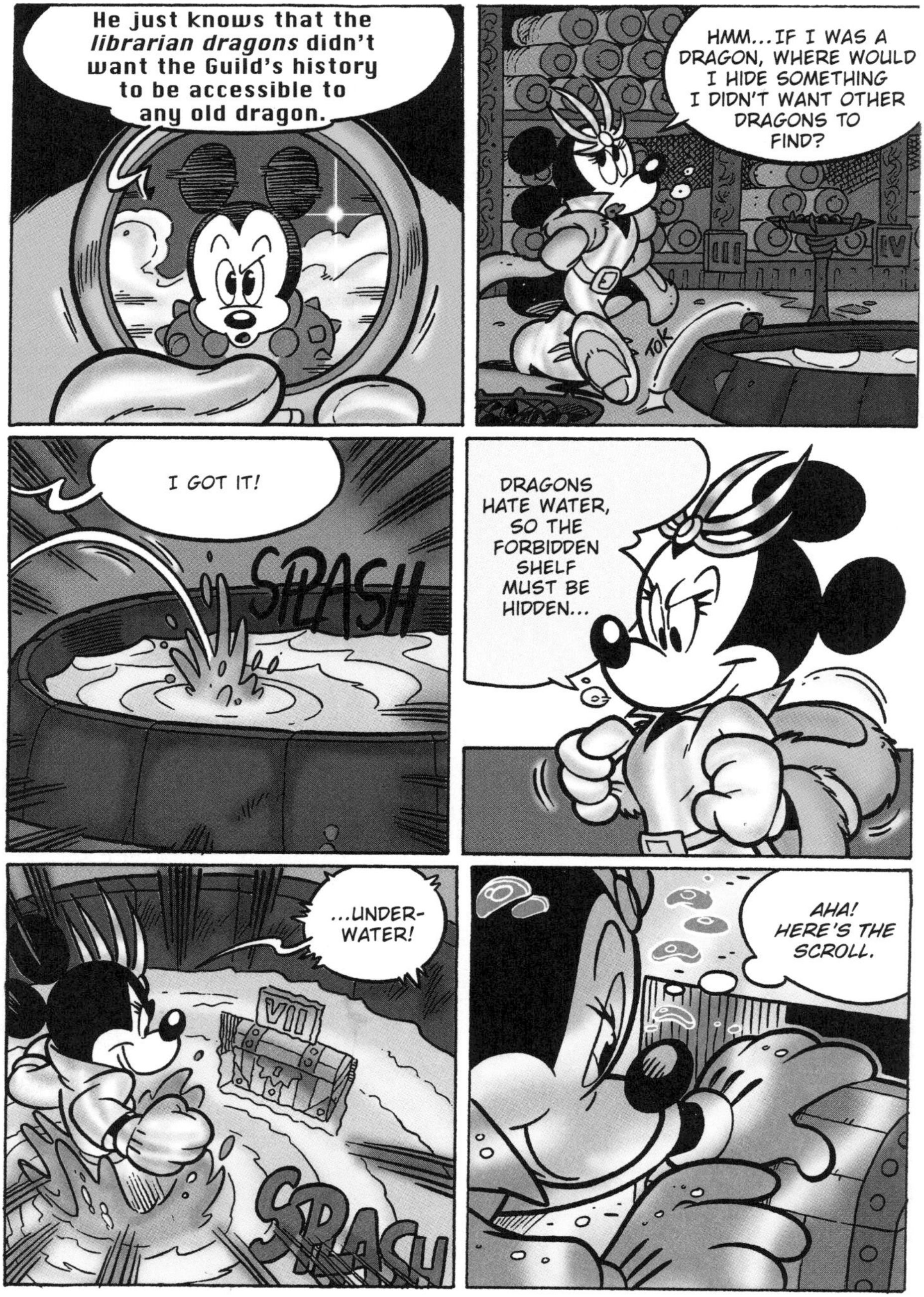
He just knows that the *librarian dragons* didn't want the Guild's history to be accessible to any old dragon.
HMM... IF I WAS A DRAGON, WHERE WOULD I HIDE SOMETHING I DIDN'T WANT OTHER DRAGONS TO FIND?
TOK
I GOT IT!
SPLASH
DRAGONS HATE WATER, SO THE FORBIDDEN SHELF MUST BE HIDDEN...
...UNDER-WATER!
VII
SPLASH
AHA! HERE'S THE SCROLL.

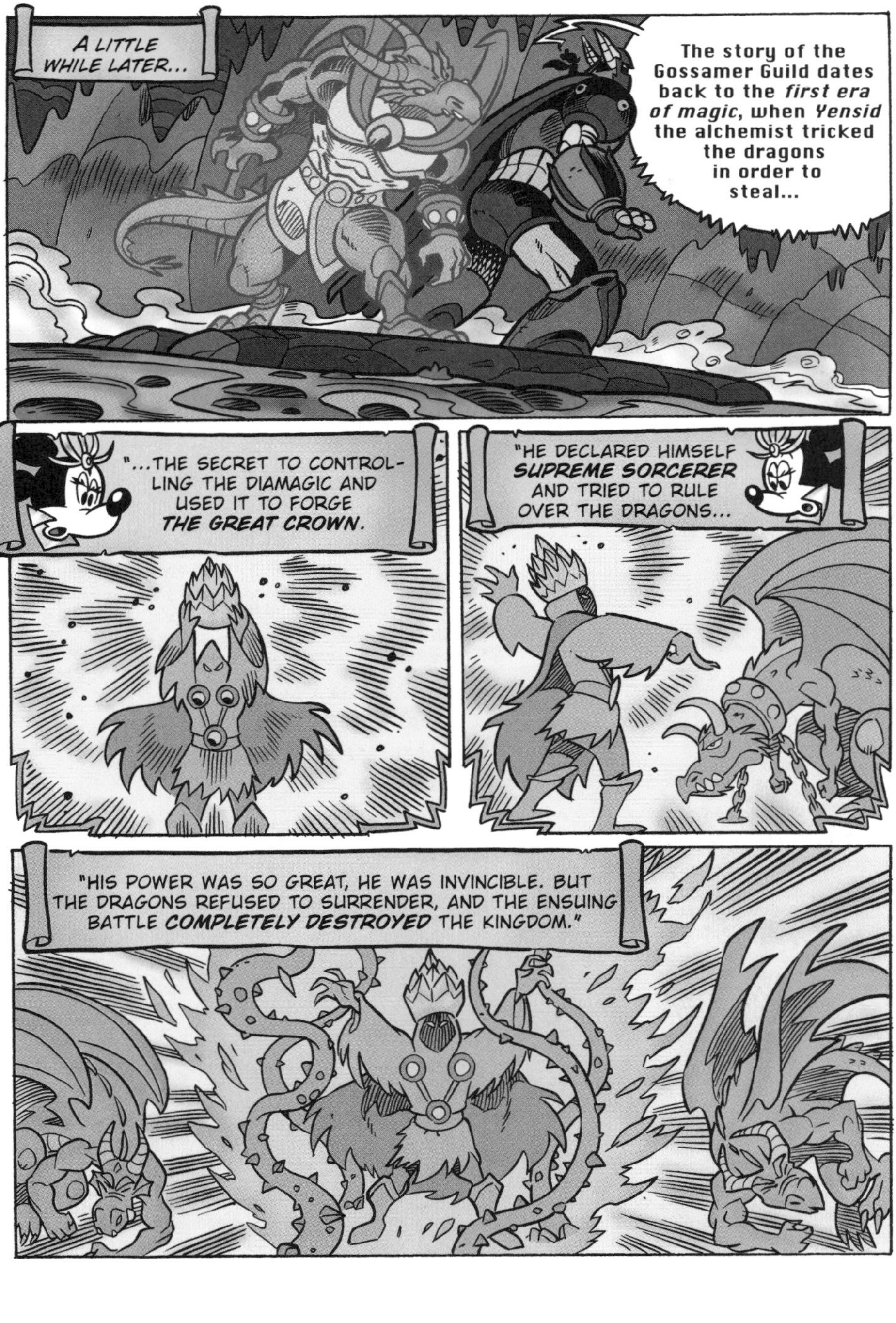
A LITTLE WHILE LATER...
The story of the Gossamer Guild dates back to the *first era of magic*, when *Yensid* the alchemist tricked the dragons in order to steal...
"...THE SECRET TO CONTROLLING THE DIAMAGIC AND USED IT TO FORGE ***THE GREAT CROWN***.
"HE DECLARED HIMSELF ***SUPREME SORCERER*** AND TRIED TO RULE OVER THE DRAGONS...
"HIS POWER WAS SO GREAT, HE WAS INVINCIBLE. BUT THE DRAGONS REFUSED TO SURRENDER, AND THE ENSUING BATTLE ***COMPLETELY DESTROYED*** THE KINGDOM."

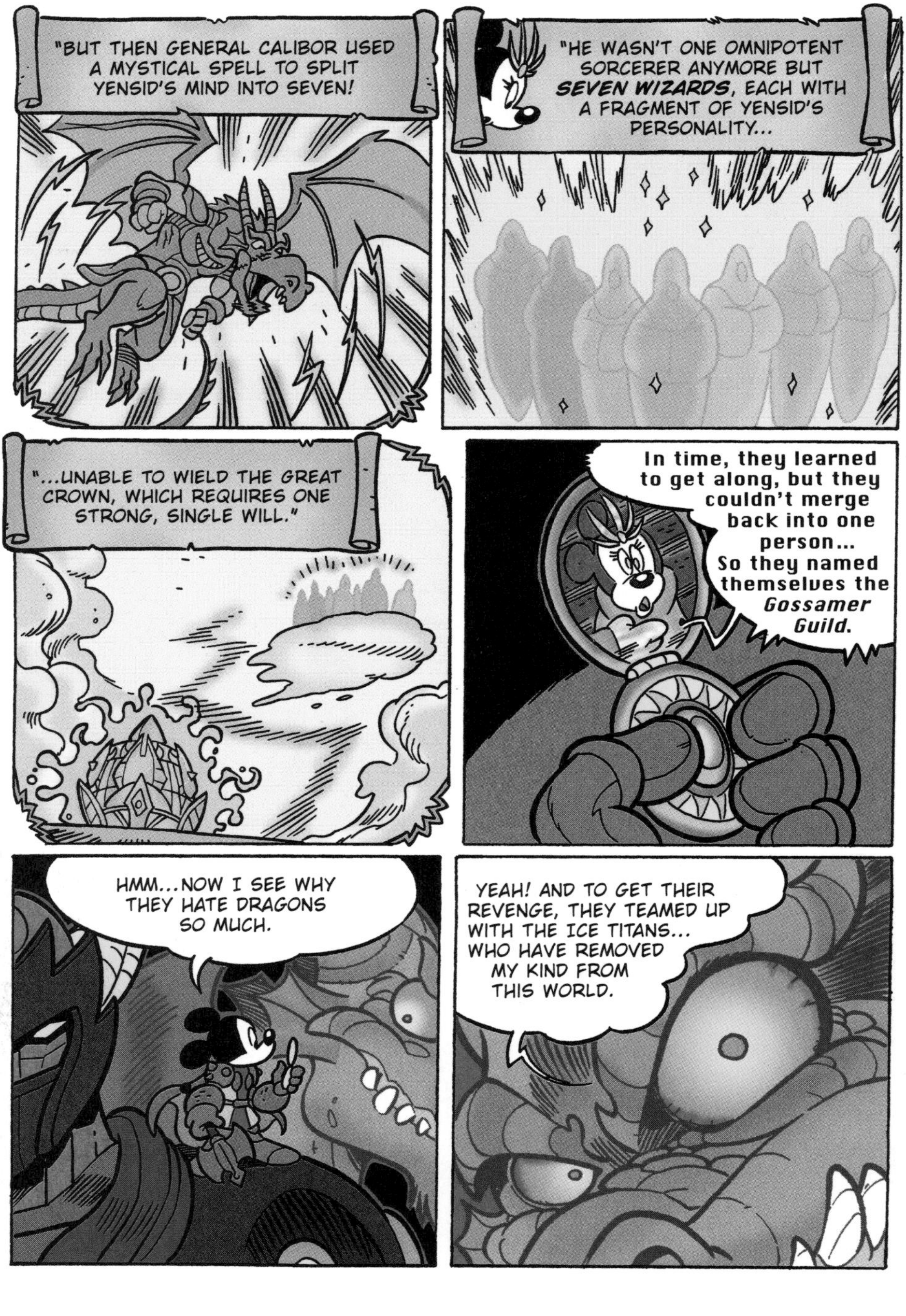
"BUT THEN GENERAL CALIBOR USED A MYSTICAL SPELL TO SPLIT YENSID'S MIND INTO SEVEN!
"HE WASN'T ONE OMNIPOTENT SORCERER ANYMORE BUT SEVEN WIZARDS, EACH WITH A FRAGMENT OF YENSID'S PERSONALITY...
"...UNABLE TO WIELD THE GREAT CROWN, WHICH REQUIRES ONE STRONG, SINGLE WILL."
In time, they learned to get along, but they couldn't merge back into one person... So they named themselves the Gossamer Guild.
HMM...NOW I SEE WHY THEY HATE DRAGONS SO MUCH.
YEAH! AND TO GET THEIR REVENGE, THEY TEAMED UP WITH THE ICE TITANS... WHO HAVE REMOVED MY KIND FROM THIS WORLD.

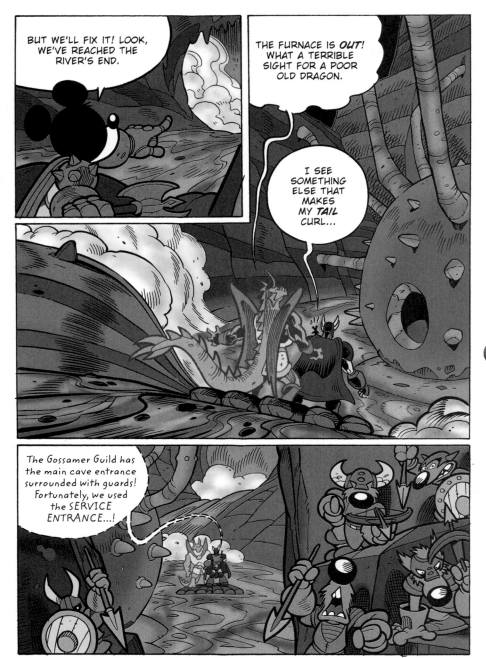

BUT WE'LL FIX IT! LOOK, WE'VE REACHED THE RIVER'S END.

THE FURNACE IS *OUT!* WHAT A TERRIBLE SIGHT FOR A POOR OLD DRAGON.

I SEE SOMETHING ELSE THAT MAKES MY *TAIL* CURL...

The Gossamer Guild has the main cave entrance surrounded with guards! Fortunately, we used the SERVICE ENTRANCE...!

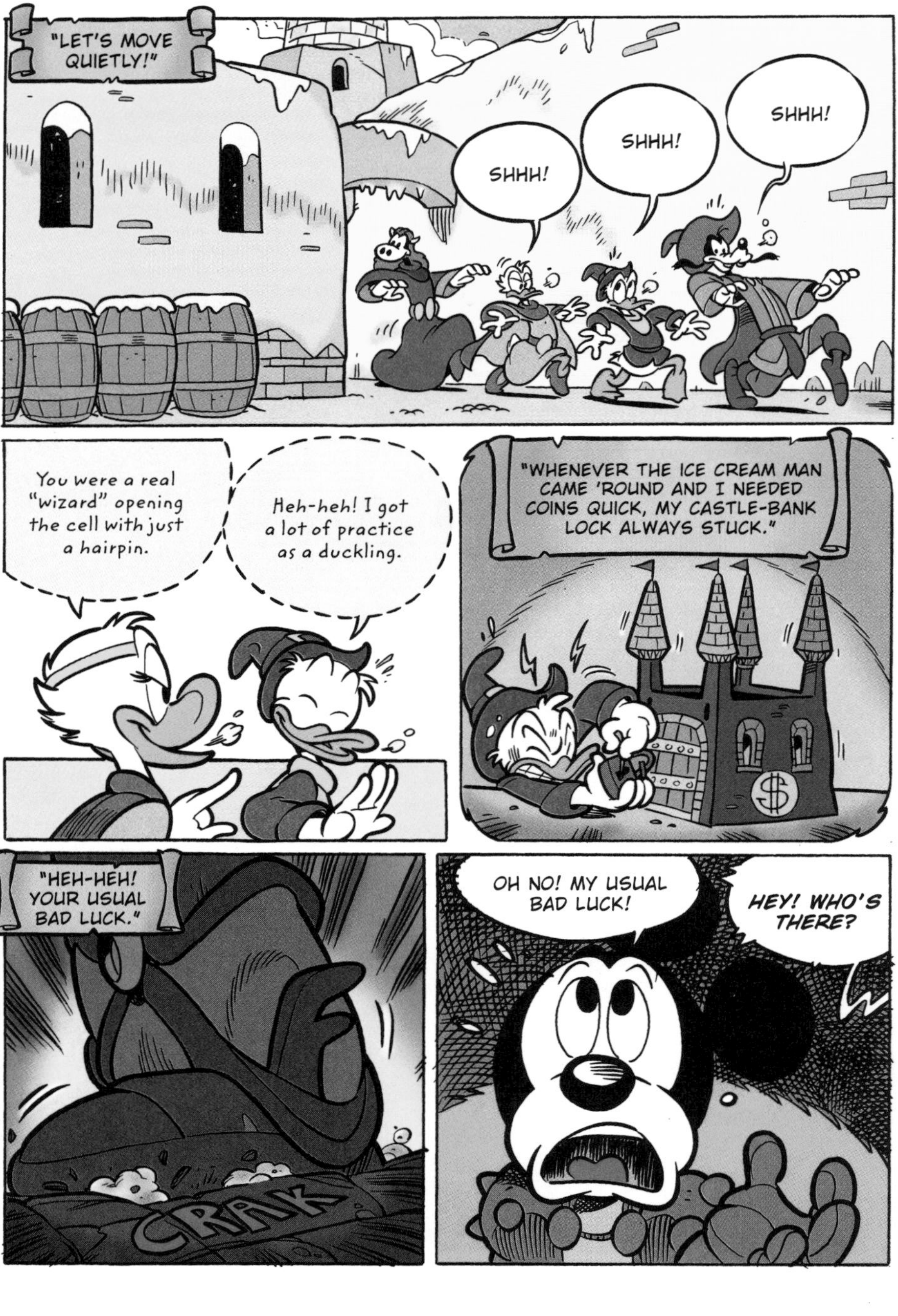
"LET'S MOVE QUIETLY!"
SHHH!
SHHH!
SHHH!
You were a real "wizard" opening the cell with just a hairpin.
Heh-heh! I got a lot of practice as a duckling.
"WHENEVER THE ICE CREAM MAN CAME 'ROUND AND I NEEDED COINS QUICK, MY CASTLE-BANK LOCK ALWAYS STUCK."
"HEH-HEH! YOUR USUAL BAD LUCK."
CRAK
OH NO! MY USUAL BAD LUCK!
HEY! WHO'S THERE?

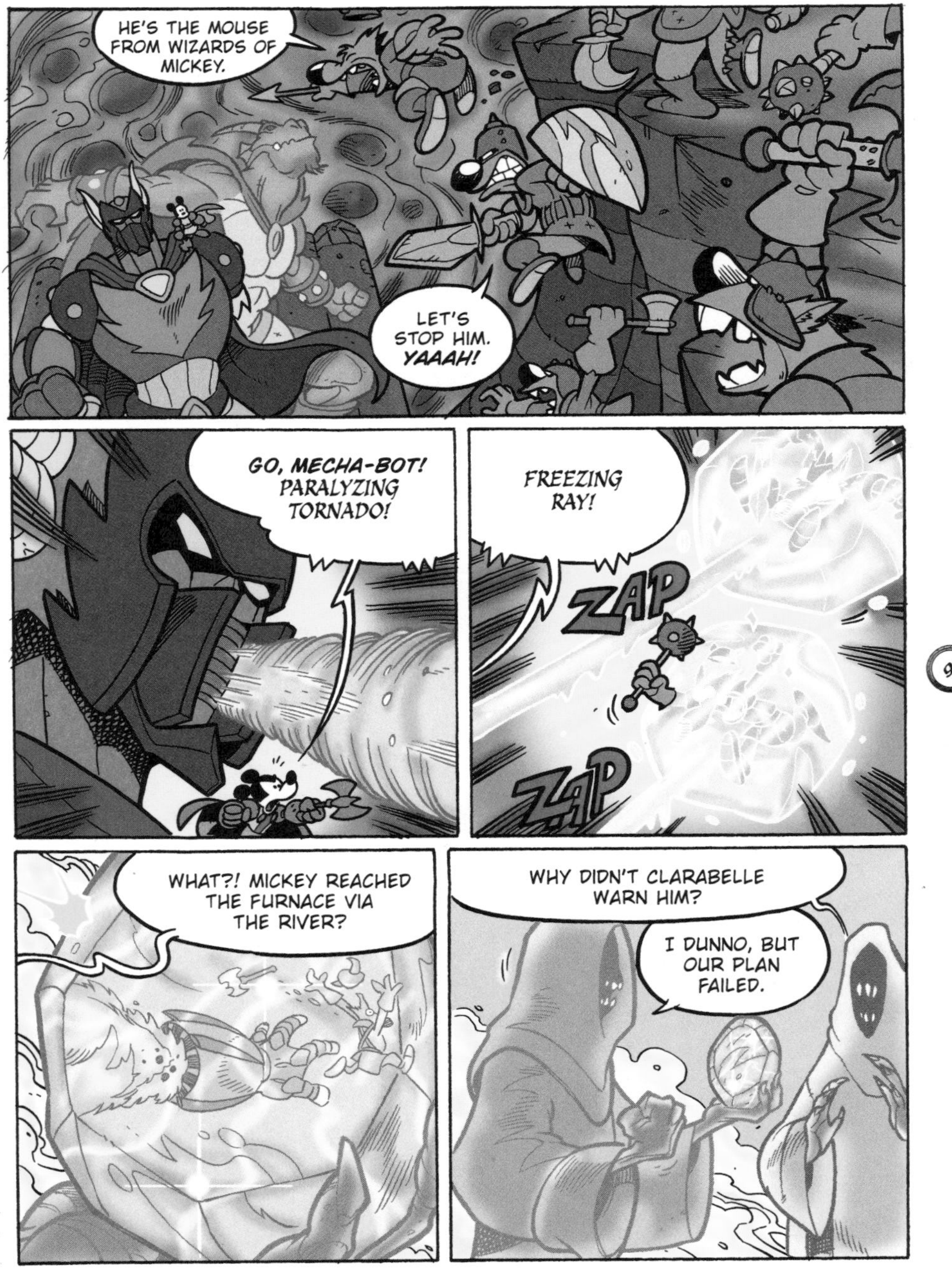
HE'S THE MOUSE FROM WIZARDS OF MICKEY.
LET'S STOP HIM. YAAAH!
GO, MECHA-BOT! PARALYZING TORNADO!
FREEZING RAY!
ZAP
ZAP
WHAT?! MICKEY REACHED THE FURNACE VIA THE RIVER?
WHY DIDN'T CLARABELLE WARN HIM?
I DUNNO, BUT OUR PLAN FAILED.

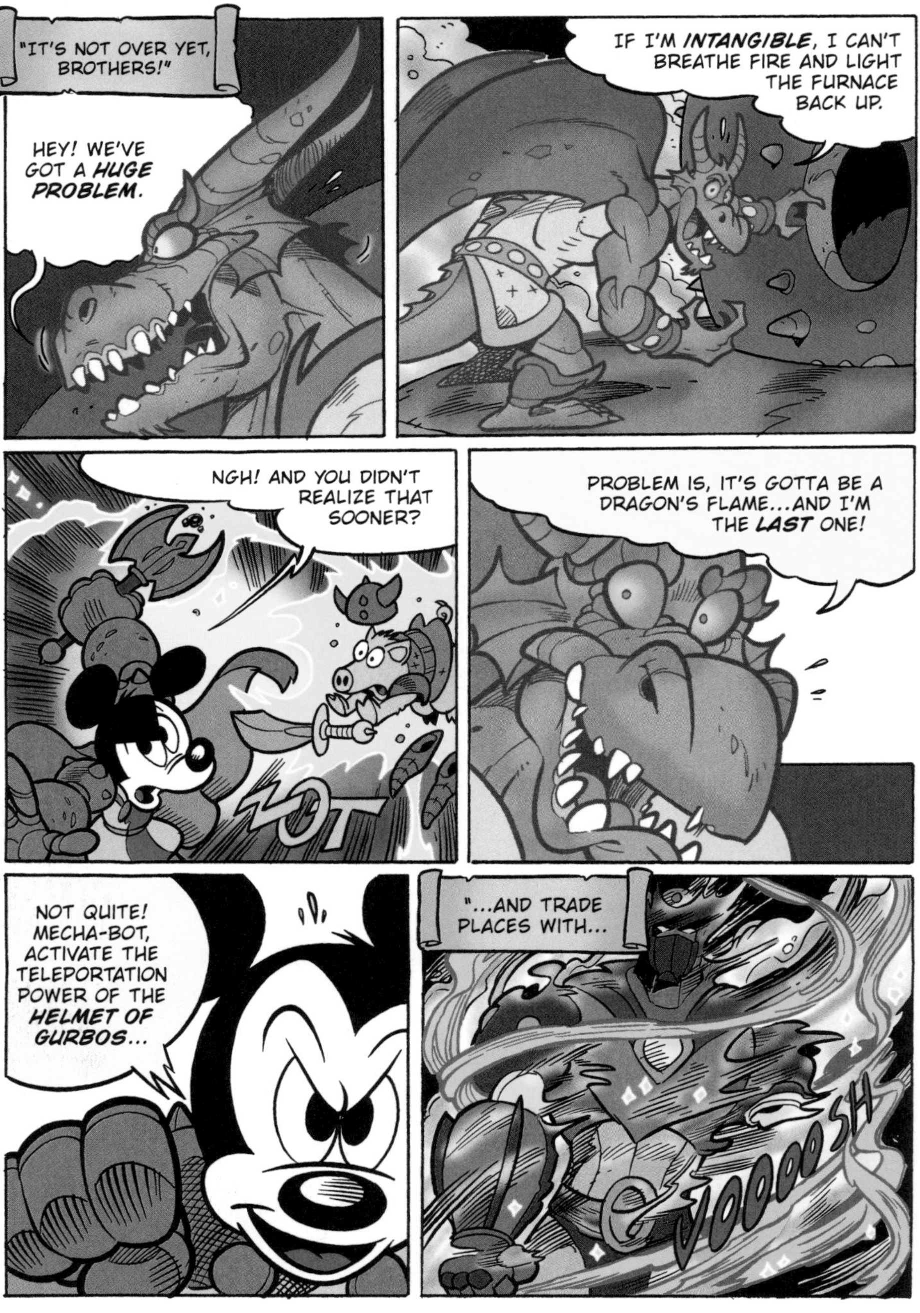
"IT'S NOT OVER YET, BROTHERS!"
HEY! WE'VE GOT A HUGE PROBLEM.
IF I'M INTANGIBLE, I CAN'T BREATHE FIRE AND LIGHT THE FURNACE BACK UP.
NGH! AND YOU DIDN'T REALIZE THAT SOONER?
ZOT
PROBLEM IS, IT'S GOTTA BE A DRAGON'S FLAME...AND I'M THE LAST ONE!
NOT QUITE! MECHA-BOT, ACTIVATE THE TELEPORTATION POWER OF THE HELMET OF GURBOS...
"...AND TRADE PLACES WITH...
VOOOOOSH

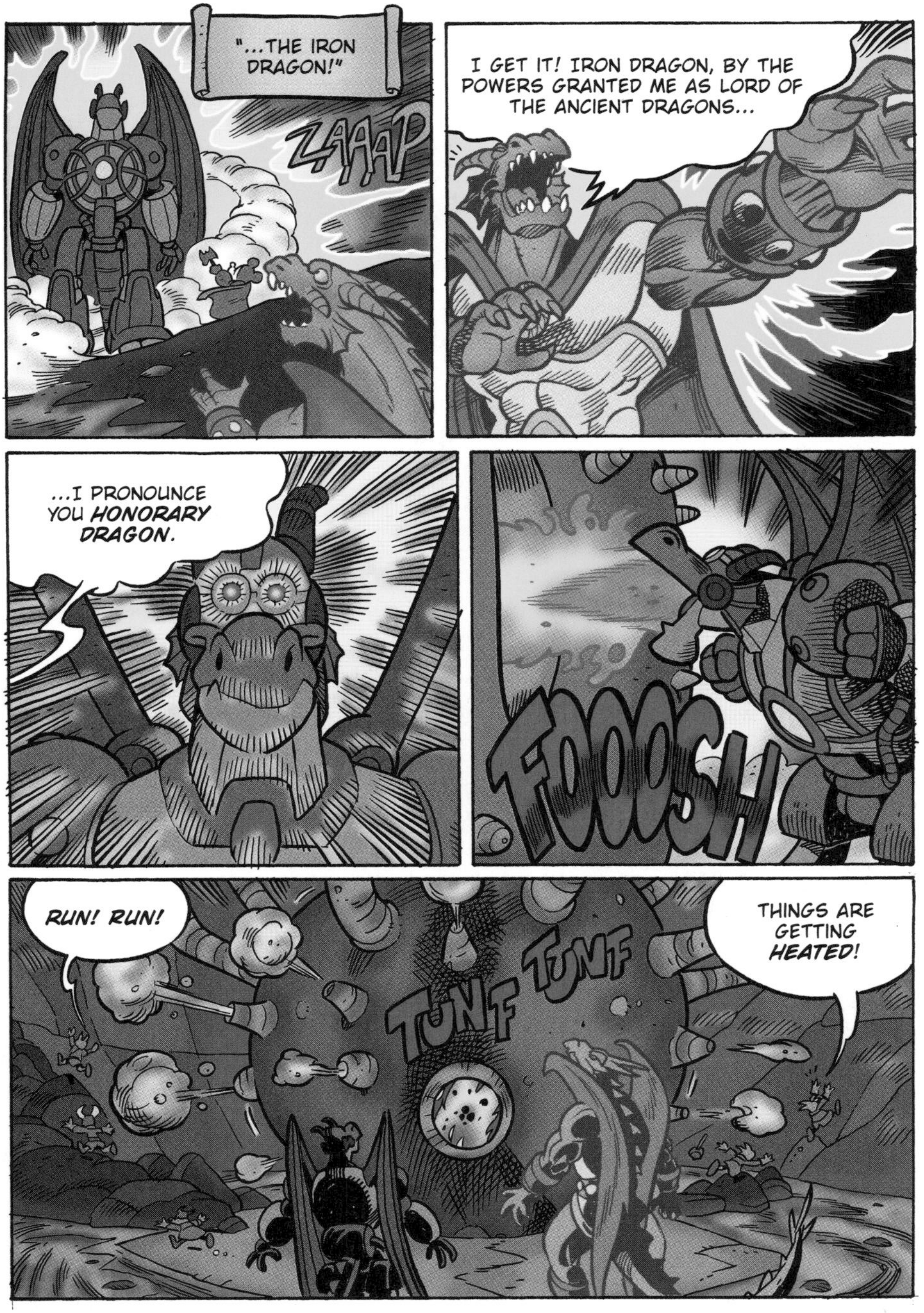
"...THE IRON DRAGON!"
ZAAAP
I GET IT! IRON DRAGON, BY THE POWERS GRANTED ME AS LORD OF THE ANCIENT DRAGONS...
...I PRONOUNCE YOU HONORARY DRAGON.
FOOOSH
RUN! RUN!
TUNF TUNF
THINGS ARE GETTING HEATED!

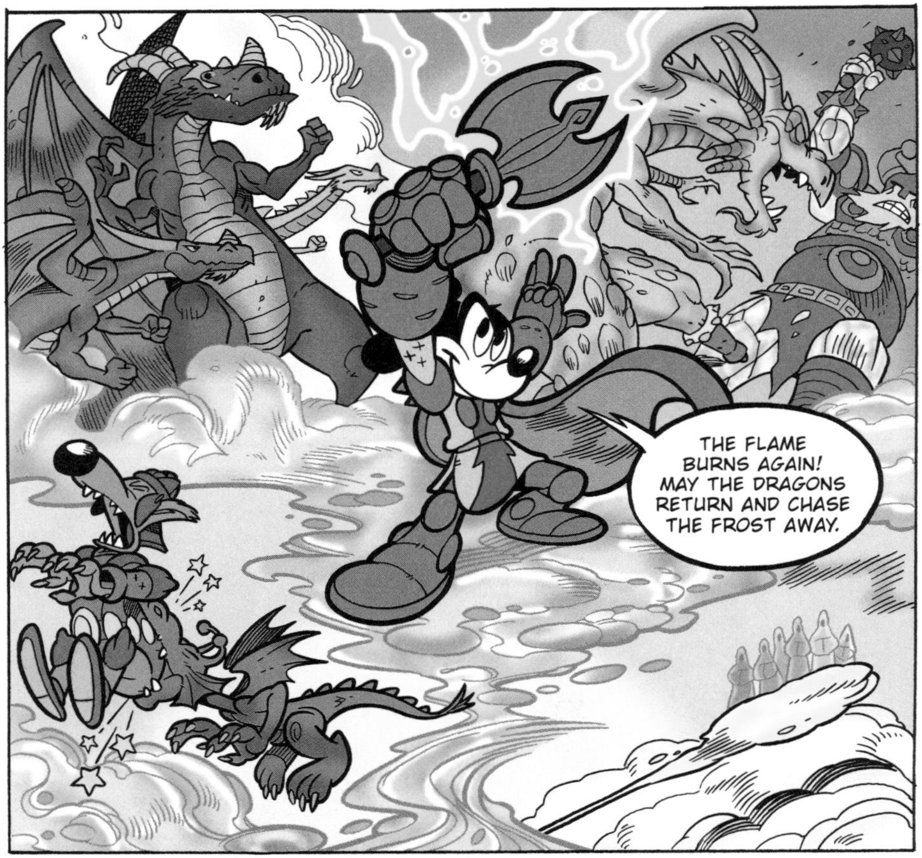
THE FLAME BURNS AGAIN! MAY THE DRAGONS RETURN AND CHASE THE FROST AWAY.

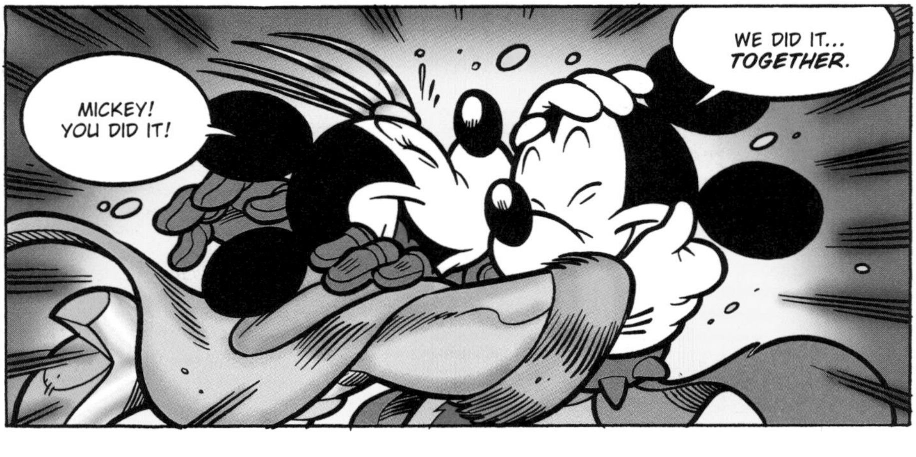
MICKEY! YOU DID IT!
WE DID IT... TOGETHER.

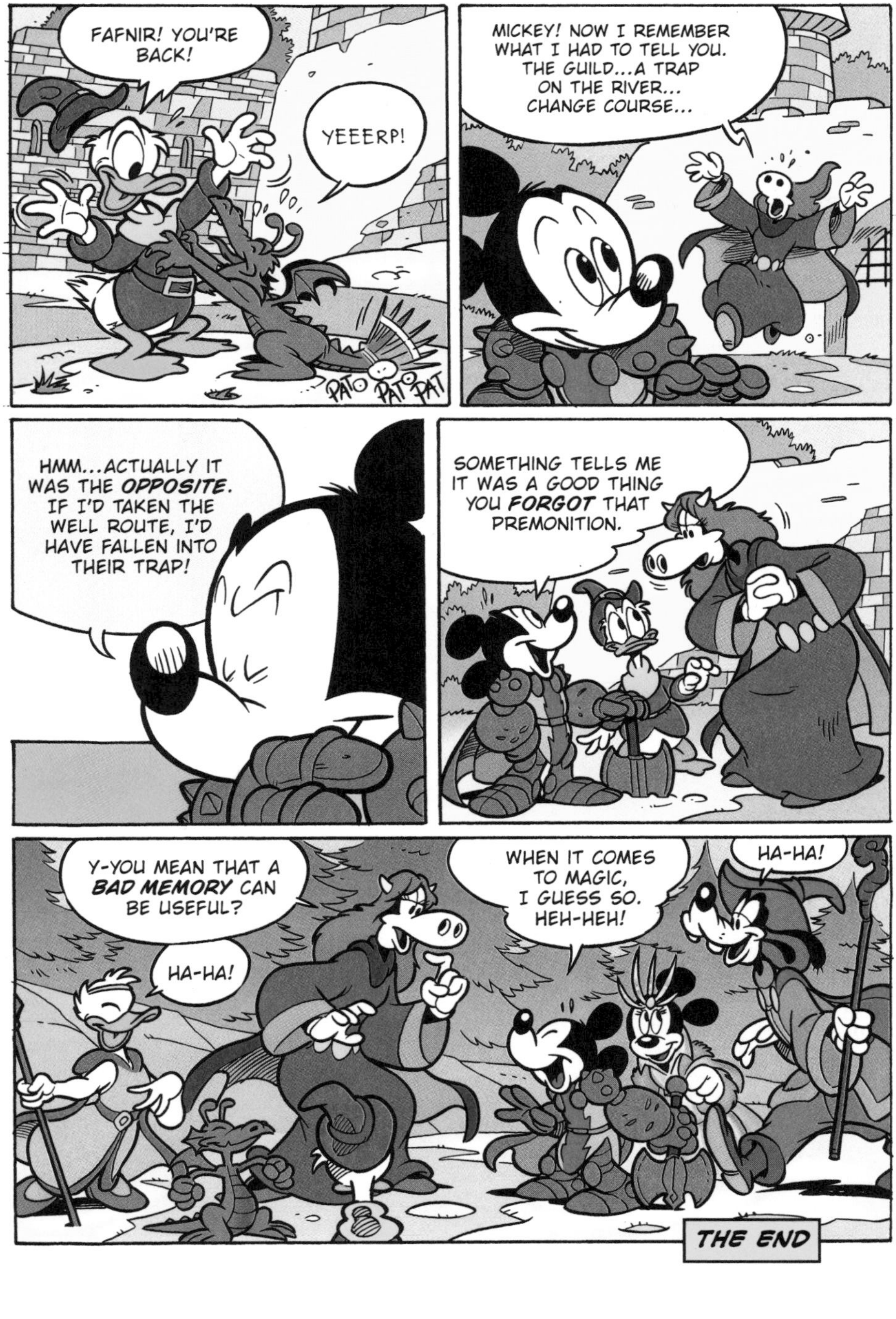
FAFNIR! YOU'RE BACK!
YEEERP!
PAT PAT PAT
MICKEY! NOW I REMEMBER WHAT I HAD TO TELL YOU. THE GUILD...A TRAP ON THE RIVER... CHANGE COURSE...
HMM...ACTUALLY IT WAS THE *OPPOSITE*. IF I'D TAKEN THE WELL ROUTE, I'D HAVE FALLEN INTO THEIR TRAP!
SOMETHING TELLS ME IT WAS A GOOD THING YOU *FORGOT* THAT PREMONITION.
Y-YOU MEAN THAT A *BAD MEMORY* CAN BE USEFUL?
HA-HA!
WHEN IT COMES TO MAGIC, I GUESS SO. HEH-HEH!
HA-HA!
THE END

Wizards of Mickey

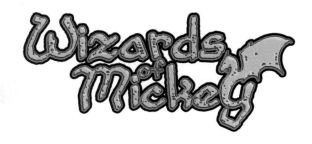

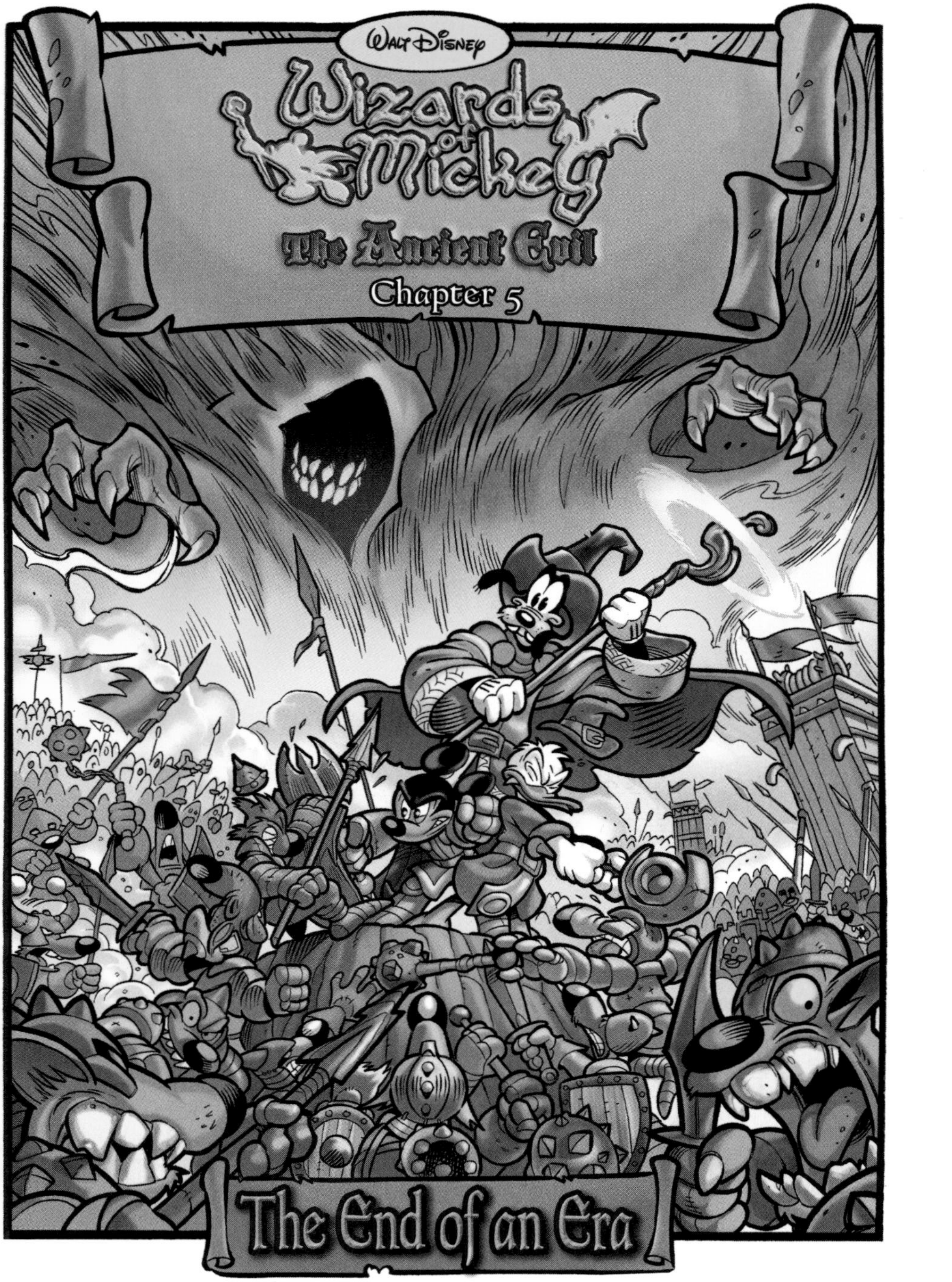
Walt Disney
Wizards of Mickey
The Ancient Evil
Chapter 5
The End of an Era

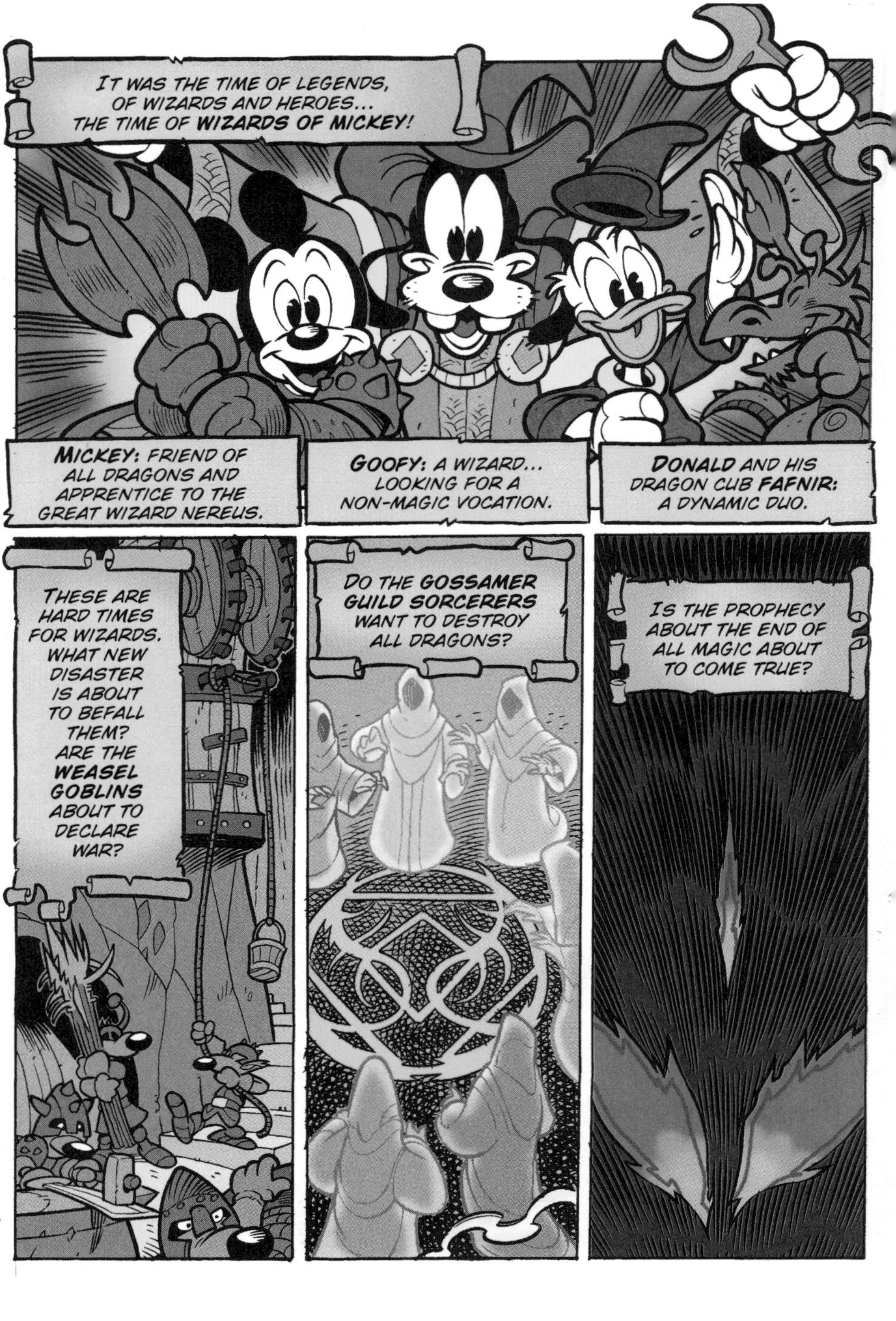
IT WAS THE TIME OF LEGENDS, OF WIZARDS AND HEROES... THE TIME OF **WIZARDS OF MICKEY**!
MICKEY: FRIEND OF ALL DRAGONS AND APPRENTICE TO THE GREAT WIZARD NEREUS.
GOOFY: A WIZARD... LOOKING FOR A NON-MAGIC VOCATION.
DONALD AND HIS DRAGON CUB **FAFNIR**: A DYNAMIC DUO.
THESE ARE HARD TIMES FOR WIZARDS. WHAT NEW DISASTER IS ABOUT TO BEFALL THEM? ARE THE **WEASEL GOBLINS** ABOUT TO DECLARE WAR?
DO THE **GOSSAMER GUILD SORCERERS** WANT TO DESTROY ALL DRAGONS?
IS THE PROPHECY ABOUT THE END OF ALL MAGIC ABOUT TO COME TRUE?

98

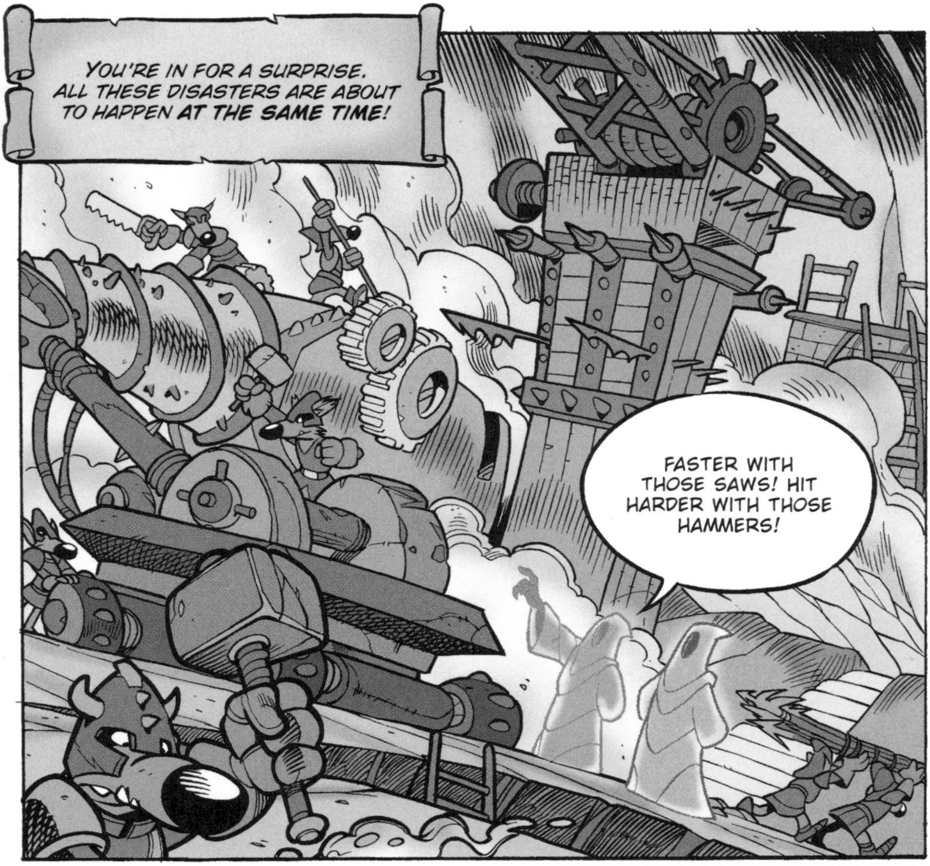
YOU'RE IN FOR A SURPRISE. ALL THESE DISASTERS ARE ABOUT TO HAPPEN AT THE SAME TIME!
FASTER WITH THOSE SAWS! HIT HARDER WITH THOSE HAMMERS!

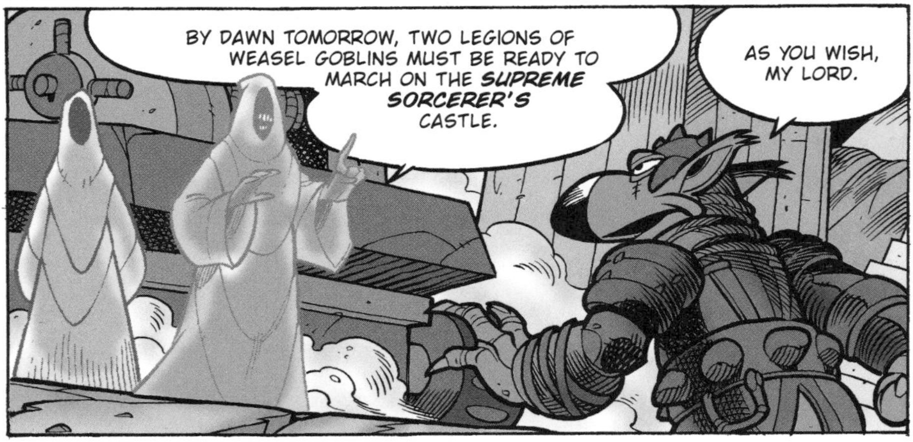
BY DAWN TOMORROW, TWO LEGIONS OF WEASEL GOBLINS MUST BE READY TO MARCH ON THE SUPREME SORCERER'S CASTLE.
AS YOU WISH, MY LORD.

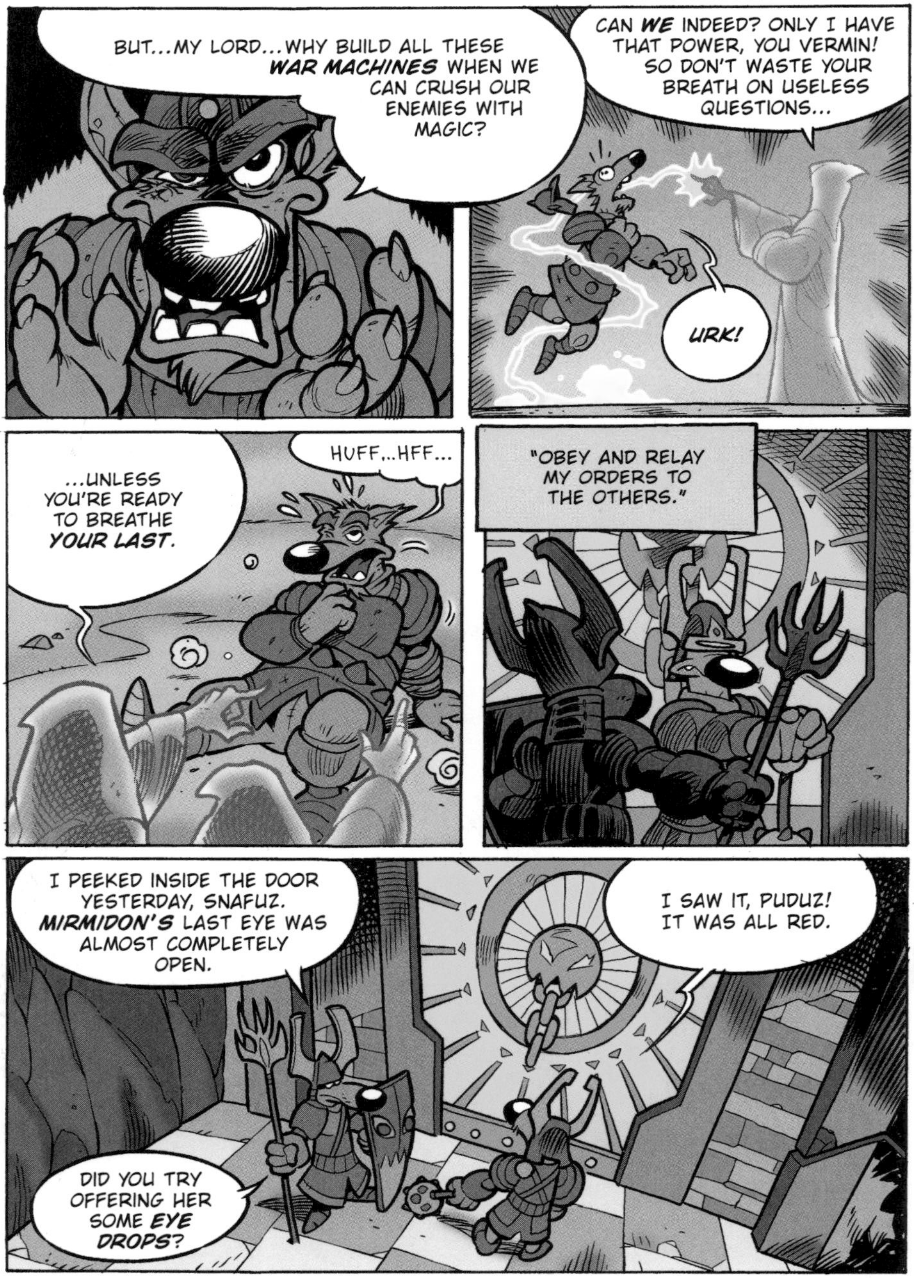
BUT...MY LORD...WHY BUILD ALL THESE WAR MACHINES WHEN WE CAN CRUSH OUR ENEMIES WITH MAGIC?
CAN WE INDEED? ONLY I HAVE THAT POWER, YOU VERMIN! SO DON'T WASTE YOUR BREATH ON USELESS QUESTIONS...
URK!
...UNLESS YOU'RE READY TO BREATHE YOUR LAST.
HUFF...HFF...
"OBEY AND RELAY MY ORDERS TO THE OTHERS."
I PEEKED INSIDE THE DOOR YESTERDAY, SNAFUZ. MIRMIDON'S LAST EYE WAS ALMOST COMPLETELY OPEN.
I SAW IT, PUDUZ! IT WAS ALL RED.
DID YOU TRY OFFERING HER SOME EYE DROPS?

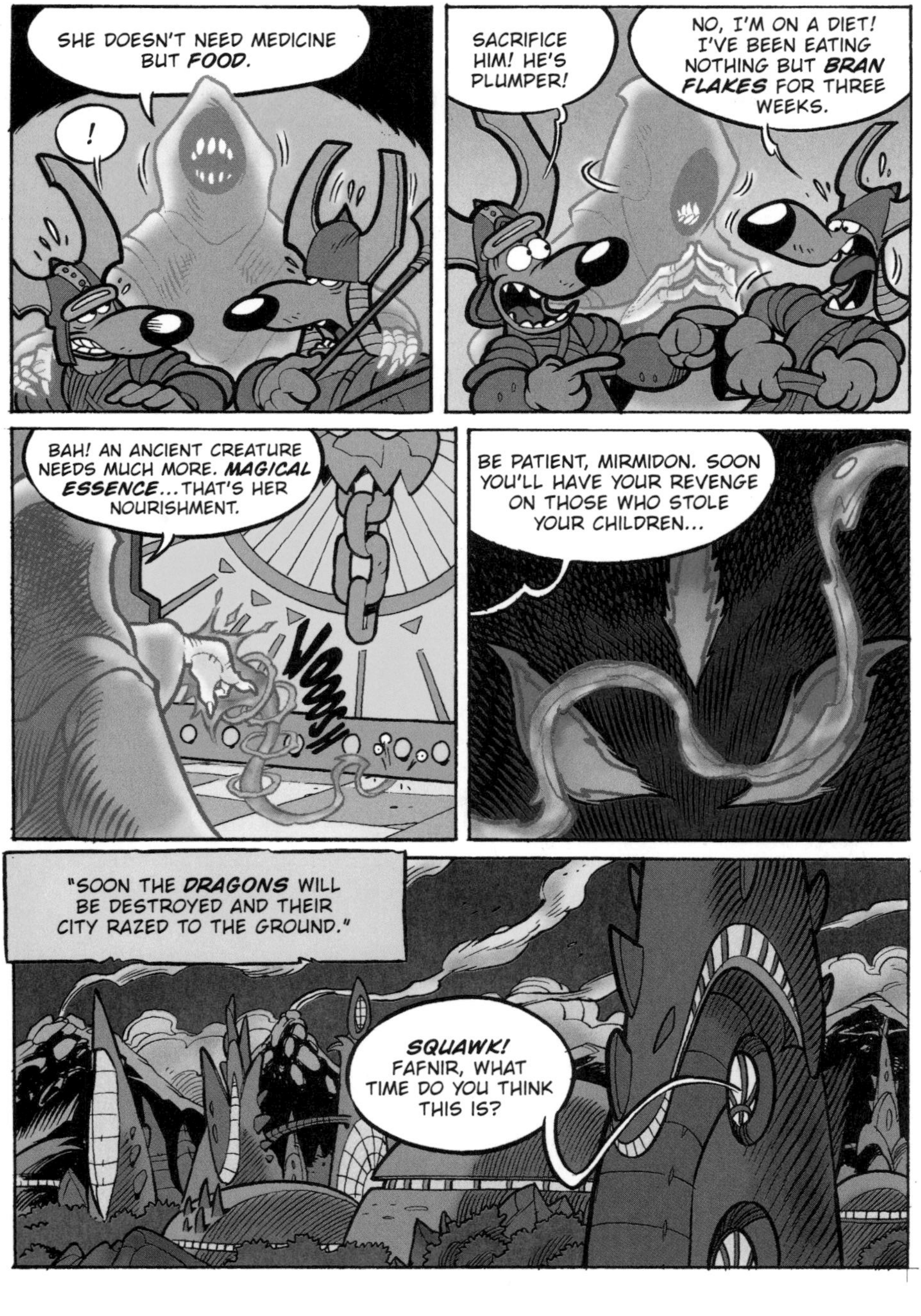
SHE DOESN'T NEED MEDICINE BUT FOOD.
!
SACRIFICE HIM! HE'S PLUMPER!
NO, I'M ON A DIET! I'VE BEEN EATING NOTHING BUT BRAN FLAKES FOR THREE WEEKS.
BAH! AN ANCIENT CREATURE NEEDS MUCH MORE. MAGICAL ESSENCE...THAT'S HER NOURISHMENT.
BE PATIENT, MIRMIDON. SOON YOU'LL HAVE YOUR REVENGE ON THOSE WHO STOLE YOUR CHILDREN...
"SOON THE DRAGONS WILL BE DESTROYED AND THEIR CITY RAZED TO THE GROUND."
SQUAWK! FAFNIR, WHAT TIME DO YOU THINK THIS IS?

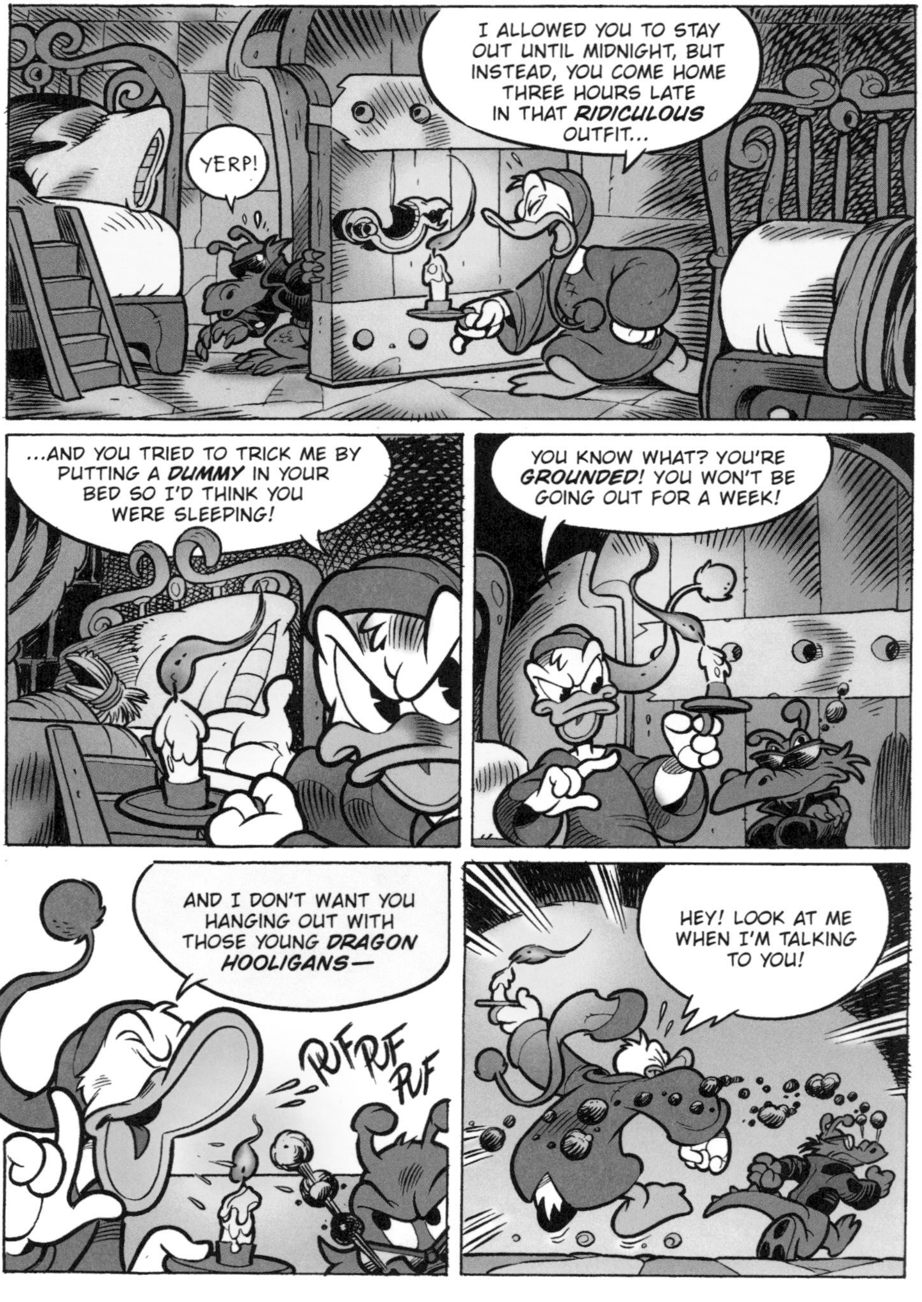
I ALLOWED YOU TO STAY OUT UNTIL MIDNIGHT, BUT INSTEAD, YOU COME HOME THREE HOURS LATE IN THAT RIDICULOUS OUTFIT...
YERP!
...AND YOU TRIED TO TRICK ME BY PUTTING A DUMMY IN YOUR BED SO I'D THINK YOU WERE SLEEPING!
YOU KNOW WHAT? YOU'RE GROUNDED! YOU WON'T BE GOING OUT FOR A WEEK!
AND I DON'T WANT YOU HANGING OUT WITH THOSE YOUNG DRAGON HOOLIGANS—
PUF PUF PUF
HEY! LOOK AT ME WHEN I'M TALKING TO YOU!

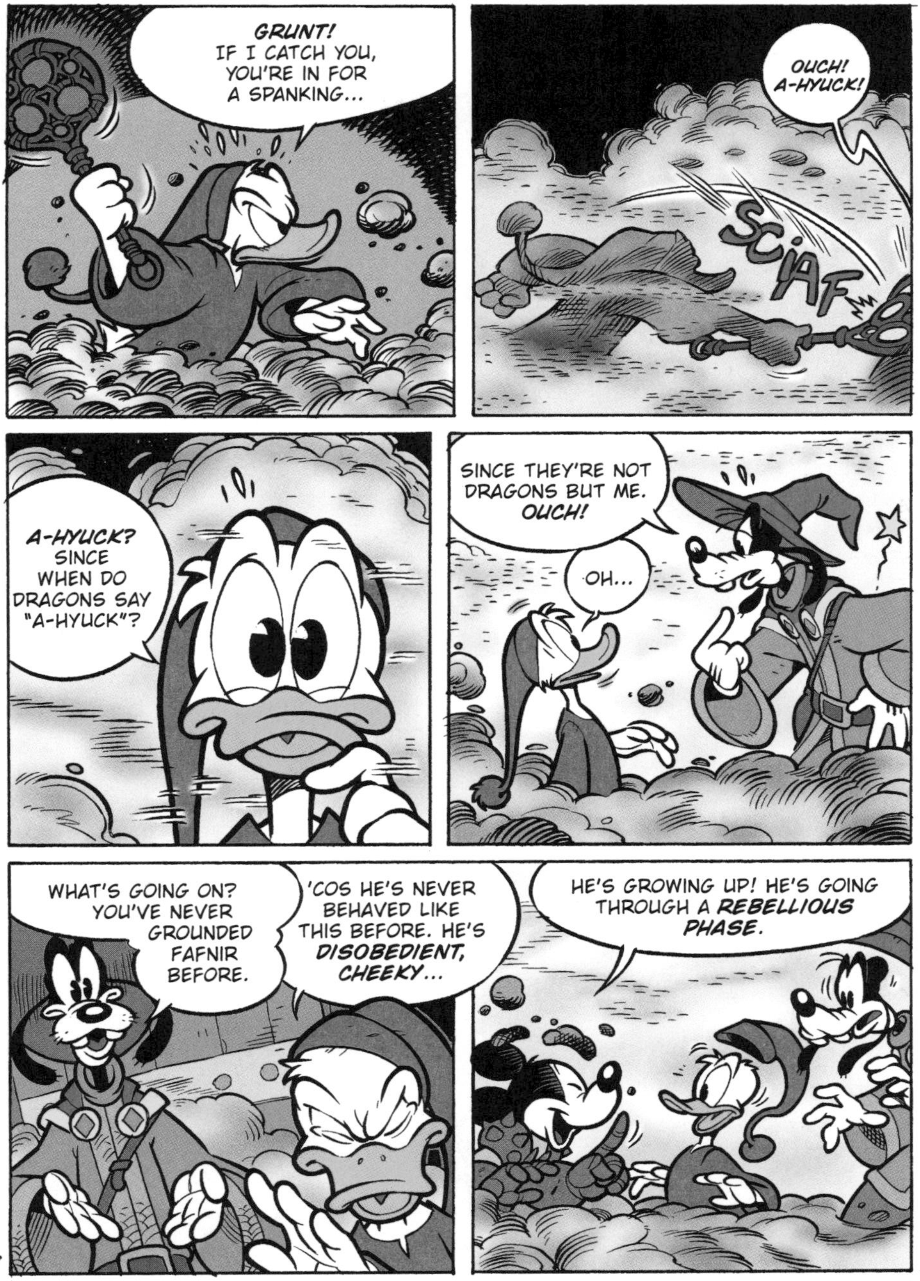
GRUNT! IF I CATCH YOU, YOU'RE IN FOR A SPANKING...
OUCH! A-HYUCK!
SCIAF
A-HYUCK? SINCE WHEN DO DRAGONS SAY "A-HYUCK"?
SINCE THEY'RE NOT DRAGONS BUT ME. OUCH!
OH...
WHAT'S GOING ON? YOU'VE NEVER GROUNDED FAFNIR BEFORE.
'COS HE'S NEVER BEHAVED LIKE THIS BEFORE. HE'S DISOBEDIENT, CHEEKY...
HE'S GROWING UP! HE'S GOING THROUGH A REBELLIOUS PHASE.

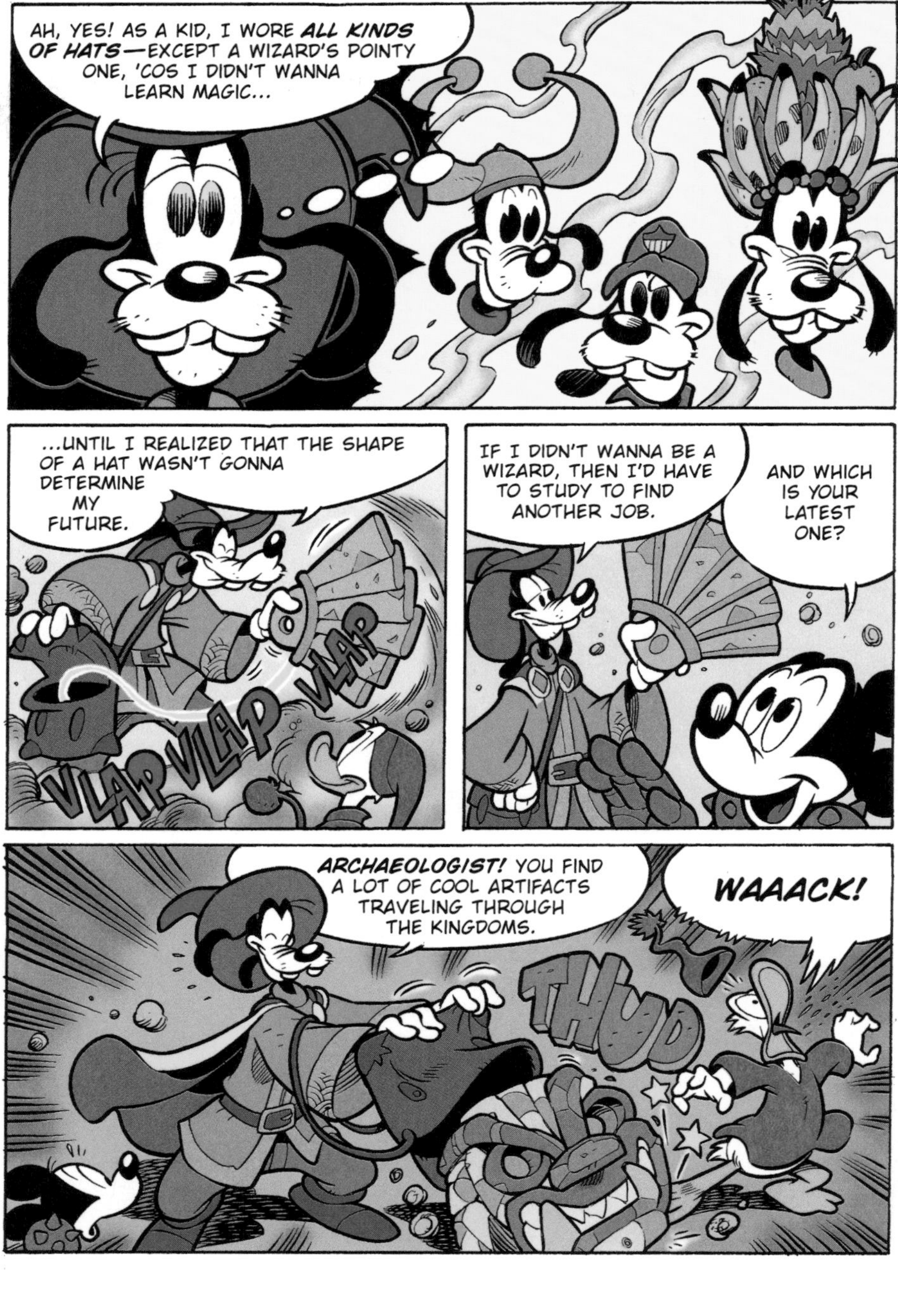
AH, YES! AS A KID, I WORE ***ALL KINDS OF HATS***—EXCEPT A WIZARD'S POINTY ONE, 'COS I DIDN'T WANNA LEARN MAGIC...
...UNTIL I REALIZED THAT THE SHAPE OF A HAT WASN'T GONNA DETERMINE MY FUTURE.
VLAP VLAP VLAP VLAP
IF I DIDN'T WANNA BE A WIZARD, THEN I'D HAVE TO STUDY TO FIND ANOTHER JOB.
AND WHICH IS YOUR LATEST ONE?
ARCHAEOLOGIST! YOU FIND A LOT OF COOL ARTIFACTS TRAVELING THROUGH THE KINGDOMS.
WAAACK!
THUD

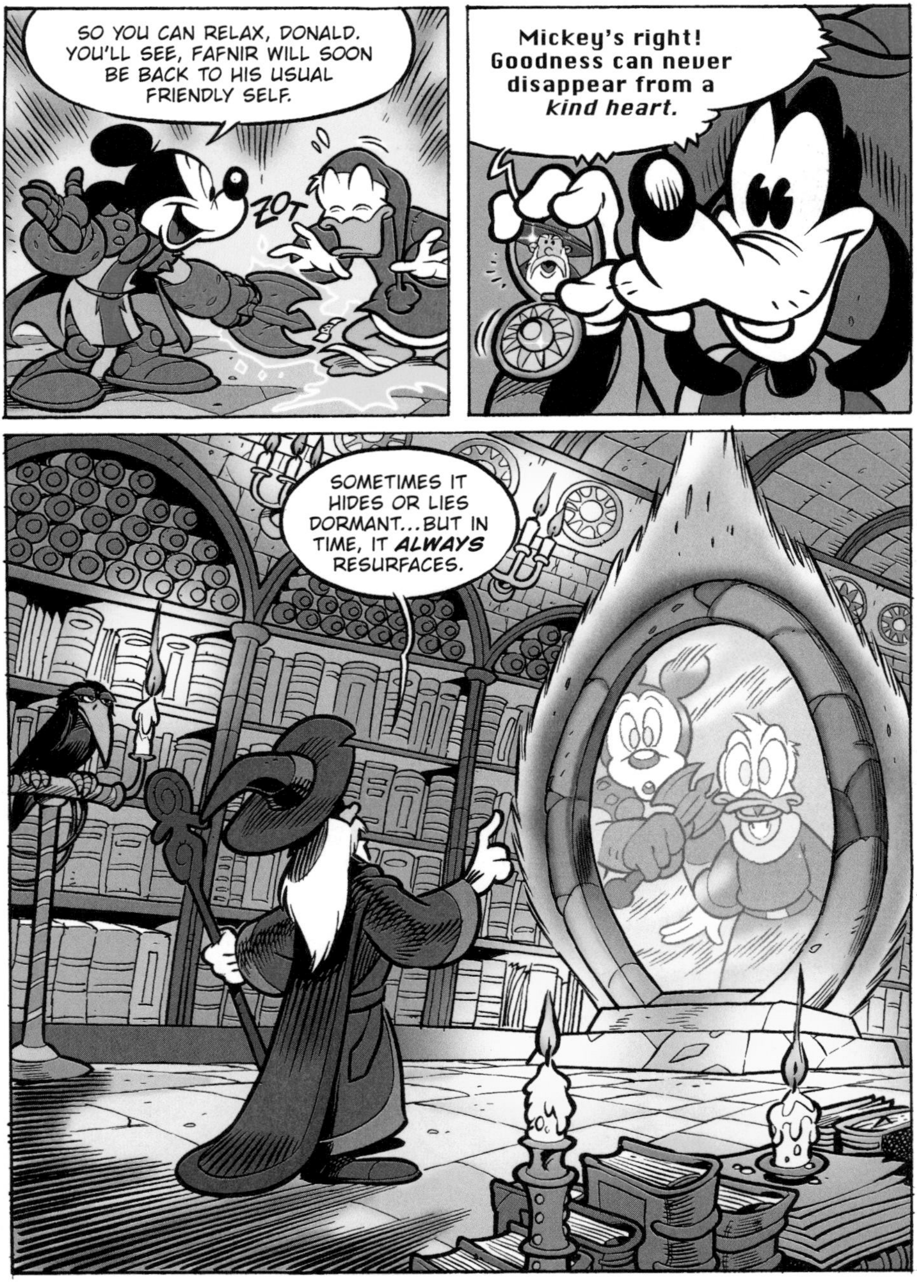
SO YOU CAN RELAX, DONALD. YOU'LL SEE, FAFNIR WILL SOON BE BACK TO HIS USUAL FRIENDLY SELF.
ZOT
Mickey's right! Goodness can never disappear from a *kind heart.*
SOMETIMES IT HIDES OR LIES DORMANT...BUT IN TIME, IT ***ALWAYS*** RESURFACES.

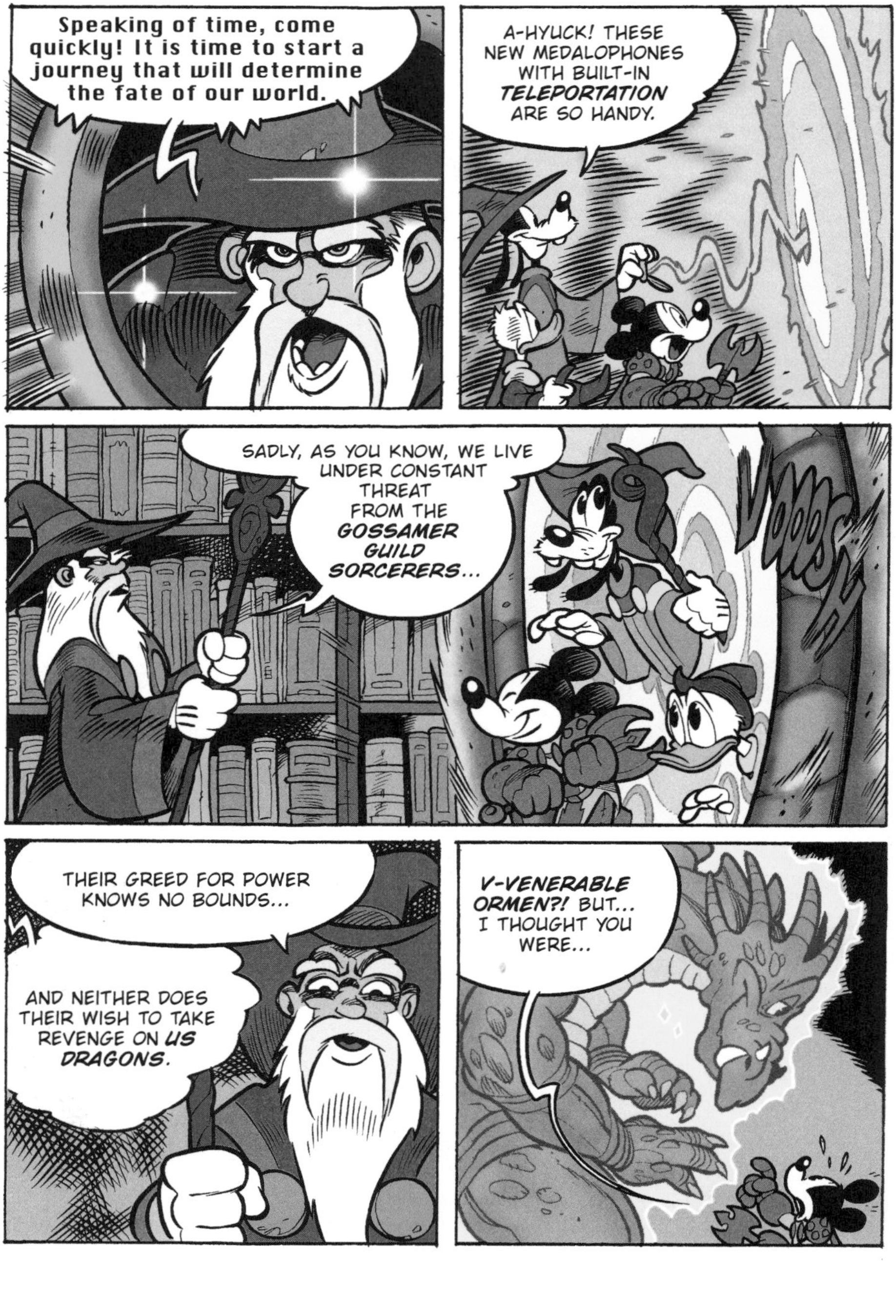

Speaking of time, come quickly! It is time to start a journey that will determine the fate of our world.
A-HYUCK! THESE NEW MEDALOPHONES WITH BUILT-IN ***TELEPORTATION*** ARE SO HANDY.
SADLY, AS YOU KNOW, WE LIVE UNDER CONSTANT THREAT FROM THE ***GOSSAMER GUILD SORCERERS...***
VOOOSH
THEIR GREED FOR POWER KNOWS NO BOUNDS...
AND NEITHER DOES THEIR WISH TO TAKE REVENGE ON ***US DRAGONS.***
V-VENERABLE ORMEN?! BUT... I THOUGHT YOU WERE...

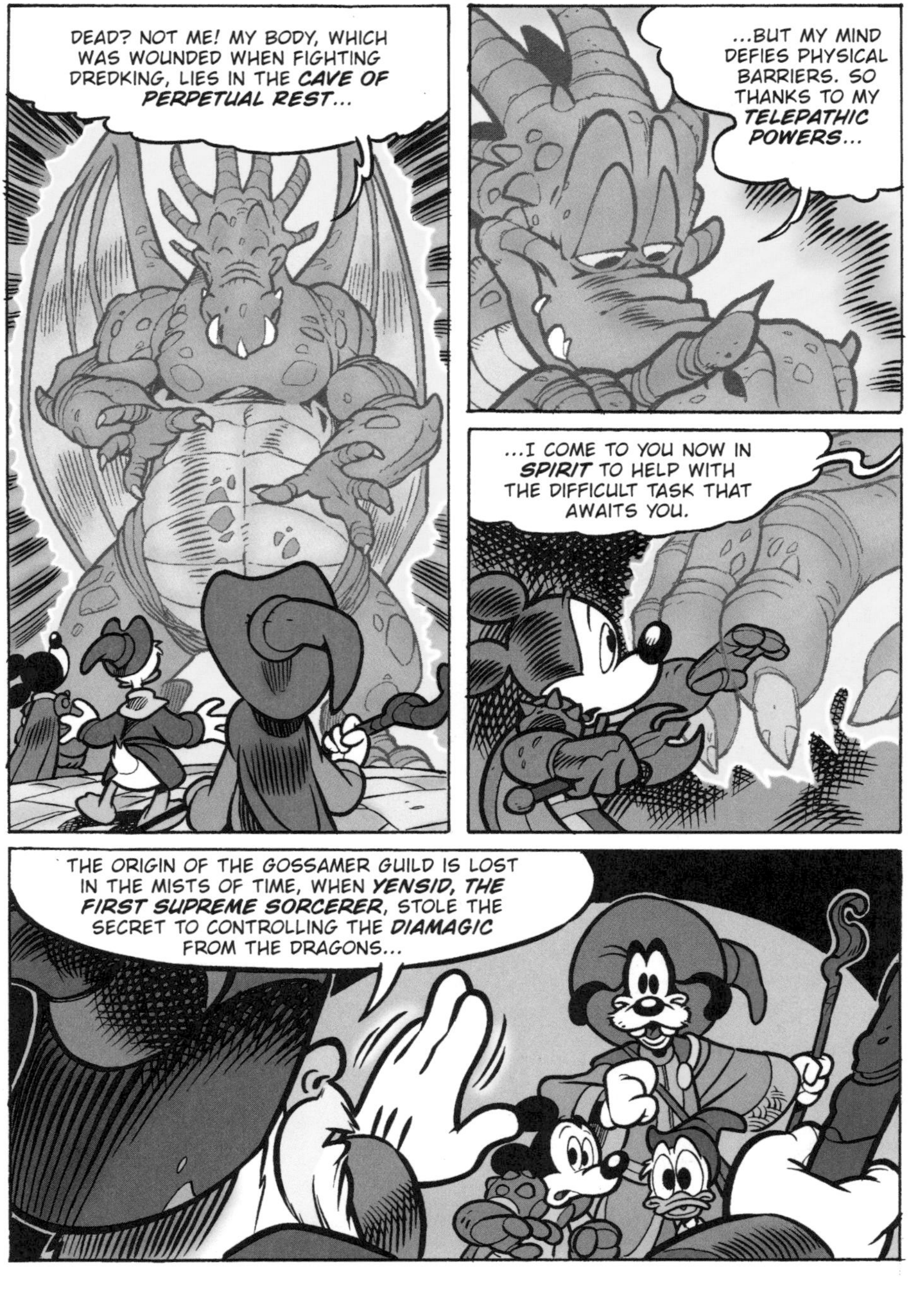
DEAD? NOT ME! MY BODY, WHICH WAS WOUNDED WHEN FIGHTING DREDKING, LIES IN THE CAVE OF PERPETUAL REST...
...BUT MY MIND DEFIES PHYSICAL BARRIERS. SO THANKS TO MY TELEPATHIC POWERS...
...I COME TO YOU NOW IN SPIRIT TO HELP WITH THE DIFFICULT TASK THAT AWAITS YOU.
THE ORIGIN OF THE GOSSAMER GUILD IS LOST IN THE MISTS OF TIME, WHEN YENSID, THE FIRST SUPREME SORCERER, STOLE THE SECRET TO CONTROLLING THE DIAMAGIC FROM THE DRAGONS...

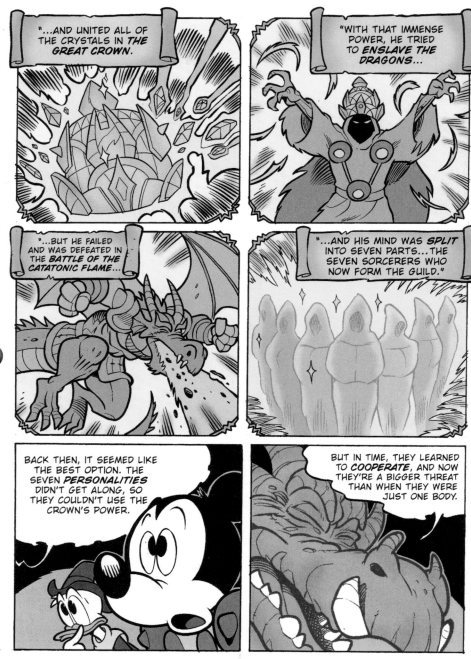

"...AND UNITED ALL OF THE CRYSTALS IN *THE GREAT CROWN*.

"WITH THAT IMMENSE POWER, HE TRIED TO *ENSLAVE THE DRAGONS*...

"...BUT HE FAILED AND WAS DEFEATED IN THE *BATTLE OF THE CATATONIC FLAME*...

"...AND HIS MIND WAS *SPLIT* INTO SEVEN PARTS...THE SEVEN SORCERERS WHO NOW FORM THE GUILD."

BACK THEN, IT SEEMED LIKE THE BEST OPTION. THE SEVEN *PERSONALITIES* DIDN'T GET ALONG, SO THEY COULDN'T USE THE CROWN'S POWER.

BUT IN TIME, THEY LEARNED TO *COOPERATE*, AND NOW THEY'RE A BIGGER THREAT THAN WHEN THEY WERE JUST ONE BODY.

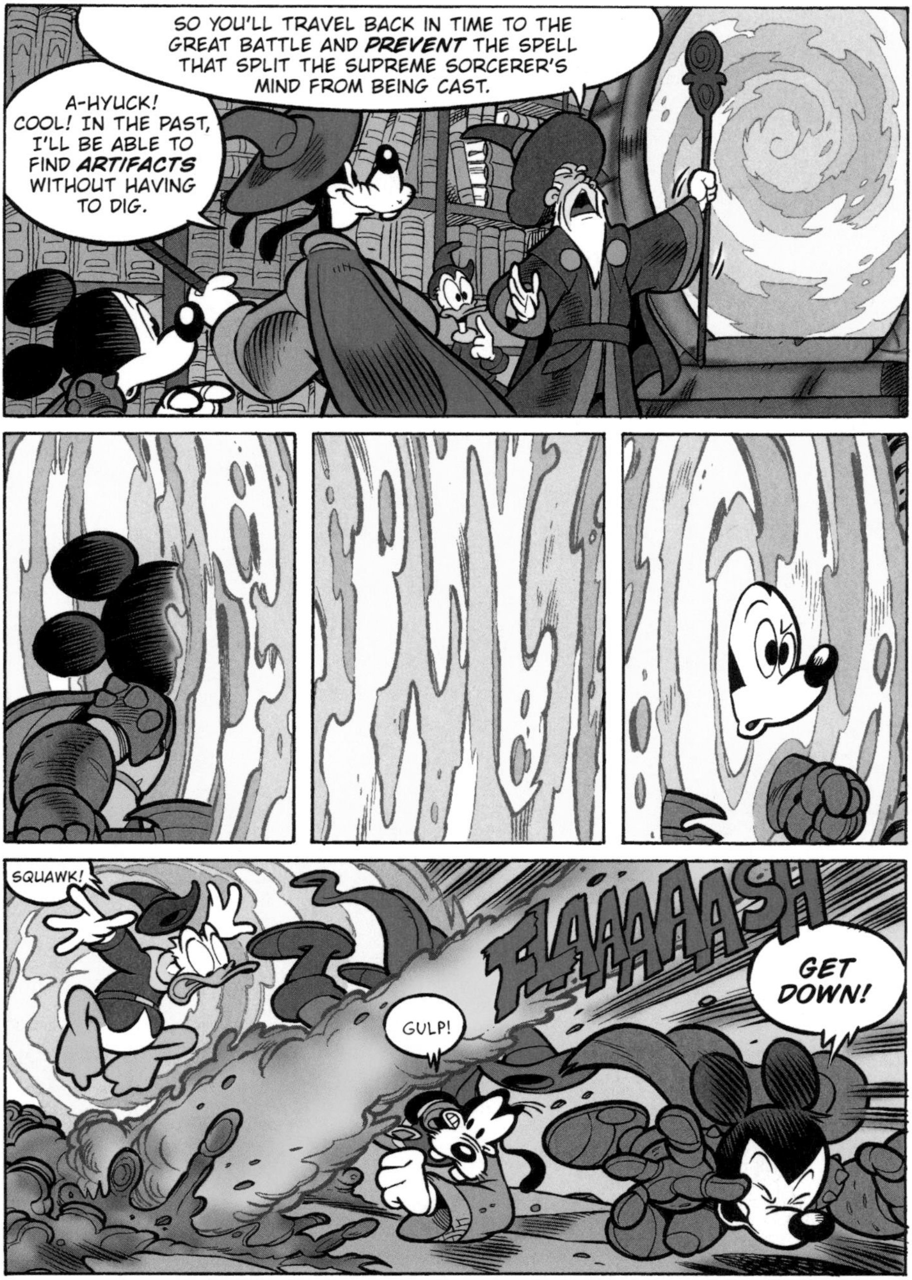
SO YOU'LL TRAVEL BACK IN TIME TO THE GREAT BATTLE AND PREVENT THE SPELL THAT SPLIT THE SUPREME SORCERER'S MIND FROM BEING CAST.
A-HYUCK! COOL! IN THE PAST, I'LL BE ABLE TO FIND ARTIFACTS WITHOUT HAVING TO DIG.
SQUAWK!
FLAAAAASH
GET DOWN!
GULP!

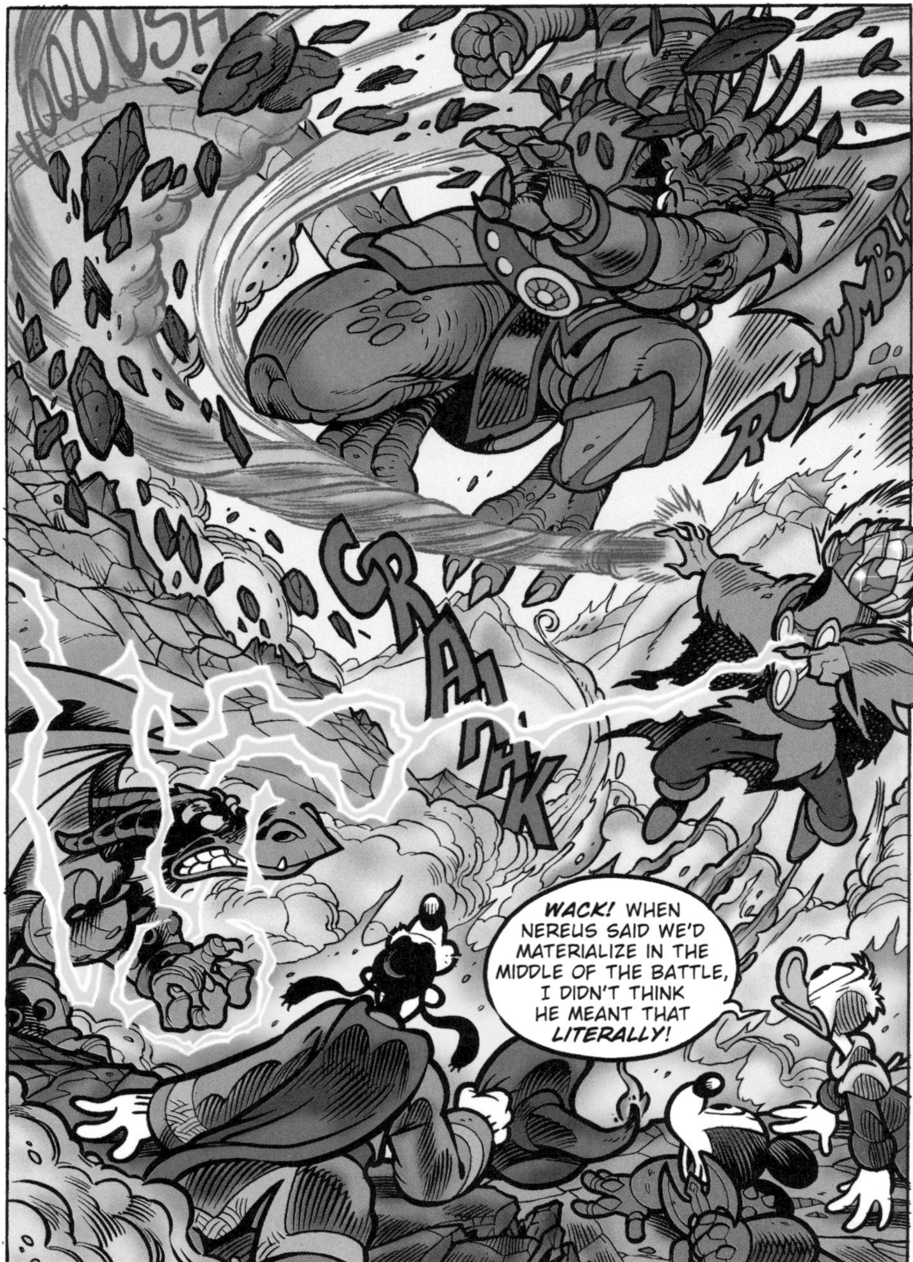

FOOOOUSH
RUUMBLE
CRAAAK
WACK! WHEN NEREUS SAID WE'D MATERIALIZE IN THE MIDDLE OF THE BATTLE, I DIDN'T THINK HE MEANT THAT LITERALLY!

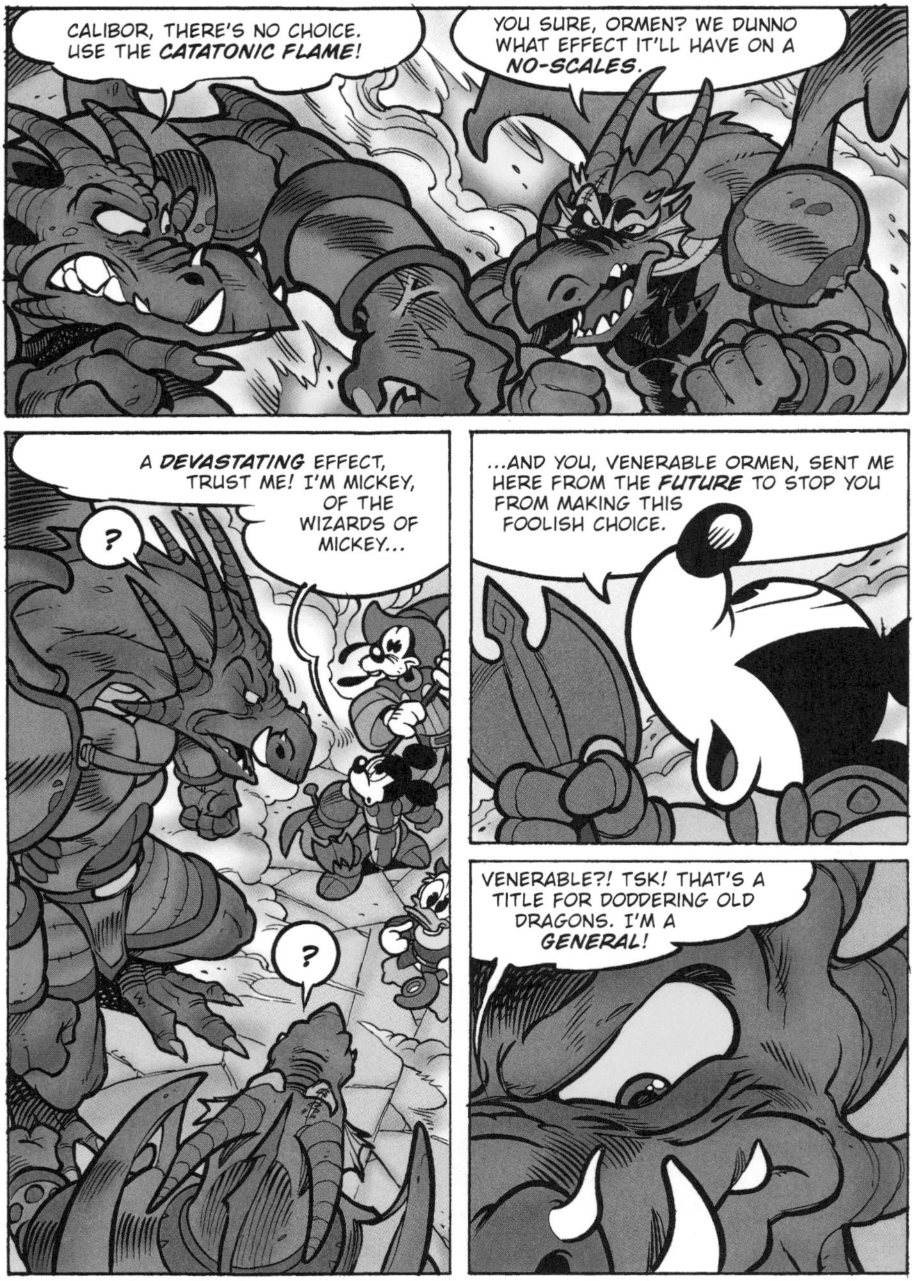
CALIBOR, THERE'S NO CHOICE. USE THE CATATONIC FLAME!
YOU SURE, ORMEN? WE DUNNO WHAT EFFECT IT'LL HAVE ON A NO-SCALES.
A DEVASTATING EFFECT, TRUST ME! I'M MICKEY, OF THE WIZARDS OF MICKEY...
?
?
...AND YOU, VENERABLE ORMEN, SENT ME HERE FROM THE FUTURE TO STOP YOU FROM MAKING THIS FOOLISH CHOICE.
VENERABLE?! TSK! THAT'S A TITLE FOR DODDERING OLD DRAGONS. I'M A GENERAL!

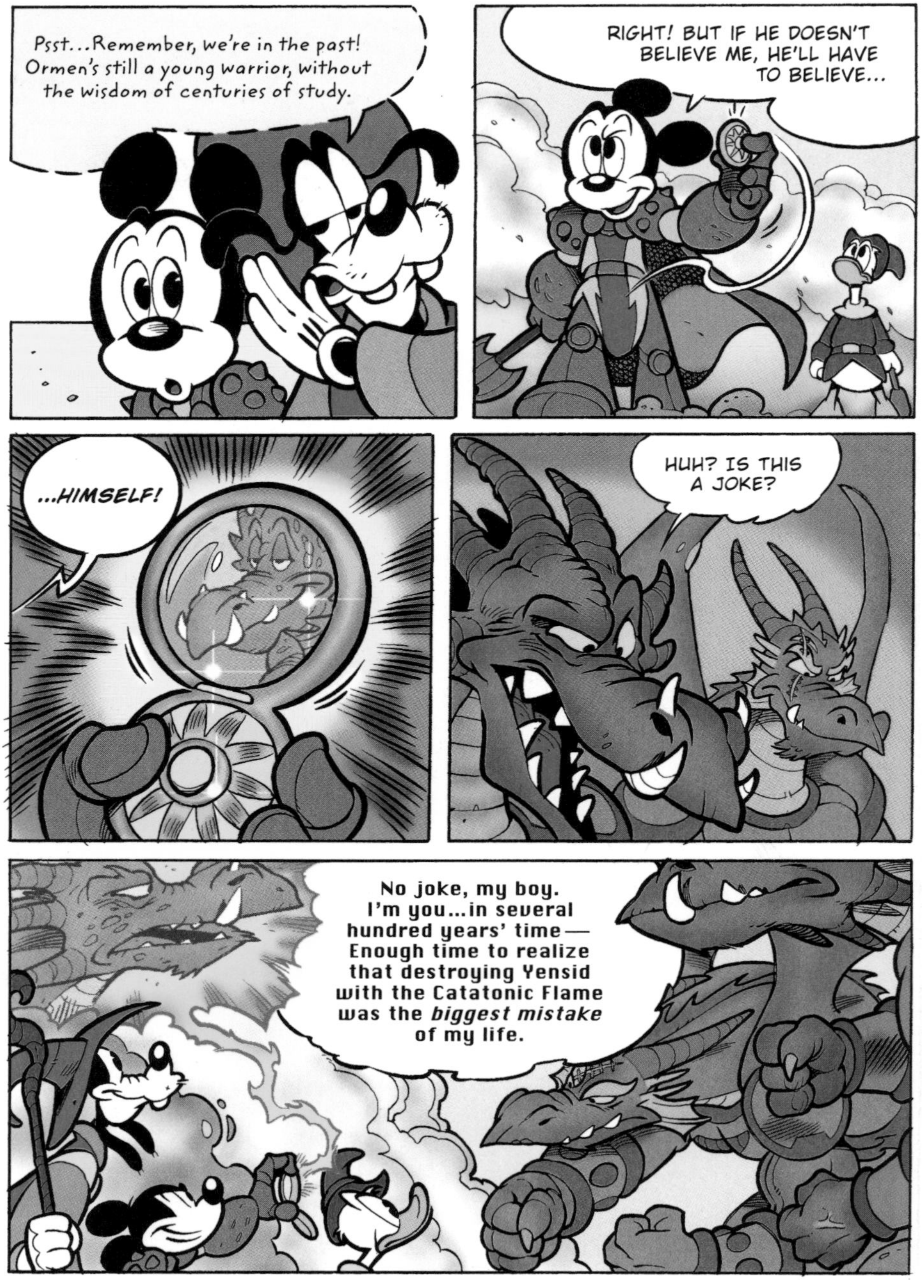
Psst...Remember, we're in the past! Ormen's still a young warrior, without the wisdom of centuries of study.
RIGHT! BUT IF HE DOESN'T BELIEVE ME, HE'LL HAVE TO BELIEVE...
...HIMSELF!
HUH? IS THIS A JOKE?
No joke, my boy. I'm you...in several hundred years' time—Enough time to realize that destroying Yensid with the Catatonic Flame was the *biggest mistake* of my life.

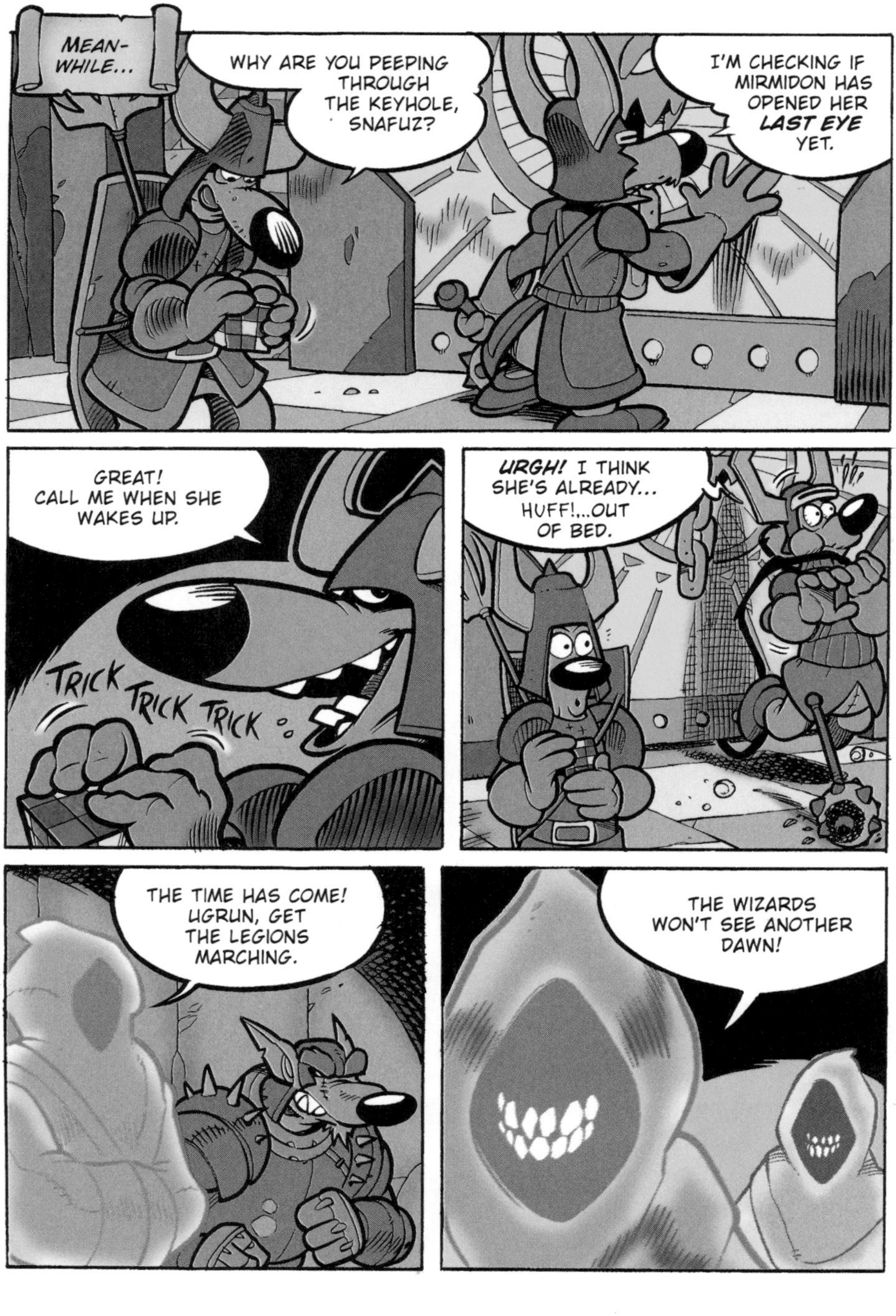
MEAN-WHILE...
WHY ARE YOU PEEPING THROUGH THE KEYHOLE, SNAFUZ?
I'M CHECKING IF MIRMIDON HAS OPENED HER LAST EYE YET.
GREAT! CALL ME WHEN SHE WAKES UP.
TRICK TRICK TRICK
URGH! I THINK SHE'S ALREADY... HUFF!...OUT OF BED.
THE TIME HAS COME! UGRUN, GET THE LEGIONS MARCHING.
THE WIZARDS WON'T SEE ANOTHER DAWN!

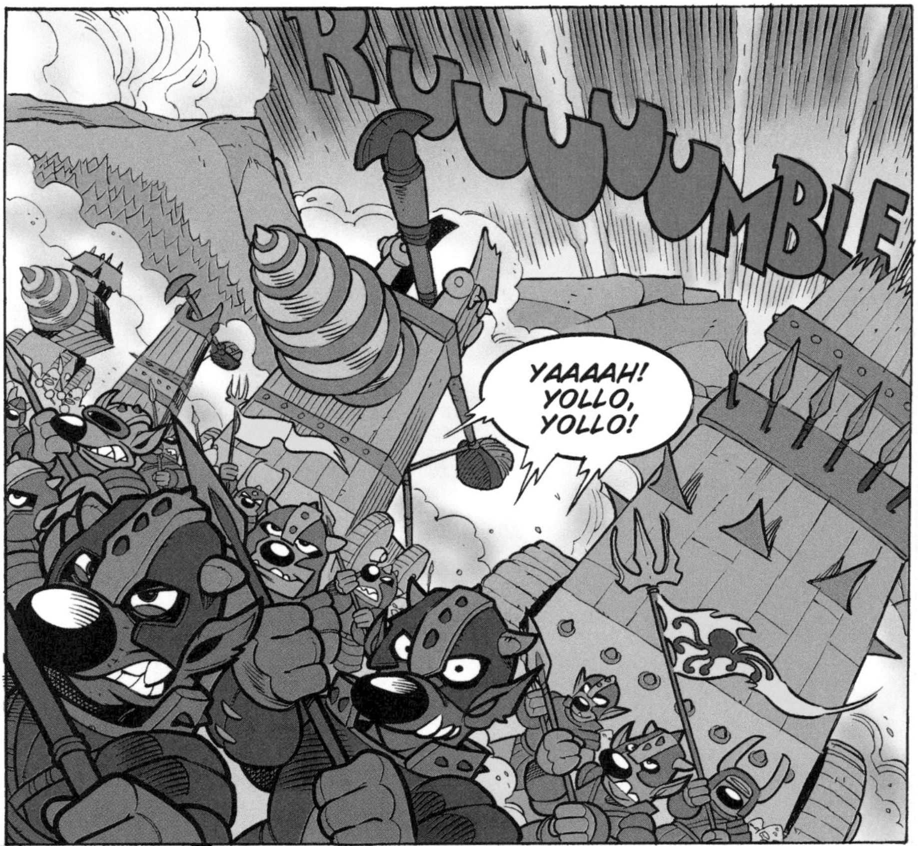
RUUUUUUMBLE
YAAAAH! YOLLO, YOLLO!

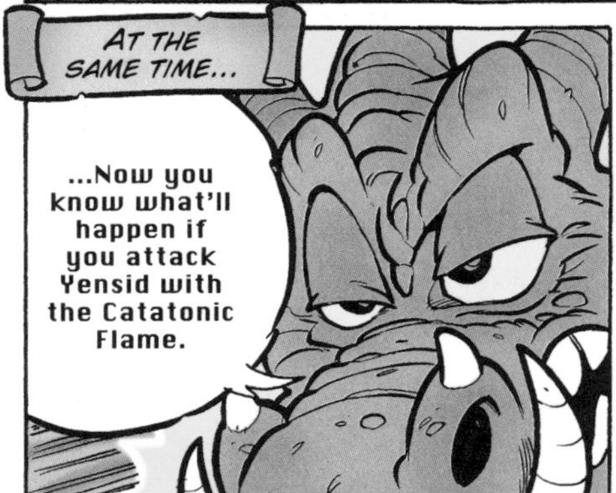
AT THE SAME TIME...
...Now you know what'll happen if you attack Yensid with the Catatonic Flame.

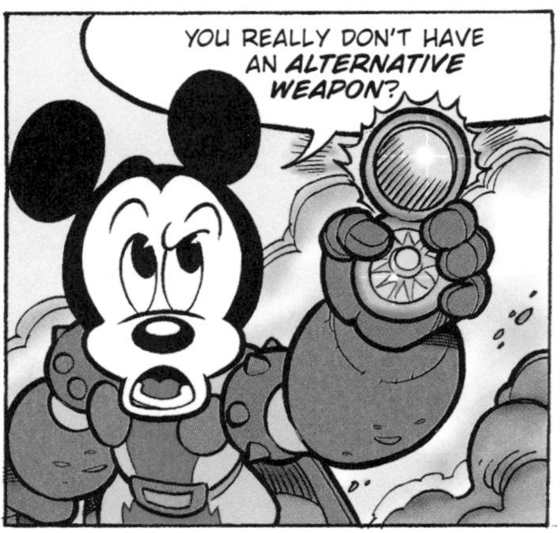
YOU REALLY DON'T HAVE AN ALTERNATIVE WEAPON?

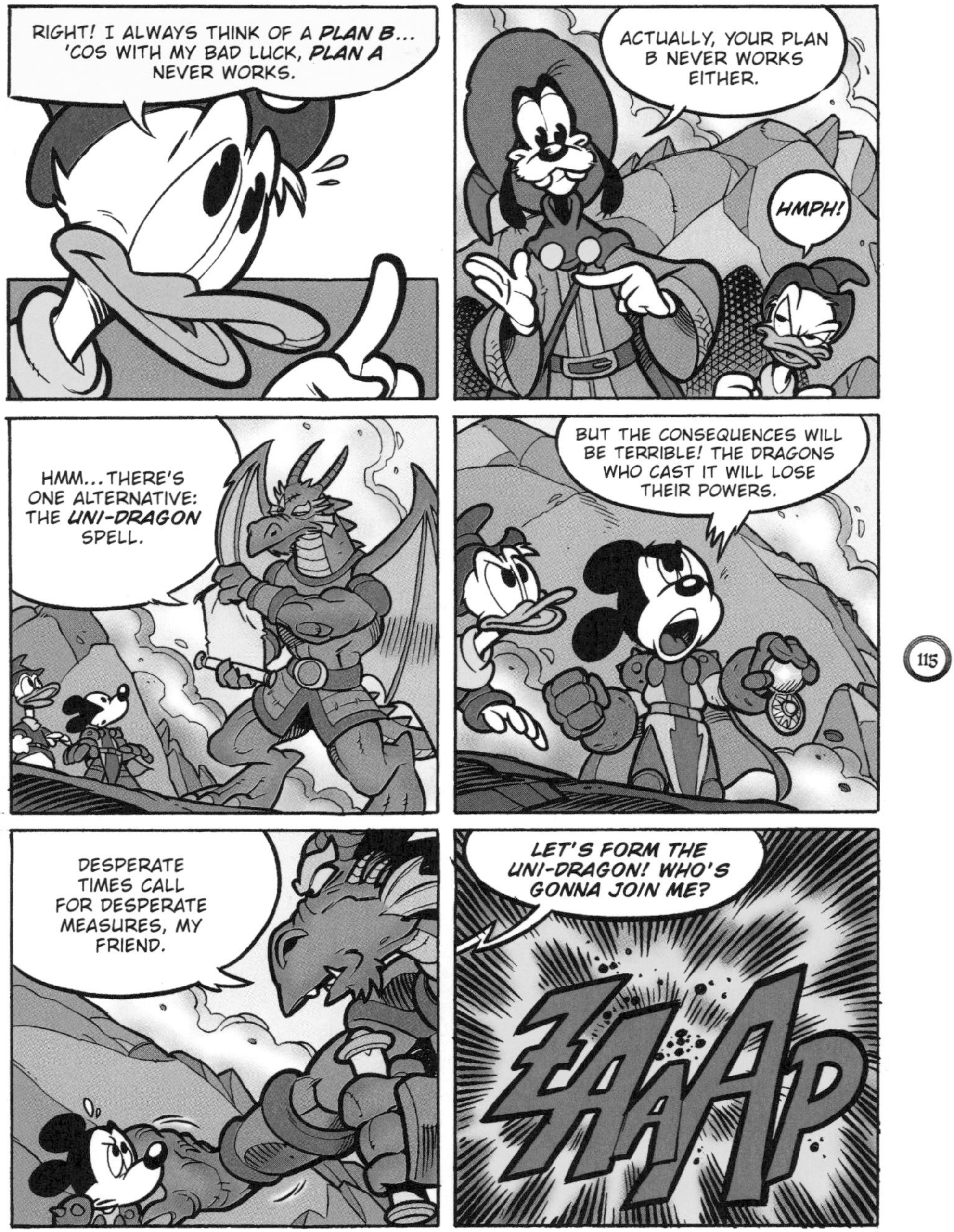
RIGHT! I ALWAYS THINK OF A PLAN B... 'COS WITH MY BAD LUCK, PLAN A NEVER WORKS.
ACTUALLY, YOUR PLAN B NEVER WORKS EITHER.
HMPH!
HMM... THERE'S ONE ALTERNATIVE: THE UNI-DRAGON SPELL.
BUT THE CONSEQUENCES WILL BE TERRIBLE! THE DRAGONS WHO CAST IT WILL LOSE THEIR POWERS.
DESPERATE TIMES CALL FOR DESPERATE MEASURES, MY FRIEND.
LET'S FORM THE UNI-DRAGON! WHO'S GONNA JOIN ME?
ZAAAAP

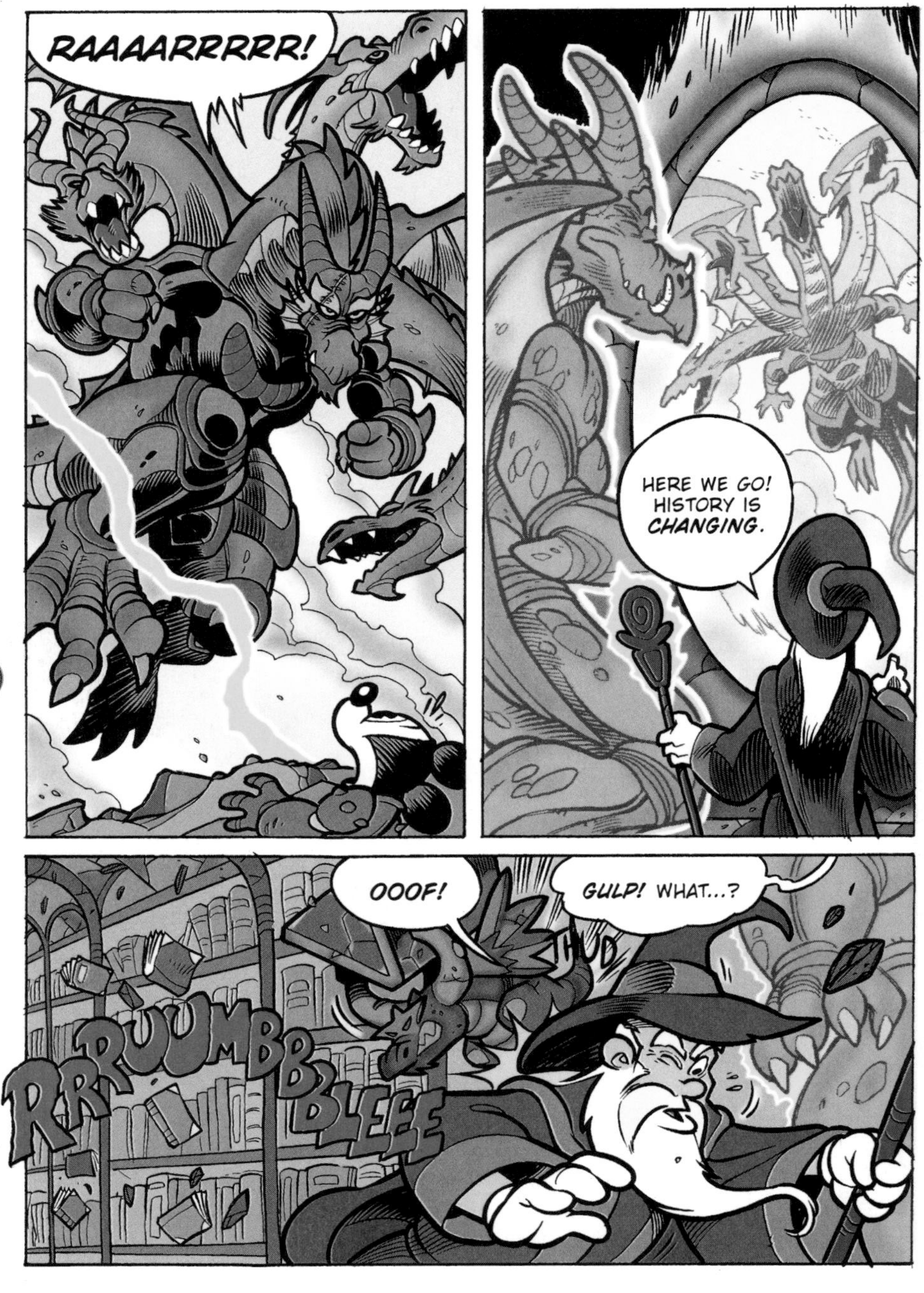
RAAAARRRRR!
HERE WE GO! HISTORY IS *CHANGING*.
OOOF!
GULP! WHAT...?
THUD
RRRUUMBBBLEEE

THE GOBLINS! EEEEEEEK!

WHAT A DISASTER! I'VE NEVER SEEN SO MANY WEASEL GOBLINS.

AND SO *HOSTILE.*

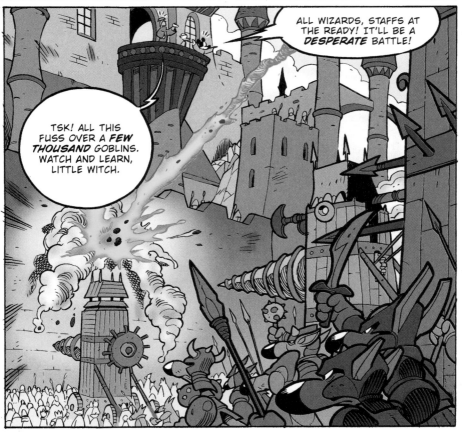

ALL WIZARDS, STAFFS AT THE READY! IT'LL BE A *DESPERATE* BATTLE!

TSK! ALL THIS FUSS OVER A *FEW THOUSAND* GOBLINS. WATCH AND LEARN, LITTLE WITCH.

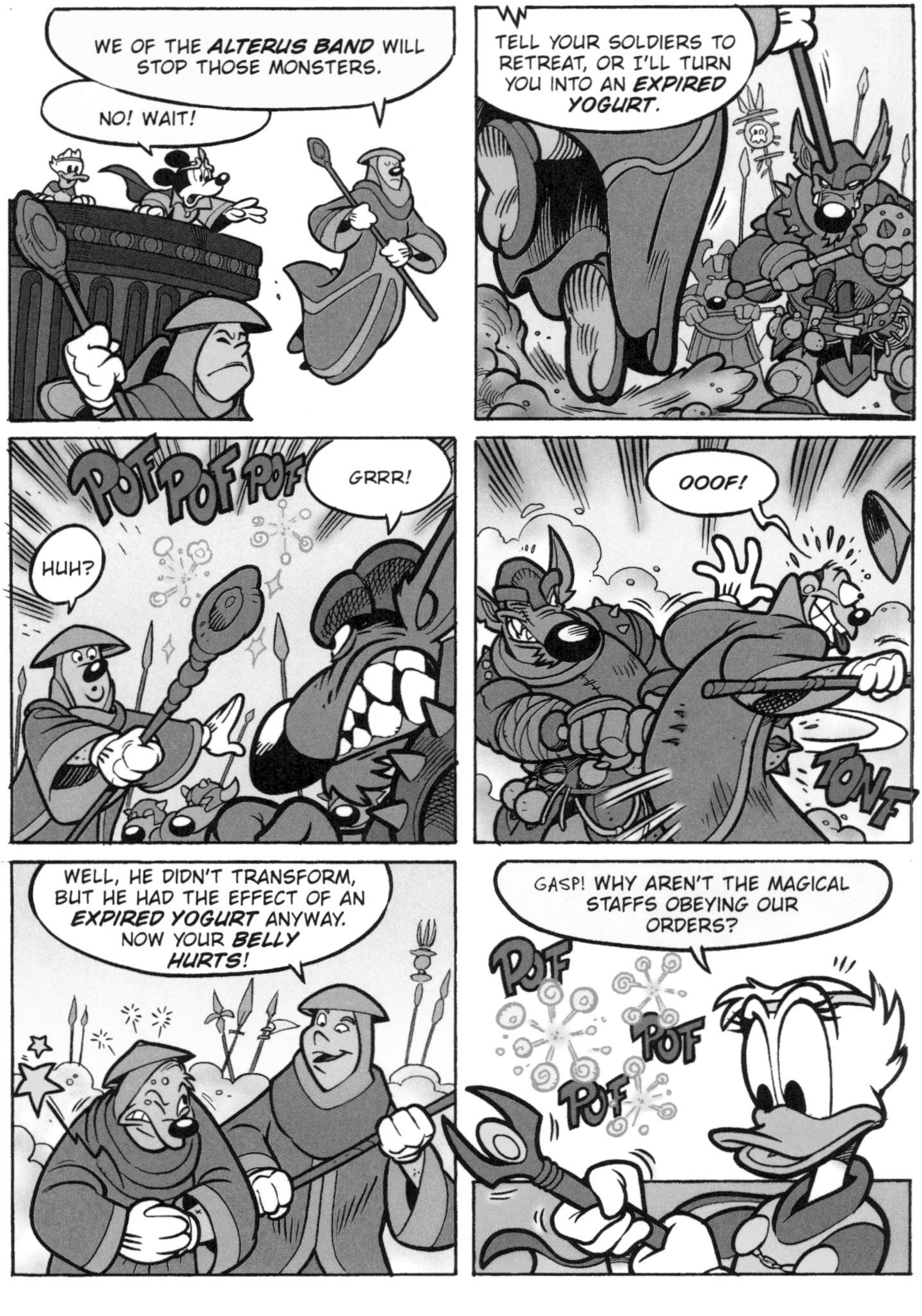

WE OF THE ALTERUS BAND WILL STOP THOSE MONSTERS.
NO! WAIT!
TELL YOUR SOLDIERS TO RETREAT, OR I'LL TURN YOU INTO AN EXPIRED YOGURT.
POF POF POF
GRRR!
HUH?
OOOF!
TONF
WELL, HE DIDN'T TRANSFORM, BUT HE HAD THE EFFECT OF AN EXPIRED YOGURT ANYWAY. NOW YOUR BELLY HURTS!
GASP! WHY AREN'T THE MAGICAL STAFFS OBEYING OUR ORDERS?
POF
POF
POF

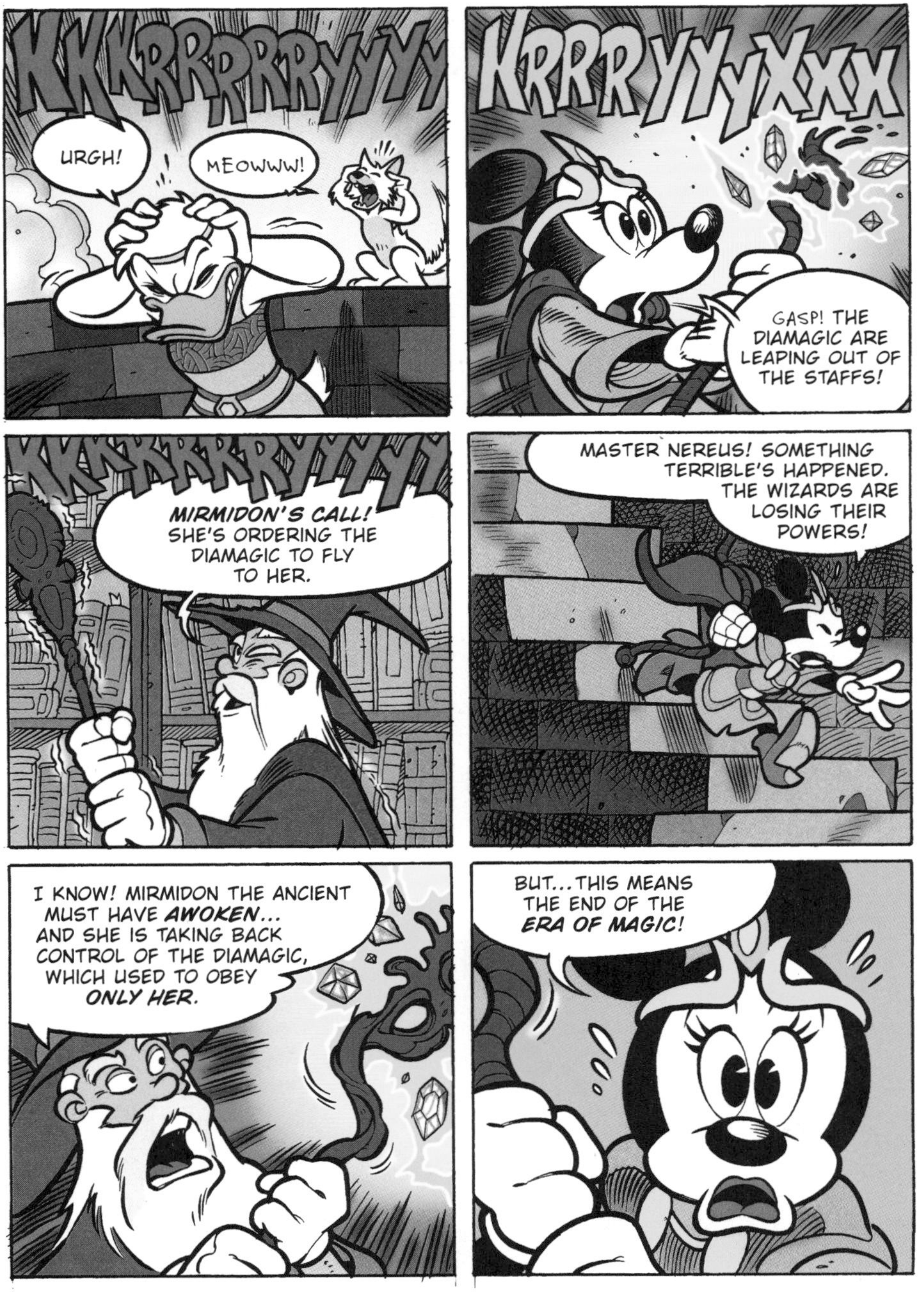
KKKRRRRRRYYYY
URGH!
MEOWWW!
KRRRYYYYXXX
GASP! THE DIAMAGIC ARE LEAPING OUT OF THE STAFFS!
KKKRRRRRRYYYYY
MIRMIDON'S CALL! SHE'S ORDERING THE DIAMAGIC TO FLY TO HER.
MASTER NEREUS! SOMETHING TERRIBLE'S HAPPENED. THE WIZARDS ARE LOSING THEIR POWERS!
I KNOW! MIRMIDON THE ANCIENT MUST HAVE AWOKEN... AND SHE IS TAKING BACK CONTROL OF THE DIAMAGIC, WHICH USED TO OBEY ONLY HER.
BUT... THIS MEANS THE END OF THE ERA OF MAGIC!

THE WIZARDS OF MICKEY ARE OUR ONLY HOPE! IF THEY STOP THE GOSSAMER GUILD FROM FORMING, MIRMIDON WILL NOT BE AWOKEN... THE FUTURE WILL BE ALTERED, AND ALL THIS WILL *NEVER HAPPEN.*

SO? HOW'S THE BATTLE GOING?

120

BAD! THE UNI-DRAGON CAN'T GET CLOSE TO YENSID.

AND NOW, WITH THE *CHANT OF SEPARATION*, I'LL BREAK YOUR STRENGTH AND YOUR MIND!

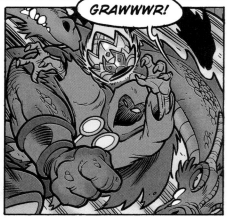

GRAWWWR!

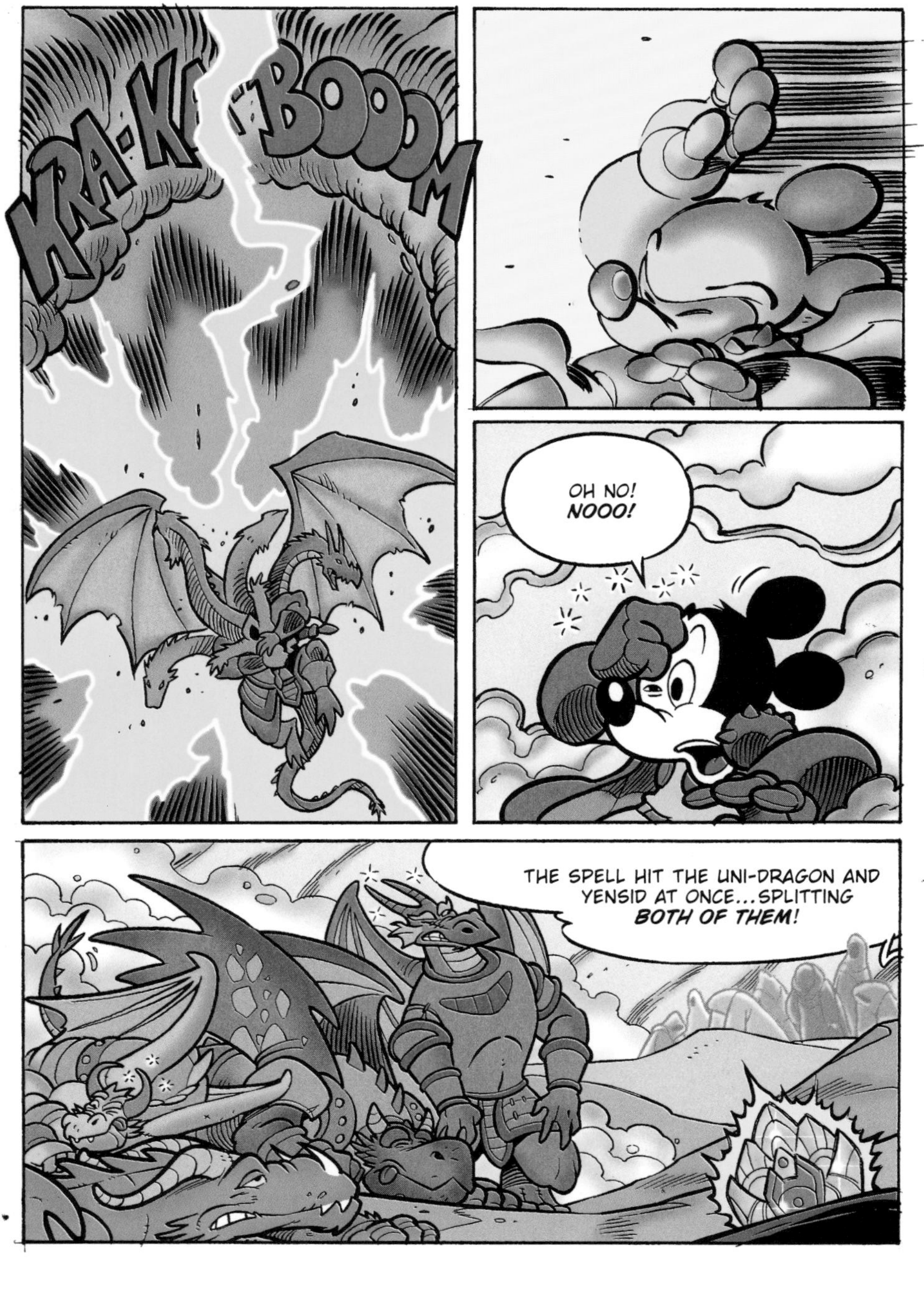
KRA-K BOOOOM
OH NO! NOOO!
THE SPELL HIT THE UNI-DRAGON AND YENSID AT ONCE...SPLITTING BOTH OF THEM!

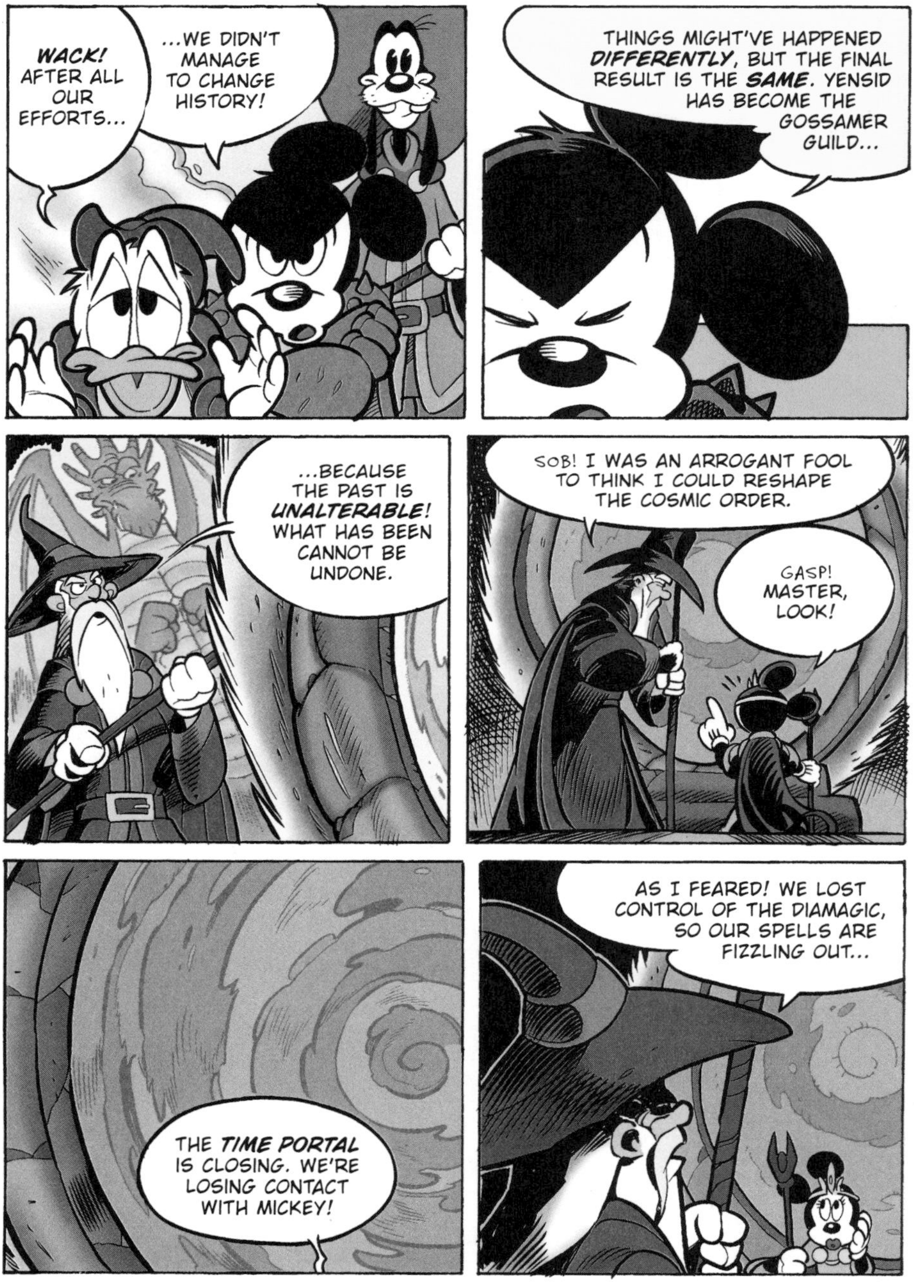
WACK! AFTER ALL OUR EFFORTS...
...WE DIDN'T MANAGE TO CHANGE HISTORY!
THINGS MIGHT'VE HAPPENED DIFFERENTLY, BUT THE FINAL RESULT IS THE SAME. YENSID HAS BECOME THE GOSSAMER GUILD...
...BECAUSE THE PAST IS UNALTERABLE! WHAT HAS BEEN CANNOT BE UNDONE.
SOB! I WAS AN ARROGANT FOOL TO THINK I COULD RESHAPE THE COSMIC ORDER.
GASP! MASTER, LOOK!
THE TIME PORTAL IS CLOSING. WE'RE LOSING CONTACT WITH MICKEY!
AS I FEARED! WE LOST CONTROL OF THE DIAMAGIC, SO OUR SPELLS ARE FIZZLING OUT...

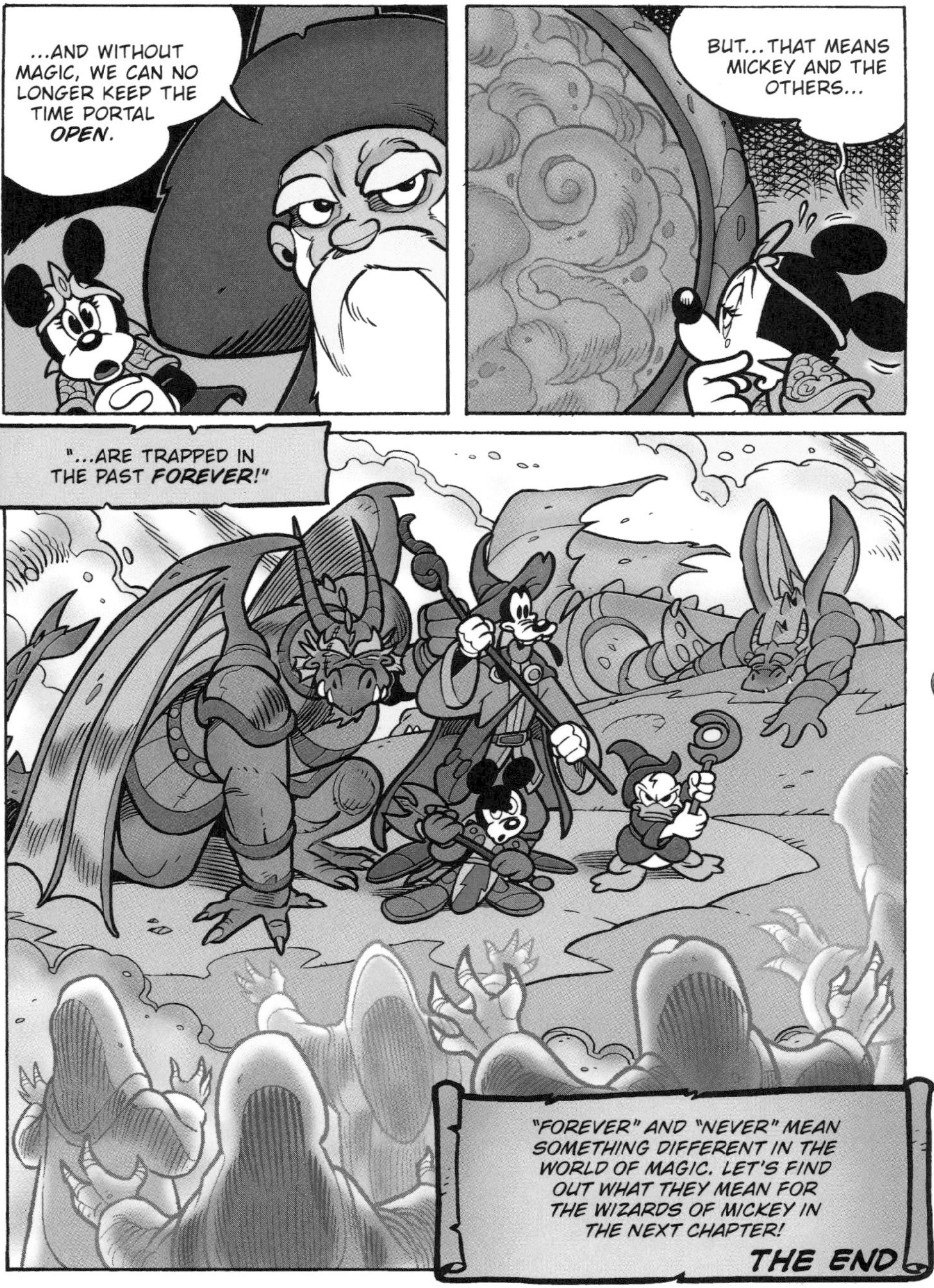

...AND WITHOUT MAGIC, WE CAN NO LONGER KEEP THE TIME PORTAL **OPEN**.
BUT... THAT MEANS MICKEY AND THE OTHERS...
"...ARE TRAPPED IN THE PAST **FOREVER**!"
"FOREVER" AND "NEVER" MEAN SOMETHING DIFFERENT IN THE WORLD OF MAGIC. LET'S FIND OUT WHAT THEY MEAN FOR THE WIZARDS OF MICKEY IN THE NEXT CHAPTER!
THE END

Wizards of Mickey

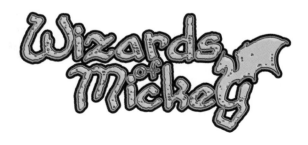

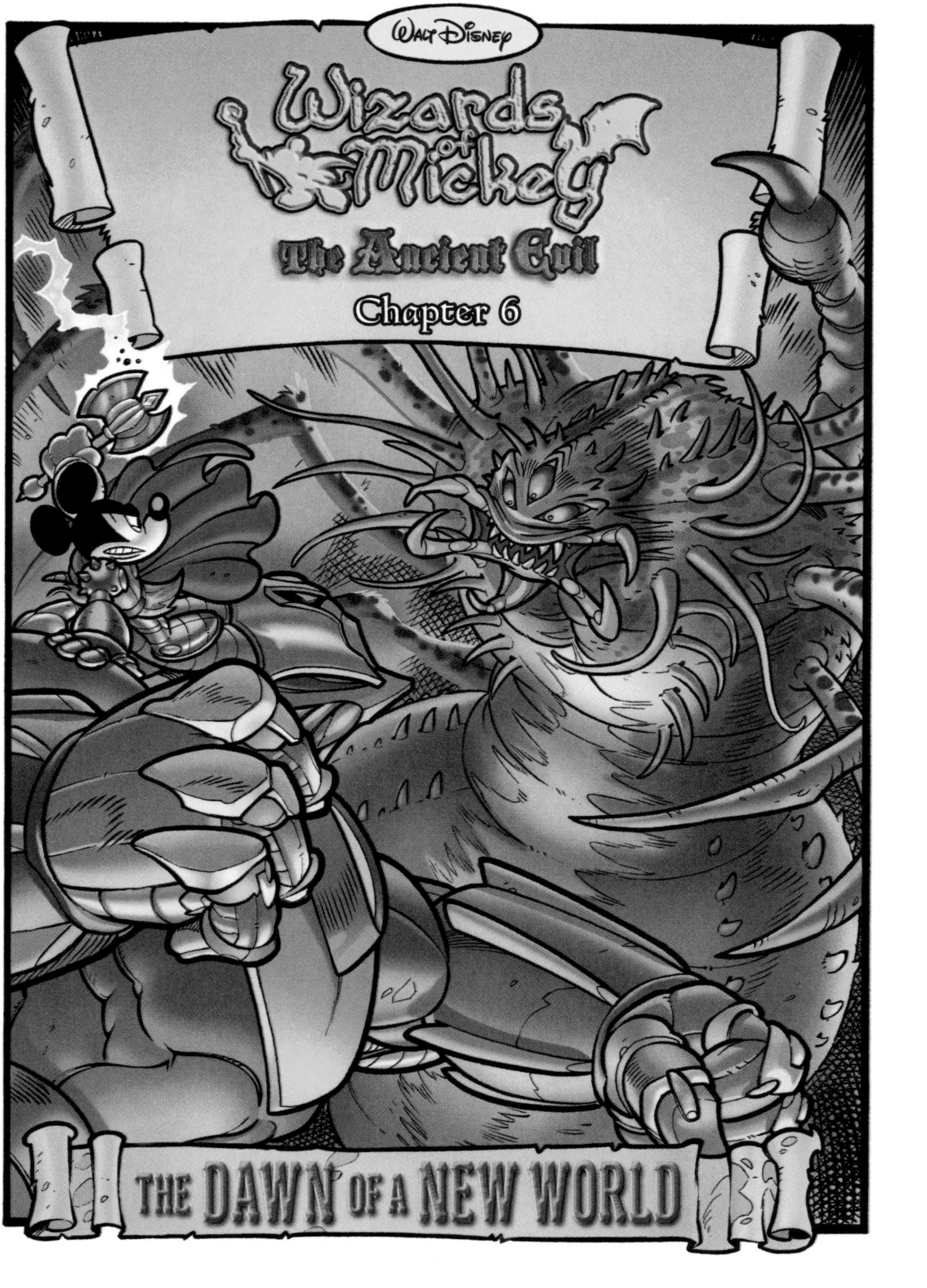
Walt Disney
Wizards of Mickey
The Ancient Evil
Chapter 6
THE DAWN OF A NEW WORLD

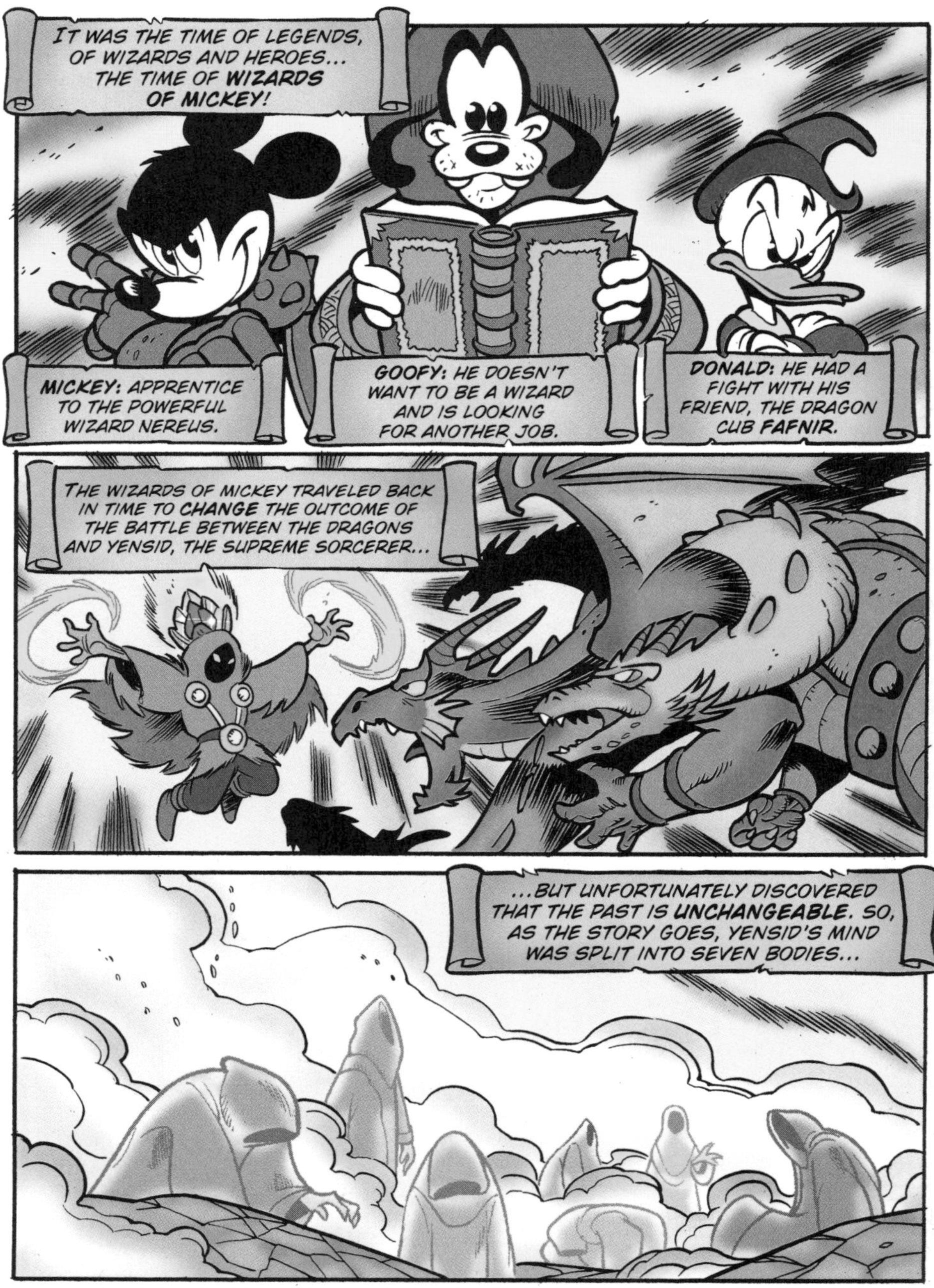
IT WAS THE TIME OF LEGENDS, OF WIZARDS AND HEROES... THE TIME OF WIZARDS OF MICKEY!
MICKEY: APPRENTICE TO THE POWERFUL WIZARD NEREUS.
GOOFY: HE DOESN'T WANT TO BE A WIZARD AND IS LOOKING FOR ANOTHER JOB.
DONALD: HE HAD A FIGHT WITH HIS FRIEND, THE DRAGON CUB FAFNIR.
THE WIZARDS OF MICKEY TRAVELED BACK IN TIME TO CHANGE THE OUTCOME OF THE BATTLE BETWEEN THE DRAGONS AND YENSID, THE SUPREME SORCERER...
...BUT UNFORTUNATELY DISCOVERED THAT THE PAST IS UNCHANGEABLE. SO, AS THE STORY GOES, YENSID'S MIND WAS SPLIT INTO SEVEN BODIES...

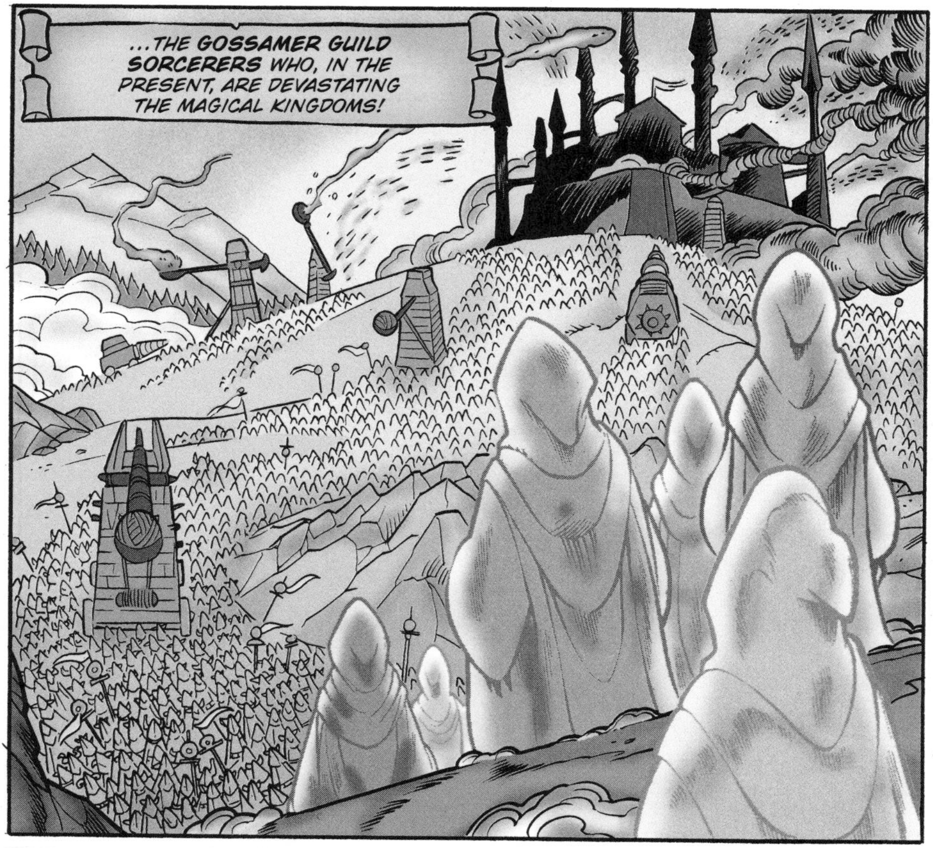
...THE GOSSAMER GUILD SORCERERS WHO, IN THE PRESENT, ARE DEVASTATING THE MAGICAL KINGDOMS!

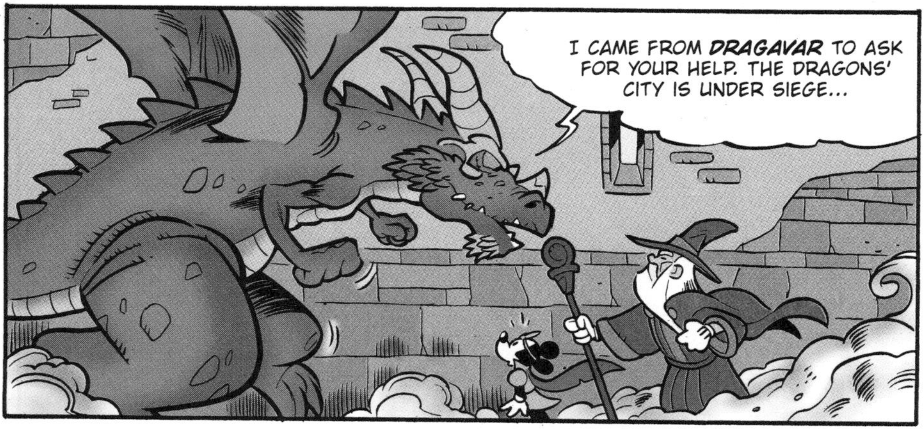
I CAME FROM DRAGAVAR TO ASK FOR YOUR HELP. THE DRAGONS' CITY IS UNDER SIEGE...

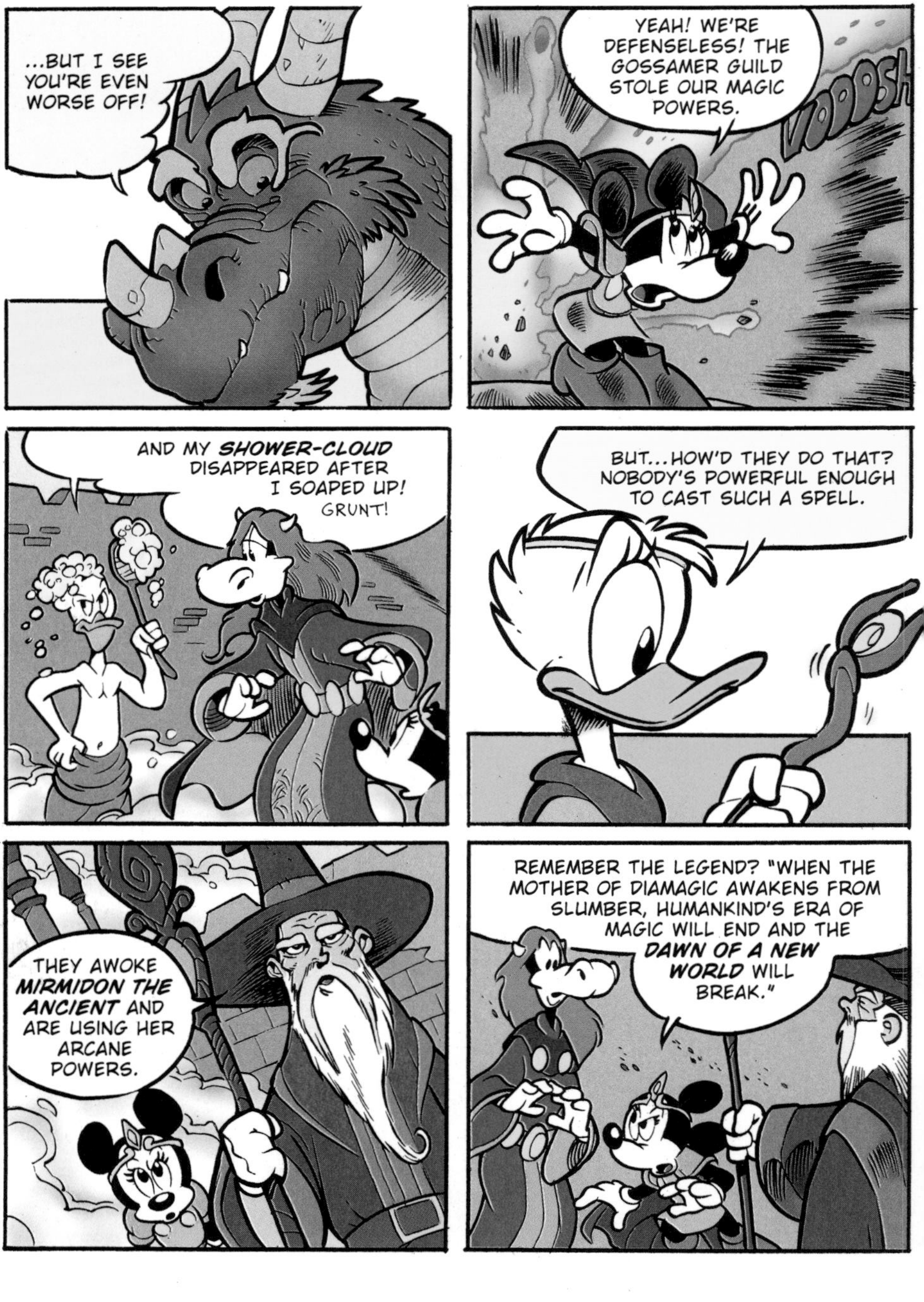
...BUT I SEE YOU'RE EVEN WORSE OFF!
YEAH! WE'RE DEFENSELESS! THE GOSSAMER GUILD STOLE OUR MAGIC POWERS.
AND MY **SHOWER-CLOUD** DISAPPEARED AFTER I SOAPED UP!
GRUNT!
BUT...HOW'D THEY DO THAT? NOBODY'S POWERFUL ENOUGH TO CAST SUCH A SPELL.
THEY AWOKE **MIRMIDON THE ANCIENT** AND ARE USING HER ARCANE POWERS.
REMEMBER THE LEGEND? "WHEN THE MOTHER OF DIAMAGIC AWAKENS FROM SLUMBER, HUMANKIND'S ERA OF MAGIC WILL END AND THE **DAWN OF A NEW WORLD** WILL BREAK."

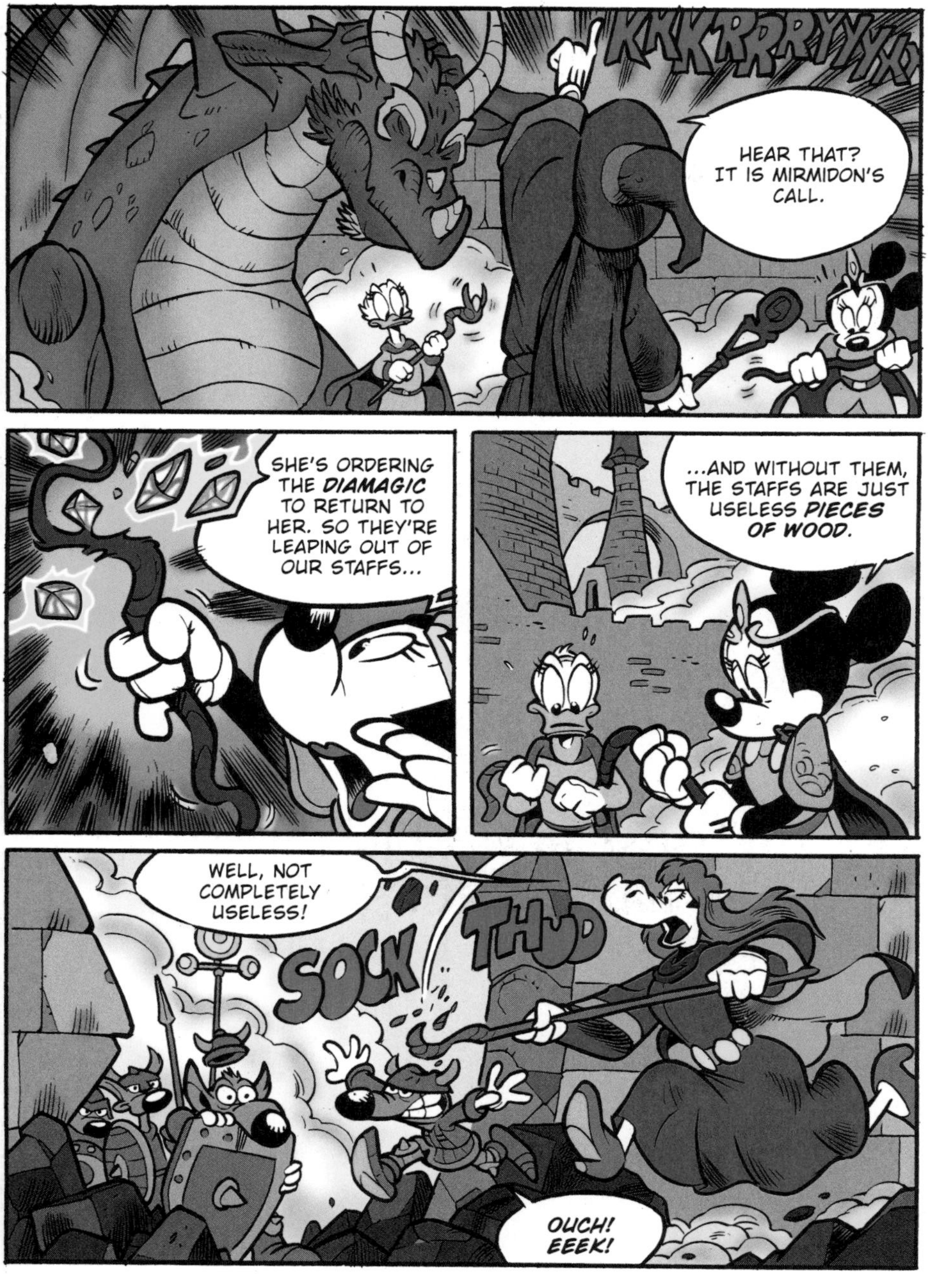

KKKRRRRYYYXX
HEAR THAT? IT IS MIRMIDON'S CALL.
SHE'S ORDERING THE DIAMAGIC TO RETURN TO HER. SO THEY'RE LEAPING OUT OF OUR STAFFS...
...AND WITHOUT THEM, THE STAFFS ARE JUST USELESS PIECES OF WOOD.
WELL, NOT COMPLETELY USELESS!
SOCK
THUD
OUCH! EEEK!

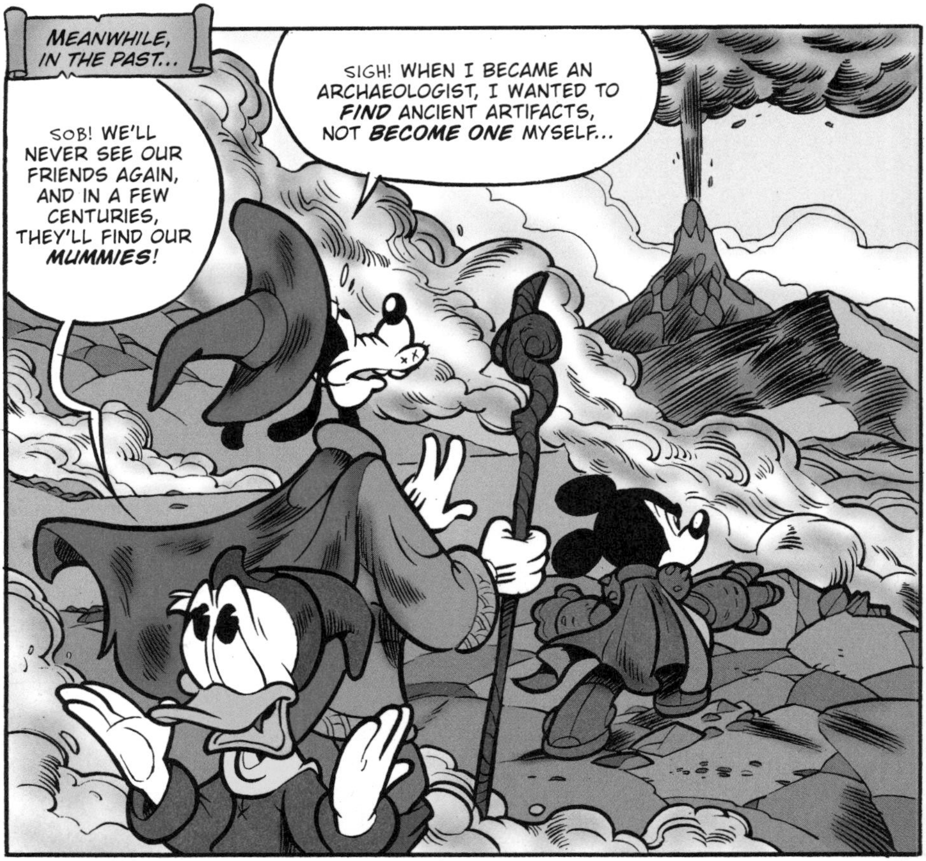
MEANWHILE, IN THE PAST...
SOB! WE'LL NEVER SEE OUR FRIENDS AGAIN, AND IN A FEW CENTURIES, THEY'LL FIND OUR ***MUMMIES***!
SIGH! WHEN I BECAME AN ARCHAEOLOGIST, I WANTED TO ***FIND*** ANCIENT ARTIFACTS, NOT ***BECOME ONE*** MYSELF...

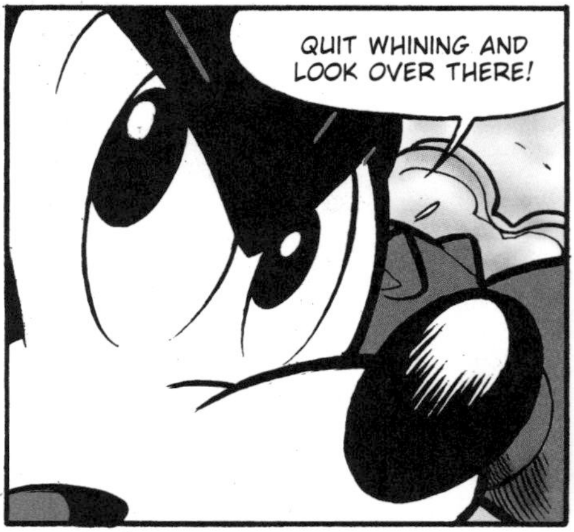
QUIT WHINING AND LOOK OVER THERE!

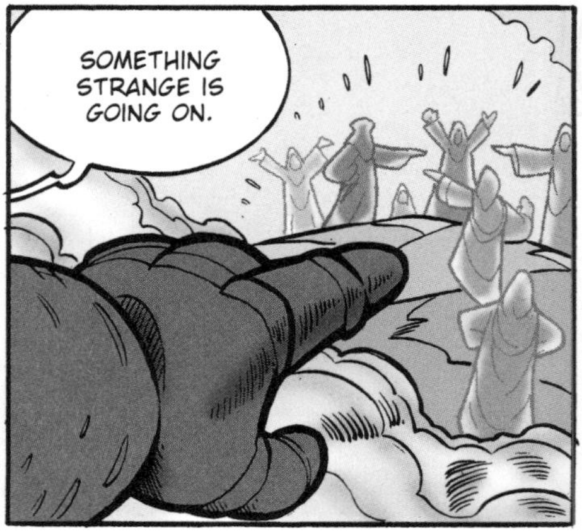
SOMETHING STRANGE IS GOING ON.

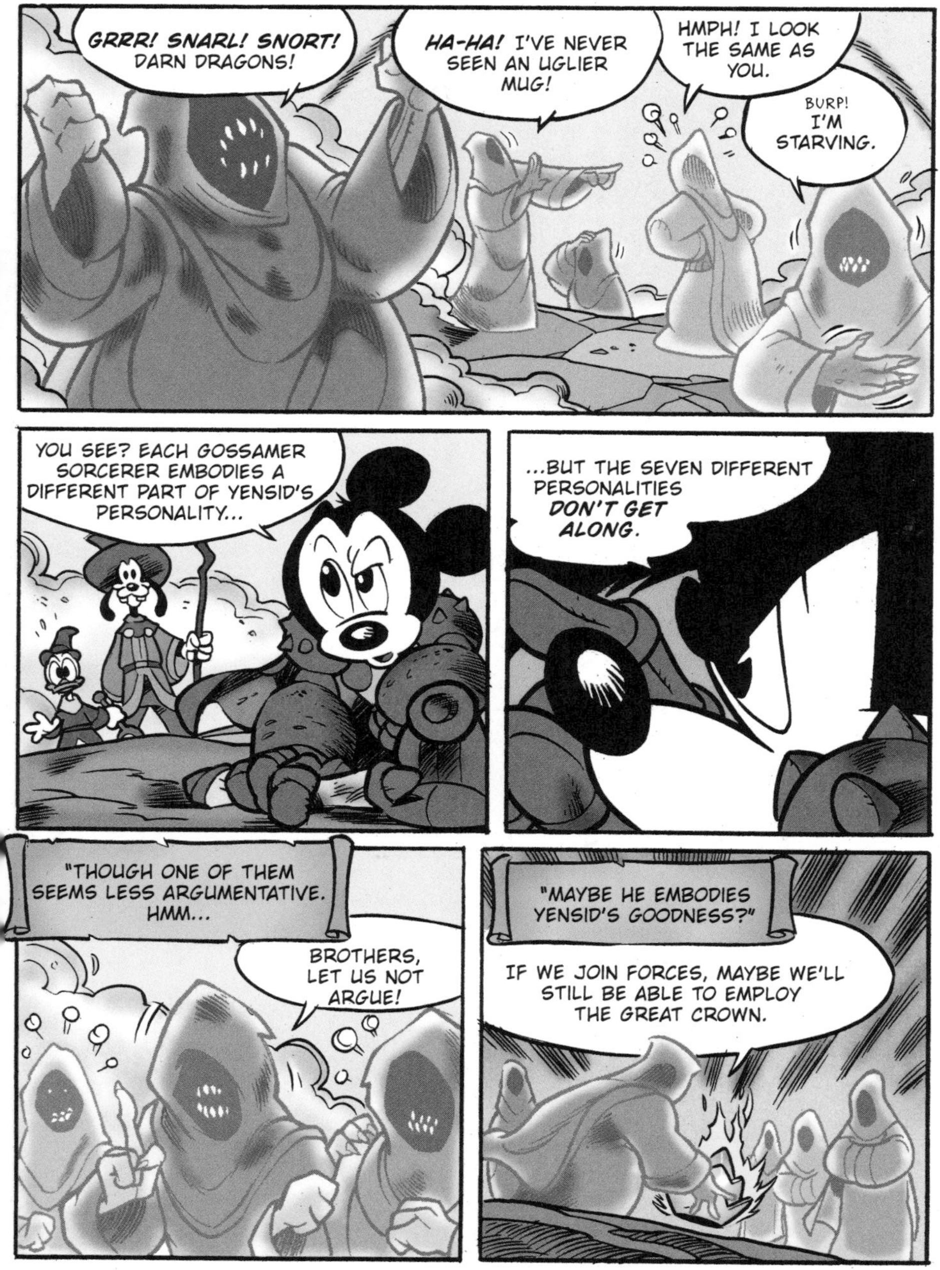
GRRR! SNARL! SNORT! DARN DRAGONS!
HA-HA! I'VE NEVER SEEN AN UGLIER MUG!
HMPH! I LOOK THE SAME AS YOU.
BURP! I'M STARVING.
YOU SEE? EACH GOSSAMER SORCERER EMBODIES A DIFFERENT PART OF YENSID'S PERSONALITY...
...BUT THE SEVEN DIFFERENT PERSONALITIES DON'T GET ALONG.
"THOUGH ONE OF THEM SEEMS LESS ARGUMENTATIVE. HMM...
BROTHERS, LET US NOT ARGUE!
"MAYBE HE EMBODIES YENSID'S GOODNESS?"
IF WE JOIN FORCES, MAYBE WE'LL STILL BE ABLE TO EMPLOY THE GREAT CROWN.

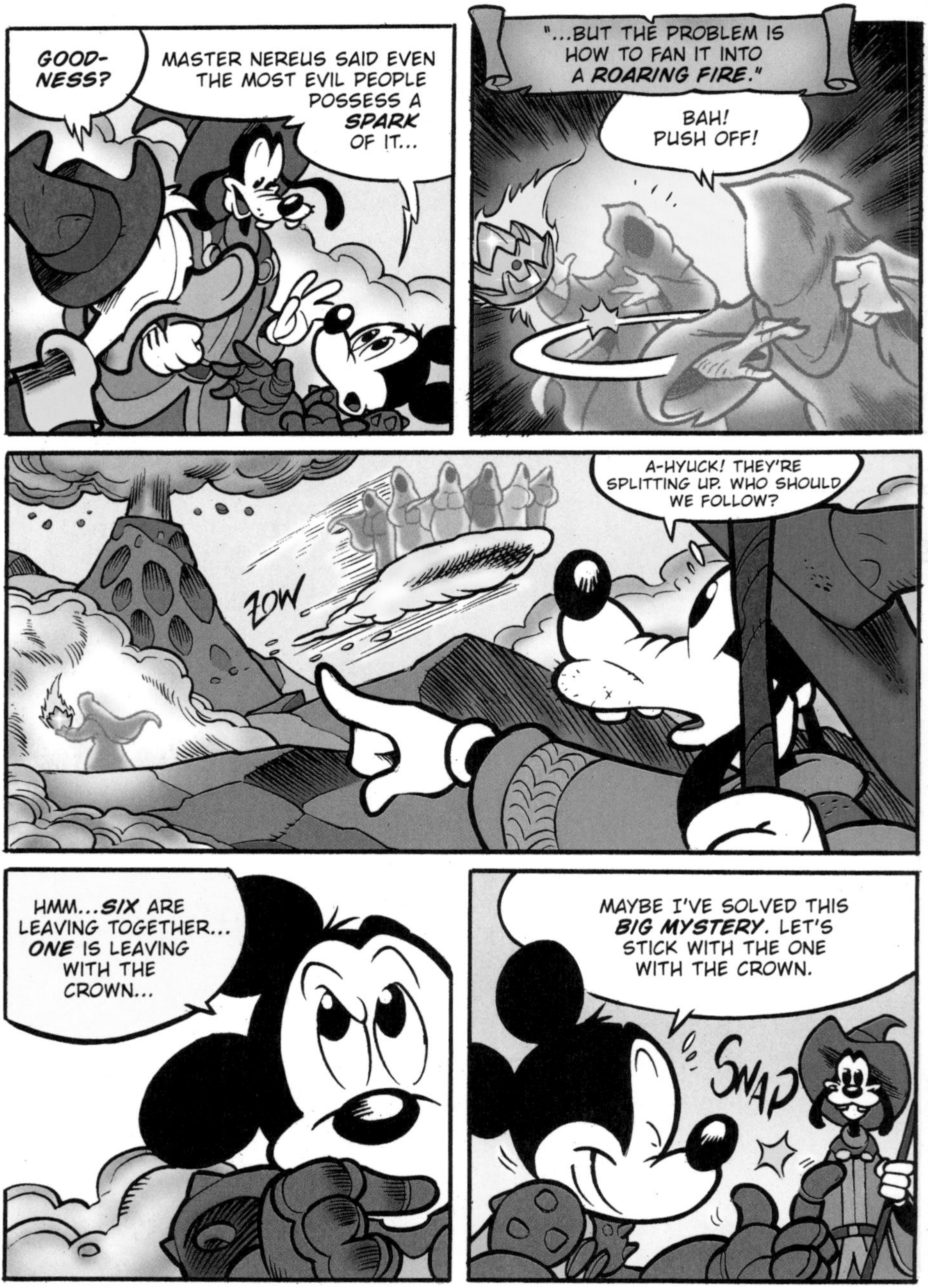
GOOD-NESS?
MASTER NEREUS SAID EVEN THE MOST EVIL PEOPLE POSSESS A SPARK OF IT...
"...BUT THE PROBLEM IS HOW TO FAN IT INTO A ROARING FIRE."
BAH! PUSH OFF!
A-HYUCK! THEY'RE SPLITTING UP. WHO SHOULD WE FOLLOW?
ZOW
HMM...SIX ARE LEAVING TOGETHER... ONE IS LEAVING WITH THE CROWN...
MAYBE I'VE SOLVED THIS BIG MYSTERY. LET'S STICK WITH THE ONE WITH THE CROWN.
SNAP

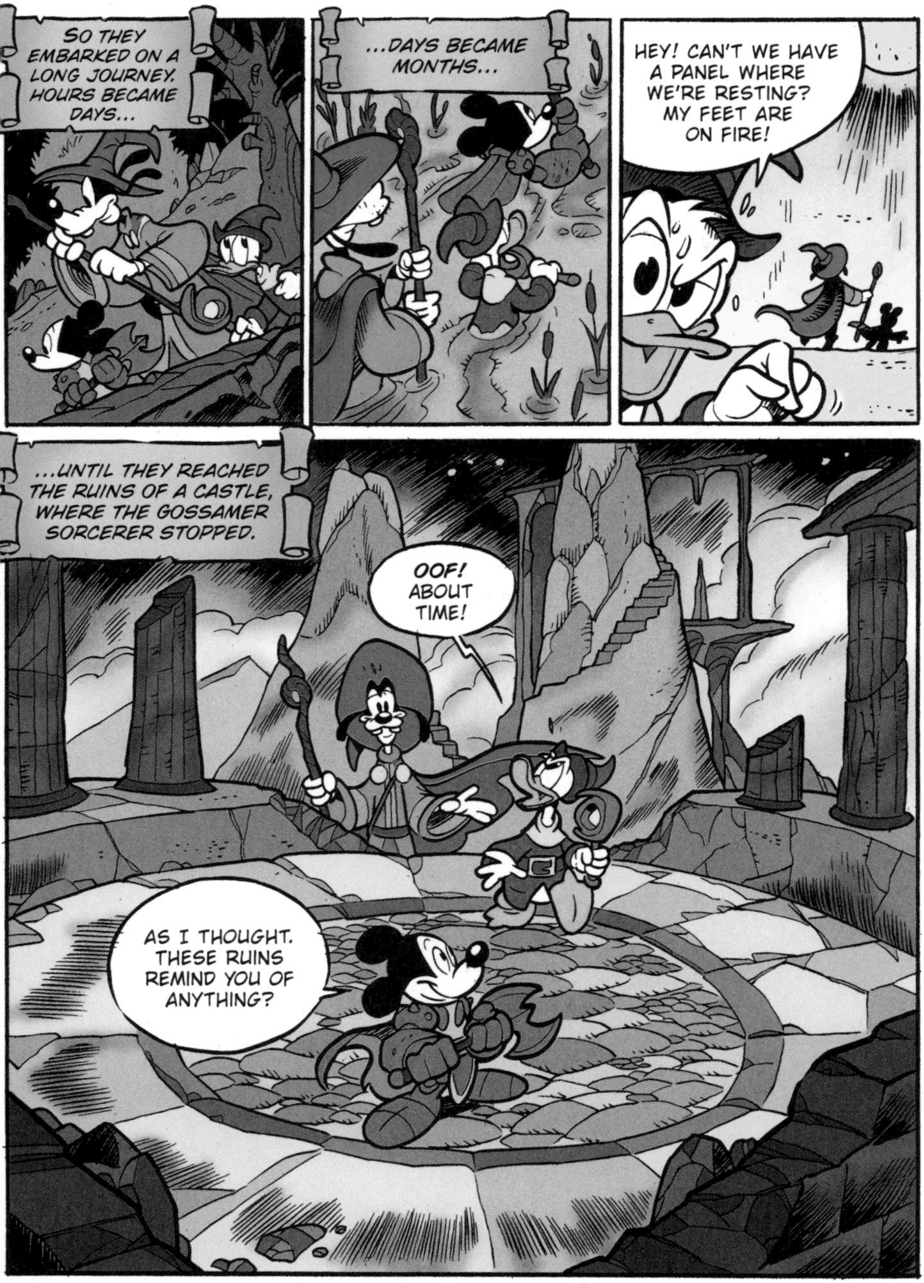
SO THEY EMBARKED ON A LONG JOURNEY. HOURS BECAME DAYS...
...DAYS BECAME MONTHS...
HEY! CAN'T WE HAVE A PANEL WHERE WE'RE RESTING? MY FEET ARE ON FIRE!
...UNTIL THEY REACHED THE RUINS OF A CASTLE, WHERE THE GOSSAMER SORCERER STOPPED.
OOF! ABOUT TIME!
AS I THOUGHT. THESE RUINS REMIND YOU OF ANYTHING?

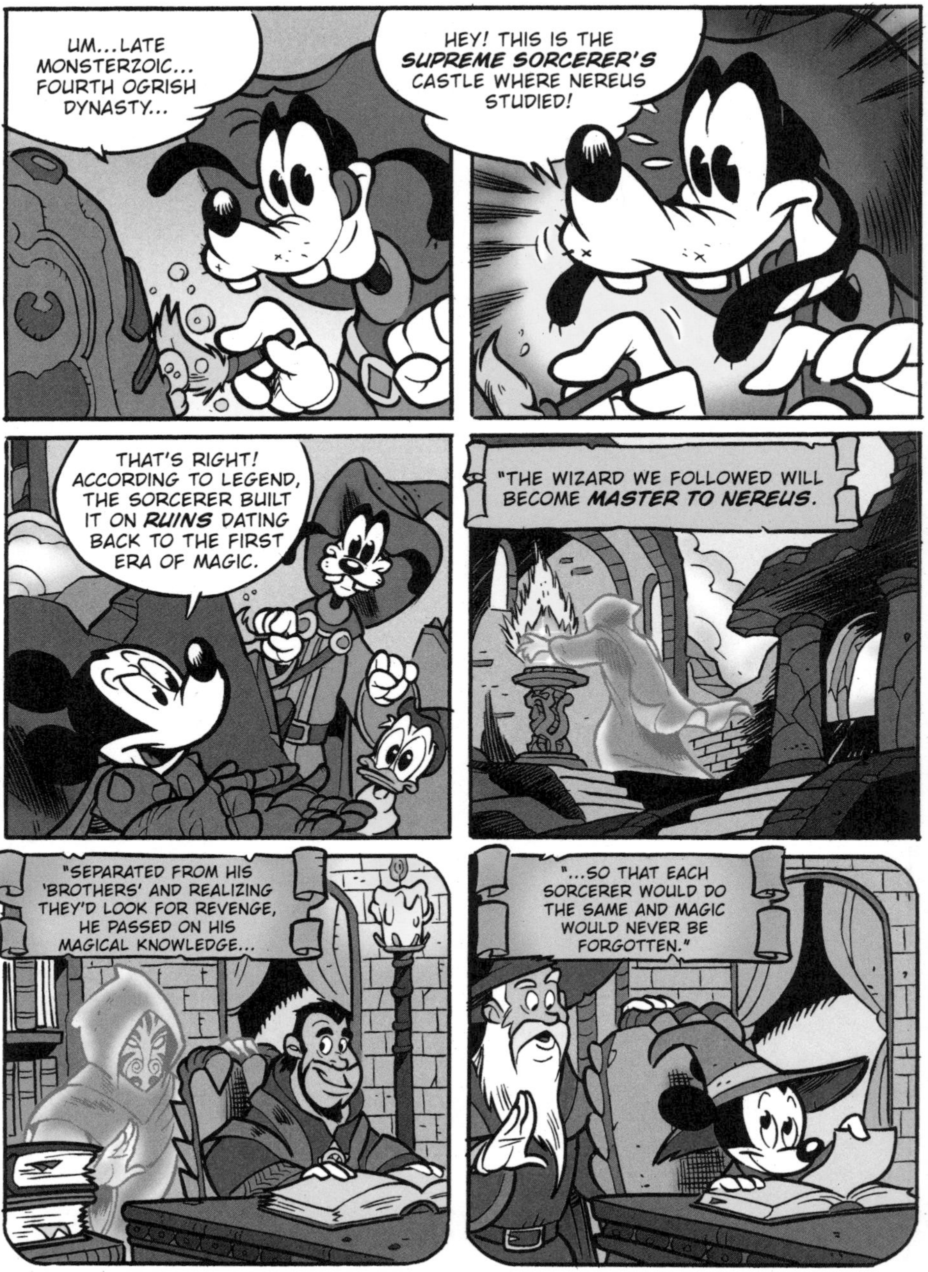
UM...LATE MONSTERZOIC... FOURTH OGRISH DYNASTY...
HEY! THIS IS THE SUPREME SORCERER'S CASTLE WHERE NEREUS STUDIED!
THAT'S RIGHT! ACCORDING TO LEGEND, THE SORCERER BUILT IT ON RUINS DATING BACK TO THE FIRST ERA OF MAGIC.
"THE WIZARD WE FOLLOWED WILL BECOME MASTER TO NEREUS.
"SEPARATED FROM HIS 'BROTHERS' AND REALIZING THEY'D LOOK FOR REVENGE, HE PASSED ON HIS MAGICAL KNOWLEDGE...
"...SO THAT EACH SORCERER WOULD DO THE SAME AND MAGIC WOULD NEVER BE FORGOTTEN."

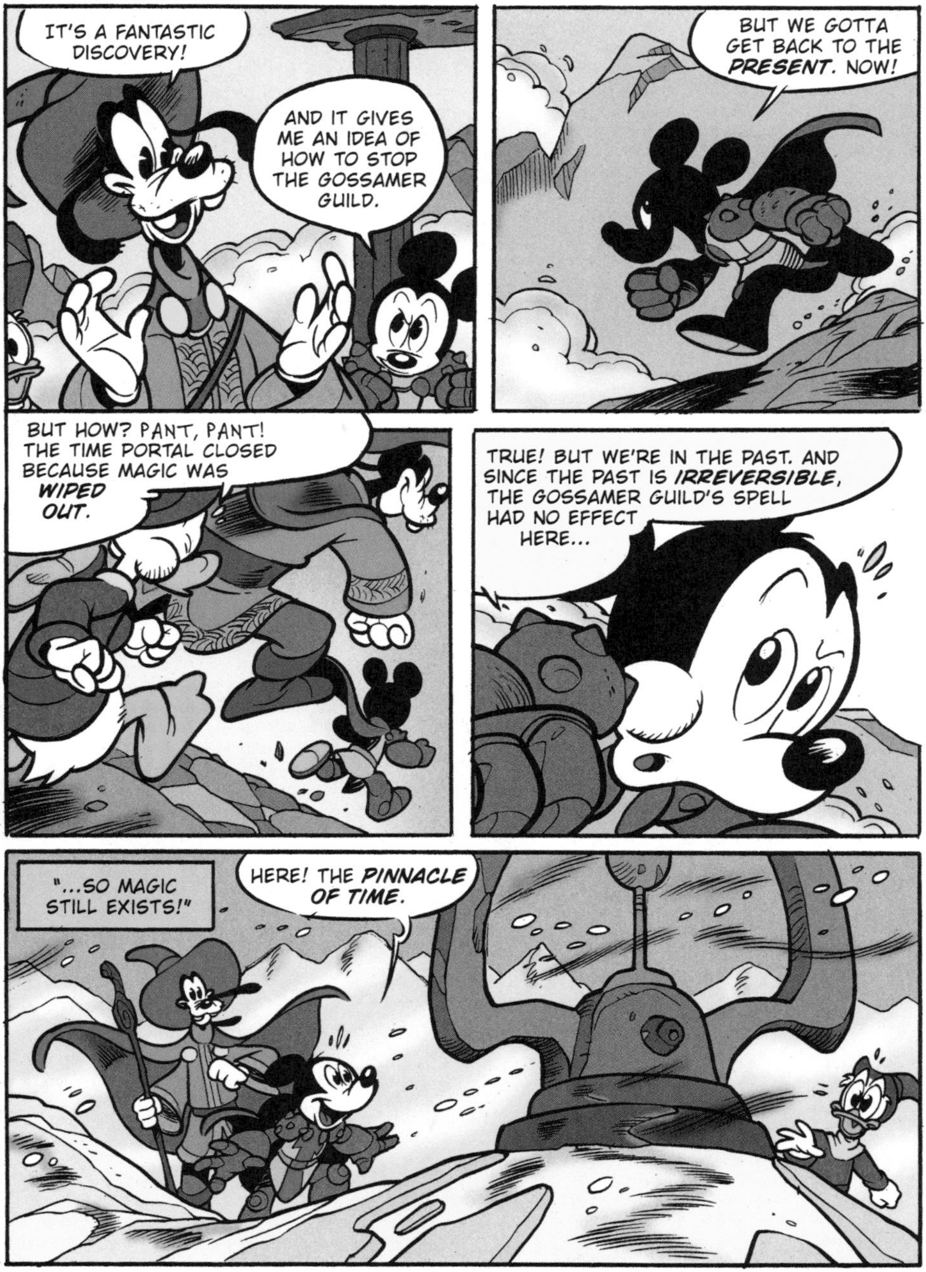
IT'S A FANTASTIC DISCOVERY!
AND IT GIVES ME AN IDEA OF HOW TO STOP THE GOSSAMER GUILD.
BUT WE GOTTA GET BACK TO THE PRESENT. NOW!
BUT HOW? PANT, PANT! THE TIME PORTAL CLOSED BECAUSE MAGIC WAS WIPED OUT.
TRUE! BUT WE'RE IN THE PAST. AND SINCE THE PAST IS IRREVERSIBLE, THE GOSSAMER GUILD'S SPELL HAD NO EFFECT HERE...
"...SO MAGIC STILL EXISTS!"
HERE! THE PINNACLE OF TIME.

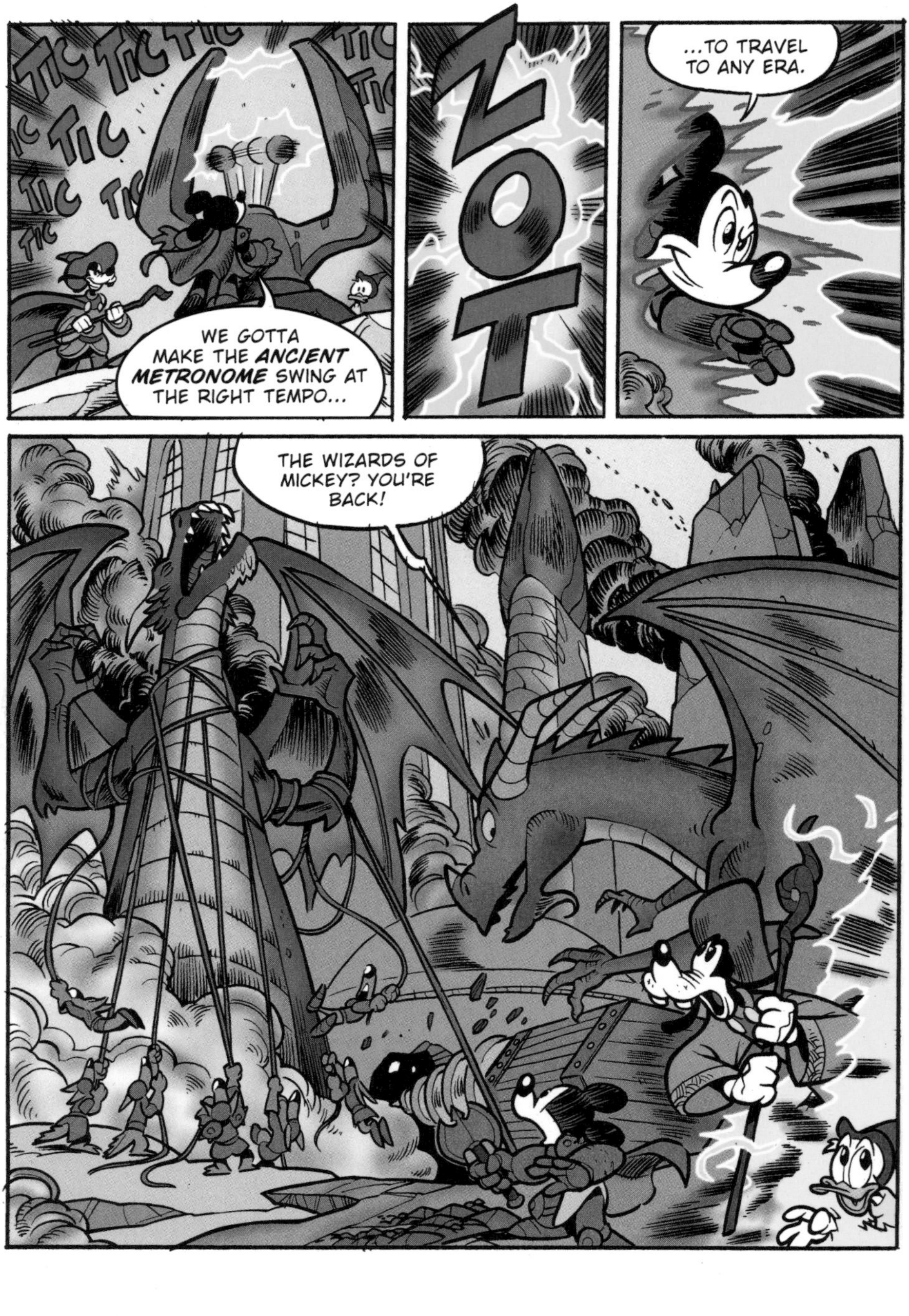
TIC TIC TIC TIC TIC TIC TIC TIC TIC TIC TIC
WE GOTTA MAKE THE ANCIENT METRONOME SWING AT THE RIGHT TEMPO...
ZOT
...TO TRAVEL TO ANY ERA.
THE WIZARDS OF MICKEY? YOU'RE BACK!

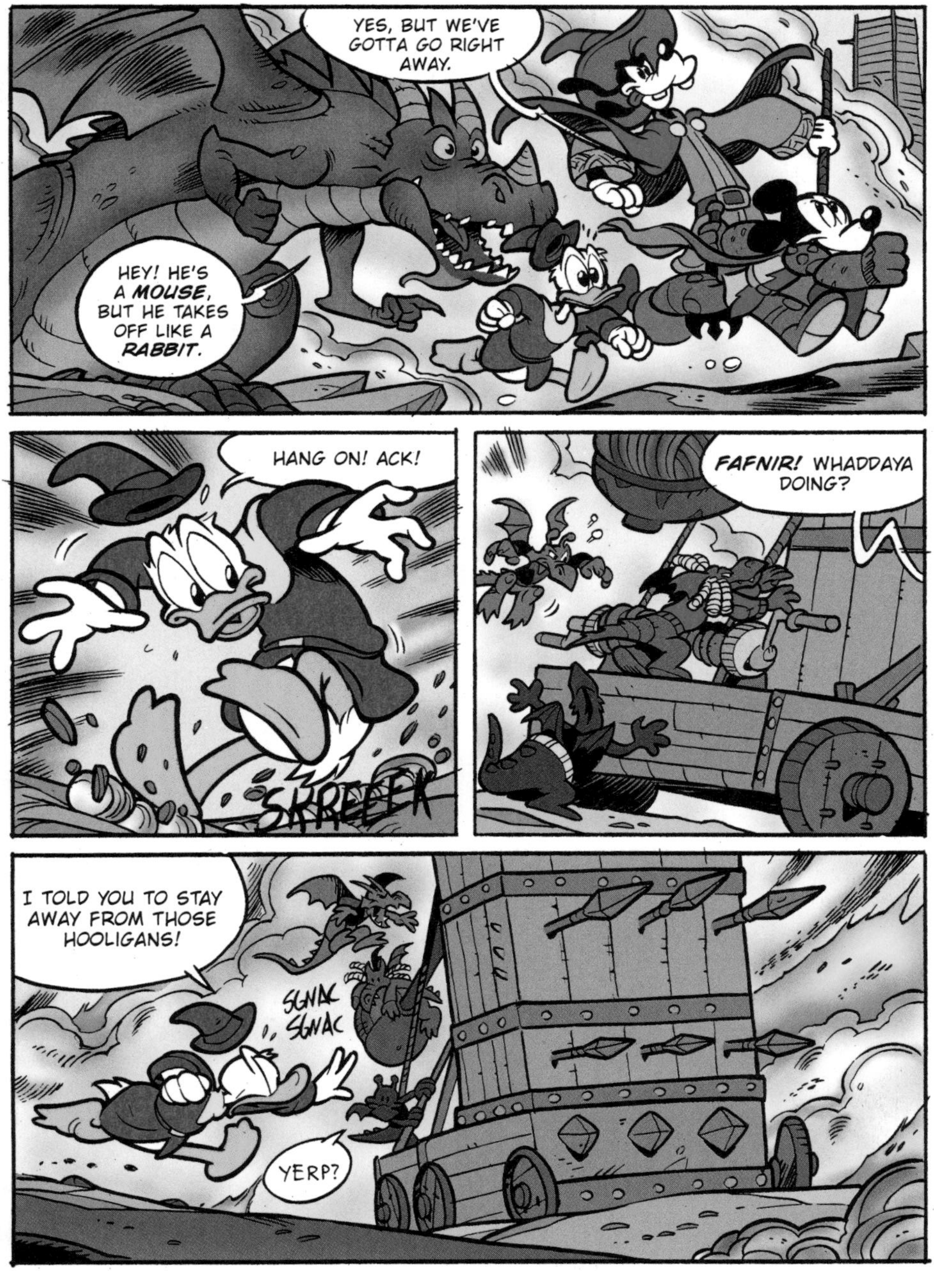
YES, BUT WE'VE GOTTA GO RIGHT AWAY.
HEY! HE'S A ***MOUSE***, BUT HE TAKES OFF LIKE A ***RABBIT***.
HANG ON! ACK!
SKREEEK
FAFNIR! WHADDAYA DOING?
I TOLD YOU TO STAY AWAY FROM THOSE HOOLIGANS!
SGNAC SGNAC
YERP?

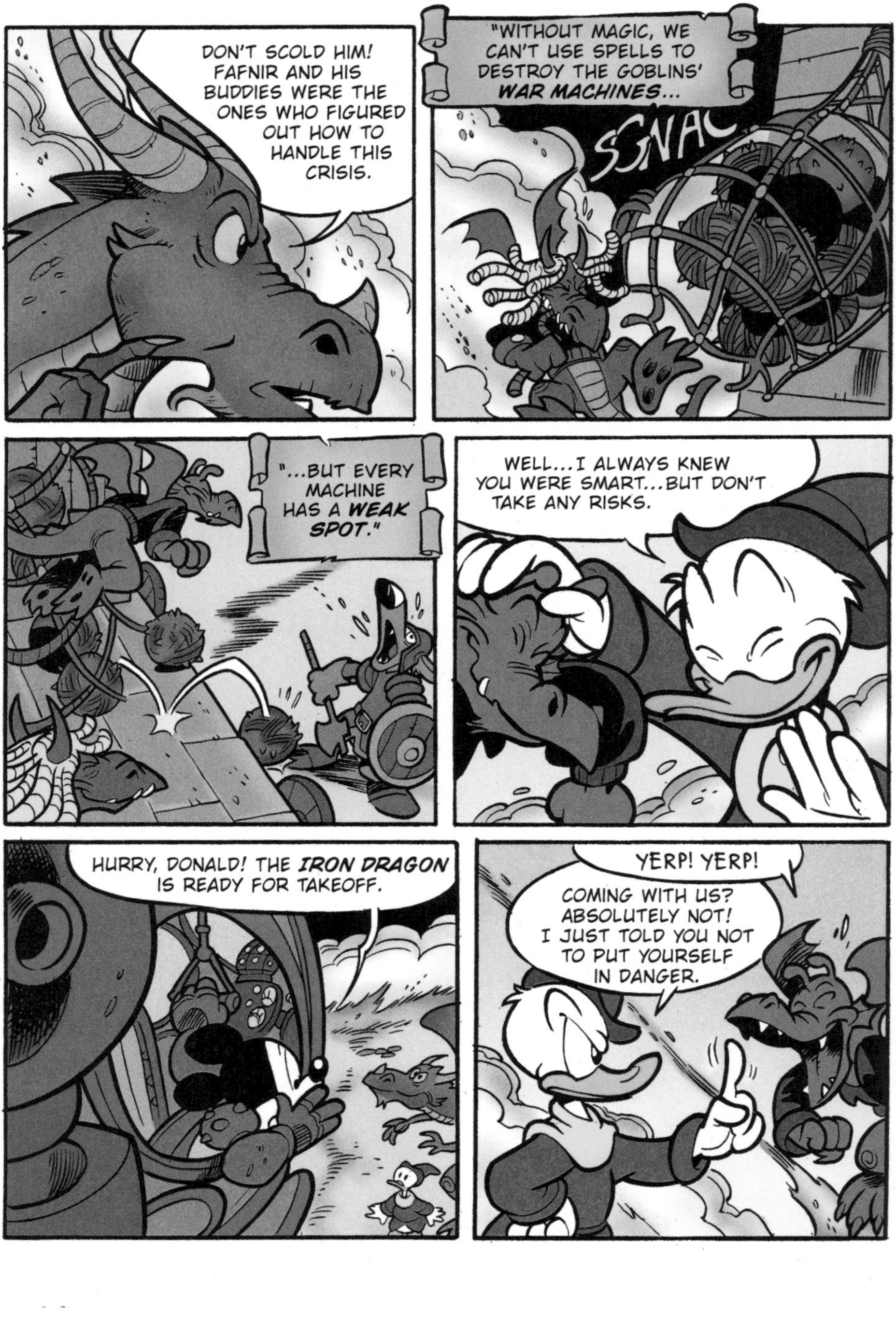
DON'T SCOLD HIM! FAFNIR AND HIS BUDDIES WERE THE ONES WHO FIGURED OUT HOW TO HANDLE THIS CRISIS.
"WITHOUT MAGIC, WE CAN'T USE SPELLS TO DESTROY THE GOBLINS' WAR MACHINES...
SGNAC
"...BUT EVERY MACHINE HAS A WEAK SPOT."
WELL...I ALWAYS KNEW YOU WERE SMART...BUT DON'T TAKE ANY RISKS.
HURRY, DONALD! THE IRON DRAGON IS READY FOR TAKEOFF.
YERP! YERP!
COMING WITH US? ABSOLUTELY NOT! I JUST TOLD YOU NOT TO PUT YOURSELF IN DANGER.

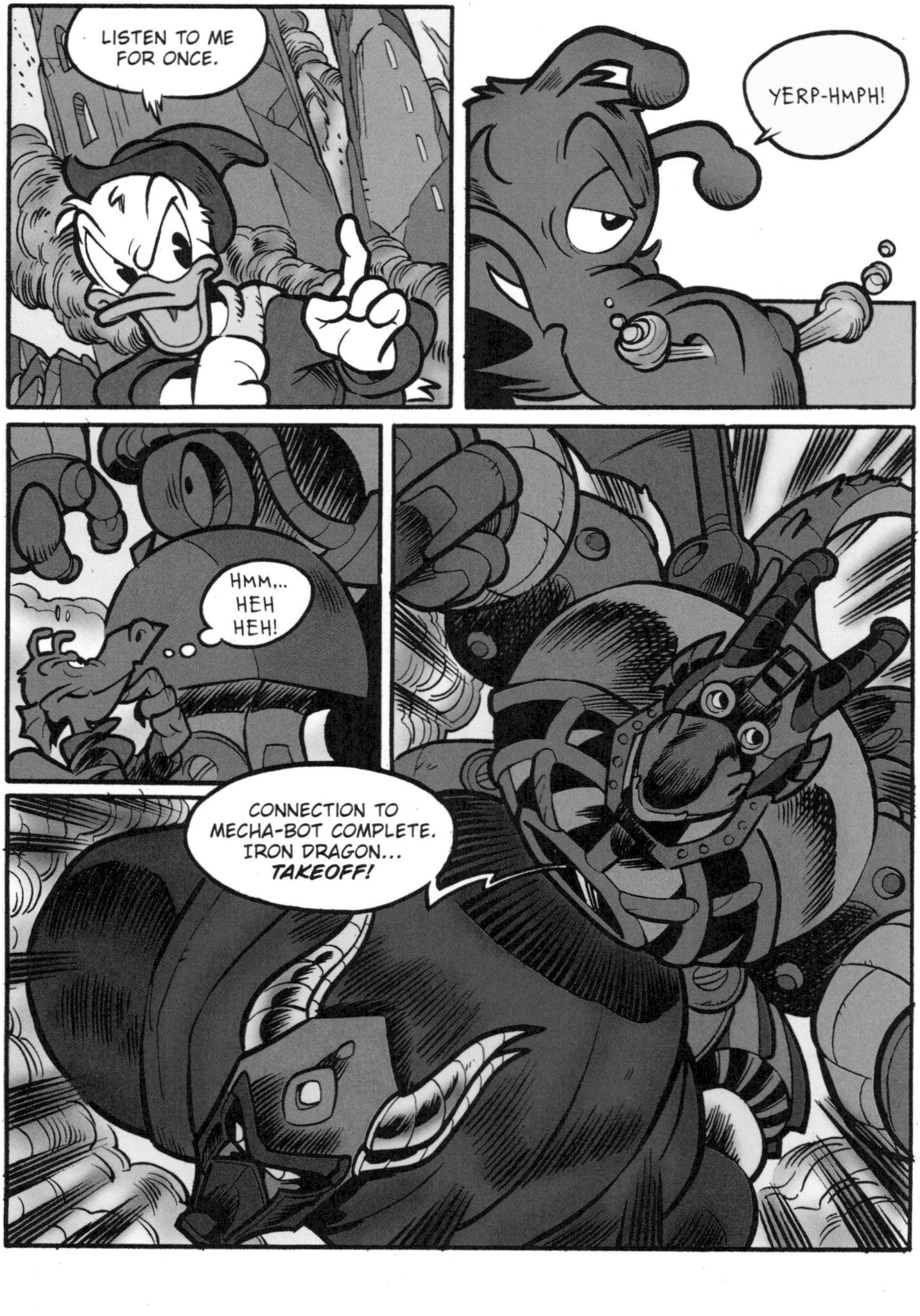
LISTEN TO ME FOR ONCE.
YERP-HMPH!
HMM... HEH HEH!
CONNECTION TO MECHA-BOT COMPLETE. IRON DRAGON... *TAKEOFF!*

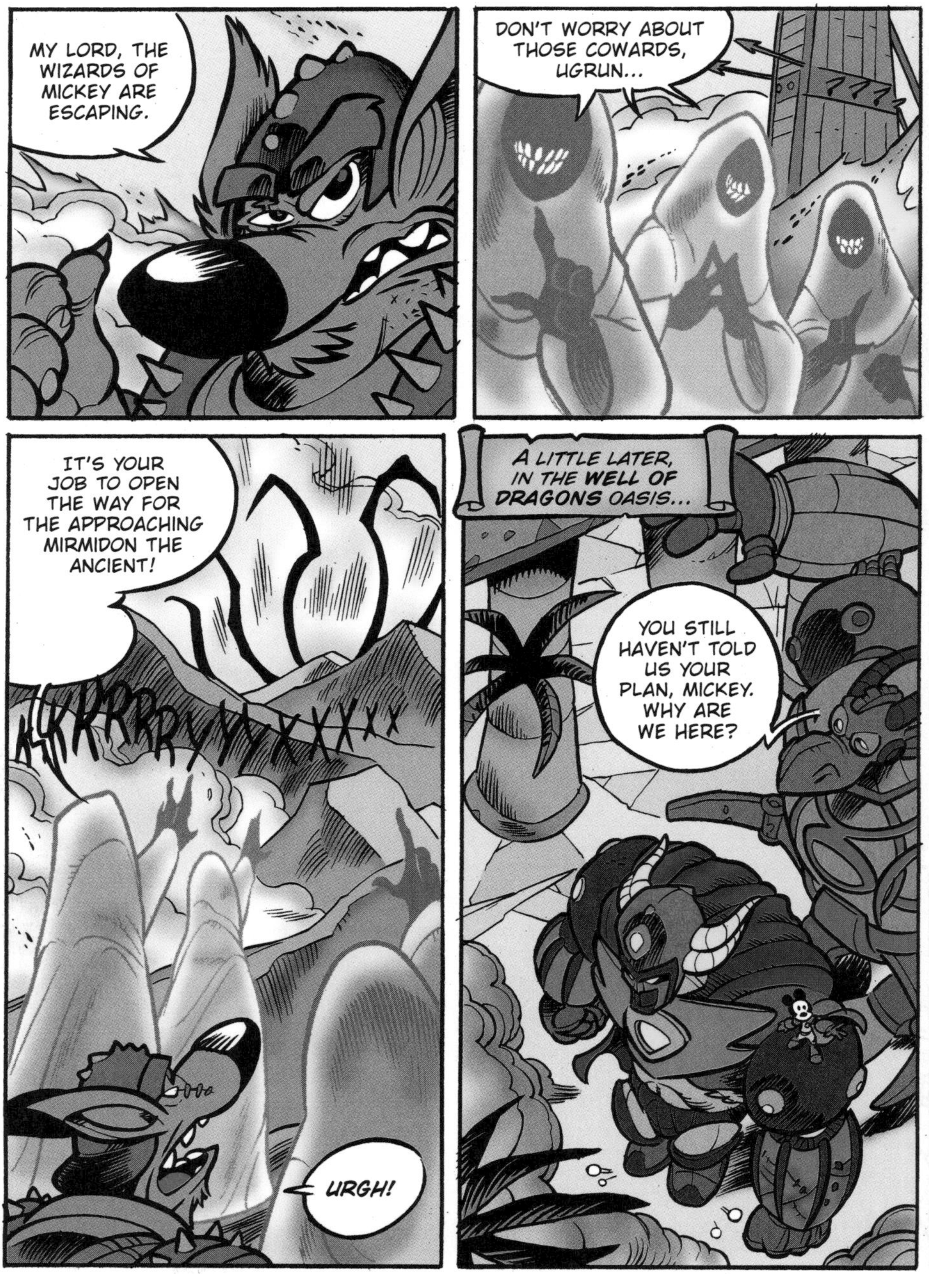
MY LORD, THE WIZARDS OF MICKEY ARE ESCAPING.
DON'T WORRY ABOUT THOSE COWARDS, UGRUN...
IT'S YOUR JOB TO OPEN THE WAY FOR THE APPROACHING MIRMIDON THE ANCIENT!
KKRRRRYYYXXXXX
URGH!
A LITTLE LATER, IN THE WELL OF DRAGONS OASIS...
YOU STILL HAVEN'T TOLD US YOUR PLAN, MICKEY. WHY ARE WE HERE?

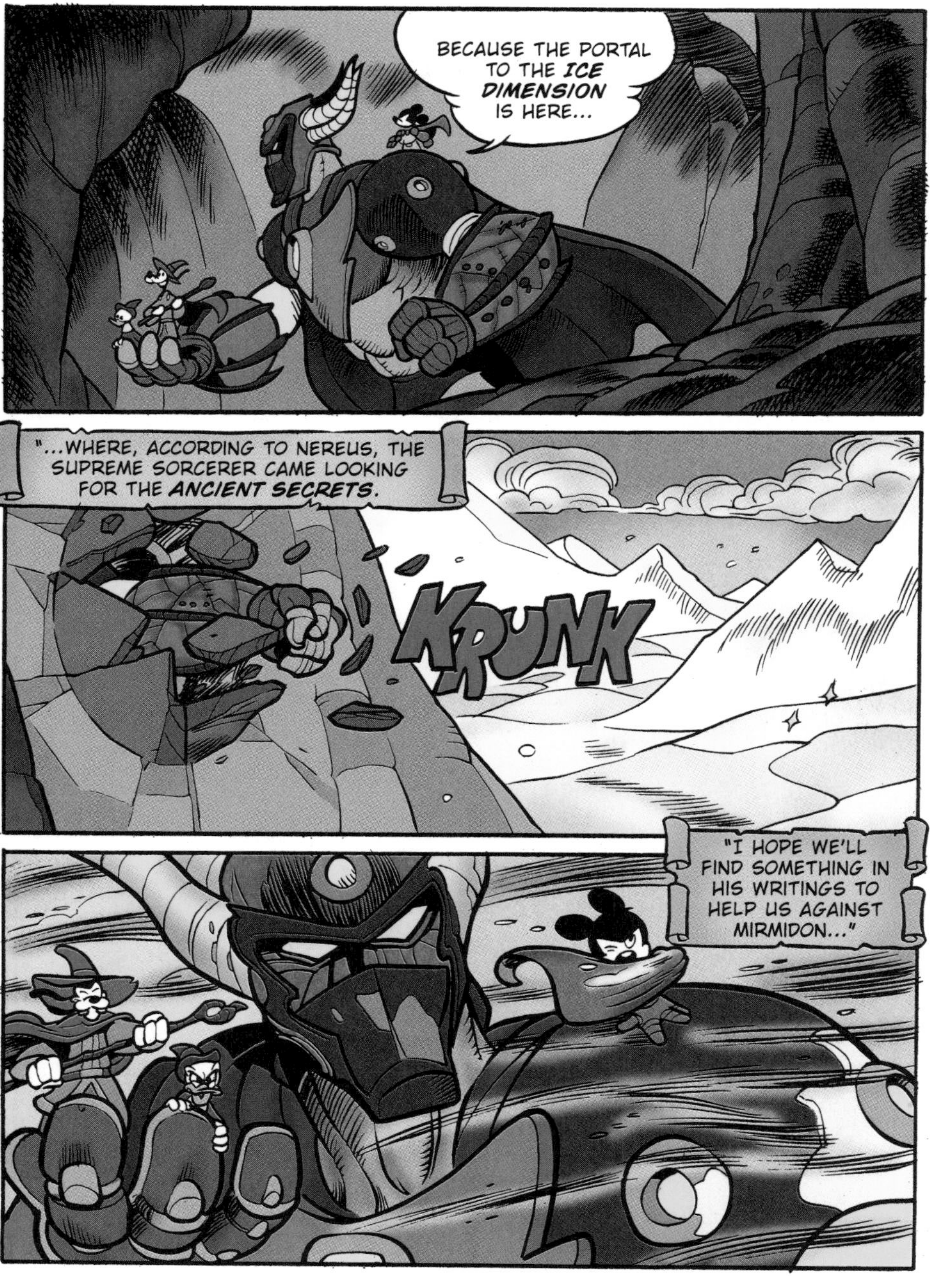

BECAUSE THE PORTAL TO THE *ICE DIMENSION* IS HERE...
"...WHERE, ACCORDING TO NEREUS, THE SUPREME SORCERER CAME LOOKING FOR THE *ANCIENT SECRETS*.
KRUNK
"I HOPE WE'LL FIND SOMETHING IN HIS WRITINGS TO HELP US AGAINST MIRMIDON..."

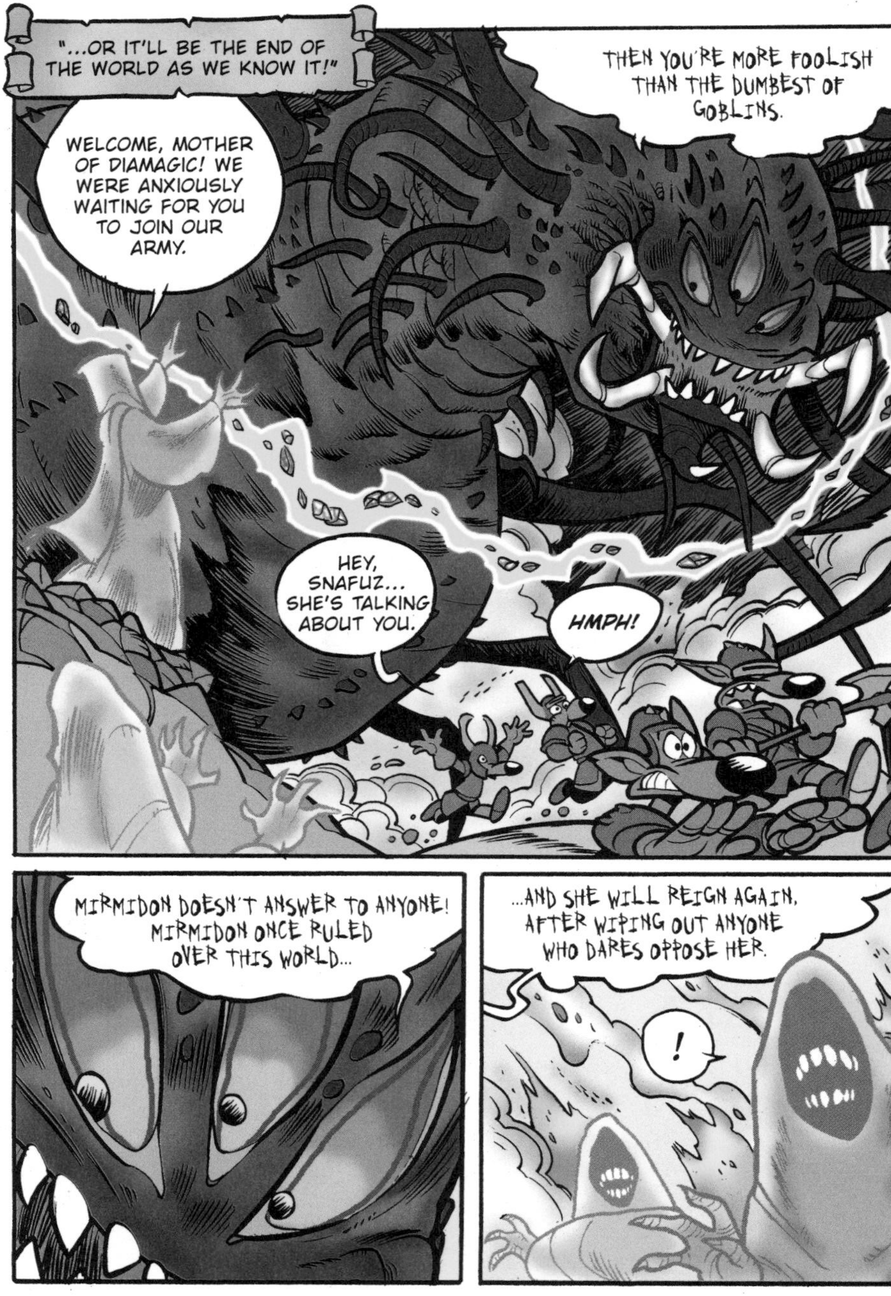
"...OR IT'LL BE THE END OF THE WORLD AS WE KNOW IT!"
WELCOME, MOTHER OF DIAMAGIC! WE WERE ANXIOUSLY WAITING FOR YOU TO JOIN OUR ARMY.
THEN YOU'RE MORE FOOLISH THAN THE DUMBEST OF GOBLINS.
HEY, SNAFUZ... SHE'S TALKING ABOUT YOU.
HMPH!
MIRMIDON DOESN'T ANSWER TO ANYONE! MIRMIDON ONCE RULED OVER THIS WORLD...
...AND SHE WILL REIGN AGAIN, AFTER WIPING OUT ANYONE WHO DARES OPPOSE HER.
!

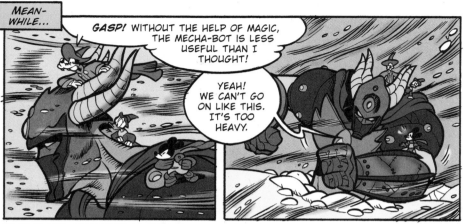

GASP! WITHOUT THE HELP OF MAGIC, THE MECHA-BOT IS LESS USEFUL THAN I THOUGHT!

YEAH! WE CAN'T GO ON LIKE THIS. IT'S TOO HEAVY.

WE'D BETTER CONTI-NUE ON FOOT.

CHATTER, CHATTER! NEXT TIME YOU WANNA CROSS A *FROZEN WORLD*, WARN ME SO I CAN WEAR *WOOL SOCKS*.

LET'S SHELTER IN THERE. WE'LL WARM UP A LITTLE.

GULP! THE GROUND IS SO SLIMY...

SGUISH SGUISH

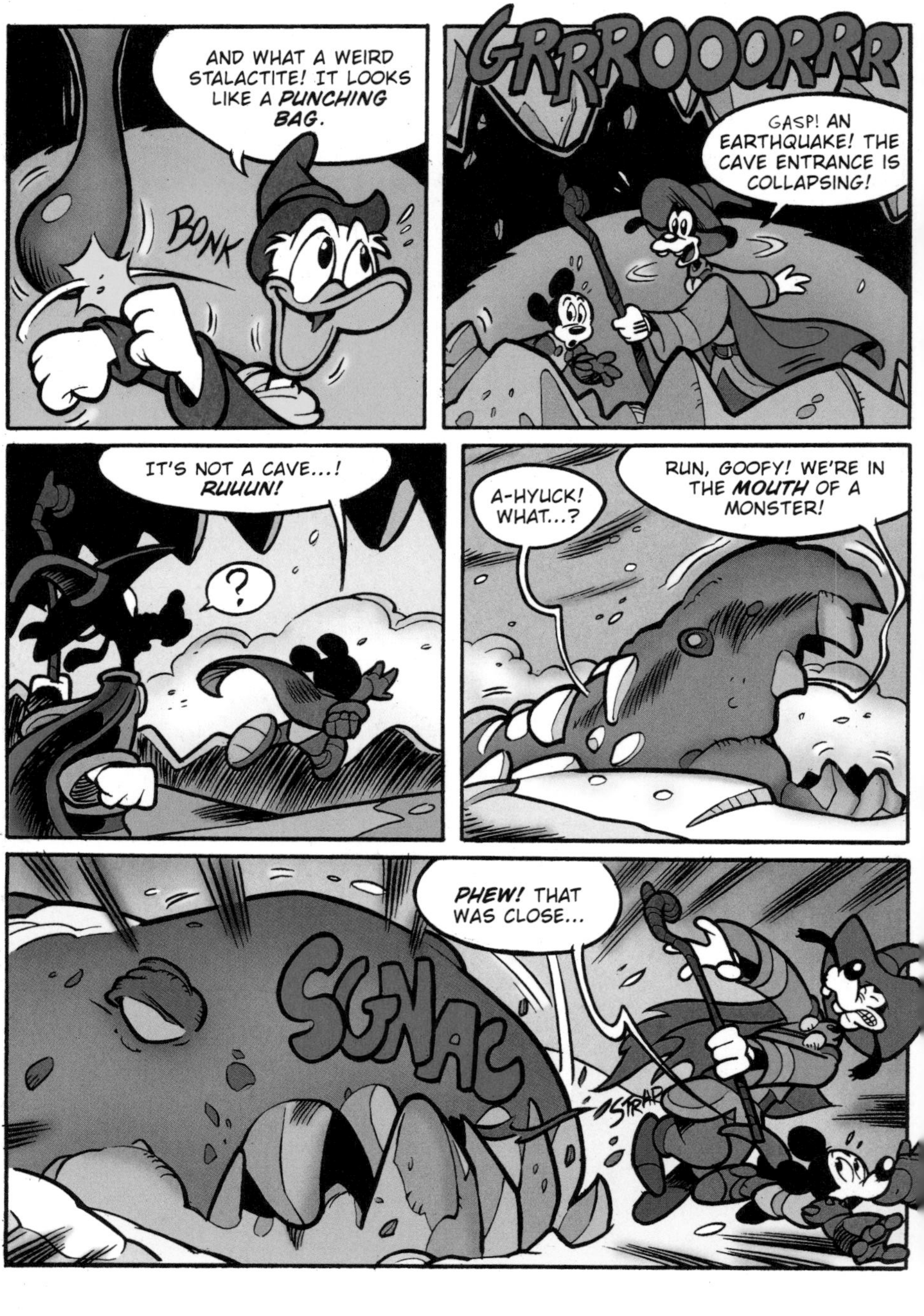

AND WHAT A WEIRD STALACTITE! IT LOOKS LIKE A PUNCHING BAG.
BONK
GRRROOORRR
GASP! AN EARTHQUAKE! THE CAVE ENTRANCE IS COLLAPSING!
IT'S NOT A CAVE...! RUUUN!
?
RUN, GOOFY! WE'RE IN THE MOUTH OF A MONSTER!
A-HYUCK! WHAT...?
PHEW! THAT WAS CLOSE...
SGNAC
STRAP

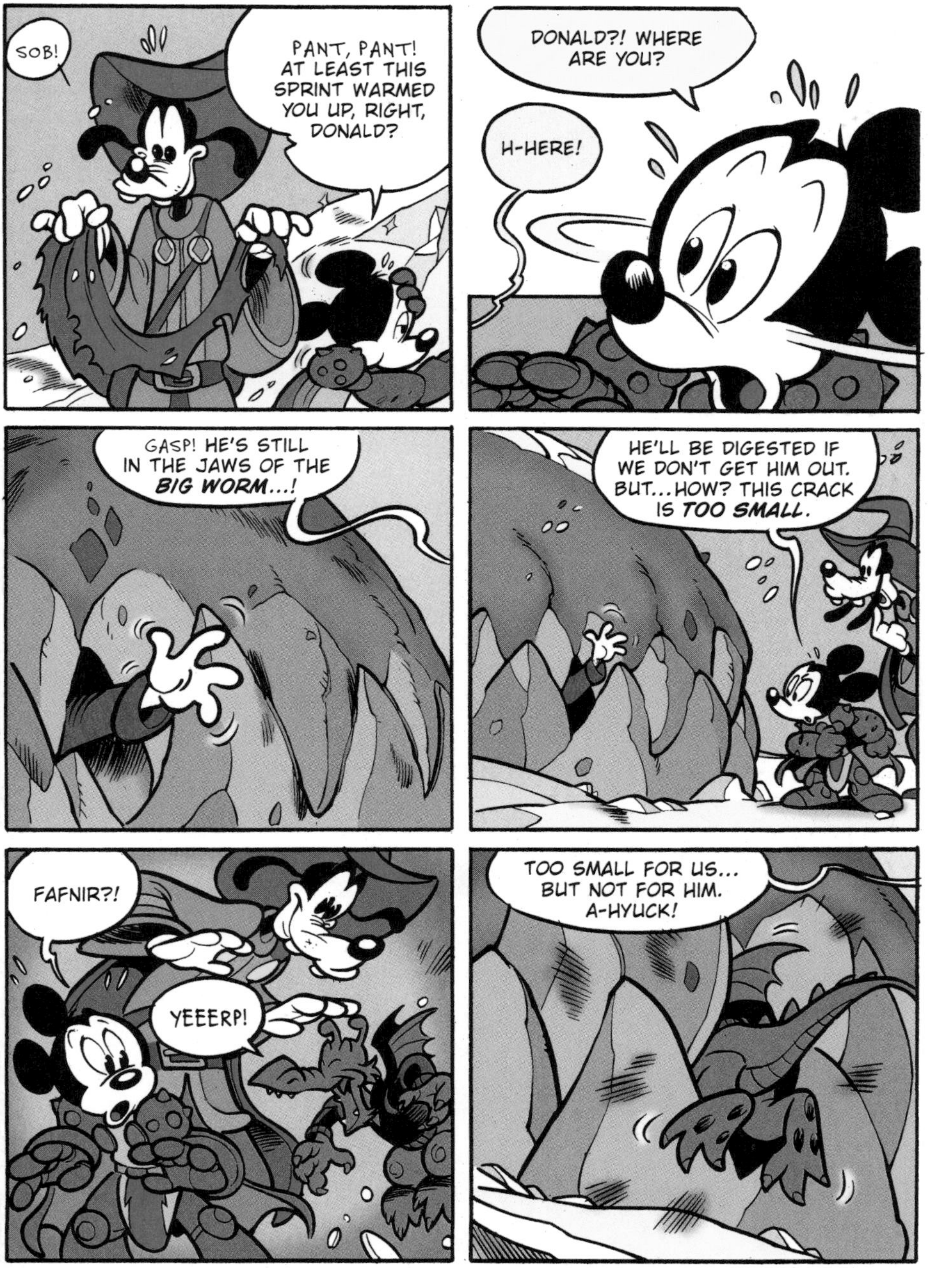
SOB!
PANT, PANT! AT LEAST THIS SPRINT WARMED YOU UP, RIGHT, DONALD?
DONALD?! WHERE ARE YOU?
H-HERE!
GASP! HE'S STILL IN THE JAWS OF THE BIG WORM...!
HE'LL BE DIGESTED IF WE DON'T GET HIM OUT. BUT...HOW? THIS CRACK IS TOO SMALL.
FAFNIR?!
YEEERP!
TOO SMALL FOR US... BUT NOT FOR HIM. A-HYUCK!

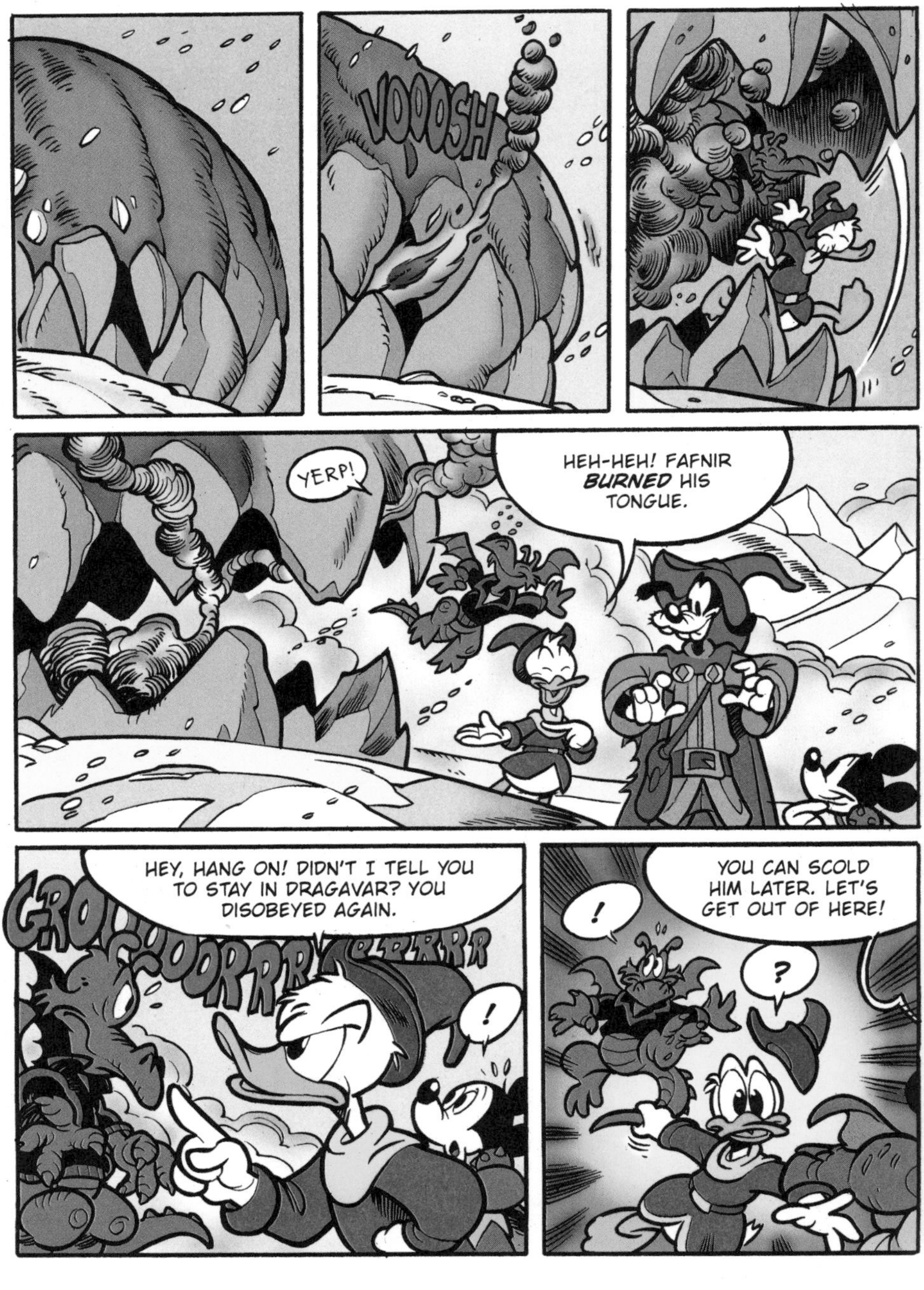
VOOOSH
YERP!
HEH-HEH! FAFNIR **BURNED** HIS TONGUE.
HEY, HANG ON! DIDN'T I TELL YOU TO STAY IN DRAGAVAR? YOU DISOBEYED AGAIN.
!
!
YOU CAN SCOLD HIM LATER. LET'S GET OUT OF HERE!
?

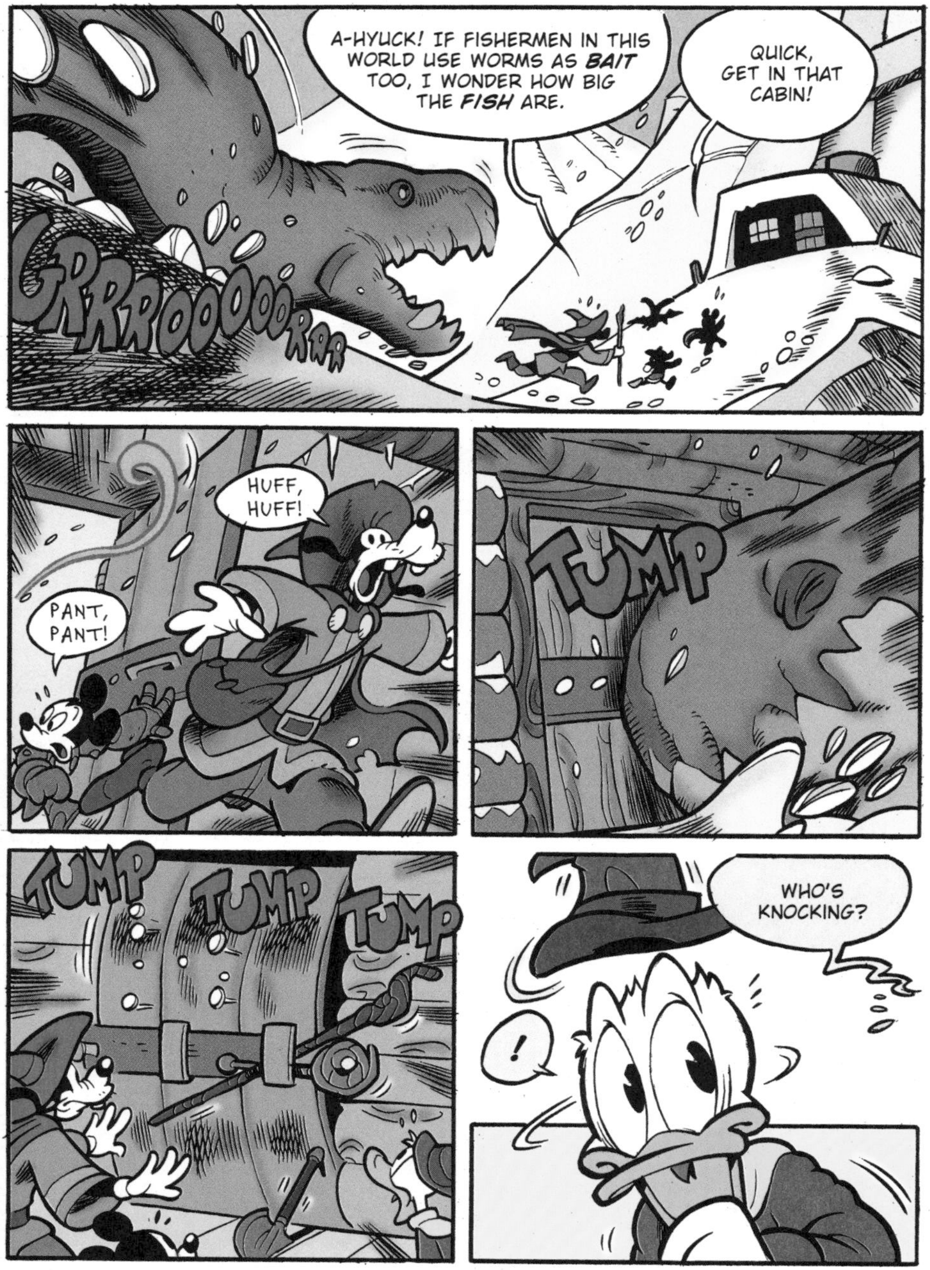
A-HYUCK! IF FISHERMEN IN THIS WORLD USE WORMS AS BAIT TOO, I WONDER HOW BIG THE FISH ARE.
QUICK, GET IN THAT CABIN!
GRRROOOOORRR
HUFF, HUFF!
PANT, PANT!
TUMP
TUMP TUMP TUMP
WHO'S KNOCKING?
!

YAWN! WHAT A NICE NAP. I FEEL GREAT AND *FULL OF LIFE.*

F-FULL OF LIFE INDEED...!

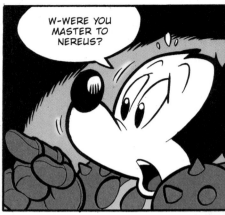

W-WERE YOU MASTER TO NEREUS?

OF COURSE, DON'T YOU RECOG— GULP! MAYBE I LOST A LITTLE *TOO* MUCH WEIGHT.

HMM...AS SOON AS I GET HOME, I'LL EAT A TON OF *CANNOLI.*

THERE WON'T BE A WORLD TO GO BACK TO IF YOU DON'T HELP US.

HUH? TELL ME EVERYTHING WHILE I...

TUMP TUMP TUMP

...GET RID OF THIS BIG WORM! ALL OF ITS NOISY HEADBUTTING IS GIVING ME A SKULL-SPLITTING HEADACHE.

ZAP

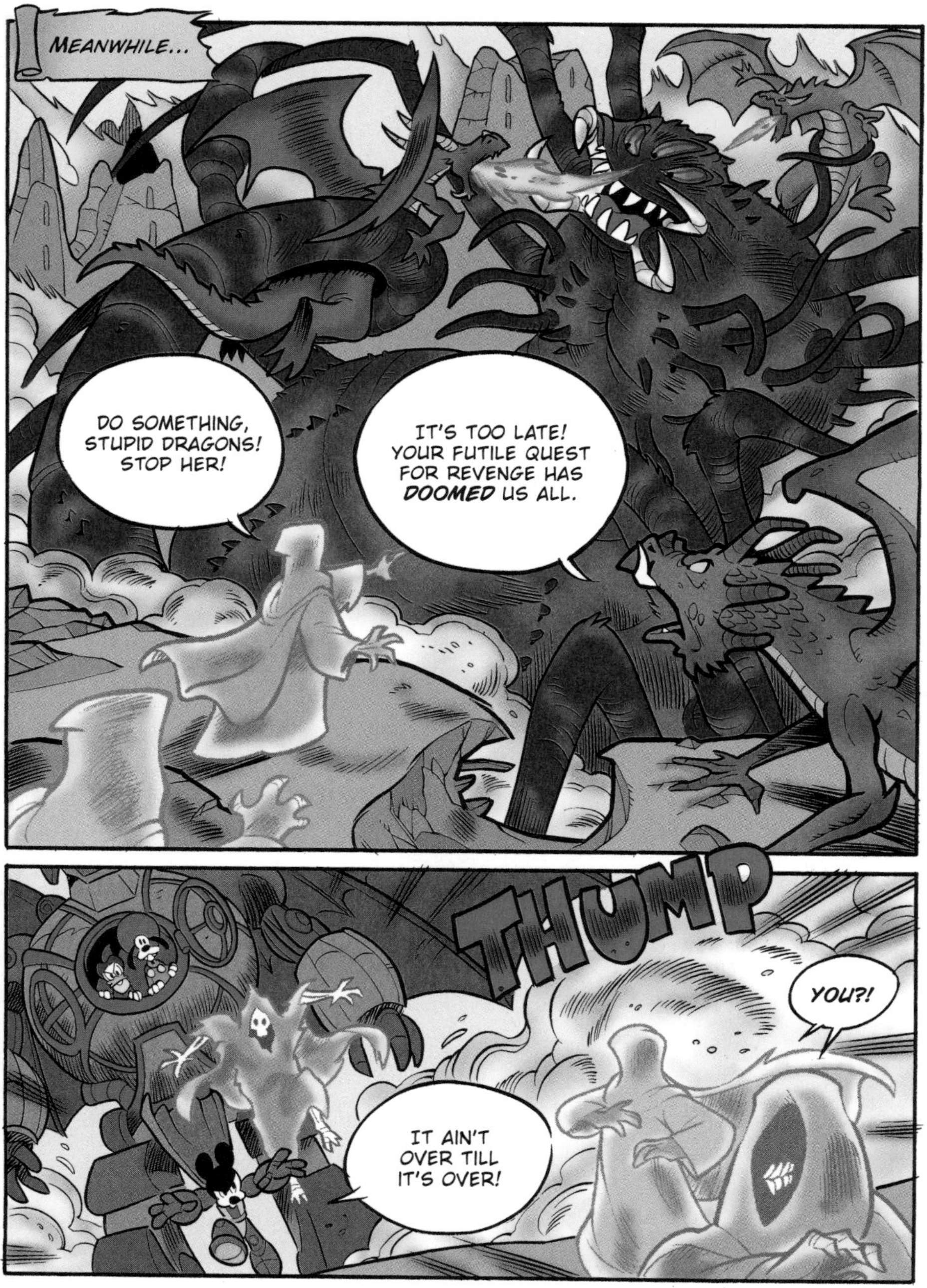
MEANWHILE...
DO SOMETHING, STUPID DRAGONS! STOP HER!
IT'S TOO LATE! YOUR FUTILE QUEST FOR REVENGE HAS DOOMED US ALL.
THUMP
YOU?!
IT AIN'T OVER TILL IT'S OVER!

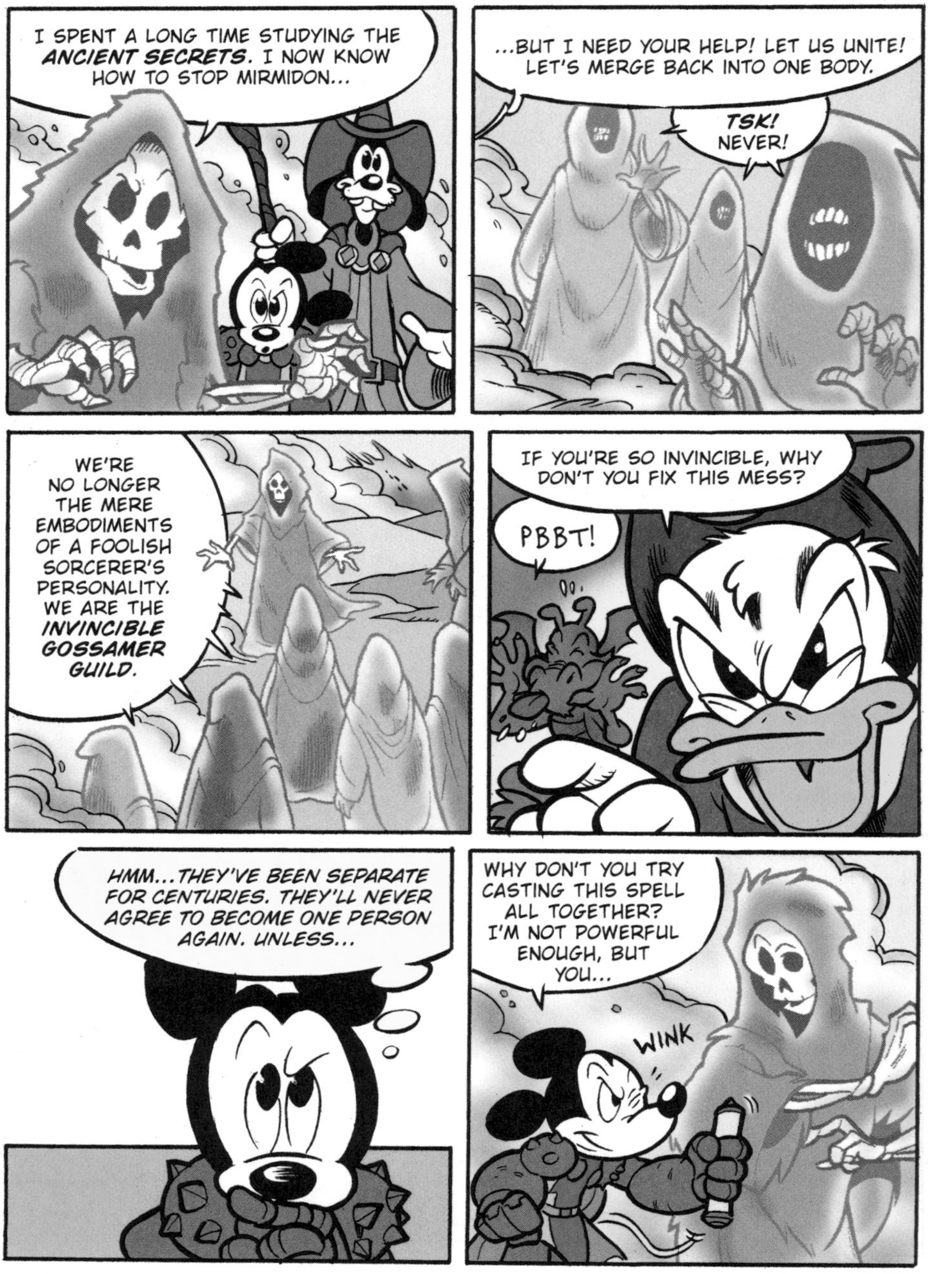
I SPENT A LONG TIME STUDYING THE ANCIENT SECRETS. I NOW KNOW HOW TO STOP MIRMIDON...
...BUT I NEED YOUR HELP! LET US UNITE! LET'S MERGE BACK INTO ONE BODY.
TSK! NEVER!
WE'RE NO LONGER THE MERE EMBODIMENTS OF A FOOLISH SORCERER'S PERSONALITY. WE ARE THE INVINCIBLE GOSSAMER GUILD.
IF YOU'RE SO INVINCIBLE, WHY DON'T YOU FIX THIS MESS?
PBBT!
HMM...THEY'VE BEEN SEPARATE FOR CENTURIES. THEY'LL NEVER AGREE TO BECOME ONE PERSON AGAIN. UNLESS...
WHY DON'T YOU TRY CASTING THIS SPELL ALL TOGETHER? I'M NOT POWERFUL ENOUGH, BUT YOU...
WINK

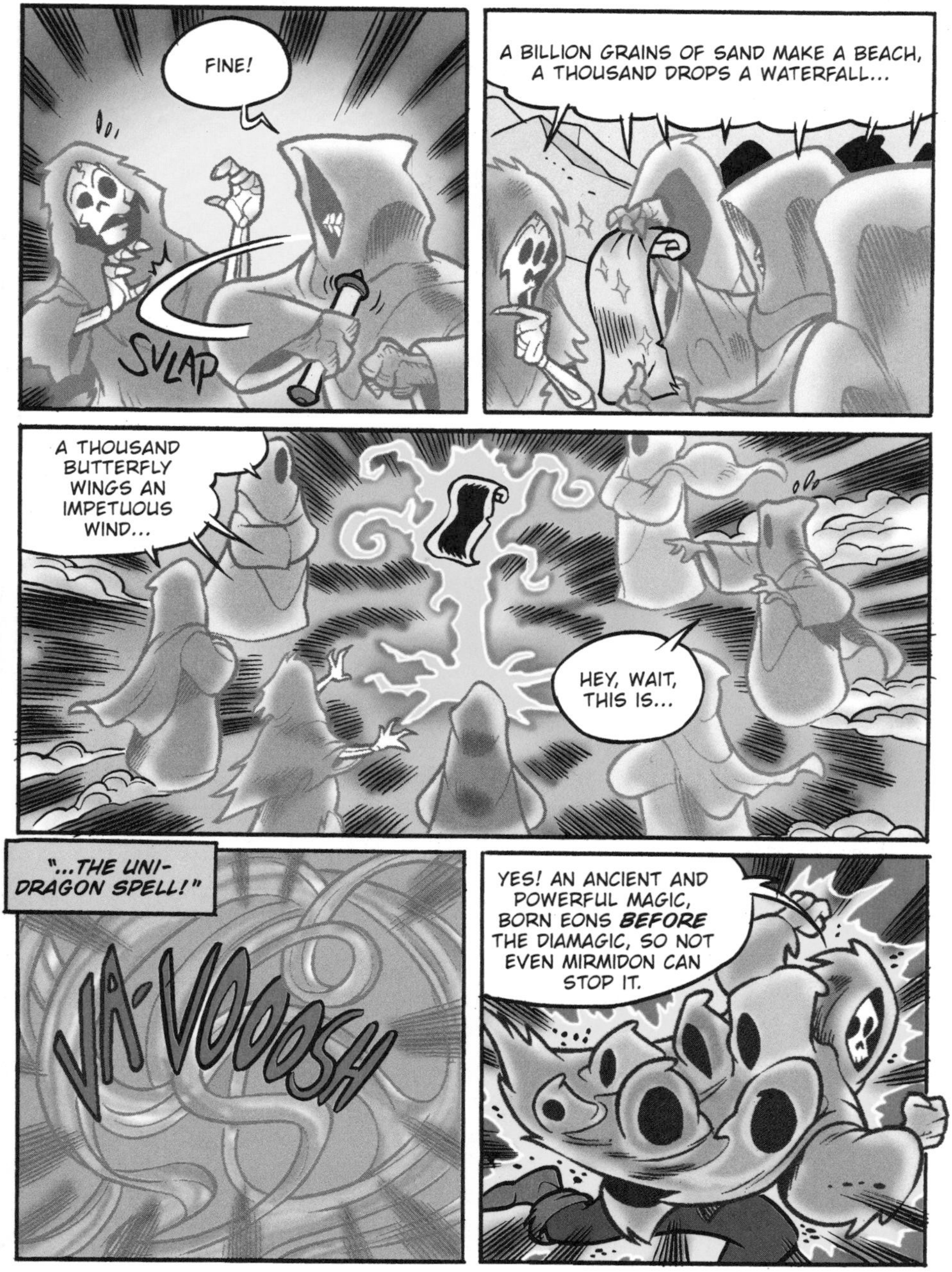
FINE!
SVLAP
A BILLION GRAINS OF SAND MAKE A BEACH, A THOUSAND DROPS A WATERFALL...
A THOUSAND BUTTERFLY WINGS AN IMPETUOUS WIND...
HEY, WAIT, THIS IS...
"...THE UNI-DRAGON SPELL!"
VA-VOOOSH
YES! AN ANCIENT AND POWERFUL MAGIC, BORN EONS BEFORE THE DIAMAGIC, SO NOT EVEN MIRMIDON CAN STOP IT.

IT WORKED! NOW THAT THE SUPREME SORCERER'S *GOOD SIDE* HAS JOINED THE OTHERS, LET'S HOPE MASTER NEREUS WAS RIGHT...

*THERE IS A **SPARK** OF GOODNESS IN EVERYONE'S HEART. YOU JUST NEED THE RIGHT FUEL TO FAN IT INTO A **RAGING FIRE**.*

WELL, IT WORKED FOR FAFNIR. EVEN THOUGH HE WAS BEING REBELLIOUS...

HMPH!

...WHEN HE SAW ME IN TROUBLE, HE RAN TO SAVE ME, REGARDLESS OF THE DANGER.

YERP!

MIRMIDON, CONTAIN YOUR ANGER AND LISTEN TO ME! I KNOW WHAT FILLS YOUR ANCIENT HEART WITH HATRED.

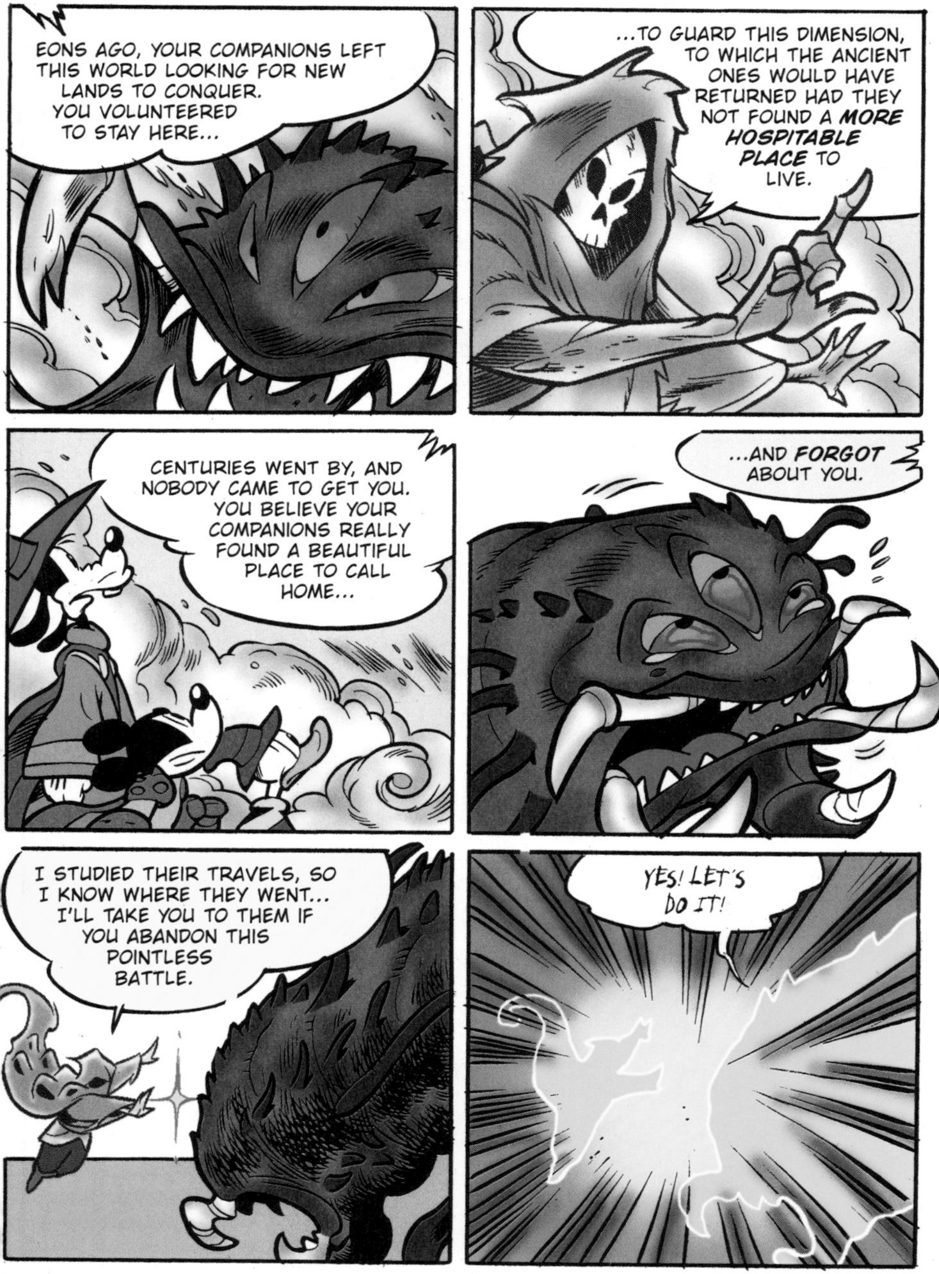
EONS AGO, YOUR COMPANIONS LEFT THIS WORLD LOOKING FOR NEW LANDS TO CONQUER. YOU VOLUNTEERED TO STAY HERE...
...TO GUARD THIS DIMENSION, TO WHICH THE ANCIENT ONES WOULD HAVE RETURNED HAD THEY NOT FOUND A **MORE HOSPITABLE PLACE** TO LIVE.
CENTURIES WENT BY, AND NOBODY CAME TO GET YOU. YOU BELIEVE YOUR COMPANIONS REALLY FOUND A BEAUTIFUL PLACE TO CALL HOME...
...AND **FORGOT** ABOUT YOU.
I STUDIED THEIR TRAVELS, SO I KNOW WHERE THEY WENT... I'LL TAKE YOU TO THEM IF YOU ABANDON THIS POINTLESS BATTLE.
YES! LET'S DO IT!

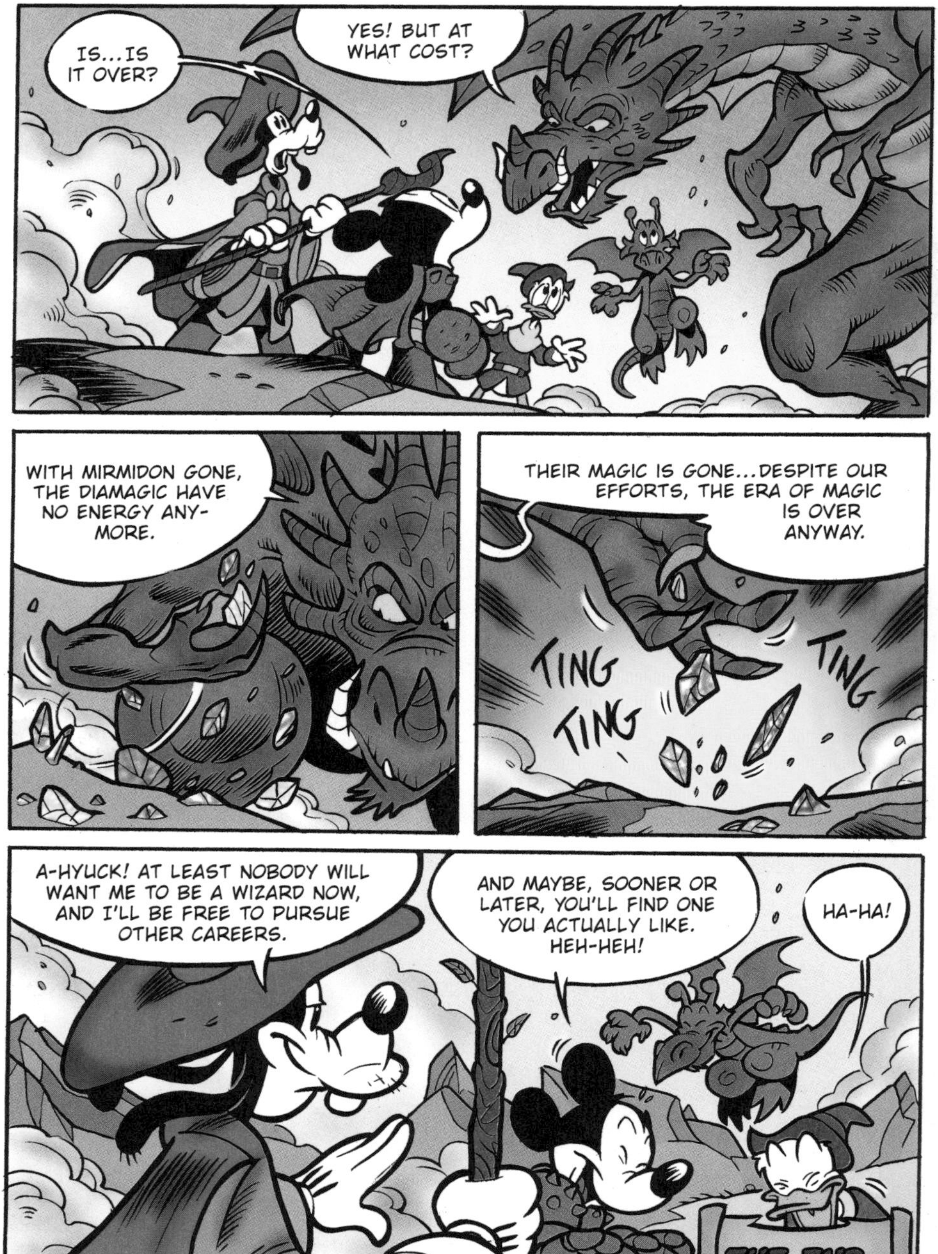
IS...IS IT OVER?
YES! BUT AT WHAT COST?
WITH MIRMIDON GONE, THE DIAMAGIC HAVE NO ENERGY ANY-MORE.
THEIR MAGIC IS GONE...DESPITE OUR EFFORTS, THE ERA OF MAGIC IS OVER ANYWAY.
TING
TING
TING
A-HYUCK! AT LEAST NOBODY WILL WANT ME TO BE A WIZARD NOW, AND I'LL BE FREE TO PURSUE OTHER CAREERS.
AND MAYBE, SOONER OR LATER, YOU'LL FIND ONE YOU ACTUALLY LIKE. HEH-HEH!
HA-HA!
THE END...

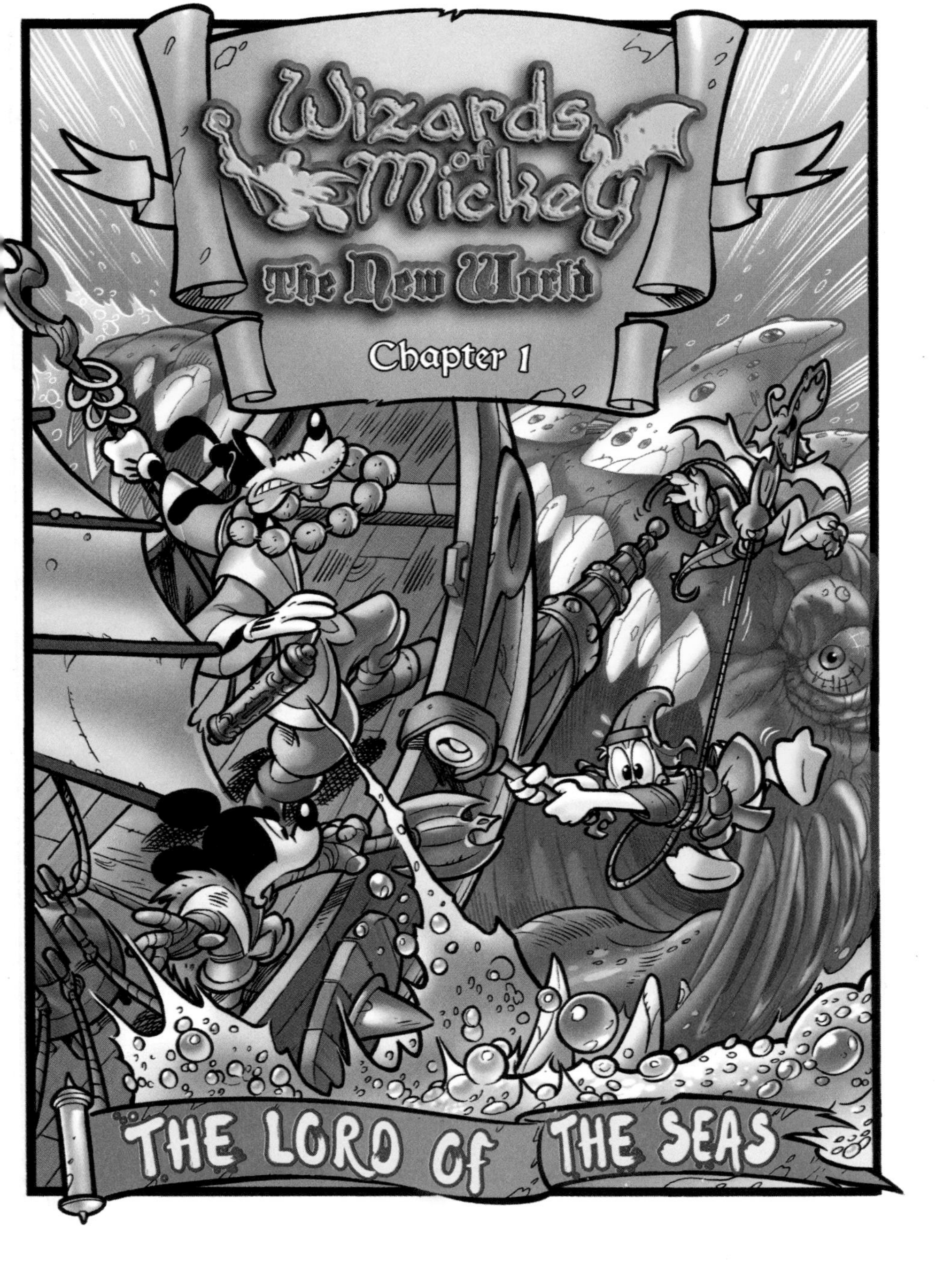
Wizards of Mickey
The New World
Chapter 1
THE LORD OF THE SEAS

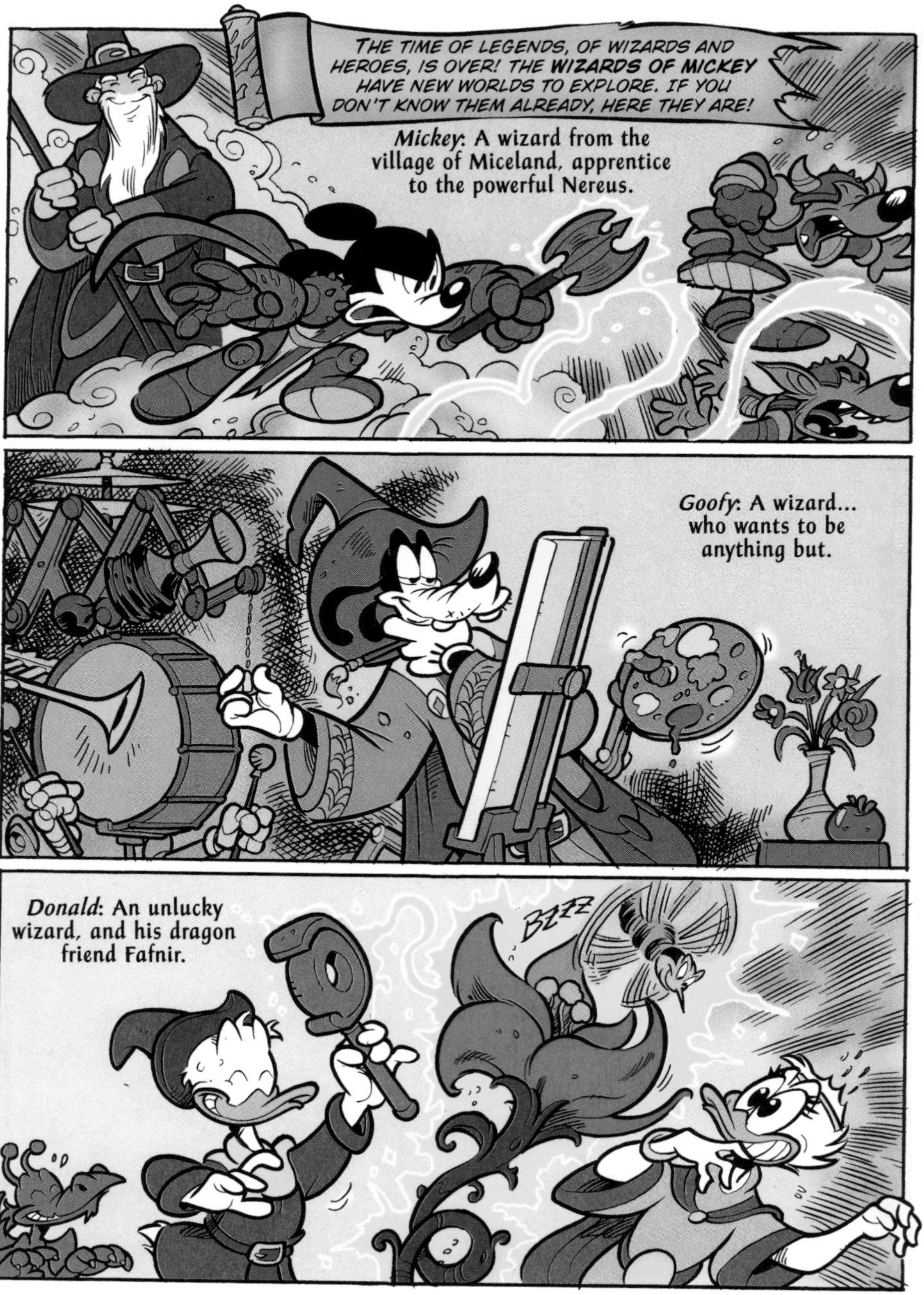
THE TIME OF LEGENDS, OF WIZARDS AND HEROES, IS OVER! THE WIZARDS OF MICKEY HAVE NEW WORLDS TO EXPLORE. IF YOU DON'T KNOW THEM ALREADY, HERE THEY ARE!
Mickey: A wizard from the village of Miceland, apprentice to the powerful Nereus.
Goofy: A wizard... who wants to be anything but.
Donald: An unlucky wizard, and his dragon friend Fafnir.
BZZZ

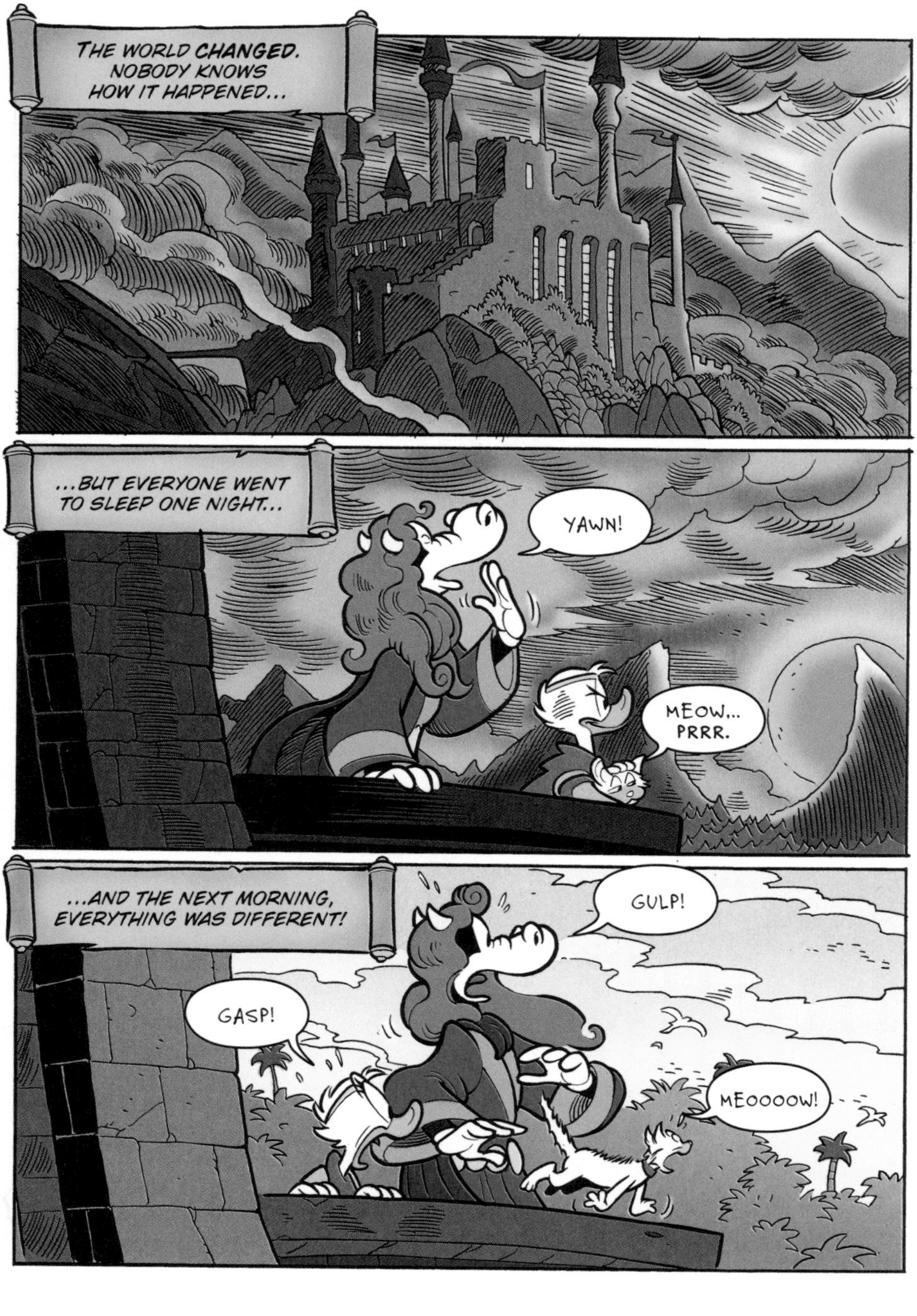
THE WORLD CHANGED. NOBODY KNOWS HOW IT HAPPENED...
...BUT EVERYONE WENT TO SLEEP ONE NIGHT...
YAWN!
MEOW... PRRR.
...AND THE NEXT MORNING, EVERYTHING WAS DIFFERENT!
GULP!
GASP!
MEOOOOW!

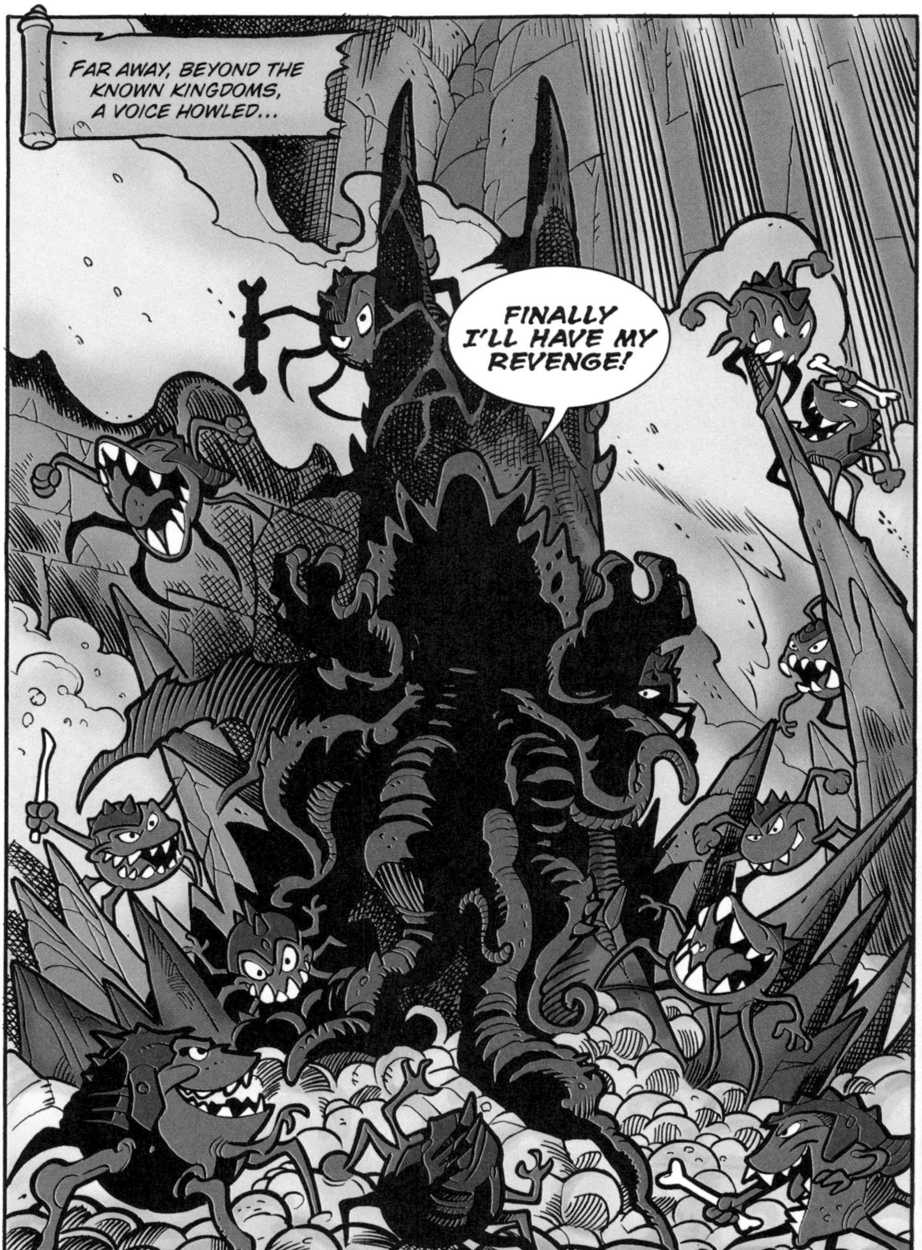
FAR AWAY, BEYOND THE KNOWN KINGDOMS, A VOICE HOWLED...
FINALLY I'LL HAVE MY REVENGE!

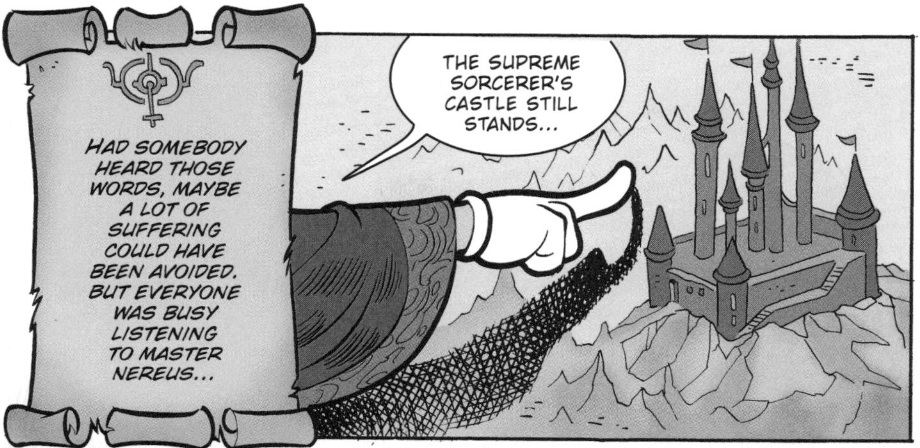
HAD SOMEBODY HEARD THOSE WORDS, MAYBE A LOT OF SUFFERING COULD HAVE BEEN AVOIDED. BUT EVERYONE WAS BUSY LISTENING TO MASTER NEREUS...
THE SUPREME SORCERER'S CASTLE STILL STANDS...

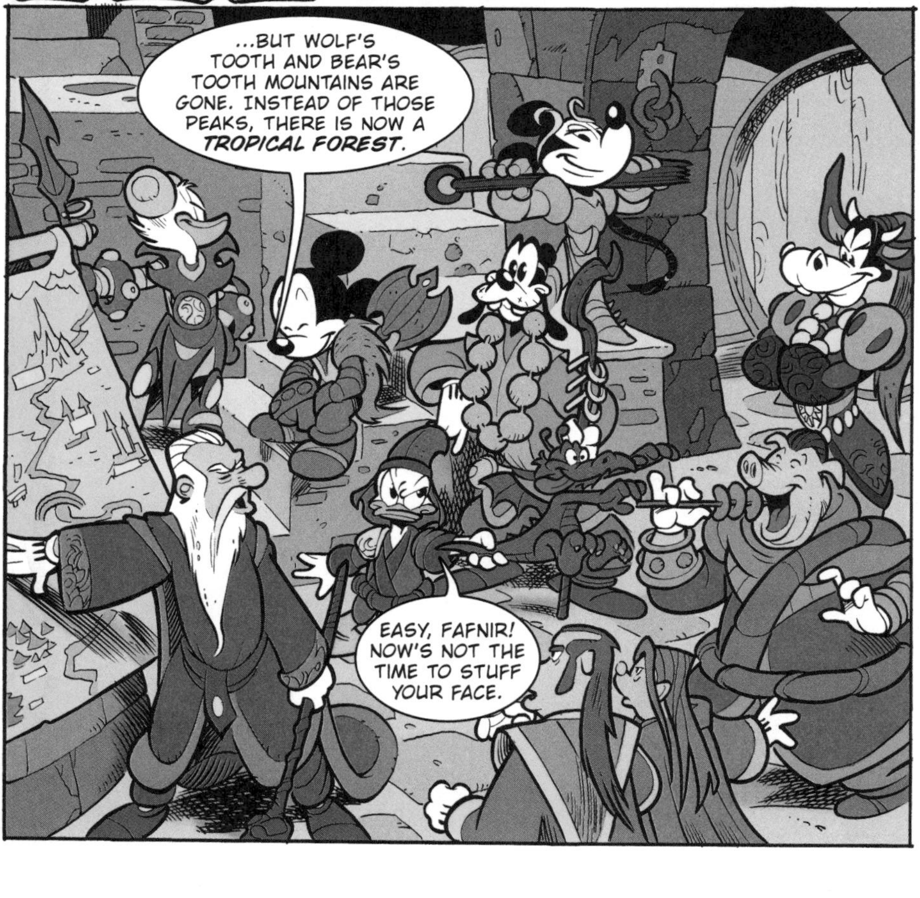
...BUT WOLF'S TOOTH AND BEAR'S TOOTH MOUNTAINS ARE GONE. INSTEAD OF THOSE PEAKS, THERE IS NOW A **TROPICAL FOREST**.
EASY, FAFNIR! NOW'S NOT THE TIME TO STUFF YOUR FACE.

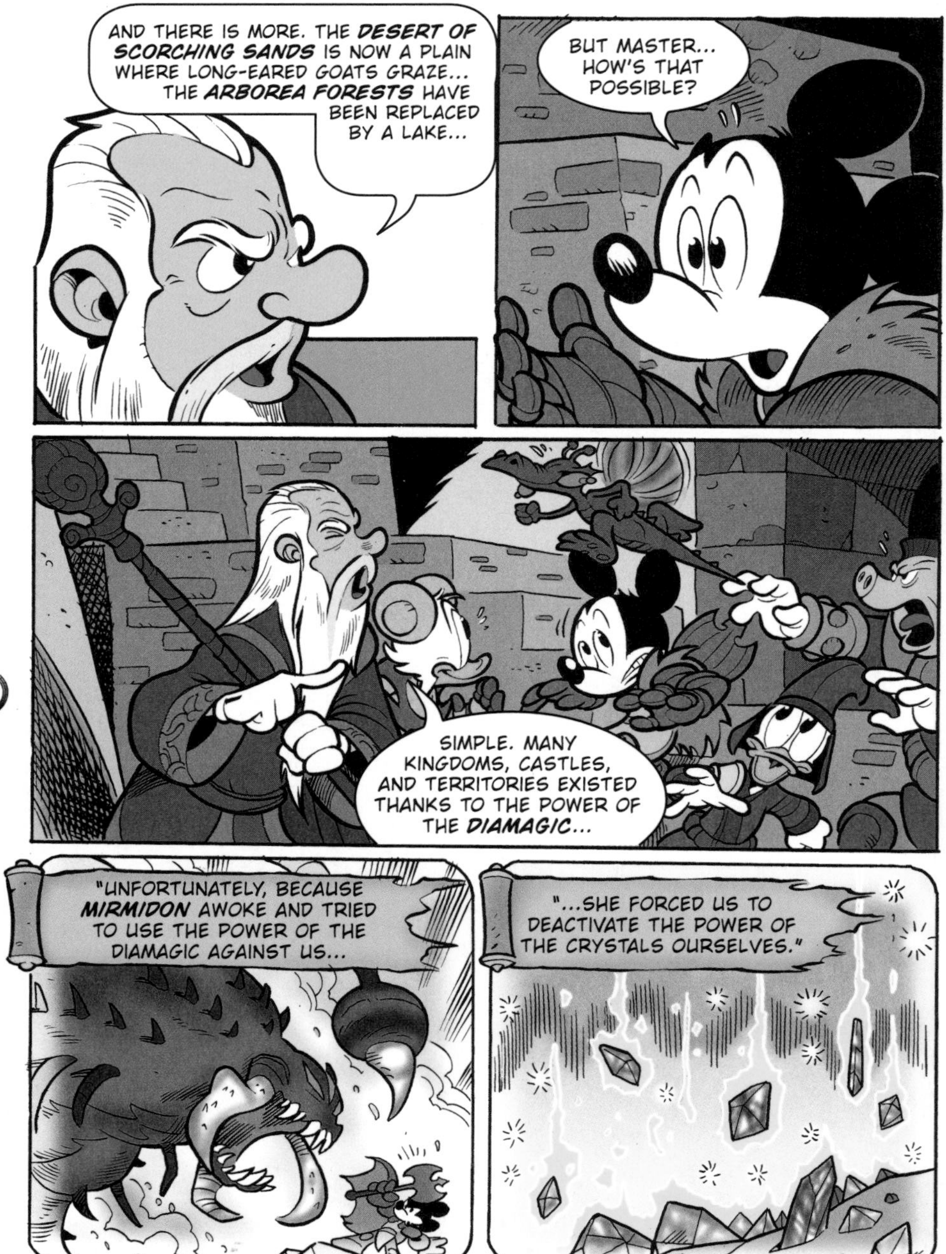
AND THERE IS MORE. THE DESERT OF SCORCHING SANDS IS NOW A PLAIN WHERE LONG-EARED GOATS GRAZE... THE ARBOREA FORESTS HAVE BEEN REPLACED BY A LAKE...
BUT MASTER... HOW'S THAT POSSIBLE?
SIMPLE. MANY KINGDOMS, CASTLES, AND TERRITORIES EXISTED THANKS TO THE POWER OF THE DIAMAGIC...
"UNFORTUNATELY, BECAUSE MIRMIDON AWOKE AND TRIED TO USE THE POWER OF THE DIAMAGIC AGAINST US...
"...SHE FORCED US TO DEACTIVATE THE POWER OF THE CRYSTALS OURSELVES."

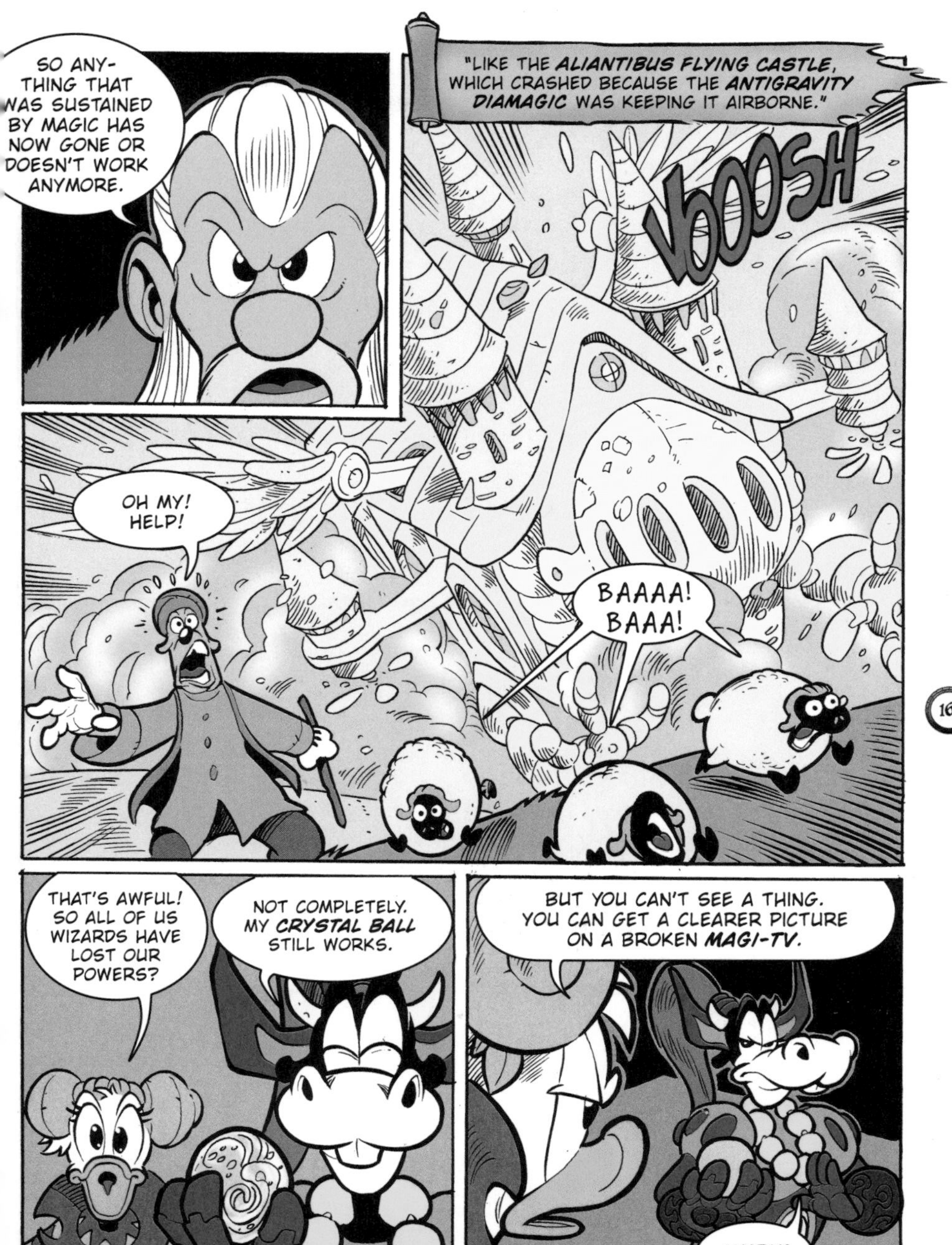

SO ANYTHING THAT WAS SUSTAINED BY MAGIC HAS NOW GONE OR DOESN'T WORK ANYMORE.
"LIKE THE ALIANTIBUS FLYING CASTLE, WHICH CRASHED BECAUSE THE ANTIGRAVITY DIAMAGIC WAS KEEPING IT AIRBORNE."
VOOOSH
OH MY! HELP!
BAAAA! BAAA!
THAT'S AWFUL! SO ALL OF US WIZARDS HAVE LOST OUR POWERS?
NOT COMPLETELY. MY CRYSTAL BALL STILL WORKS.
BUT YOU CAN'T SEE A THING. YOU CAN GET A CLEARER PICTURE ON A BROKEN MAGI-TV.
HMPH!

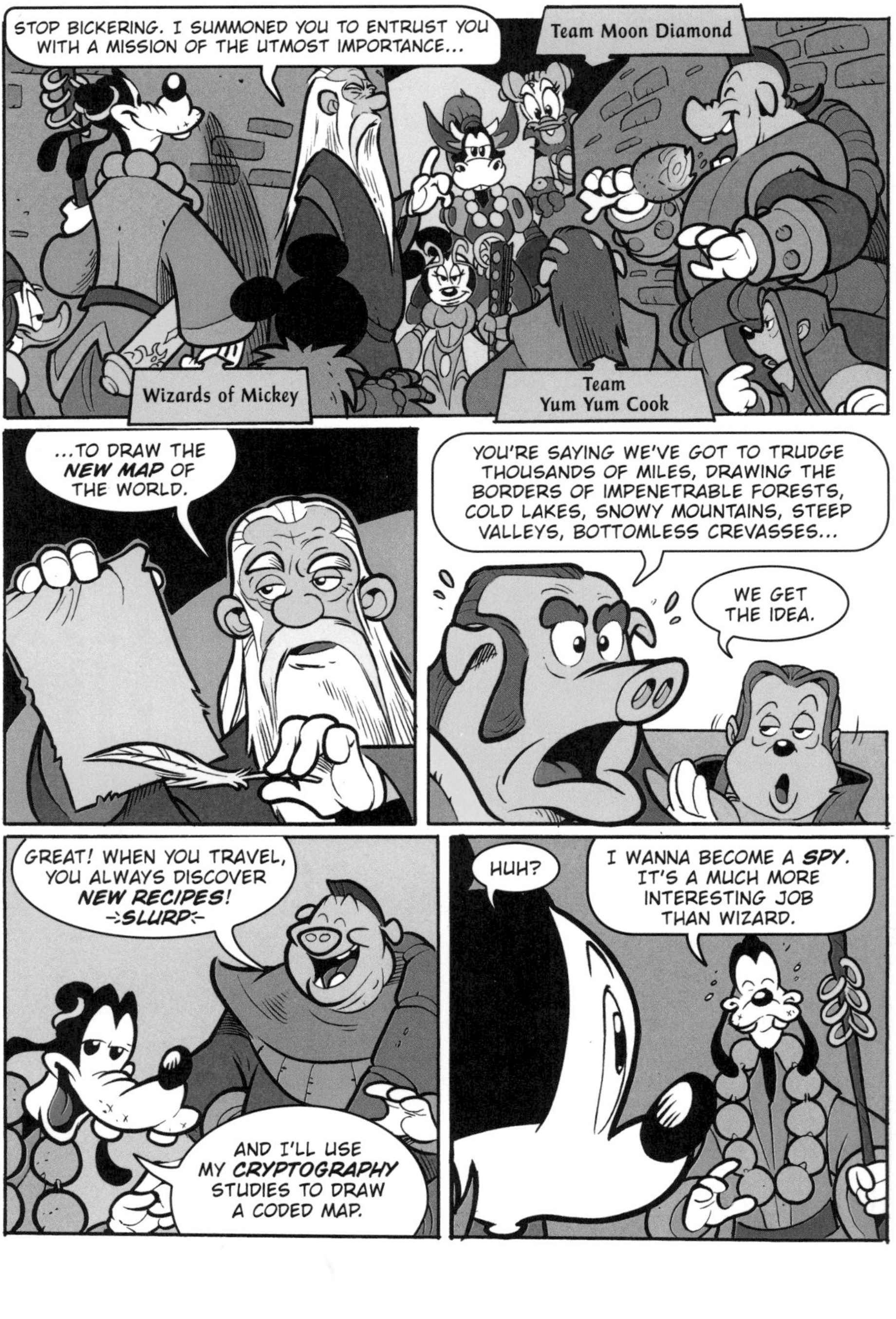
STOP BICKERING. I SUMMONED YOU TO ENTRUST YOU WITH A MISSION OF THE UTMOST IMPORTANCE...
Team Moon Diamond
Wizards of Mickey
Team Yum Yum Cook
...TO DRAW THE NEW MAP OF THE WORLD.
YOU'RE SAYING WE'VE GOT TO TRUDGE THOUSANDS OF MILES, DRAWING THE BORDERS OF IMPENETRABLE FORESTS, COLD LAKES, SNOWY MOUNTAINS, STEEP VALLEYS, BOTTOMLESS CREVASSES...
WE GET THE IDEA.
GREAT! WHEN YOU TRAVEL, YOU ALWAYS DISCOVER NEW RECIPES! -SLURP-
AND I'LL USE MY CRYPTOGRAPHY STUDIES TO DRAW A CODED MAP.
HUH?
I WANNA BECOME A SPY. IT'S A MUCH MORE INTERESTING JOB THAN WIZARD.

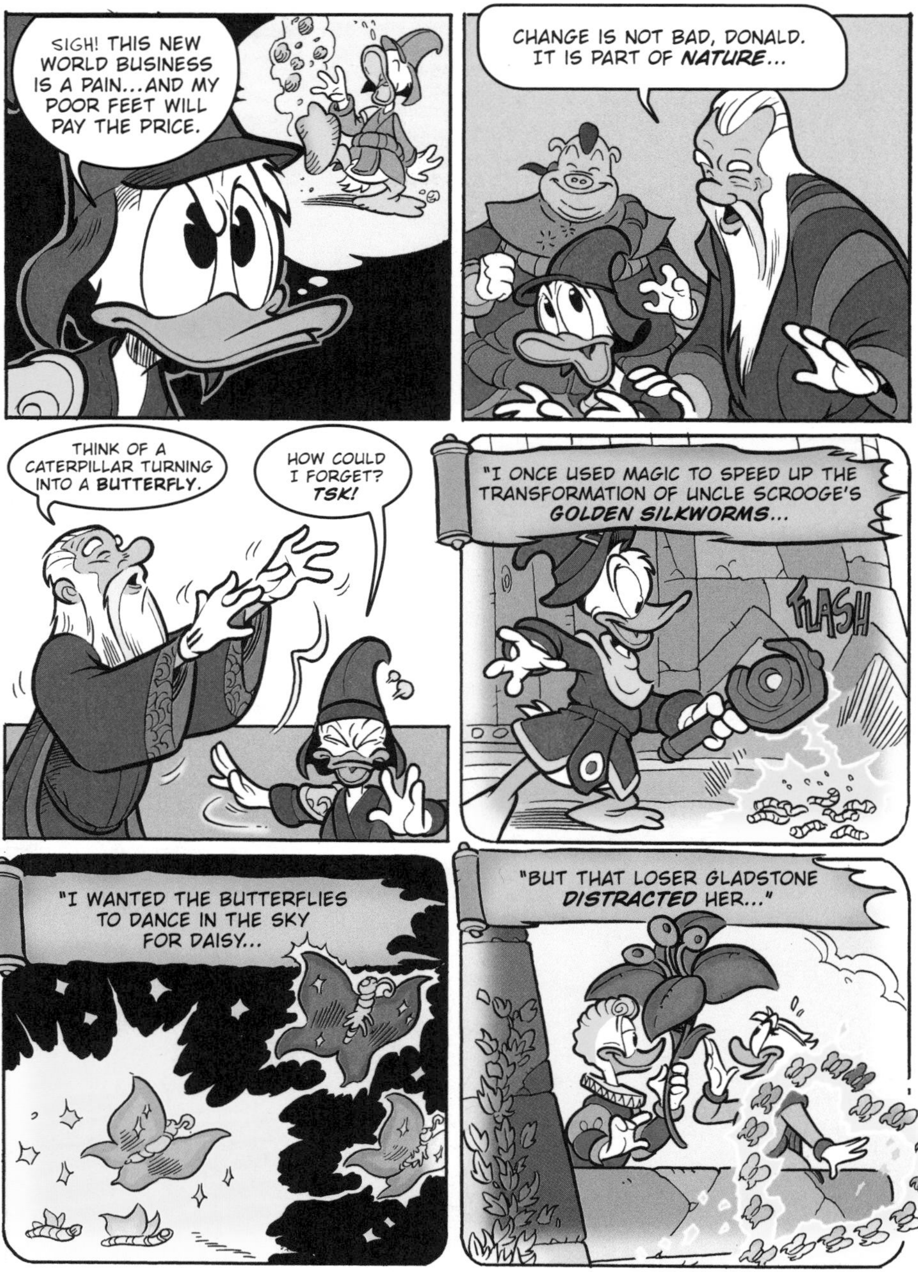

SIGH! THIS NEW WORLD BUSINESS IS A PAIN...AND MY POOR FEET WILL PAY THE PRICE.
CHANGE IS NOT BAD, DONALD. IT IS PART OF NATURE...
THINK OF A CATERPILLAR TURNING INTO A BUTTERFLY.
HOW COULD I FORGET? TSK!
"I ONCE USED MAGIC TO SPEED UP THE TRANSFORMATION OF UNCLE SCROOGE'S GOLDEN SILKWORMS...
FLASH
"I WANTED THE BUTTERFLIES TO DANCE IN THE SKY FOR DAISY...
"BUT THAT LOSER GLADSTONE DISTRACTED HER..."

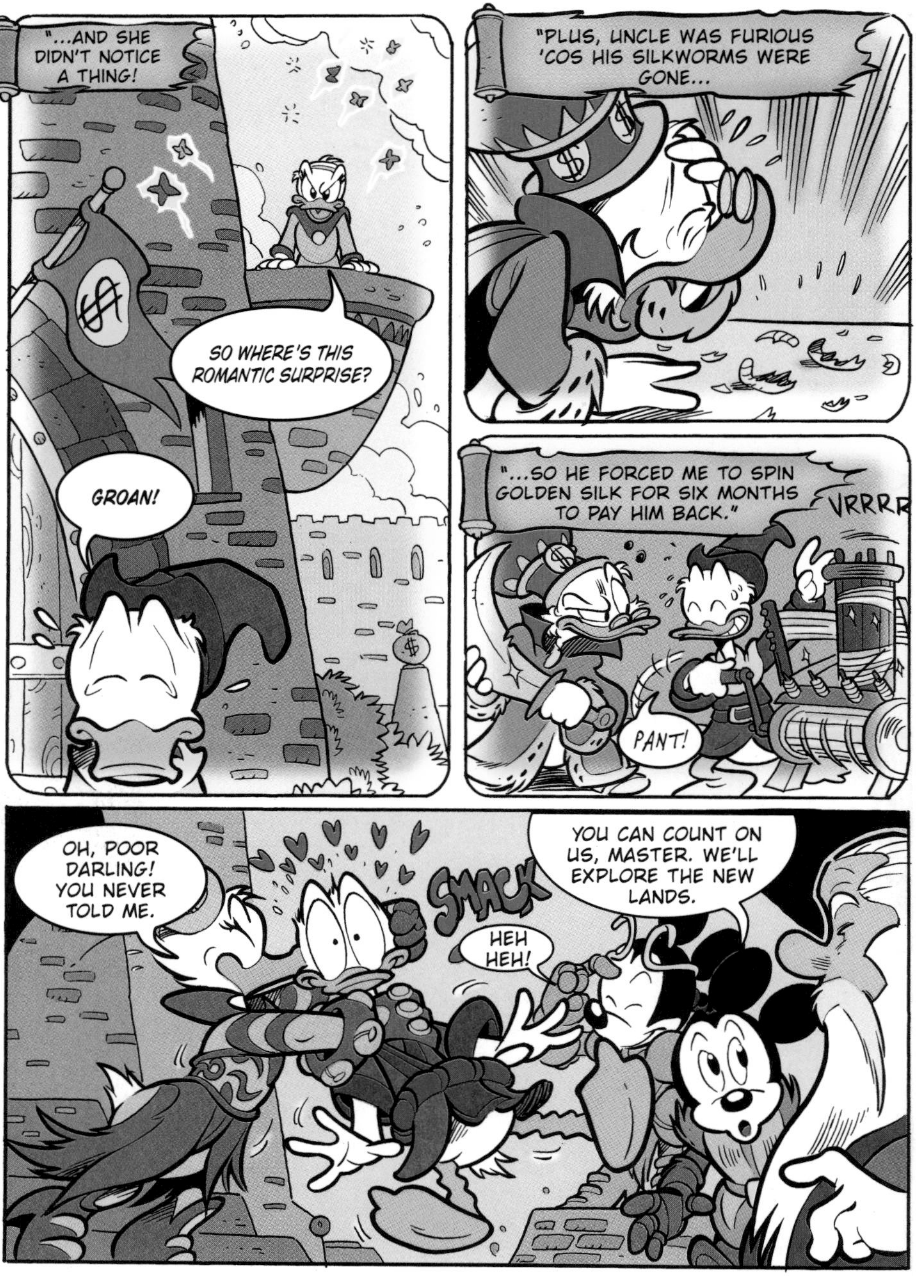
"...AND SHE DIDN'T NOTICE A THING!
SO WHERE'S THIS ROMANTIC SURPRISE?
GROAN!
"PLUS, UNCLE WAS FURIOUS 'COS HIS SILKWORMS WERE GONE...
"...SO HE FORCED ME TO SPIN GOLDEN SILK FOR SIX MONTHS TO PAY HIM BACK."
VRRRR
PANT!
OH, POOR DARLING! YOU NEVER TOLD ME.
SMACK
HEH HEH!
YOU CAN COUNT ON US, MASTER. WE'LL EXPLORE THE NEW LANDS.

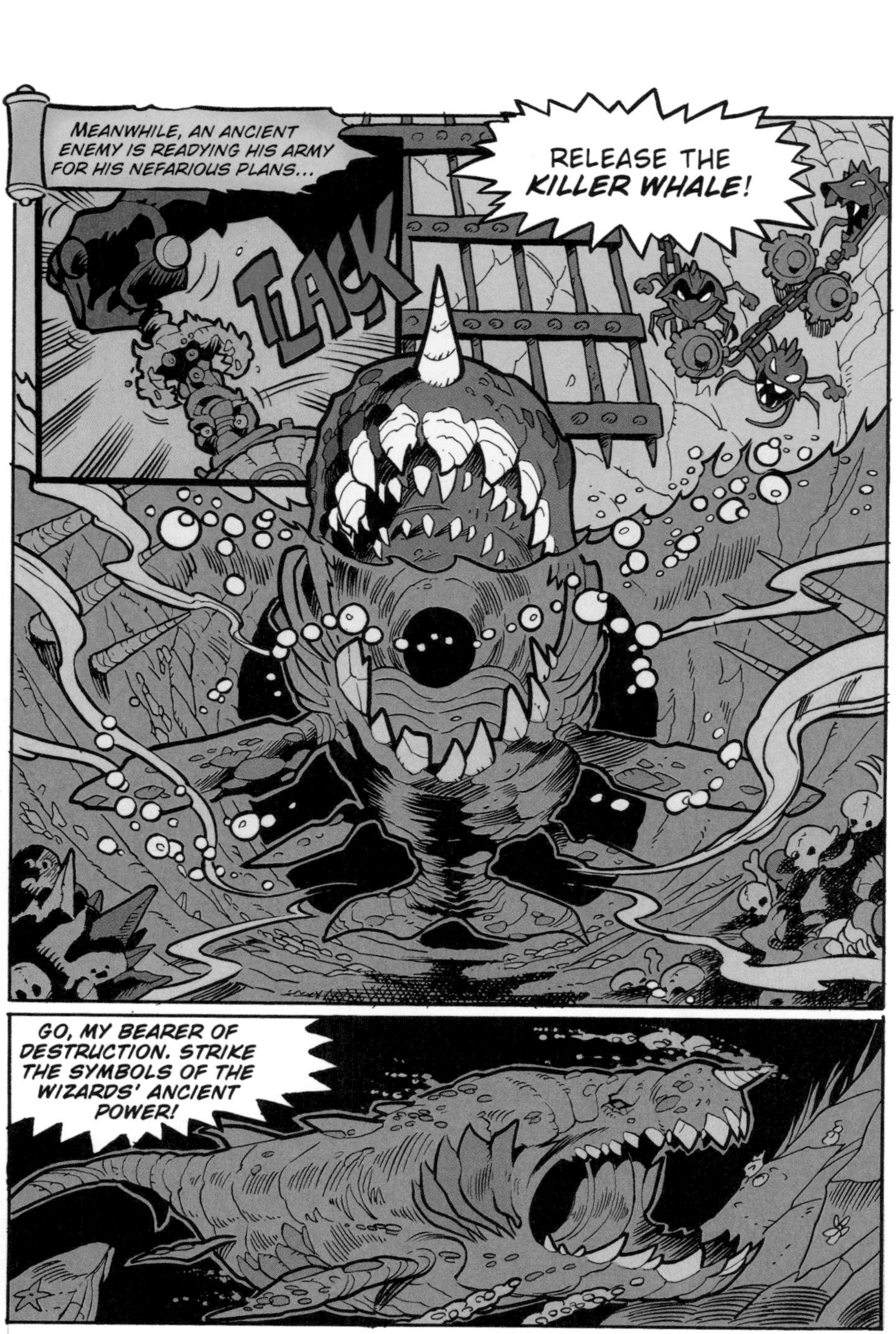
MEANWHILE, AN ANCIENT ENEMY IS READYING HIS ARMY FOR HIS NEFARIOUS PLANS...
RELEASE THE KILLER WHALE!
TLACK
GO, MY BEARER OF DESTRUCTION. STRIKE THE SYMBOLS OF THE WIZARDS' ANCIENT POWER!

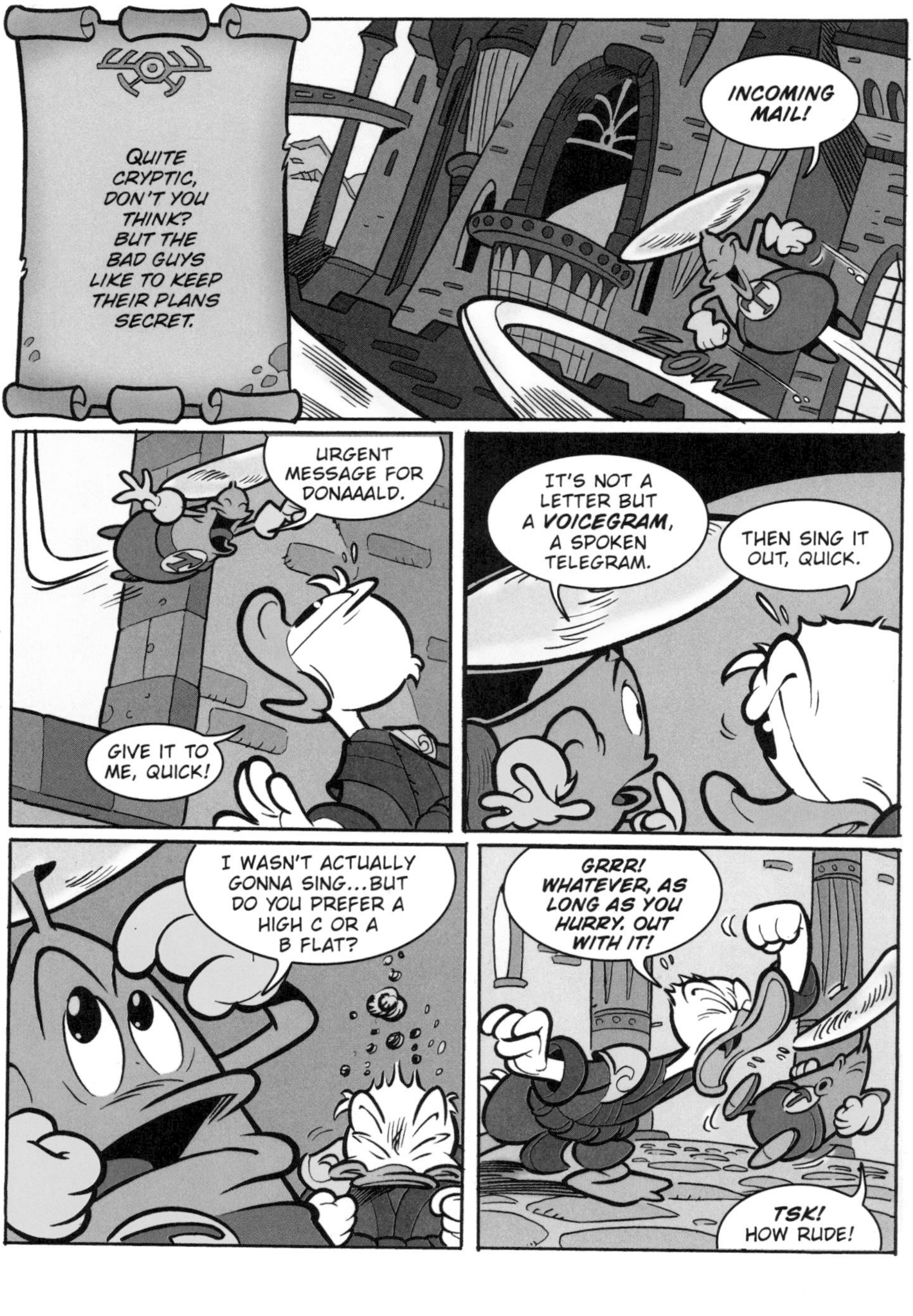
QUITE CRYPTIC, DON'T YOU THINK? BUT THE BAD GUYS LIKE TO KEEP THEIR PLANS SECRET.
INCOMING MAIL!
ZOOM
URGENT MESSAGE FOR DONAAALD.
GIVE IT TO ME, QUICK!
IT'S NOT A LETTER BUT A VOICEGRAM, A SPOKEN TELEGRAM.
THEN SING IT OUT, QUICK.
I WASN'T ACTUALLY GONNA SING...BUT DO YOU PREFER A HIGH C OR A B FLAT?
GRRR! WHATEVER, AS LONG AS YOU HURRY. OUT WITH IT!
TSK! HOW RUDE!

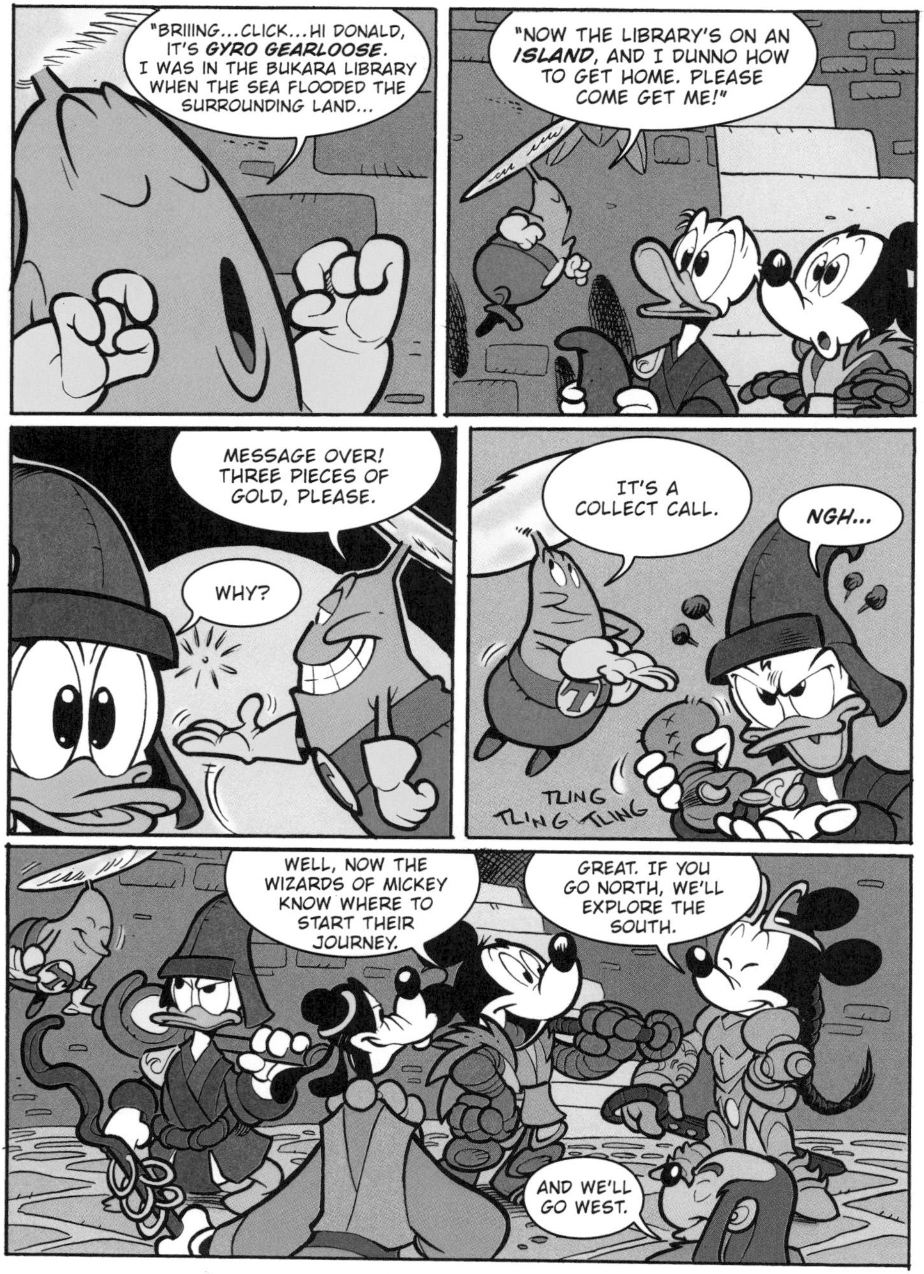
"BRIIING...CLICK...HI DONALD, IT'S GYRO GEARLOOSE. I WAS IN THE BUKARA LIBRARY WHEN THE SEA FLOODED THE SURROUNDING LAND...
"NOW THE LIBRARY'S ON AN ISLAND, AND I DUNNO HOW TO GET HOME. PLEASE COME GET ME!"
MESSAGE OVER! THREE PIECES OF GOLD, PLEASE.
WHY?
IT'S A COLLECT CALL.
NGH...
TLING TLING TLING
WELL, NOW THE WIZARDS OF MICKEY KNOW WHERE TO START THEIR JOURNEY.
GREAT. IF YOU GO NORTH, WE'LL EXPLORE THE SOUTH.
AND WE'LL GO WEST.

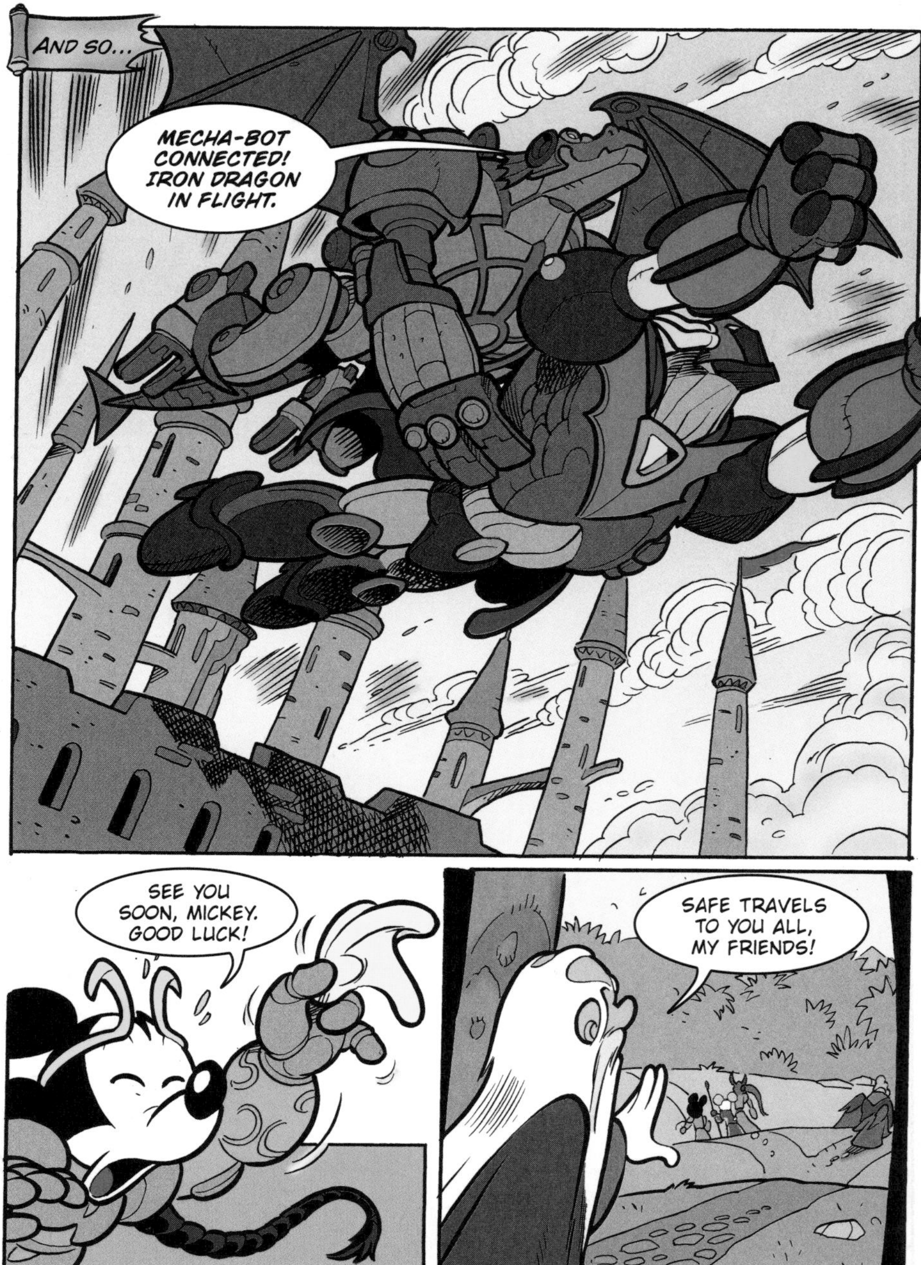
AND SO...
MECHA-BOT CONNECTED! IRON DRAGON IN FLIGHT.
SEE YOU SOON, MICKEY. GOOD LUCK!
SAFE TRAVELS TO YOU ALL, MY FRIENDS!

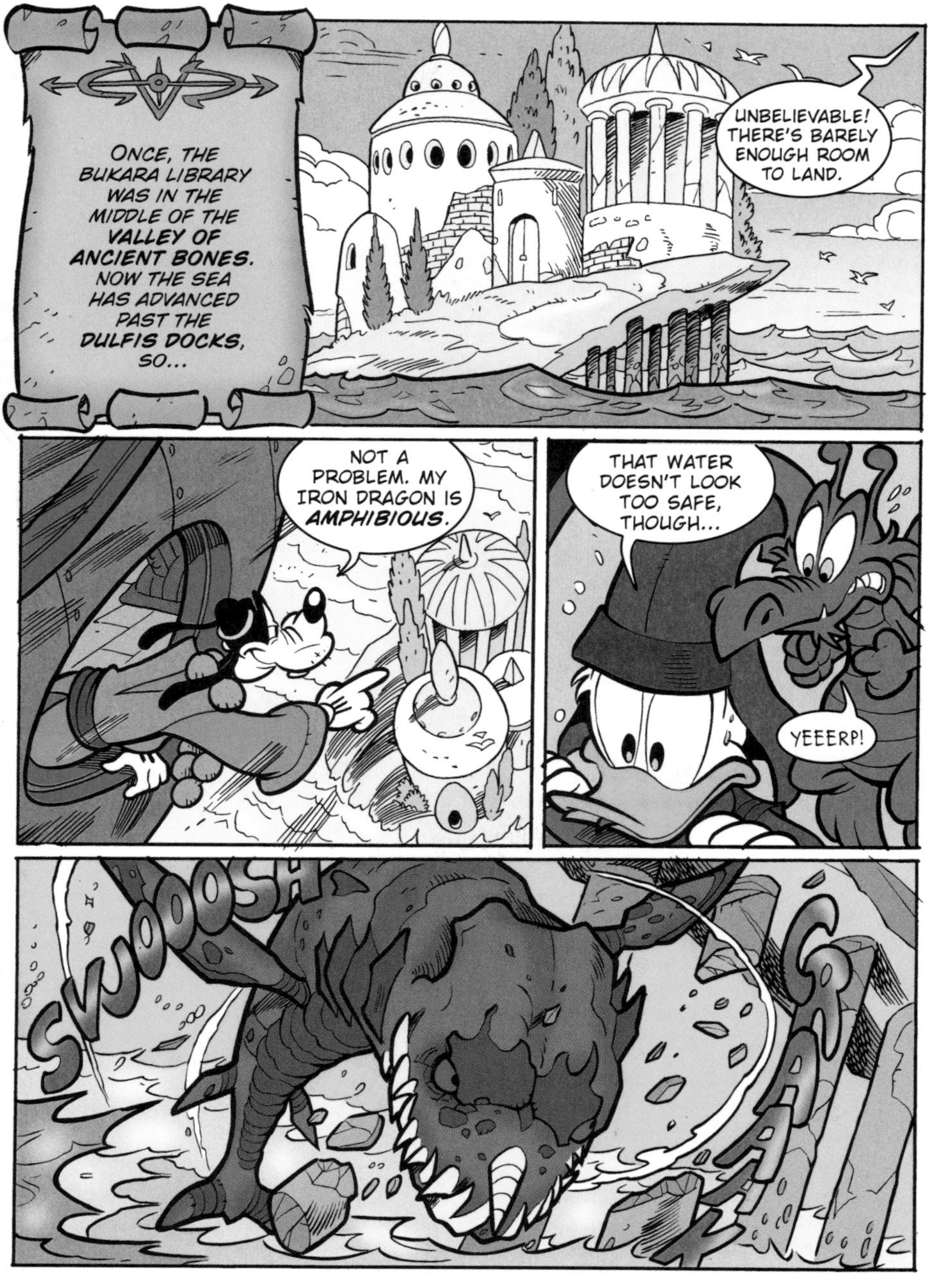
ONCE, THE BUKARA LIBRARY WAS IN THE MIDDLE OF THE VALLEY OF ANCIENT BONES. NOW THE SEA HAS ADVANCED PAST THE DULFIS DOCKS, SO...
UNBELIEVABLE! THERE'S BARELY ENOUGH ROOM TO LAND.
NOT A PROBLEM. MY IRON DRAGON IS AMPHIBIOUS.
THAT WATER DOESN'T LOOK TOO SAFE, THOUGH...
YEEERP!
SWOOOSH

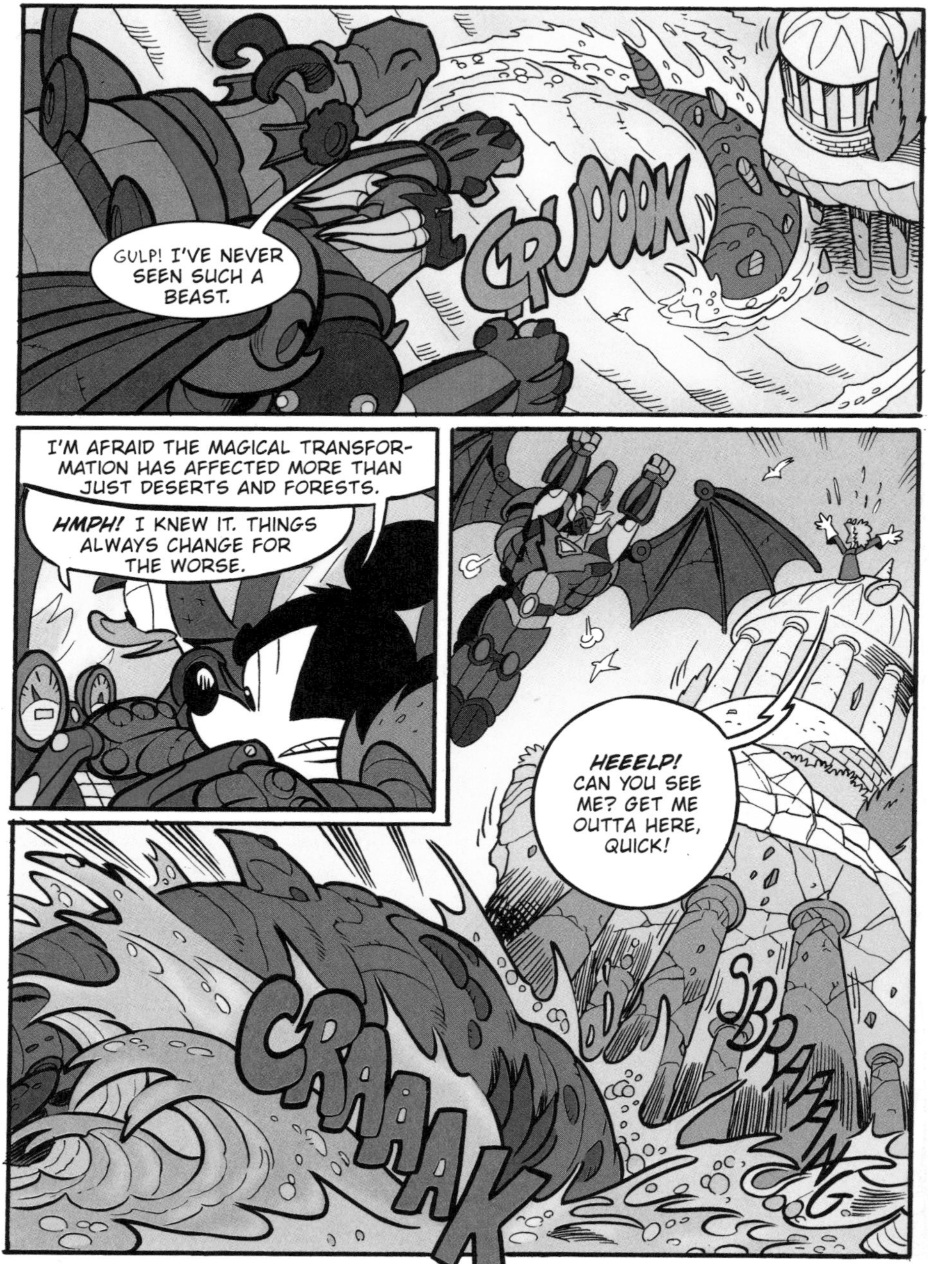
GULP! I'VE NEVER SEEN SUCH A BEAST.
CRUOOOK
I'M AFRAID THE MAGICAL TRANSFORMATION HAS AFFECTED MORE THAN JUST DESERTS AND FORESTS.
HMPH! I KNEW IT. THINGS ALWAYS CHANGE FOR THE WORSE.
HEEELP! CAN YOU SEE ME? GET ME OUTTA HERE, QUICK!
CRAAAAK
SBRAAANG

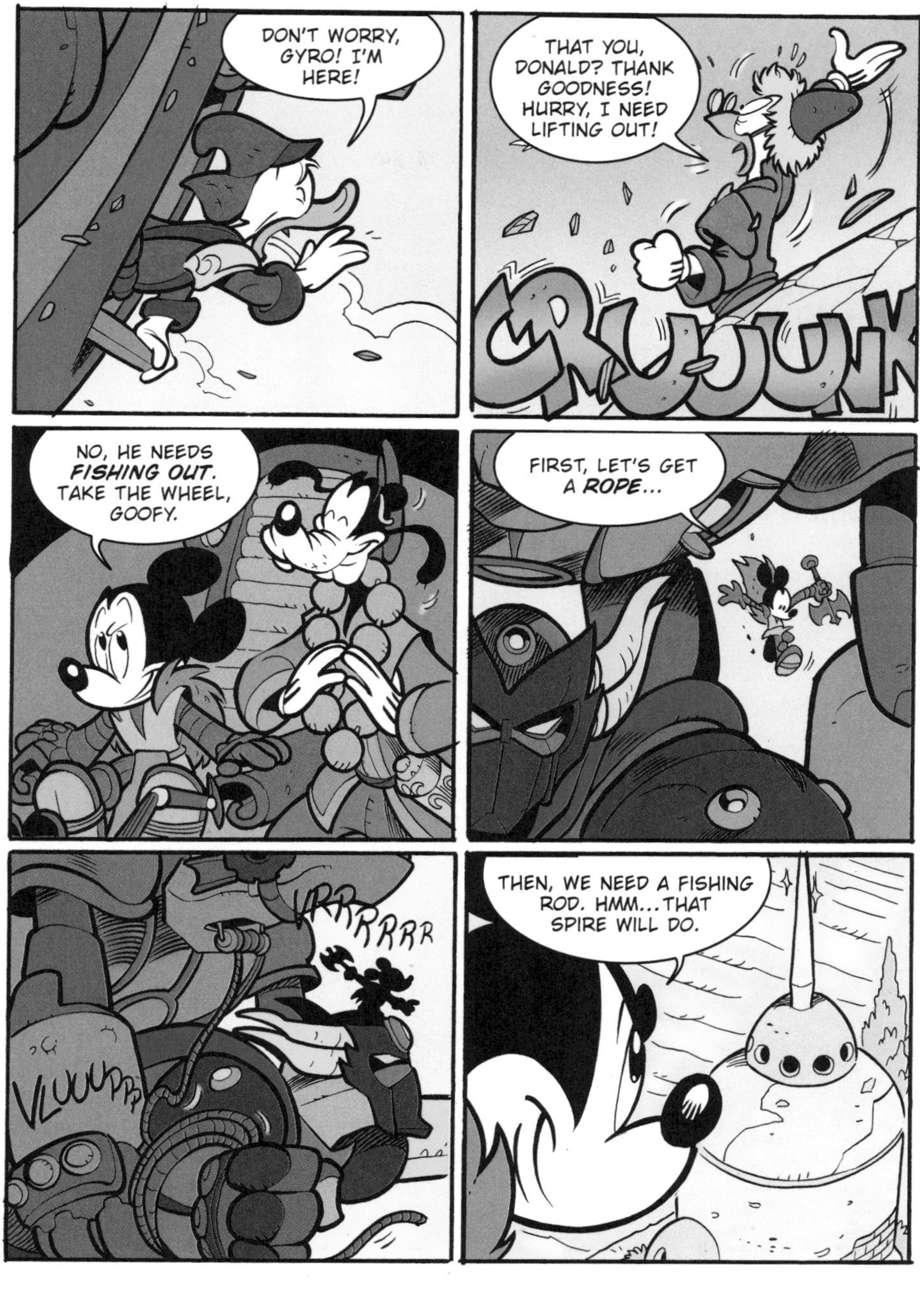
DON'T WORRY, GYRO! I'M HERE!
THAT YOU, DONALD? THANK GOODNESS! HURRY, I NEED LIFTING OUT!
CRUUUNK
NO, HE NEEDS *FISHING OUT*. TAKE THE WHEEL, GOOFY.
FIRST, LET'S GET A *ROPE*...
VRRRRRRR
VLUUUPPP
THEN, WE NEED A FISHING ROD. HMM...THAT SPIRE WILL DO.

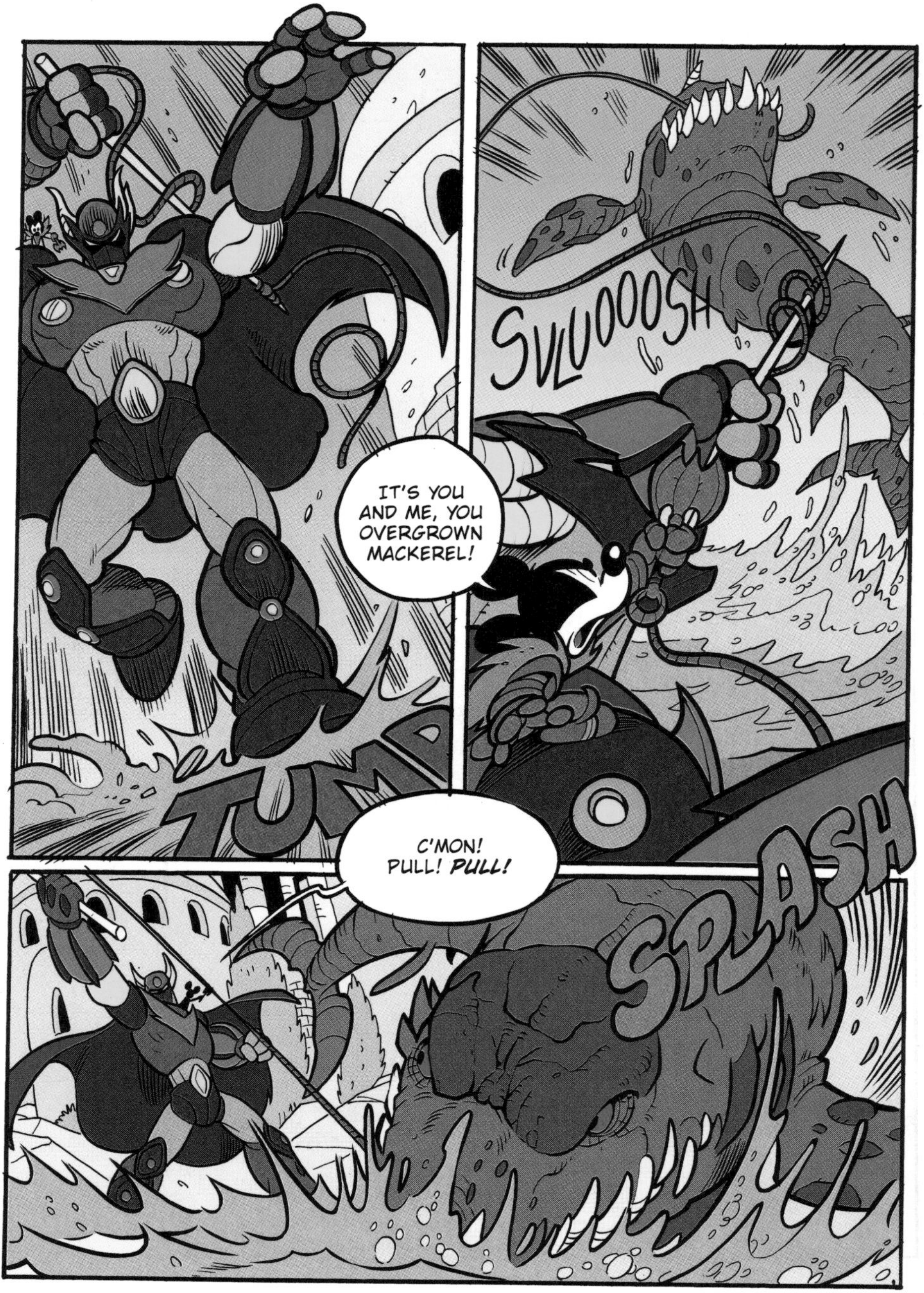

SVLUOOOSH
IT'S YOU AND ME, YOU OVERGROWN MACKEREL!
TUMP
C'MON! PULL! PULL!
SPLASH

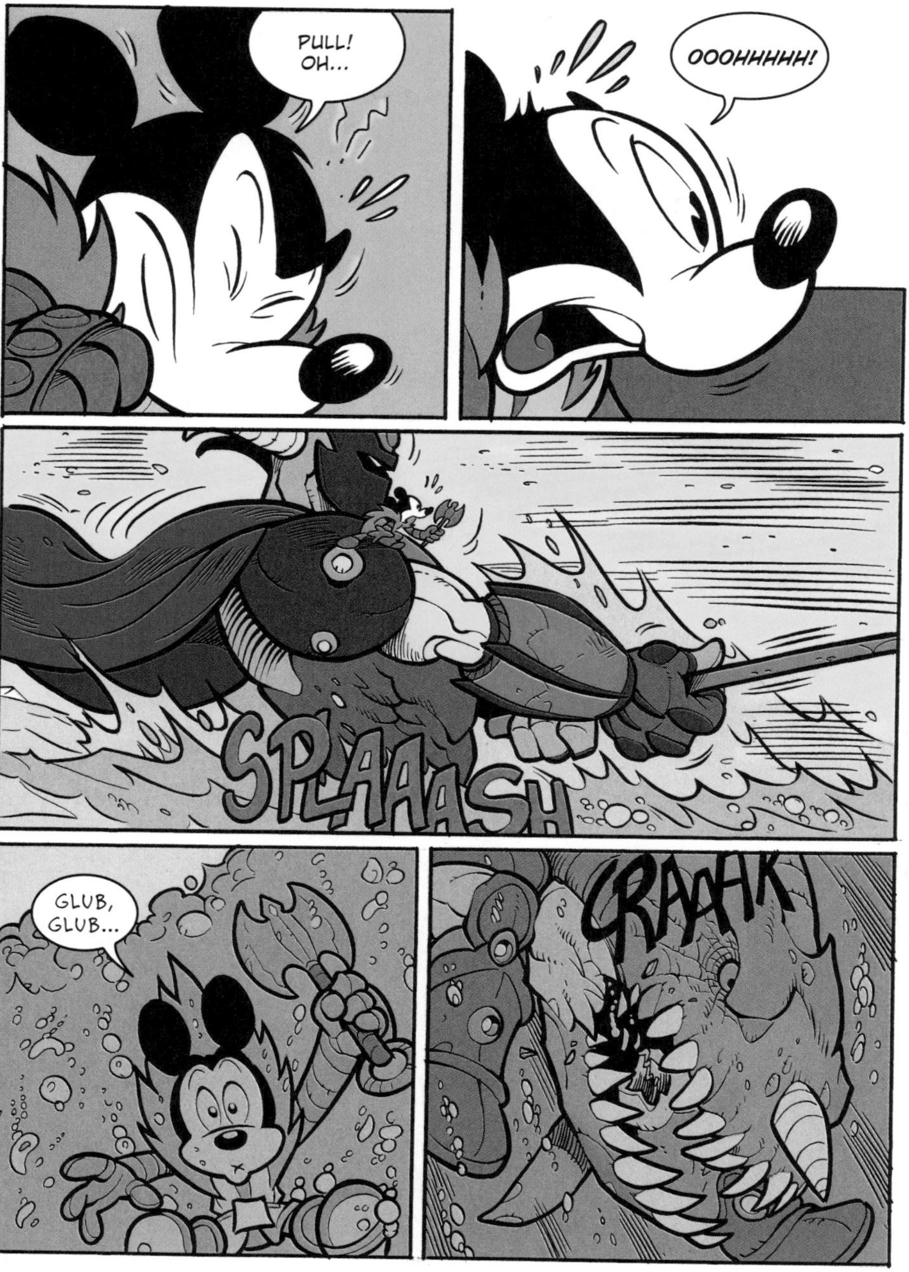
PULL! OH...
OOOHHHHH!
SPLAAASH
GLUB, GLUB...
CRAAAK

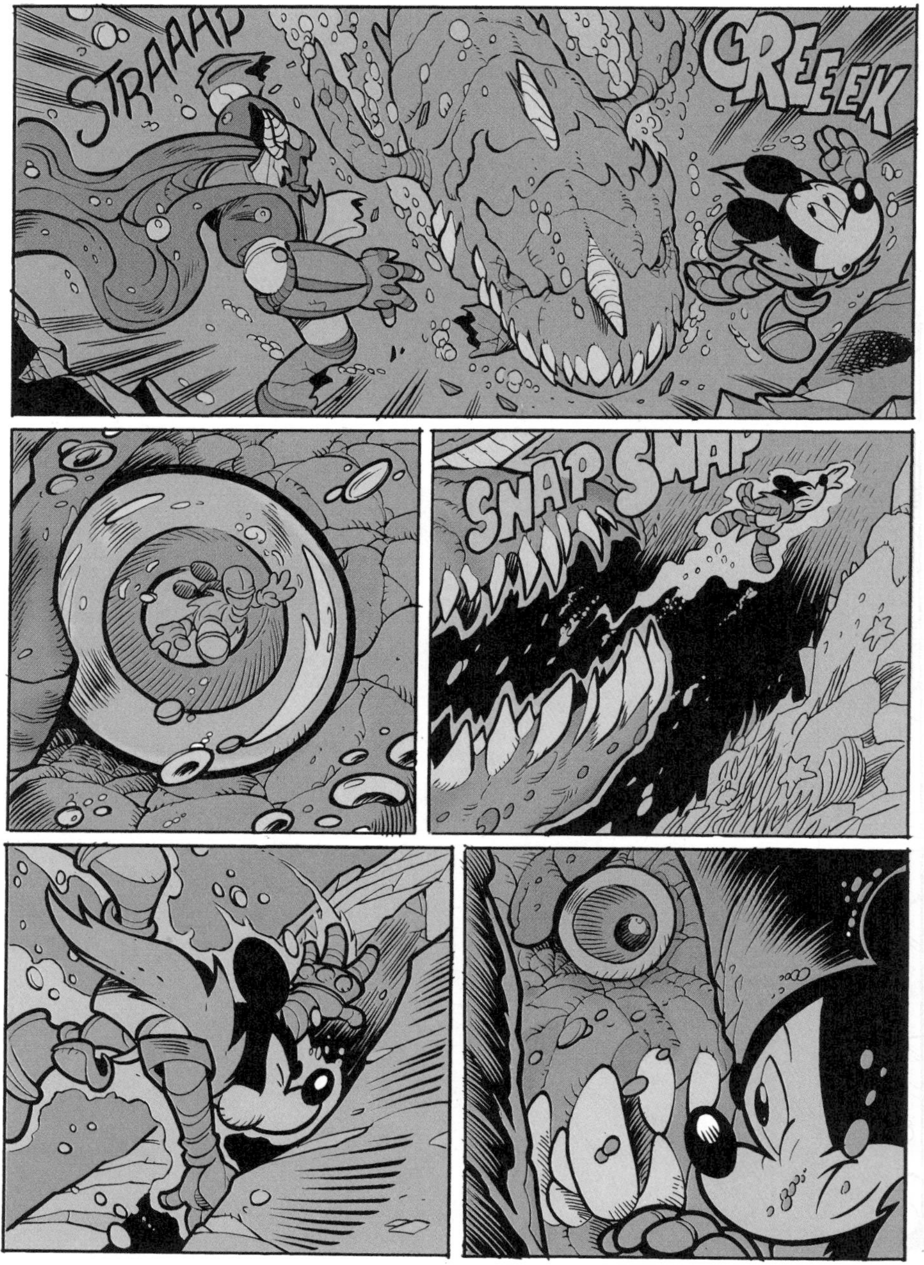
STRAAAP
CREEEK
SNAP SNAP

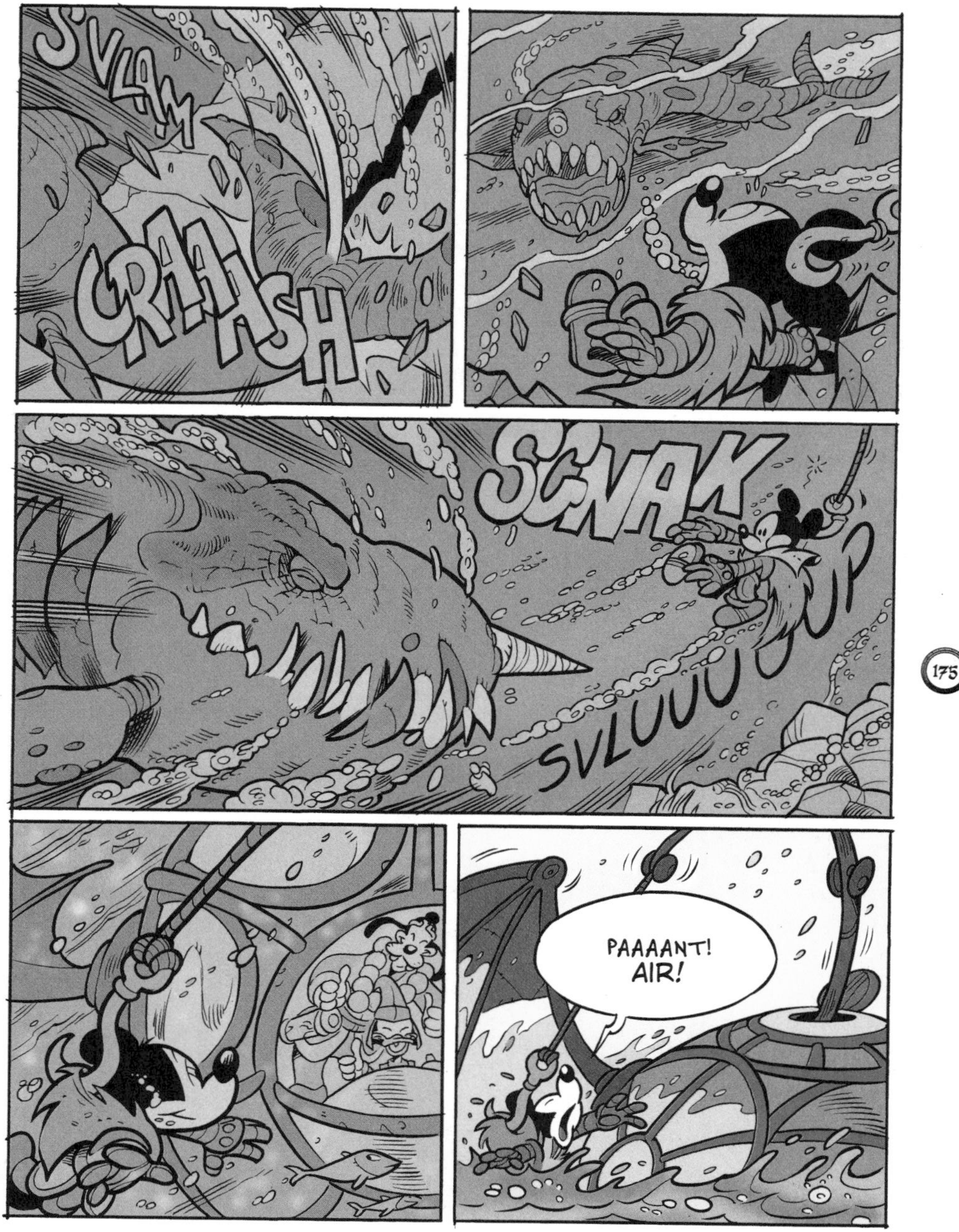
SVLAM
CRAAASH
SCNAK
SVLUUUUUUP
PAAAANT!
AIR!

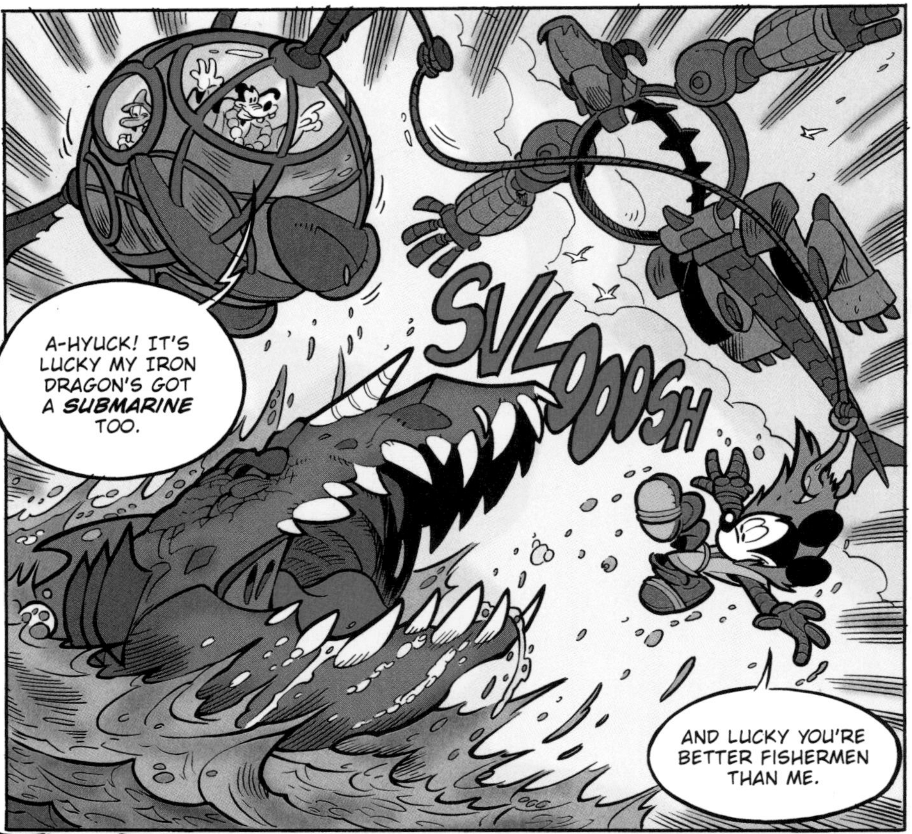
A-HYUCK! IT'S LUCKY MY IRON DRAGON'S GOT A **SUBMARINE** TOO.
SVLOOOSH
AND LUCKY YOU'RE BETTER FISHERMEN THAN ME.

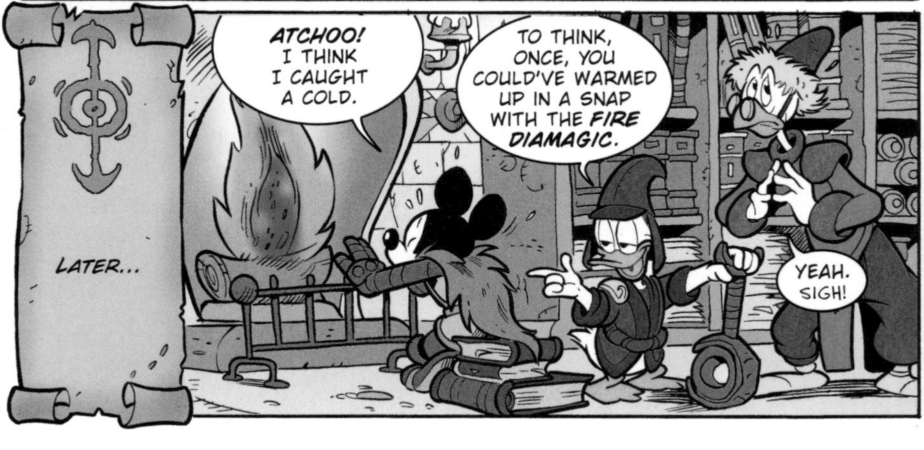
LATER...
ATCHOO! I THINK I CAUGHT A COLD.
TO THINK, ONCE, YOU COULD'VE WARMED UP IN A SNAP WITH THE ***FIRE DIAMAGIC***.
YEAH. SIGH!

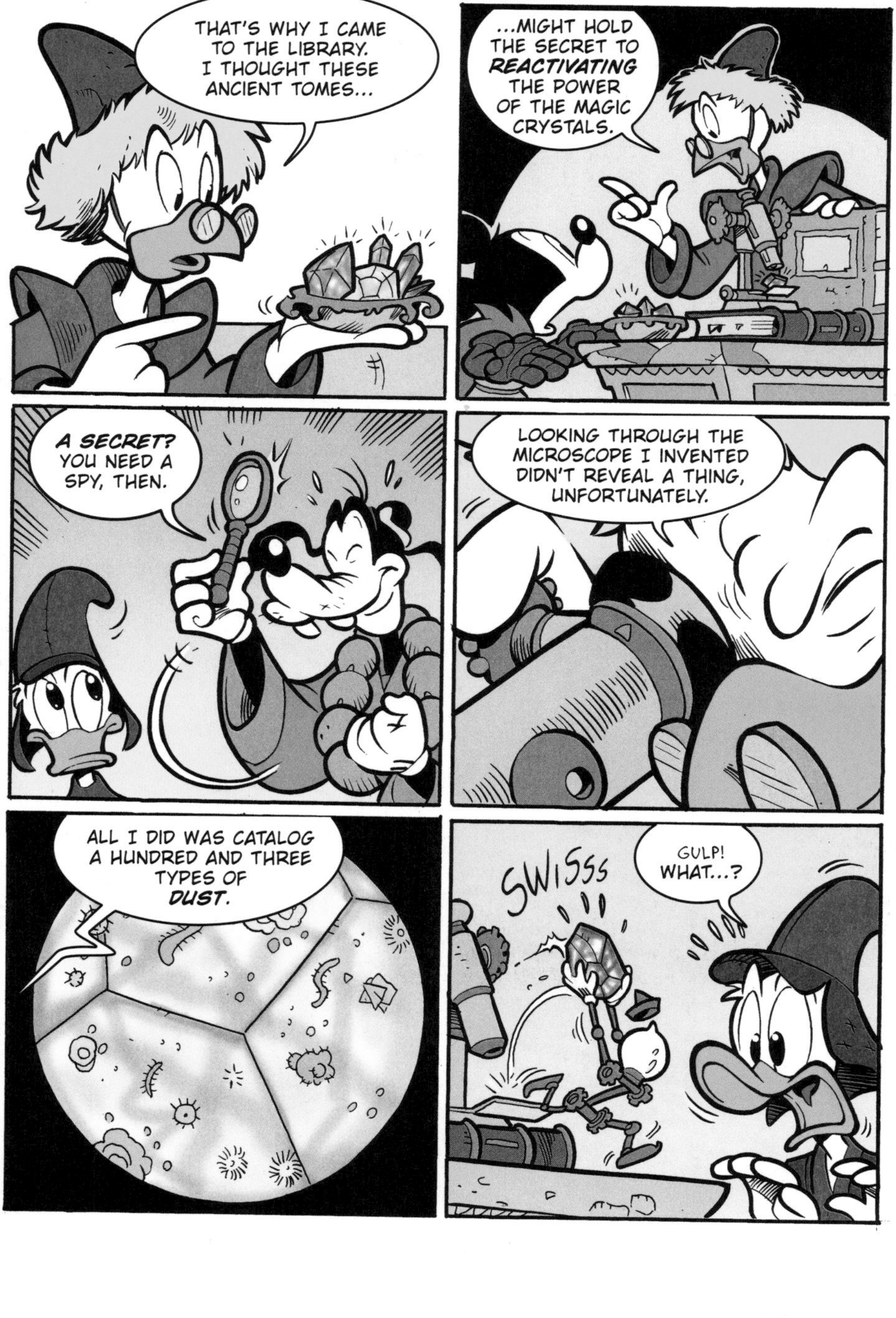
THAT'S WHY I CAME TO THE LIBRARY. I THOUGHT THESE ANCIENT TOMES...
...MIGHT HOLD THE SECRET TO *REACTIVATING* THE POWER OF THE MAGIC CRYSTALS.
A SECRET? YOU NEED A SPY, THEN.
LOOKING THROUGH THE MICROSCOPE I INVENTED DIDN'T REVEAL A THING, UNFORTUNATELY.
ALL I DID WAS CATALOG A HUNDRED AND THREE TYPES OF *DUST*.
SWISSS
GULP! WHAT...?

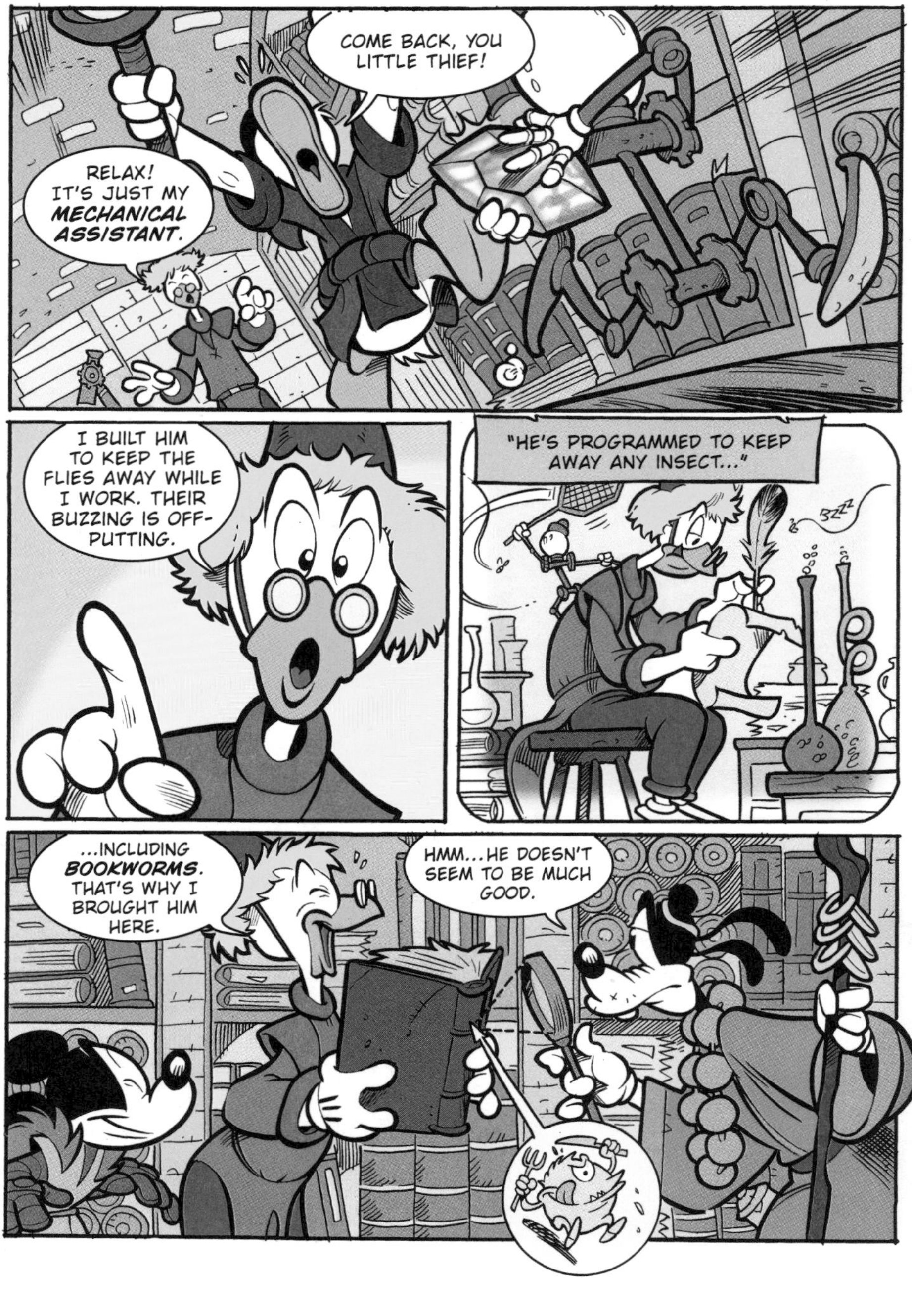
COME BACK, YOU LITTLE THIEF!
RELAX! IT'S JUST MY **MECHANICAL ASSISTANT**.
I BUILT HIM TO KEEP THE FLIES AWAY WHILE I WORK. THEIR BUZZING IS OFF-PUTTING.
"HE'S PROGRAMMED TO KEEP AWAY ANY INSECT..."
ZZZ
...INCLUDING **BOOKWORMS**. THAT'S WHY I BROUGHT HIM HERE.
HMM...HE DOESN'T SEEM TO BE MUCH GOOD.

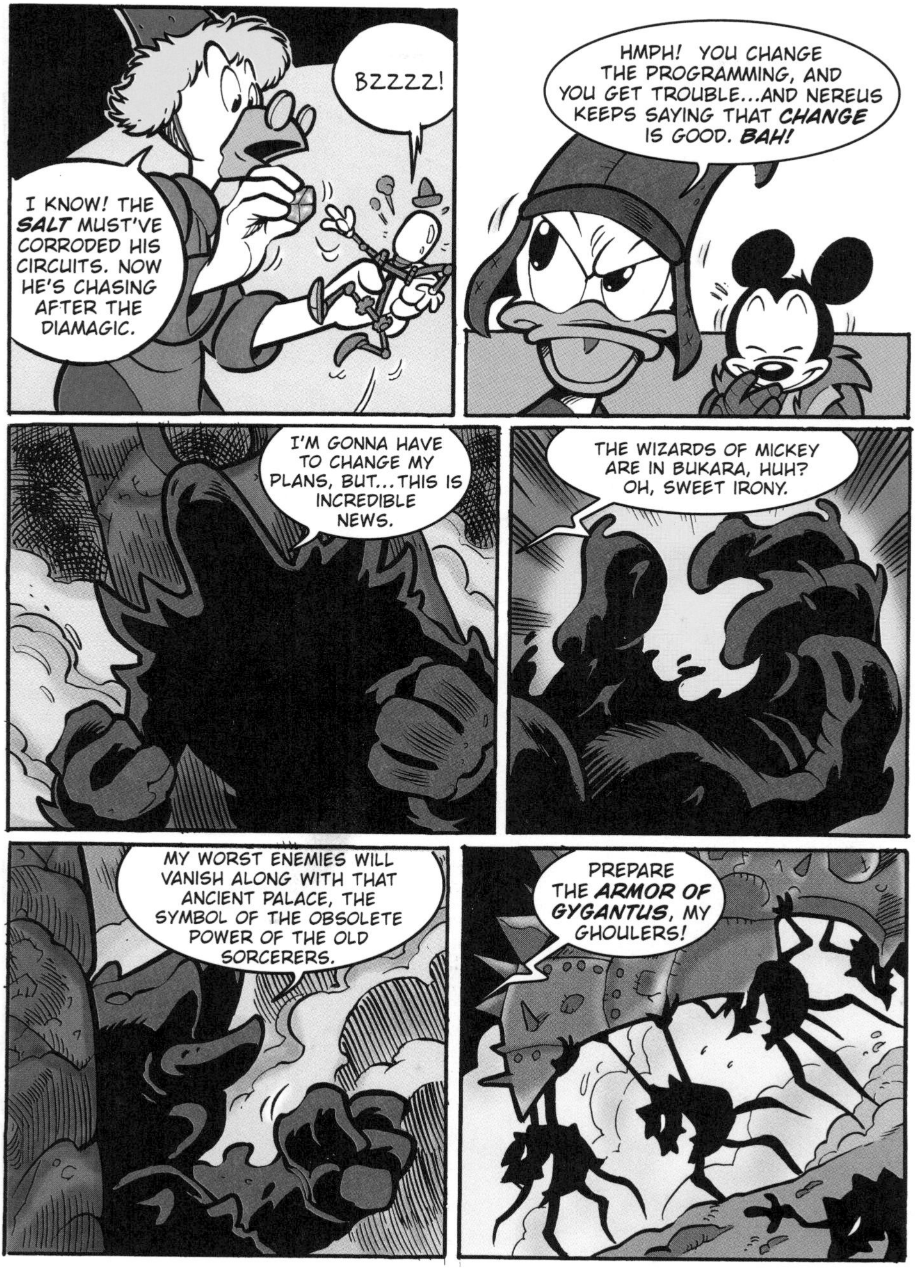
BZZZZ!
I KNOW! THE SALT MUST'VE CORRODED HIS CIRCUITS. NOW HE'S CHASING AFTER THE DIAMAGIC.
HMPH! YOU CHANGE THE PROGRAMMING, AND YOU GET TROUBLE...AND NEREUS KEEPS SAYING THAT CHANGE IS GOOD. BAH!
I'M GONNA HAVE TO CHANGE MY PLANS, BUT...THIS IS INCREDIBLE NEWS.
THE WIZARDS OF MICKEY ARE IN BUKARA, HUH? OH, SWEET IRONY.
MY WORST ENEMIES WILL VANISH ALONG WITH THAT ANCIENT PALACE, THE SYMBOL OF THE OBSOLETE POWER OF THE OLD SORCERERS.
PREPARE THE ARMOR OF GYGANTUS, MY GHOULERS!

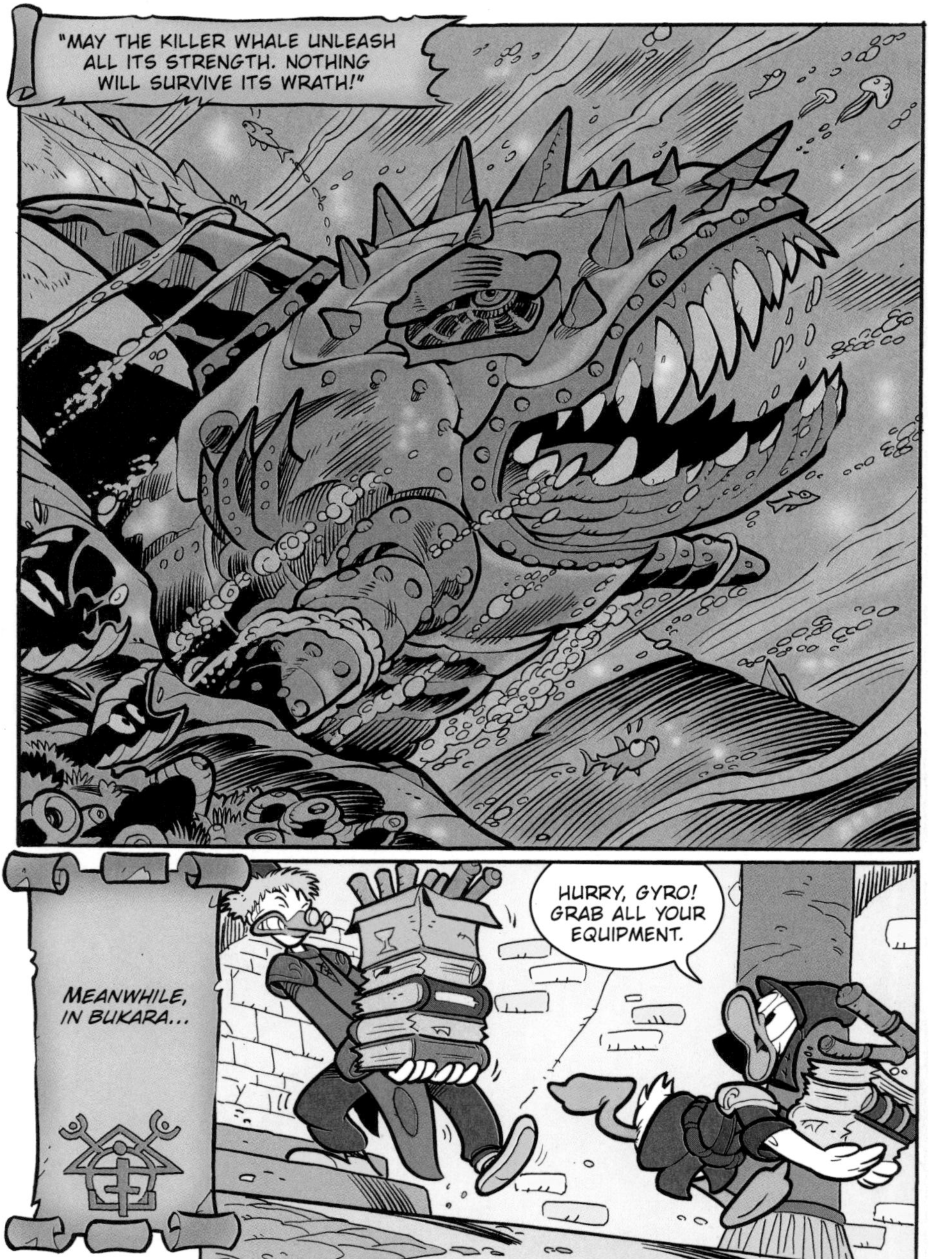
"MAY THE KILLER WHALE UNLEASH ALL ITS STRENGTH. NOTHING WILL SURVIVE ITS WRATH!"
MEANWHILE, IN BUKARA...
HURRY, GYRO! GRAB ALL YOUR EQUIPMENT.

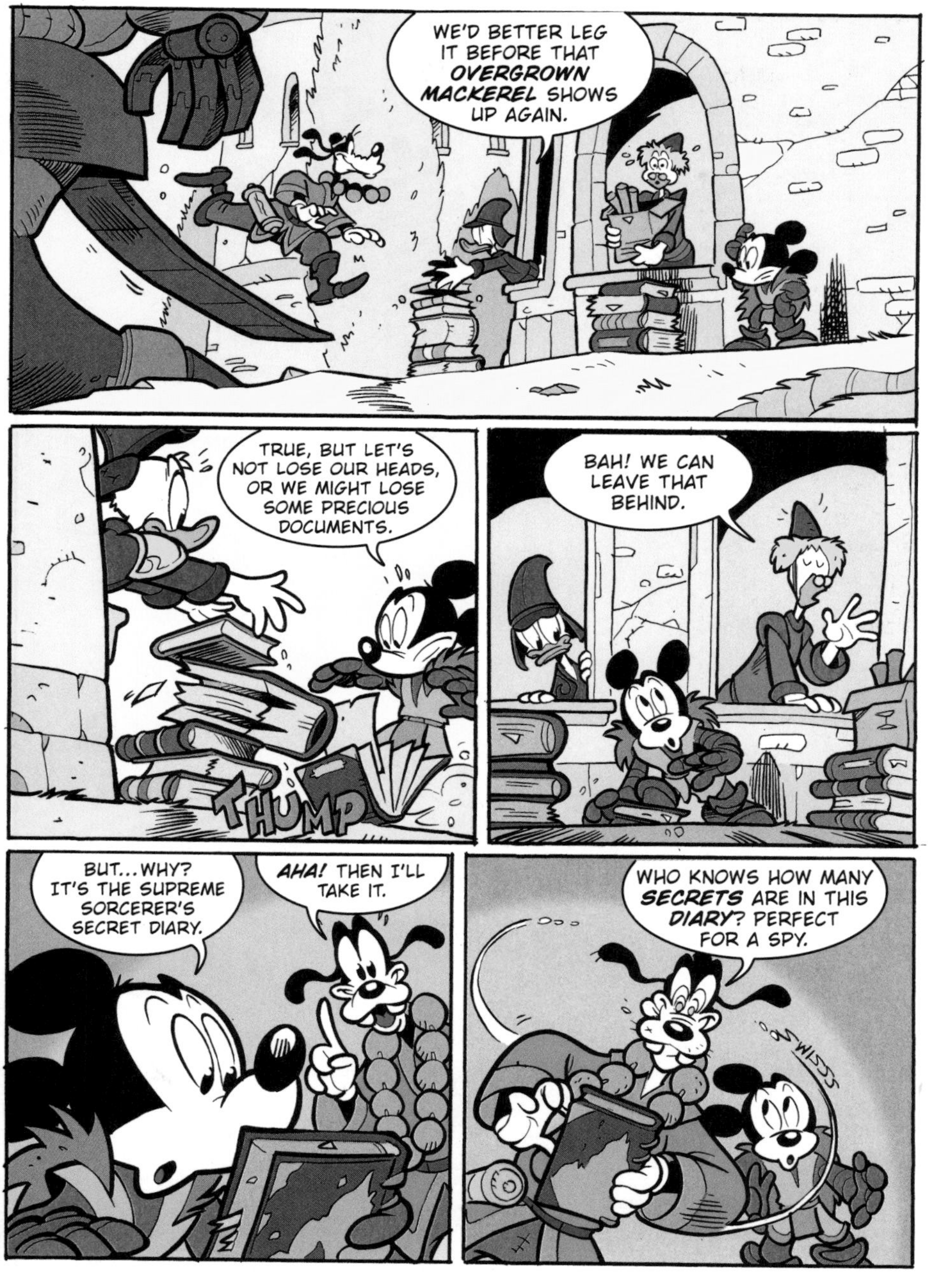

WE'D BETTER LEG IT BEFORE THAT **OVERGROWN MACKEREL** SHOWS UP AGAIN.
TRUE, BUT LET'S NOT LOSE OUR HEADS, OR WE MIGHT LOSE SOME PRECIOUS DOCUMENTS.
THUMP
BAH! WE CAN LEAVE THAT BEHIND.
BUT...WHY? IT'S THE SUPREME SORCERER'S SECRET DIARY.
AHA! THEN I'LL TAKE IT.
WHO KNOWS HOW MANY **SECRETS** ARE IN THIS **DIARY**? PERFECT FOR A SPY.
SWISSS

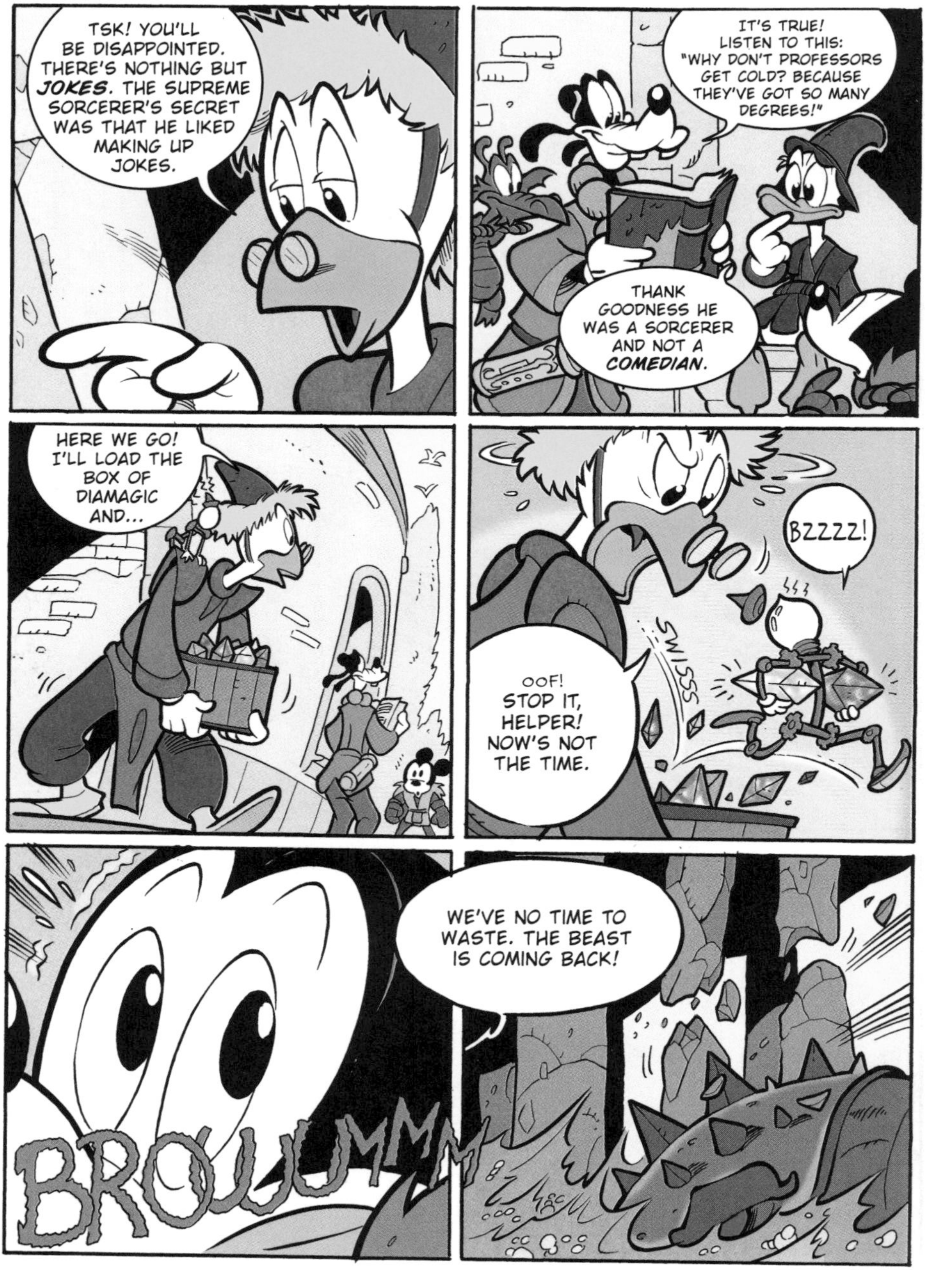
TSK! YOU'LL BE DISAPPOINTED. THERE'S NOTHING BUT **JOKES**. THE SUPREME SORCERER'S SECRET WAS THAT HE LIKED MAKING UP JOKES.
IT'S TRUE! LISTEN TO THIS: "WHY DON'T PROFESSORS GET COLD? BECAUSE THEY'VE GOT SO MANY DEGREES!"
THANK GOODNESS HE WAS A SORCERER AND NOT A **COMEDIAN**.
HERE WE GO! I'LL LOAD THE BOX OF DIAMAGIC AND...
BZZZZ!
SWISSS
OOF! STOP IT, HELPER! NOW'S NOT THE TIME.
WE'VE NO TIME TO WASTE. THE BEAST IS COMING BACK!
BROUUMMM

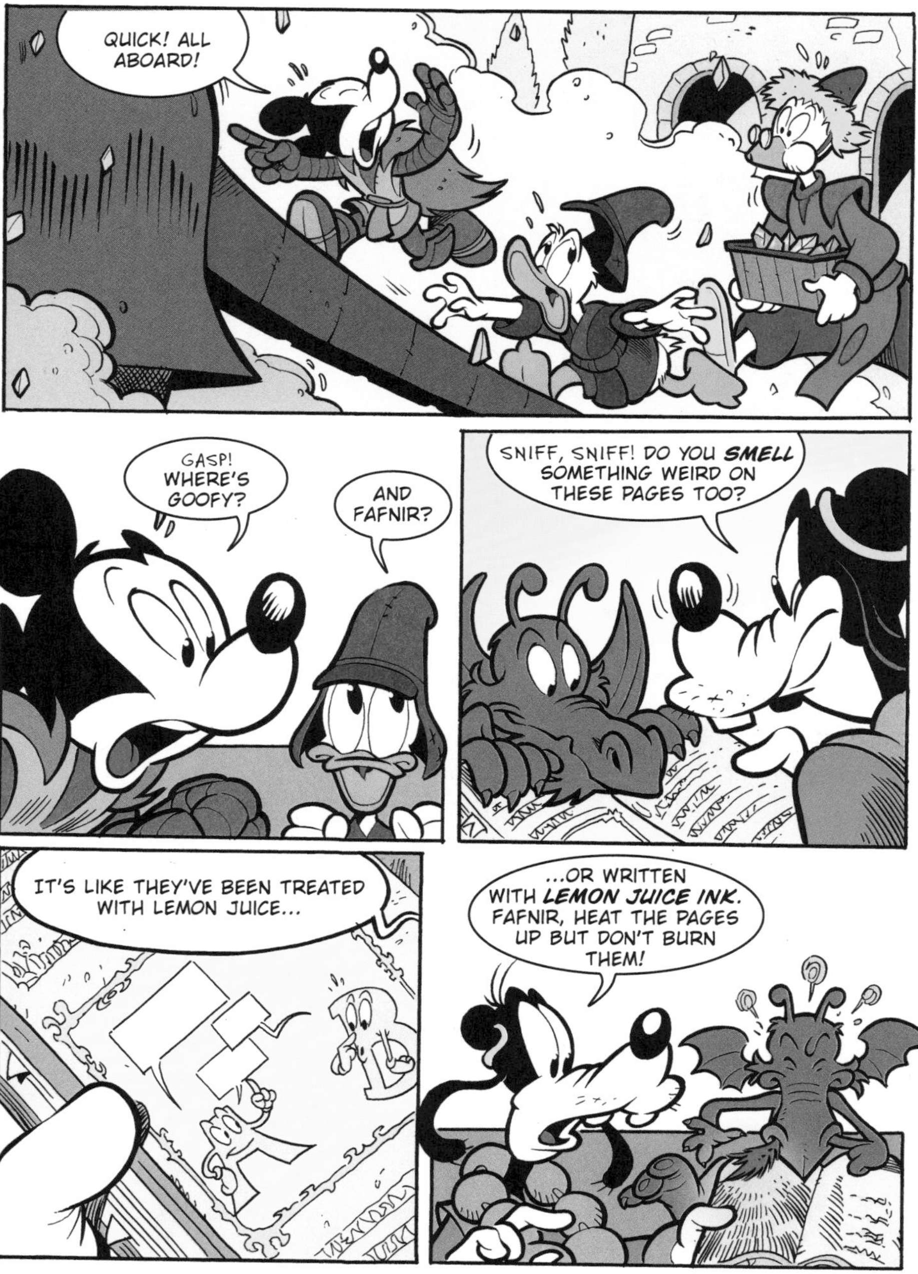
QUICK! ALL ABOARD!
GASP! WHERE'S GOOFY?
AND FAFNIR?
SNIFF, SNIFF! DO YOU SMELL SOMETHING WEIRD ON THESE PAGES TOO?
IT'S LIKE THEY'VE BEEN TREATED WITH LEMON JUICE...
...OR WRITTEN WITH LEMON JUICE INK. FAFNIR, HEAT THE PAGES UP BUT DON'T BURN THEM!

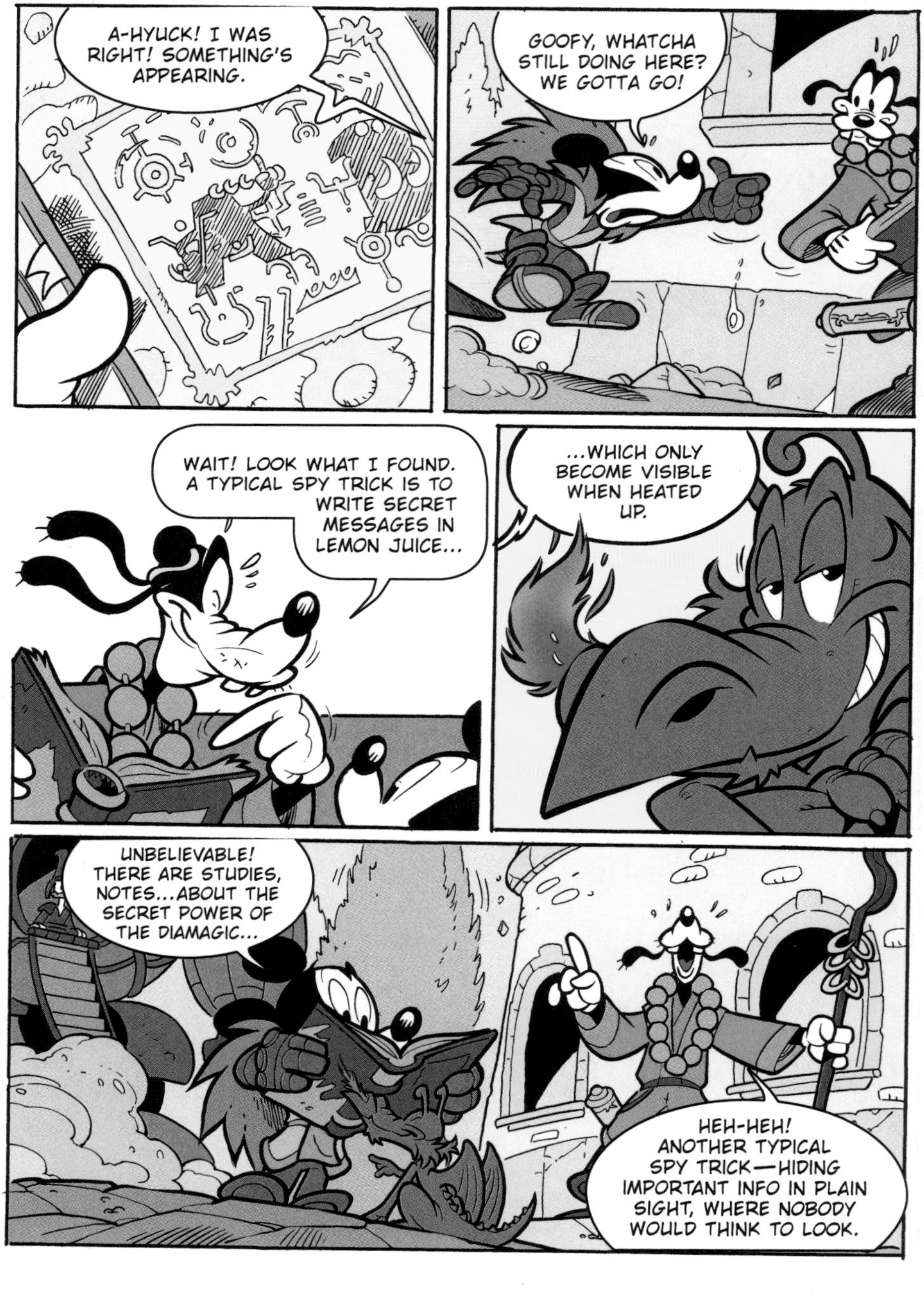
A-HYUCK! I WAS RIGHT! SOMETHING'S APPEARING.
GOOFY, WHATCHA STILL DOING HERE? WE GOTTA GO!
WAIT! LOOK WHAT I FOUND. A TYPICAL SPY TRICK IS TO WRITE SECRET MESSAGES IN LEMON JUICE...
...WHICH ONLY BECOME VISIBLE WHEN HEATED UP.
UNBELIEVABLE! THERE ARE STUDIES, NOTES...ABOUT THE SECRET POWER OF THE DIAMAGIC...
HEH-HEH! ANOTHER TYPICAL SPY TRICK—HIDING IMPORTANT INFO IN PLAIN SIGHT, WHERE NOBODY WOULD THINK TO LOOK.

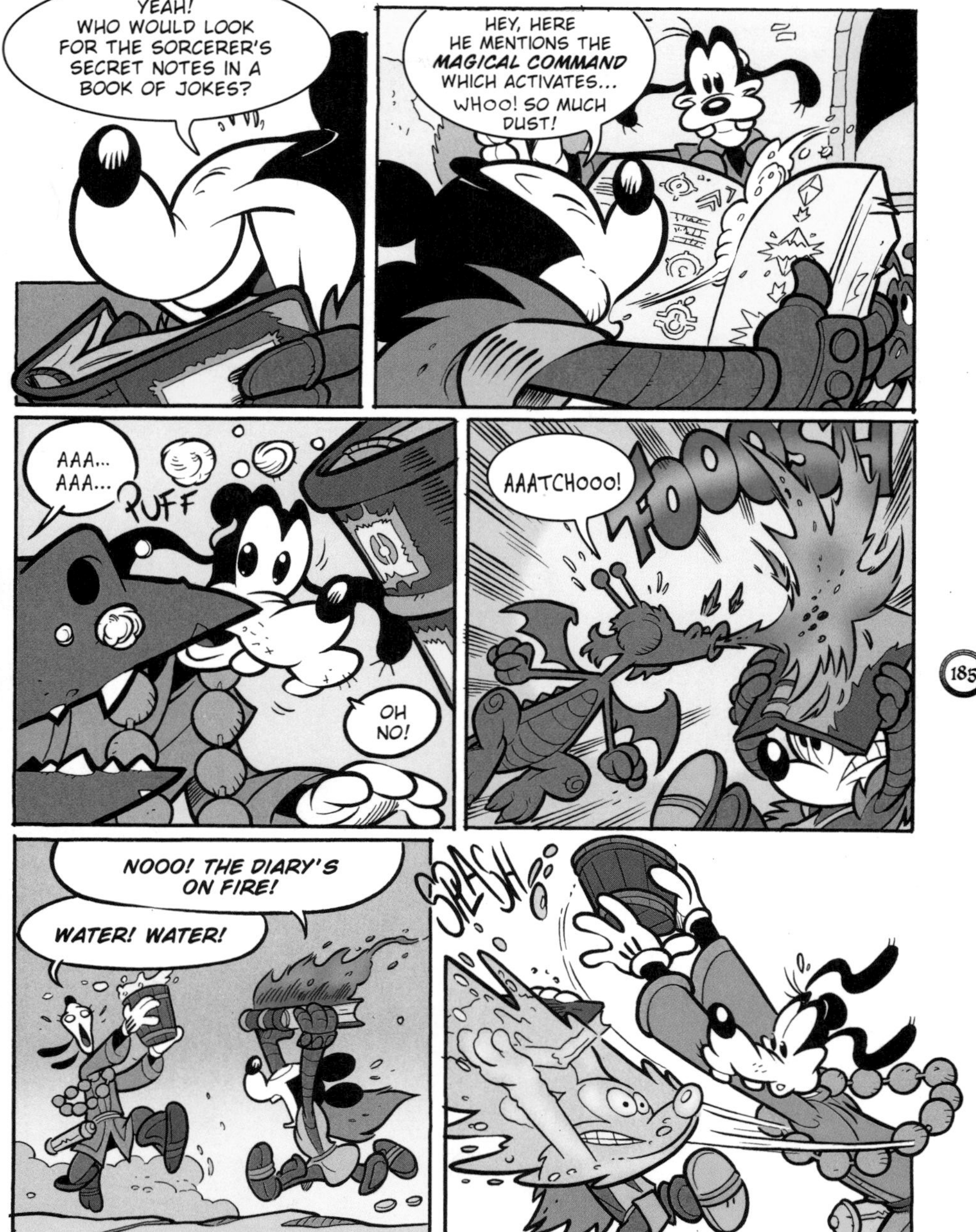
YEAH! WHO WOULD LOOK FOR THE SORCERER'S SECRET NOTES IN A BOOK OF JOKES?
HEY, HERE HE MENTIONS THE MAGICAL COMMAND WHICH ACTIVATES... WHOO! SO MUCH DUST!
AAA... AAA...
PUFF
OH NO!
AAATCHOOO!
FOOOSH
NOOO! THE DIARY'S ON FIRE!
WATER! WATER!
SPLASH

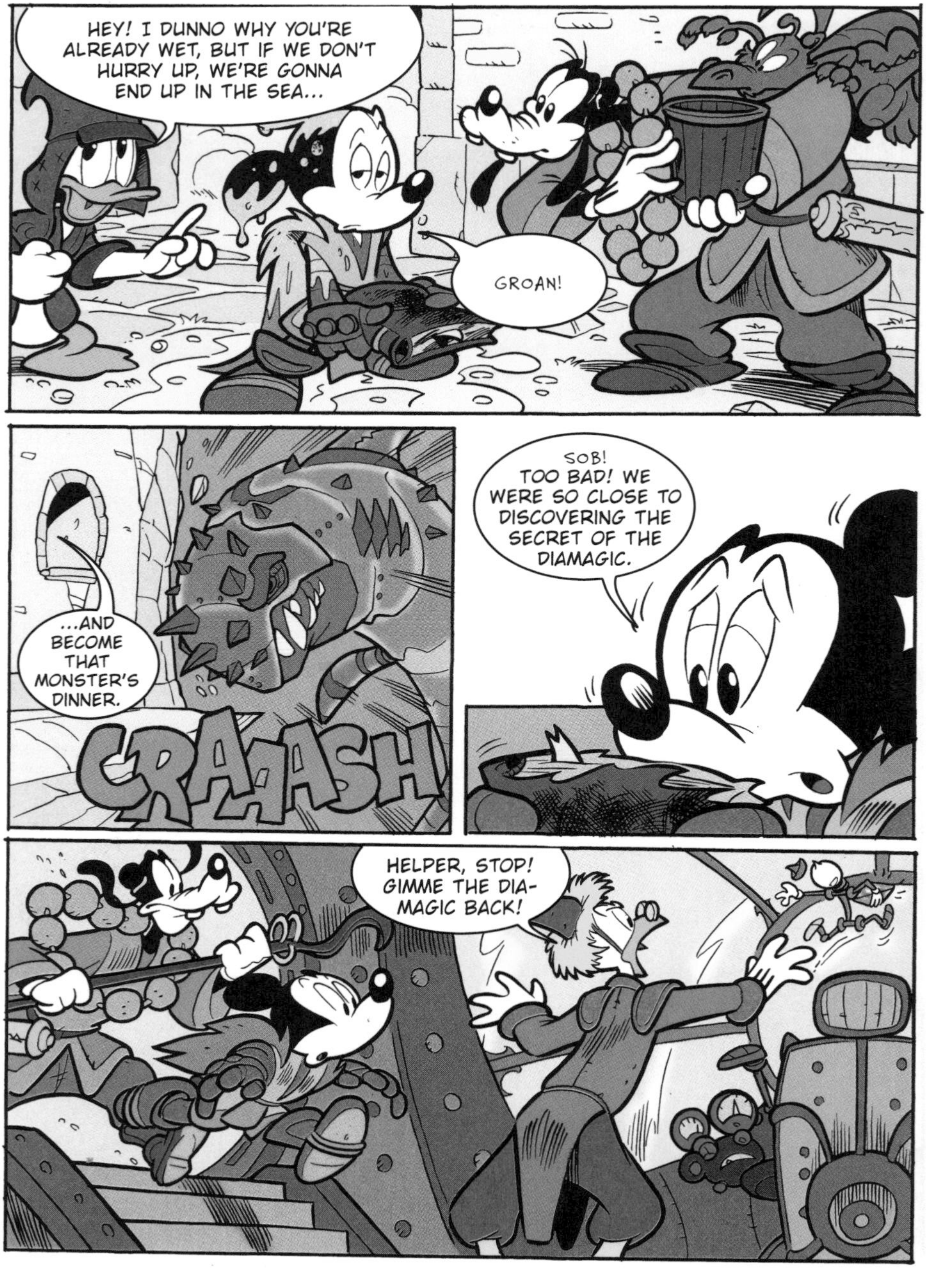

HEY! I DUNNO WHY YOU'RE ALREADY WET, BUT IF WE DON'T HURRY UP, WE'RE GONNA END UP IN THE SEA...
GROAN!
...AND BECOME THAT MONSTER'S DINNER.
CRAAASH
SOB! TOO BAD! WE WERE SO CLOSE TO DISCOVERING THE SECRET OF THE DIAMAGIC.
HELPER, STOP! GIMME THE DIA-MAGIC BACK!

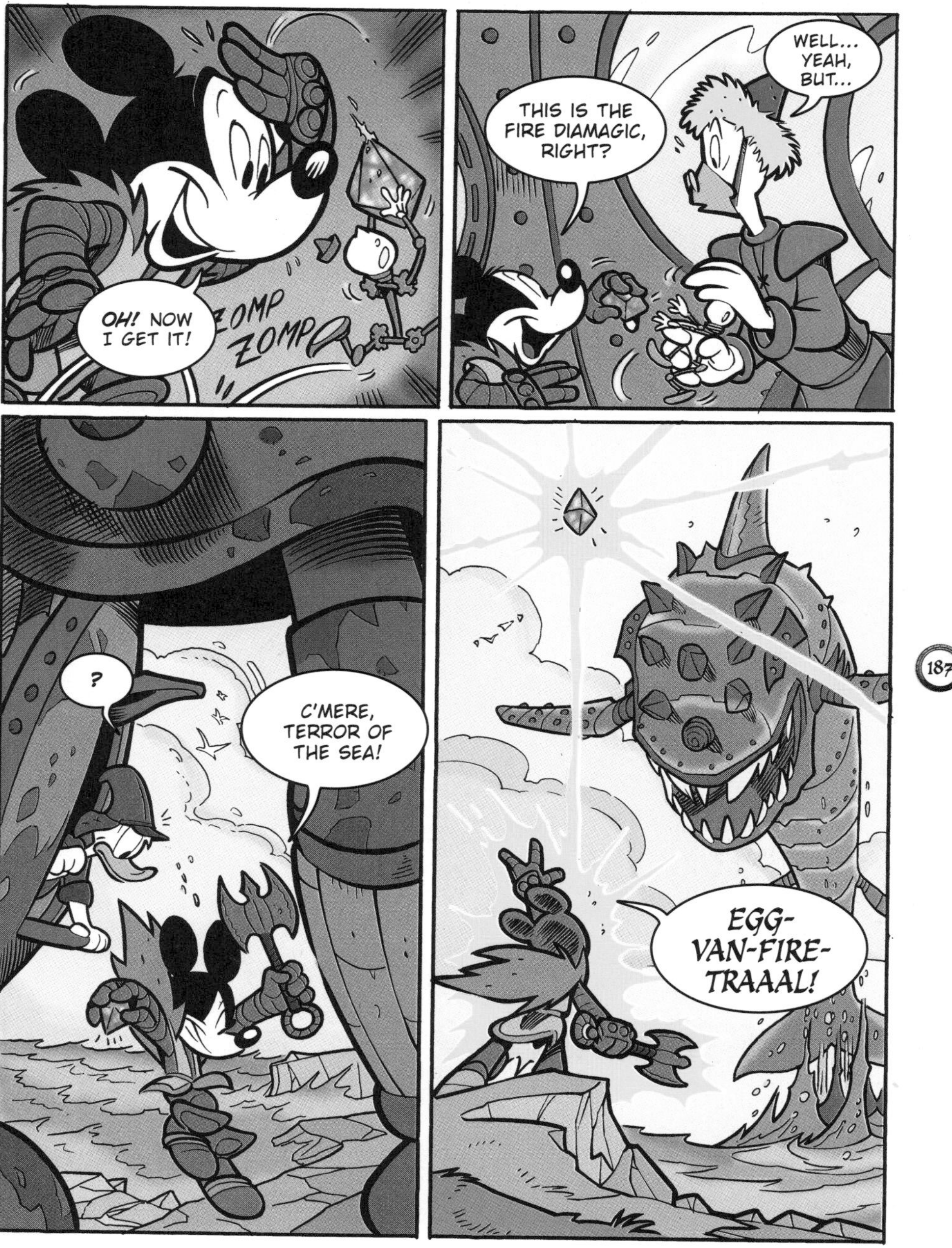
OH! NOW I GET IT!
ZOMP ZOMP
THIS IS THE FIRE DIAMAGIC, RIGHT?
WELL... YEAH, BUT...
?
C'MERE, TERROR OF THE SEA!
EGG-VAN-FIRE-TRAAAL!

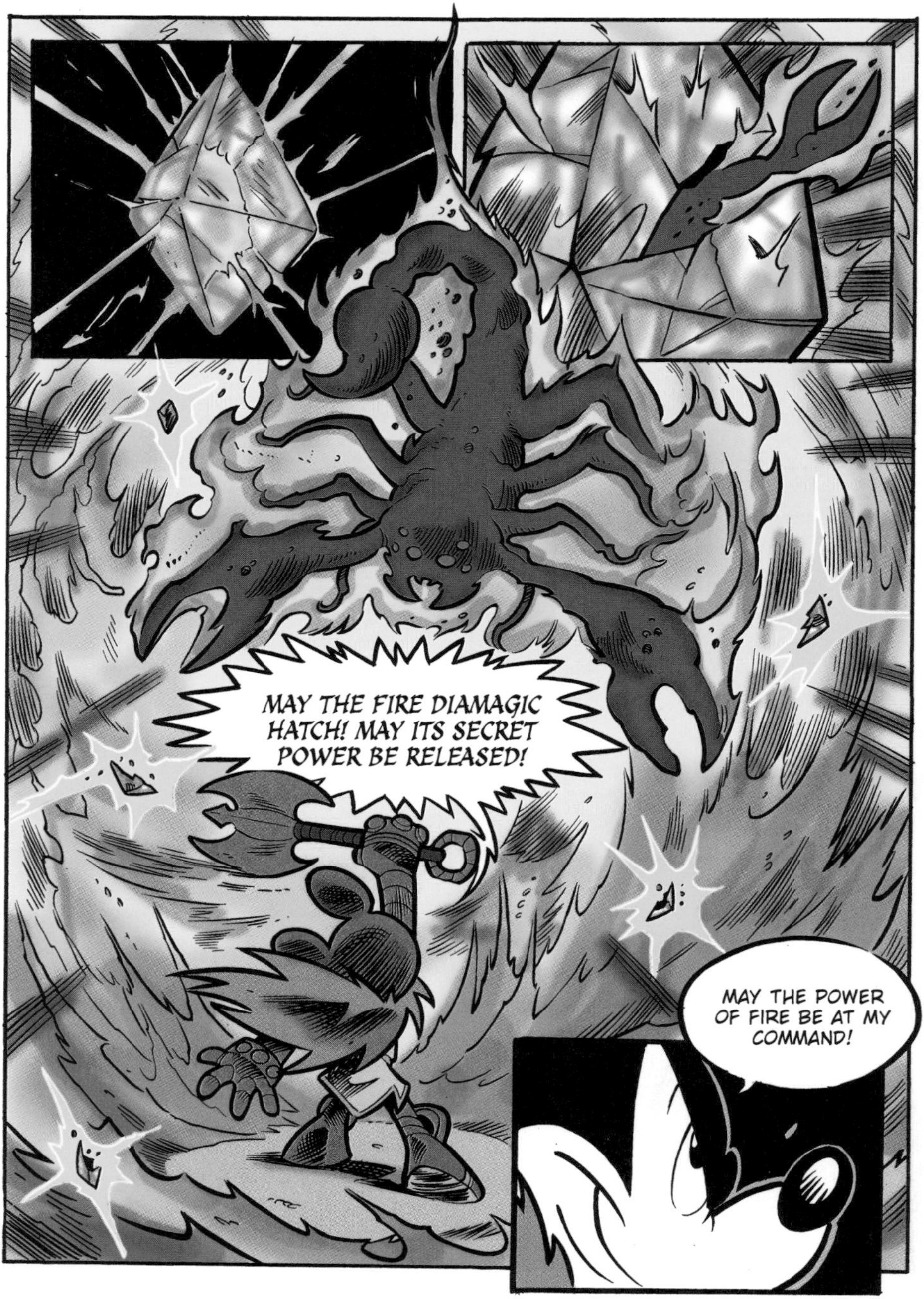
MAY THE FIRE DIAMAGIC HATCH! MAY ITS SECRET POWER BE RELEASED!
MAY THE POWER OF FIRE BE AT MY COMMAND!

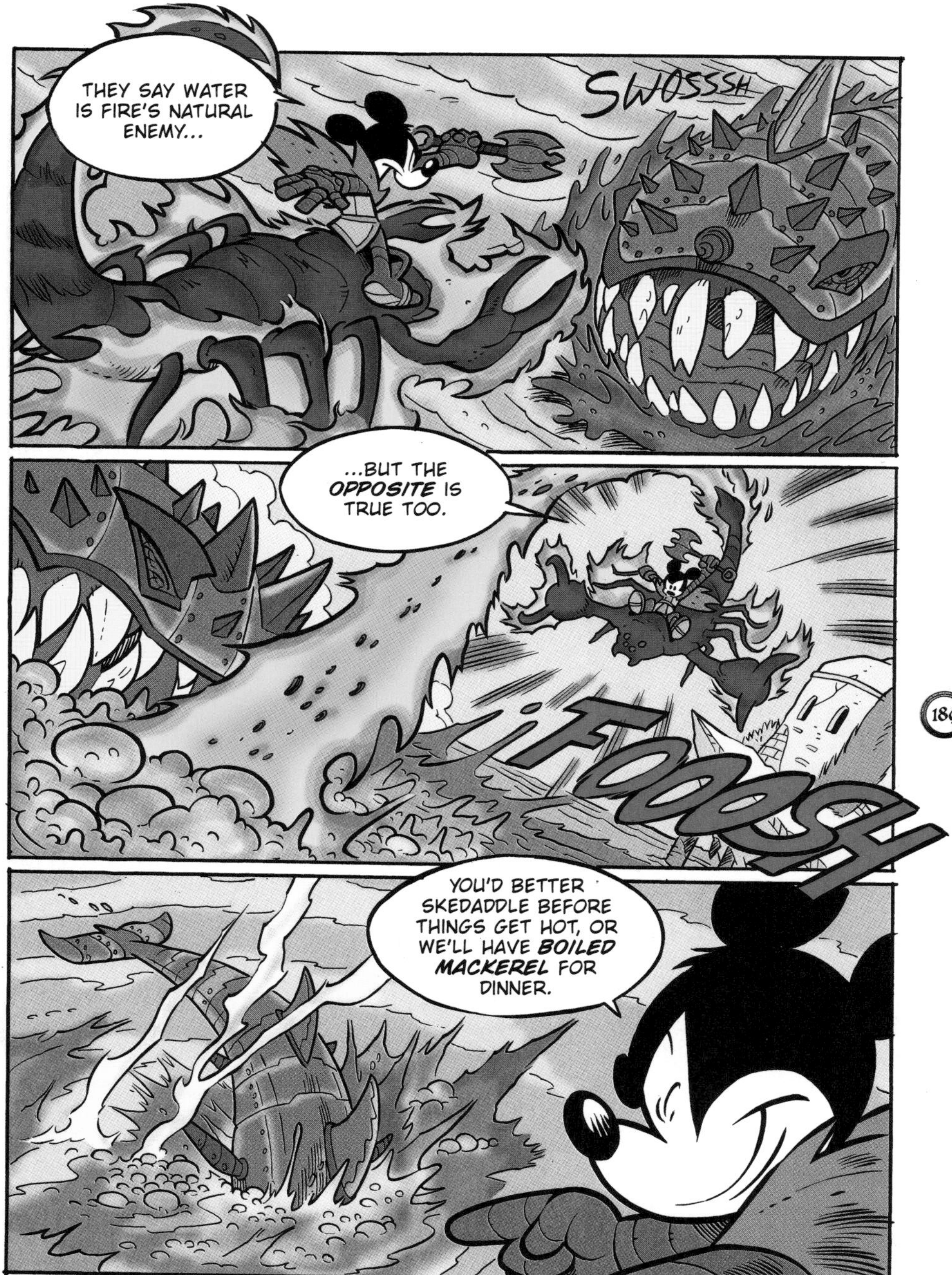
THEY SAY WATER IS FIRE'S NATURAL ENEMY...
SWOSSSH
...BUT THE OPPOSITE IS TRUE TOO.
FOOOSH
YOU'D BETTER SKEDADDLE BEFORE THINGS GET HOT, OR WE'LL HAVE BOILED MACKEREL FOR DINNER.

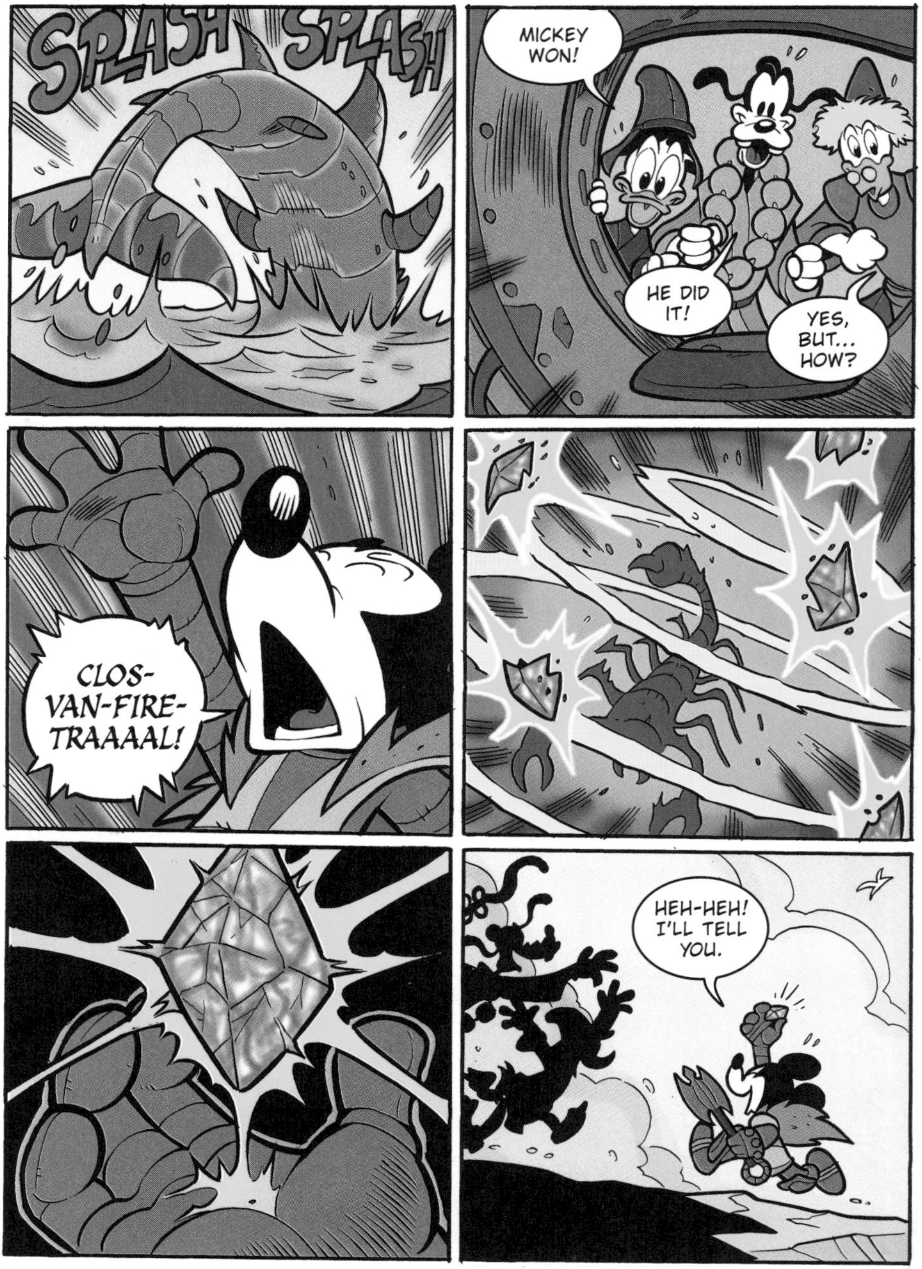
SPLASH SPLASH
MICKEY WON!
HE DID IT!
YES, BUT... HOW?
CLOS-VAN-FIRE-TRAAAAL!
HEH-HEH! I'LL TELL YOU.

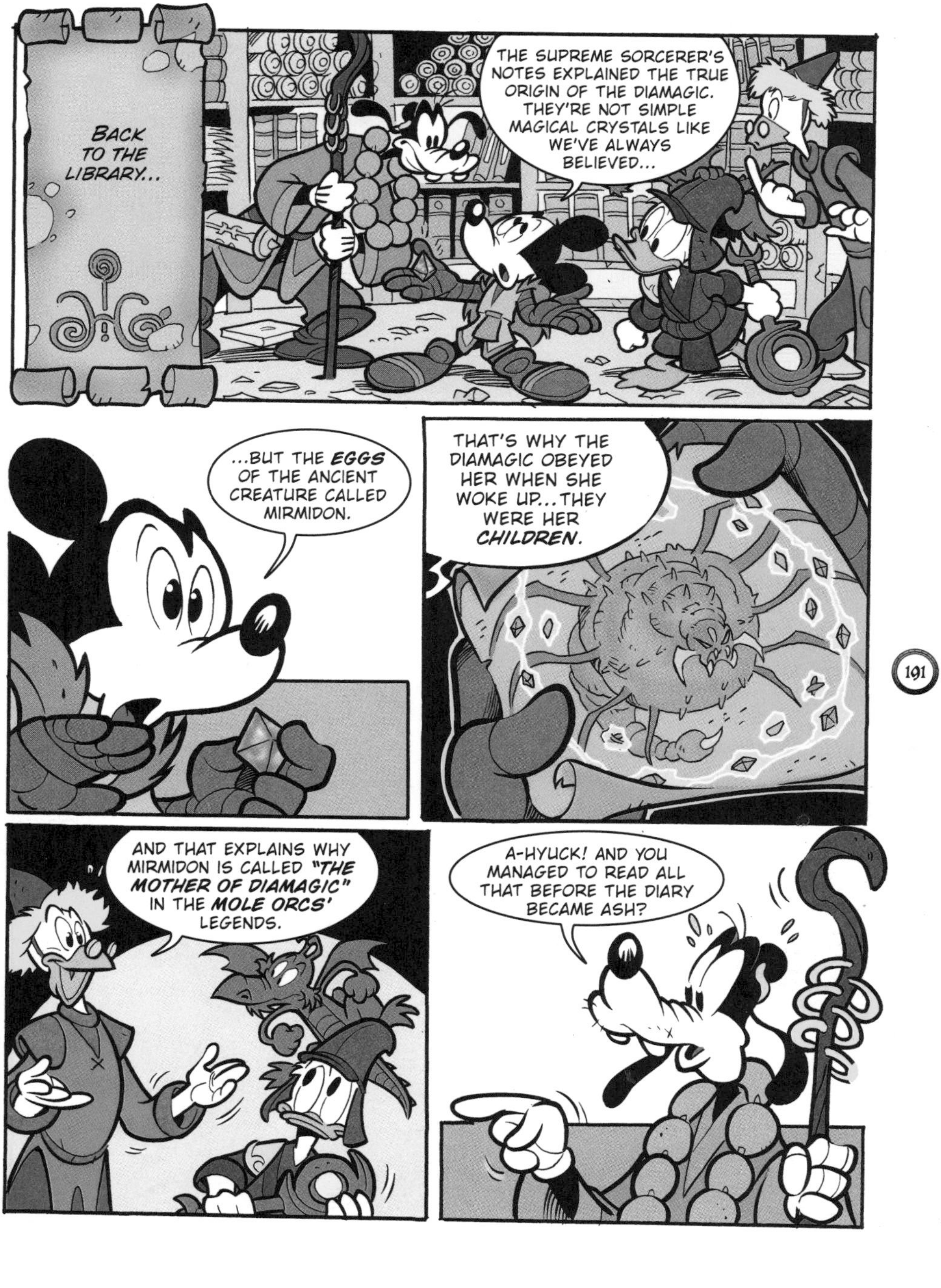
BACK TO THE LIBRARY...
THE SUPREME SORCERER'S NOTES EXPLAINED THE TRUE ORIGIN OF THE DIAMAGIC. THEY'RE NOT SIMPLE MAGICAL CRYSTALS LIKE WE'VE ALWAYS BELIEVED...
...BUT THE EGGS OF THE ANCIENT CREATURE CALLED MIRMIDON.
THAT'S WHY THE DIAMAGIC OBEYED HER WHEN SHE WOKE UP...THEY WERE HER CHILDREN.
AND THAT EXPLAINS WHY MIRMIDON IS CALLED "THE MOTHER OF DIAMAGIC" IN THE MOLE ORCS' LEGENDS.
A-HYUCK! AND YOU MANAGED TO READ ALL THAT BEFORE THE DIARY BECAME ASH?

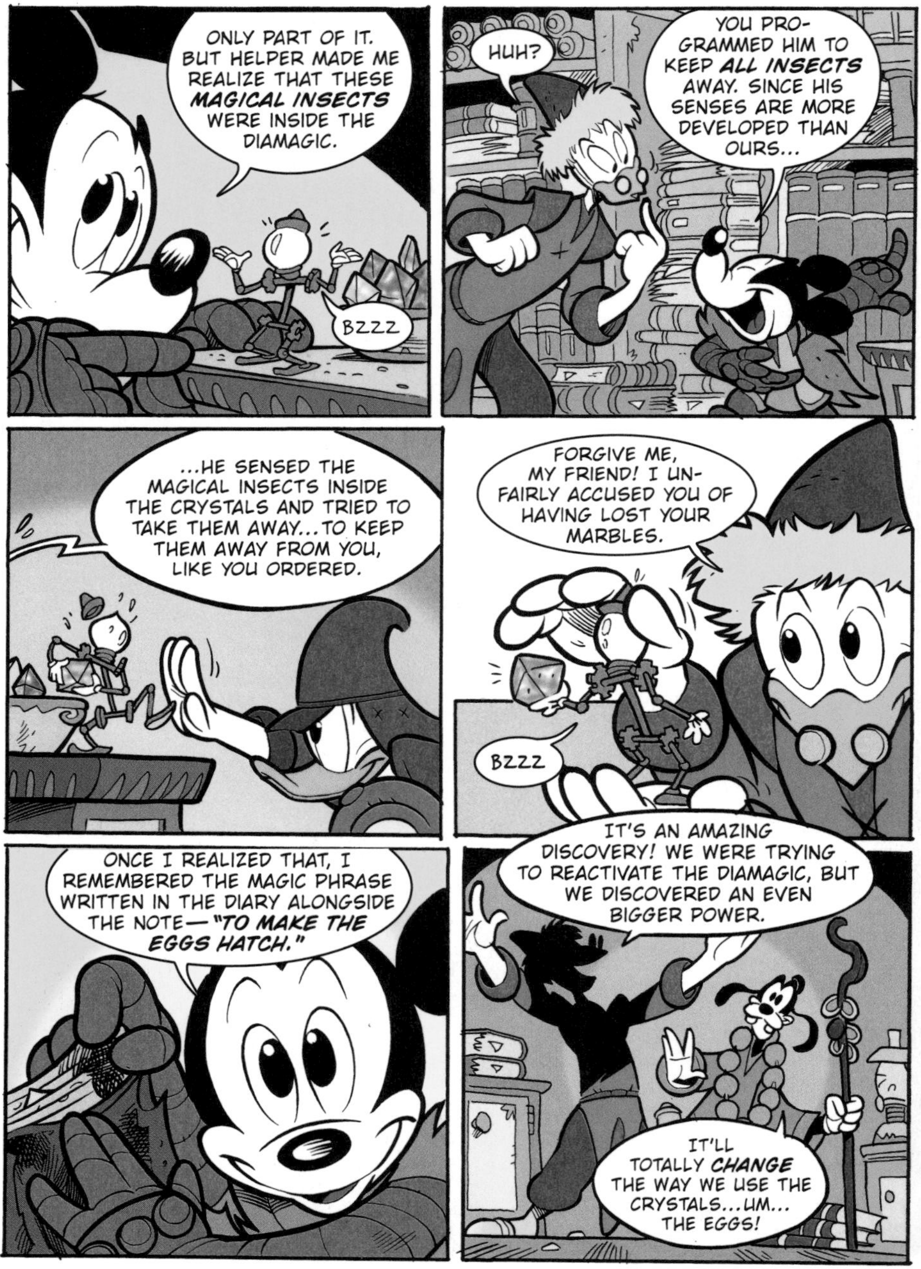
ONLY PART OF IT. BUT HELPER MADE ME REALIZE THAT THESE **MAGICAL INSECTS** WERE INSIDE THE DIAMAGIC.
BZZZ
HUH?
YOU PROGRAMMED HIM TO KEEP **ALL INSECTS** AWAY. SINCE HIS SENSES ARE MORE DEVELOPED THAN OURS...
...HE SENSED THE MAGICAL INSECTS INSIDE THE CRYSTALS AND TRIED TO TAKE THEM AWAY...TO KEEP THEM AWAY FROM YOU, LIKE YOU ORDERED.
FORGIVE ME, MY FRIEND! I UNFAIRLY ACCUSED YOU OF HAVING LOST YOUR MARBLES.
BZZZ
ONCE I REALIZED THAT, I REMEMBERED THE MAGIC PHRASE WRITTEN IN THE DIARY ALONGSIDE THE NOTE— **"TO MAKE THE EGGS HATCH."**
IT'S AN AMAZING DISCOVERY! WE WERE TRYING TO REACTIVATE THE DIAMAGIC, BUT WE DISCOVERED AN EVEN BIGGER POWER.
IT'LL TOTALLY **CHANGE** THE WAY WE USE THE CRYSTALS...UM... THE EGGS!

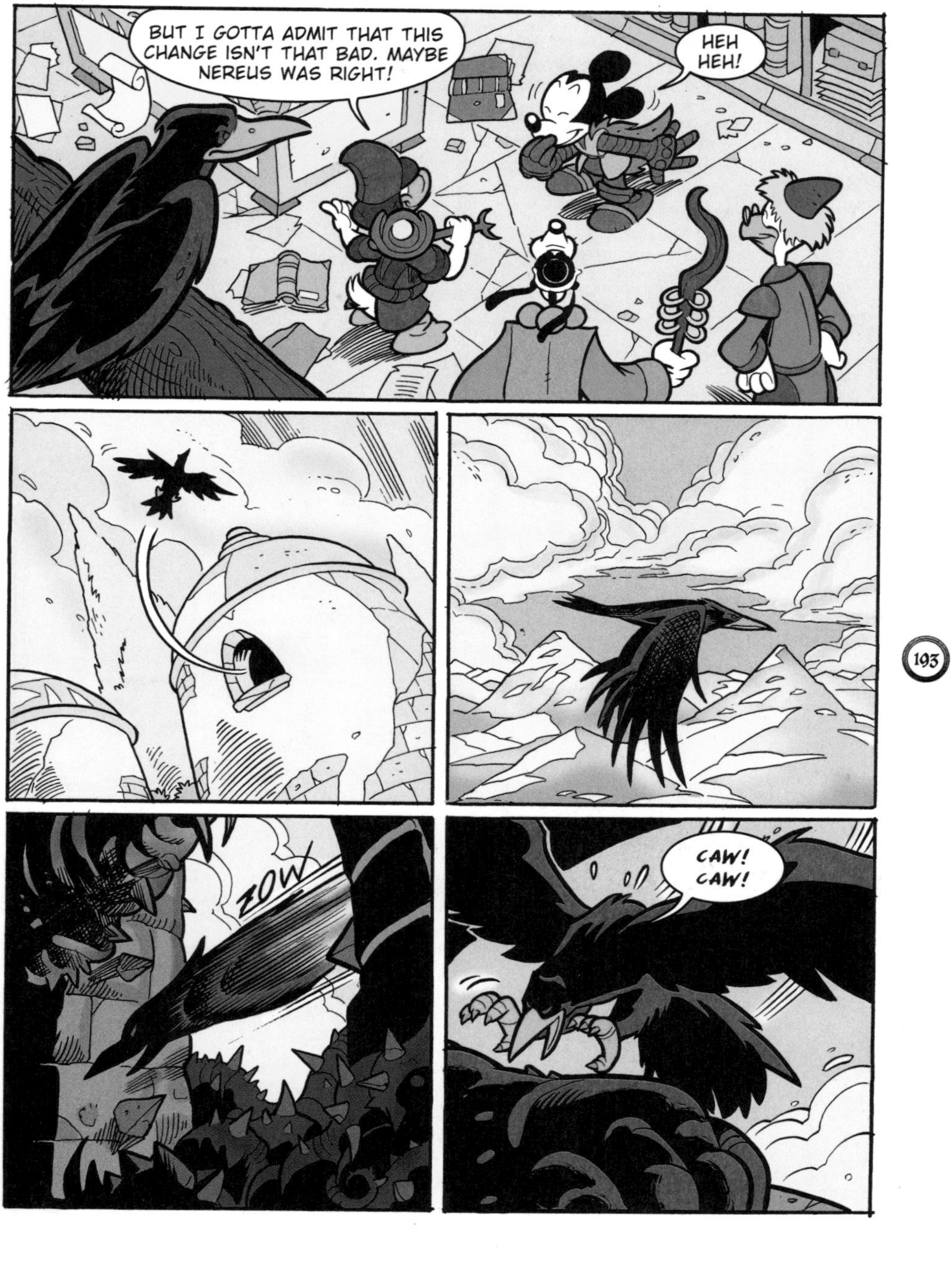
BUT I GOTTA ADMIT THAT THIS CHANGE ISN'T THAT BAD. MAYBE NEREUS WAS RIGHT!
HEH HEH!
ZOW
CAW! CAW!

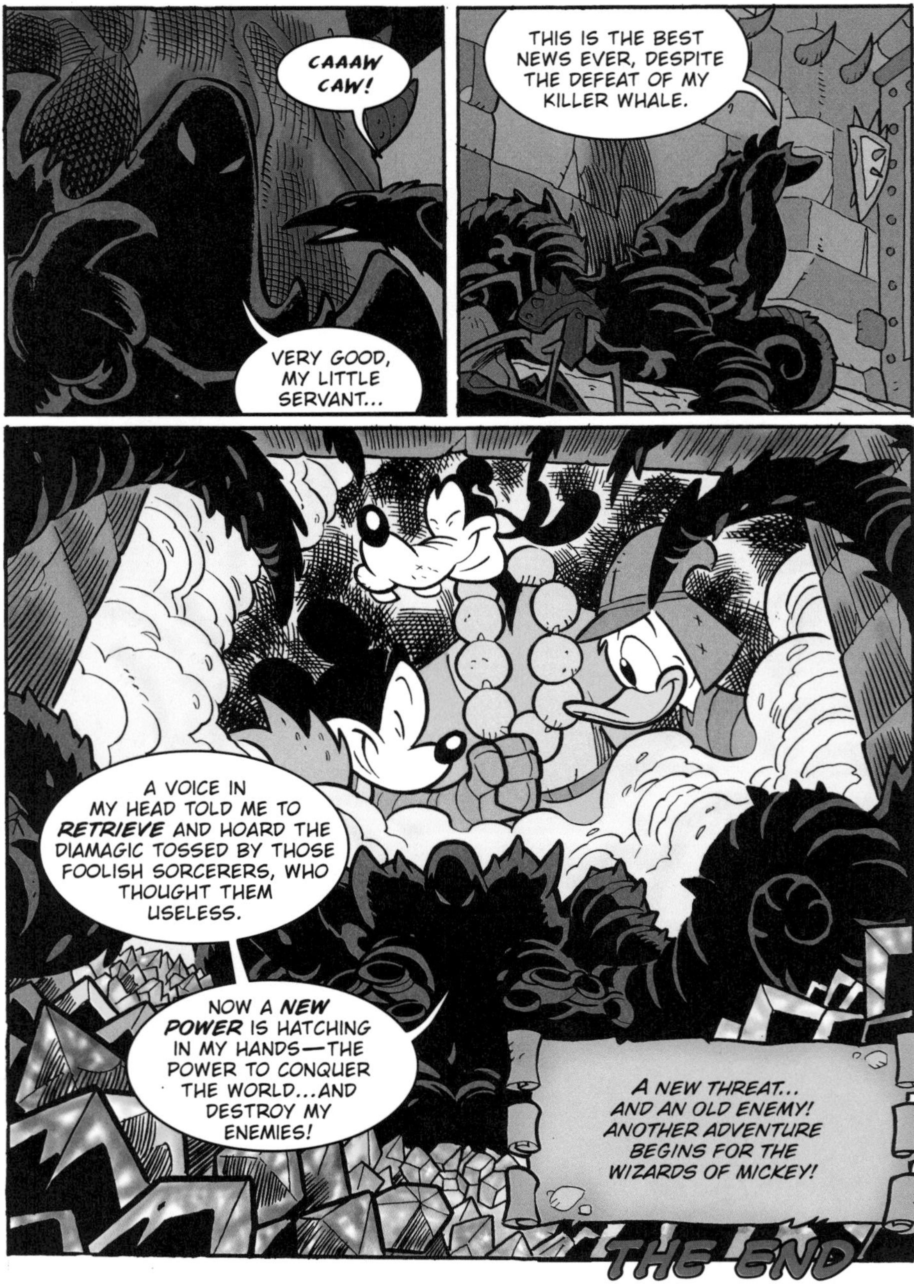
CAAAW CAW!
VERY GOOD, MY LITTLE SERVANT...
THIS IS THE BEST NEWS EVER, DESPITE THE DEFEAT OF MY KILLER WHALE.
A VOICE IN MY HEAD TOLD ME TO RETRIEVE AND HOARD THE DIAMAGIC TOSSED BY THOSE FOOLISH SORCERERS, WHO THOUGHT THEM USELESS.
NOW A NEW POWER IS HATCHING IN MY HANDS—THE POWER TO CONQUER THE WORLD...AND DESTROY MY ENEMIES!
A NEW THREAT... AND AN OLD ENEMY! ANOTHER ADVENTURE BEGINS FOR THE WIZARDS OF MICKEY!
THE END

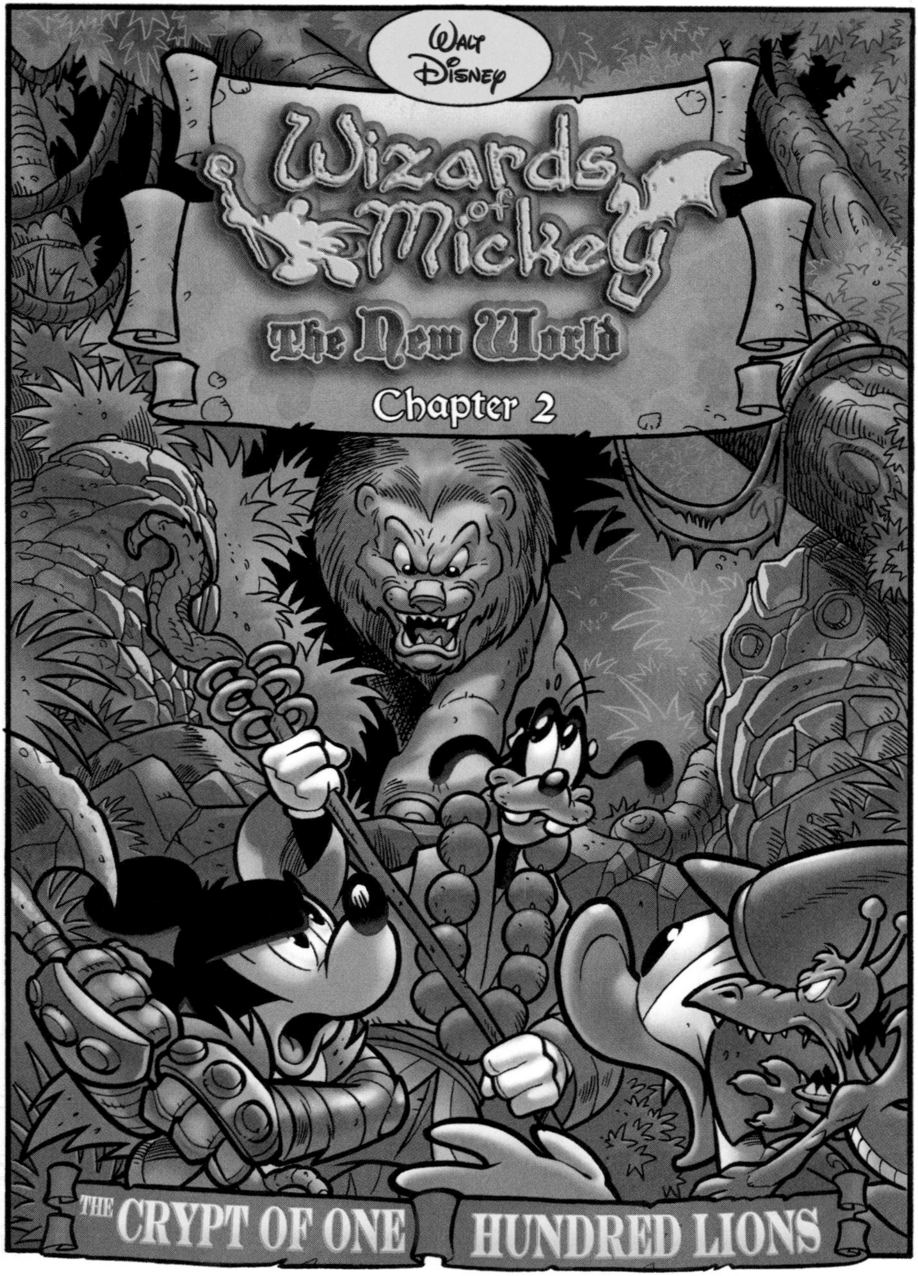
Walt Disney
Wizards of Mickey
The New World
Chapter 2
THE CRYPT OF ONE HUNDRED LIONS

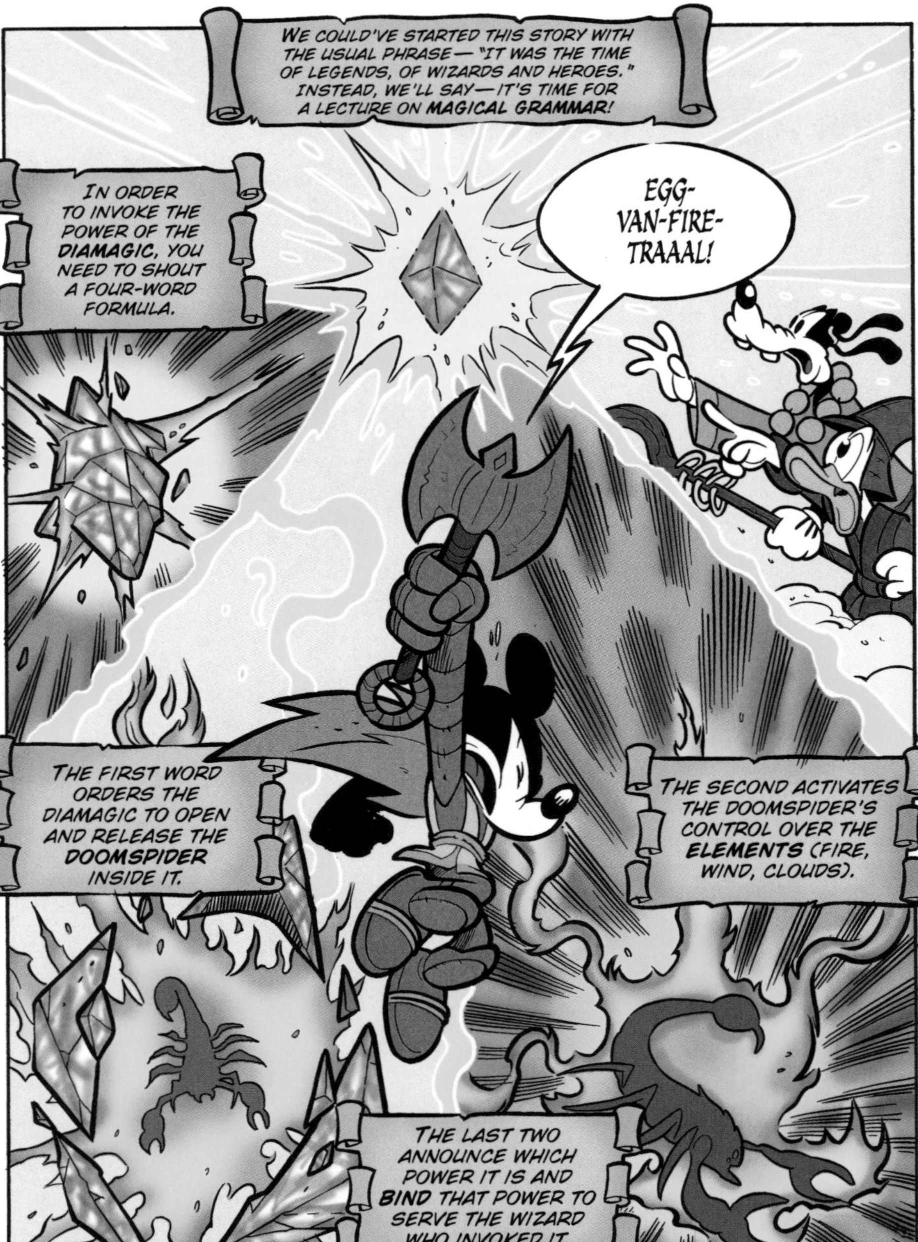
WE COULD'VE STARTED THIS STORY WITH THE USUAL PHRASE—"IT WAS THE TIME OF LEGENDS, OF WIZARDS AND HEROES." INSTEAD, WE'LL SAY—IT'S TIME FOR A LECTURE ON MAGICAL GRAMMAR!
IN ORDER TO INVOKE THE POWER OF THE DIAMAGIC, YOU NEED TO SHOUT A FOUR-WORD FORMULA.
EGG-VAN-FIRE-TRAAAL!
THE FIRST WORD ORDERS THE DIAMAGIC TO OPEN AND RELEASE THE DOOMSPIDER INSIDE IT.
THE SECOND ACTIVATES THE DOOMSPIDER'S CONTROL OVER THE ELEMENTS (FIRE, WIND, CLOUDS).
THE LAST TWO ANNOUNCE WHICH POWER IT IS AND BIND THAT POWER TO SERVE THE WIZARD WHO INVOKED IT.

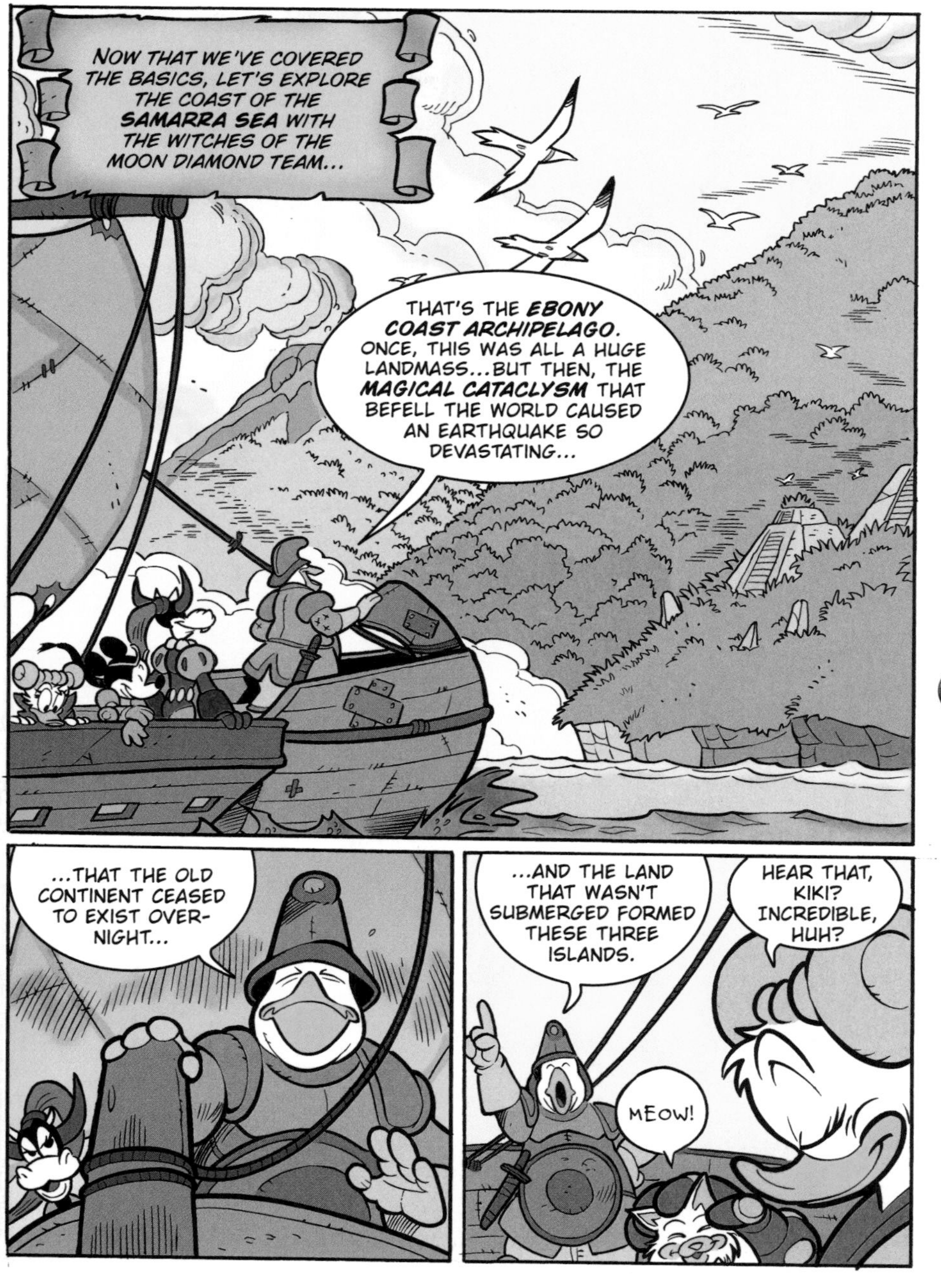
NOW THAT WE'VE COVERED THE BASICS, LET'S EXPLORE THE COAST OF THE SAMARRA SEA WITH THE WITCHES OF THE MOON DIAMOND TEAM...
THAT'S THE EBONY COAST ARCHIPELAGO. ONCE, THIS WAS ALL A HUGE LANDMASS...BUT THEN, THE MAGICAL CATACLYSM THAT BEFELL THE WORLD CAUSED AN EARTHQUAKE SO DEVASTATING...
...THAT THE OLD CONTINENT CEASED TO EXIST OVER-NIGHT...
...AND THE LAND THAT WASN'T SUBMERGED FORMED THESE THREE ISLANDS.
HEAR THAT, KIKI? INCREDIBLE, HUH?
MEOW!

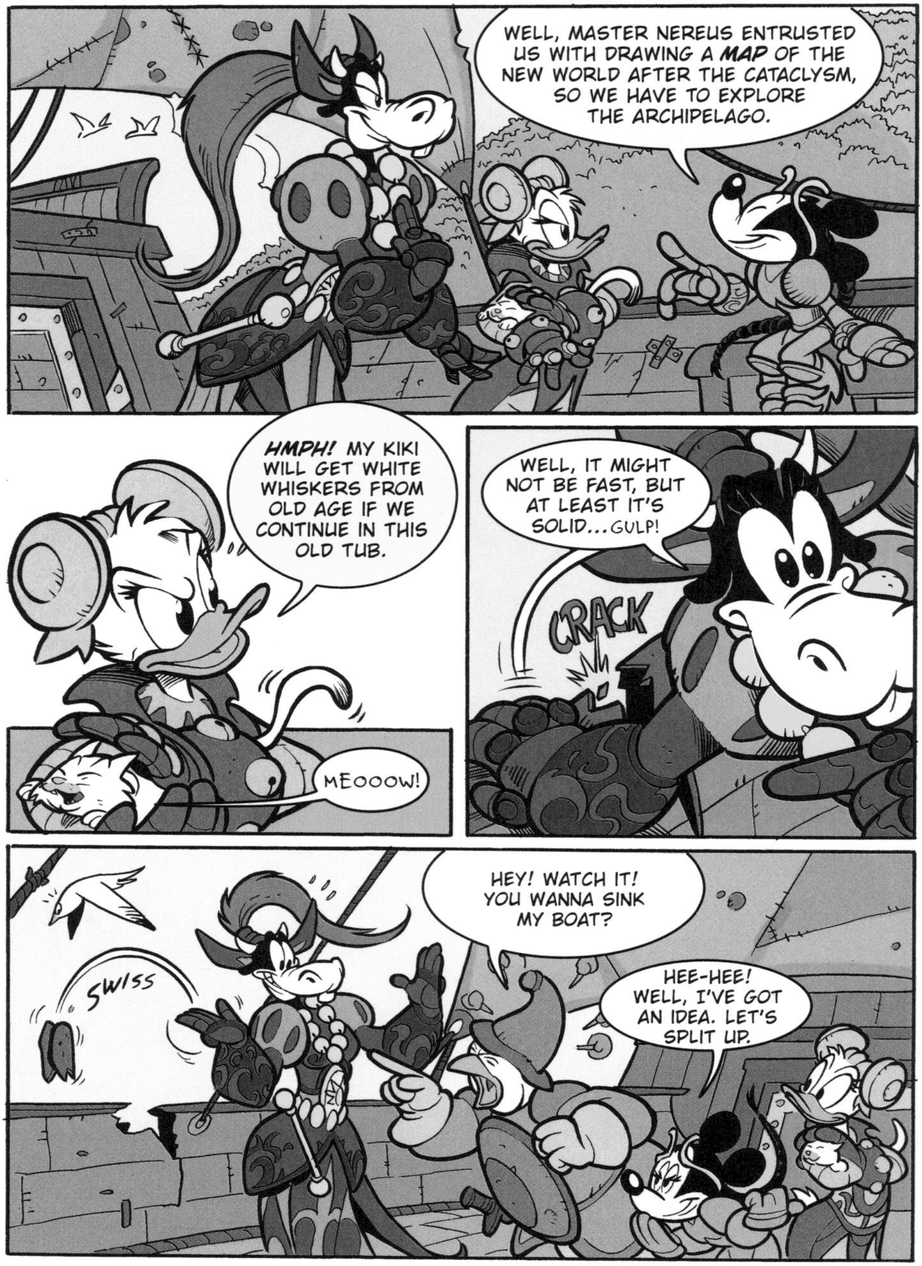
WELL, MASTER NEREUS ENTRUSTED US WITH DRAWING A MAP OF THE NEW WORLD AFTER THE CATACLYSM, SO WE HAVE TO EXPLORE THE ARCHIPELAGO.
HMPH! MY KIKI WILL GET WHITE WHISKERS FROM OLD AGE IF WE CONTINUE IN THIS OLD TUB.
MEOOOW!
WELL, IT MIGHT NOT BE FAST, BUT AT LEAST IT'S SOLID... GULP!
CRACK
SWISS
HEY! WATCH IT! YOU WANNA SINK MY BOAT?
HEE-HEE! WELL, I'VE GOT AN IDEA. LET'S SPLIT UP.

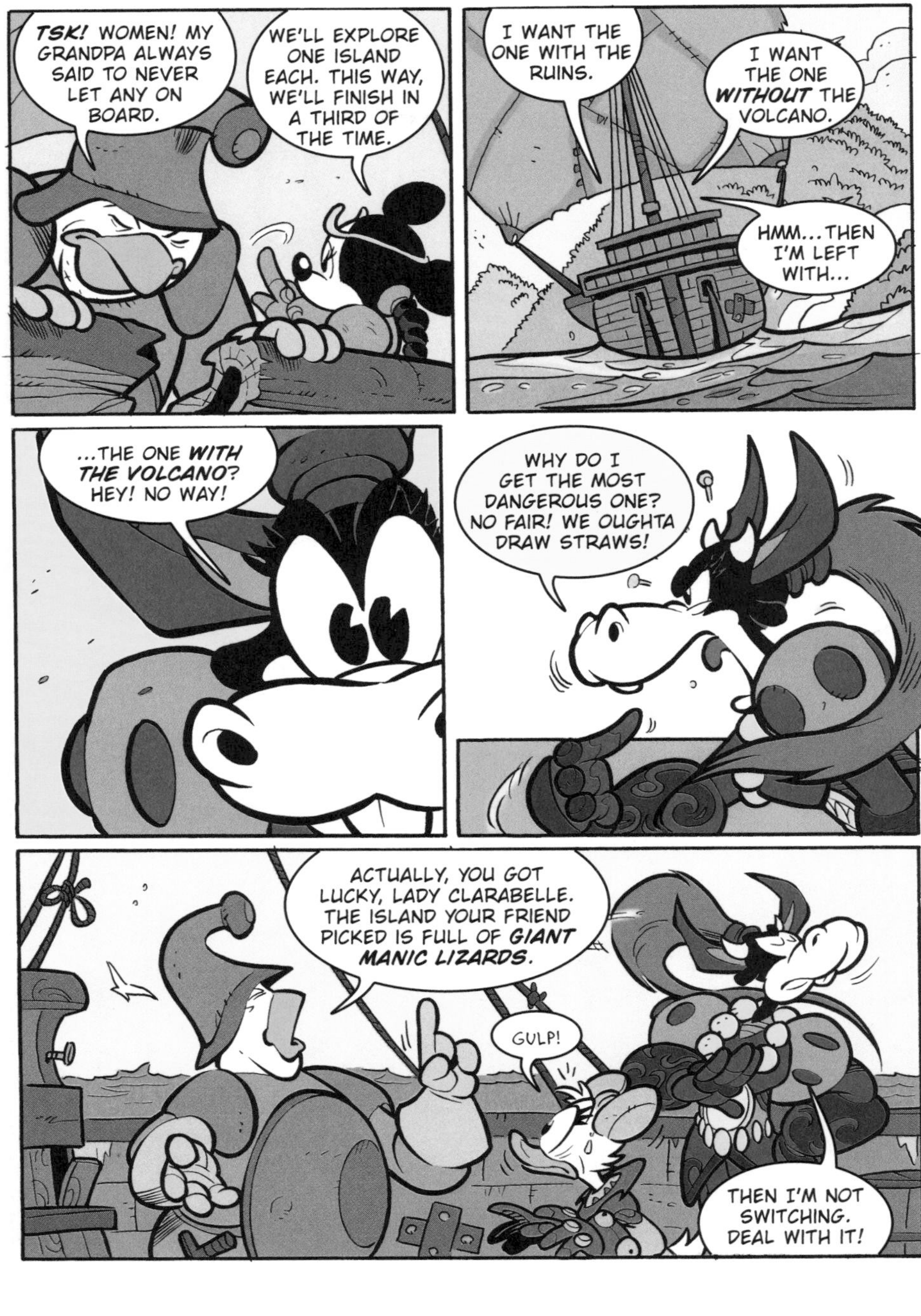

TSK! WOMEN! MY GRANDPA ALWAYS SAID TO NEVER LET ANY ON BOARD.
WE'LL EXPLORE ONE ISLAND EACH. THIS WAY, WE'LL FINISH IN A THIRD OF THE TIME.
I WANT THE ONE WITH THE RUINS.
I WANT THE ONE WITHOUT THE VOLCANO.
HMM... THEN I'M LEFT WITH...
...THE ONE WITH THE VOLCANO? HEY! NO WAY!
WHY DO I GET THE MOST DANGEROUS ONE? NO FAIR! WE OUGHTA DRAW STRAWS!
ACTUALLY, YOU GOT LUCKY, LADY CLARABELLE. THE ISLAND YOUR FRIEND PICKED IS FULL OF GIANT MANIC LIZARDS.
GULP!
THEN I'M NOT SWITCHING. DEAL WITH IT!

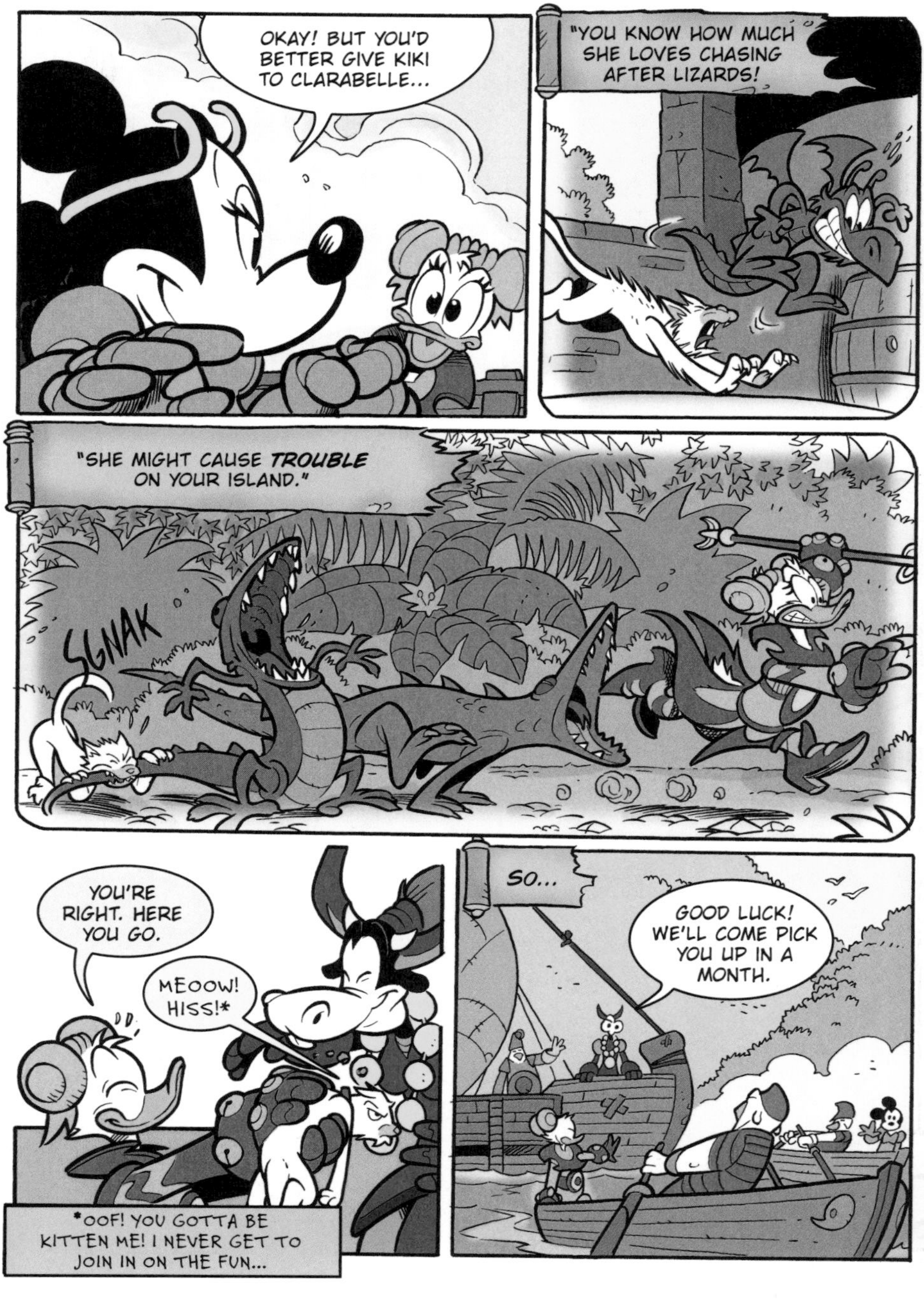

OKAY! BUT YOU'D BETTER GIVE KIKI TO CLARABELLE...
"YOU KNOW HOW MUCH SHE LOVES CHASING AFTER LIZARDS!
"SHE MIGHT CAUSE *TROUBLE* ON YOUR ISLAND."
SGNAK
YOU'RE RIGHT. HERE YOU GO.
MEOOW! HISS!*
*OOF! YOU GOTTA BE KITTEN ME! I NEVER GET TO JOIN IN ON THE FUN...
SO...
GOOD LUCK! WE'LL COME PICK YOU UP IN A MONTH.

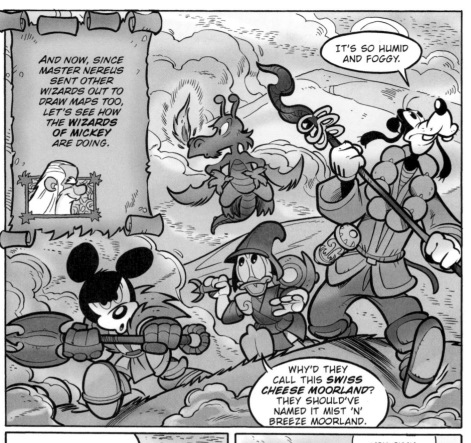

AND NOW, SINCE MASTER NEREUS SENT OTHER WIZARDS OUT TO DRAW MAPS TOO, LET'S SEE HOW THE *WIZARDS OF MICKEY* ARE DOING.

IT'S SO HUMID AND FOGGY.

WHY'D THEY CALL THIS *SWISS CHEESE MOORLAND*? THEY SHOULD'VE NAMED IT MIST 'N' BREEZE MOORLAND.

C'MON! I THINK I SEE A CASTLE OVER THERE.

STHUMP

SQUAAAWK!

YOU OKAY, DONALD?

HMPH! NOW I KNOW WHY IT'S CALLED SWISS CHEESE MOORLAND... IT'S FULL OF *HOLES!*

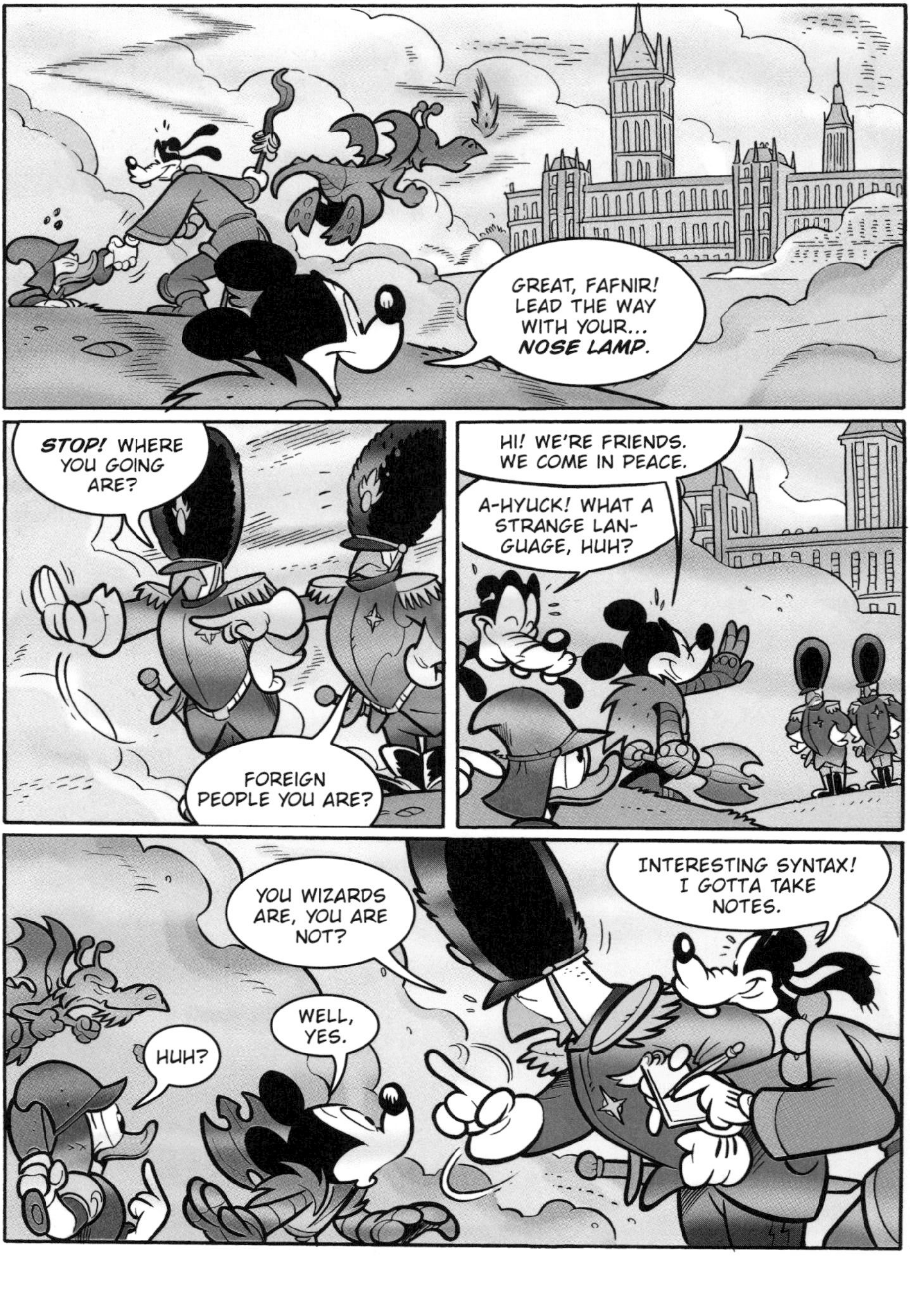

GREAT, FAFNIR! LEAD THE WAY WITH YOUR... NOSE LAMP.
STOP! WHERE YOU GOING ARE?
FOREIGN PEOPLE YOU ARE?
HI! WE'RE FRIENDS. WE COME IN PEACE.
A-HYUCK! WHAT A STRANGE LAN-GUAGE, HUH?
YOU WIZARDS ARE, YOU ARE NOT?
INTERESTING SYNTAX! I GOTTA TAKE NOTES.
WELL, YES.
HUH?

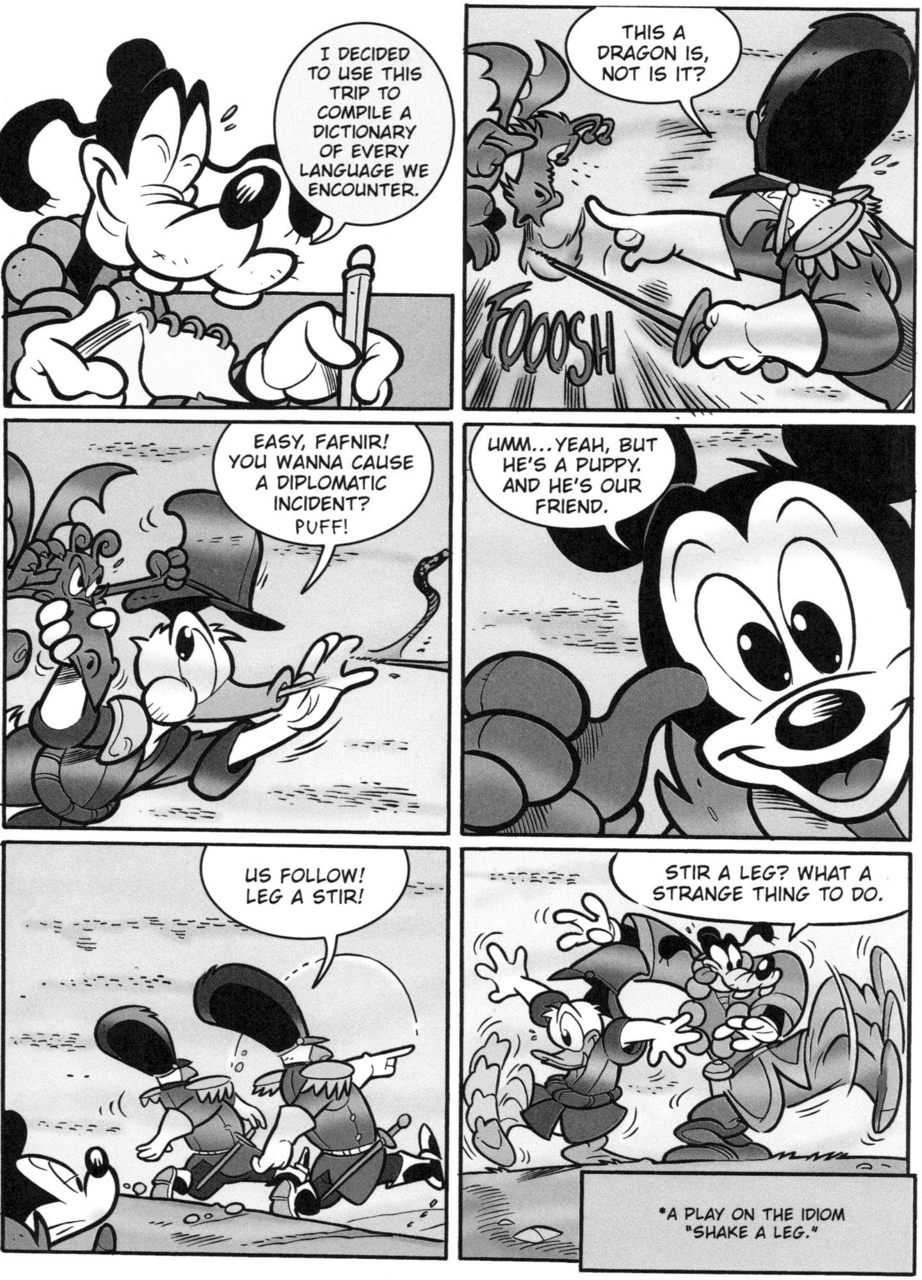
I DECIDED TO USE THIS TRIP TO COMPILE A DICTIONARY OF EVERY LANGUAGE WE ENCOUNTER.
THIS A DRAGON IS, NOT IS IT?
FOOOSH
EASY, FAFNIR! YOU WANNA CAUSE A DIPLOMATIC INCIDENT?
PUFF!
UMM...YEAH, BUT HE'S A PUPPY. AND HE'S OUR FRIEND.
US FOLLOW! LEG A STIR!
STIR A LEG? WHAT A STRANGE THING TO DO.
*A PLAY ON THE IDIOM "SHAKE A LEG."

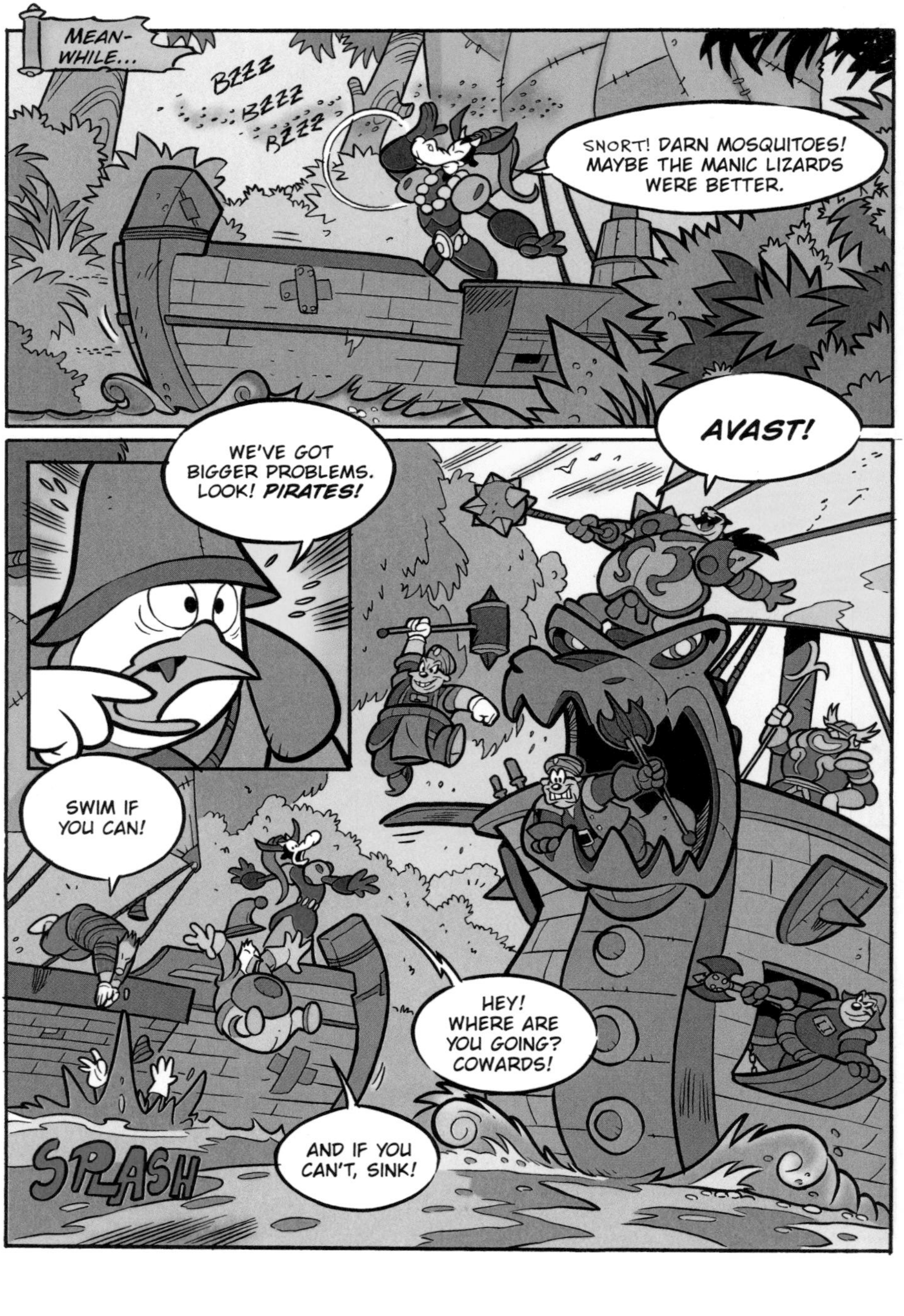
MEAN-WHILE...
BZZZ BZZZ BZZZ
SNORT! DARN MOSQUITOES! MAYBE THE MANIC LIZARDS WERE BETTER.
WE'VE GOT BIGGER PROBLEMS. LOOK! PIRATES!
AVAST!
SWIM IF YOU CAN!
HEY! WHERE ARE YOU GOING? COWARDS!
AND IF YOU CAN'T, SINK!
SPLASH

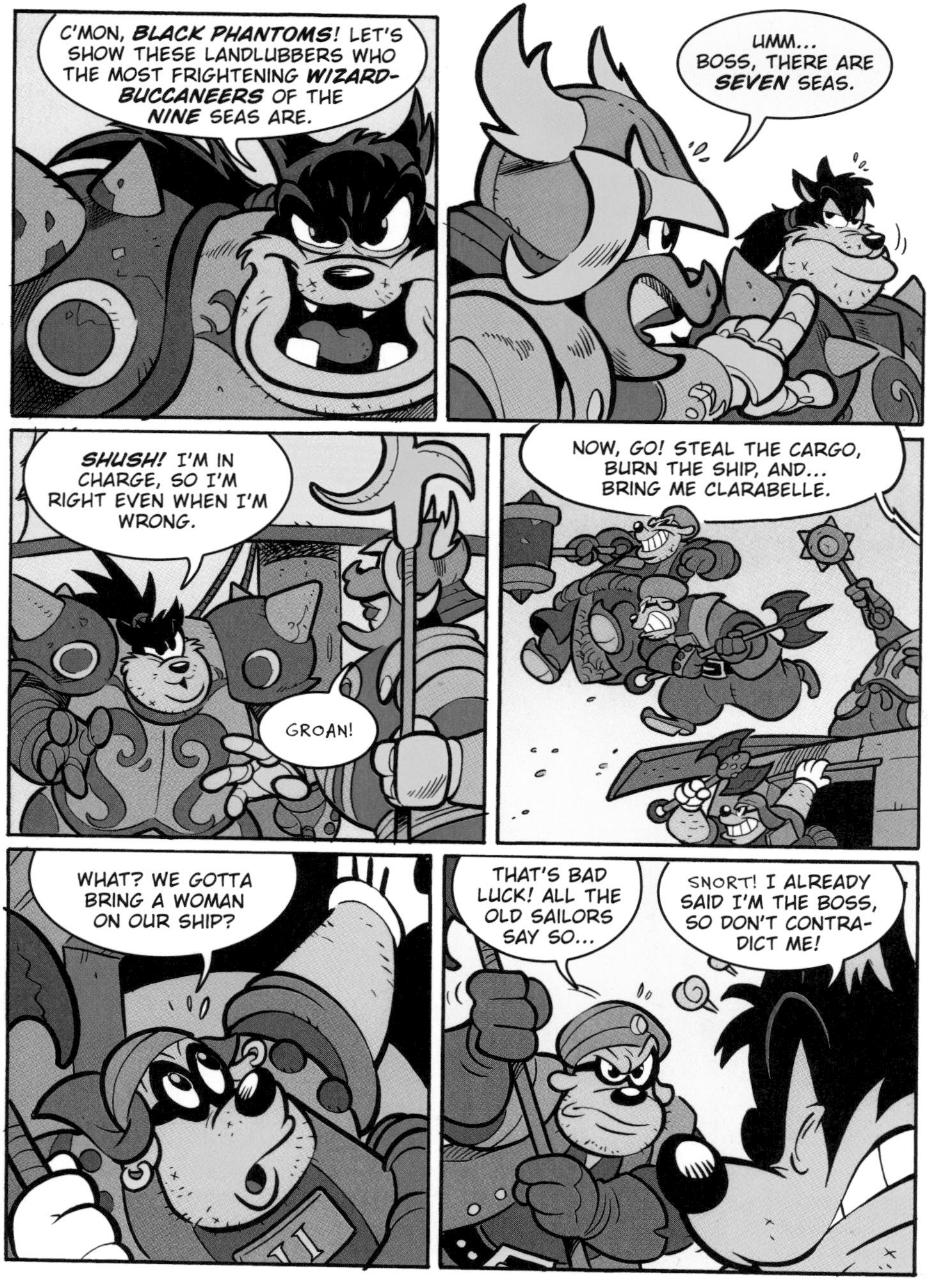

C'MON, BLACK PHANTOMS! LET'S SHOW THESE LANDLUBBERS WHO THE MOST FRIGHTENING WIZARD-BUCCANEERS OF THE NINE SEAS ARE.
UMM... BOSS, THERE ARE SEVEN SEAS.
SHUSH! I'M IN CHARGE, SO I'M RIGHT EVEN WHEN I'M WRONG.
GROAN!
NOW, GO! STEAL THE CARGO, BURN THE SHIP, AND... BRING ME CLARABELLE.
WHAT? WE GOTTA BRING A WOMAN ON OUR SHIP?
THAT'S BAD LUCK! ALL THE OLD SAILORS SAY SO...
SNORT! I ALREADY SAID I'M THE BOSS, SO DON'T CONTRA-DICT ME!

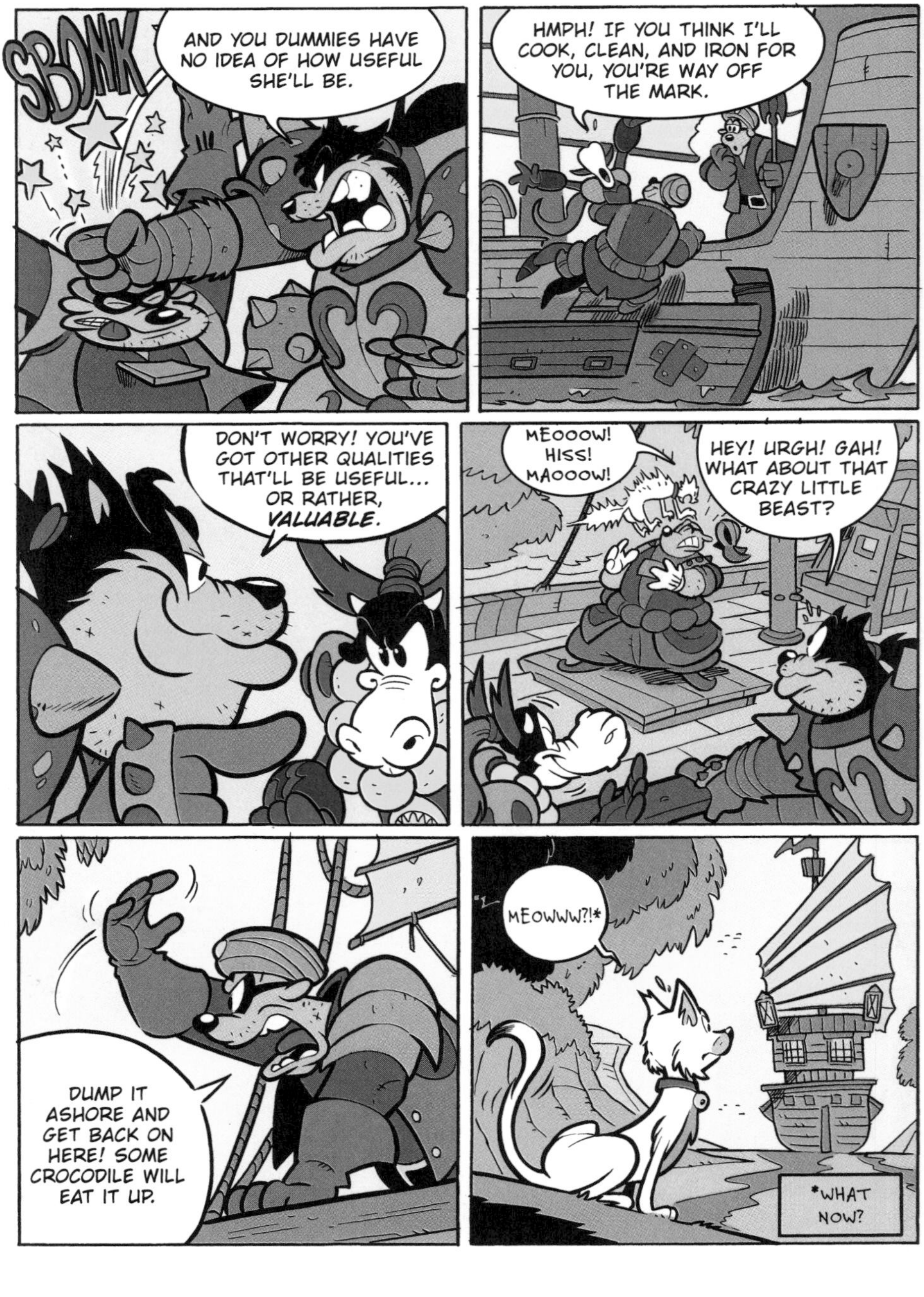
SBONK
AND YOU DUMMIES HAVE NO IDEA OF HOW USEFUL SHE'LL BE.
HMPH! IF YOU THINK I'LL COOK, CLEAN, AND IRON FOR YOU, YOU'RE WAY OFF THE MARK.
DON'T WORRY! YOU'VE GOT OTHER QUALITIES THAT'LL BE USEFUL... OR RATHER, VALUABLE.
MEOOOW! HISS! MAOOOW!
HEY! URGH! GAH! WHAT ABOUT THAT CRAZY LITTLE BEAST?
DUMP IT ASHORE AND GET BACK ON HERE! SOME CROCODILE WILL EAT IT UP.
MEOWWW?!*
*WHAT NOW?

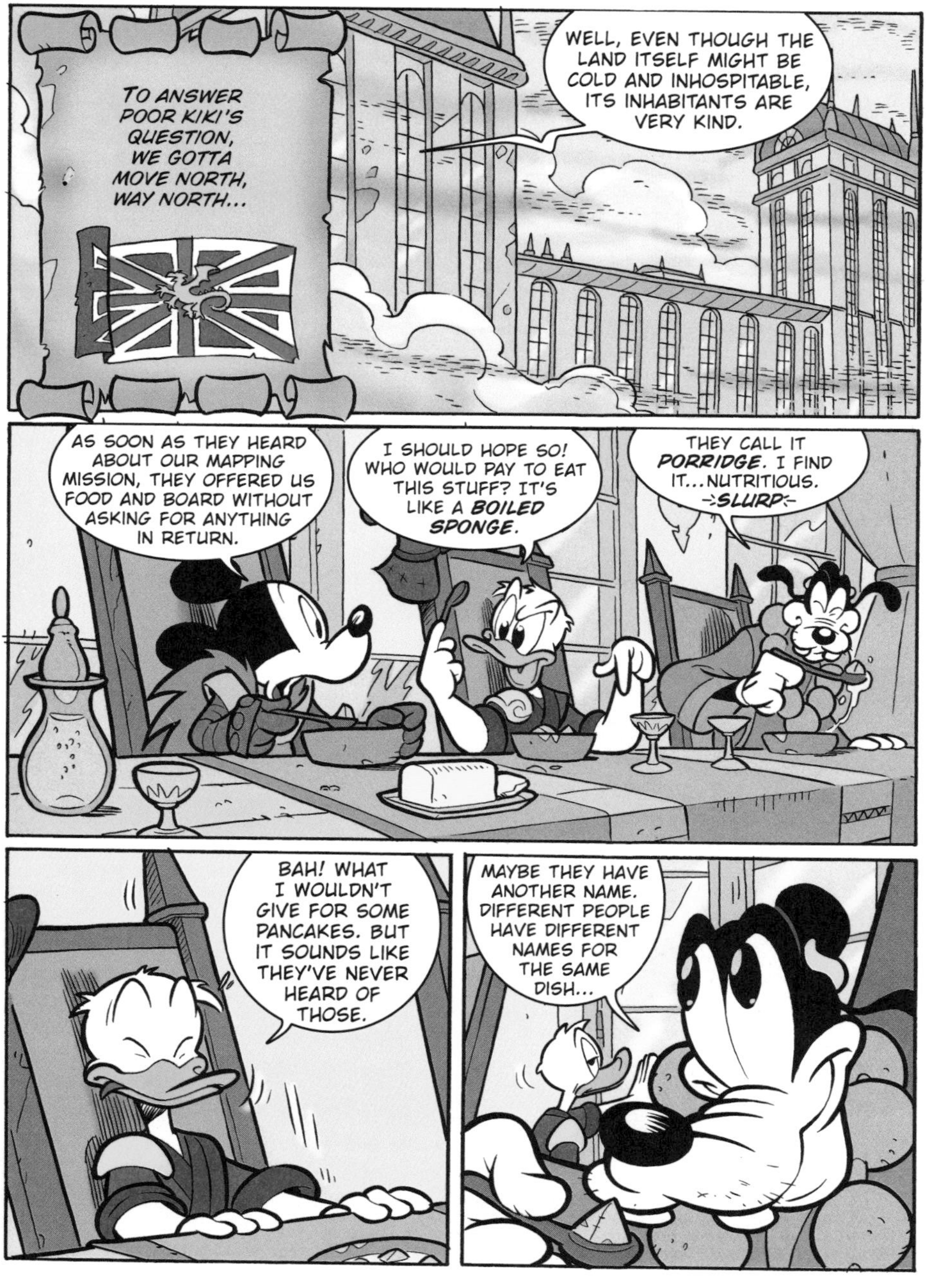
TO ANSWER POOR KIKI'S QUESTION, WE GOTTA MOVE NORTH, WAY NORTH...
WELL, EVEN THOUGH THE LAND ITSELF MIGHT BE COLD AND INHOSPITABLE, ITS INHABITANTS ARE VERY KIND.
AS SOON AS THEY HEARD ABOUT OUR MAPPING MISSION, THEY OFFERED US FOOD AND BOARD WITHOUT ASKING FOR ANYTHING IN RETURN.
I SHOULD HOPE SO! WHO WOULD PAY TO EAT THIS STUFF? IT'S LIKE A **BOILED SPONGE**.
THEY CALL IT **PORRIDGE**. I FIND IT...NUTRITIOUS. **SLURP**
BAH! WHAT I WOULDN'T GIVE FOR SOME PANCAKES. BUT IT SOUNDS LIKE THEY'VE NEVER HEARD OF THOSE.
MAYBE THEY HAVE ANOTHER NAME. DIFFERENT PEOPLE HAVE DIFFERENT NAMES FOR THE SAME DISH...

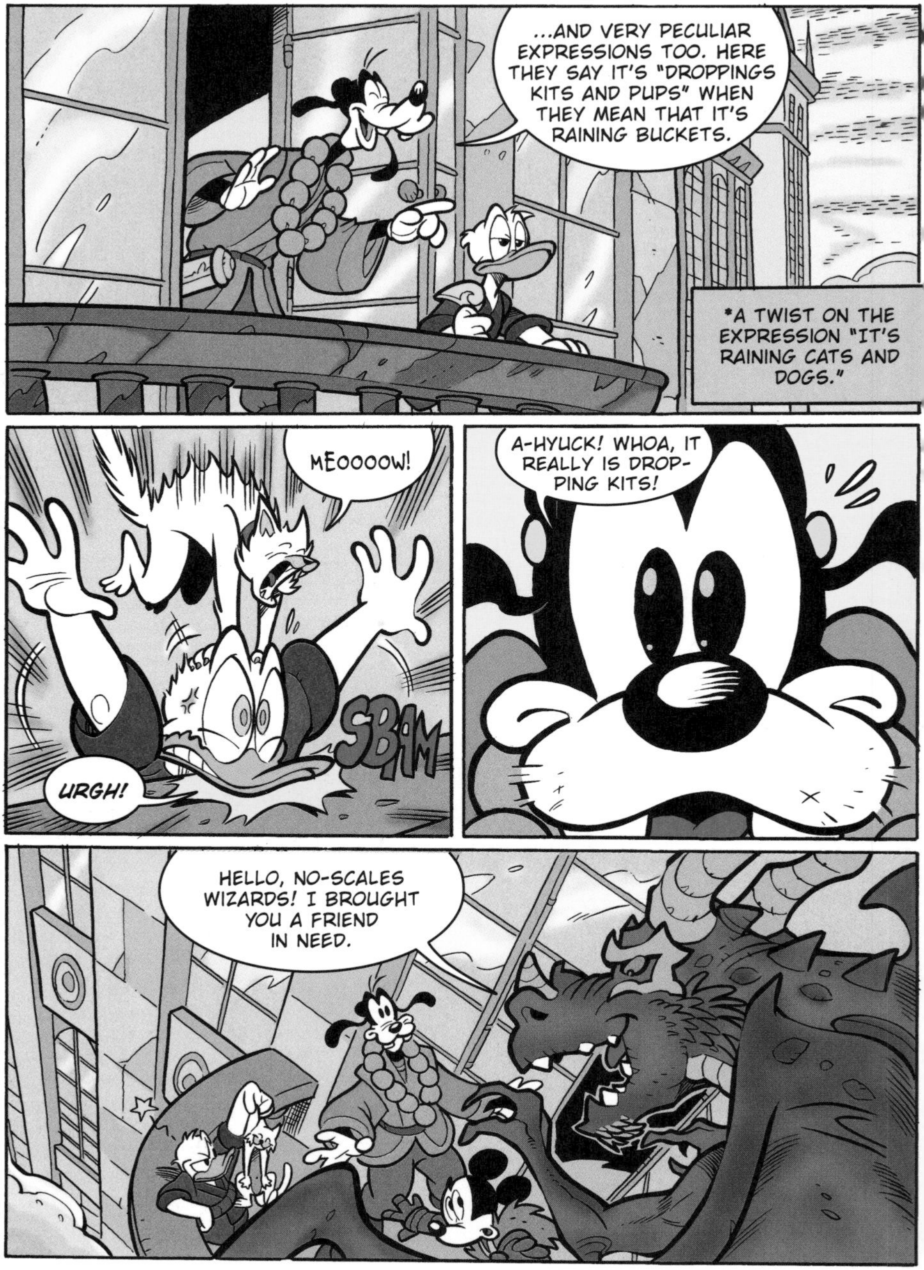
...AND VERY PECULIAR EXPRESSIONS TOO. HERE THEY SAY IT'S "DROPPINGS KITS AND PUPS" WHEN THEY MEAN THAT IT'S RAINING BUCKETS.
*A TWIST ON THE EXPRESSION "IT'S RAINING CATS AND DOGS."
MEOOOOW!
SBAM
URGH!
A-HYUCK! WHOA, IT REALLY IS DROP-PING KITS!
HELLO, NO-SCALES WIZARDS! I BROUGHT YOU A FRIEND IN NEED.

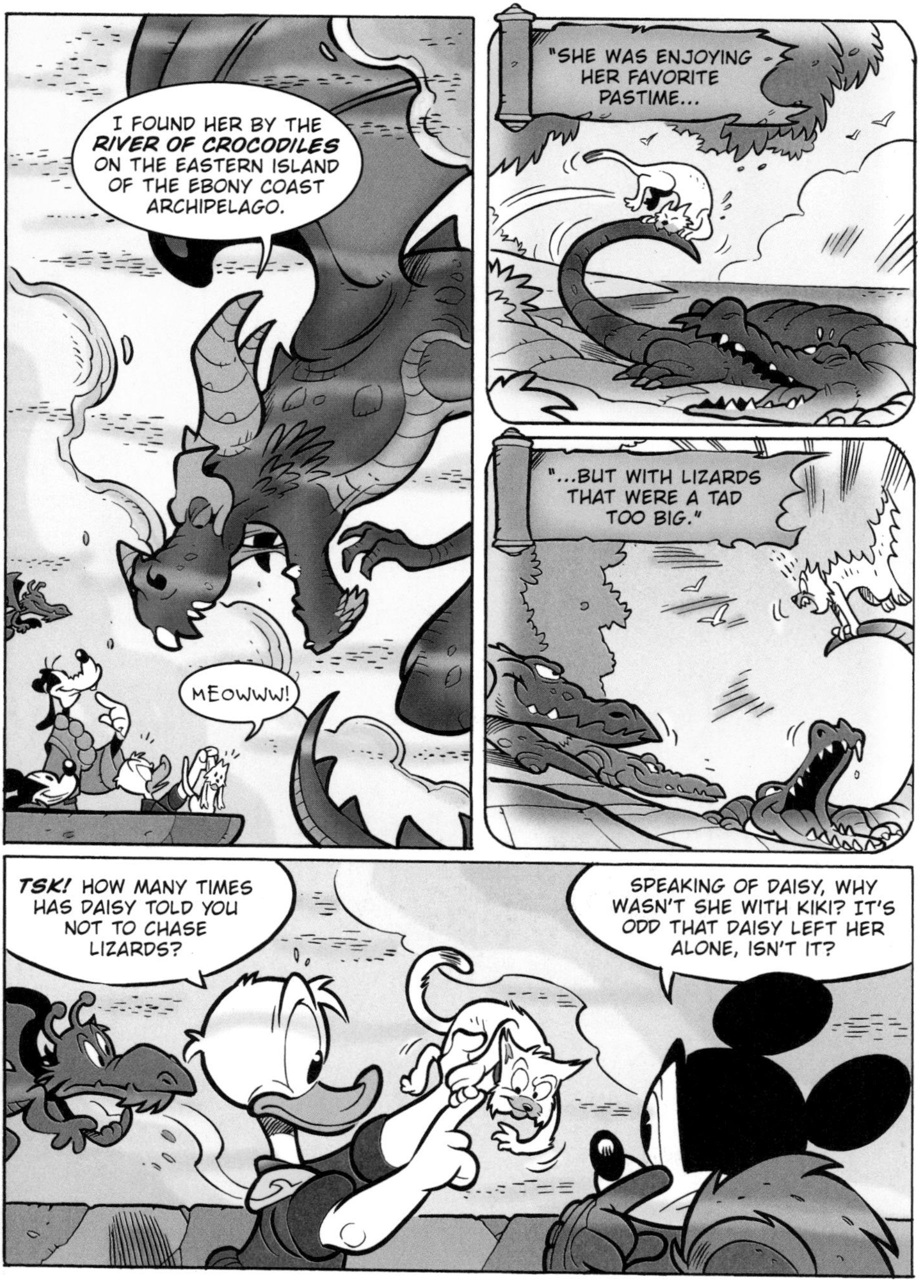
I FOUND HER BY THE ***RIVER OF CROCODILES*** ON THE EASTERN ISLAND OF THE EBONY COAST ARCHIPELAGO.
MEOWWW!
"SHE WAS ENJOYING HER FAVORITE PASTIME...
"...BUT WITH LIZARDS THAT WERE A TAD TOO BIG."
TSK! HOW MANY TIMES HAS DAISY TOLD YOU NOT TO CHASE LIZARDS?
SPEAKING OF DAISY, WHY WASN'T SHE WITH KIKI? IT'S ODD THAT DAISY LEFT HER ALONE, ISN'T IT?

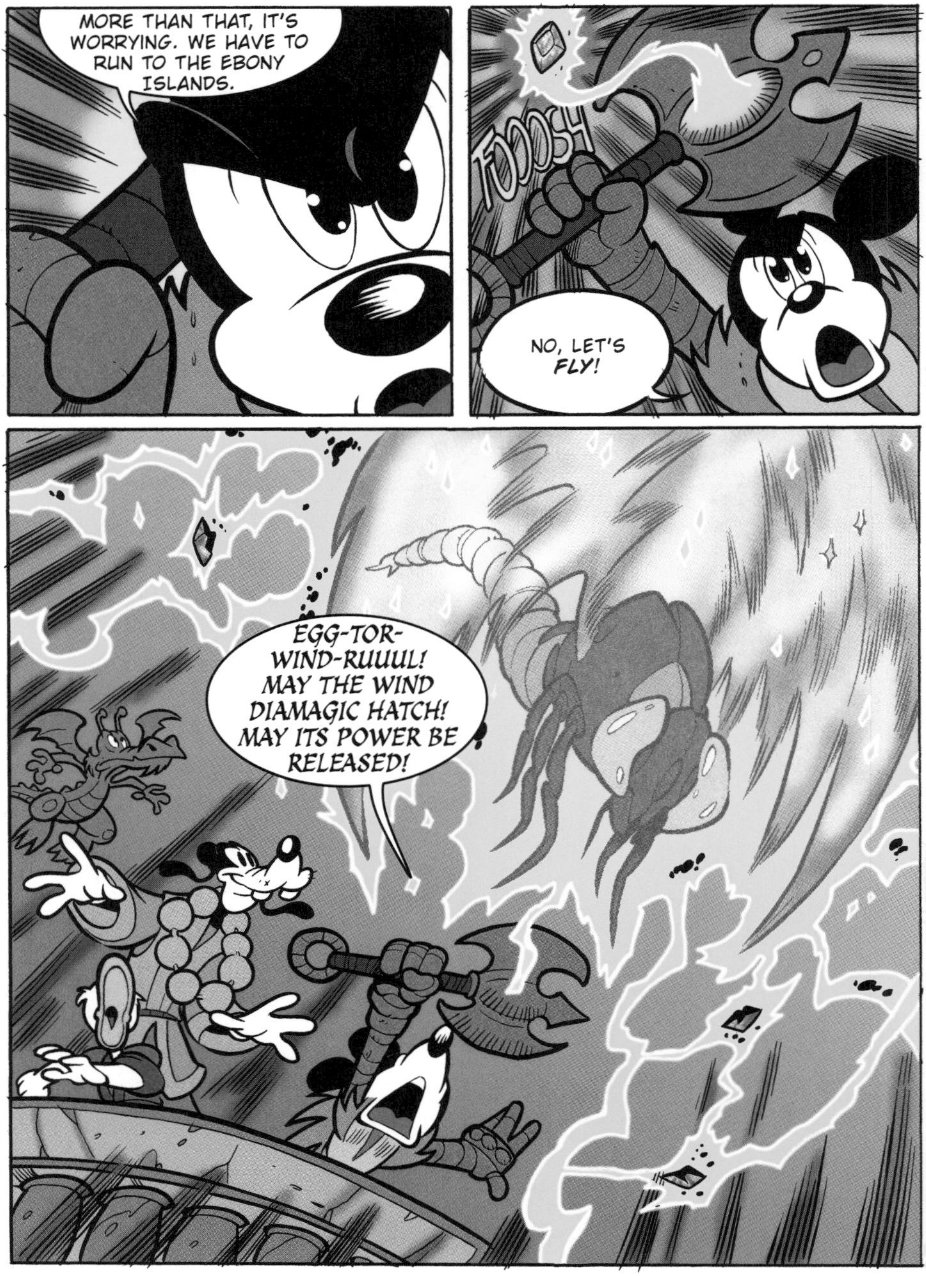
MORE THAN THAT, IT'S WORRYING. WE HAVE TO RUN TO THE EBONY ISLANDS.
FOOOSH
NO, LET'S *FLY*!
EGG-TOR-WIND-RUUUL! MAY THE WIND DIAMAGIC HATCH! MAY ITS POWER BE RELEASED!

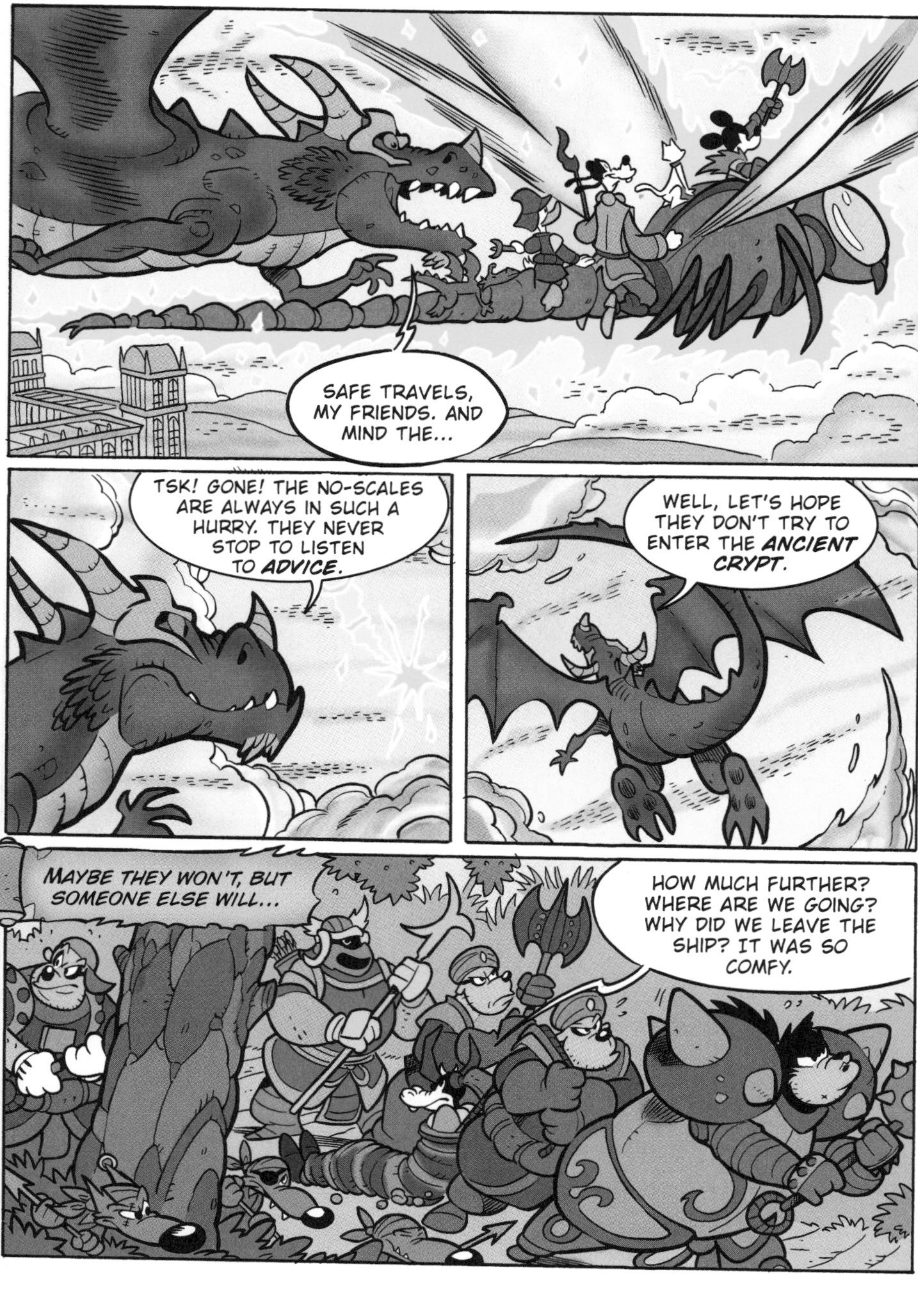
SAFE TRAVELS, MY FRIENDS. AND MIND THE...
TSK! GONE! THE NO-SCALES ARE ALWAYS IN SUCH A HURRY. THEY NEVER STOP TO LISTEN TO ADVICE.
WELL, LET'S HOPE THEY DON'T TRY TO ENTER THE ANCIENT CRYPT.
MAYBE THEY WON'T, BUT SOMEONE ELSE WILL...
HOW MUCH FURTHER? WHERE ARE WE GOING? WHY DID WE LEAVE THE SHIP? IT WAS SO COMFY.

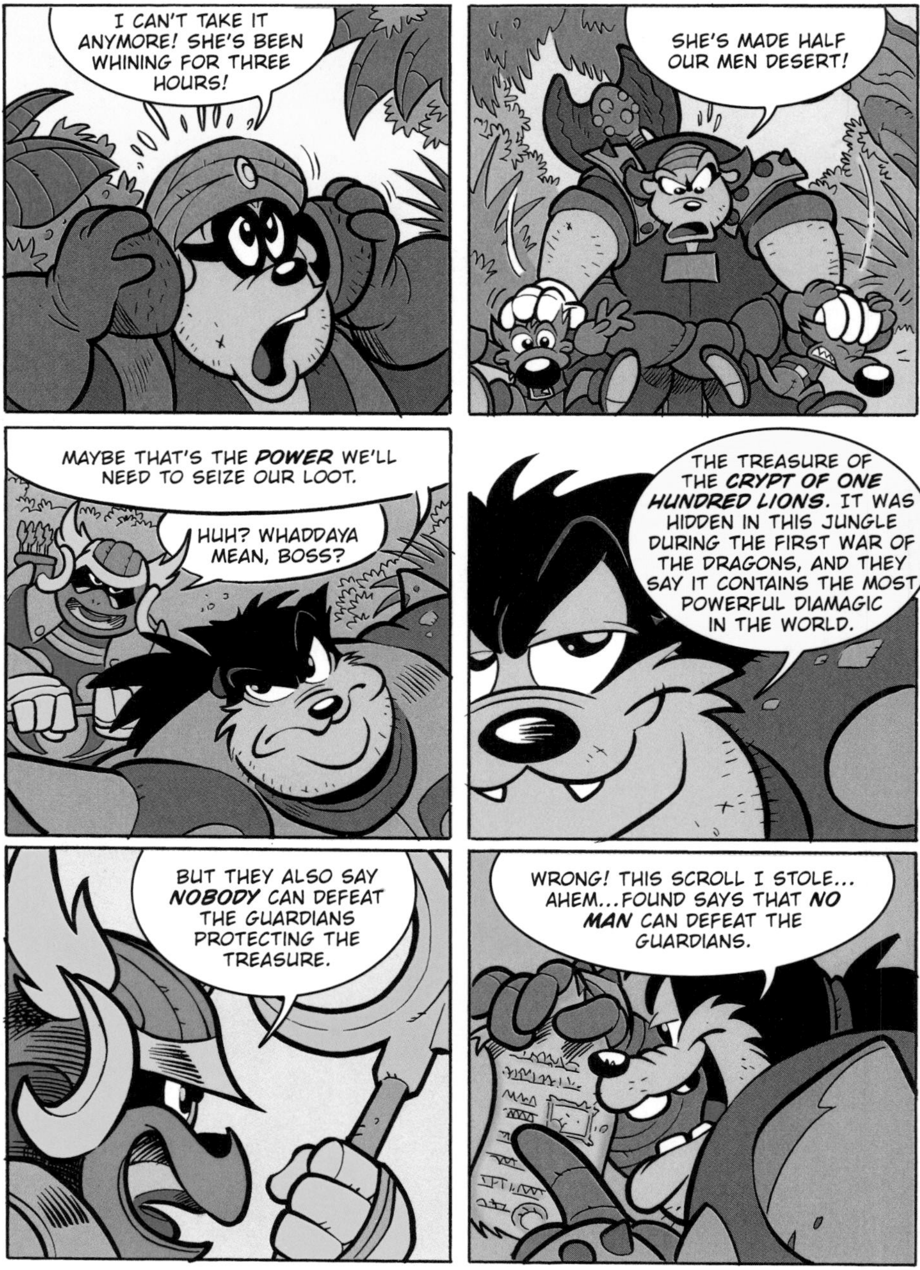
I CAN'T TAKE IT ANYMORE! SHE'S BEEN WHINING FOR THREE HOURS!
SHE'S MADE HALF OUR MEN DESERT!
MAYBE THAT'S THE **POWER** WE'LL NEED TO SEIZE OUR LOOT.
HUH? WHADDAYA MEAN, BOSS?
THE TREASURE OF THE **CRYPT OF ONE HUNDRED LIONS**. IT WAS HIDDEN IN THIS JUNGLE DURING THE FIRST WAR OF THE DRAGONS, AND THEY SAY IT CONTAINS THE MOST POWERFUL DIAMAGIC IN THE WORLD.
BUT THEY ALSO SAY **NOBODY** CAN DEFEAT THE GUARDIANS PROTECTING THE TREASURE.
WRONG! THIS SCROLL I STOLE... AHEM...FOUND SAYS THAT **NO MAN** CAN DEFEAT THE GUARDIANS.

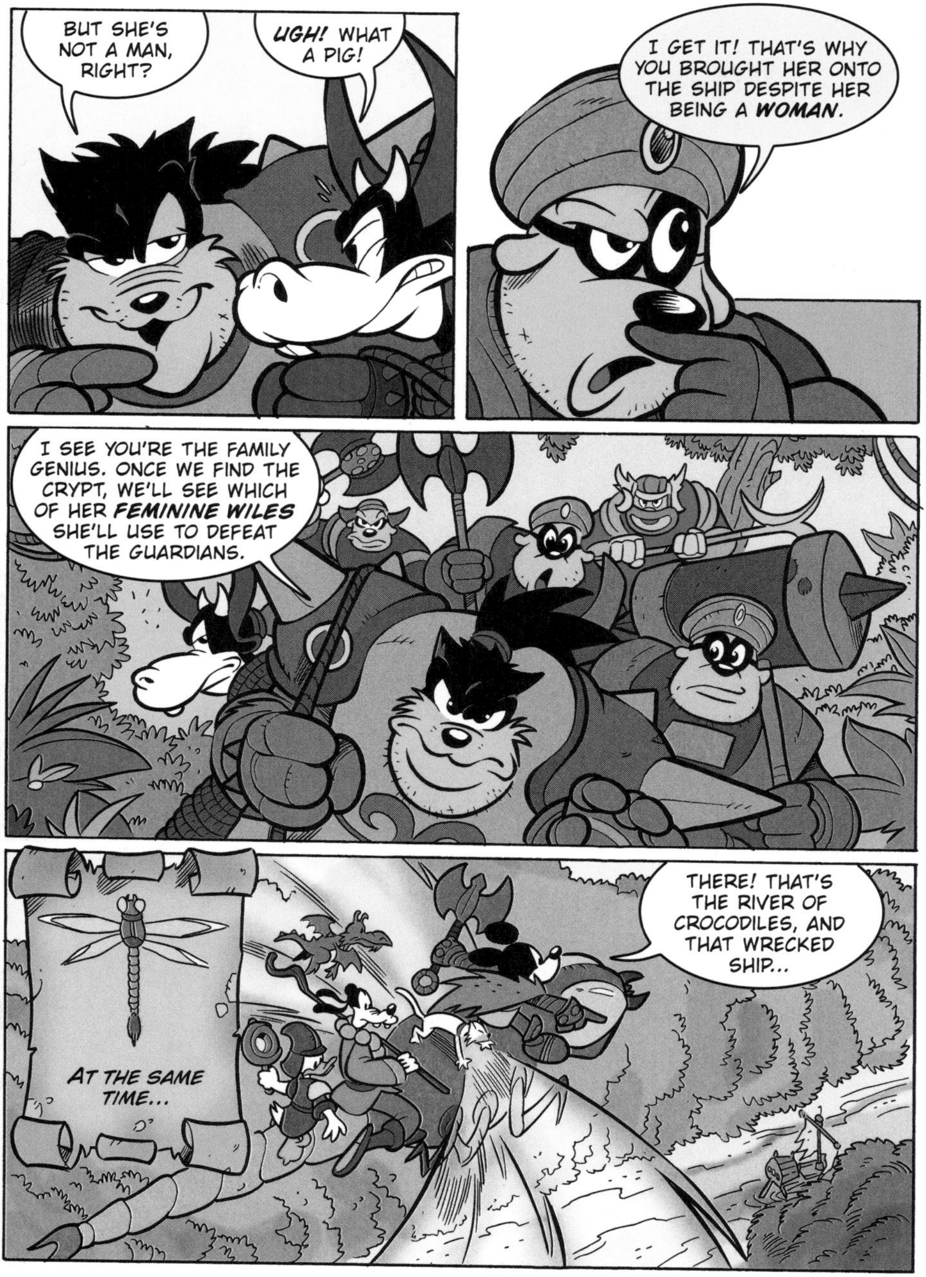
BUT SHE'S NOT A MAN, RIGHT?
UGH! WHAT A PIG!
I GET IT! THAT'S WHY YOU BROUGHT HER ONTO THE SHIP DESPITE HER BEING A WOMAN.
I SEE YOU'RE THE FAMILY GENIUS. ONCE WE FIND THE CRYPT, WE'LL SEE WHICH OF HER FEMININE WILES SHE'LL USE TO DEFEAT THE GUARDIANS.
AT THE SAME TIME...
THERE! THAT'S THE RIVER OF CROCODILES, AND THAT WRECKED SHIP...

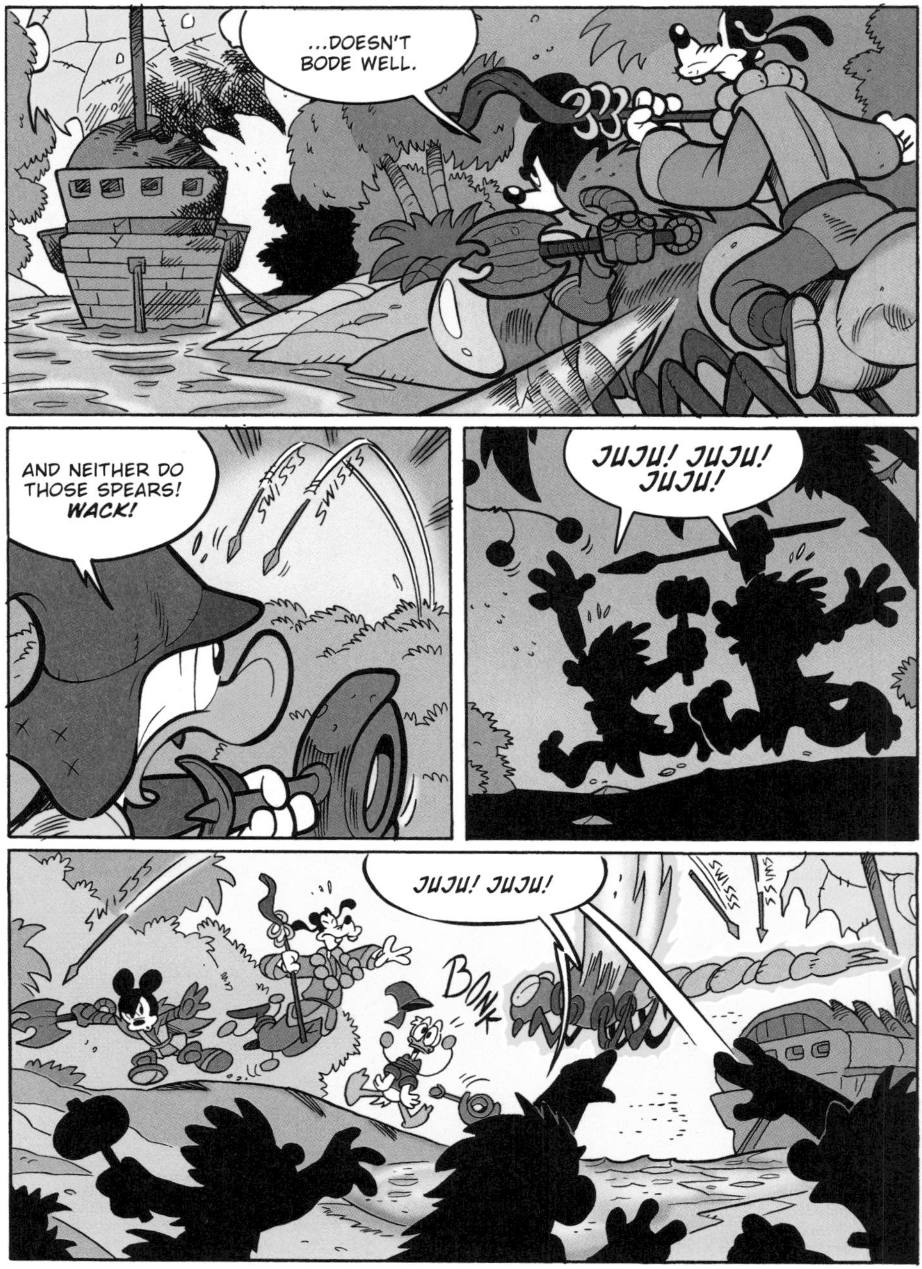

...DOESN'T BODE WELL.
AND NEITHER DO THOSE SPEARS! WACK!
SWISSS
SWISSS
JUJU! JUJU! JUJU!
SWISSSS
JUJU! JUJU!
SWISSS
SWISSS
BONK

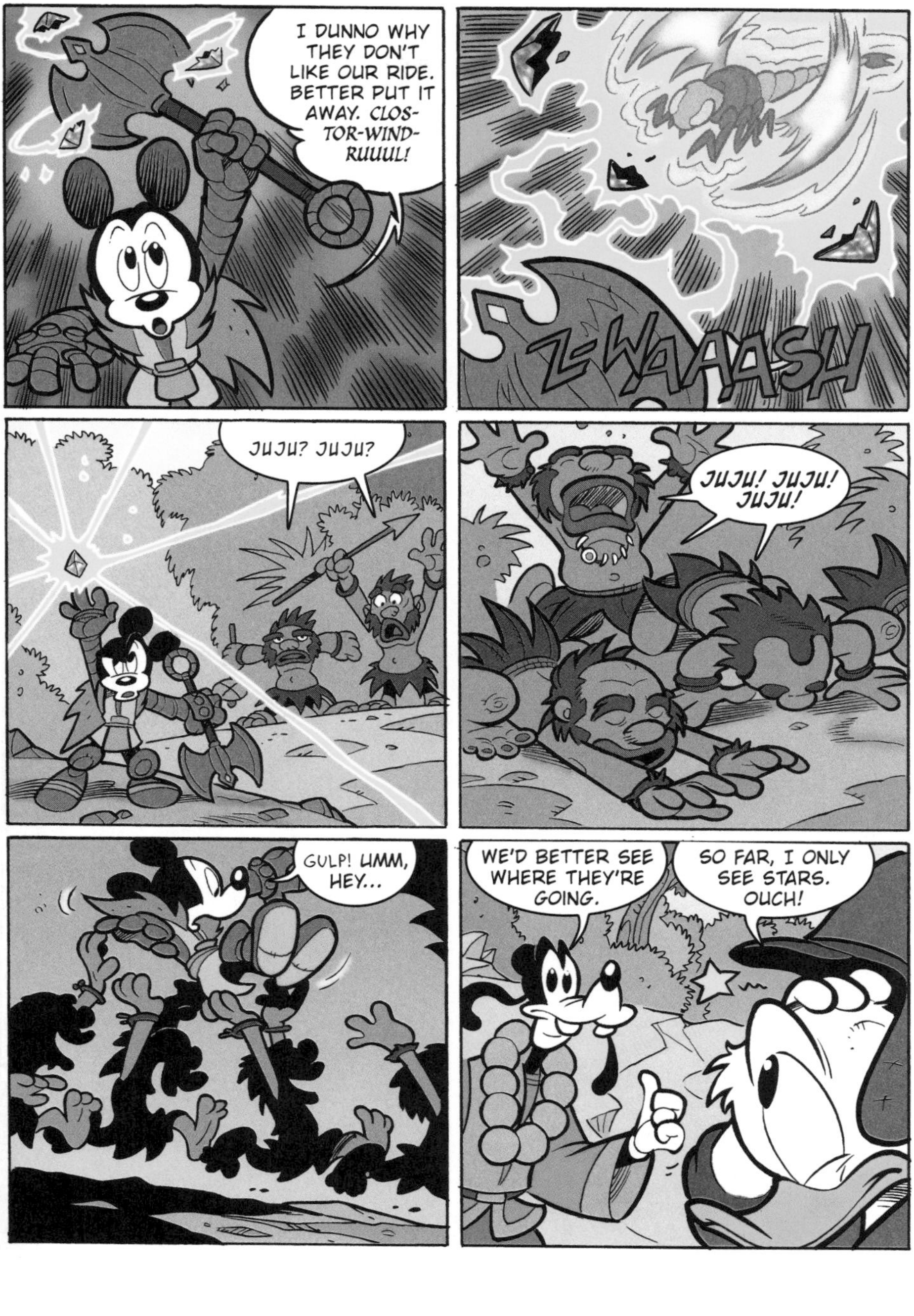
I DUNNO WHY THEY DON'T LIKE OUR RIDE. BETTER PUT IT AWAY. CLOS-TOR-WIND-RUUUL!
Z-WAAASH
JUJU? JUJU?
JUJU! JUJU! JUJU!
GULP! UMM, HEY...
WE'D BETTER SEE WHERE THEY'RE GOING.
SO FAR, I ONLY SEE STARS. OUCH!

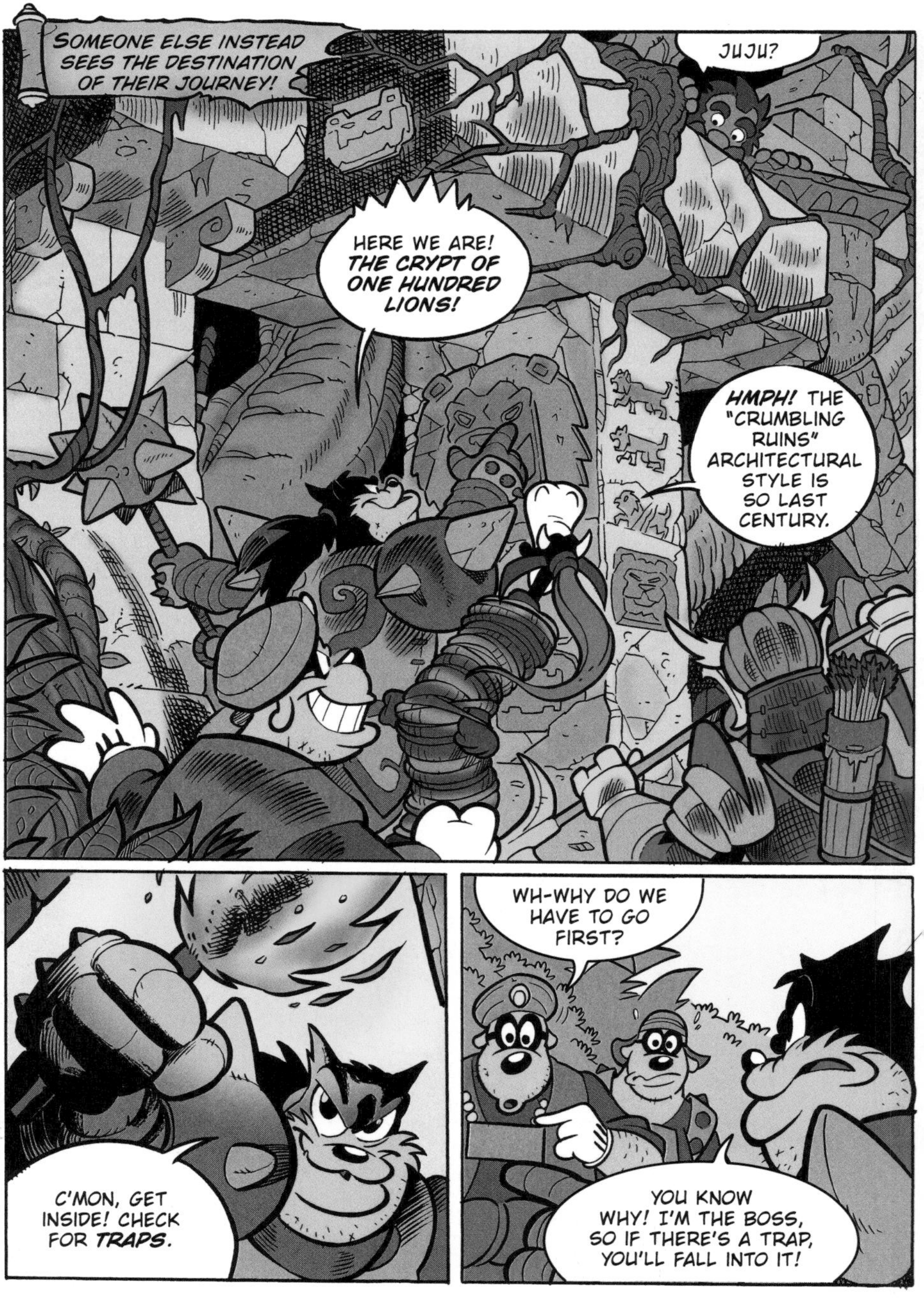
SOMEONE ELSE INSTEAD SEES THE DESTINATION OF THEIR JOURNEY!
JUJU?
HERE WE ARE! ***THE CRYPT OF ONE HUNDRED LIONS!***
HMPH! THE "CRUMBLING RUINS" ARCHITECTURAL STYLE IS SO LAST CENTURY.
C'MON, GET INSIDE! CHECK FOR ***TRAPS***.
WH-WHY DO WE HAVE TO GO FIRST?
YOU KNOW WHY! I'M THE BOSS, SO IF THERE'S A TRAP, YOU'LL FALL INTO IT!

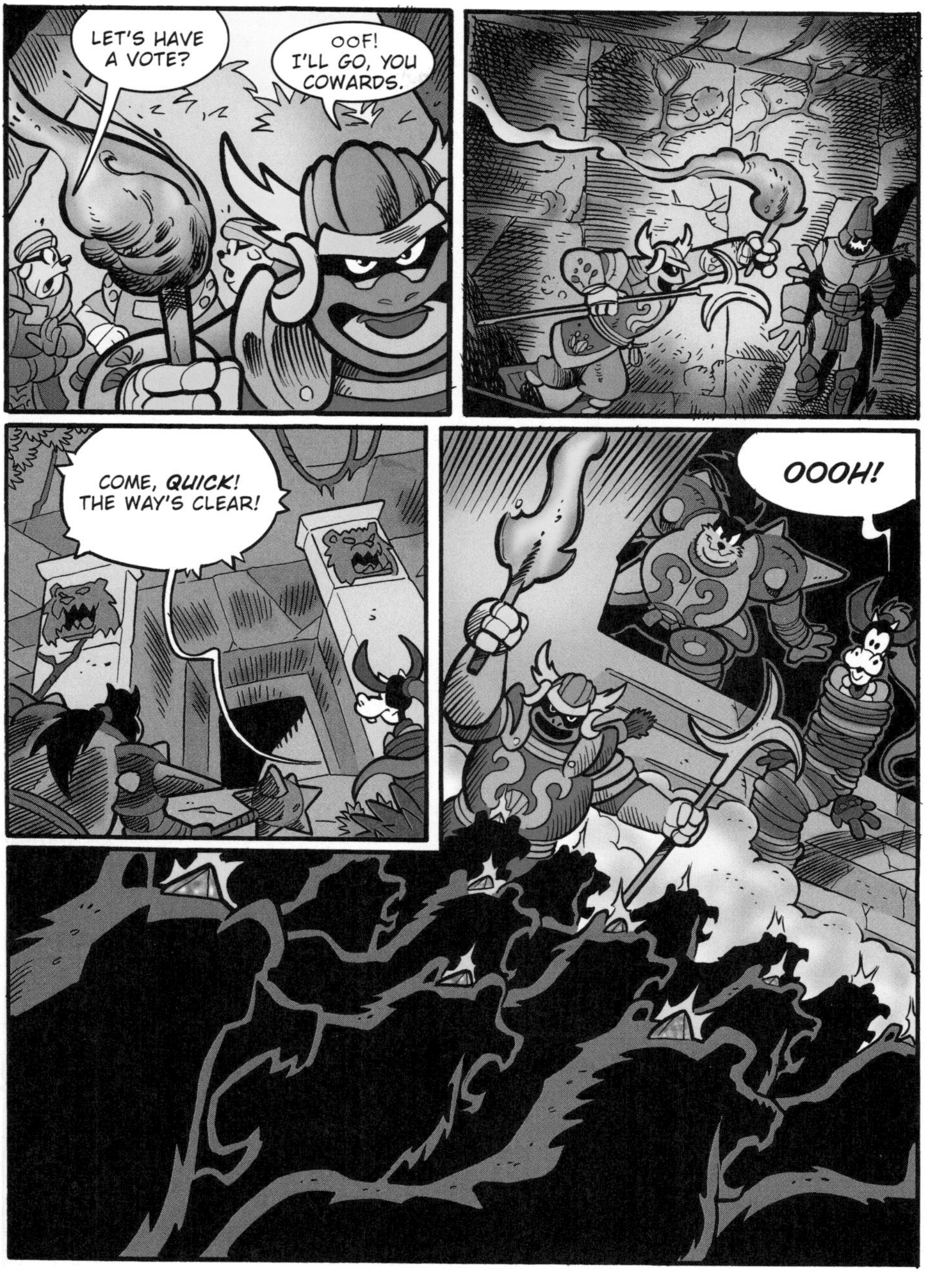
LET'S HAVE A VOTE?
OOF! I'LL GO, YOU COWARDS.
COME, QUICK! THE WAY'S CLEAR!
OOOH!

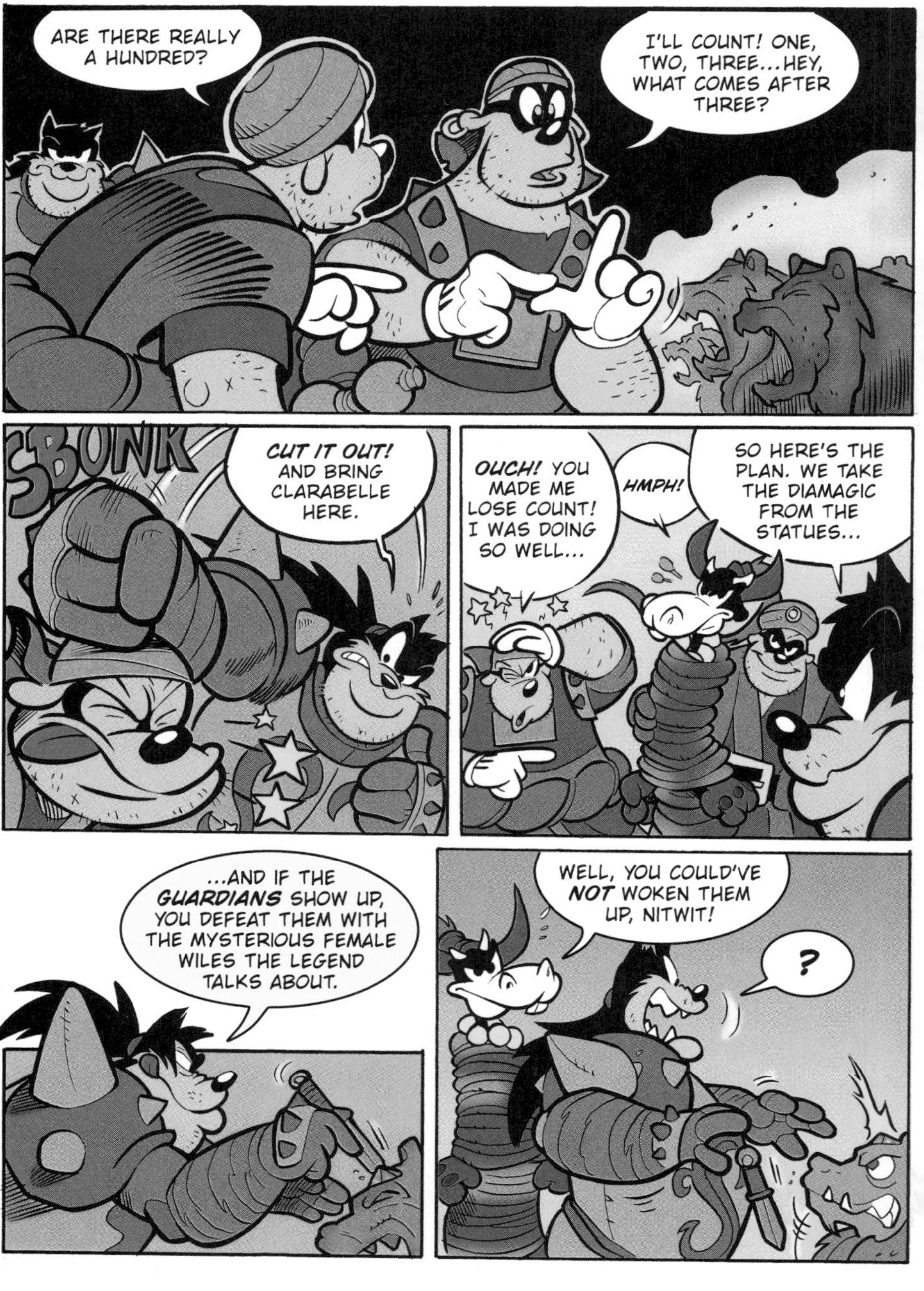
ARE THERE REALLY A HUNDRED?
I'LL COUNT! ONE, TWO, THREE...HEY, WHAT COMES AFTER THREE?
SBONK
CUT IT OUT! AND BRING CLARABELLE HERE.
OUCH! YOU MADE ME LOSE COUNT! I WAS DOING SO WELL...
HMPH!
SO HERE'S THE PLAN. WE TAKE THE DIAMAGIC FROM THE STATUES...
...AND IF THE GUARDIANS SHOW UP, YOU DEFEAT THEM WITH THE MYSTERIOUS FEMALE WILES THE LEGEND TALKS ABOUT.
WELL, YOU COULD'VE NOT WOKEN THEM UP, NITWIT!
?

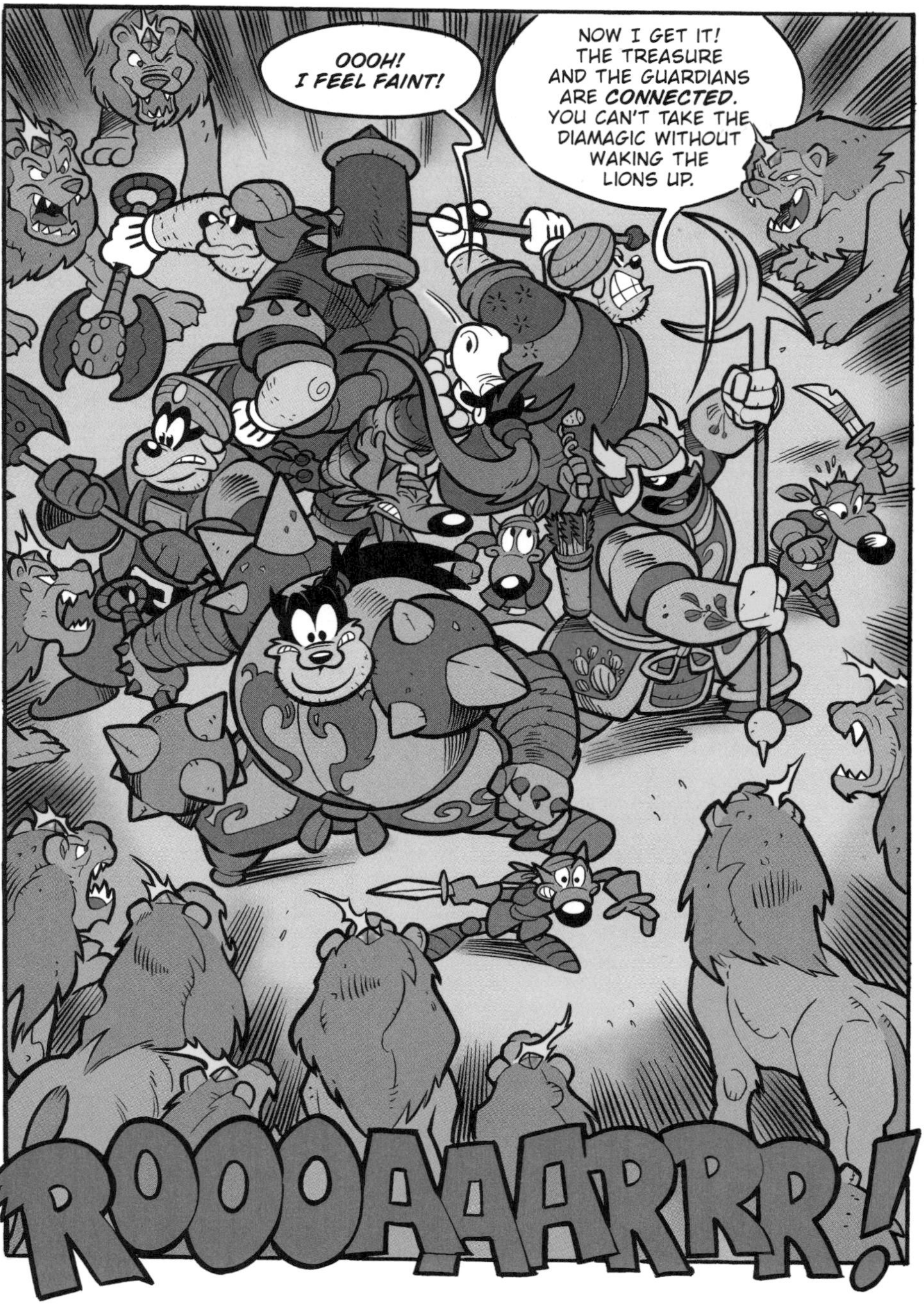
OOOH! I FEEL FAINT!
NOW I GET IT! THE TREASURE AND THE GUARDIANS ARE **CONNECTED.** YOU CAN'T TAKE THE DIAMAGIC WITHOUT WAKING THE LIONS UP.
ROOOAAARRR!

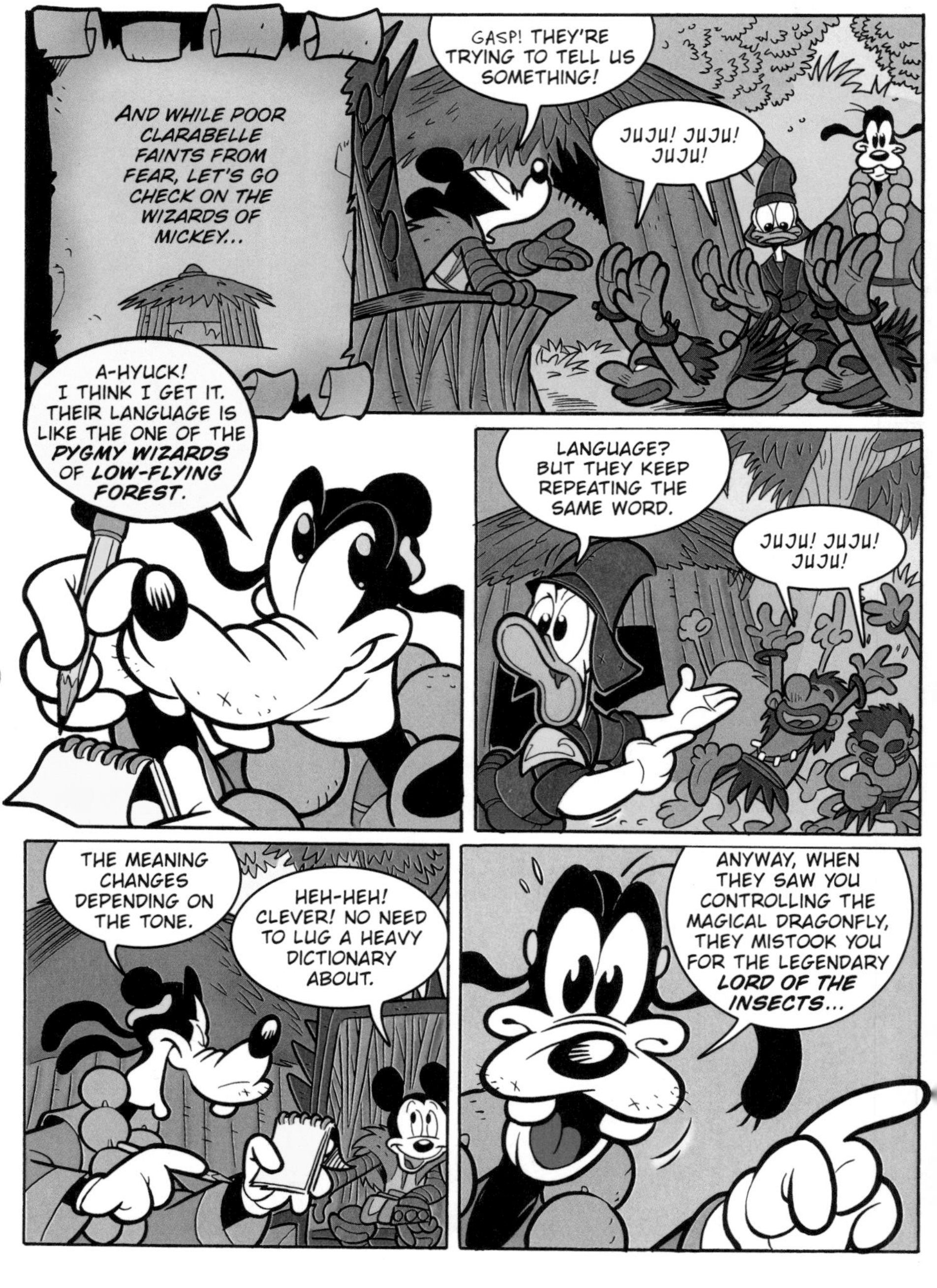

AND WHILE POOR CLARABELLE FAINTS FROM FEAR, LET'S GO CHECK ON THE WIZARDS OF MICKEY...
GASP! THEY'RE TRYING TO TELL US SOMETHING!
JUJU! JUJU! JUJU!
A-HYUCK! I THINK I GET IT. THEIR LANGUAGE IS LIKE THE ONE OF THE PYGMY WIZARDS OF LOW-FLYING FOREST.
LANGUAGE? BUT THEY KEEP REPEATING THE SAME WORD.
JUJU! JUJU! JUJU!
THE MEANING CHANGES DEPENDING ON THE TONE.
HEH-HEH! CLEVER! NO NEED TO LUG A HEAVY DICTIONARY ABOUT.
ANYWAY, WHEN THEY SAW YOU CONTROLLING THE MAGICAL DRAGONFLY, THEY MISTOOK YOU FOR THE LEGENDARY LORD OF THE INSECTS...

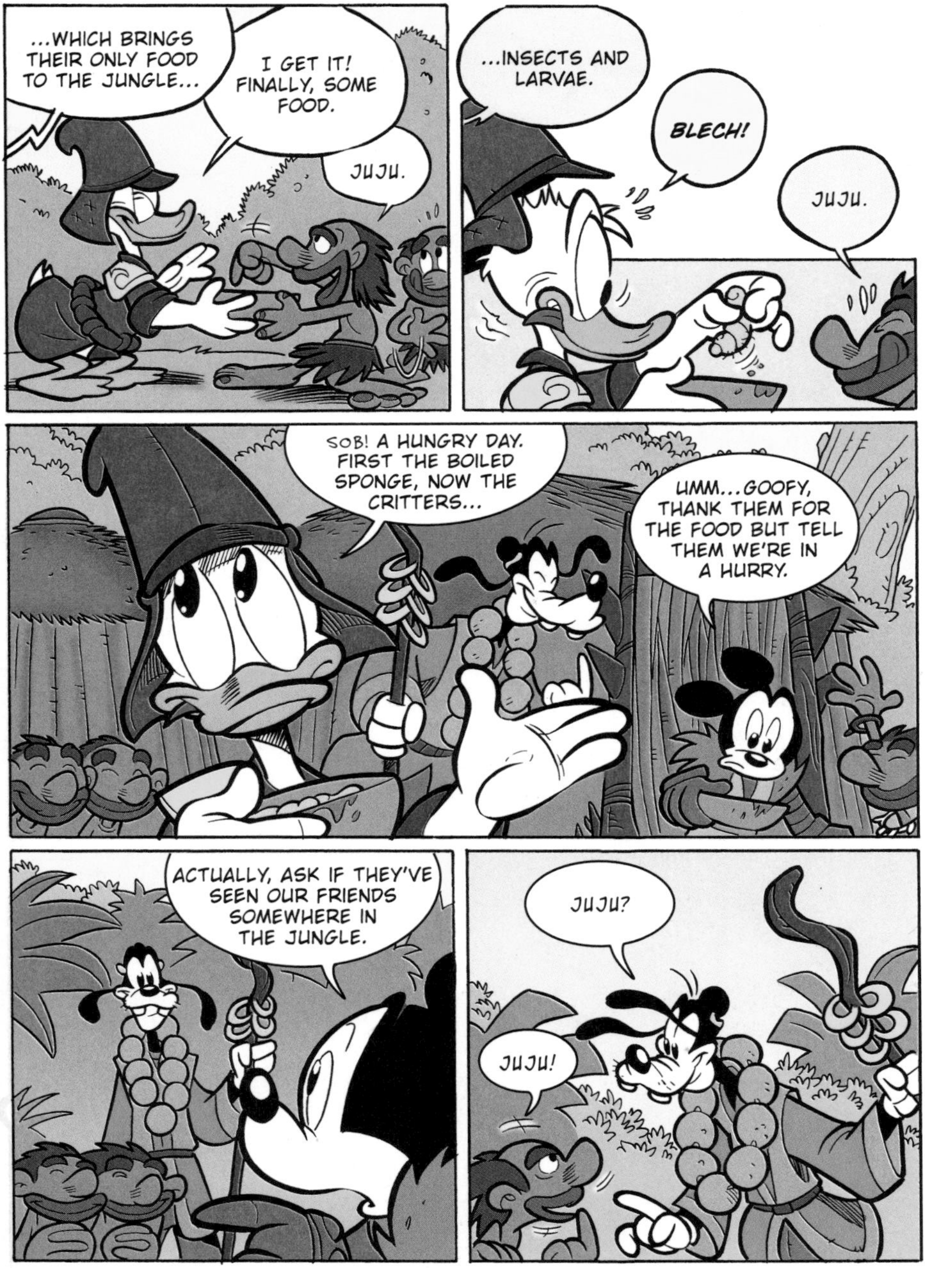
...WHICH BRINGS THEIR ONLY FOOD TO THE JUNGLE...
I GET IT! FINALLY, SOME FOOD.
JUJU.
...INSECTS AND LARVAE.
BLECH!
JUJU.
SOB! A HUNGRY DAY. FIRST THE BOILED SPONGE, NOW THE CRITTERS...
UMM...GOOFY, THANK THEM FOR THE FOOD BUT TELL THEM WE'RE IN A HURRY.
ACTUALLY, ASK IF THEY'VE SEEN OUR FRIENDS SOMEWHERE IN THE JUNGLE.
JUJU?
JUJU!

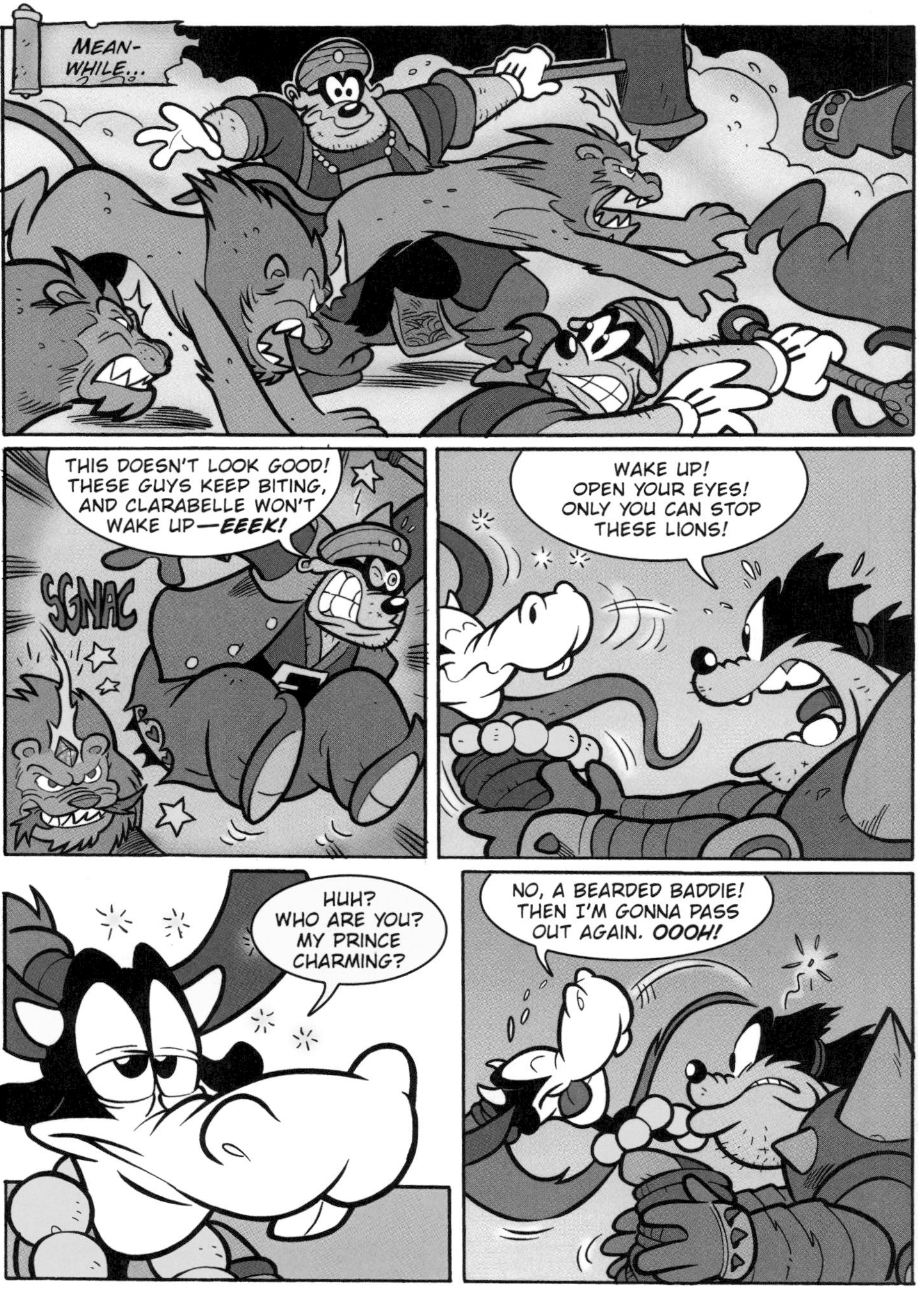
MEAN-WHILE...
THIS DOESN'T LOOK GOOD! THESE GUYS KEEP BITING, AND CLARABELLE WON'T WAKE UP—EEEK!
SGNAC
WAKE UP! OPEN YOUR EYES! ONLY YOU CAN STOP THESE LIONS!
HUH? WHO ARE YOU? MY PRINCE CHARMING?
NO, A BEARDED BADDIE! THEN I'M GONNA PASS OUT AGAIN. OOOH!

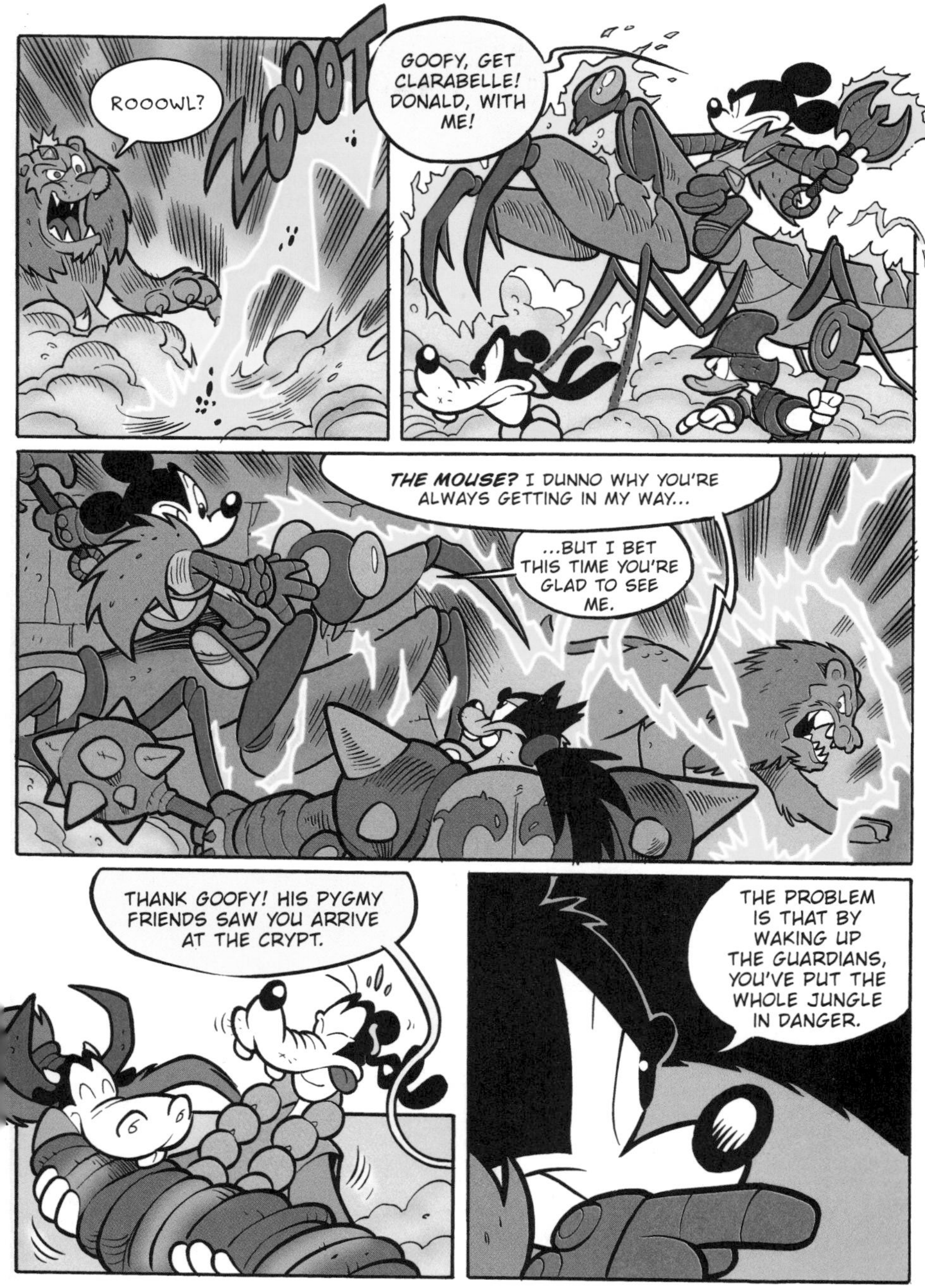
ROOOWL?
ZOOOT
GOOFY, GET CLARABELLE! DONALD, WITH ME!
THE MOUSE? I DUNNO WHY YOU'RE ALWAYS GETTING IN MY WAY...
...BUT I BET THIS TIME YOU'RE GLAD TO SEE ME.
THANK GOOFY! HIS PYGMY FRIENDS SAW YOU ARRIVE AT THE CRYPT.
THE PROBLEM IS THAT BY WAKING UP THE GUARDIANS, YOU'VE PUT THE WHOLE JUNGLE IN DANGER.

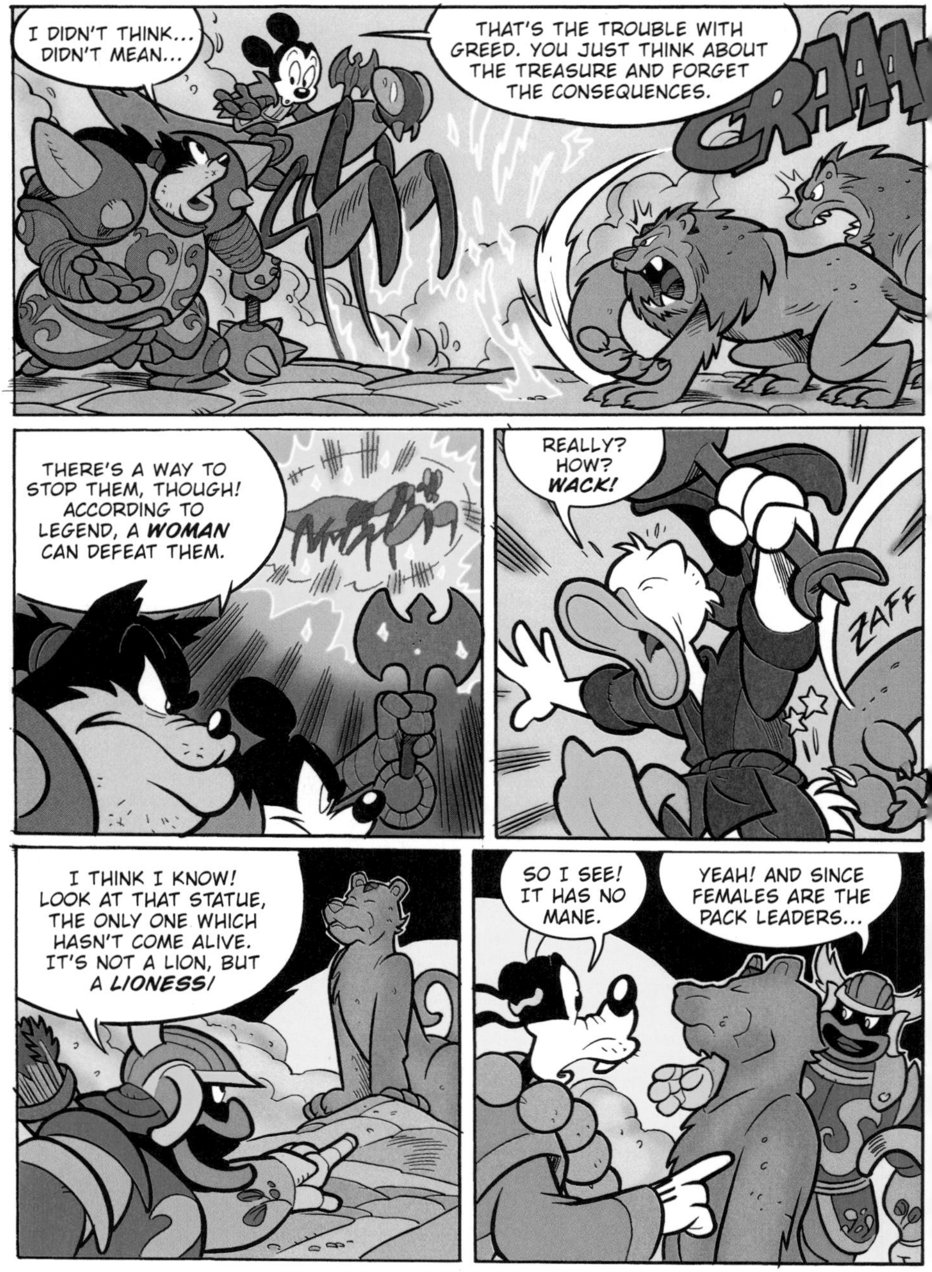

I DIDN'T THINK... DIDN'T MEAN...
THAT'S THE TROUBLE WITH GREED. YOU JUST THINK ABOUT THE TREASURE AND FORGET THE CONSEQUENCES.
CRAAA
THERE'S A WAY TO STOP THEM, THOUGH! ACCORDING TO LEGEND, A WOMAN CAN DEFEAT THEM.
REALLY? HOW? WACK!
ZAFF
I THINK I KNOW! LOOK AT THAT STATUE, THE ONLY ONE WHICH HASN'T COME ALIVE. IT'S NOT A LION, BUT A LIONESS!
SO I SEE! IT HAS NO MANE.
YEAH! AND SINCE FEMALES ARE THE PACK LEADERS...

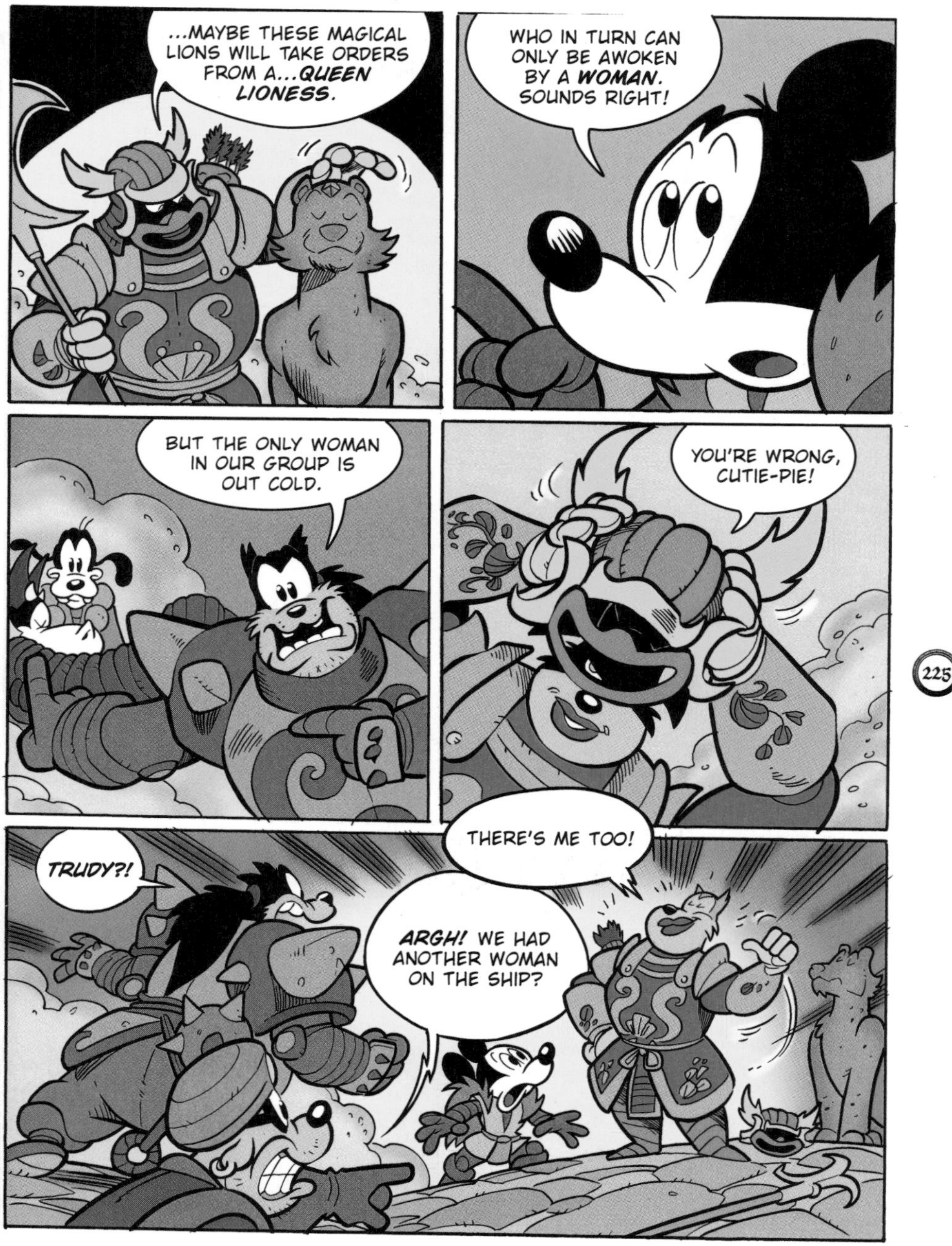
...MAYBE THESE MAGICAL LIONS WILL TAKE ORDERS FROM A...QUEEN LIONESS.
WHO IN TURN CAN ONLY BE AWOKEN BY A WOMAN. SOUNDS RIGHT!
BUT THE ONLY WOMAN IN OUR GROUP IS OUT COLD.
YOU'RE WRONG, CUTIE-PIE!
TRUDY?!
THERE'S ME TOO!
ARGH! WE HAD ANOTHER WOMAN ON THE SHIP?

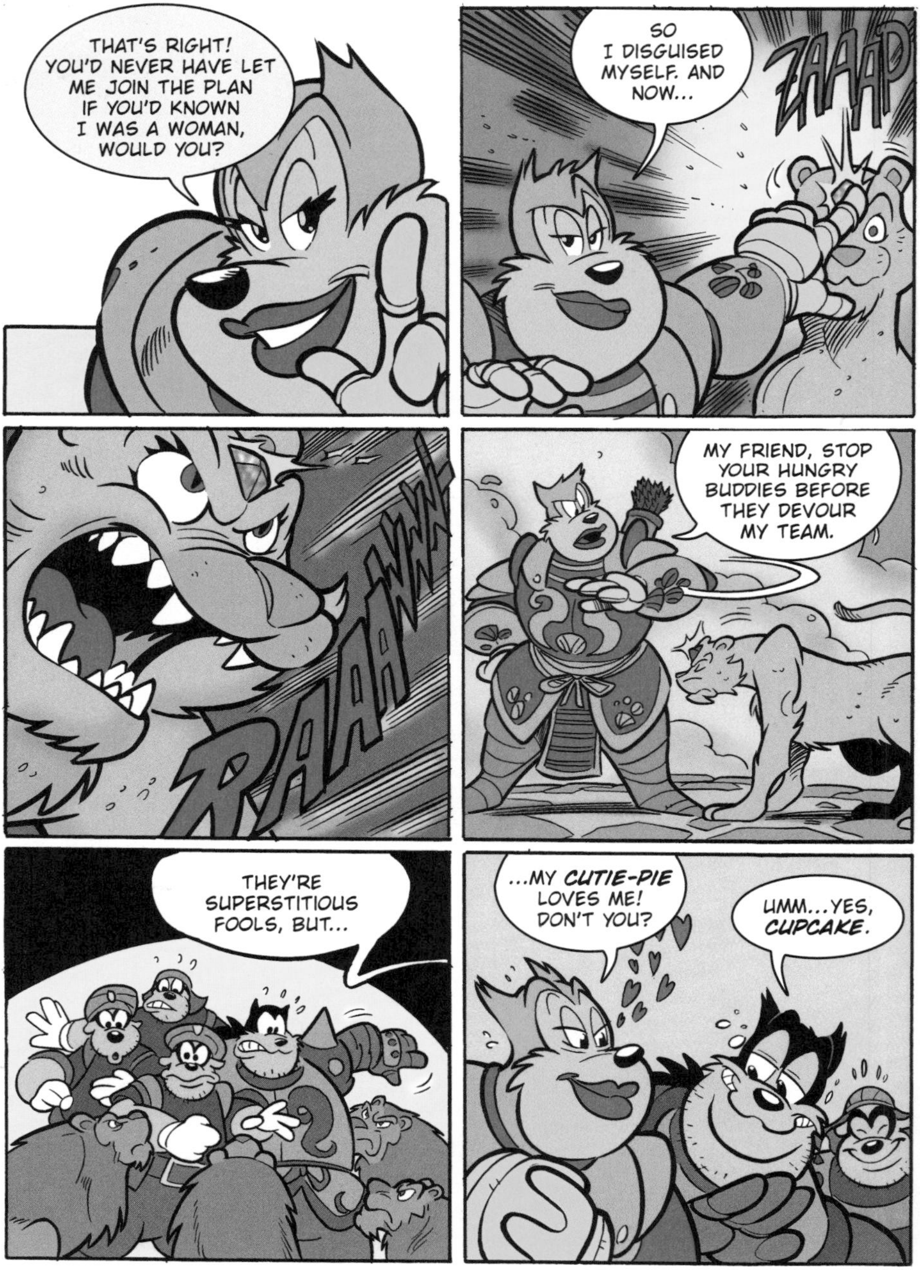
THAT'S RIGHT! YOU'D NEVER HAVE LET ME JOIN THE PLAN IF YOU'D KNOWN I WAS A WOMAN, WOULD YOU?
SO I DISGUISED MYSELF. AND NOW...
ZAAAP
RAAAWWK
MY FRIEND, STOP YOUR HUNGRY BUDDIES BEFORE THEY DEVOUR MY TEAM.
THEY'RE SUPERSTITIOUS FOOLS, BUT...
...MY CUTIE-PIE LOVES ME! DON'T YOU?
UMM...YES, CUPCAKE.

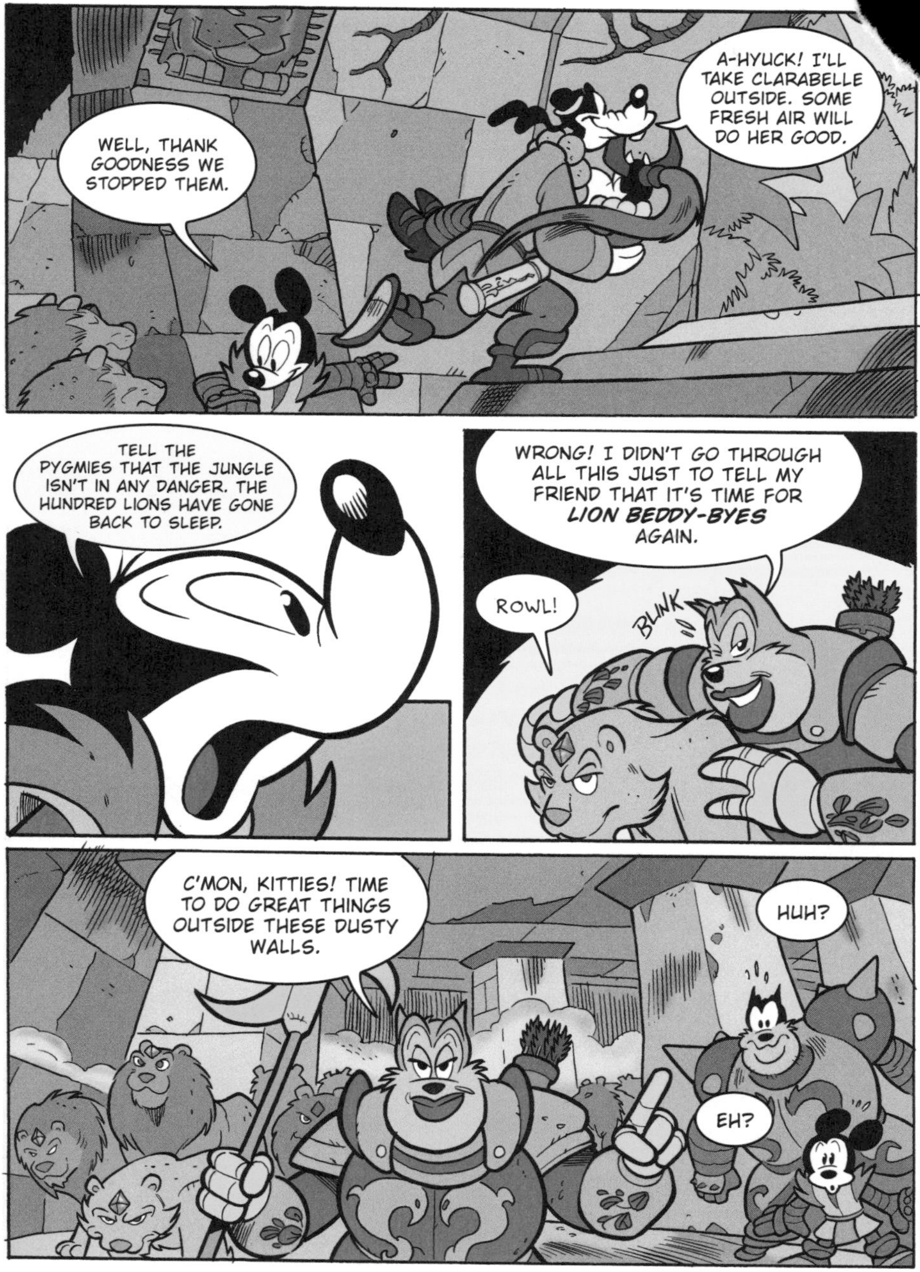
WELL, THANK GOODNESS WE STOPPED THEM.
A-HYUCK! I'LL TAKE CLARABELLE OUTSIDE. SOME FRESH AIR WILL DO HER GOOD.
TELL THE PYGMIES THAT THE JUNGLE ISN'T IN ANY DANGER. THE HUNDRED LIONS HAVE GONE BACK TO SLEEP.
WRONG! I DIDN'T GO THROUGH ALL THIS JUST TO TELL MY FRIEND THAT IT'S TIME FOR ***LION BEDDY-BYES*** AGAIN.
ROWL!
BLINK
C'MON, KITTIES! TIME TO DO GREAT THINGS OUTSIDE THESE DUSTY WALLS.
HUH?
EH?

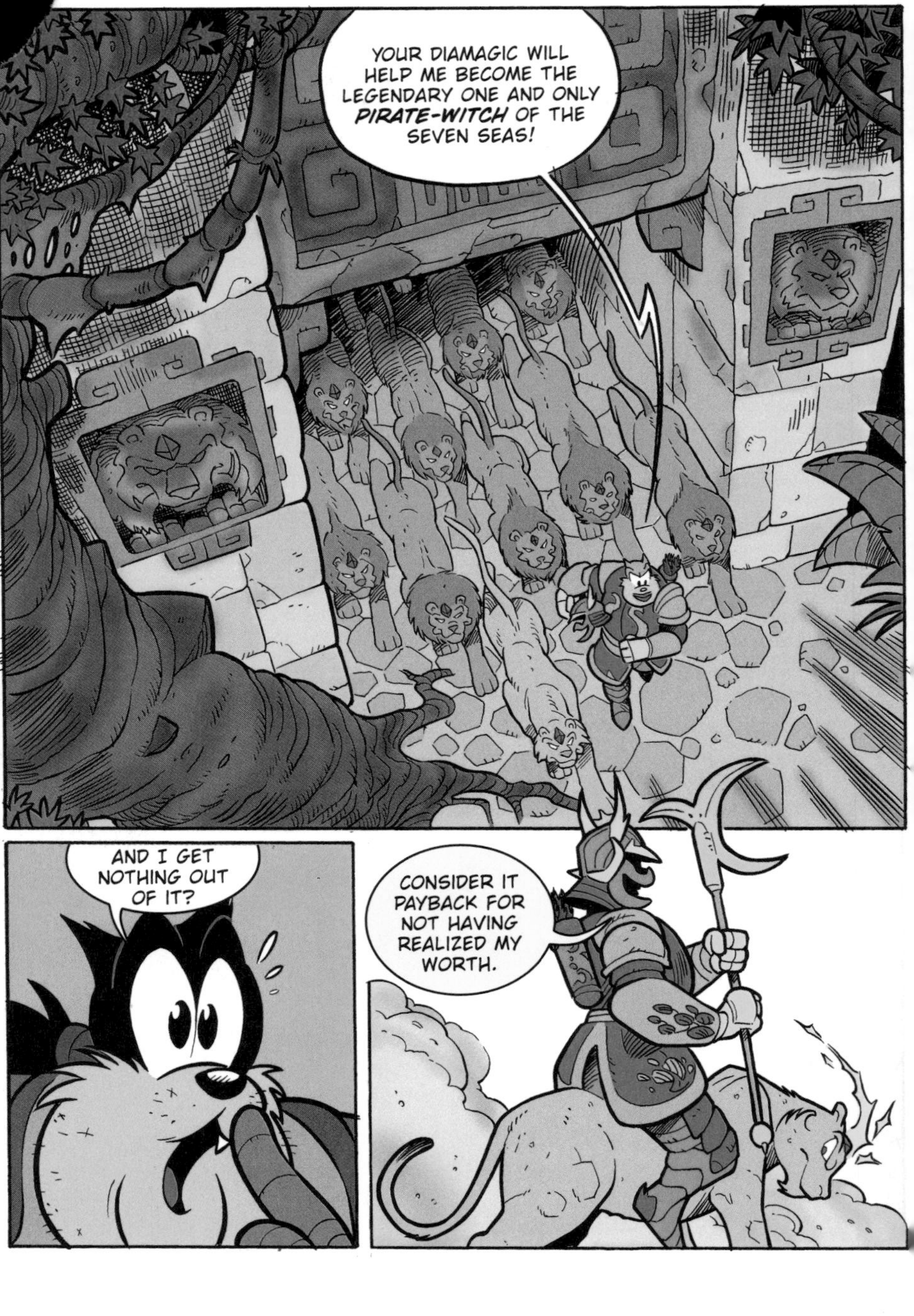
YOUR DIAMAGIC WILL HELP ME BECOME THE LEGENDARY ONE AND ONLY ***PIRATE-WITCH*** OF THE SEVEN SEAS!
AND I GET NOTHING OUT OF IT?
CONSIDER IT PAYBACK FOR NOT HAVING REALIZED MY WORTH.

GIDDY UP! LET'S FLY!

GASP! NOW I SEE WHY BRINGING A WOMAN ON BOARD IS BAD LUCK.

'COS THEY GET SEASICK?

'COS THEY DROP THE ANCHOR ON YOUR FEET?

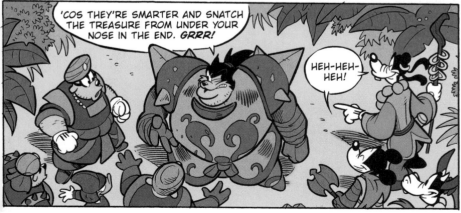

'COS THEY'RE SMARTER AND SNATCH THE TREASURE FROM UNDER YOUR NOSE IN THE END. *GRRR!*

HEH-HEH-HEH!

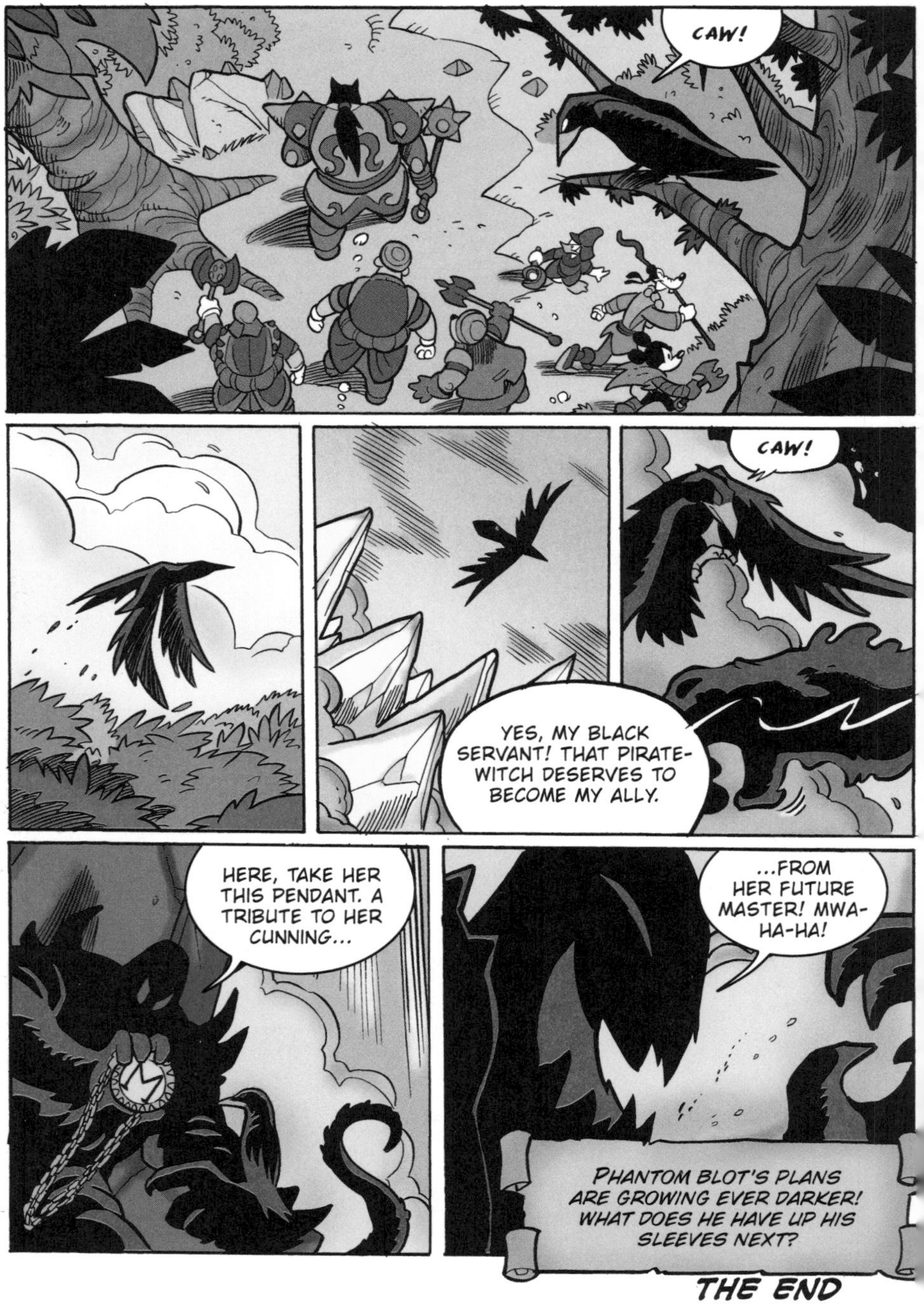
CAW!
CAW!
YES, MY BLACK SERVANT! THAT PIRATE-WITCH DESERVES TO BECOME MY ALLY.
HERE, TAKE HER THIS PENDANT. A TRIBUTE TO HER CUNNING...
...FROM HER FUTURE MASTER! MWA-HA-HA!
PHANTOM BLOT'S PLANS ARE GROWING EVER DARKER! WHAT DOES HE HAVE UP HIS SLEEVES NEXT?
THE END

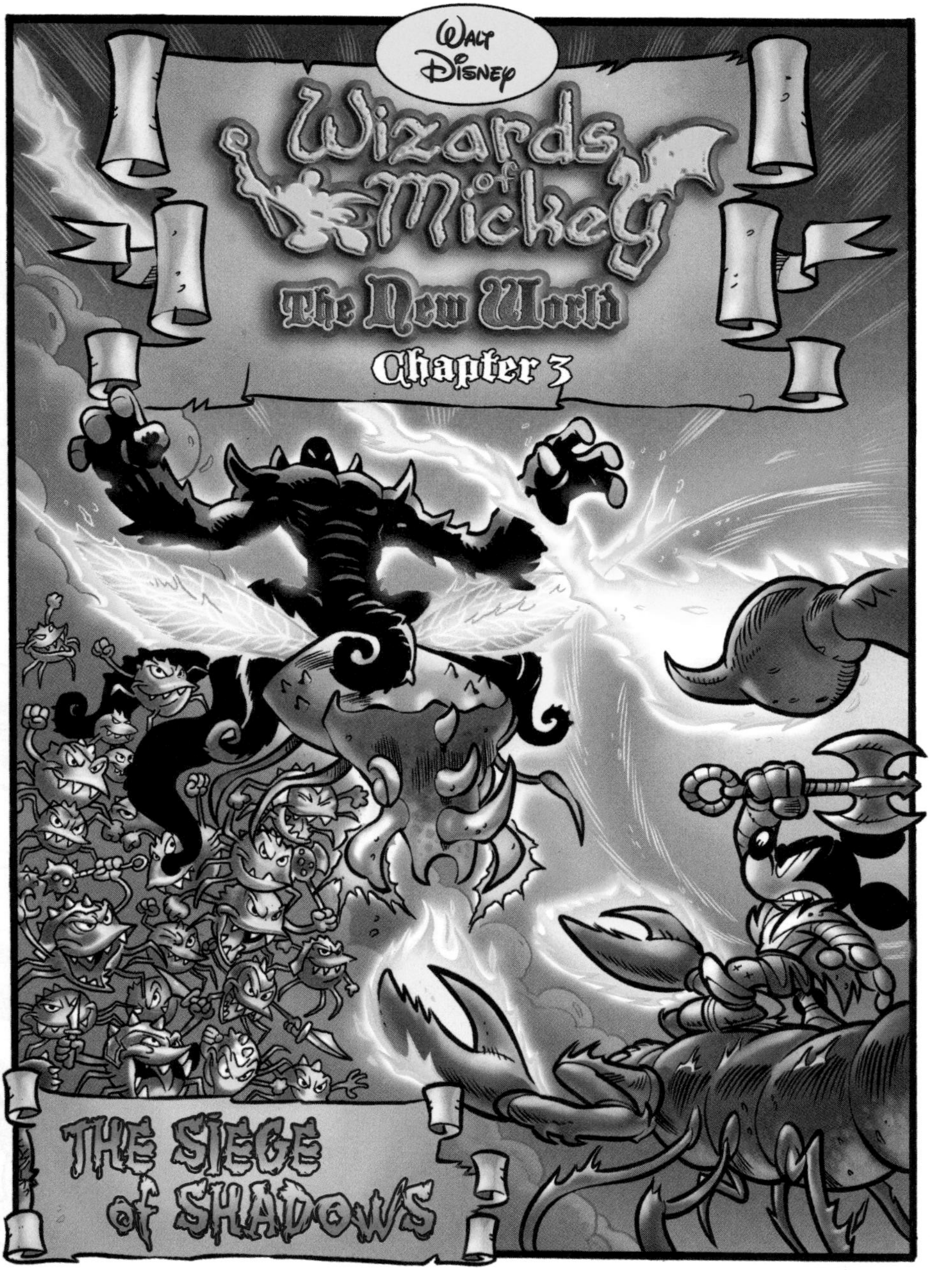

Walt Disney
Wizards of Mickey
The New World
Chapter 3
THE SIEGE of SHADOWS

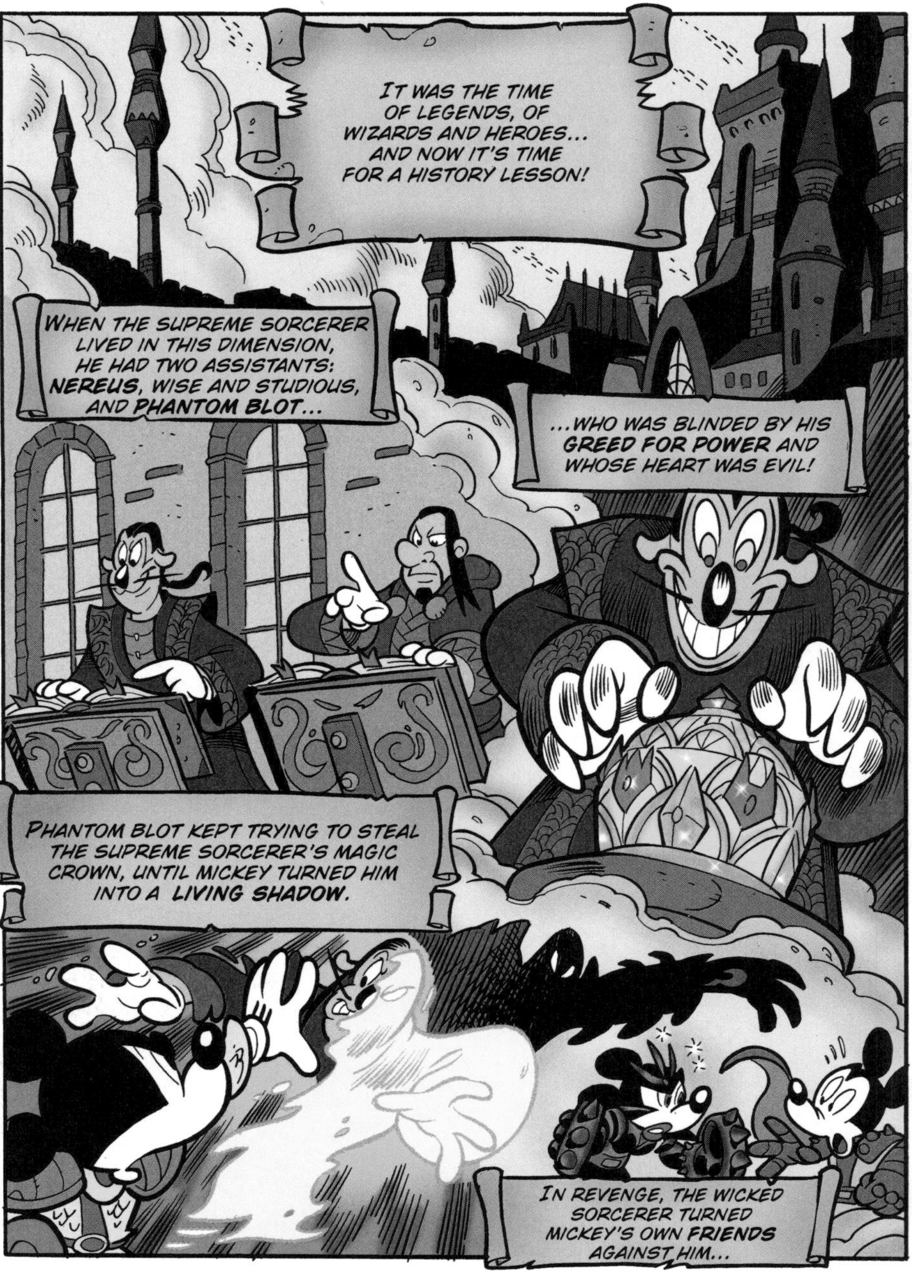

IT WAS THE TIME OF LEGENDS, OF WIZARDS AND HEROES... AND NOW IT'S TIME FOR A HISTORY LESSON!
WHEN THE SUPREME SORCERER LIVED IN THIS DIMENSION, HE HAD TWO ASSISTANTS: NEREUS, WISE AND STUDIOUS, AND PHANTOM BLOT...
...WHO WAS BLINDED BY HIS GREED FOR POWER AND WHOSE HEART WAS EVIL!
PHANTOM BLOT KEPT TRYING TO STEAL THE SUPREME SORCERER'S MAGIC CROWN, UNTIL MICKEY TURNED HIM INTO A LIVING SHADOW.
IN REVENGE, THE WICKED SORCERER TURNED MICKEY'S OWN FRIENDS AGAINST HIM...

232

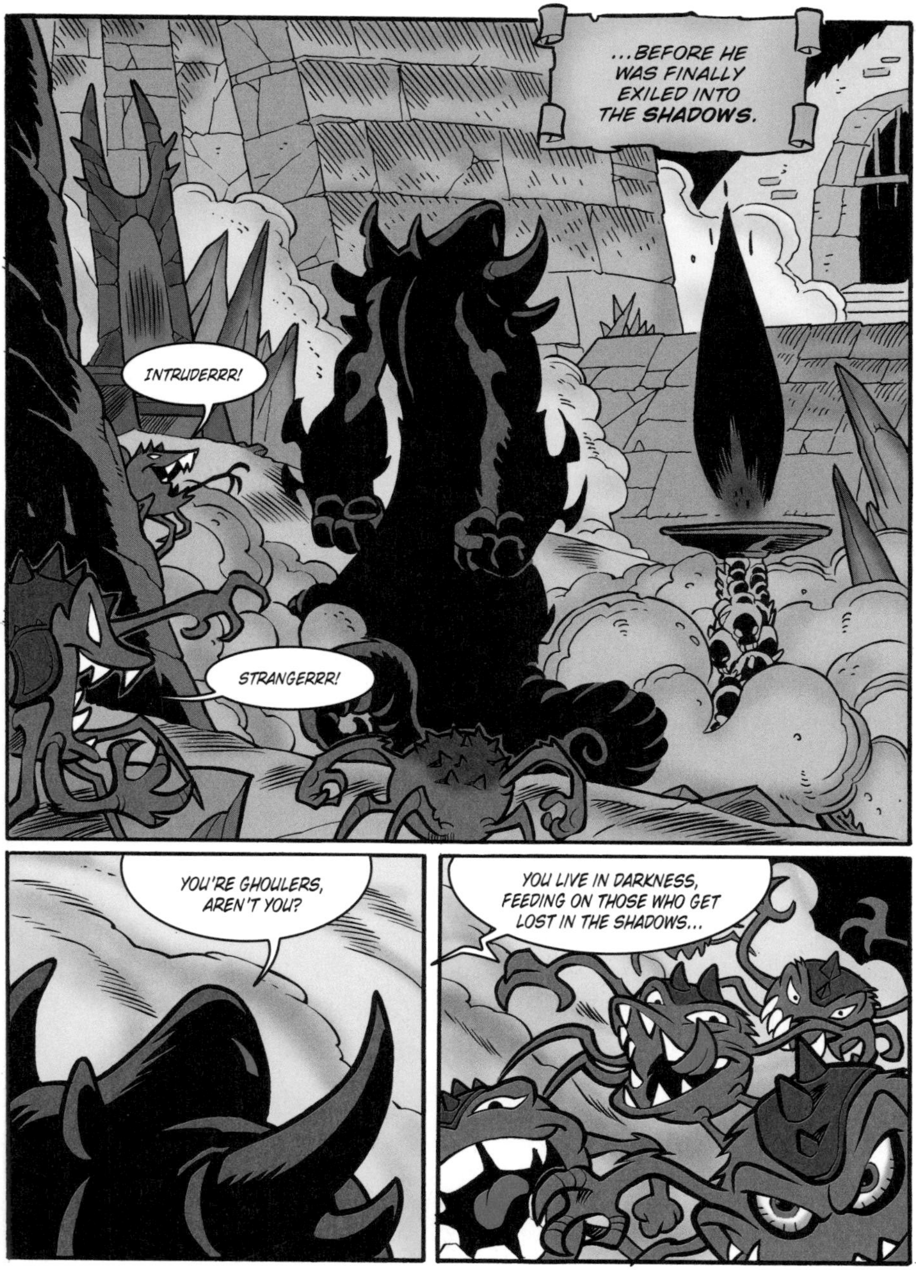

...BEFORE HE WAS FINALLY EXILED INTO THE SHADOWS.
INTRUDERRR!
STRANGERRR!
YOU'RE GHOULERS, AREN'T YOU?
YOU LIVE IN DARKNESS, FEEDING ON THOSE WHO GET LOST IN THE SHADOWS...

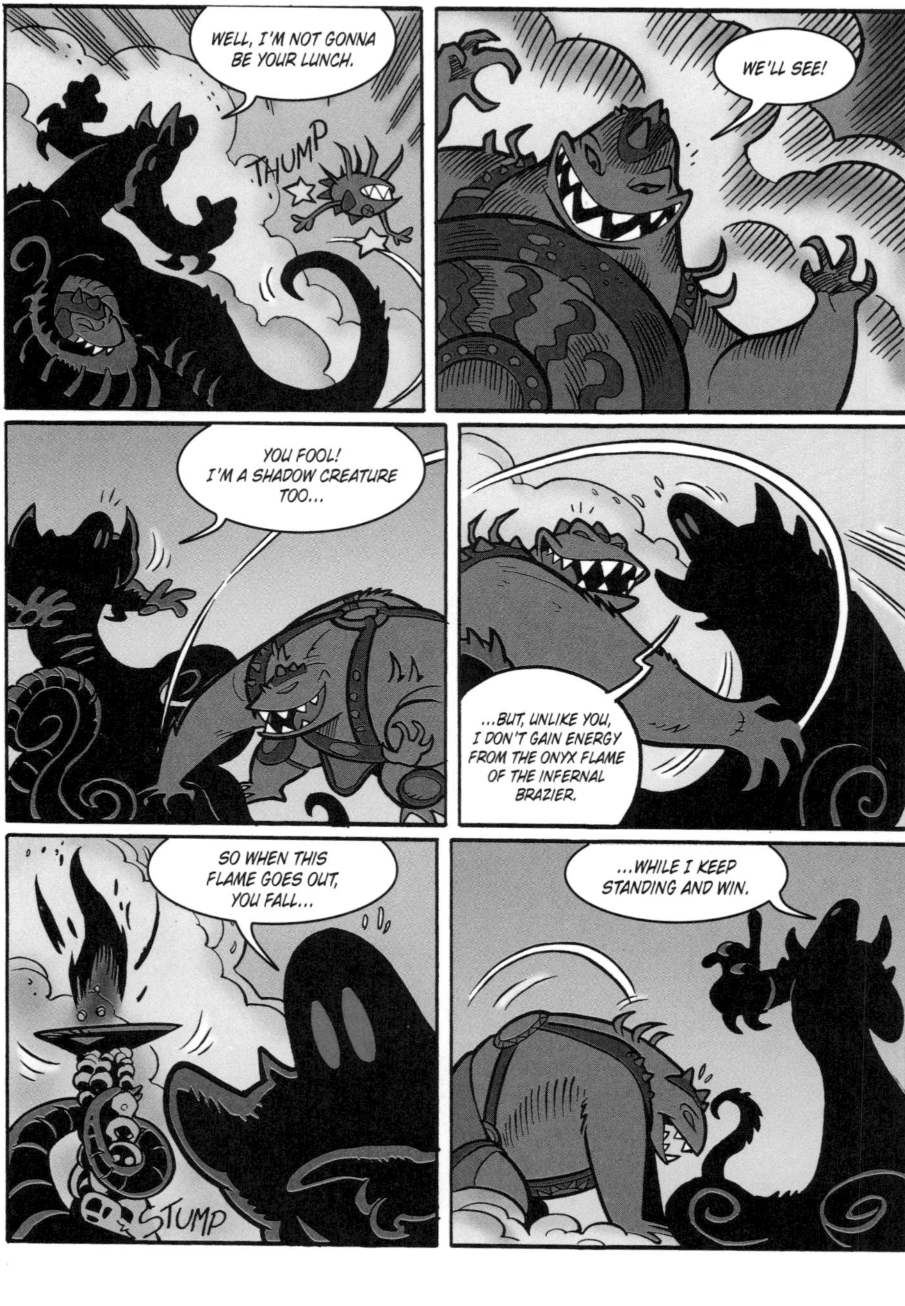
WELL, I'M NOT GONNA BE YOUR LUNCH.
THUMP
WE'LL SEE!
YOU FOOL! I'M A SHADOW CREATURE TOO...
...BUT, UNLIKE YOU, I DON'T GAIN ENERGY FROM THE ONYX FLAME OF THE INFERNAL BRAZIER.
SO WHEN THIS FLAME GOES OUT, YOU FALL...
STUMP
...WHILE I KEEP STANDING AND WIN.

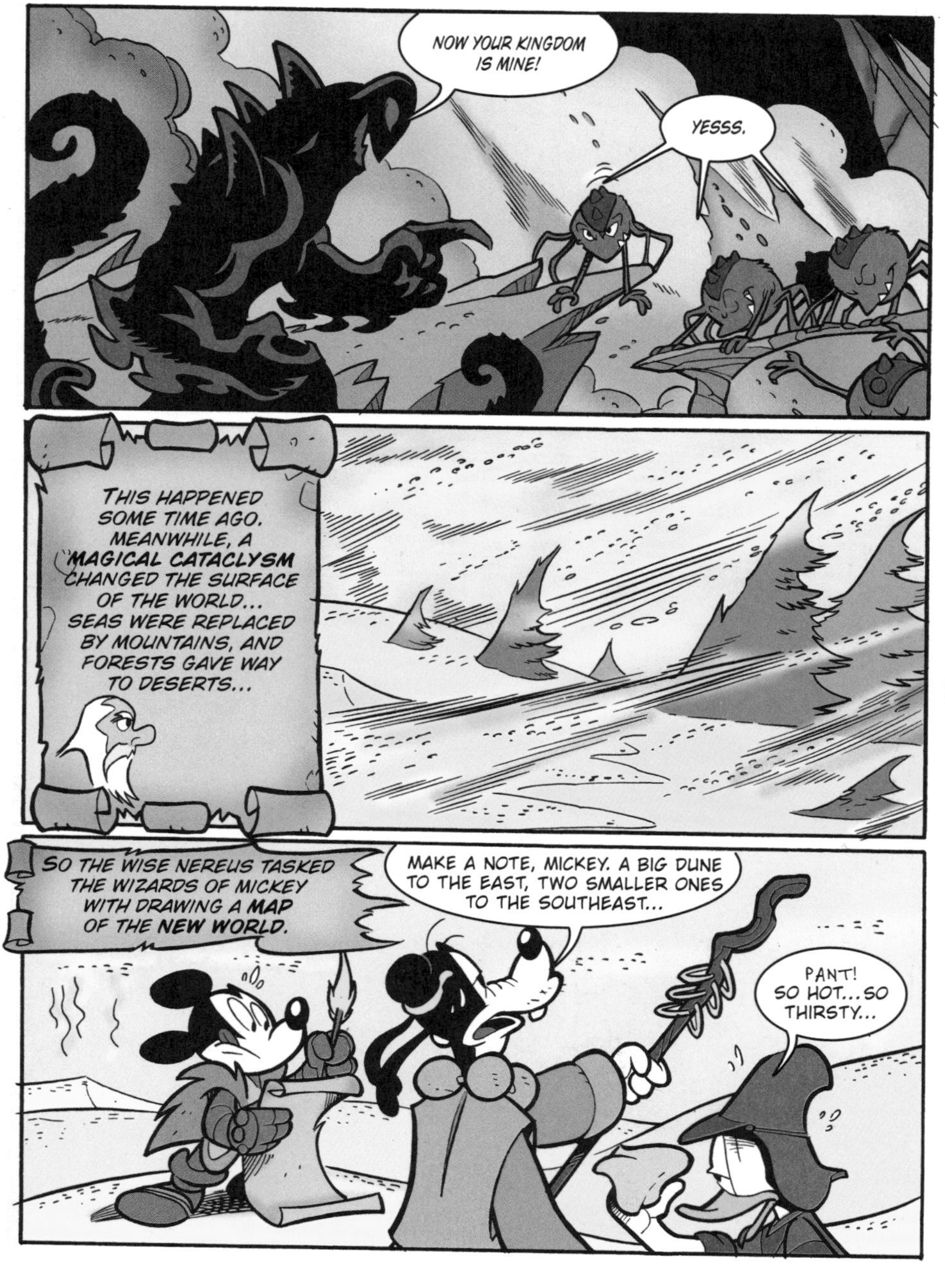

NOW YOUR KINGDOM IS MINE!
YESSS.
THIS HAPPENED SOME TIME AGO. MEANWHILE, A **MAGICAL CATACLYSM** CHANGED THE SURFACE OF THE WORLD... SEAS WERE REPLACED BY MOUNTAINS, AND FORESTS GAVE WAY TO DESERTS...
SO THE WISE NEREUS TASKED THE WIZARDS OF MICKEY WITH DRAWING A **MAP** OF THE **NEW WORLD**.
MAKE A NOTE, MICKEY. A BIG DUNE TO THE EAST, TWO SMALLER ONES TO THE SOUTHEAST...
PANT! SO HOT...SO THIRSTY...

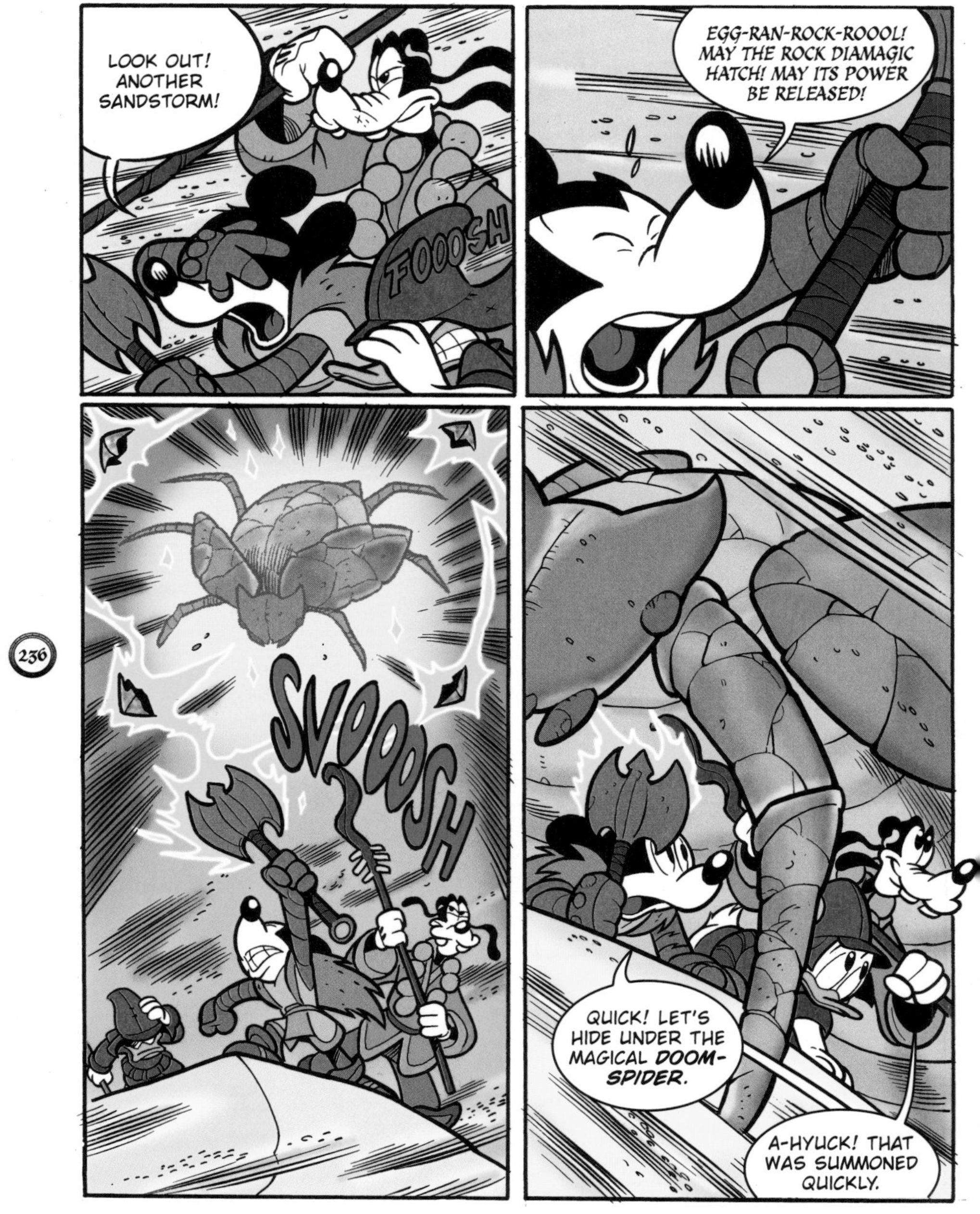
LOOK OUT! ANOTHER SANDSTORM!
FOOOSH
EGG-RAN-ROCK-ROOOL! MAY THE ROCK DIAMAGIC HATCH! MAY ITS POWER BE RELEASED!
SVOOOSH
QUICK! LET'S HIDE UNDER THE MAGICAL DOOM-SPIDER.
A-HYUCK! THAT WAS SUMMONED QUICKLY.

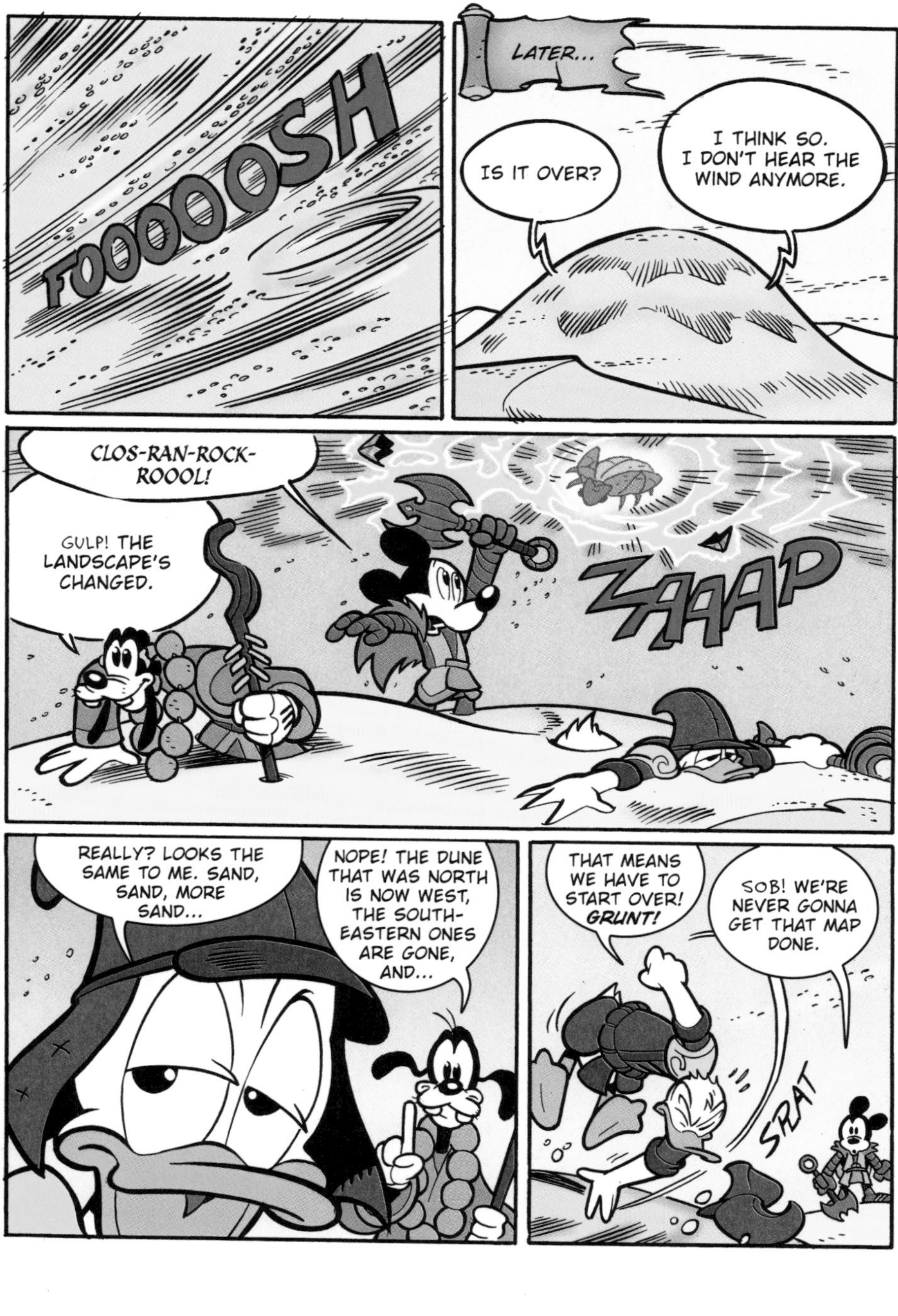
FOOOOOSH
LATER...
IS IT OVER?
I THINK SO. I DON'T HEAR THE WIND ANYMORE.
CLOS-RAN-ROCK-ROOOL!
GULP! THE LANDSCAPE'S CHANGED.
ZAAAP
REALLY? LOOKS THE SAME TO ME. SAND, SAND, MORE SAND...
NOPE! THE DUNE THAT WAS NORTH IS NOW WEST, THE SOUTH-EASTERN ONES ARE GONE, AND...
THAT MEANS WE HAVE TO START OVER! GRUNT!
SOB! WE'RE NEVER GONNA GET THAT MAP DONE.
SPLAT

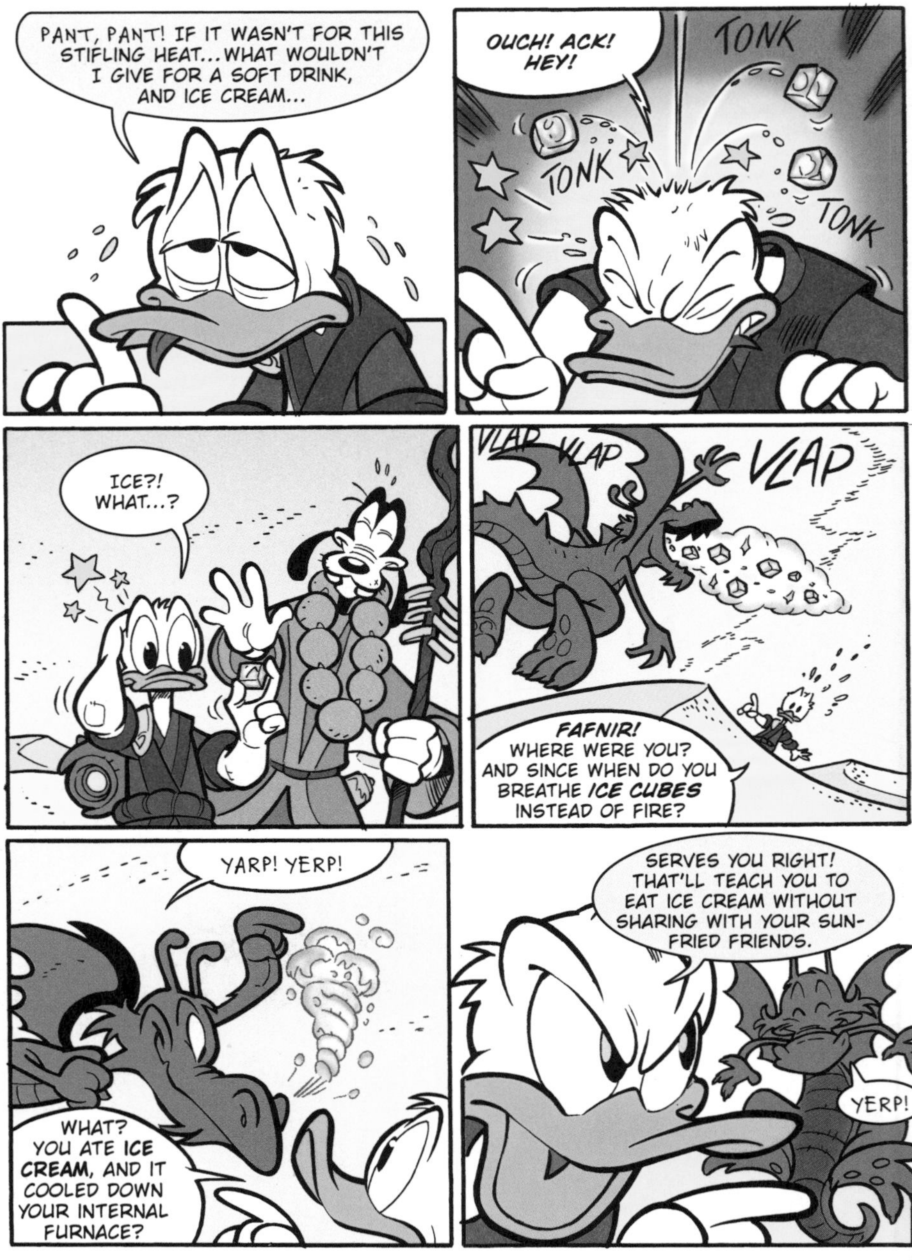
PANT, PANT! IF IT WASN'T FOR THIS STIFLING HEAT...WHAT WOULDN'T I GIVE FOR A SOFT DRINK, AND ICE CREAM...
OUCH! ACK! HEY!
TONK
TONK
TONK
ICE?! WHAT...?
VLAP
VLAP
VLAP
FAFNIR! WHERE WERE YOU? AND SINCE WHEN DO YOU BREATHE ICE CUBES INSTEAD OF FIRE?
YARP! YERP!
WHAT? YOU ATE ICE CREAM, AND IT COOLED DOWN YOUR INTERNAL FURNACE?
SERVES YOU RIGHT! THAT'LL TEACH YOU TO EAT ICE CREAM WITHOUT SHARING WITH YOUR SUN-FRIED FRIENDS.
YERP!

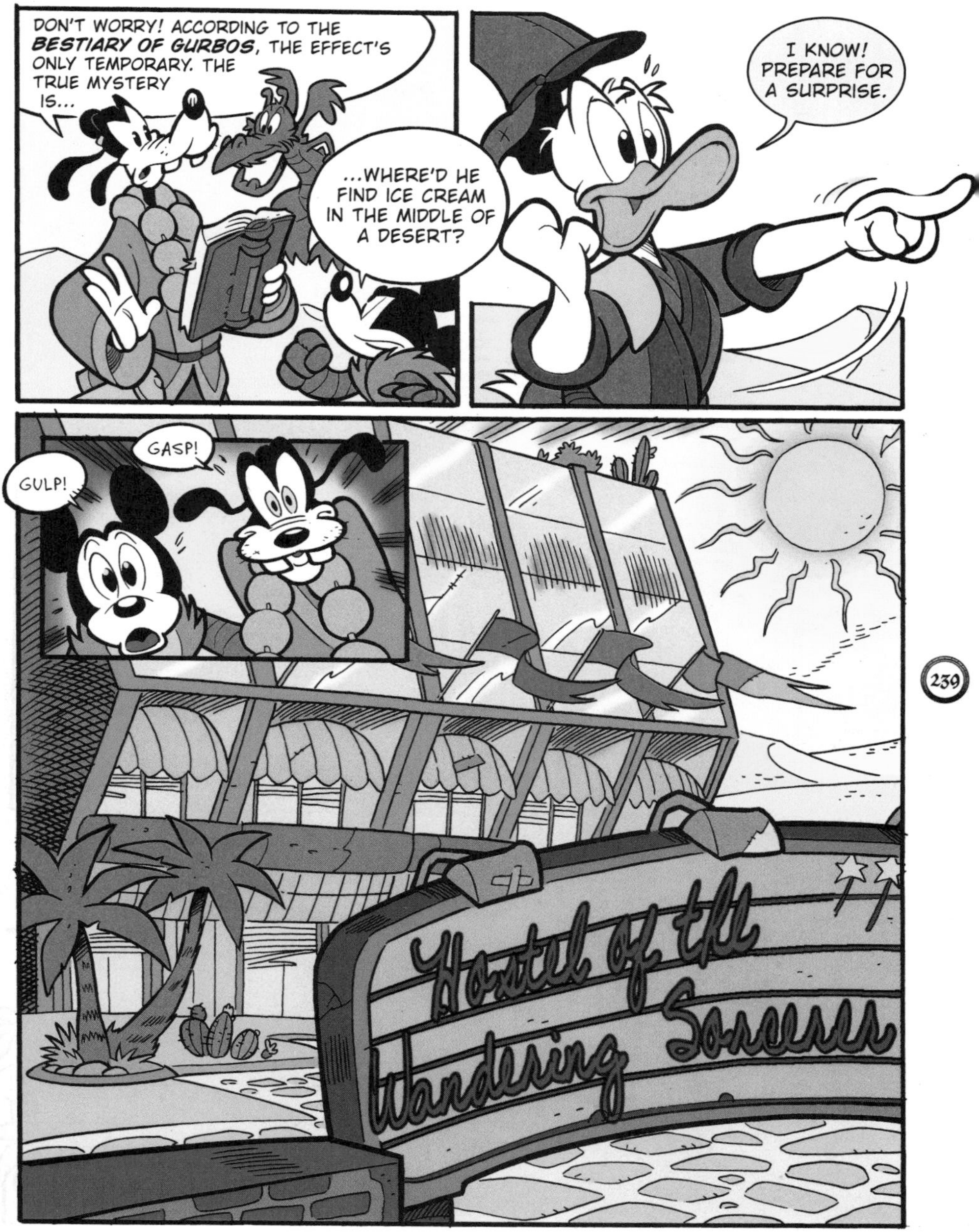
DON'T WORRY! ACCORDING TO THE BESTIARY OF GURBOS, THE EFFECT'S ONLY TEMPORARY. THE TRUE MYSTERY IS...
...WHERE'D HE FIND ICE CREAM IN THE MIDDLE OF A DESERT?
I KNOW! PREPARE FOR A SURPRISE.
GULP!
GASP!
Hostel of the Wandering Sorcerer

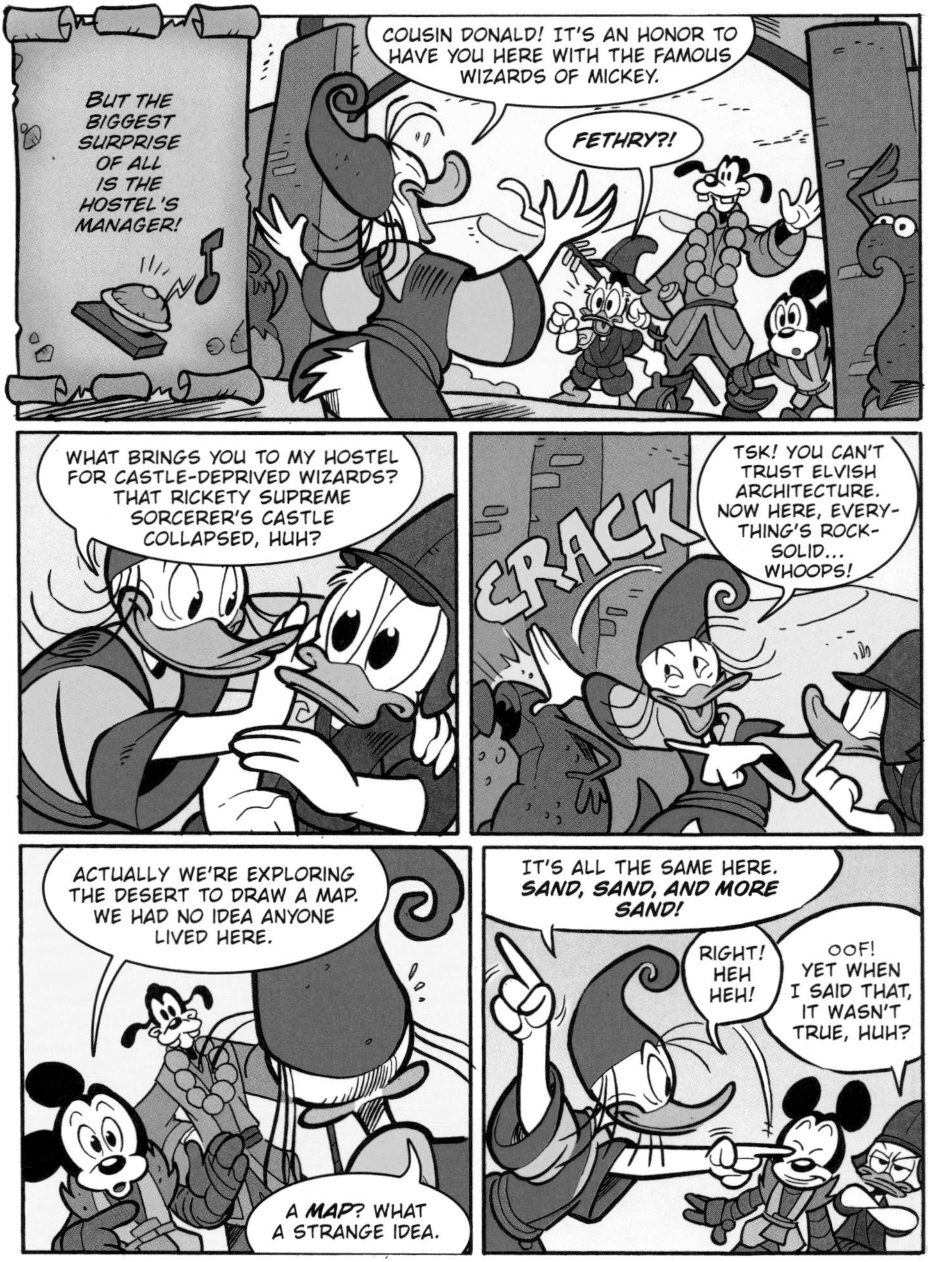
BUT THE BIGGEST SURPRISE OF ALL IS THE HOSTEL'S MANAGER!
COUSIN DONALD! IT'S AN HONOR TO HAVE YOU HERE WITH THE FAMOUS WIZARDS OF MICKEY.
FETHRY?!
WHAT BRINGS YOU TO MY HOSTEL FOR CASTLE-DEPRIVED WIZARDS? THAT RICKETY SUPREME SORCERER'S CASTLE COLLAPSED, HUH?
CRACK
TSK! YOU CAN'T TRUST ELVISH ARCHITECTURE. NOW HERE, EVERY-THING'S ROCK-SOLID... WHOOPS!
ACTUALLY WE'RE EXPLORING THE DESERT TO DRAW A MAP. WE HAD NO IDEA ANYONE LIVED HERE.
A MAP? WHAT A STRANGE IDEA.
IT'S ALL THE SAME HERE. SAND, SAND, AND MORE SAND!
RIGHT! HEH HEH!
OOF! YET WHEN I SAID THAT, IT WASN'T TRUE, HUH?

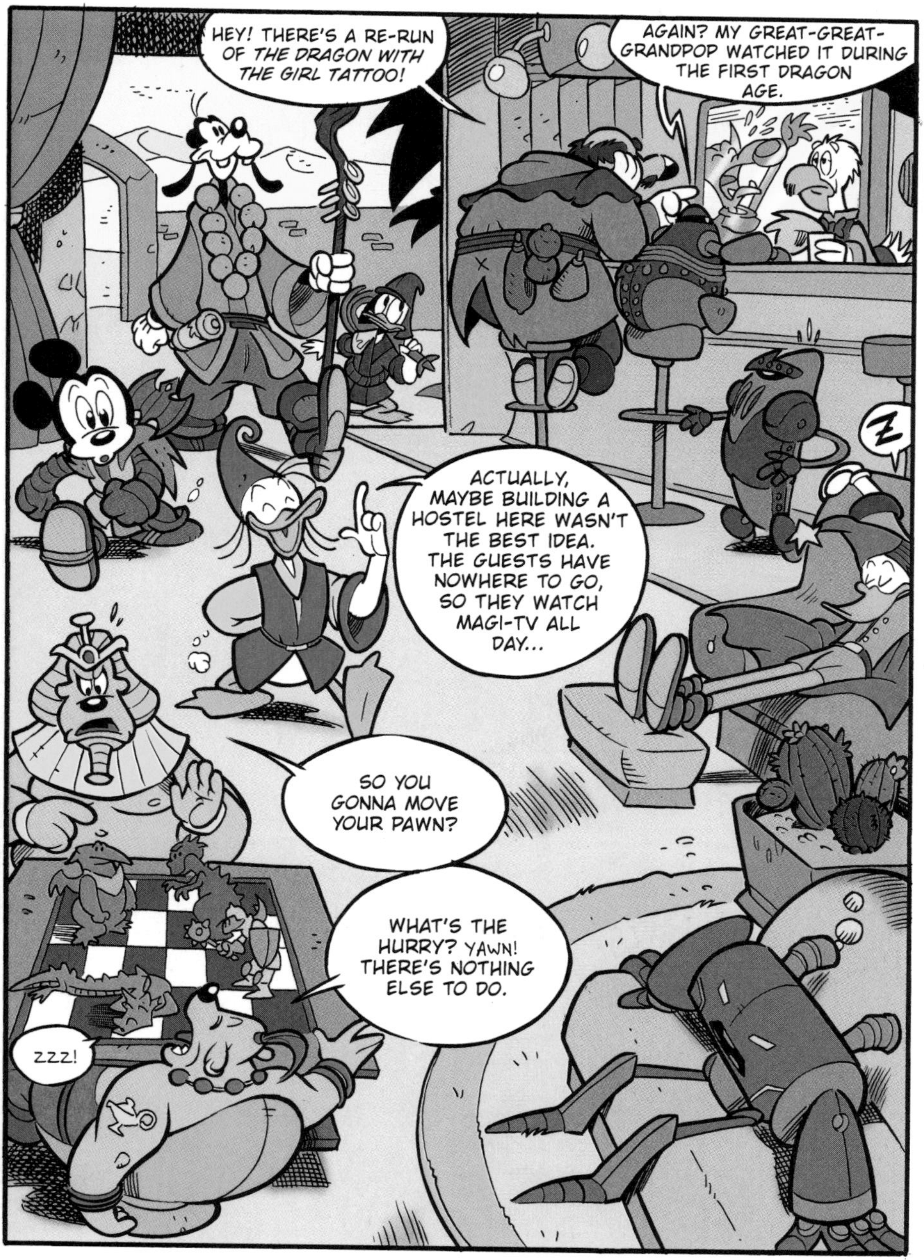
HEY! THERE'S A RE-RUN OF THE DRAGON WITH THE GIRL TATTOO!
AGAIN? MY GREAT-GREAT-GRANDPOP WATCHED IT DURING THE FIRST DRAGON AGE.
Z
ACTUALLY, MAYBE BUILDING A HOSTEL HERE WASN'T THE BEST IDEA. THE GUESTS HAVE NOWHERE TO GO, SO THEY WATCH MAGI-TV ALL DAY...
SO YOU GONNA MOVE YOUR PAWN?
WHAT'S THE HURRY? YAWN! THERE'S NOTHING ELSE TO DO.
ZZZ!

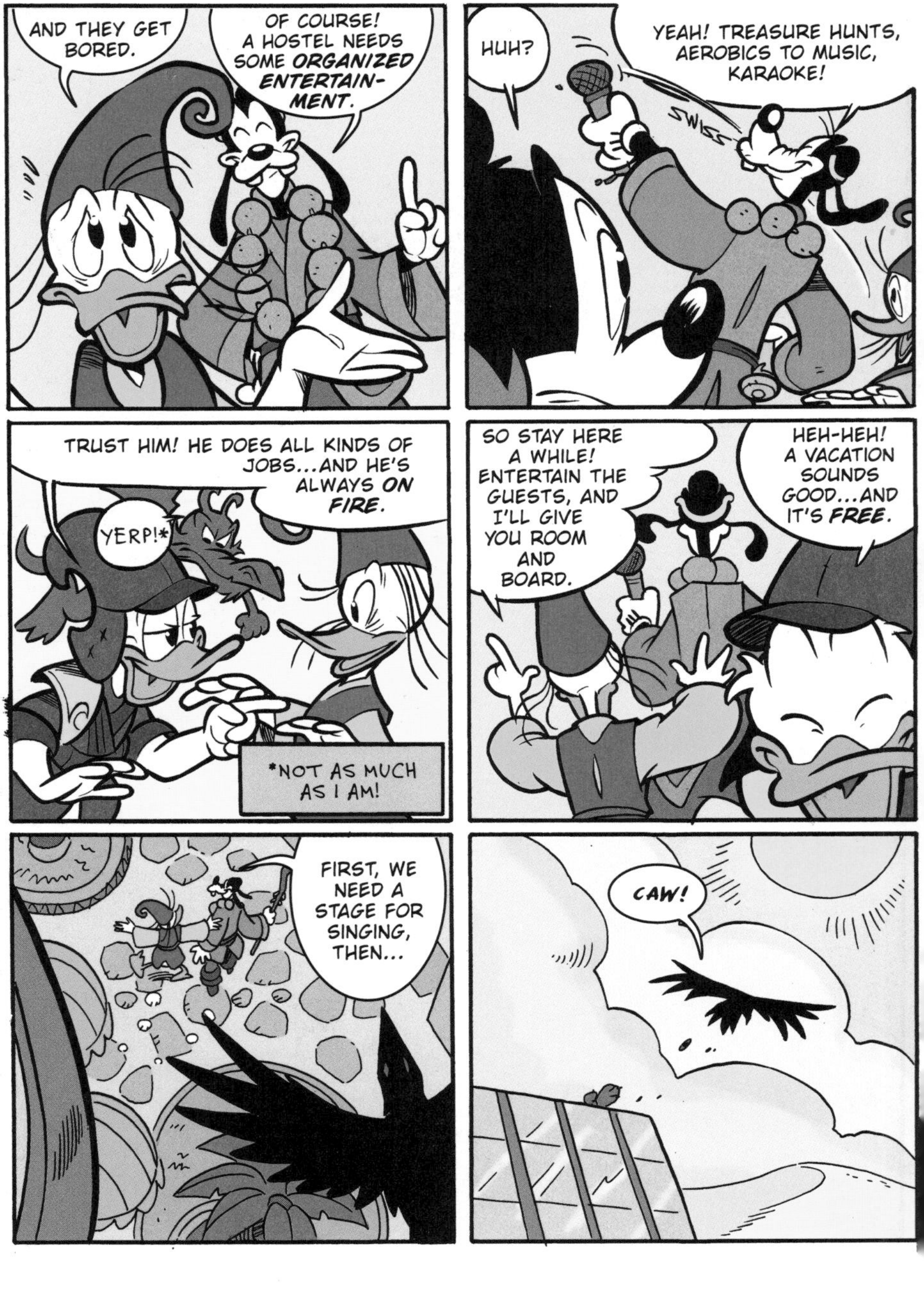

AND THEY GET BORED.
OF COURSE! A HOSTEL NEEDS SOME ORGANIZED ENTERTAIN-MENT.
HUH?
YEAH! TREASURE HUNTS, AEROBICS TO MUSIC, KARAOKE!
SWISS
TRUST HIM! HE DOES ALL KINDS OF JOBS...AND HE'S ALWAYS ON FIRE.
YERP!*
*NOT AS MUCH AS I AM!
SO STAY HERE A WHILE! ENTERTAIN THE GUESTS, AND I'LL GIVE YOU ROOM AND BOARD.
HEH-HEH! A VACATION SOUNDS GOOD...AND IT'S FREE.
FIRST, WE NEED A STAGE FOR SINGING, THEN...
CAW!

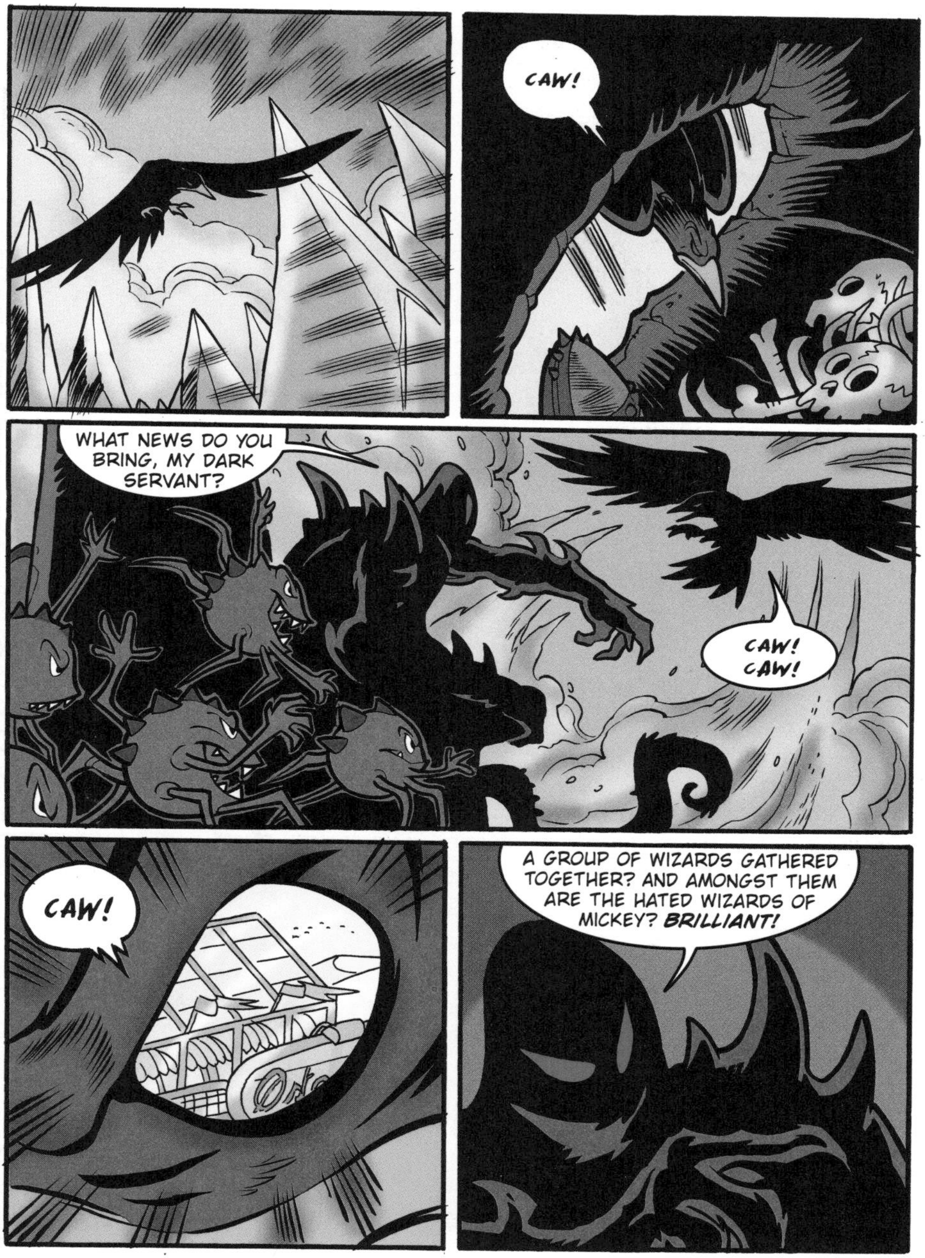
CAW!
WHAT NEWS DO YOU BRING, MY DARK SERVANT?
CAW! CAW!
CAW!
A GROUP OF WIZARDS GATHERED TOGETHER? AND AMONGST THEM ARE THE HATED WIZARDS OF MICKEY? *BRILLIANT!*

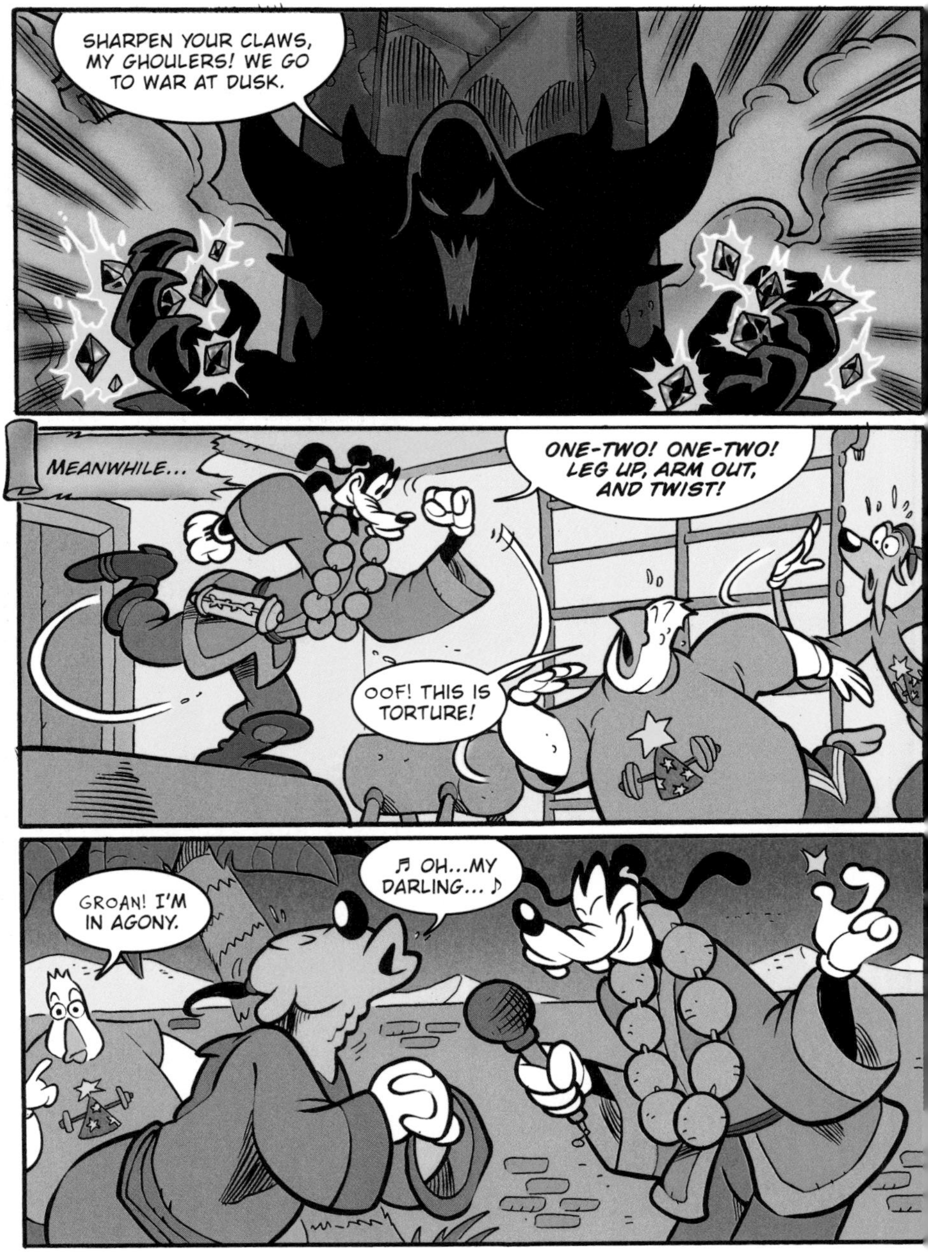
SHARPEN YOUR CLAWS, MY GHOULERS! WE GO TO WAR AT DUSK.
MEANWHILE...
ONE-TWO! ONE-TWO! LEG UP, ARM OUT, AND TWIST!
OOF! THIS IS TORTURE!
GROAN! I'M IN AGONY.
♬ OH...MY DARLING... ♪

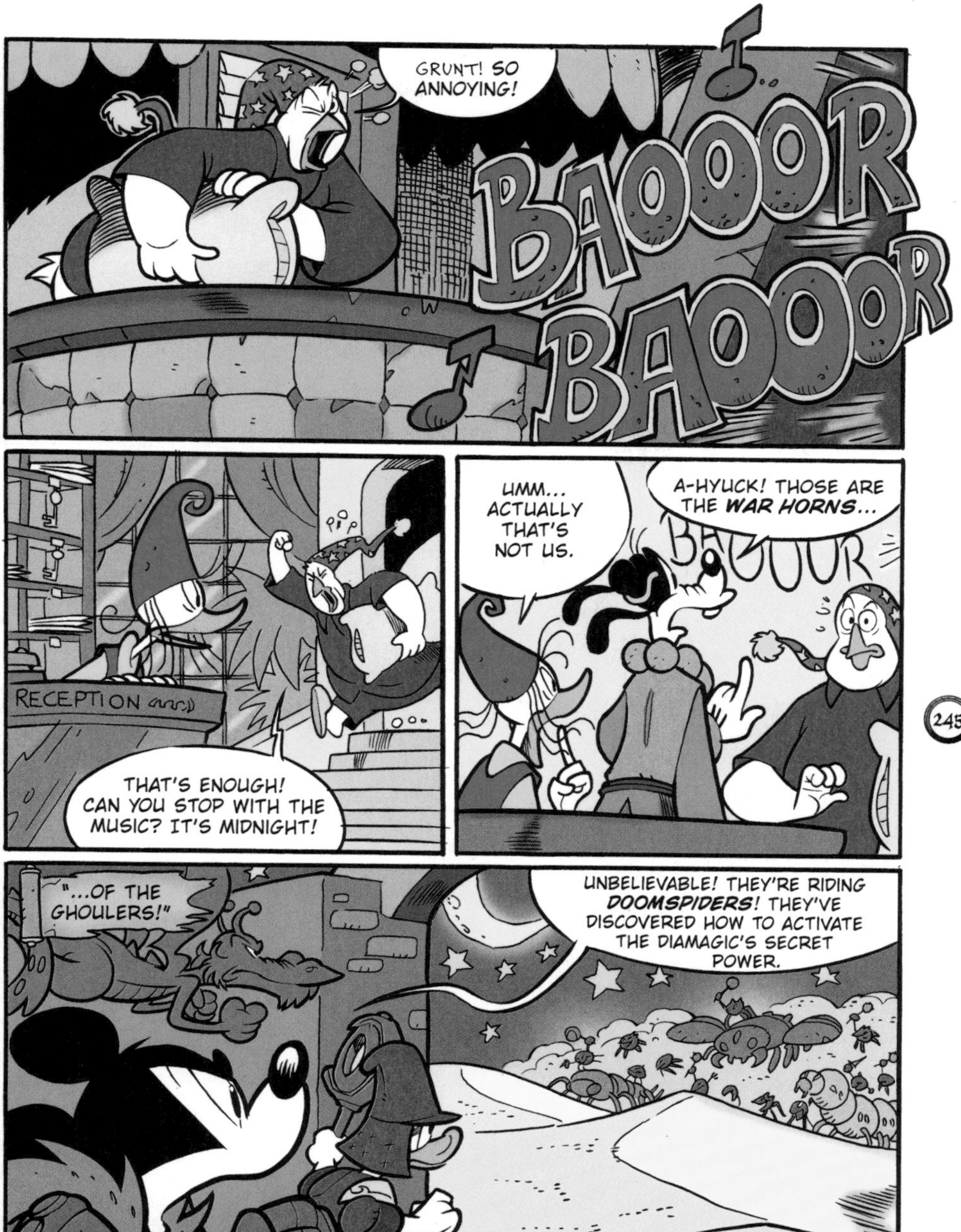
GRUNT! SO ANNOYING!
BAOOOR BAOOOR
UMM... ACTUALLY THAT'S NOT US.
A-HYUCK! THOSE ARE THE **WAR HORNS**...
BAOOOR
RECEPTION
THAT'S ENOUGH! CAN YOU STOP WITH THE MUSIC? IT'S MIDNIGHT!
"...OF THE GHOULERS!"
UNBELIEVABLE! THEY'RE RIDING **DOOMSPIDERS**! THEY'VE DISCOVERED HOW TO ACTIVATE THE DIAMAGIC'S SECRET POWER.

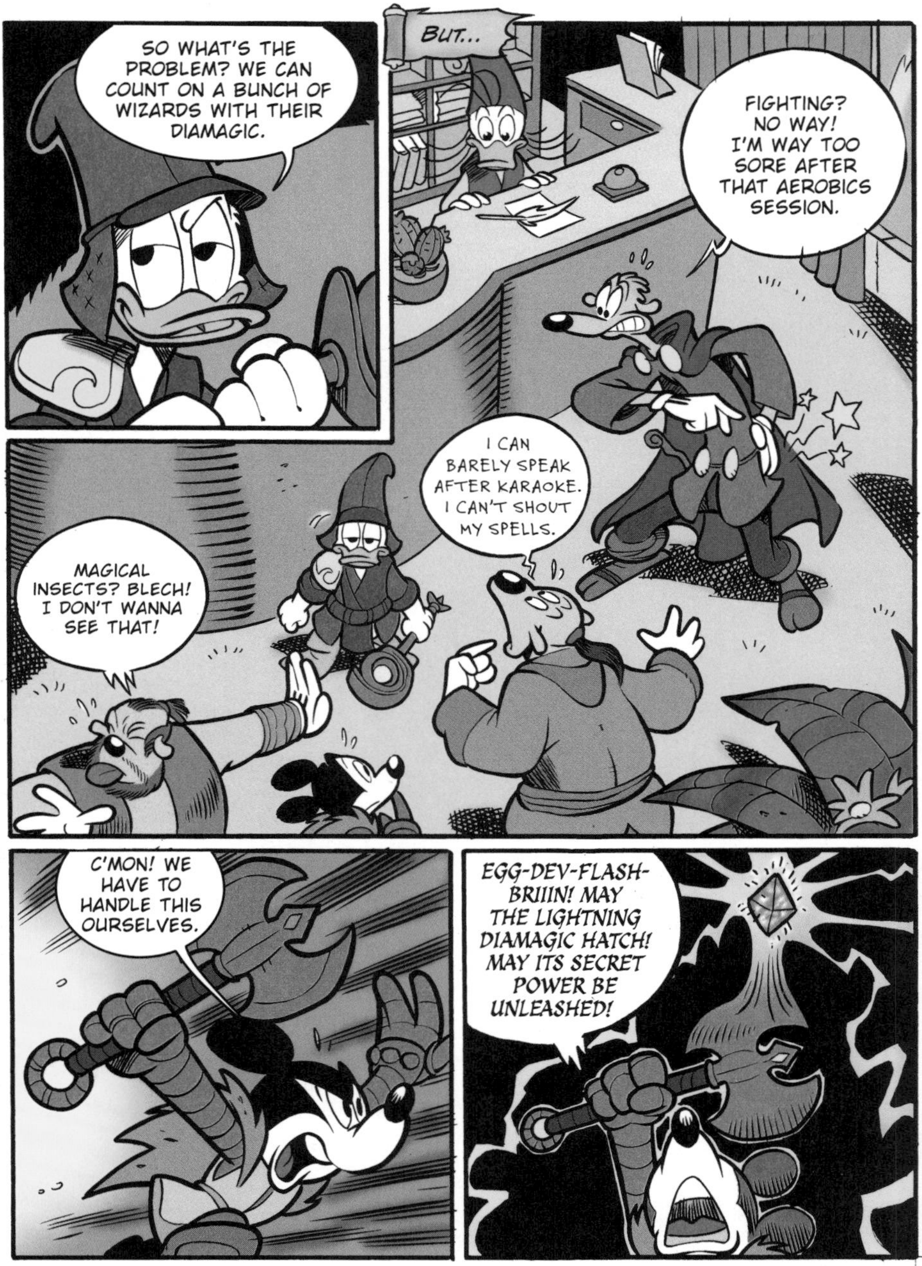
SO WHAT'S THE PROBLEM? WE CAN COUNT ON A BUNCH OF WIZARDS WITH THEIR DIAMAGIC.
BUT...
FIGHTING? NO WAY! I'M WAY TOO SORE AFTER THAT AEROBICS SESSION.
I CAN BARELY SPEAK AFTER KARAOKE. I CAN'T SHOUT MY SPELLS.
MAGICAL INSECTS? BLECH! I DON'T WANNA SEE THAT!
C'MON! WE HAVE TO HANDLE THIS OURSELVES.
EGG-DEV-FLASH-BRIIIN! MAY THE LIGHTNING DIAMAGIC HATCH! MAY ITS SECRET POWER BE UNLEASHED!

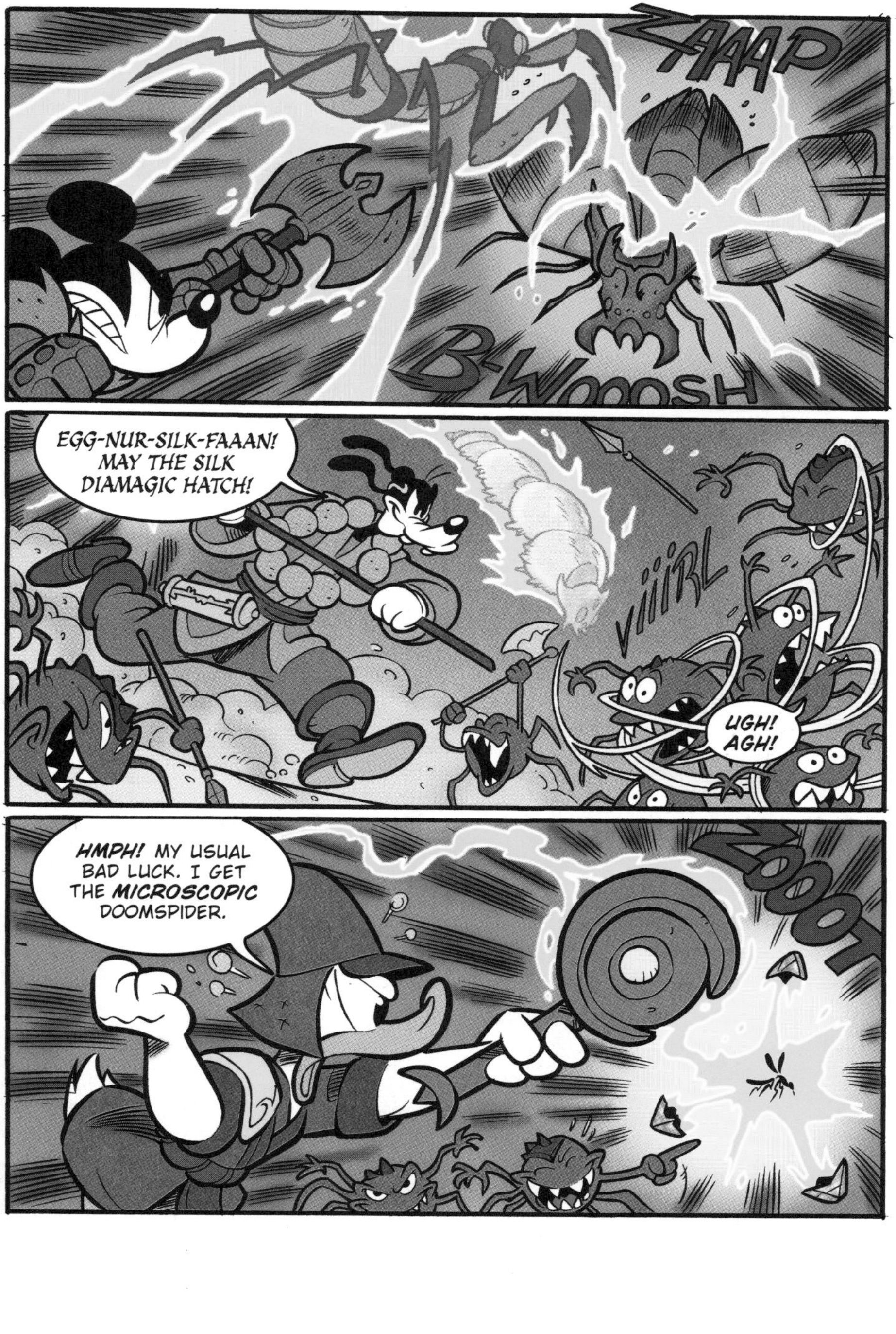
ZAAAP
B-WOOOSH
EGG-NUR-SILK-FAAAN! MAY THE SILK DIAMAGIC HATCH!
VIIIRL
UGH! AGH!
HMPH! MY USUAL BAD LUCK. I GET THE MICROSCOPIC DOOMSPIDER.
ZOOOT

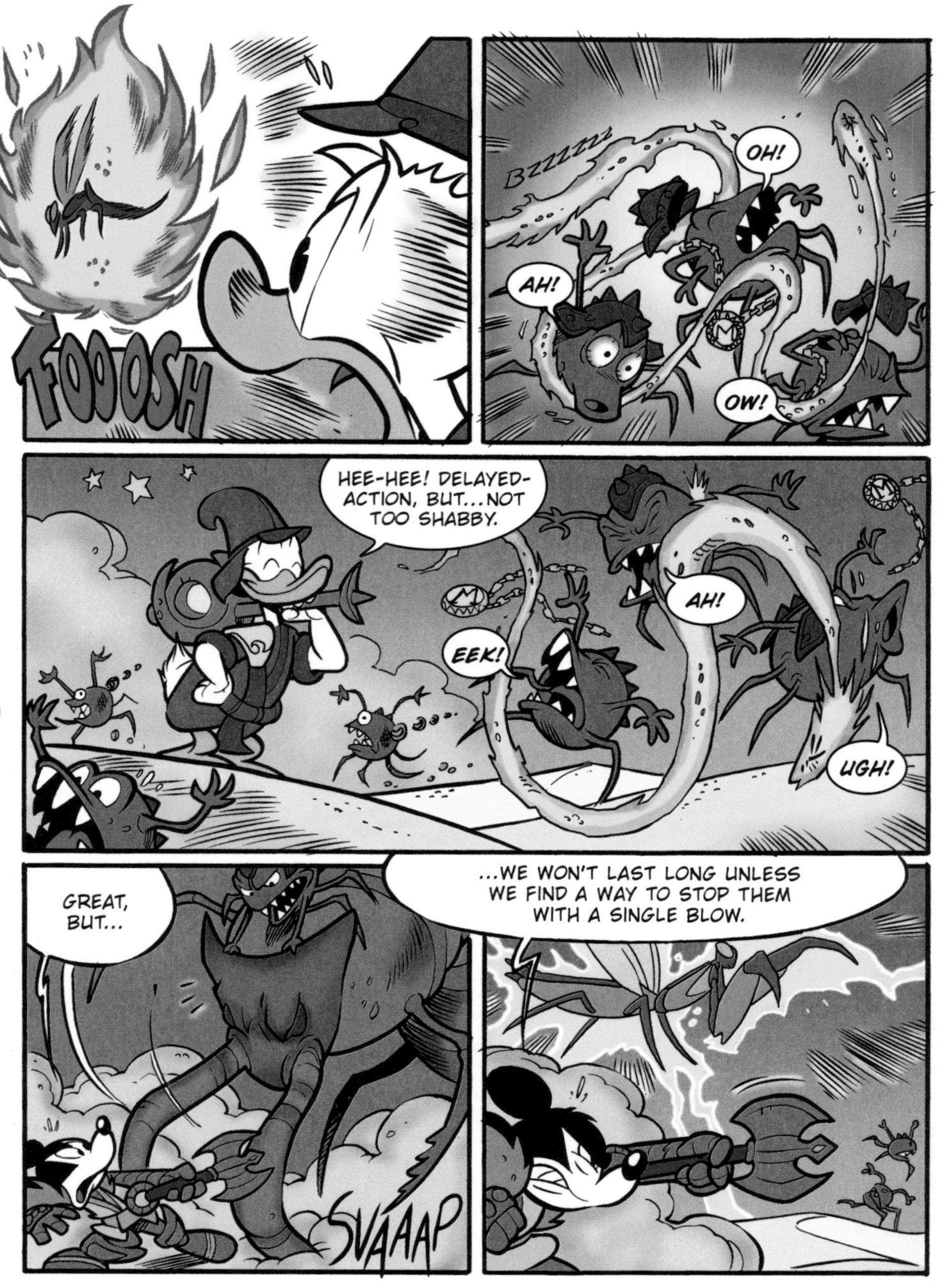
FOOOSH
BZZZZZZ
OH!
AH!
OW!
HEE-HEE! DELAYED-ACTION, BUT...NOT TOO SHABBY.
AH!
EEK!
UGH!
GREAT, BUT...
...WE WON'T LAST LONG UNLESS WE FIND A WAY TO STOP THEM WITH A SINGLE BLOW.
SVAAAP

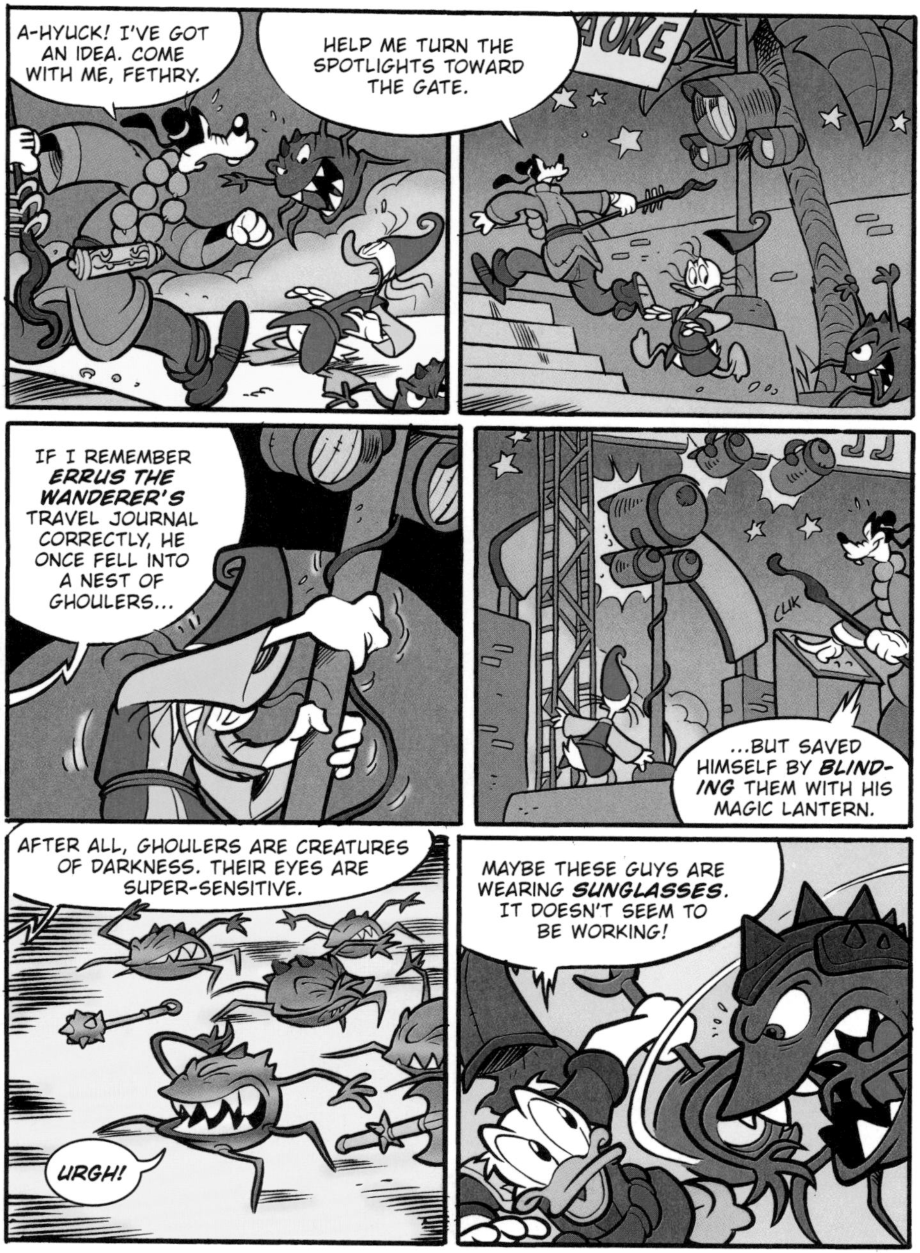
A-HYUCK! I'VE GOT AN IDEA. COME WITH ME, FETHRY.
HELP ME TURN THE SPOTLIGHTS TOWARD THE GATE.
AOKE
IF I REMEMBER ERRUS THE WANDERER'S TRAVEL JOURNAL CORRECTLY, HE ONCE FELL INTO A NEST OF GHOULERS...
CLIK
...BUT SAVED HIMSELF BY BLINDING THEM WITH HIS MAGIC LANTERN.
AFTER ALL, GHOULERS ARE CREATURES OF DARKNESS. THEIR EYES ARE SUPER-SENSITIVE.
URGH!
MAYBE THESE GUYS ARE WEARING SUNGLASSES. IT DOESN'T SEEM TO BE WORKING!

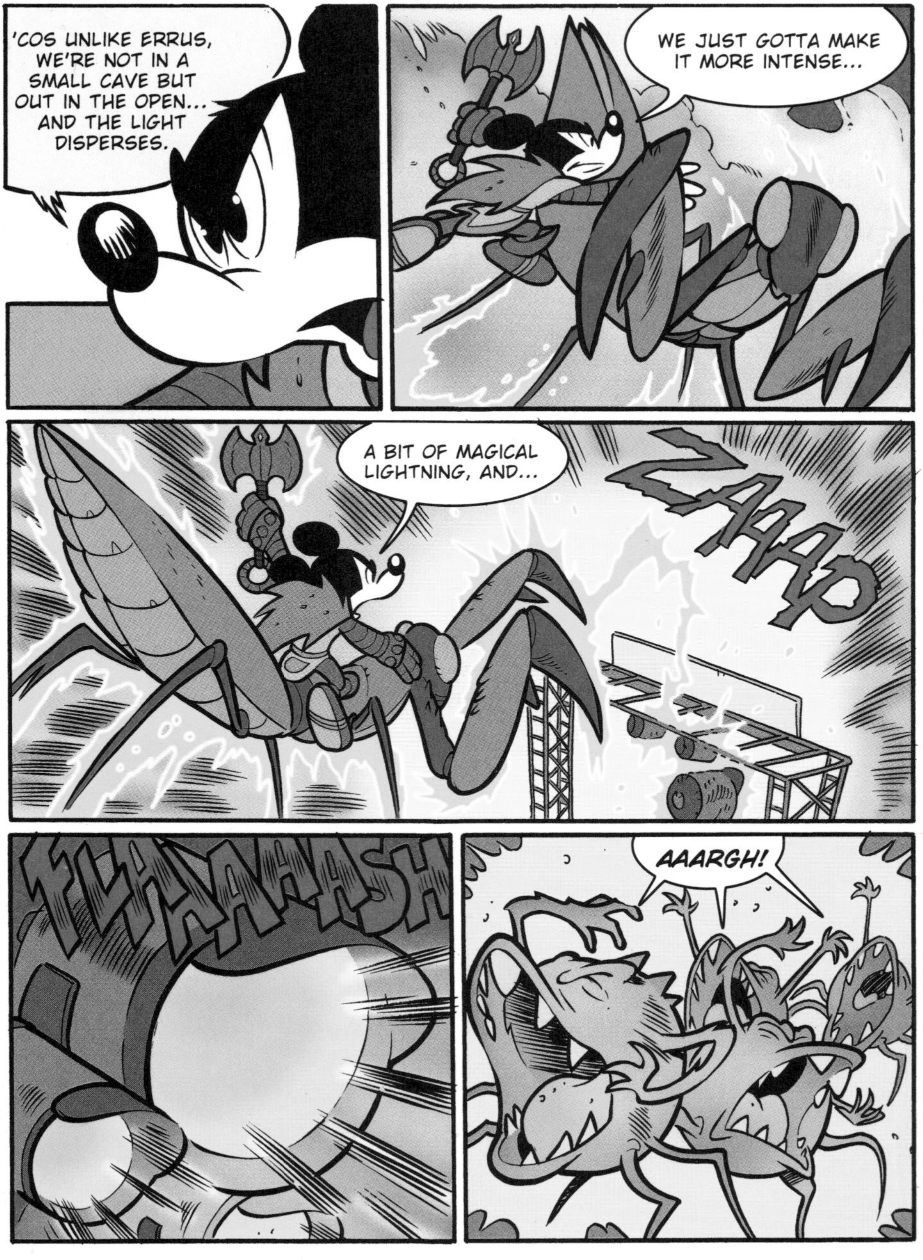
'COS UNLIKE ERRUS, WE'RE NOT IN A SMALL CAVE BUT OUT IN THE OPEN... AND THE LIGHT DISPERSES.
WE JUST GOTTA MAKE IT MORE INTENSE...
A BIT OF MAGICAL LIGHTNING, AND...
ZAAAP
FLAAAAASH
AAARGH!

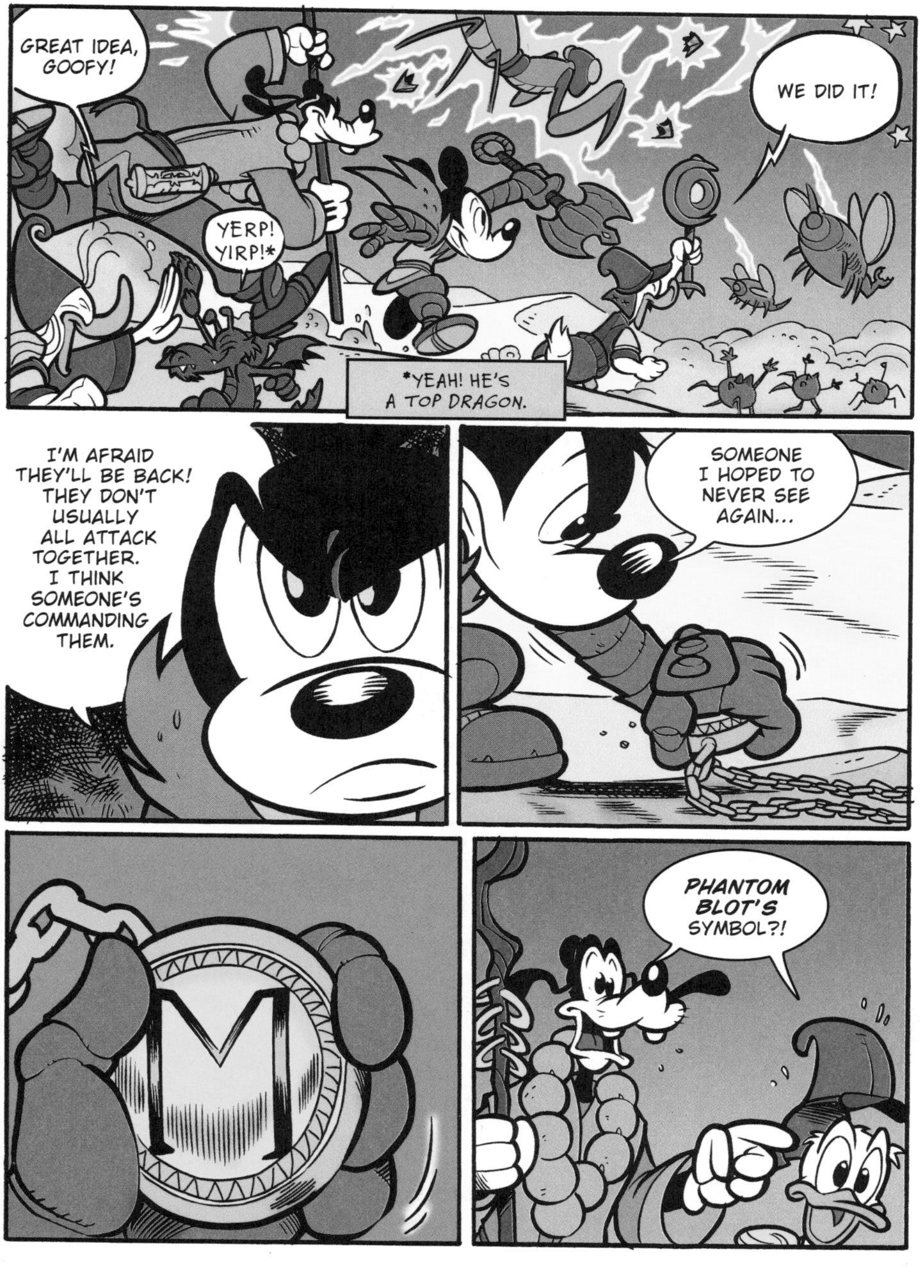
GREAT IDEA, GOOFY!
WE DID IT!
YERP! YIRP!*
*YEAH! HE'S A TOP DRAGON.
I'M AFRAID THEY'LL BE BACK! THEY DON'T USUALLY ALL ATTACK TOGETHER. I THINK SOMEONE'S COMMANDING THEM.
SOMEONE I HOPED TO NEVER SEE AGAIN...
PHANTOM BLOT'S SYMBOL?!

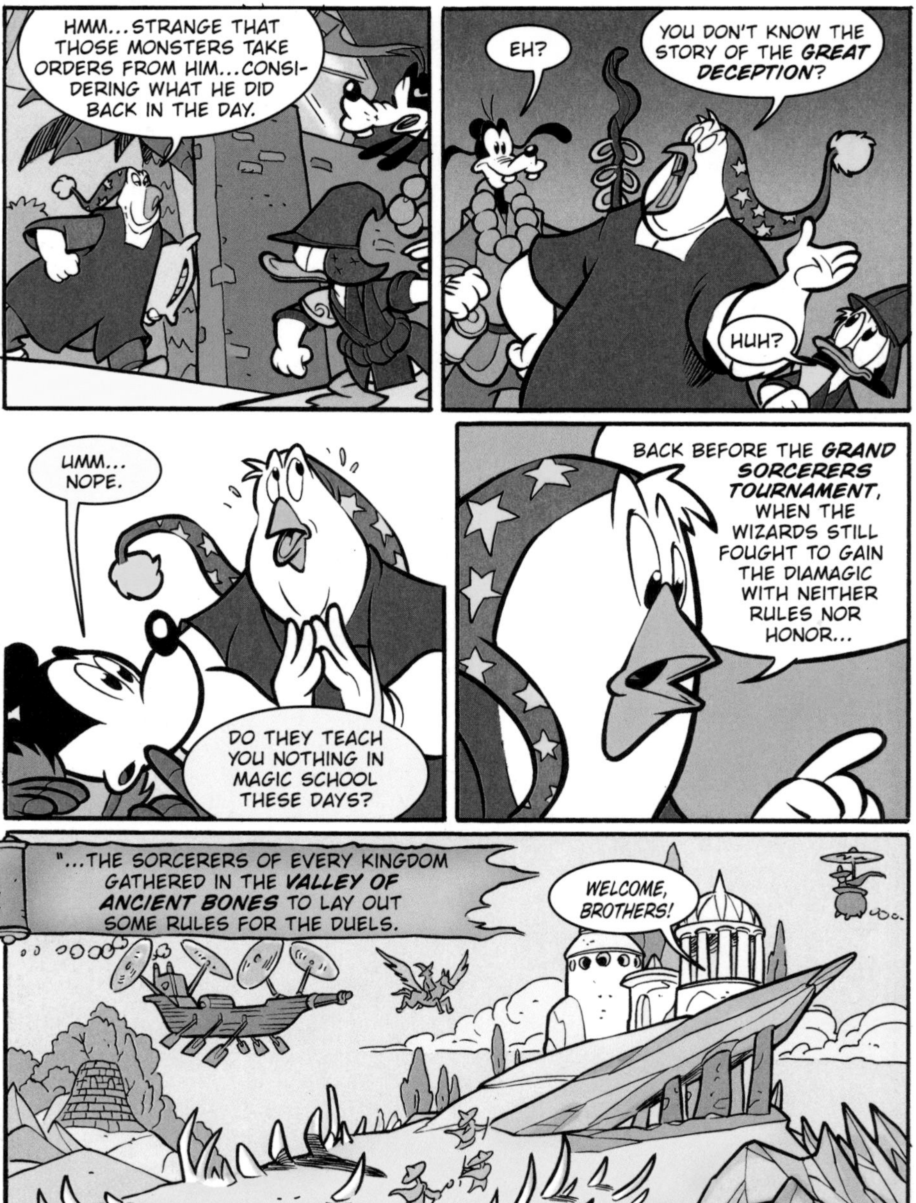
HMM... STRANGE THAT THOSE MONSTERS TAKE ORDERS FROM HIM... CONSI-DERING WHAT HE DID BACK IN THE DAY.
EH?
YOU DON'T KNOW THE STORY OF THE GREAT DECEPTION?
HUH?
UMM... NOPE.
DO THEY TEACH YOU NOTHING IN MAGIC SCHOOL THESE DAYS?
BACK BEFORE THE GRAND SORCERERS TOURNAMENT, WHEN THE WIZARDS STILL FOUGHT TO GAIN THE DIAMAGIC WITH NEITHER RULES NOR HONOR...
"...THE SORCERERS OF EVERY KINGDOM GATHERED IN THE VALLEY OF ANCIENT BONES TO LAY OUT SOME RULES FOR THE DUELS.
WELCOME, BROTHERS!

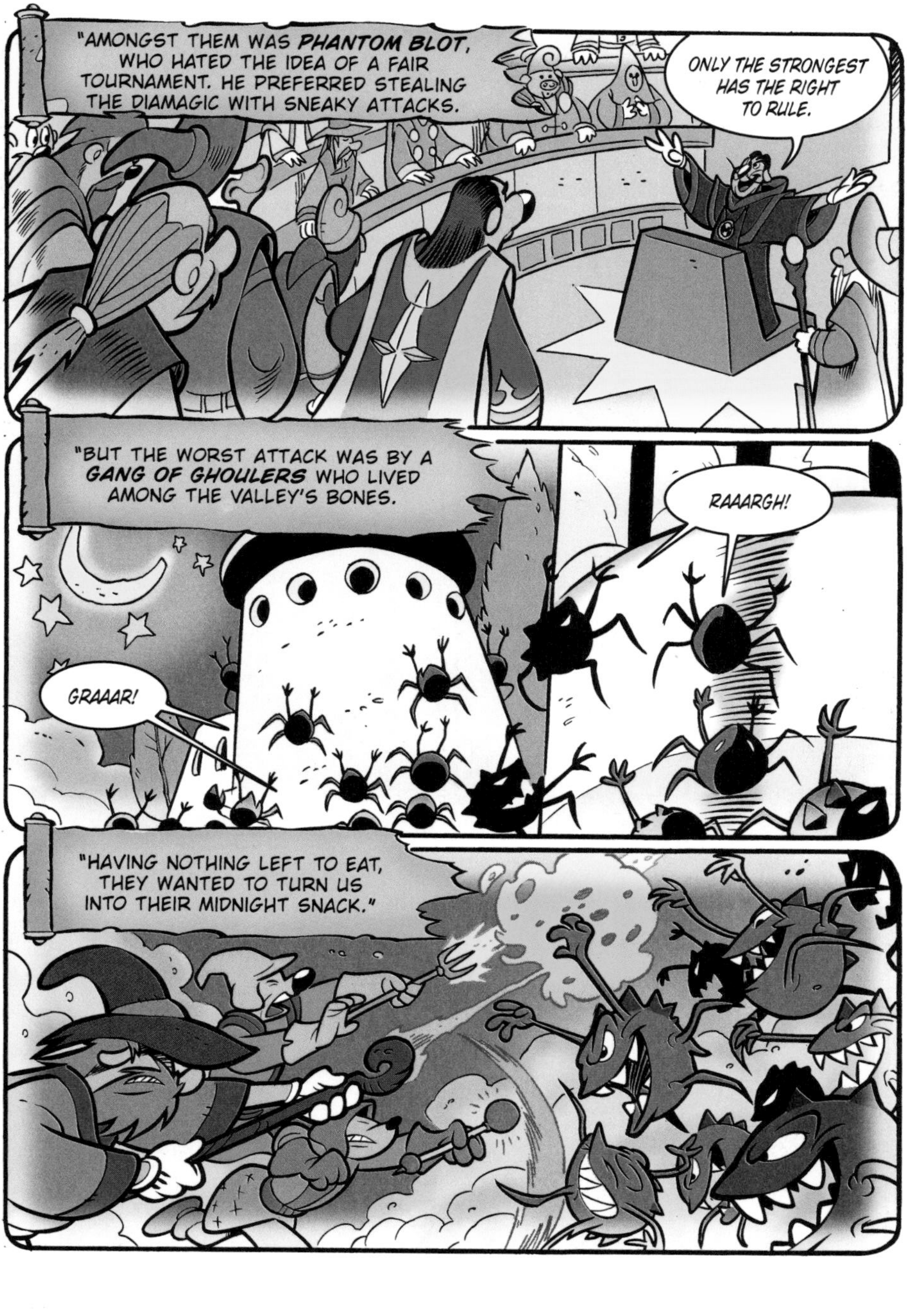
"AMONGST THEM WAS PHANTOM BLOT, WHO HATED THE IDEA OF A FAIR TOURNAMENT. HE PREFERRED STEALING THE DIAMAGIC WITH SNEAKY ATTACKS.
ONLY THE STRONGEST HAS THE RIGHT TO RULE.
"BUT THE WORST ATTACK WAS BY A GANG OF GHOULERS WHO LIVED AMONG THE VALLEY'S BONES.
GRAAAR!
RAAARGH!
"HAVING NOTHING LEFT TO EAT, THEY WANTED TO TURN US INTO THEIR MIDNIGHT SNACK."

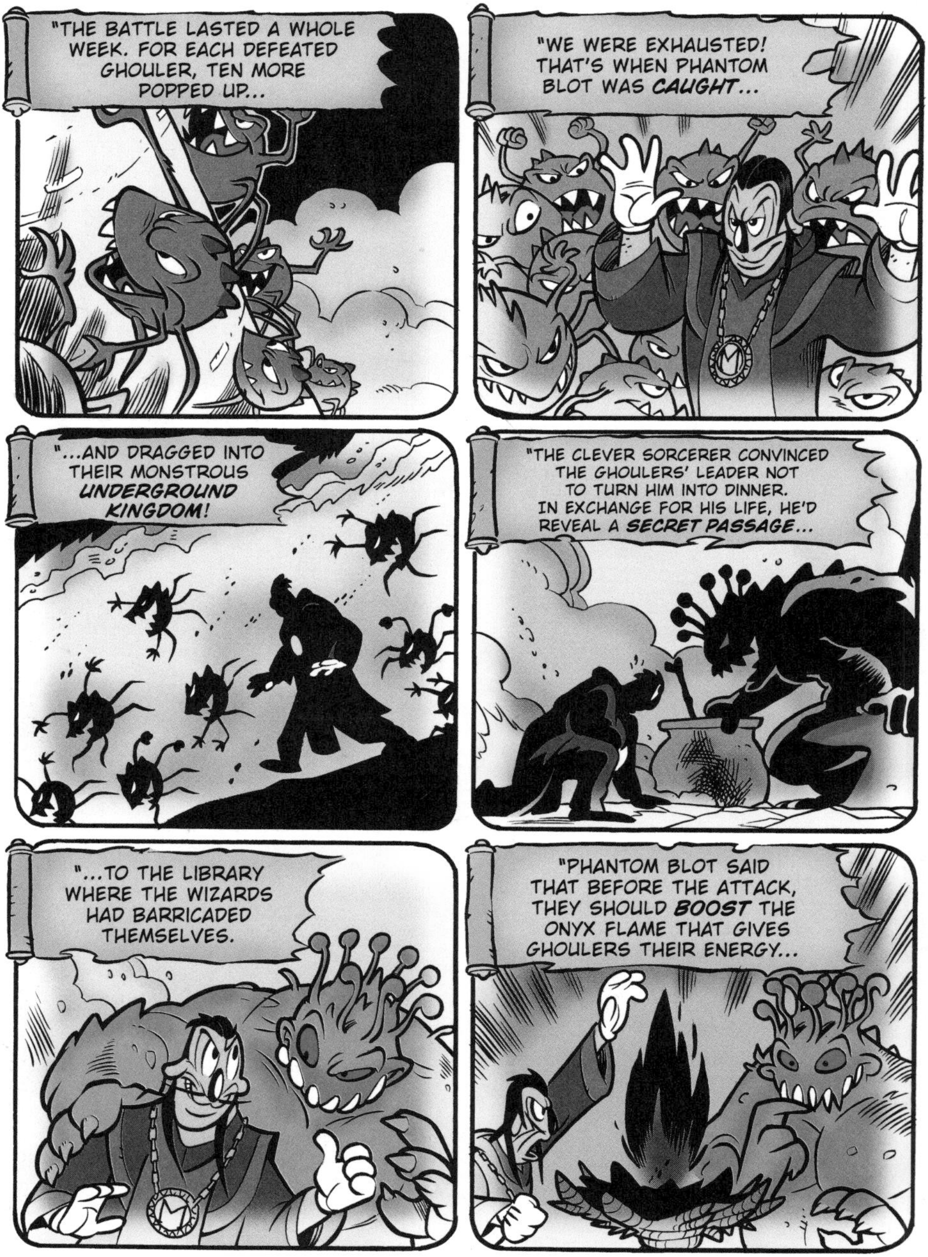
"THE BATTLE LASTED A WHOLE WEEK. FOR EACH DEFEATED GHOULER, TEN MORE POPPED UP...
"WE WERE EXHAUSTED! THAT'S WHEN PHANTOM BLOT WAS CAUGHT...
"...AND DRAGGED INTO THEIR MONSTROUS UNDERGROUND KINGDOM!
"THE CLEVER SORCERER CONVINCED THE GHOULERS' LEADER NOT TO TURN HIM INTO DINNER. IN EXCHANGE FOR HIS LIFE, HE'D REVEAL A SECRET PASSAGE...
"...TO THE LIBRARY WHERE THE WIZARDS HAD BARRICADED THEMSELVES.
"PHANTOM BLOT SAID THAT BEFORE THE ATTACK, THEY SHOULD BOOST THE ONYX FLAME THAT GIVES GHOULERS THEIR ENERGY...

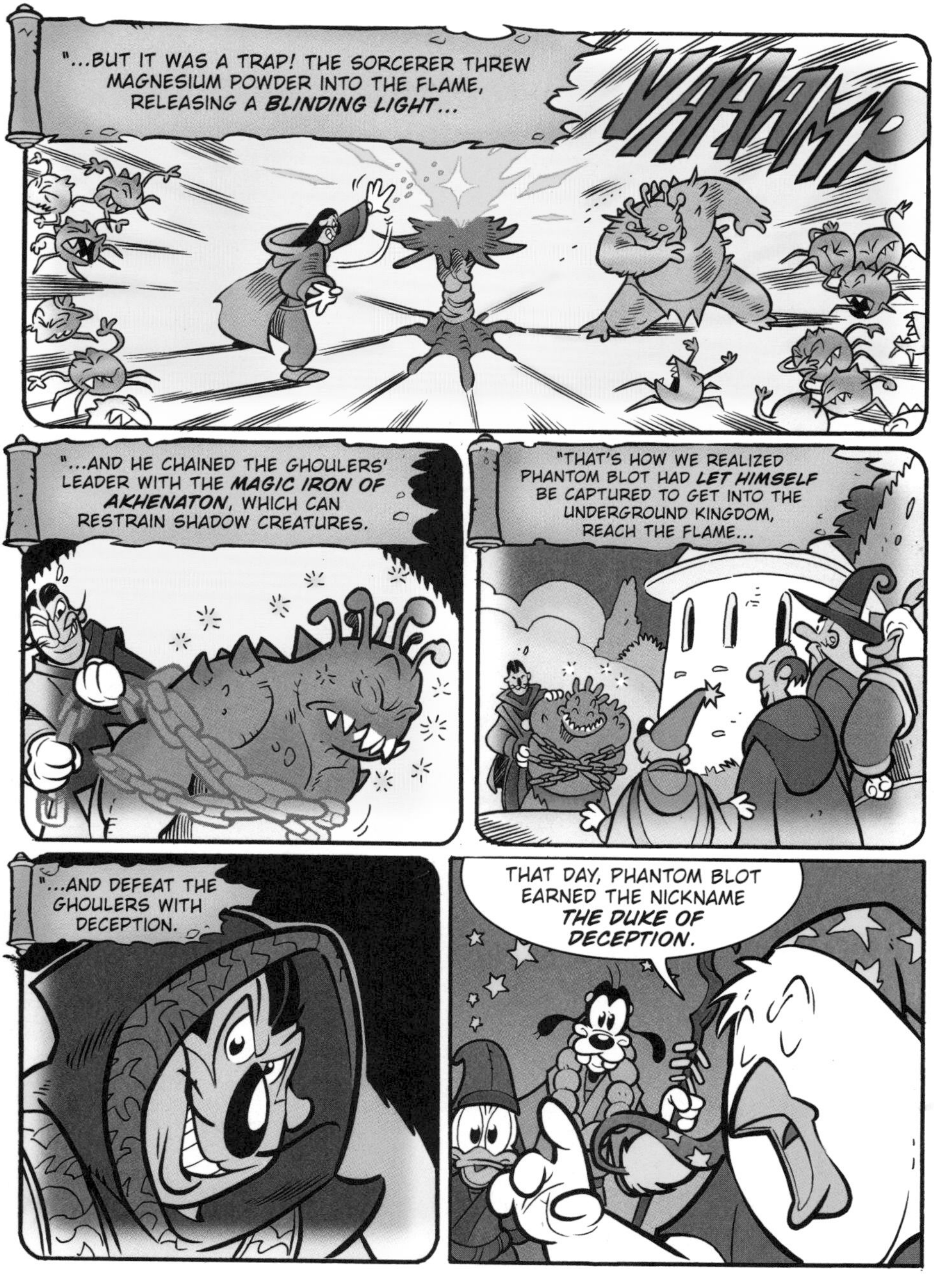
"...BUT IT WAS A TRAP! THE SORCERER THREW MAGNESIUM POWDER INTO THE FLAME, RELEASING A BLINDING LIGHT...
VAAAMP
"...AND HE CHAINED THE GHOULERS' LEADER WITH THE MAGIC IRON OF AKHENATON, WHICH CAN RESTRAIN SHADOW CREATURES.
"THAT'S HOW WE REALIZED PHANTOM BLOT HAD LET HIMSELF BE CAPTURED TO GET INTO THE UNDERGROUND KINGDOM, REACH THE FLAME...
"...AND DEFEAT THE GHOULERS WITH DECEPTION.
THAT DAY, PHANTOM BLOT EARNED THE NICKNAME THE DUKE OF DECEPTION.

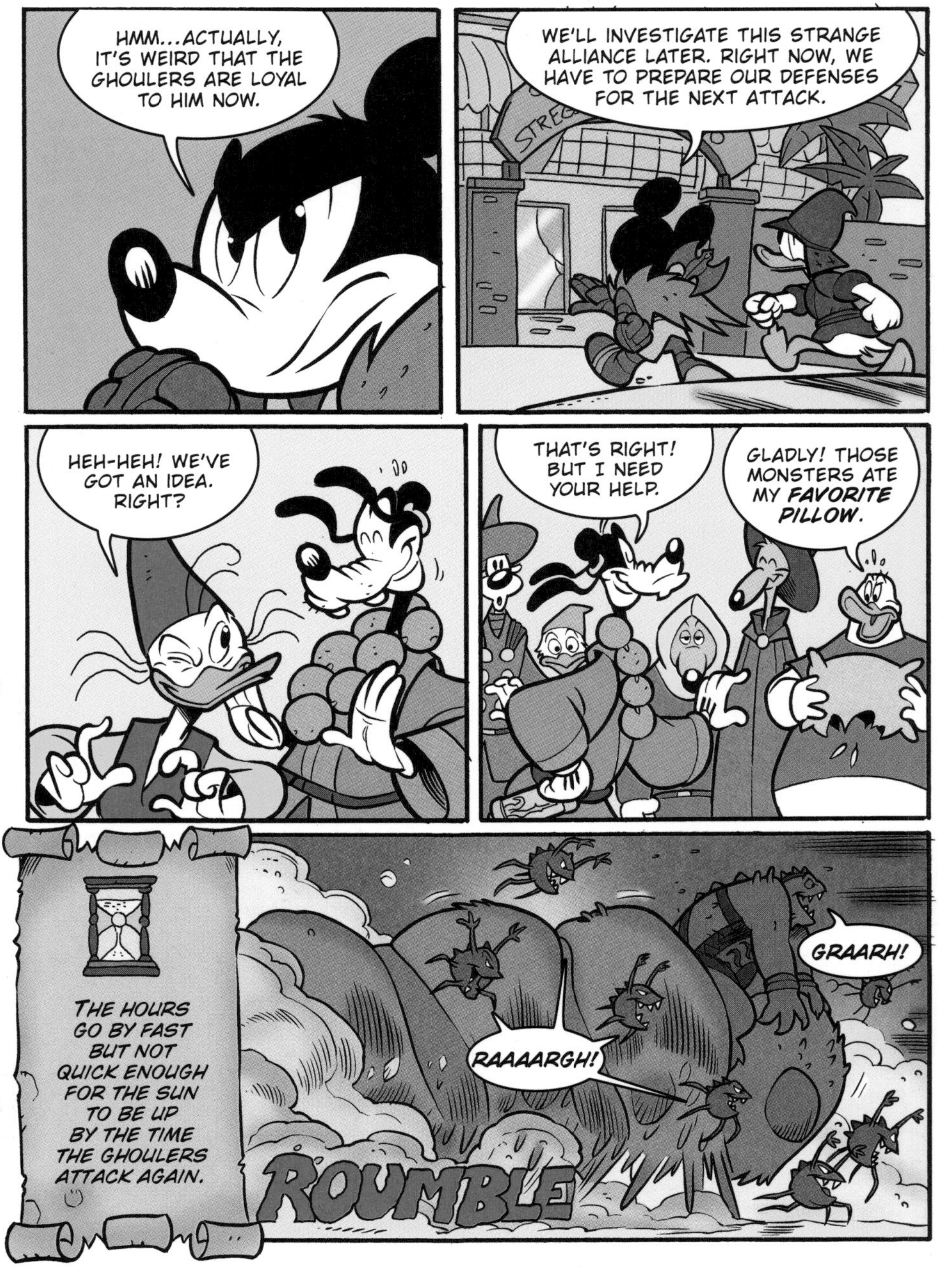
HMM...ACTUALLY, IT'S WEIRD THAT THE GHOULERS ARE LOYAL TO HIM NOW.
WE'LL INVESTIGATE THIS STRANGE ALLIANCE LATER. RIGHT NOW, WE HAVE TO PREPARE OUR DEFENSES FOR THE NEXT ATTACK.
HEH-HEH! WE'VE GOT AN IDEA. RIGHT?
THAT'S RIGHT! BUT I NEED YOUR HELP.
GLADLY! THOSE MONSTERS ATE MY *FAVORITE PILLOW*.
THE HOURS GO BY FAST BUT NOT QUICK ENOUGH FOR THE SUN TO BE UP BY THE TIME THE GHOULERS ATTACK AGAIN.
GRAARH!
RAAAARGH!
ROUMBLE

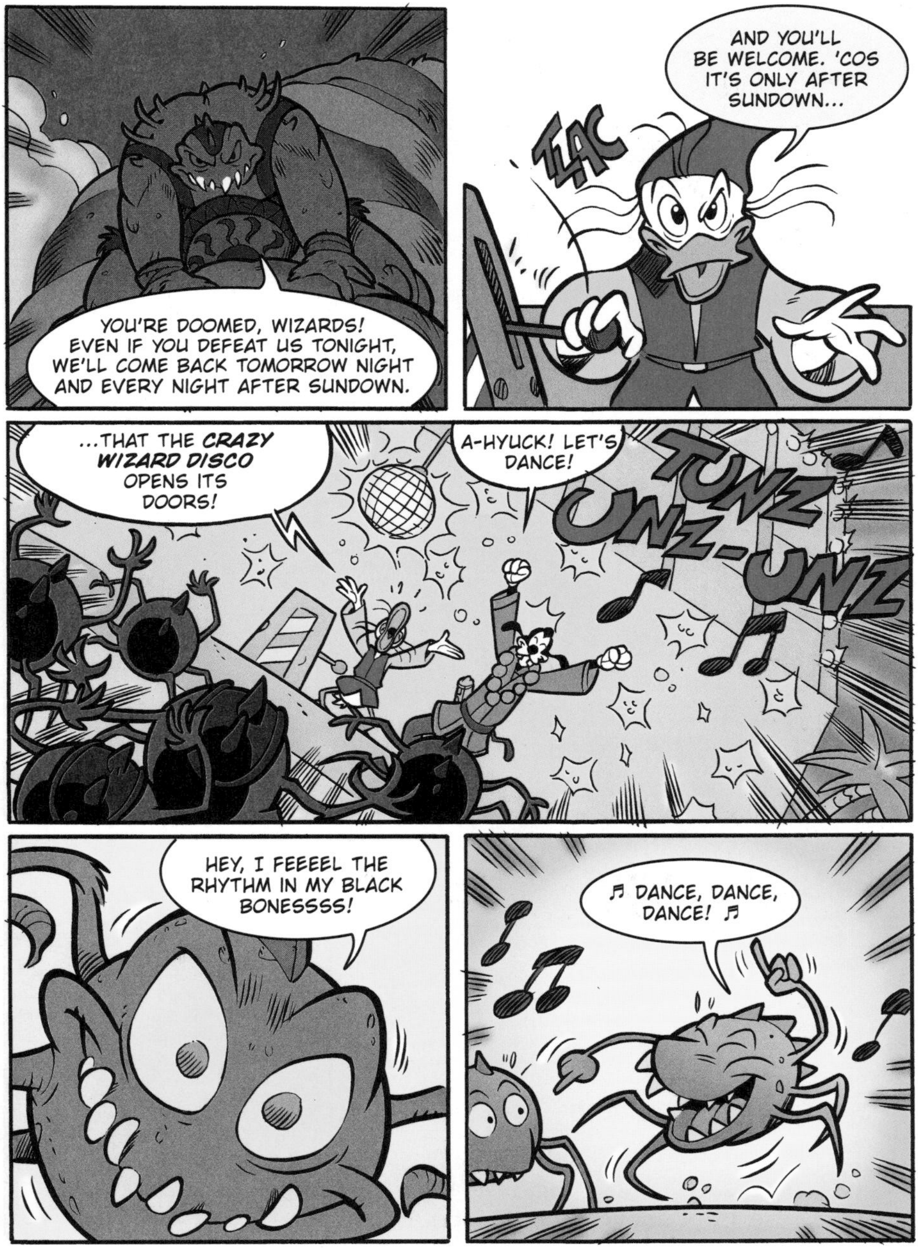
YOU'RE DOOMED, WIZARDS! EVEN IF YOU DEFEAT US TONIGHT, WE'LL COME BACK TOMORROW NIGHT AND EVERY NIGHT AFTER SUNDOWN.
AND YOU'LL BE WELCOME. 'COS IT'S ONLY AFTER SUNDOWN...
TLAC
...THAT THE CRAZY WIZARD DISCO OPENS ITS DOORS!
A-HYUCK! LET'S DANCE!
TUNZ UNZ-UNZ
HEY, I FEEEEL THE RHYTHM IN MY BLACK BONESSSS!
♬ DANCE, DANCE, DANCE! ♬

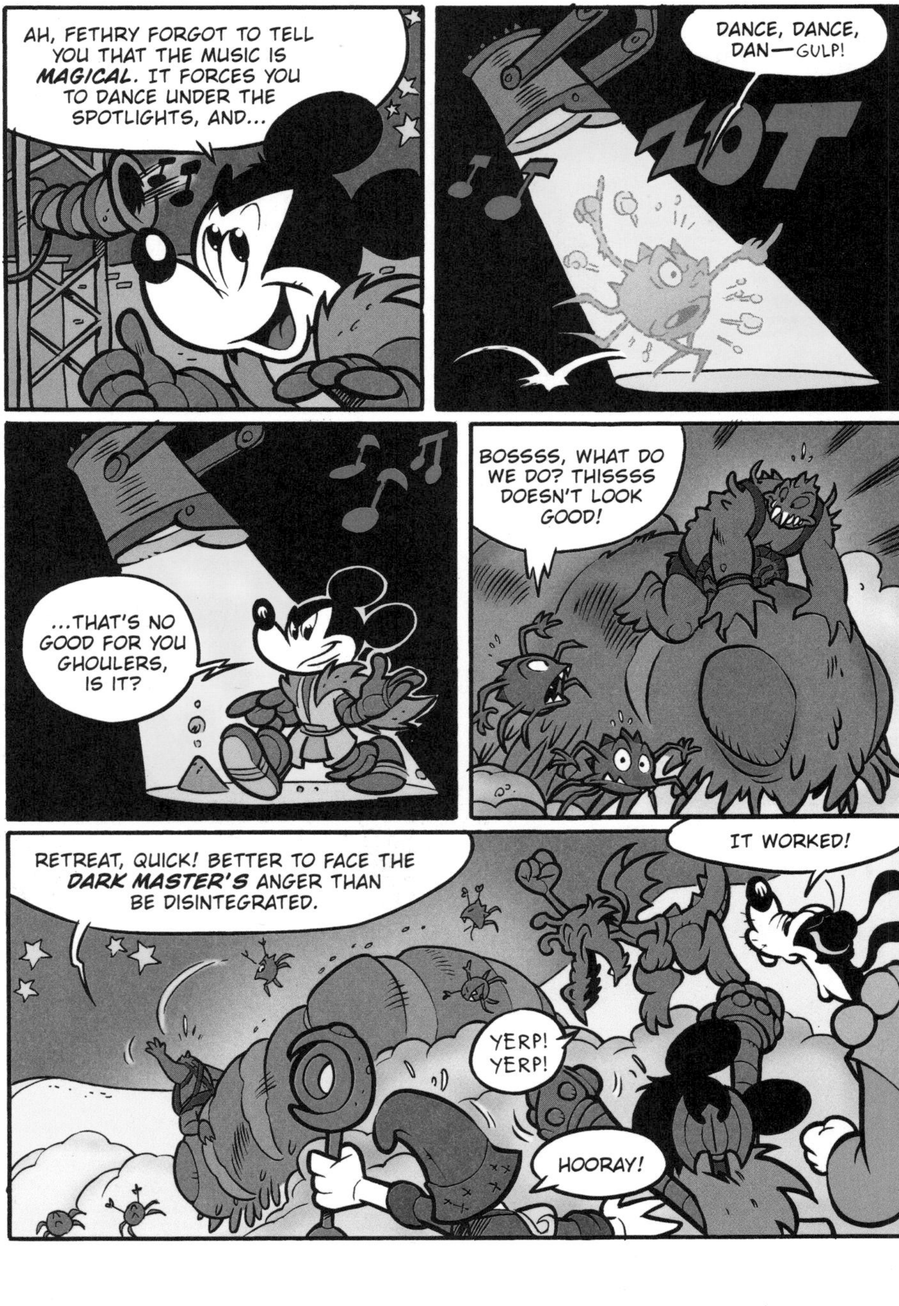
AH, FETHRY FORGOT TO TELL YOU THAT THE MUSIC IS MAGICAL. IT FORCES YOU TO DANCE UNDER THE SPOTLIGHTS, AND...
DANCE, DANCE, DAN—GULP!
ZOT
...THAT'S NO GOOD FOR YOU GHOULERS, IS IT?
BOSSSS, WHAT DO WE DO? THISSSS DOESN'T LOOK GOOD!
RETREAT, QUICK! BETTER TO FACE THE DARK MASTER'S ANGER THAN BE DISINTEGRATED.
IT WORKED!
YERP! YERP!
HOORAY!

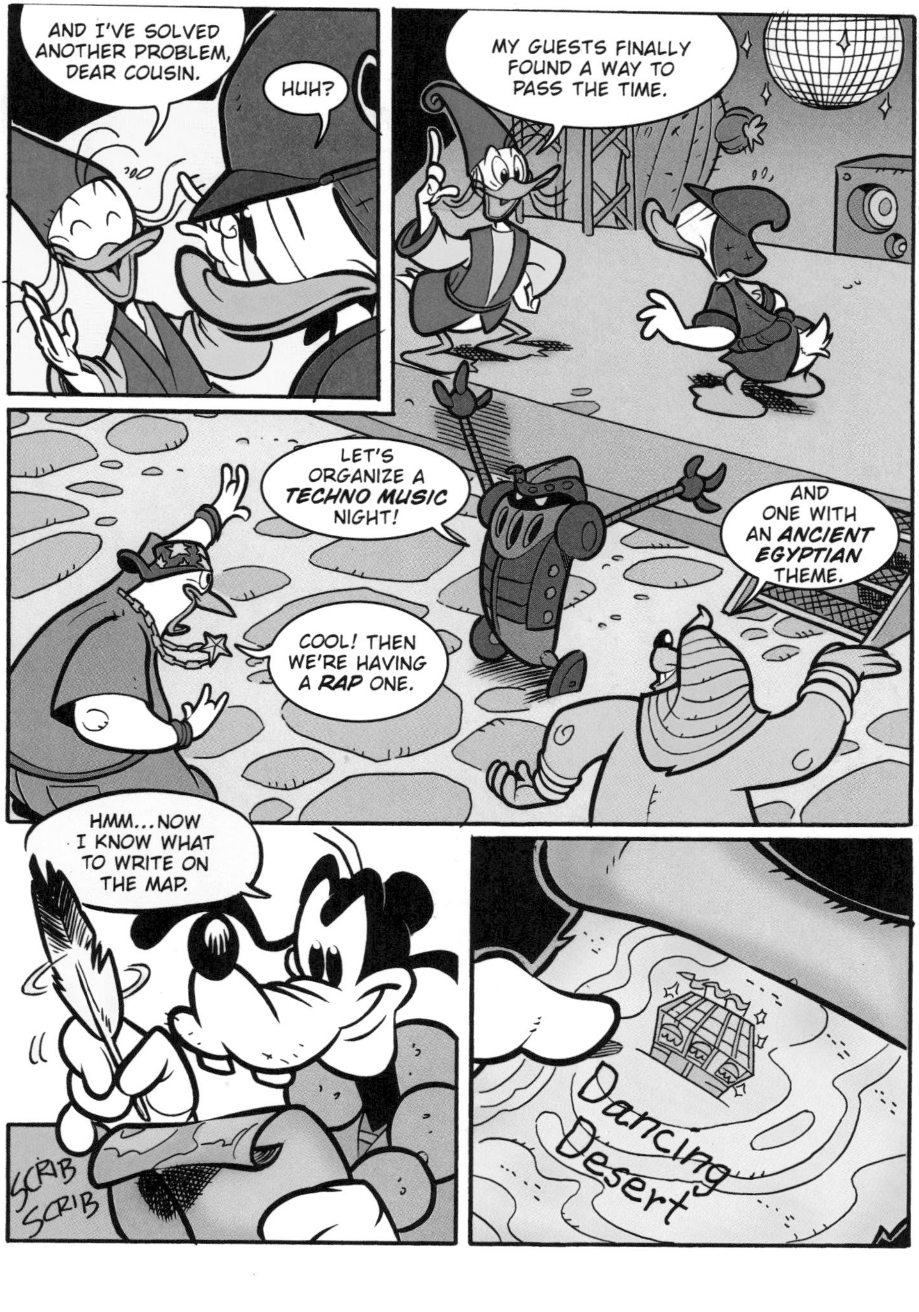
AND I'VE SOLVED ANOTHER PROBLEM, DEAR COUSIN.
HUH?
MY GUESTS FINALLY FOUND A WAY TO PASS THE TIME.
LET'S ORGANIZE A TECHNO MUSIC NIGHT!
AND ONE WITH AN ANCIENT EGYPTIAN THEME.
COOL! THEN WE'RE HAVING A RAP ONE.
HMM...NOW I KNOW WHAT TO WRITE ON THE MAP.
SCRIB SCRIB
Dancing Desert

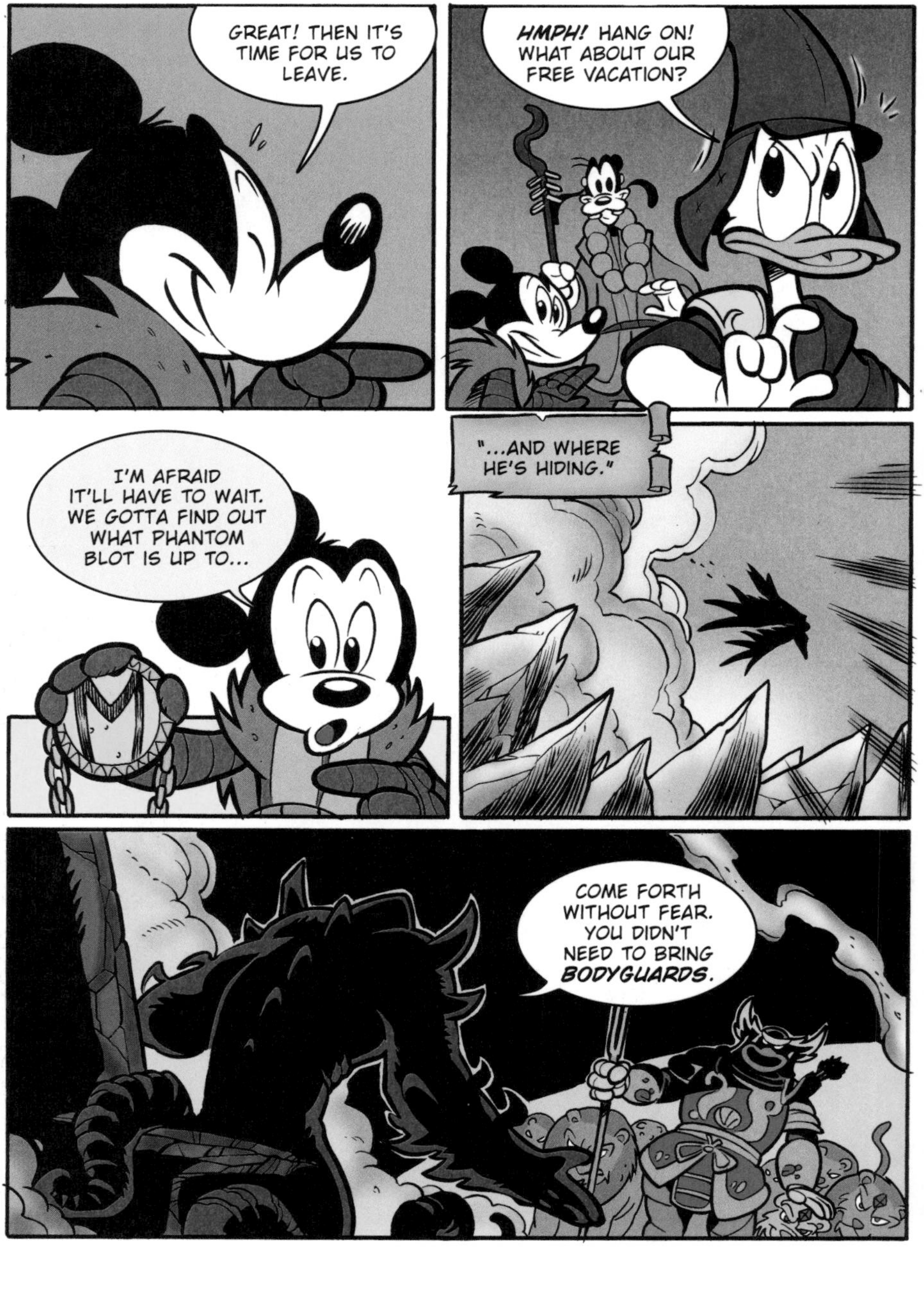
GREAT! THEN IT'S TIME FOR US TO LEAVE.
HMPH! HANG ON! WHAT ABOUT OUR FREE VACATION?
I'M AFRAID IT'LL HAVE TO WAIT. WE GOTTA FIND OUT WHAT PHANTOM BLOT IS UP TO...
"...AND WHERE HE'S HIDING."
COME FORTH WITHOUT FEAR. YOU DIDN'T NEED TO BRING BODYGUARDS.

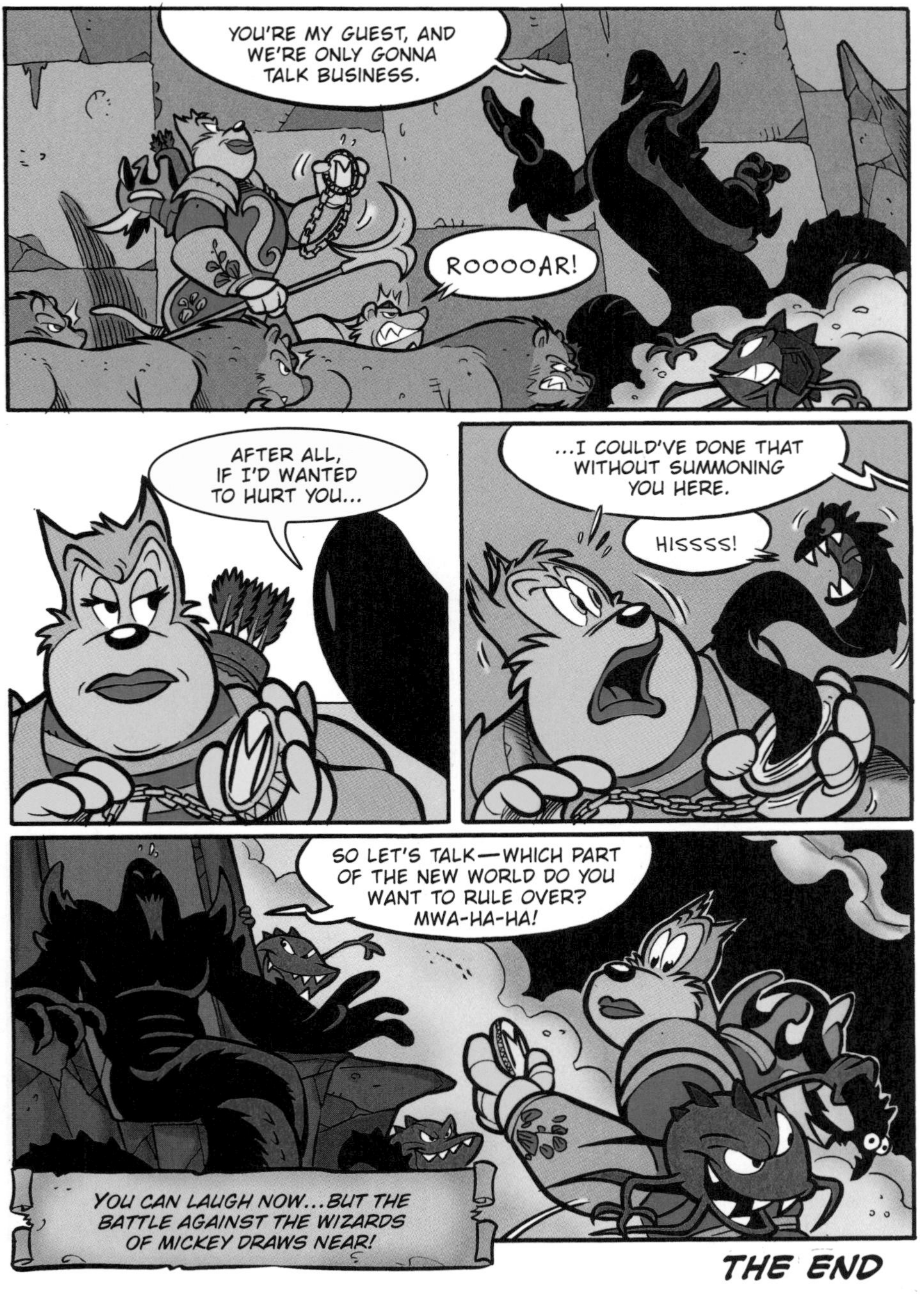
YOU'RE MY GUEST, AND WE'RE ONLY GONNA TALK BUSINESS.
ROOOOAR!
AFTER ALL, IF I'D WANTED TO HURT YOU...
...I COULD'VE DONE THAT WITHOUT SUMMONING YOU HERE.
HISSSS!
SO LET'S TALK—WHICH PART OF THE NEW WORLD DO YOU WANT TO RULE OVER? MWA-HA-HA!
YOU CAN LAUGH NOW...BUT THE BATTLE AGAINST THE WIZARDS OF MICKEY DRAWS NEAR!

THE END

Wizards of Mickey

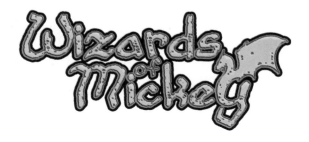

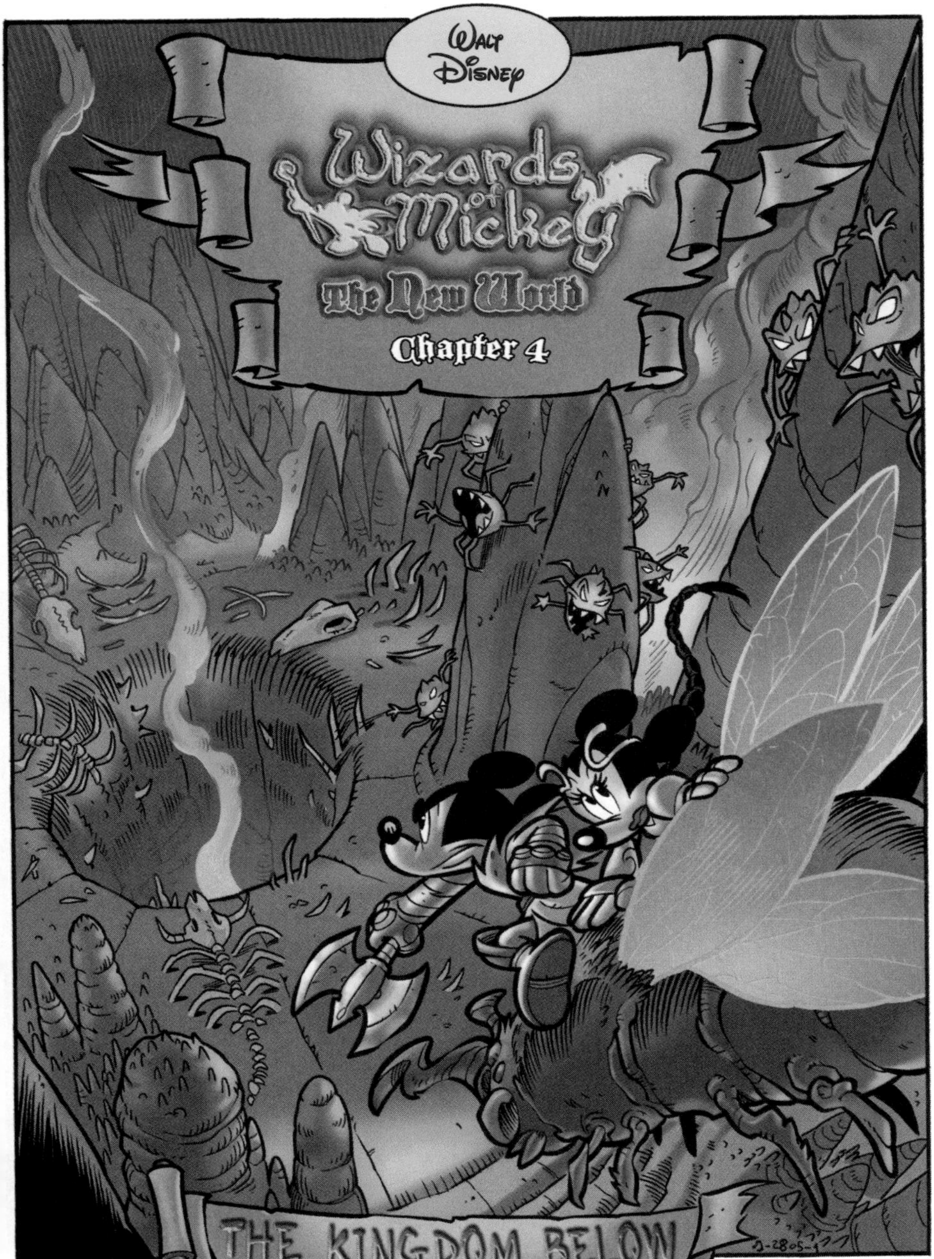
Walt Disney
Wizards of Mickey
The New World
Chapter 4
THE KINGDOM BELOW

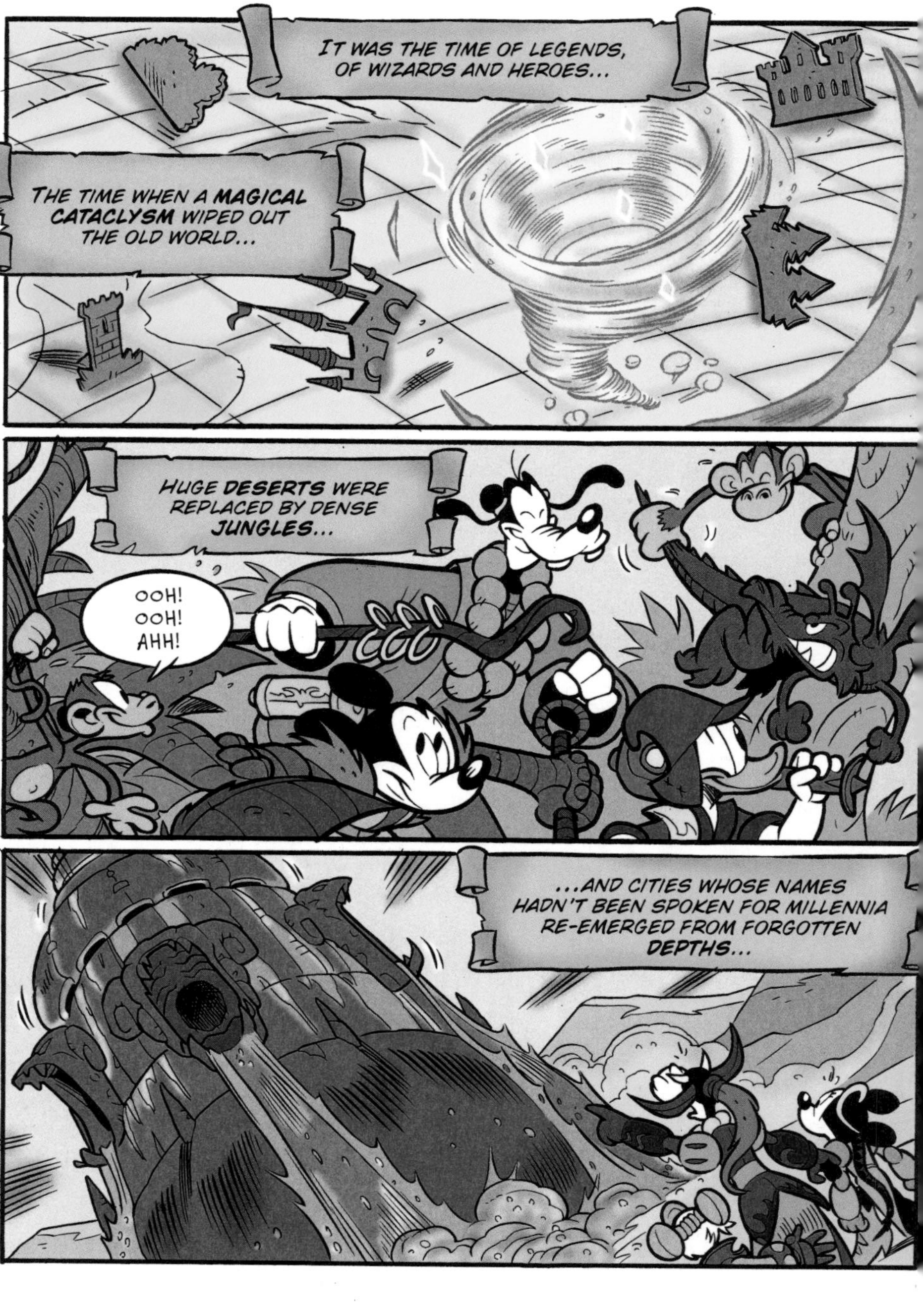
IT WAS THE TIME OF LEGENDS, OF WIZARDS AND HEROES...
THE TIME WHEN A MAGICAL CATACLYSM WIPED OUT THE OLD WORLD...
HUGE DESERTS WERE REPLACED BY DENSE JUNGLES...
OOH! OOH! AHH!
...AND CITIES WHOSE NAMES HADN'T BEEN SPOKEN FOR MILLENNIA RE-EMERGED FROM FORGOTTEN DEPTHS...

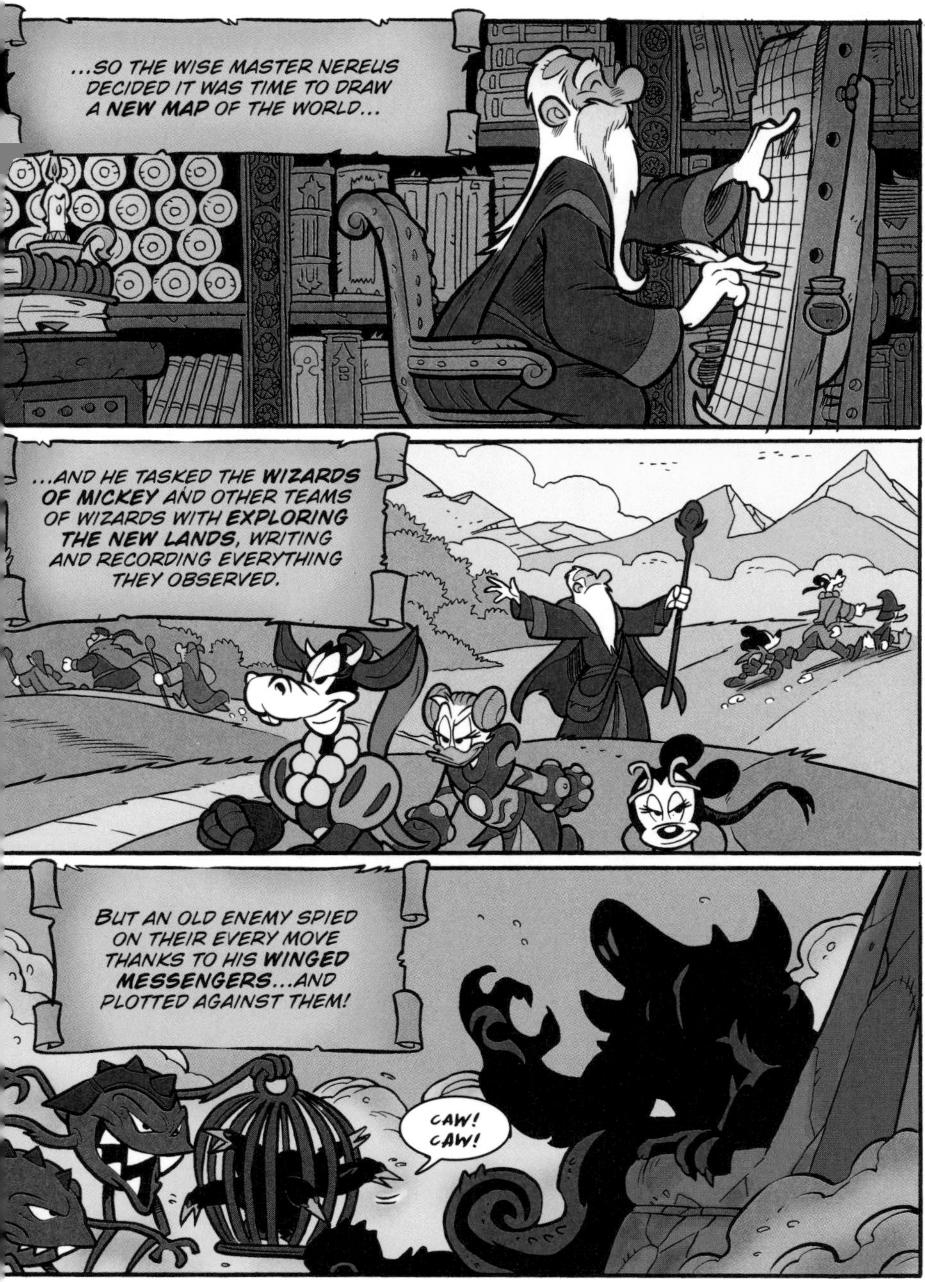

...SO THE WISE MASTER NEREUS DECIDED IT WAS TIME TO DRAW A NEW MAP OF THE WORLD...
...AND HE TASKED THE WIZARDS OF MICKEY AND OTHER TEAMS OF WIZARDS WITH EXPLORING THE NEW LANDS, WRITING AND RECORDING EVERYTHING THEY OBSERVED.
BUT AN OLD ENEMY SPIED ON THEIR EVERY MOVE THANKS TO HIS WINGED MESSENGERS...AND PLOTTED AGAINST THEM!
CAW! CAW!

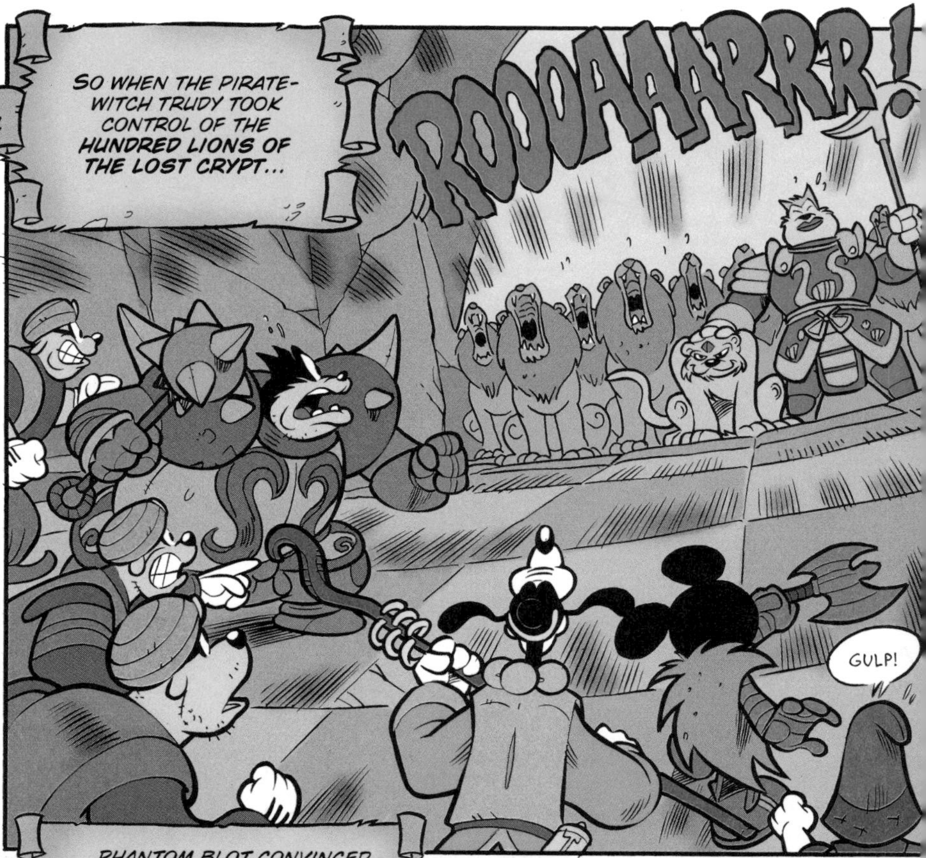
SO WHEN THE PIRATE-WITCH TRUDY TOOK CONTROL OF THE HUNDRED LIONS OF THE LOST CRYPT...
ROOOAAARRRR!
GULP!

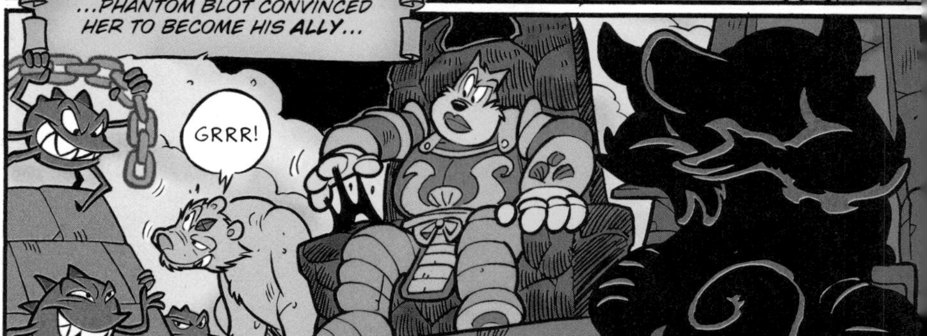
...PHANTOM BLOT CONVINCED HER TO BECOME HIS ALLY...
GRRR!

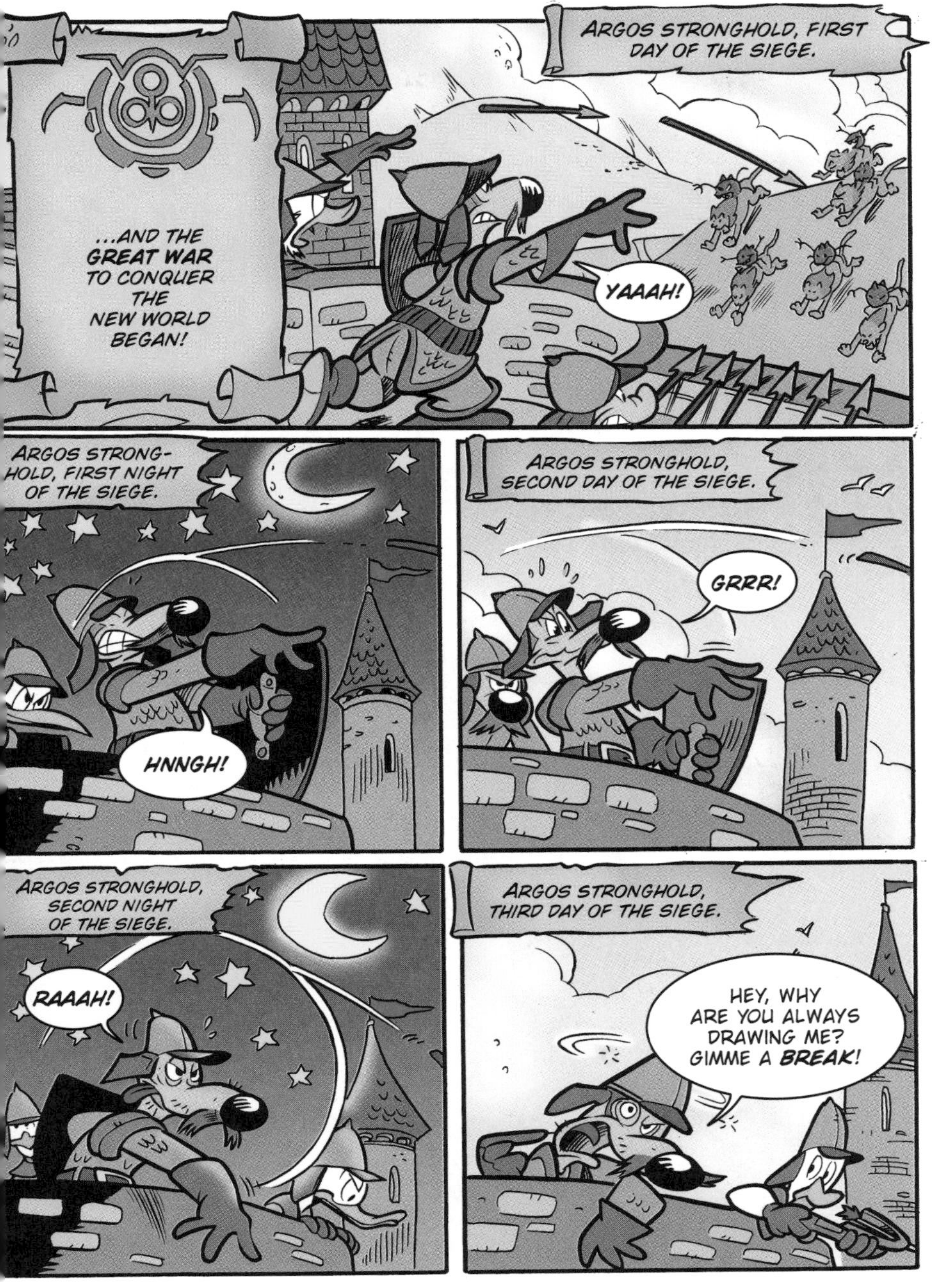
ARGOS STRONGHOLD, FIRST DAY OF THE SIEGE.
...AND THE GREAT WAR TO CONQUER THE NEW WORLD BEGAN!
YAAAH!
ARGOS STRONG-HOLD, FIRST NIGHT OF THE SIEGE.
HNNGH!
ARGOS STRONGHOLD, SECOND DAY OF THE SIEGE.
GRRR!
ARGOS STRONGHOLD, SECOND NIGHT OF THE SIEGE.
RAAAH!
ARGOS STRONGHOLD, THIRD DAY OF THE SIEGE.
HEY, WHY ARE YOU ALWAYS DRAWING ME? GIMME A BREAK!

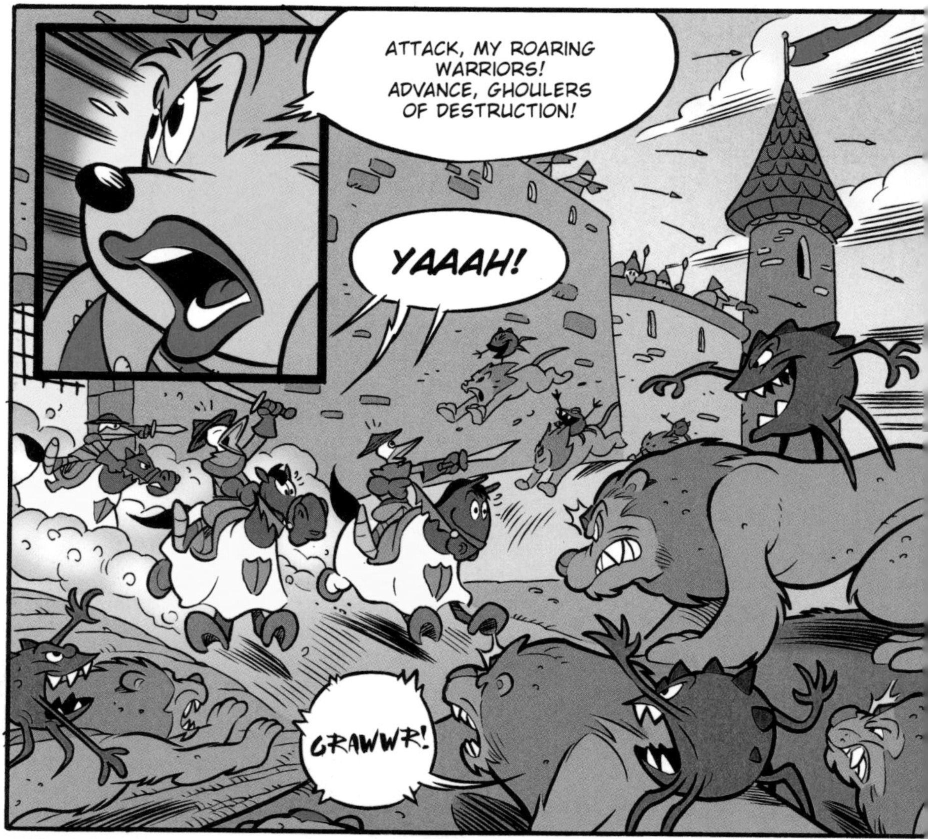
ATTACK, MY ROARING WARRIORS! ADVANCE, GHOULERS OF DESTRUCTION!
YAAAH!
GRAWWR!

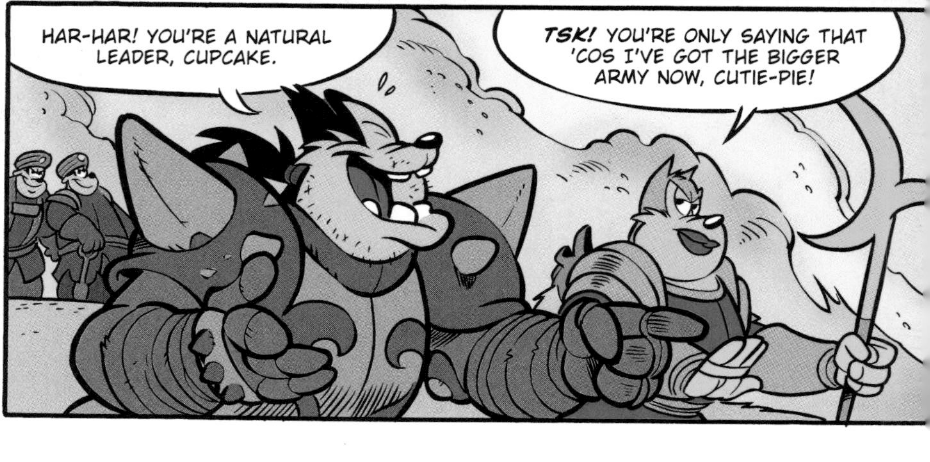
HAR-HAR! YOU'RE A NATURAL LEADER, CUPCAKE.
TSK! YOU'RE ONLY SAYING THAT 'COS I'VE GOT THE BIGGER ARMY NOW, CUTIE-PIE!

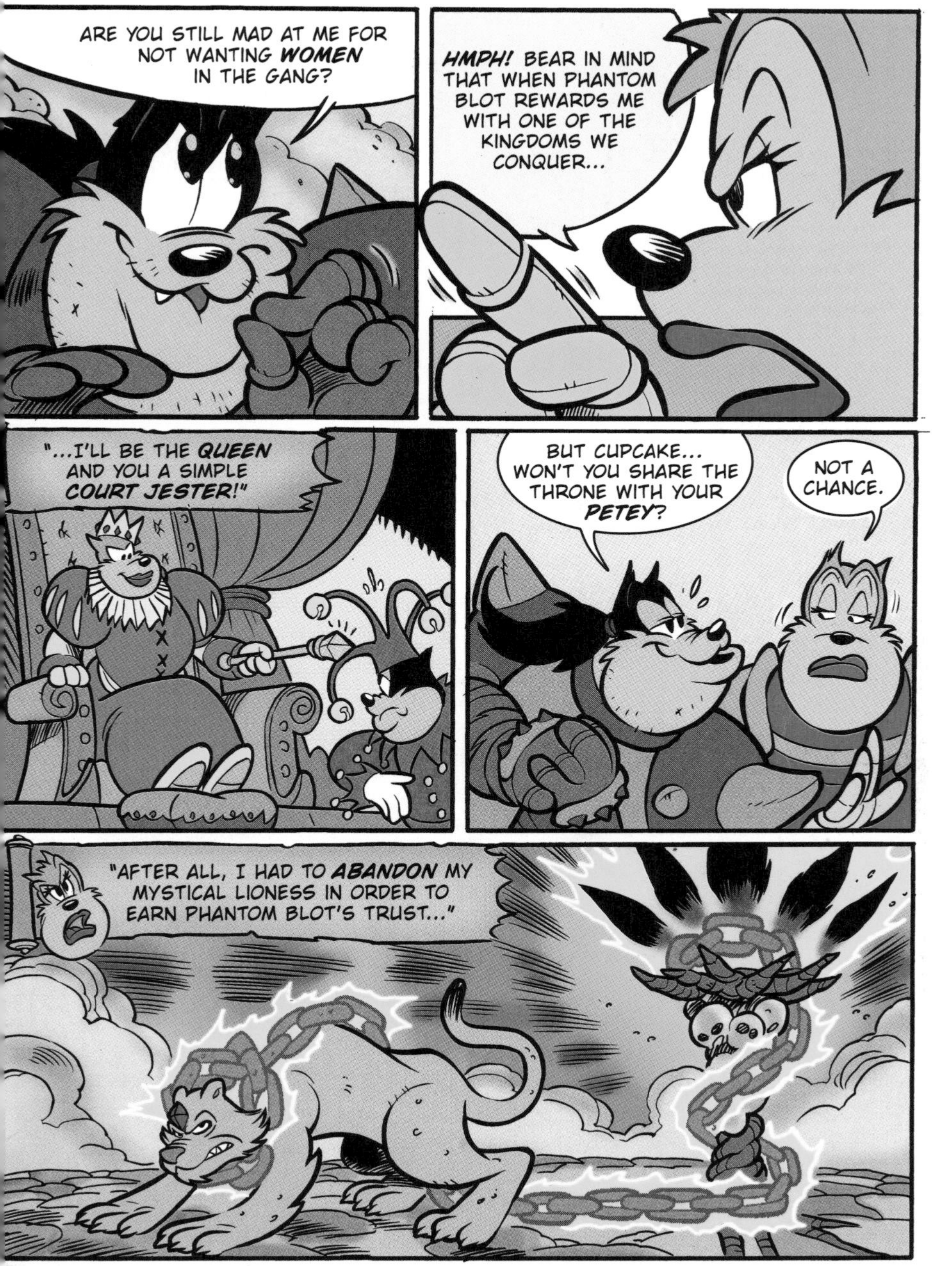
ARE YOU STILL MAD AT ME FOR NOT WANTING WOMEN IN THE GANG?
HMPH! BEAR IN MIND THAT WHEN PHANTOM BLOT REWARDS ME WITH ONE OF THE KINGDOMS WE CONQUER...
"...I'LL BE THE QUEEN AND YOU A SIMPLE COURT JESTER!"
BUT CUPCAKE... WON'T YOU SHARE THE THRONE WITH YOUR PETEY?
NOT A CHANCE.
"AFTER ALL, I HAD TO ABANDON MY MYSTICAL LIONESS IN ORDER TO EARN PHANTOM BLOT'S TRUST..."

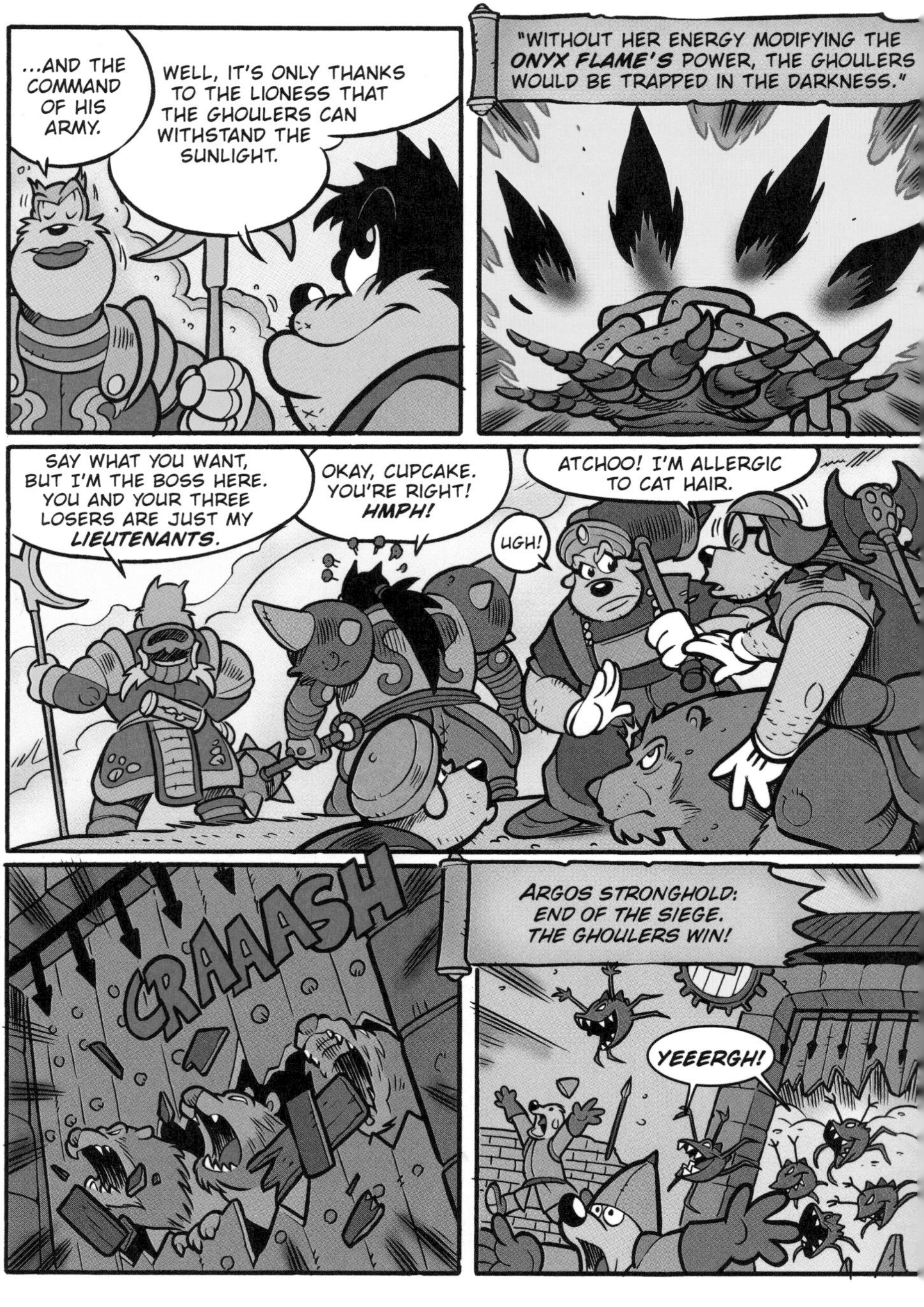
...AND THE COMMAND OF HIS ARMY.
WELL, IT'S ONLY THANKS TO THE LIONESS THAT THE GHOULERS CAN WITHSTAND THE SUNLIGHT.
"WITHOUT HER ENERGY MODIFYING THE ONYX FLAME'S POWER, THE GHOULERS WOULD BE TRAPPED IN THE DARKNESS."
SAY WHAT YOU WANT, BUT I'M THE BOSS HERE. YOU AND YOUR THREE LOSERS ARE JUST MY LIEUTENANTS.
OKAY, CUPCAKE. YOU'RE RIGHT! HMPH!
ATCHOO! I'M ALLERGIC TO CAT HAIR.
UGH!
CRAAASH
ARGOS STRONGHOLD: END OF THE SIEGE. THE GHOULERS WIN!
YEEERGH!

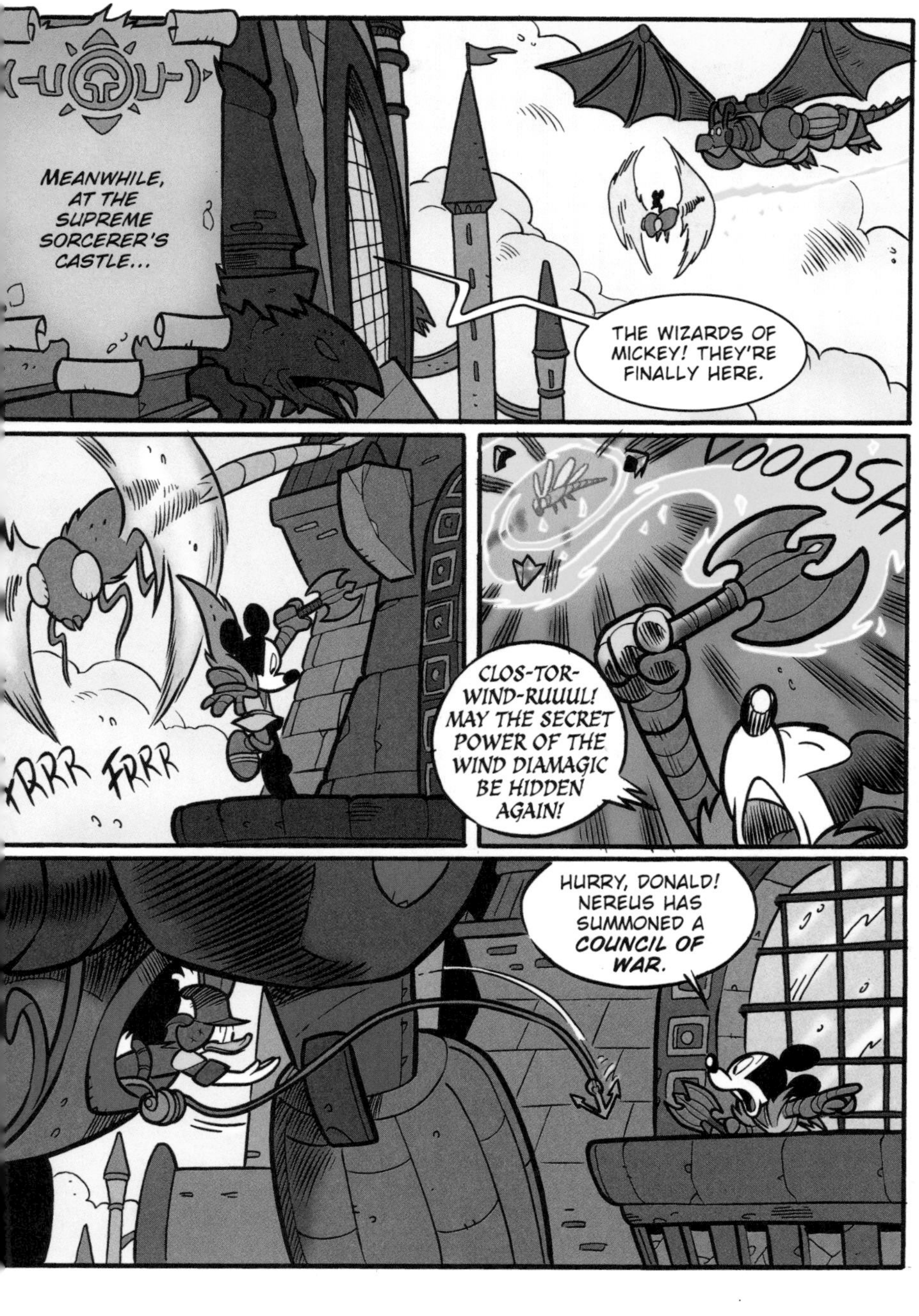
MEANWHILE, AT THE SUPREME SORCERER'S CASTLE...
THE WIZARDS OF MICKEY! THEY'RE FINALLY HERE.
FRRR FRRR
VOOOSH
CLOS-TOR-WIND-RUUUL! MAY THE SECRET POWER OF THE WIND DIAMAGIC BE HIDDEN AGAIN!
HURRY, DONALD! NEREUS HAS SUMMONED A COUNCIL OF WAR.

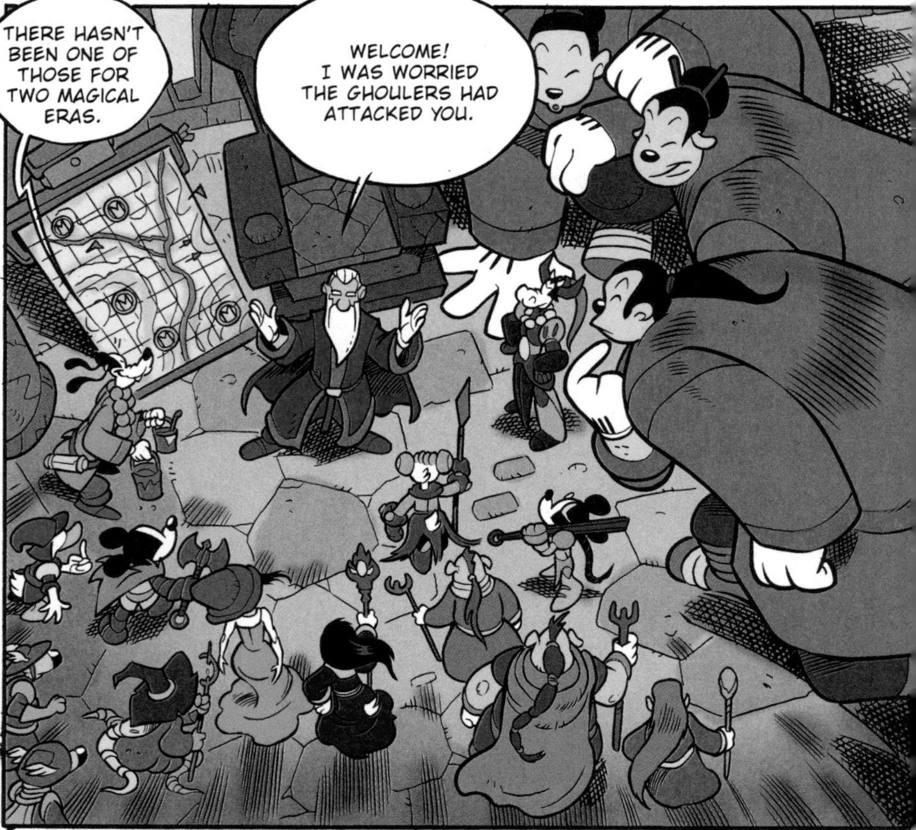
THERE HASN'T BEEN ONE OF THOSE FOR TWO MAGICAL ERAS.
WELCOME! I WAS WORRIED THE GHOULERS HAD ATTACKED YOU.

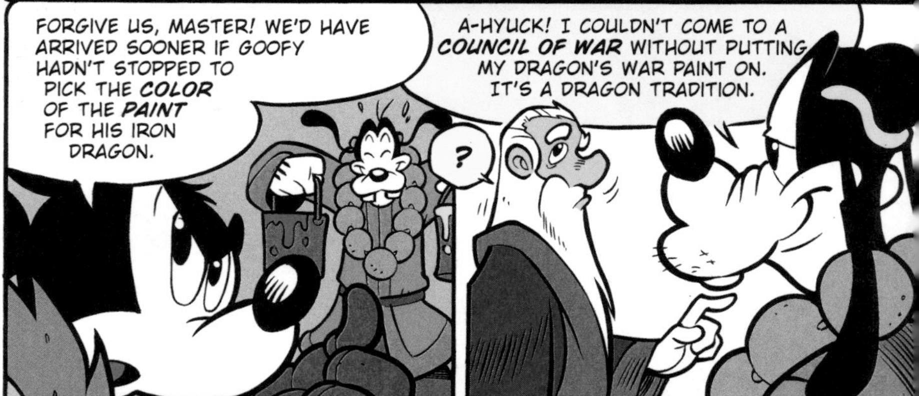
FORGIVE US, MASTER! WE'D HAVE ARRIVED SOONER IF GOOFY HADN'T STOPPED TO PICK THE COLOR OF THE PAINT FOR HIS IRON DRAGON.
?
A-HYUCK! I COULDN'T COME TO A COUNCIL OF WAR WITHOUT PUTTING MY DRAGON'S WAR PAINT ON. IT'S A DRAGON TRADITION.

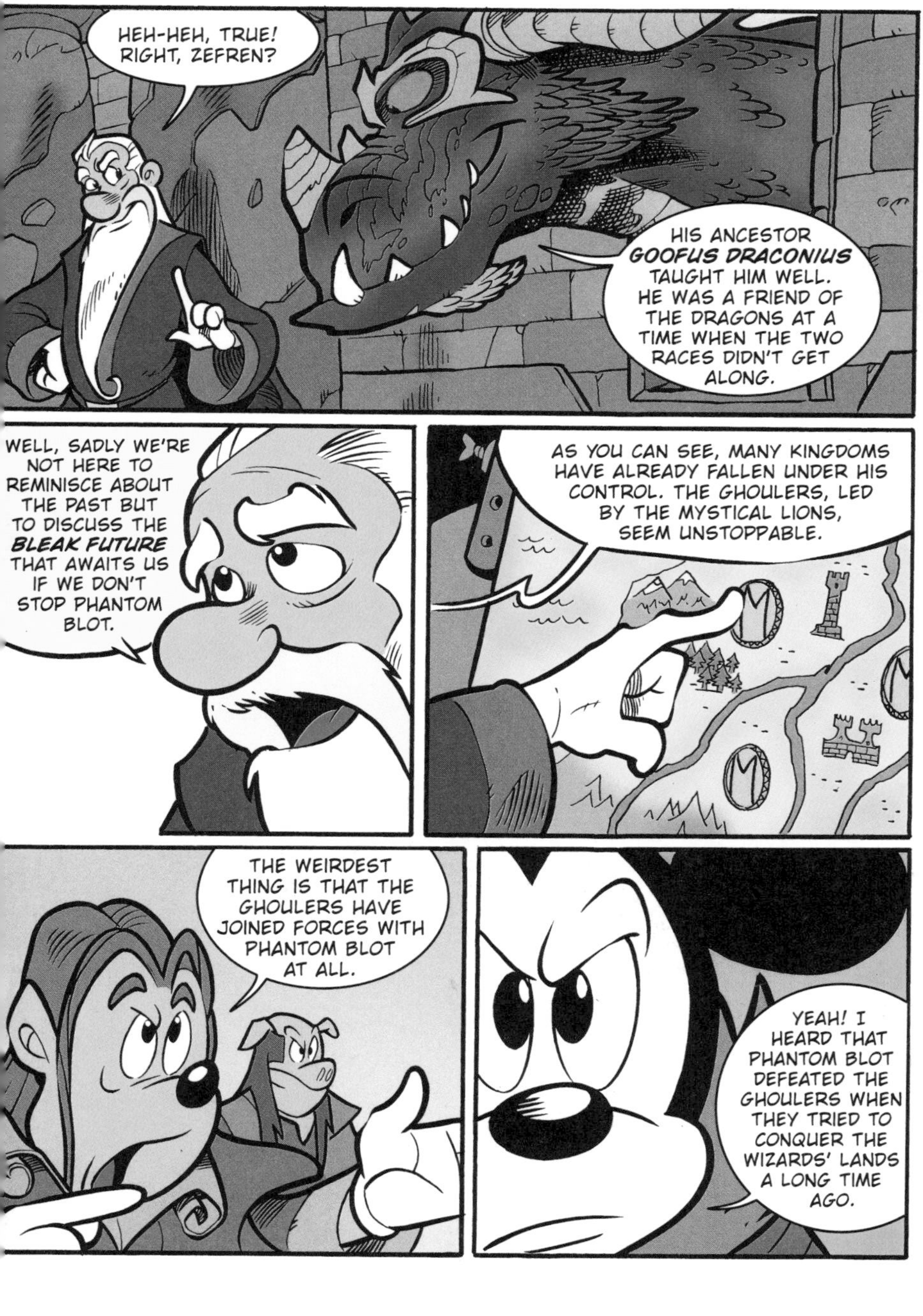
HEH-HEH, TRUE! RIGHT, ZEFREN?
HIS ANCESTOR GOOFUS DRACONIUS TAUGHT HIM WELL. HE WAS A FRIEND OF THE DRAGONS AT A TIME WHEN THE TWO RACES DIDN'T GET ALONG.
WELL, SADLY WE'RE NOT HERE TO REMINISCE ABOUT THE PAST BUT TO DISCUSS THE BLEAK FUTURE THAT AWAITS US IF WE DON'T STOP PHANTOM BLOT.
AS YOU CAN SEE, MANY KINGDOMS HAVE ALREADY FALLEN UNDER HIS CONTROL. THE GHOULERS, LED BY THE MYSTICAL LIONS, SEEM UNSTOPPABLE.
THE WEIRDEST THING IS THAT THE GHOULERS HAVE JOINED FORCES WITH PHANTOM BLOT AT ALL.
YEAH! I HEARD THAT PHANTOM BLOT DEFEATED THE GHOULERS WHEN THEY TRIED TO CONQUER THE WIZARDS' LANDS A LONG TIME AGO.

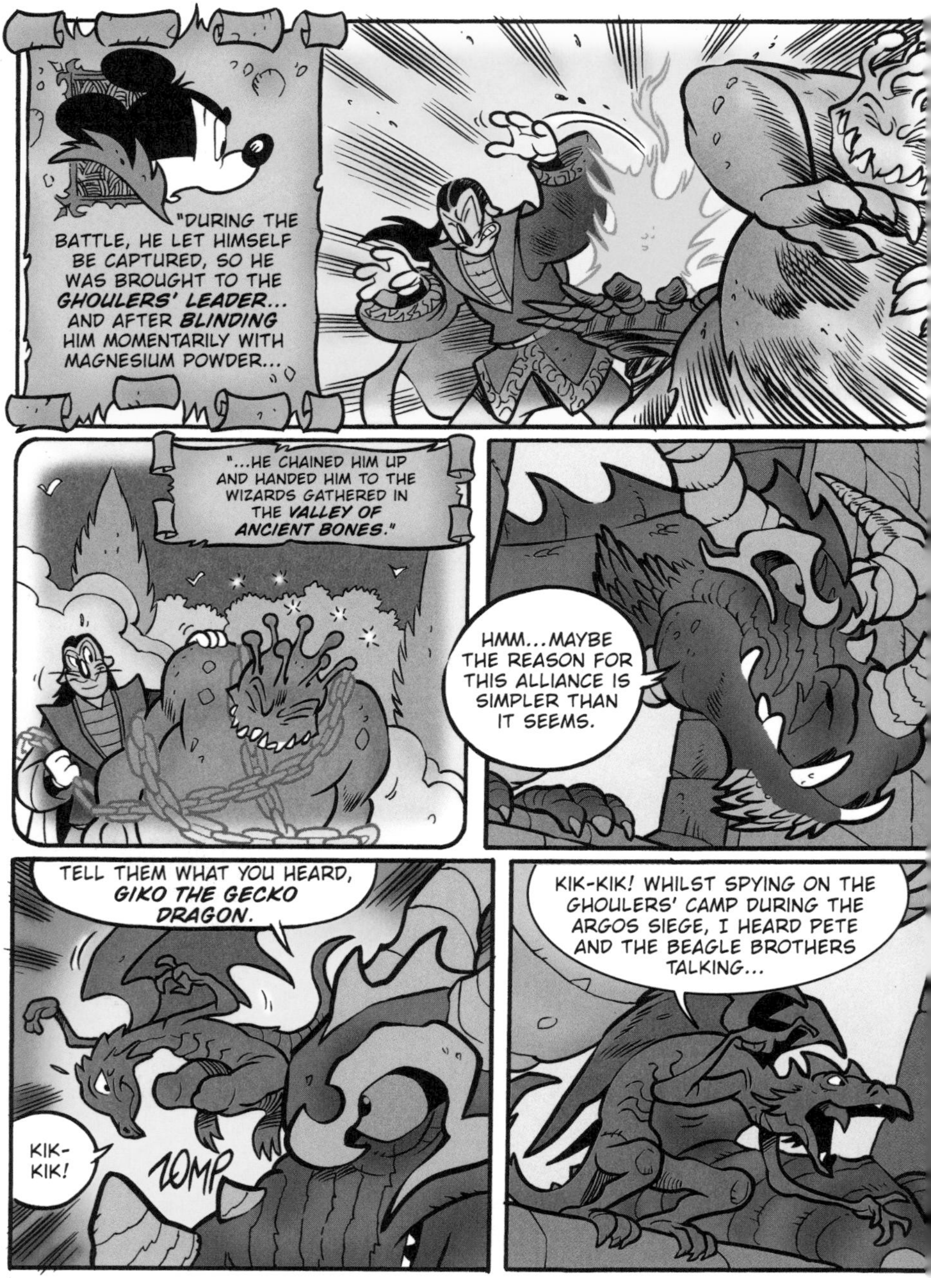
"DURING THE BATTLE, HE LET HIMSELF BE CAPTURED, SO HE WAS BROUGHT TO THE GHOULERS' LEADER... AND AFTER BLINDING HIM MOMENTARILY WITH MAGNESIUM POWDER...
"...HE CHAINED HIM UP AND HANDED HIM TO THE WIZARDS GATHERED IN THE VALLEY OF ANCIENT BONES."
HMM...MAYBE THE REASON FOR THIS ALLIANCE IS SIMPLER THAN IT SEEMS.
TELL THEM WHAT YOU HEARD, GIKO THE GECKO DRAGON.
KIK-KIK!
ZOMP
KIK-KIK! WHILST SPYING ON THE GHOULERS' CAMP DURING THE ARGOS SIEGE, I HEARD PETE AND THE BEAGLE BROTHERS TALKING...

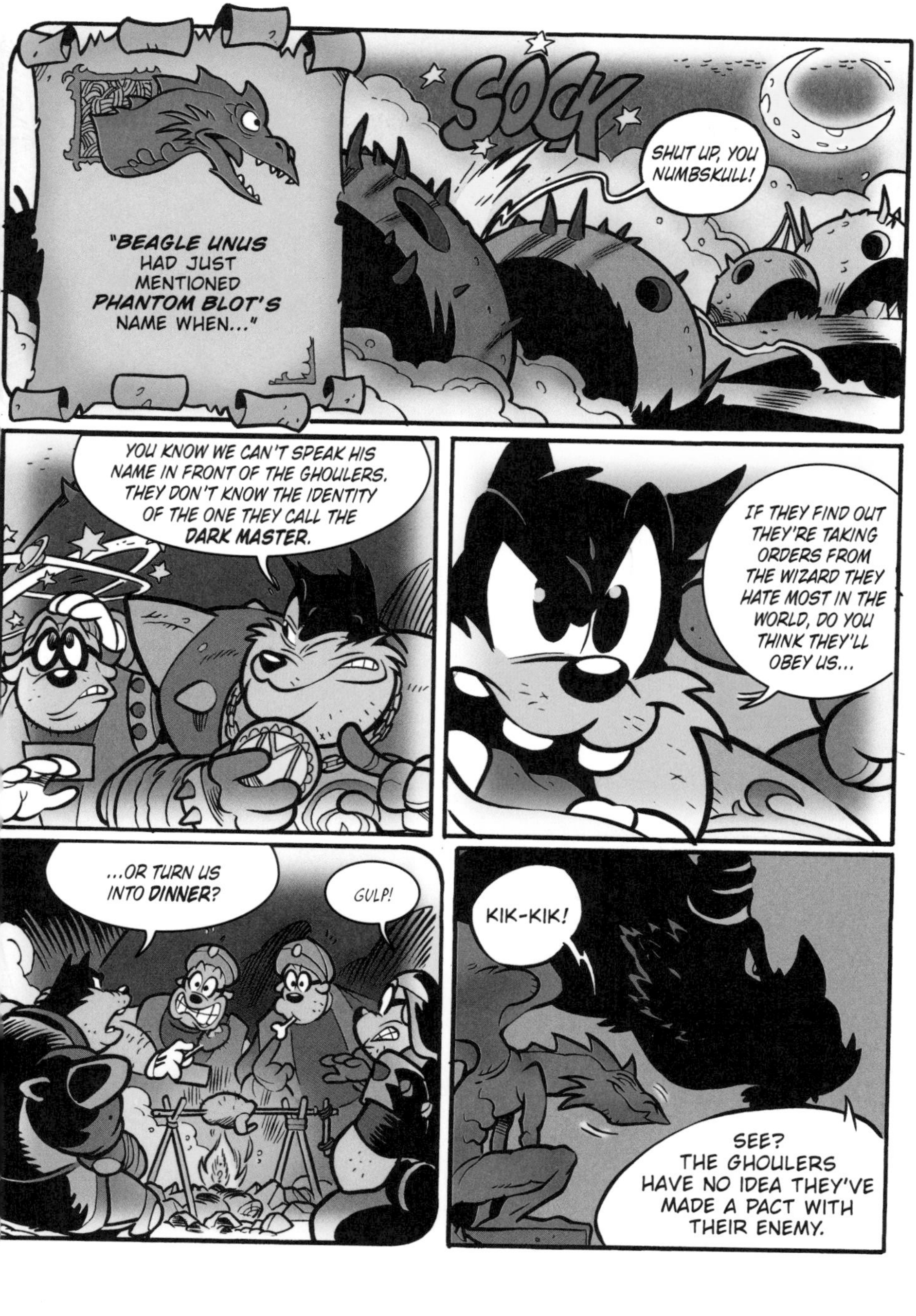

"BEAGLE UNUS HAD JUST MENTIONED PHANTOM BLOT'S NAME WHEN..."
SOCK
SHUT UP, YOU NUMBSKULL!
YOU KNOW WE CAN'T SPEAK HIS NAME IN FRONT OF THE GHOULERS. THEY DON'T KNOW THE IDENTITY OF THE ONE THEY CALL THE DARK MASTER.
IF THEY FIND OUT THEY'RE TAKING ORDERS FROM THE WIZARD THEY HATE MOST IN THE WORLD, DO YOU THINK THEY'LL OBEY US...
...OR TURN US INTO DINNER?
GULP!
KIK-KIK!
SEE? THE GHOULERS HAVE NO IDEA THEY'VE MADE A PACT WITH THEIR ENEMY.

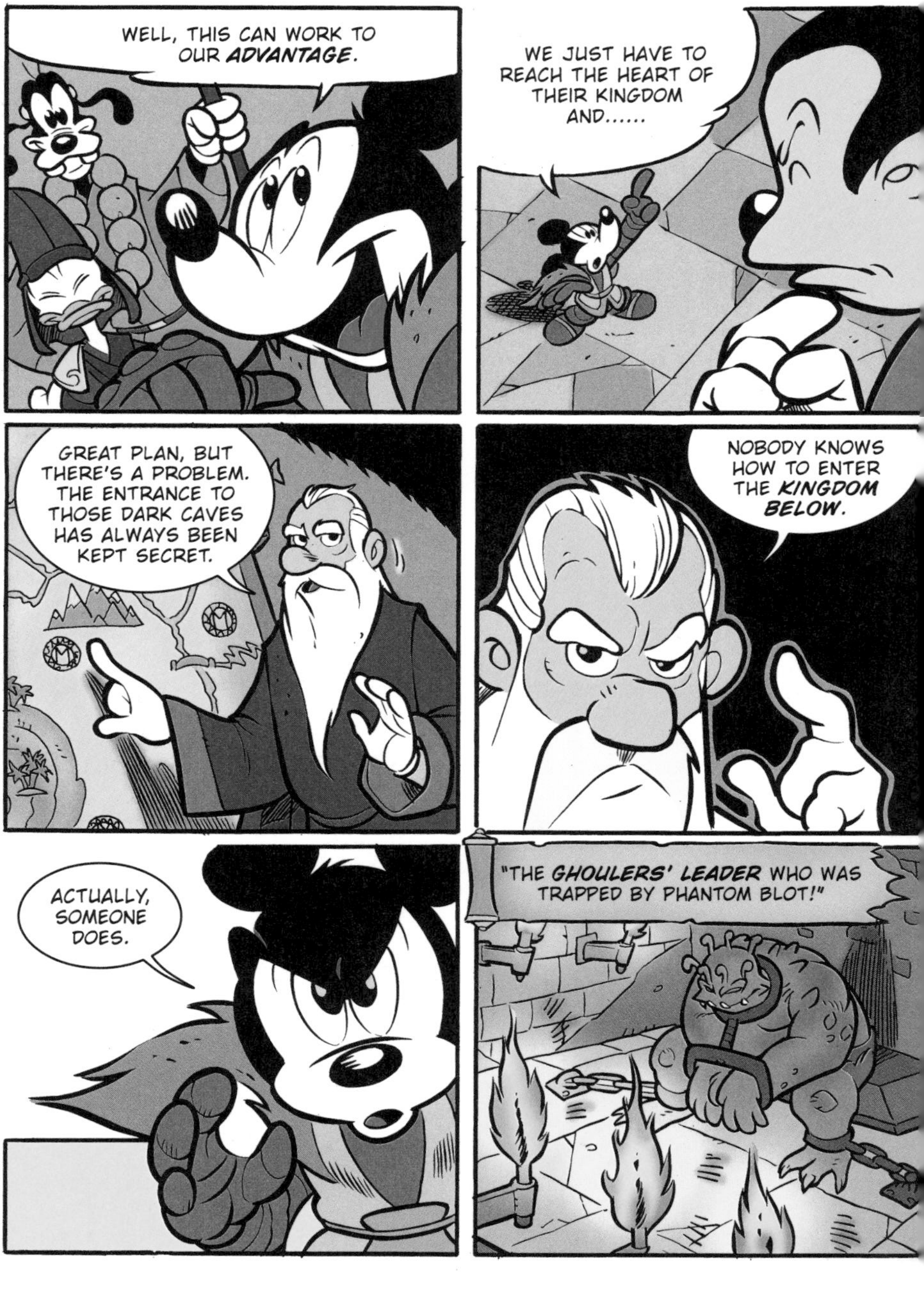
WELL, THIS CAN WORK TO OUR ADVANTAGE.
WE JUST HAVE TO REACH THE HEART OF THEIR KINGDOM AND......
GREAT PLAN, BUT THERE'S A PROBLEM. THE ENTRANCE TO THOSE DARK CAVES HAS ALWAYS BEEN KEPT SECRET.
NOBODY KNOWS HOW TO ENTER THE KINGDOM BELOW.
ACTUALLY, SOMEONE DOES.
"THE GHOULERS' LEADER WHO WAS TRAPPED BY PHANTOM BLOT!"

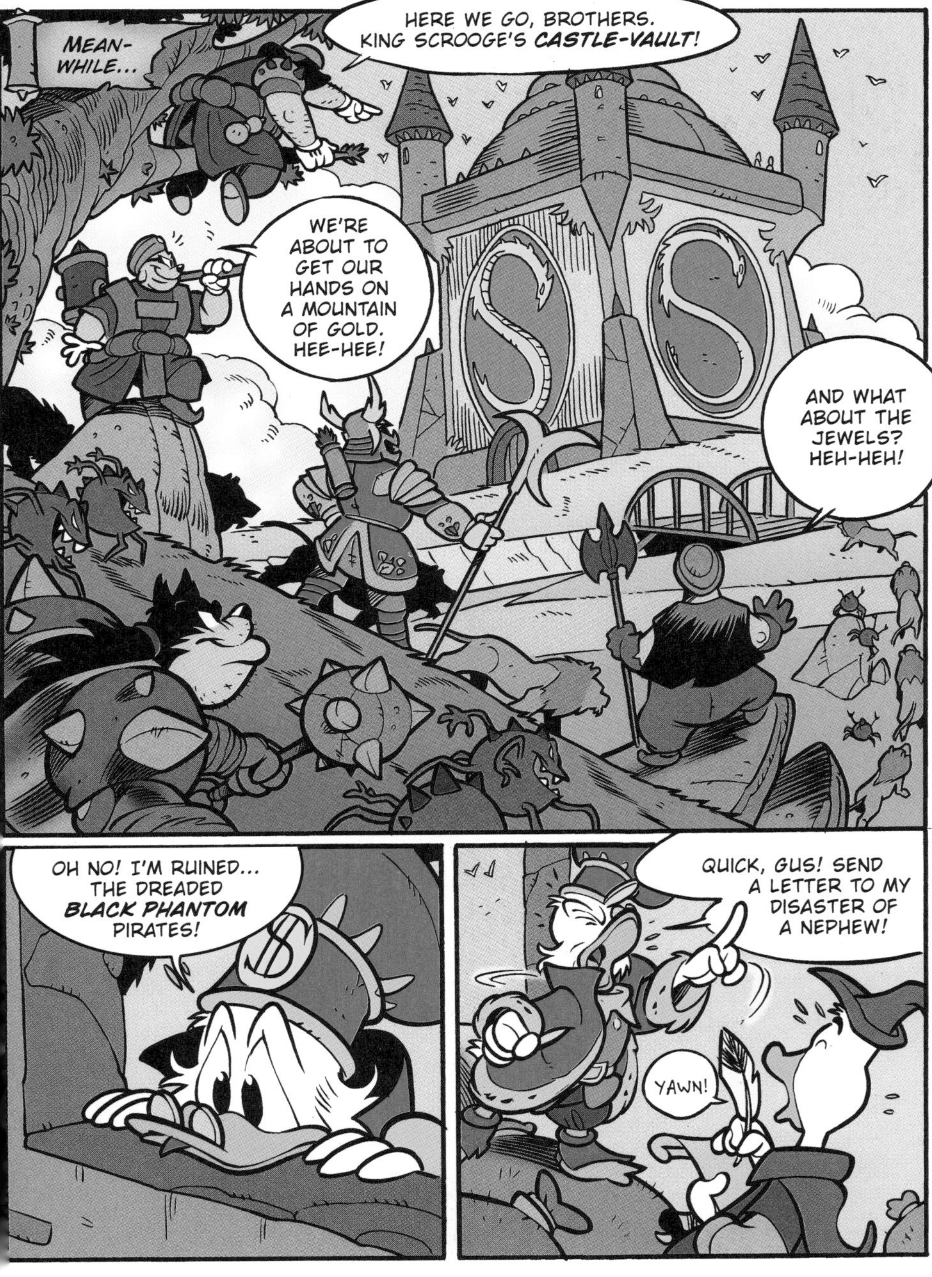

MEAN-WHILE...
HERE WE GO, BROTHERS. KING SCROOGE'S CASTLE-VAULT!
WE'RE ABOUT TO GET OUR HANDS ON A MOUNTAIN OF GOLD. HEE-HEE!
AND WHAT ABOUT THE JEWELS? HEH-HEH!
OH NO! I'M RUINED... THE DREADED BLACK PHANTOM PIRATES!
QUICK, GUS! SEND A LETTER TO MY DISASTER OF A NEPHEW!
YAWN!

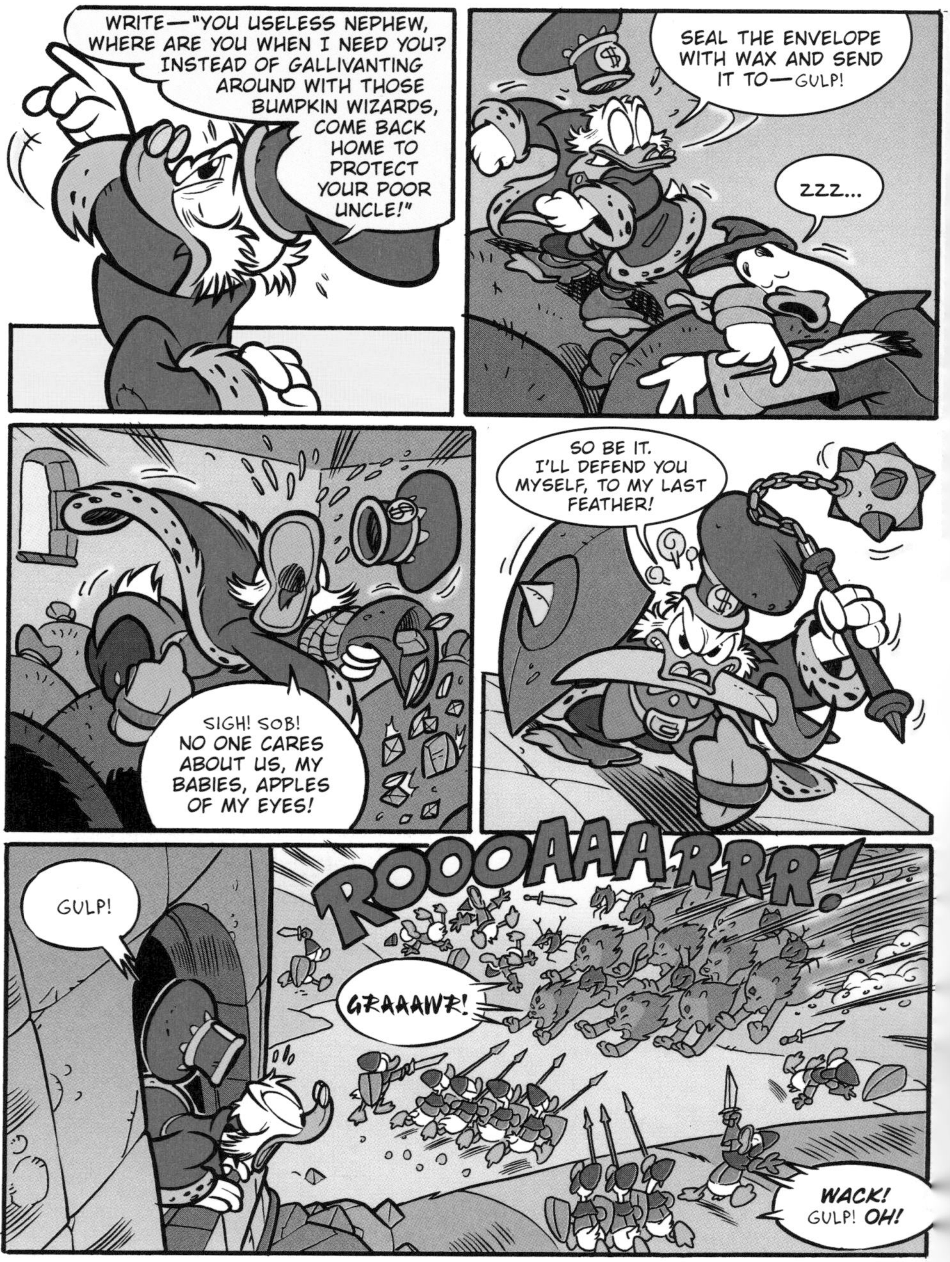
WRITE—"YOU USELESS NEPHEW, WHERE ARE YOU WHEN I NEED YOU? INSTEAD OF GALLIVANTING AROUND WITH THOSE BUMPKIN WIZARDS, COME BACK HOME TO PROTECT YOUR POOR UNCLE!"
SEAL THE ENVELOPE WITH WAX AND SEND IT TO—GULP!
ZZZ...
SIGH! SOB! NO ONE CARES ABOUT US, MY BABIES, APPLES OF MY EYES!
SO BE IT. I'LL DEFEND YOU MYSELF, TO MY LAST FEATHER!
GULP!
ROOOAAARRR!
GRAAAWR!
WACK! GULP! OH!

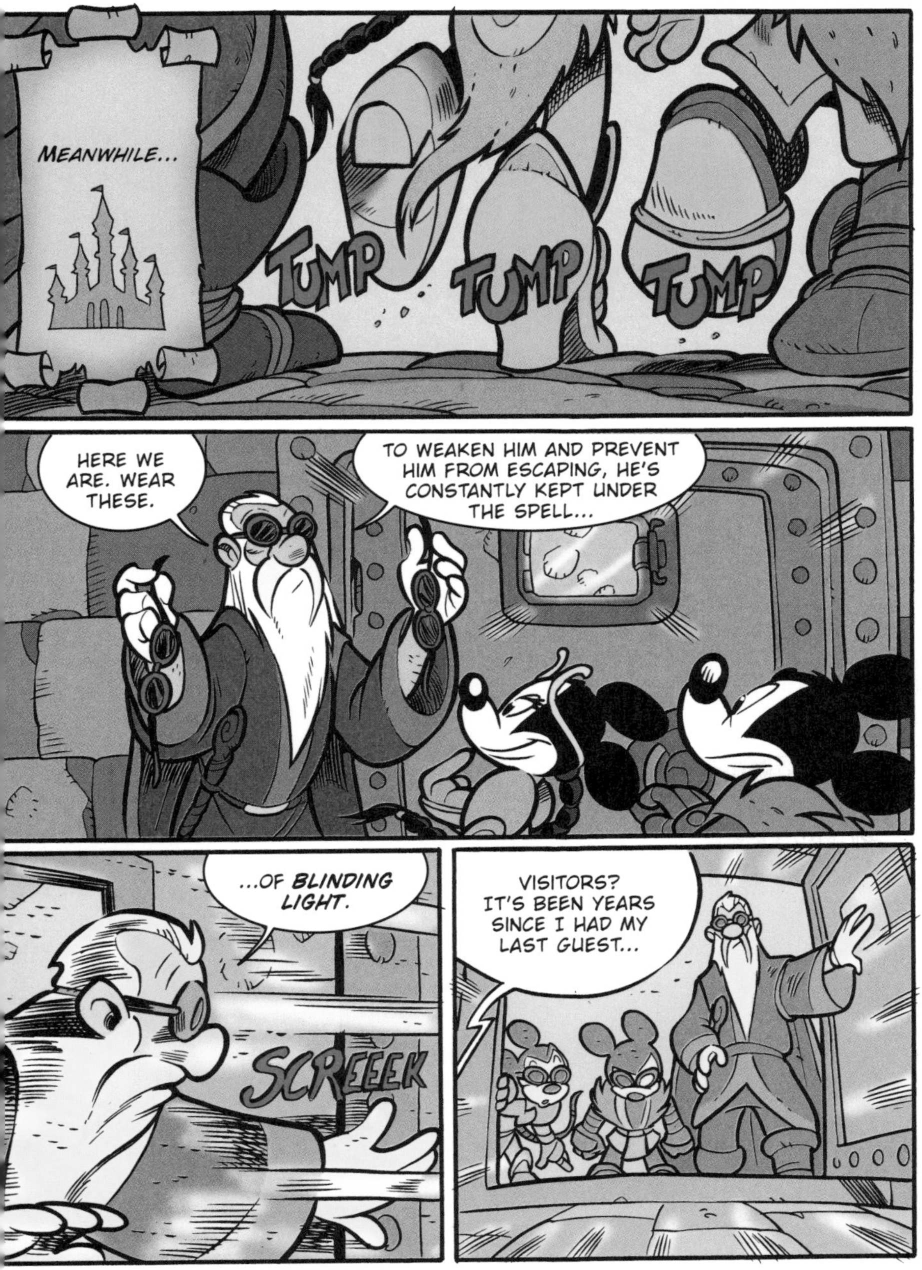

MEANWHILE...
TUMP TUMP TUMP
HERE WE ARE. WEAR THESE.
TO WEAKEN HIM AND PREVENT HIM FROM ESCAPING, HE'S CONSTANTLY KEPT UNDER THE SPELL...
...OF BLINDING LIGHT.
SCREEEK
VISITORS? IT'S BEEN YEARS SINCE I HAD MY LAST GUEST...

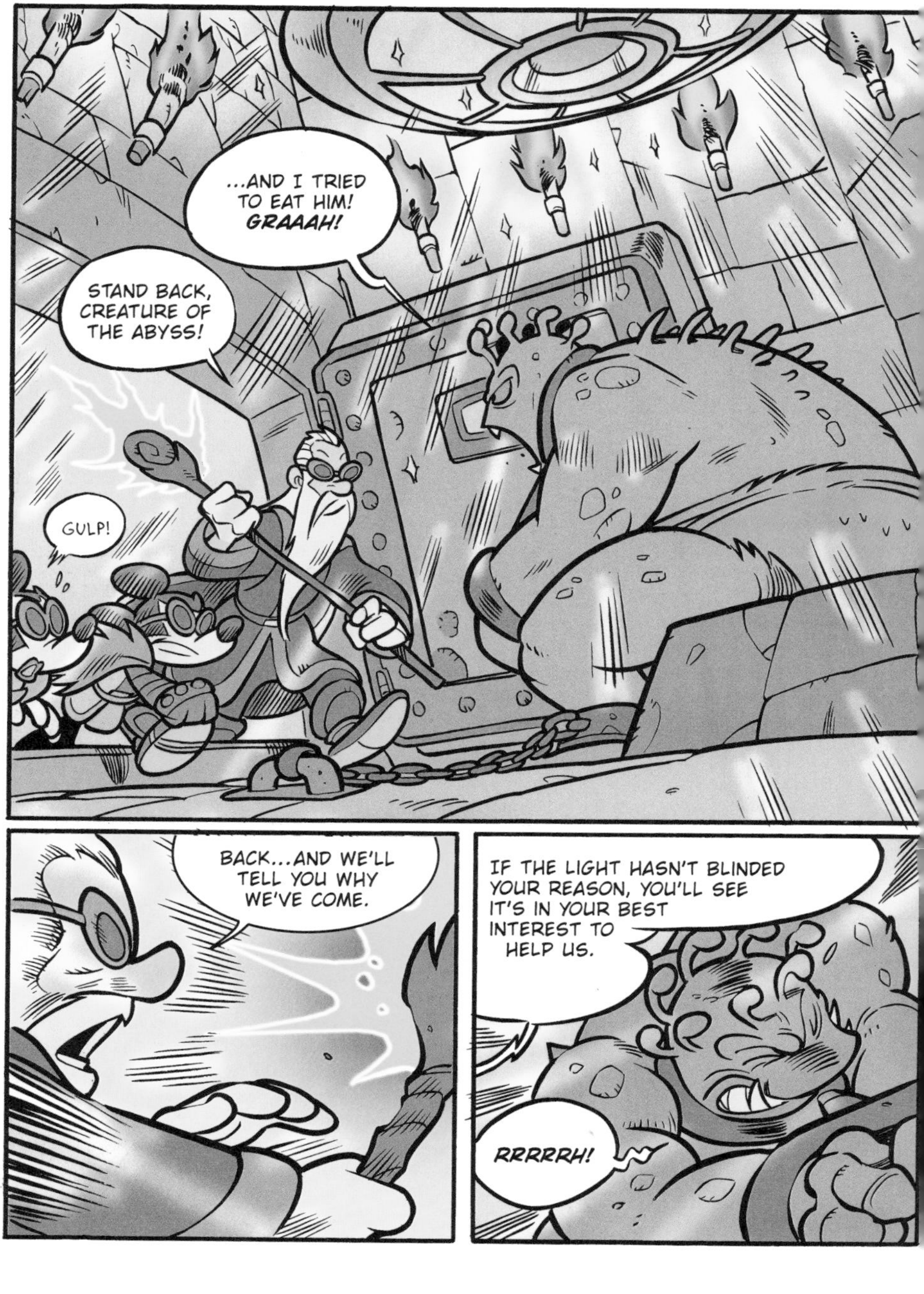
...AND I TRIED TO EAT HIM! *GRAAAH!*
STAND BACK, CREATURE OF THE ABYSS!
GULP!
BACK...AND WE'LL TELL YOU WHY WE'VE COME.
IF THE LIGHT HASN'T BLINDED YOUR REASON, YOU'LL SEE IT'S IN YOUR BEST INTEREST TO HELP US.
RRRRRH!

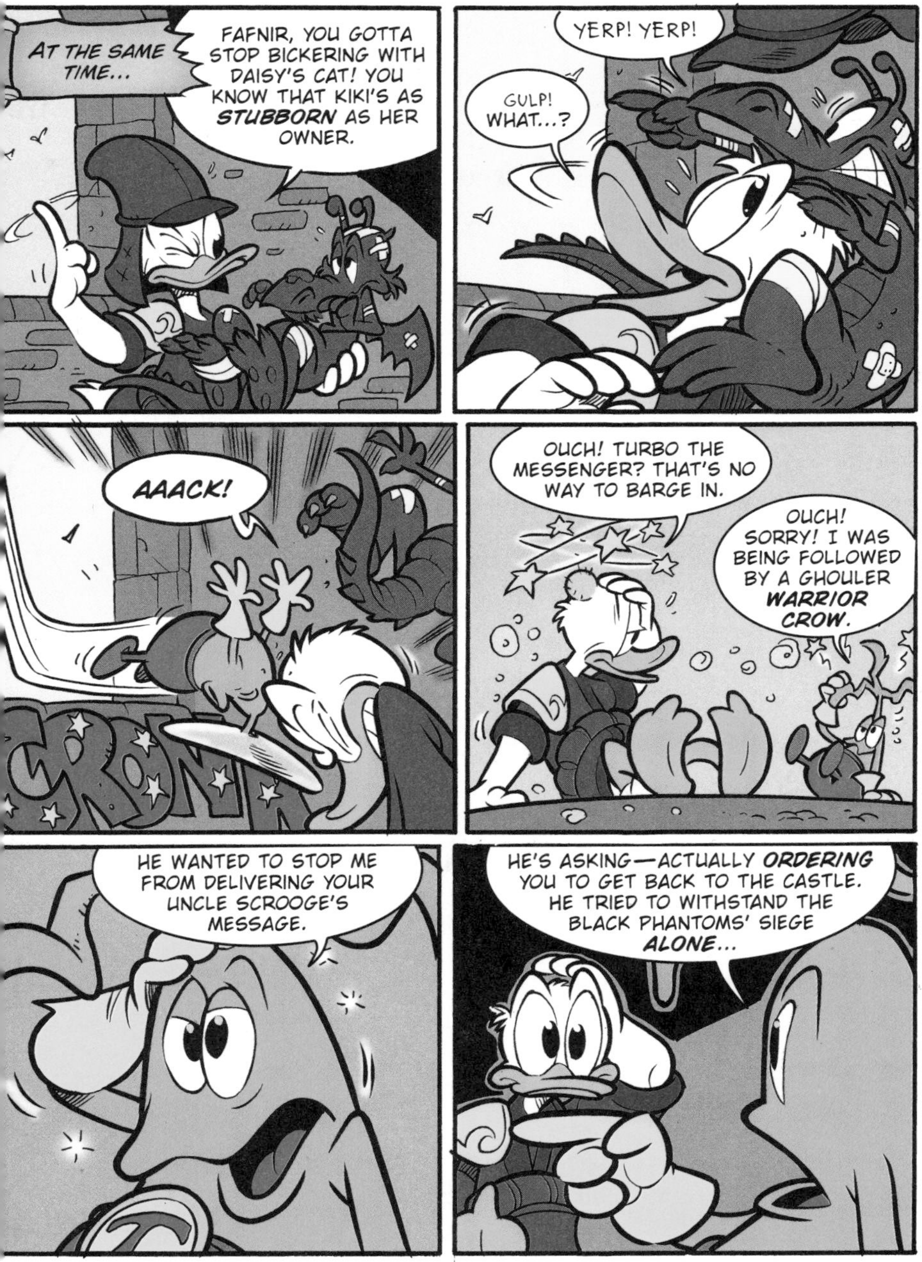

AT THE SAME TIME...
FAFNIR, YOU GOTTA STOP BICKERING WITH DAISY'S CAT! YOU KNOW THAT KIKI'S AS STUBBORN AS HER OWNER.
YERP! YERP!
GULP! WHAT...?
AAACK!
CRONK
OUCH! TURBO THE MESSENGER? THAT'S NO WAY TO BARGE IN.
OUCH! SORRY! I WAS BEING FOLLOWED BY A GHOULER WARRIOR CROW.
HE WANTED TO STOP ME FROM DELIVERING YOUR UNCLE SCROOGE'S MESSAGE.
HE'S ASKING—ACTUALLY ORDERING YOU TO GET BACK TO THE CASTLE. HE TRIED TO WITHSTAND THE BLACK PHANTOMS' SIEGE ALONE...

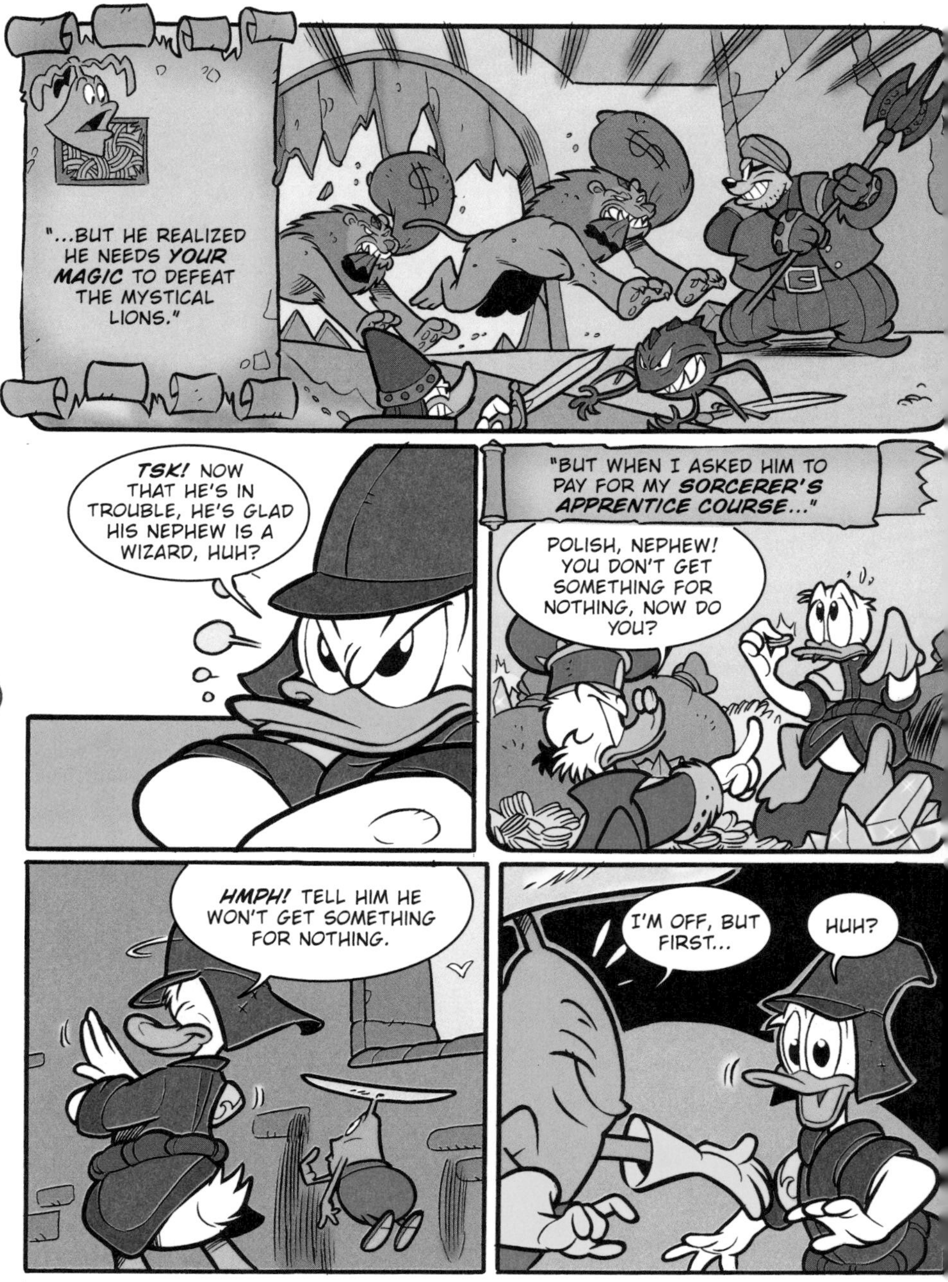
"...BUT HE REALIZED HE NEEDS YOUR MAGIC TO DEFEAT THE MYSTICAL LIONS."
TSK! NOW THAT HE'S IN TROUBLE, HE'S GLAD HIS NEPHEW IS A WIZARD, HUH?
"BUT WHEN I ASKED HIM TO PAY FOR MY SORCERER'S APPRENTICE COURSE..."
POLISH, NEPHEW! YOU DON'T GET SOMETHING FOR NOTHING, NOW DO YOU?
HMPH! TELL HIM HE WON'T GET SOMETHING FOR NOTHING.
I'M OFF, BUT FIRST...
HUH?

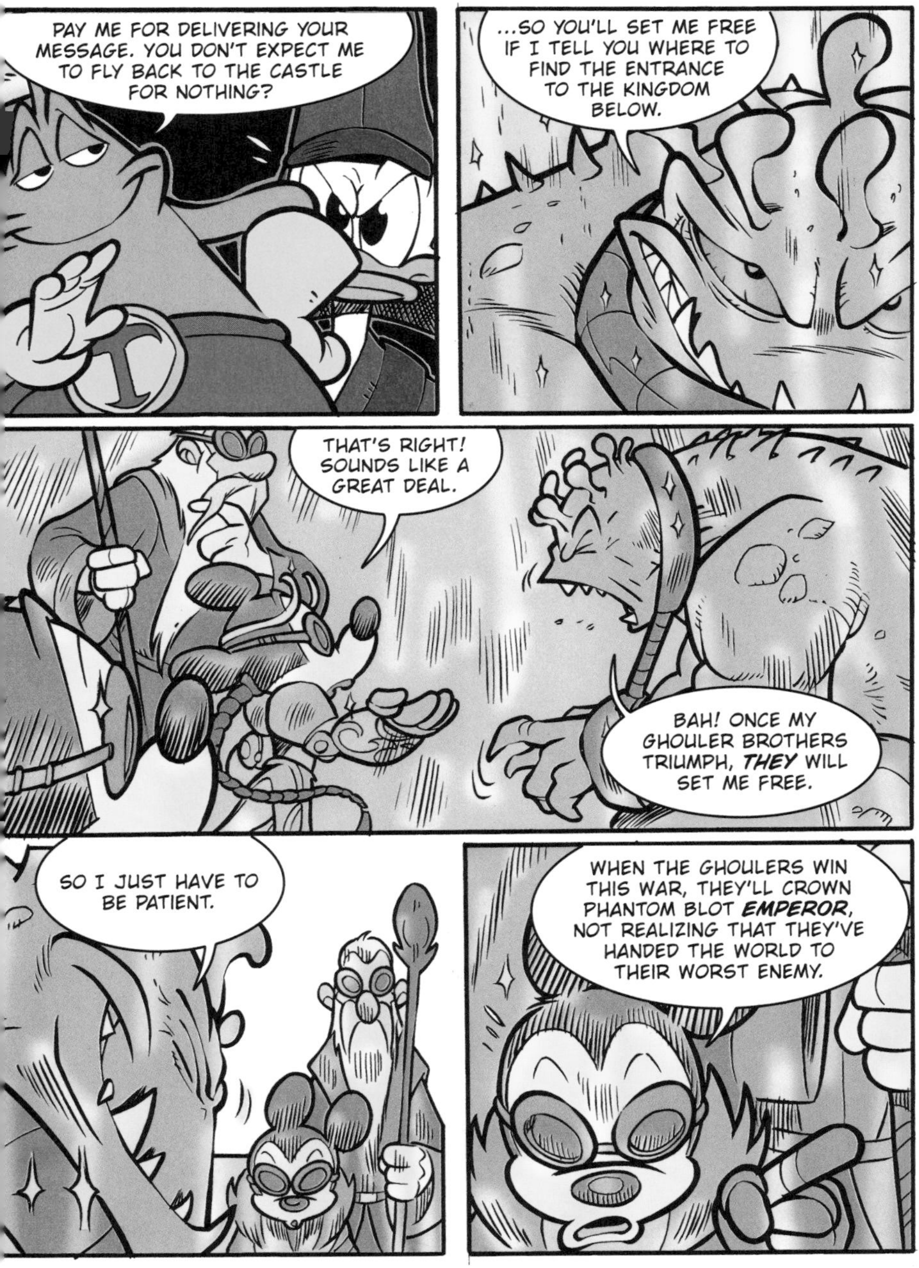
PAY ME FOR DELIVERING YOUR MESSAGE. YOU DON'T EXPECT ME TO FLY BACK TO THE CASTLE FOR NOTHING?
...SO YOU'LL SET ME FREE IF I TELL YOU WHERE TO FIND THE ENTRANCE TO THE KINGDOM BELOW.
THAT'S RIGHT! SOUNDS LIKE A GREAT DEAL.
BAH! ONCE MY GHOULER BROTHERS TRIUMPH, *THEY* WILL SET ME FREE.
SO I JUST HAVE TO BE PATIENT.
WHEN THE GHOULERS WIN THIS WAR, THEY'LL CROWN PHANTOM BLOT *EMPEROR*, NOT REALIZING THAT THEY'VE HANDED THE WORLD TO THEIR WORST ENEMY.

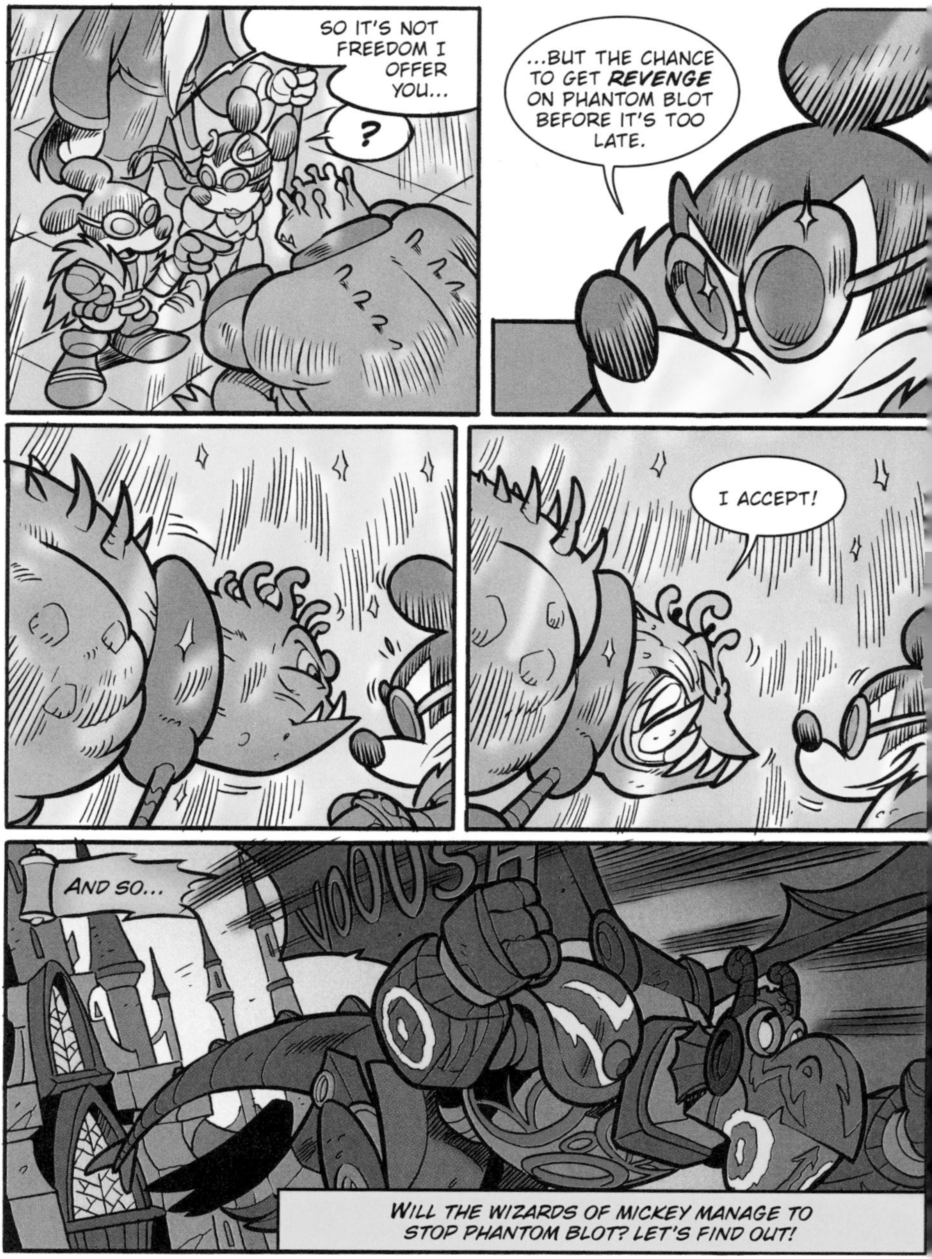
SO IT'S NOT FREEDOM I OFFER YOU...
?
...BUT THE CHANCE TO GET REVENGE ON PHANTOM BLOT BEFORE IT'S TOO LATE.
I ACCEPT!
AND SO...
VOOOSH
WILL THE WIZARDS OF MICKEY MANAGE TO STOP PHANTOM BLOT? LET'S FIND OUT!

END OF PART ONE

Wizards of Mickey

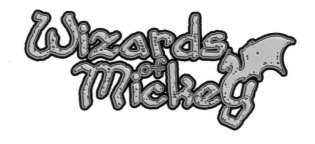

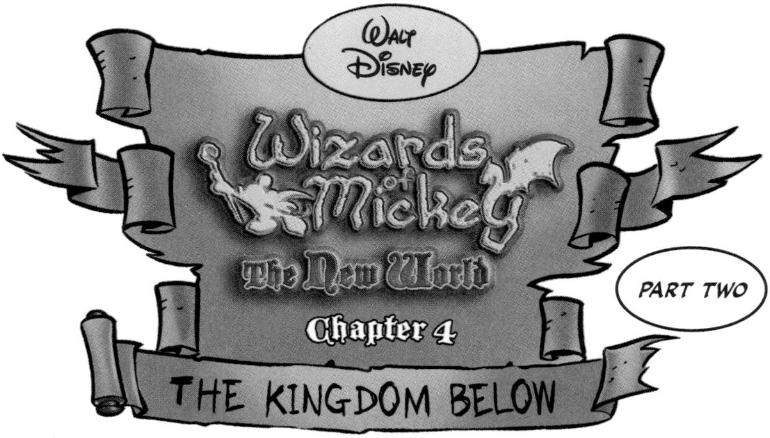
Walt Disney
Wizards of Mickey
The New World
Chapter 4
THE KINGDOM BELOW
PART TWO

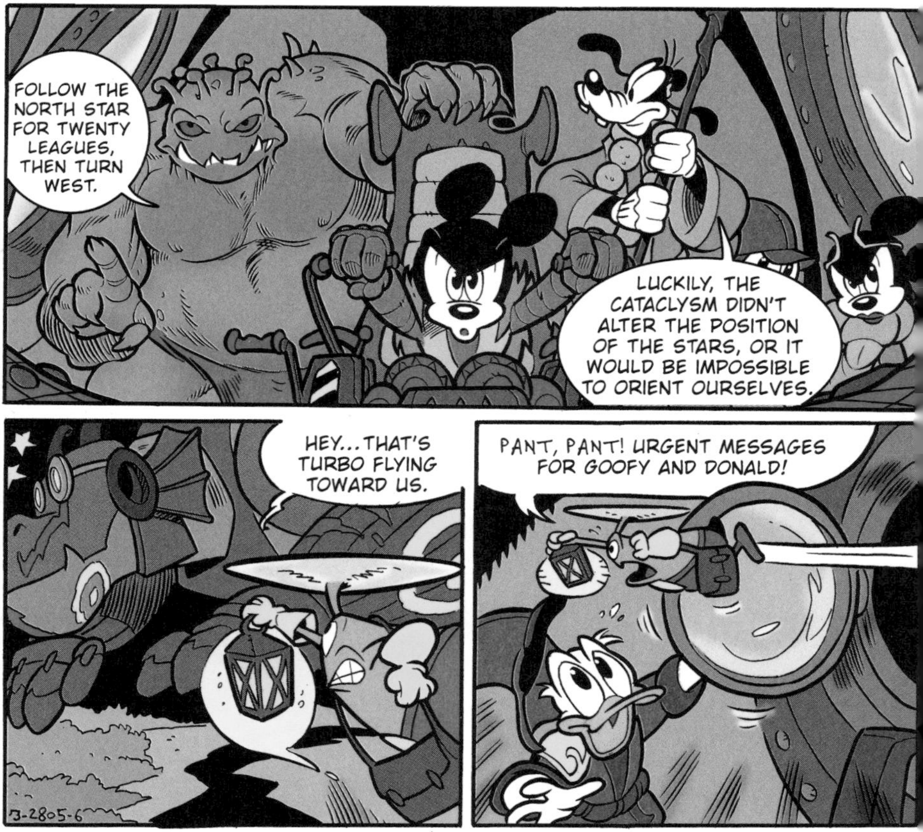
FOLLOW THE NORTH STAR FOR TWENTY LEAGUES, THEN TURN WEST.
LUCKILY, THE CATACLYSM DIDN'T ALTER THE POSITION OF THE STARS, OR IT WOULD BE IMPOSSIBLE TO ORIENT OURSELVES.
HEY...THAT'S TURBO FLYING TOWARD US.
PANT, PANT! URGENT MESSAGES FOR GOOFY AND DONALD!

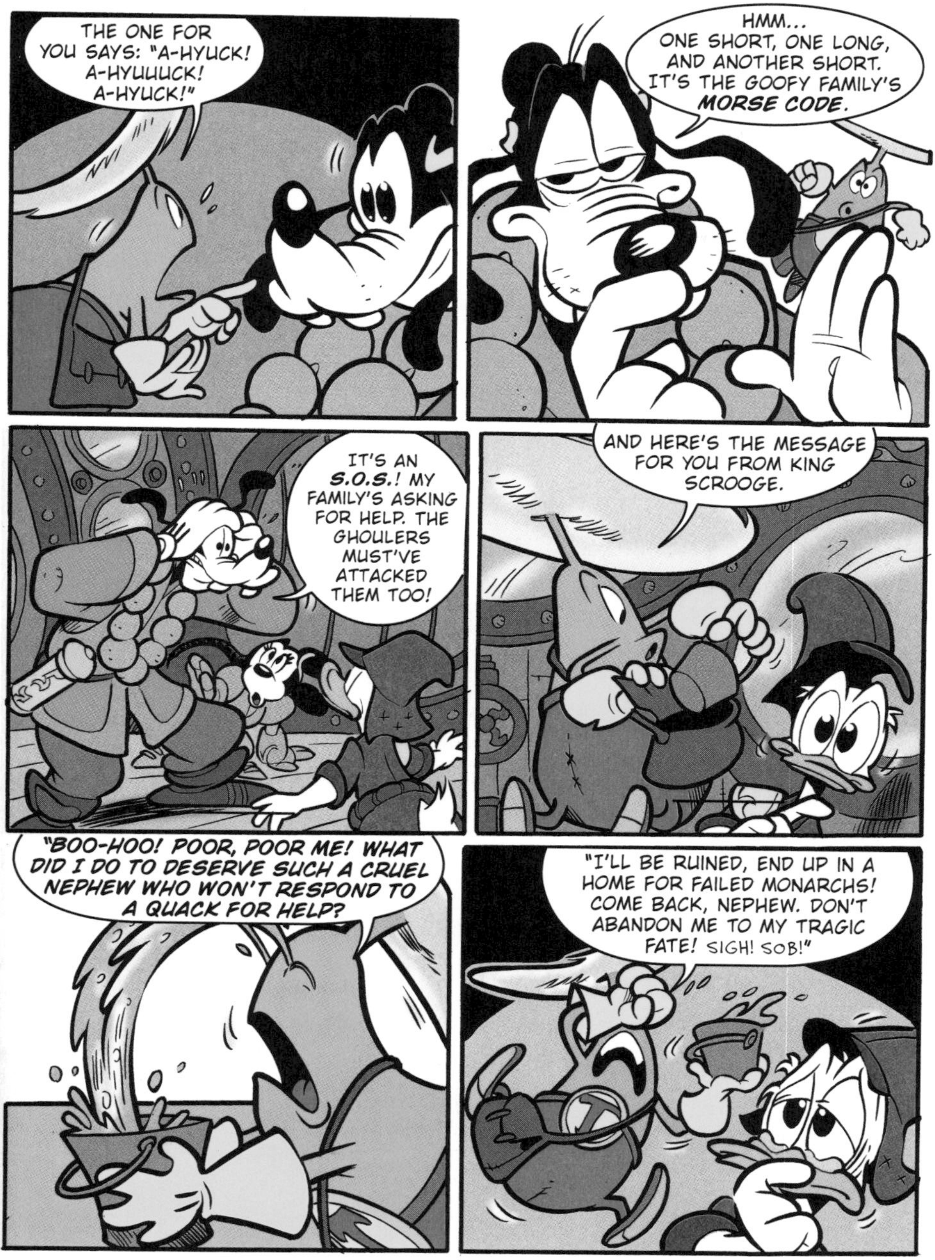
THE ONE FOR YOU SAYS: "A-HYUCK! A-HYUUUCK! A-HYUCK!"
HMM... ONE SHORT, ONE LONG, AND ANOTHER SHORT. IT'S THE GOOFY FAMILY'S MORSE CODE.
IT'S AN S.O.S.! MY FAMILY'S ASKING FOR HELP. THE GHOULERS MUST'VE ATTACKED THEM TOO!
AND HERE'S THE MESSAGE FOR YOU FROM KING SCROOGE.
"BOO-HOO! POOR, POOR ME! WHAT DID I DO TO DESERVE SUCH A CRUEL NEPHEW WHO WON'T RESPOND TO A QUACK FOR HELP?
"I'LL BE RUINED, END UP IN A HOME FOR FAILED MONARCHS! COME BACK, NEPHEW. DON'T ABANDON ME TO MY TRAGIC FATE! SIGH! SOB!"

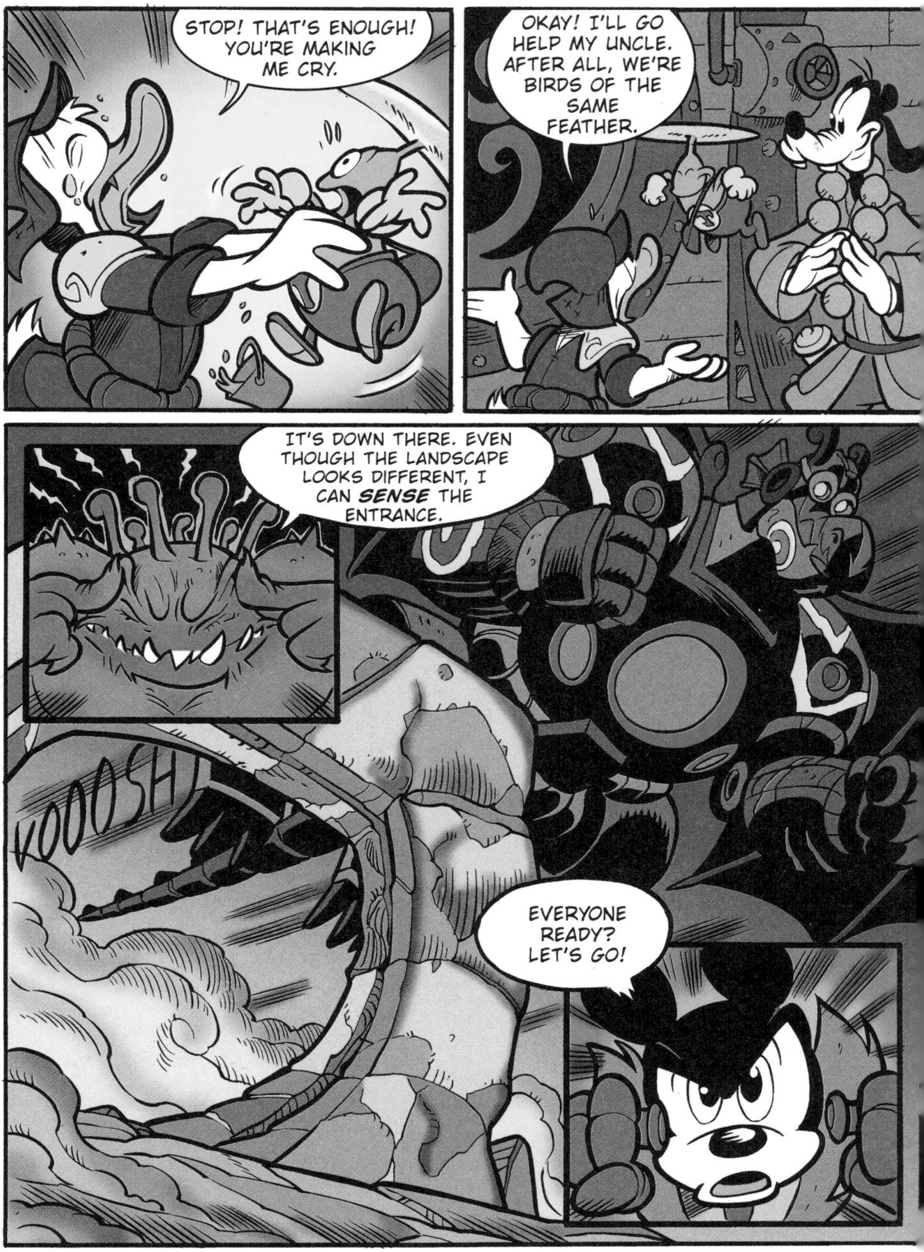
STOP! THAT'S ENOUGH! YOU'RE MAKING ME CRY.
OKAY! I'LL GO HELP MY UNCLE. AFTER ALL, WE'RE BIRDS OF THE SAME FEATHER.
IT'S DOWN THERE. EVEN THOUGH THE LANDSCAPE LOOKS DIFFERENT, I CAN SENSE THE ENTRANCE.
VOOOSH
EVERYONE READY? LET'S GO!

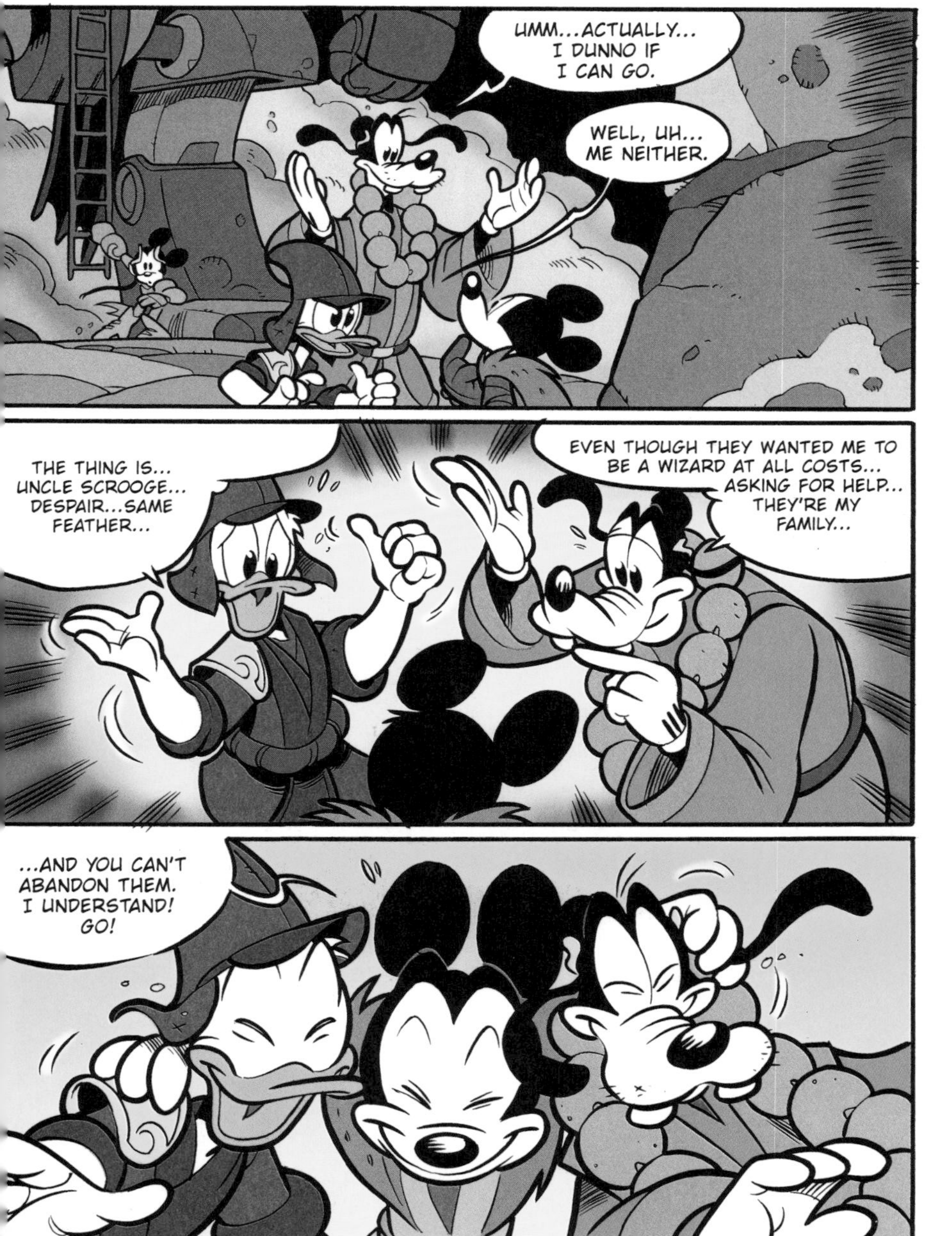
UMM...ACTUALLY... I DUNNO IF I CAN GO.
WELL, UH... ME NEITHER.
THE THING IS... UNCLE SCROOGE... DESPAIR...SAME FEATHER...
EVEN THOUGH THEY WANTED ME TO BE A WIZARD AT ALL COSTS... ASKING FOR HELP... THEY'RE MY FAMILY...
...AND YOU CAN'T ABANDON THEM. I UNDERSTAND! GO!

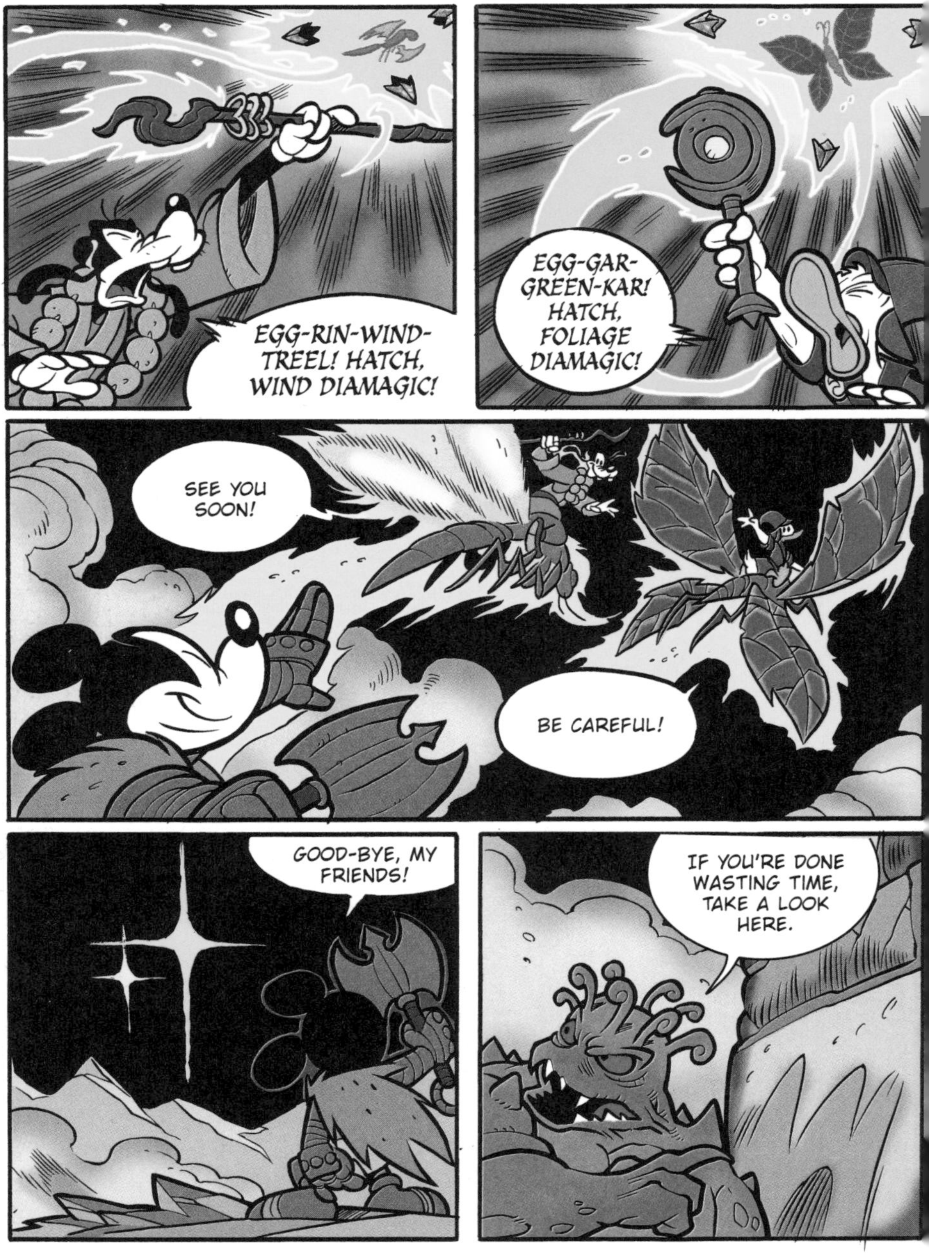
EGG-RIN-WIND-TREEL! HATCH, WIND DIAMAGIC!
EGG-GAR-GREEN-KAR! HATCH, FOLIAGE DIAMAGIC!
SEE YOU SOON!
BE CAREFUL!
GOOD-BYE, MY FRIENDS!
IF YOU'RE DONE WASTING TIME, TAKE A LOOK HERE.

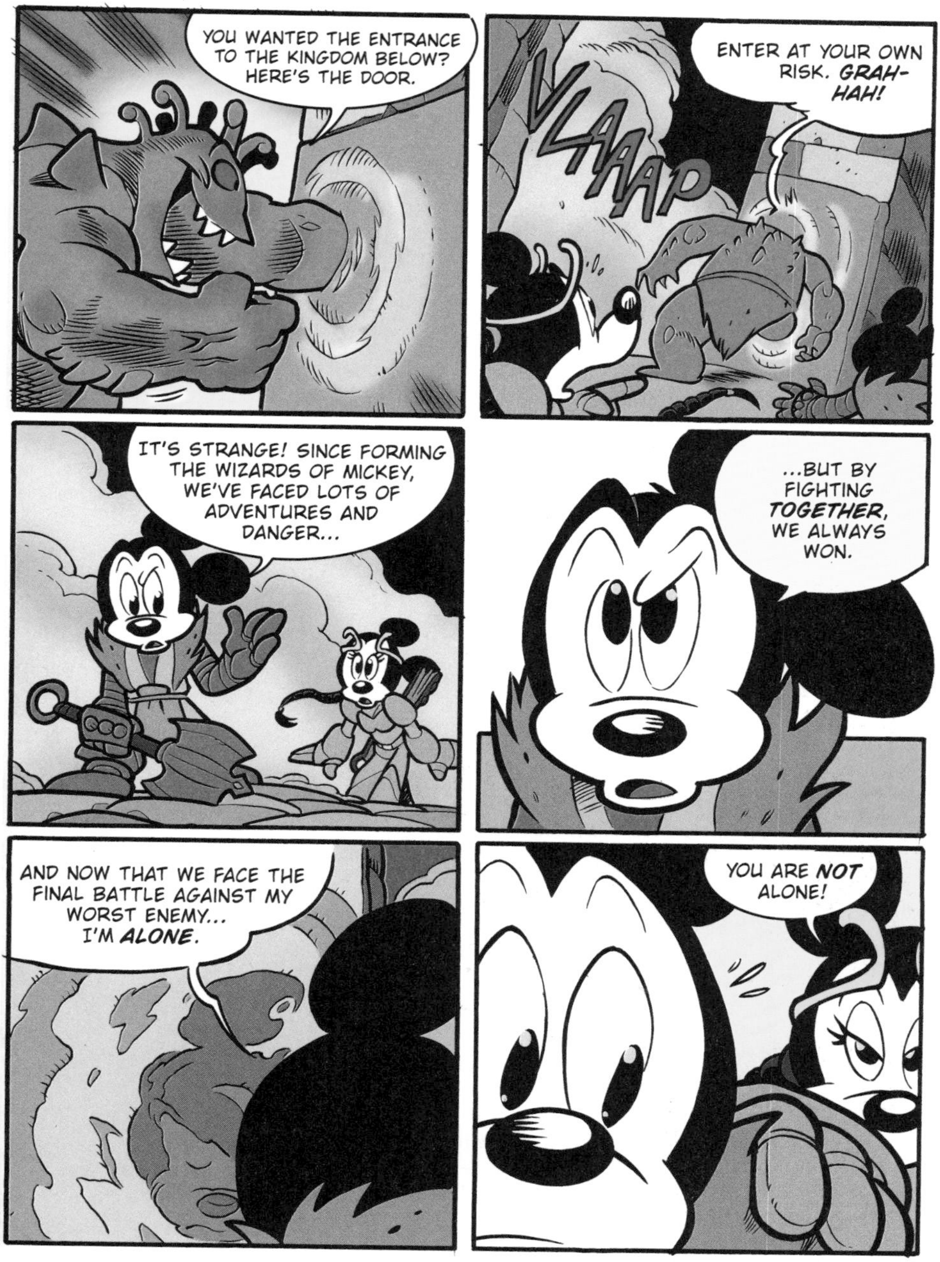
YOU WANTED THE ENTRANCE TO THE KINGDOM BELOW? HERE'S THE DOOR.
ENTER AT YOUR OWN RISK. GRAH-HAH!
VLAAAP
IT'S STRANGE! SINCE FORMING THE WIZARDS OF MICKEY, WE'VE FACED LOTS OF ADVENTURES AND DANGER...
...BUT BY FIGHTING TOGETHER, WE ALWAYS WON.
AND NOW THAT WE FACE THE FINAL BATTLE AGAINST MY WORST ENEMY... I'M ALONE.
YOU ARE NOT ALONE!

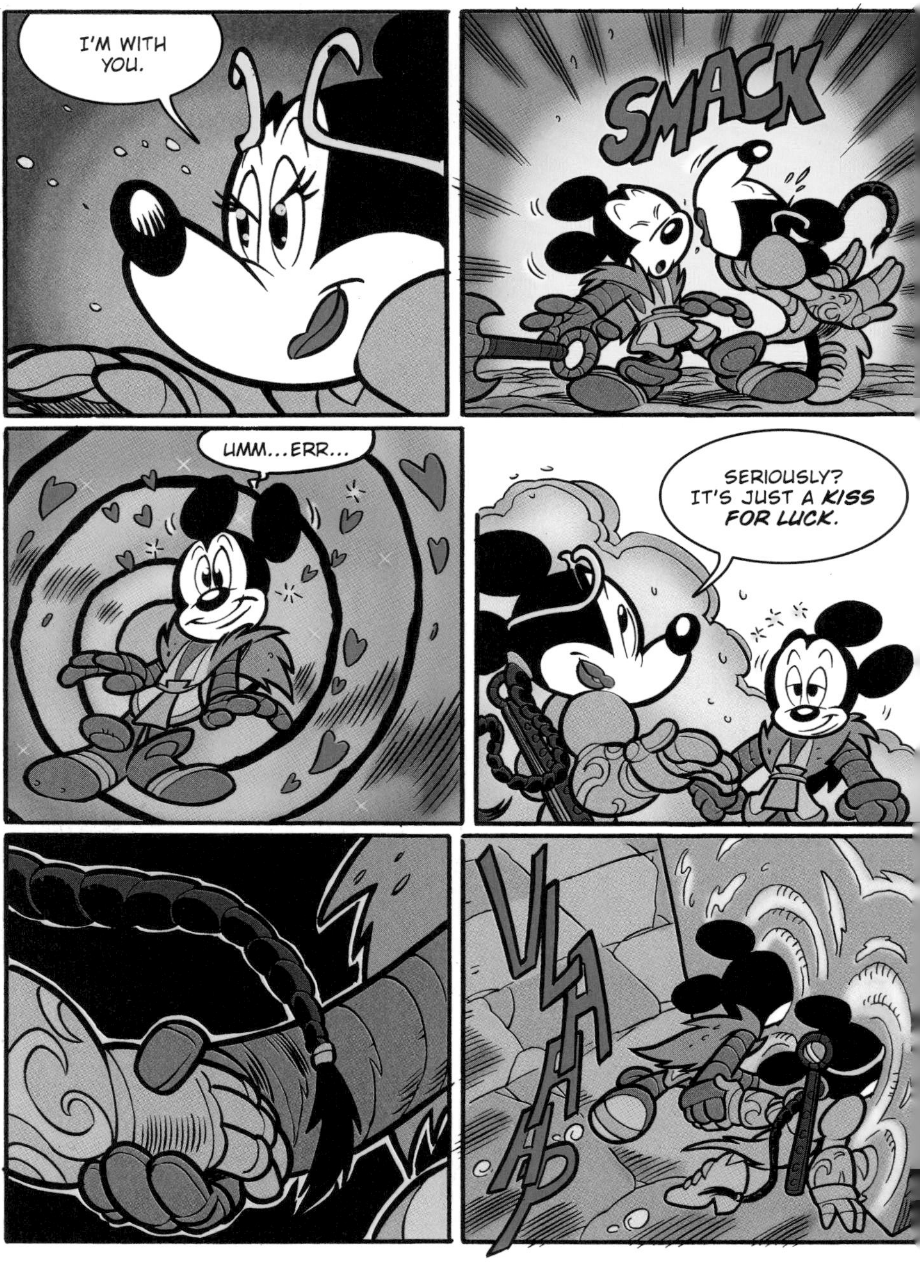
I'M WITH YOU.
SMACK
UMM...ERR...
SERIOUSLY? IT'S JUST A *KISS FOR LUCK*.
VLAAAP

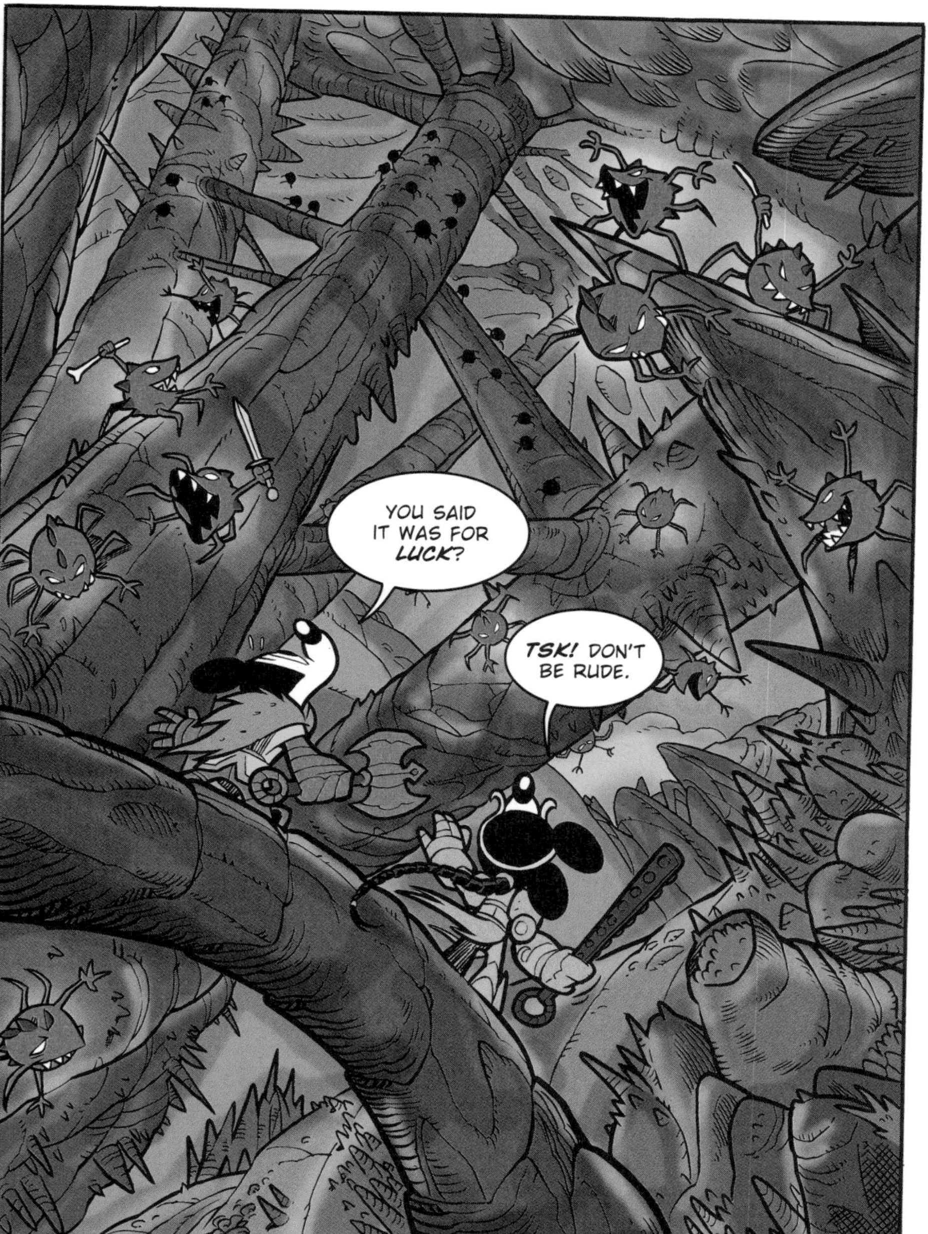
YOU SAID IT WAS FOR LUCK?
TSK! DON'T BE RUDE.

INTRUDERS! THE DARK MASTER PREDICTED YOUR ARRIVAL...

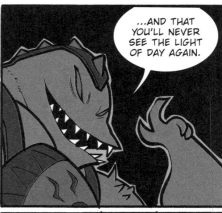

...AND THAT YOU'LL NEVER SEE THE LIGHT OF DAY AGAIN.

FOR NOW, I'LL SETTLE FOR *THIS LIGHT*. EGG-TOR-FLASH-VAAAL!

MAY THE LIGHTNING DIAMAGIC UNLEASH ITS POWER!

VAMP

VAMP

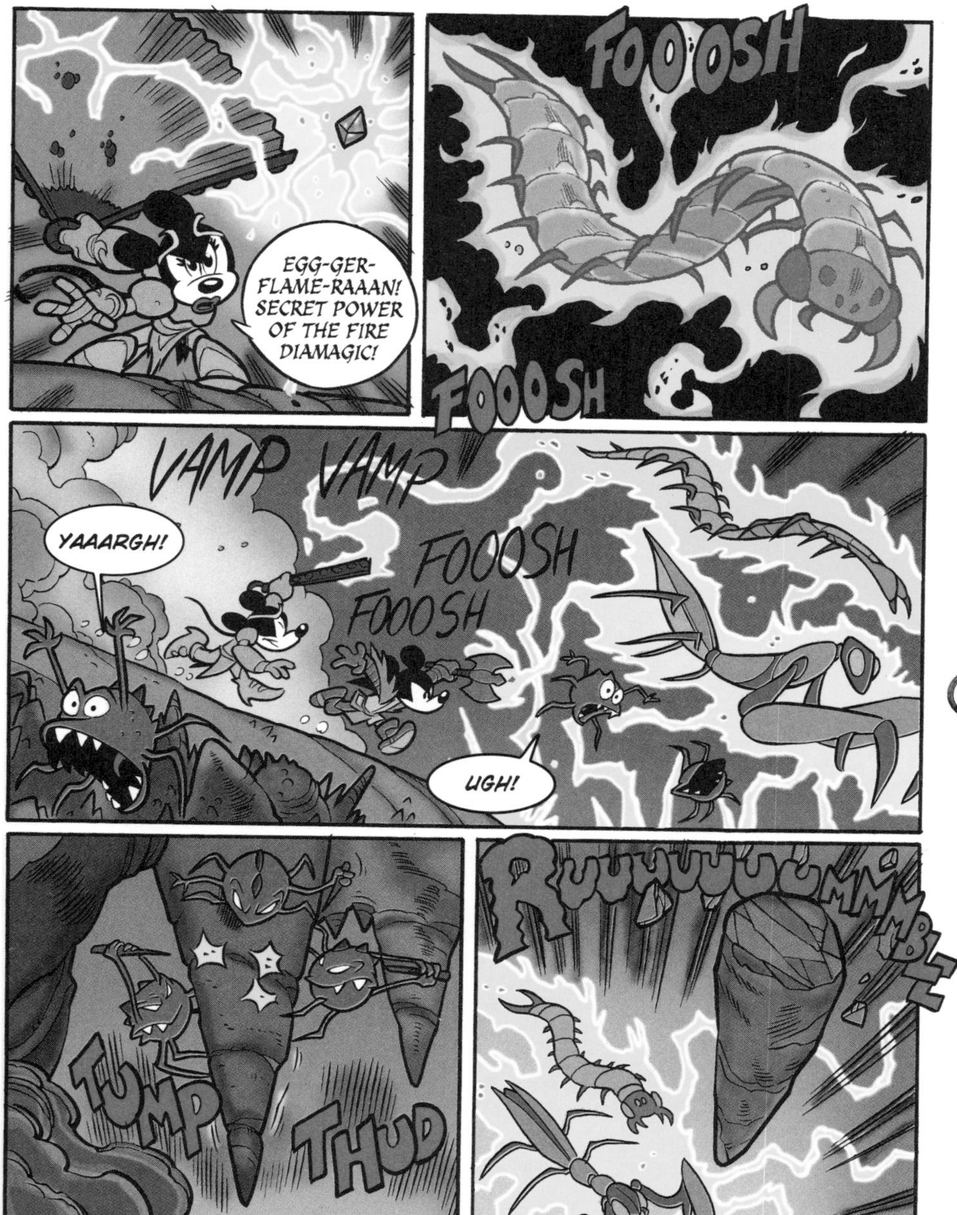
EGG-GER-FLAME-RAAAN! SECRET POWER OF THE FIRE DIAMAGIC!
FOOOSH
FOOOSH
VAMP VAMP
YAAARGH!
FOOOSH
FOOOSH
UGH!
TUMP
THUD
RUUUUUMMMBLE

LOOK OUT!

C'MERE, YOU PUNY LITTLE MOUSE! THE DARK MASTER WAS RIGHT—YOU'RE NOT EVEN GOOD FOR A *SNACK*.

THE DARK MASTER KEEPS LYING TO YOU...

...AND YOU ALL FALL FOR IT!

THE FORGOTTEN?

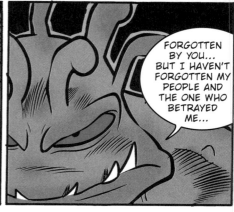

FORGOTTEN BY YOU... BUT I HAVEN'T FORGOTTEN MY PEOPLE AND THE ONE WHO BETRAYED ME...

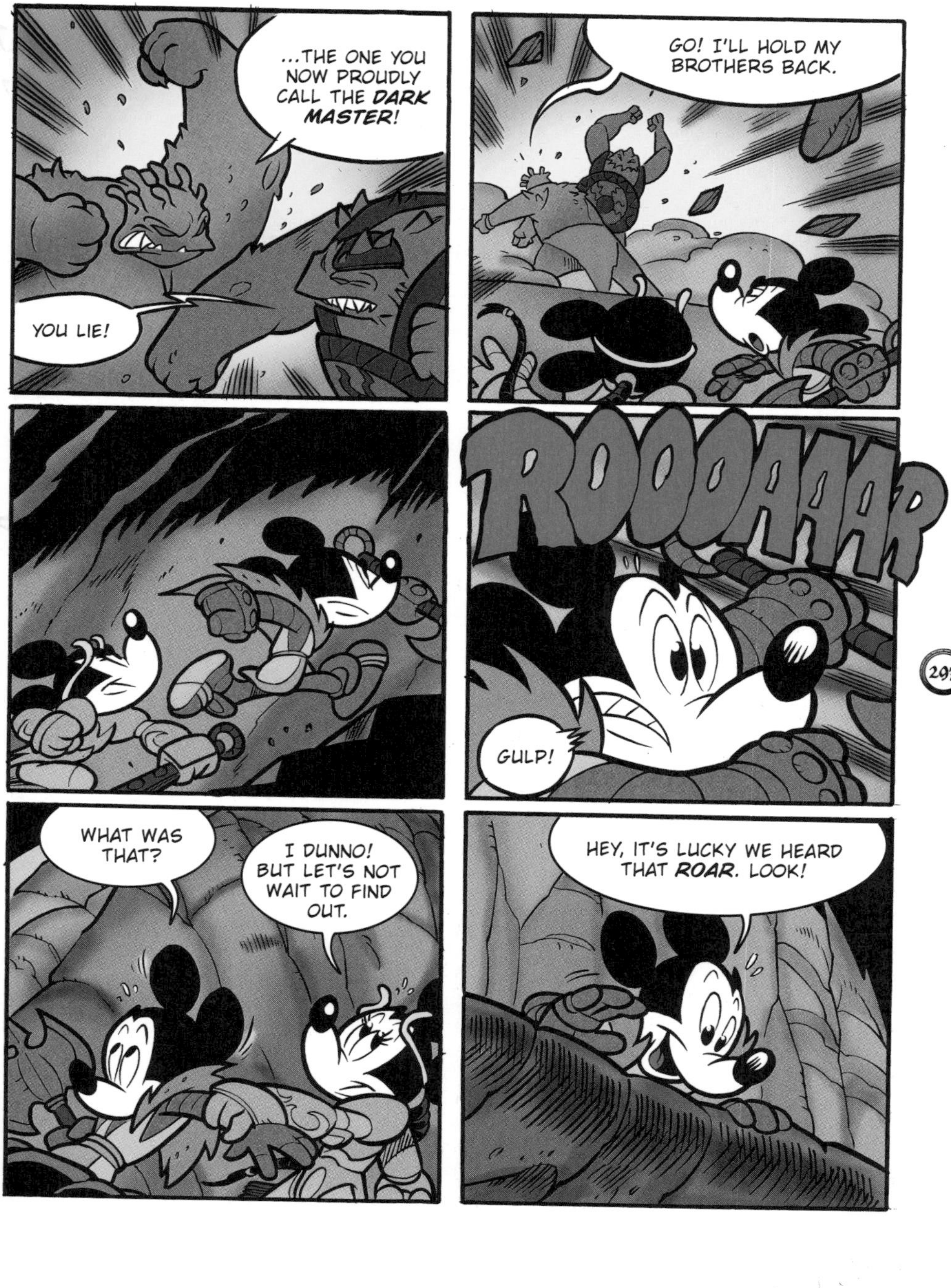
...THE ONE YOU NOW PROUDLY CALL THE DARK MASTER!
YOU LIE!
GO! I'LL HOLD MY BROTHERS BACK.
ROOOAAAR
GULP!
WHAT WAS THAT?
I DUNNO! BUT LET'S NOT WAIT TO FIND OUT.
HEY, IT'S LUCKY WE HEARD THAT ROAR. LOOK!

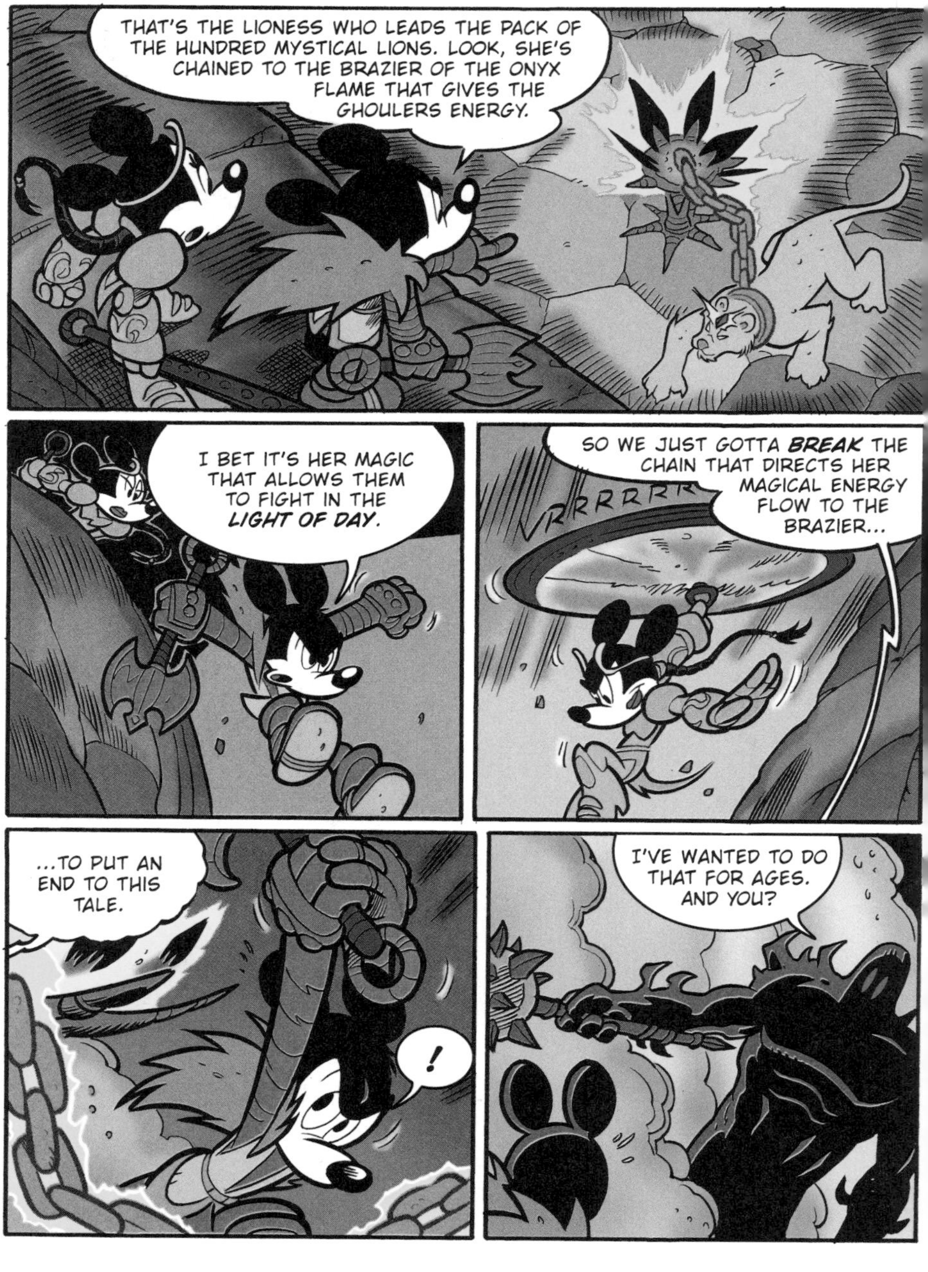

THAT'S THE LIONESS WHO LEADS THE PACK OF THE HUNDRED MYSTICAL LIONS. LOOK, SHE'S CHAINED TO THE BRAZIER OF THE ONYX FLAME THAT GIVES THE GHOULERS ENERGY.
I BET IT'S HER MAGIC THAT ALLOWS THEM TO FIGHT IN THE *LIGHT OF DAY*.
SO WE JUST GOTTA **BREAK** THE CHAIN THAT DIRECTS HER MAGICAL ENERGY FLOW TO THE BRAZIER...
VRRRRRR
...TO PUT AN END TO THIS TALE.
!
I'VE WANTED TO DO THAT FOR AGES. AND YOU?

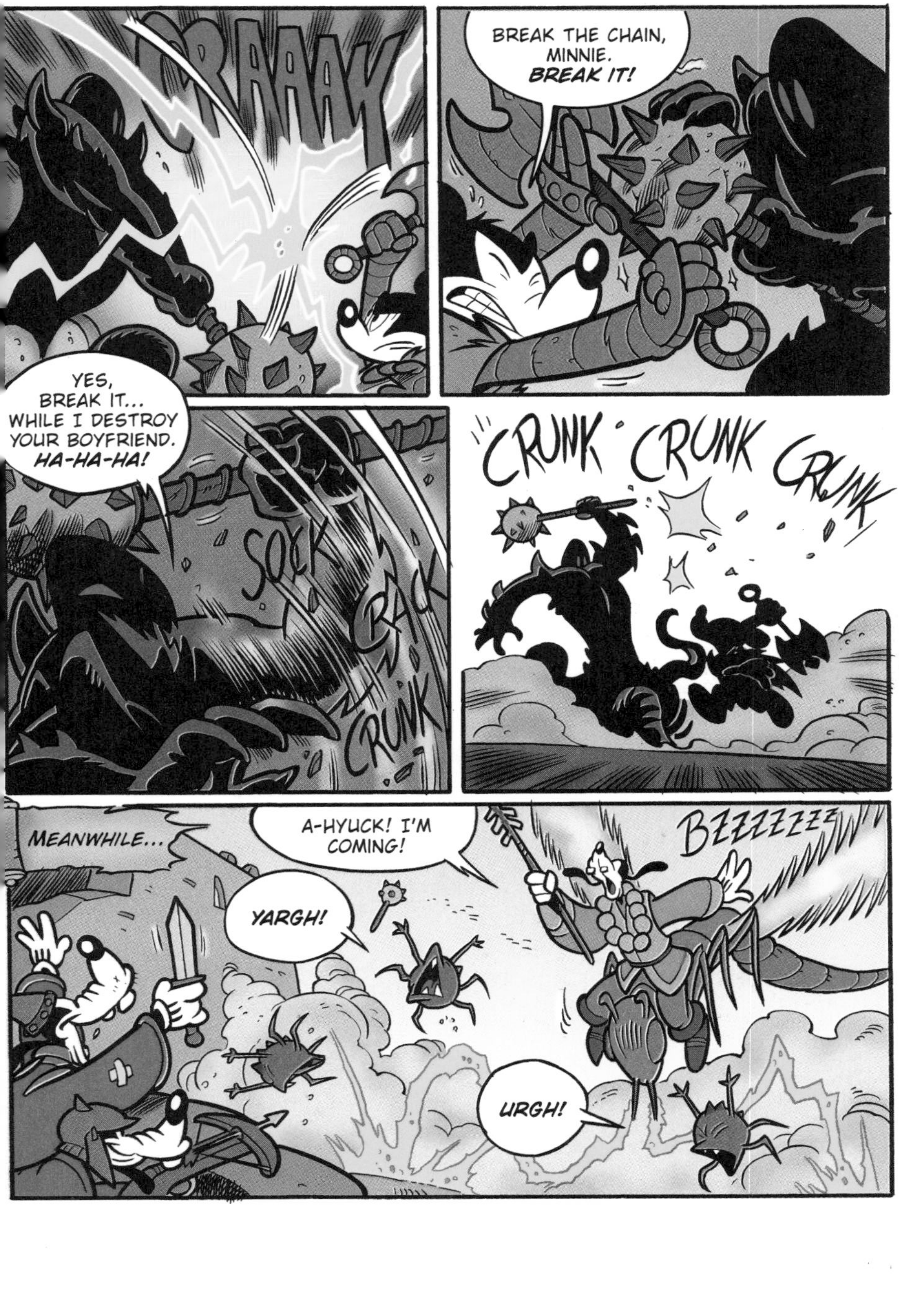
BRAAAK
BREAK THE CHAIN, MINNIE. BREAK IT!
YES, BREAK IT... WHILE I DESTROY YOUR BOYFRIEND. HA-HA-HA!
SOCK
CRACK
CRUNK
CRUNK CRUNK CRUNK
MEANWHILE...
A-HYUCK! I'M COMING!
BZZZZZZZ
YARGH!
URGH!

WELCOME BACK, GOOFY!
UNCLE PIPPO, UNCLE GOODEN! IT'S SO GOOD TO SEE YOU SAFE AND SOUND.
WELL, MORE OR LESS!
A-HYUCK!
DON'T WORRY. I'M HERE! ASIDE FROM BEING A WIZARD, I CAN DO MARTIAL ARTS. HI-YAAAH!
THUD
POK
IN KING SCROOGE'S KINGDOM...
HANG IN THERE, UNCLE. I'M COMING...
...AS LONG AS THE WINGS HOLD UP! MY USUAL BAD LUCK... I JUST HAD TO GET A FAULTY MAGICAL INSECT.

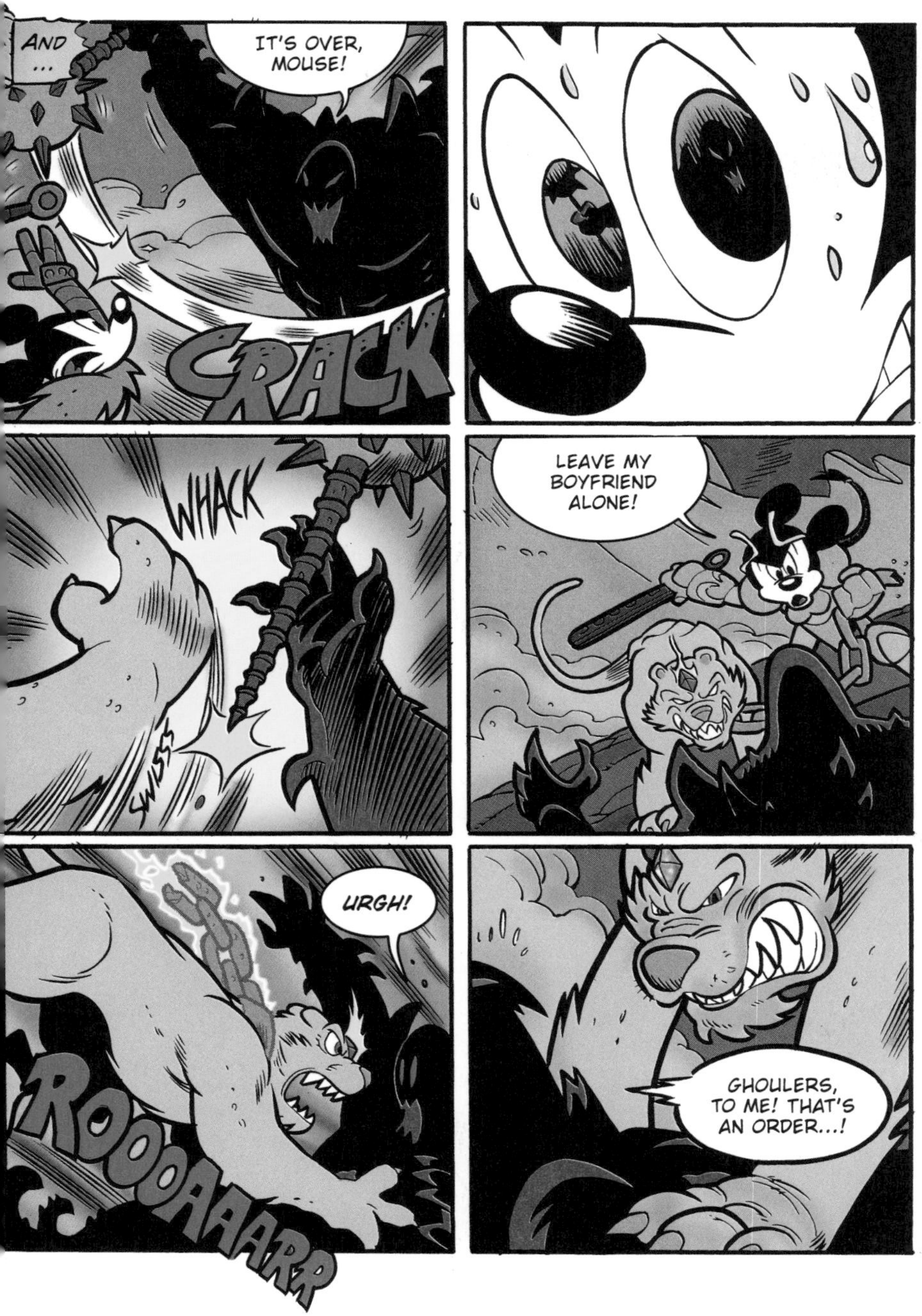
AND ...
IT'S OVER, MOUSE!
CRACK
WHACK
SWISSS
LEAVE MY BOYFRIEND ALONE!
URGH!
ROOOAAARR
GHOULERS, TO ME! THAT'S AN ORDER...!

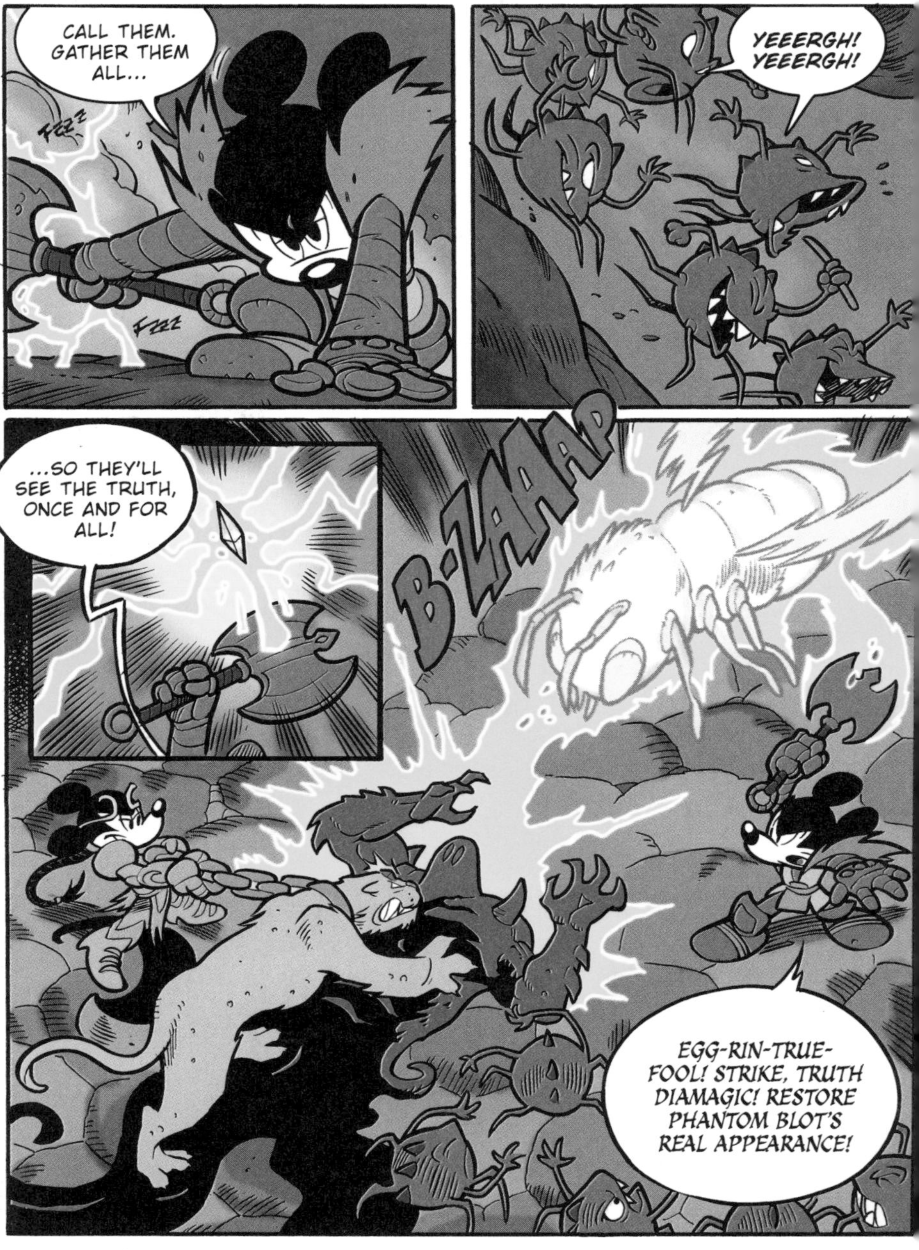
CALL THEM. GATHER THEM ALL...
FZZZ
FZZZ
YEEERGH! YEEERGH!
...SO THEY'LL SEE THE TRUTH, ONCE AND FOR ALL!
B-ZAAAP
EGG-RIN-TRUE-FOOL! STRIKE, TRUTH DIAMAGIC! RESTORE PHANTOM BLOT'S REAL APPEARANCE!

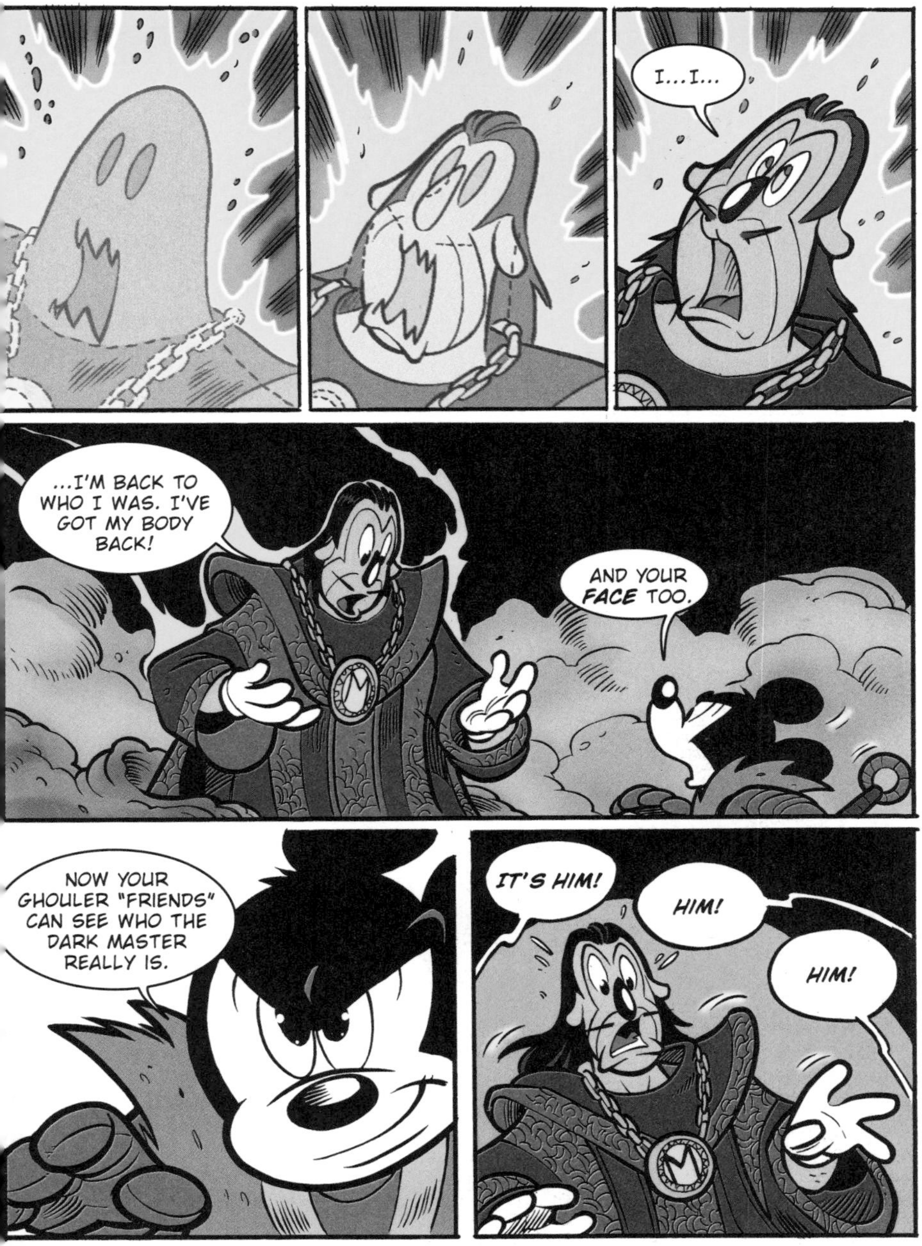
I...I...
...I'M BACK TO WHO I WAS. I'VE GOT MY BODY BACK!
AND YOUR FACE TOO.
NOW YOUR GHOULER "FRIENDS" CAN SEE WHO THE DARK MASTER REALLY IS.
IT'S HIM!
HIM!
HIM!

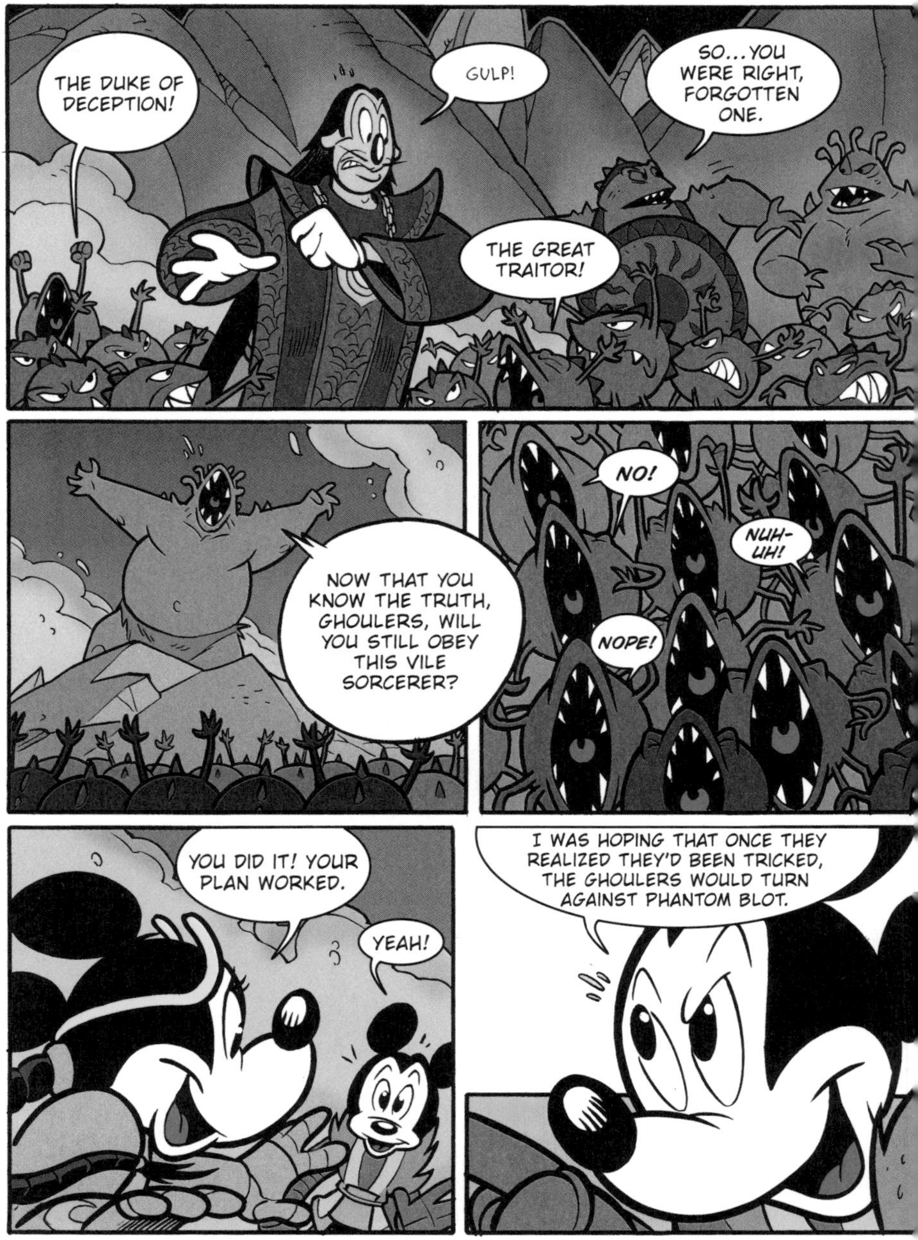
THE DUKE OF DECEPTION!
GULP!
SO...YOU WERE RIGHT, FORGOTTEN ONE.
THE GREAT TRAITOR!
NOW THAT YOU KNOW THE TRUTH, GHOULERS, WILL YOU STILL OBEY THIS VILE SORCERER?
NO!
NUH-UH!
NOPE!
YOU DID IT! YOUR PLAN WORKED.
YEAH!
I WAS HOPING THAT ONCE THEY REALIZED THEY'D BEEN TRICKED, THE GHOULERS WOULD TURN AGAINST PHANTOM BLOT.

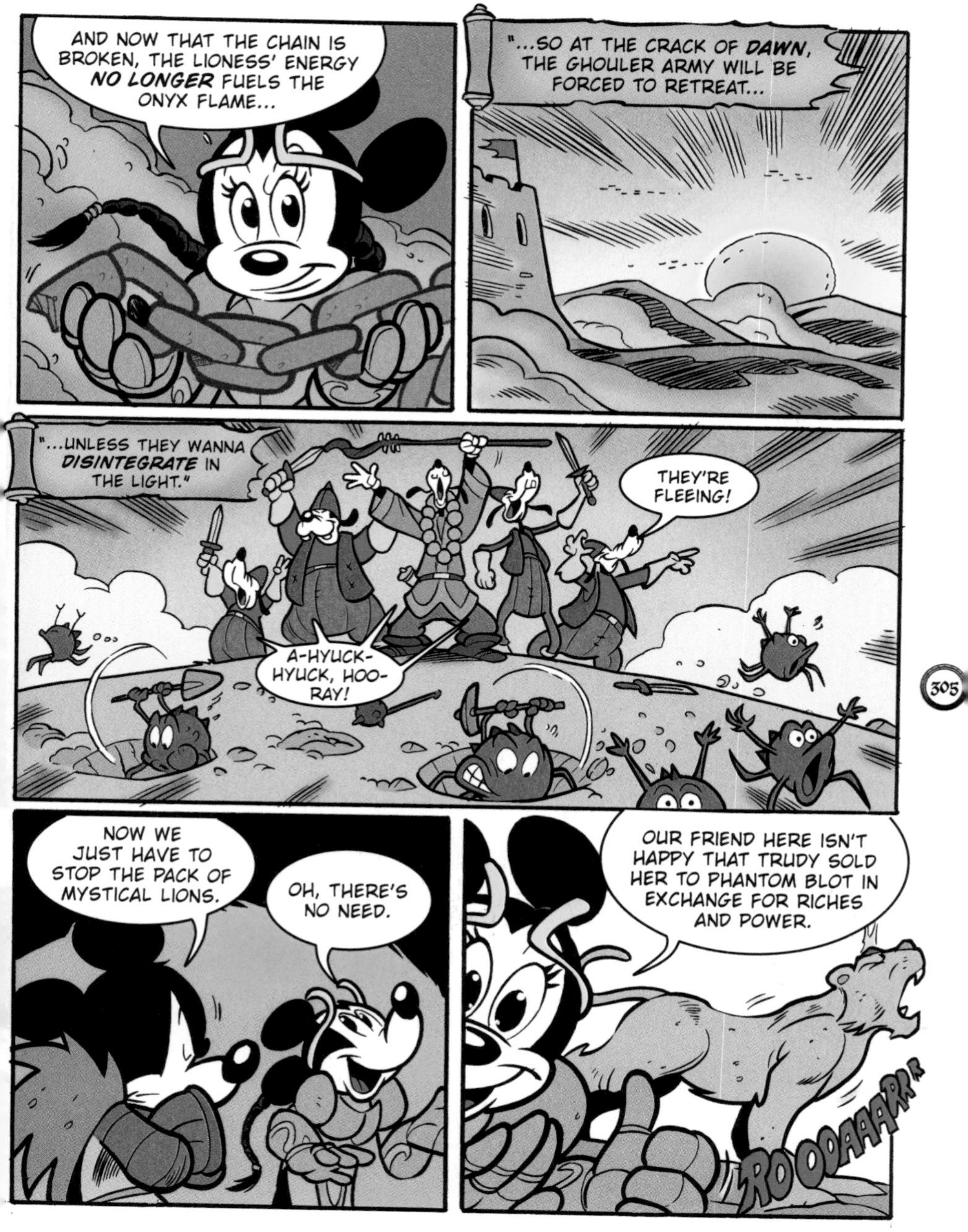

AND NOW THAT THE CHAIN IS BROKEN, THE LIONESS' ENERGY NO LONGER FUELS THE ONYX FLAME...
"...SO AT THE CRACK OF DAWN, THE GHOULER ARMY WILL BE FORCED TO RETREAT...
"...UNLESS THEY WANNA DISINTEGRATE IN THE LIGHT."
THEY'RE FLEEING!
A-HYUCK-HYUCK, HOO-RAY!
NOW WE JUST HAVE TO STOP THE PACK OF MYSTICAL LIONS.
OH, THERE'S NO NEED.
OUR FRIEND HERE ISN'T HAPPY THAT TRUDY SOLD HER TO PHANTOM BLOT IN EXCHANGE FOR RICHES AND POWER.
ROOOAAARRR

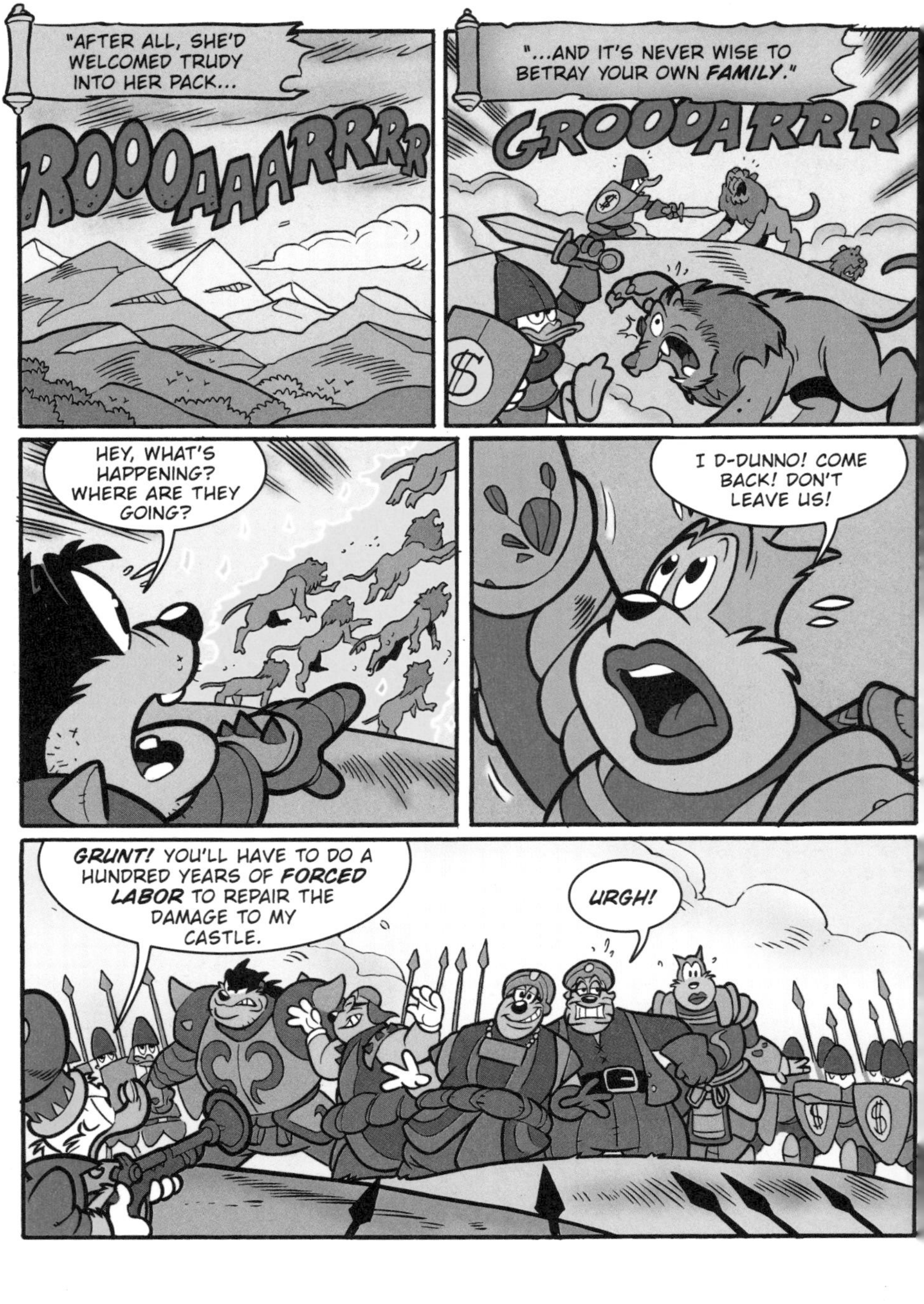
"AFTER ALL, SHE'D WELCOMED TRUDY INTO HER PACK...
ROOOAAARRRR
"...AND IT'S NEVER WISE TO BETRAY YOUR OWN FAMILY."
GROOOARRR
HEY, WHAT'S HAPPENING? WHERE ARE THEY GOING?
I D-DUNNO! COME BACK! DON'T LEAVE US!
GRUNT! YOU'LL HAVE TO DO A HUNDRED YEARS OF FORCED LABOR TO REPAIR THE DAMAGE TO MY CASTLE.
URGH!

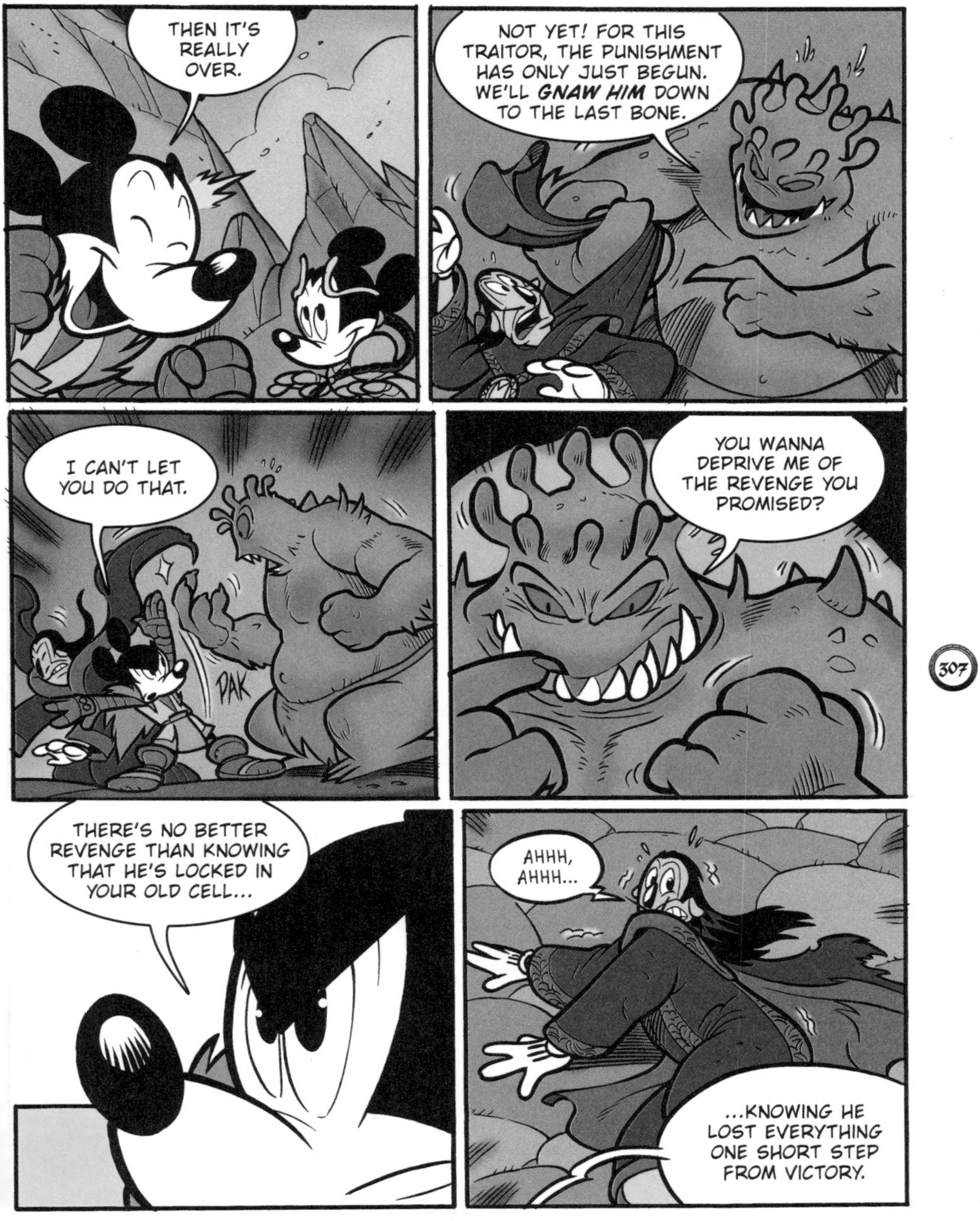
THEN IT'S REALLY OVER.
NOT YET! FOR THIS TRAITOR, THE PUNISHMENT HAS ONLY JUST BEGUN. WE'LL GNAW HIM DOWN TO THE LAST BONE.
I CAN'T LET YOU DO THAT.
DAK
YOU WANNA DEPRIVE ME OF THE REVENGE YOU PROMISED?
THERE'S NO BETTER REVENGE THAN KNOWING THAT HE'S LOCKED IN YOUR OLD CELL...
AHHH, AHHH...
...KNOWING HE LOST EVERYTHING ONE SHORT STEP FROM VICTORY.

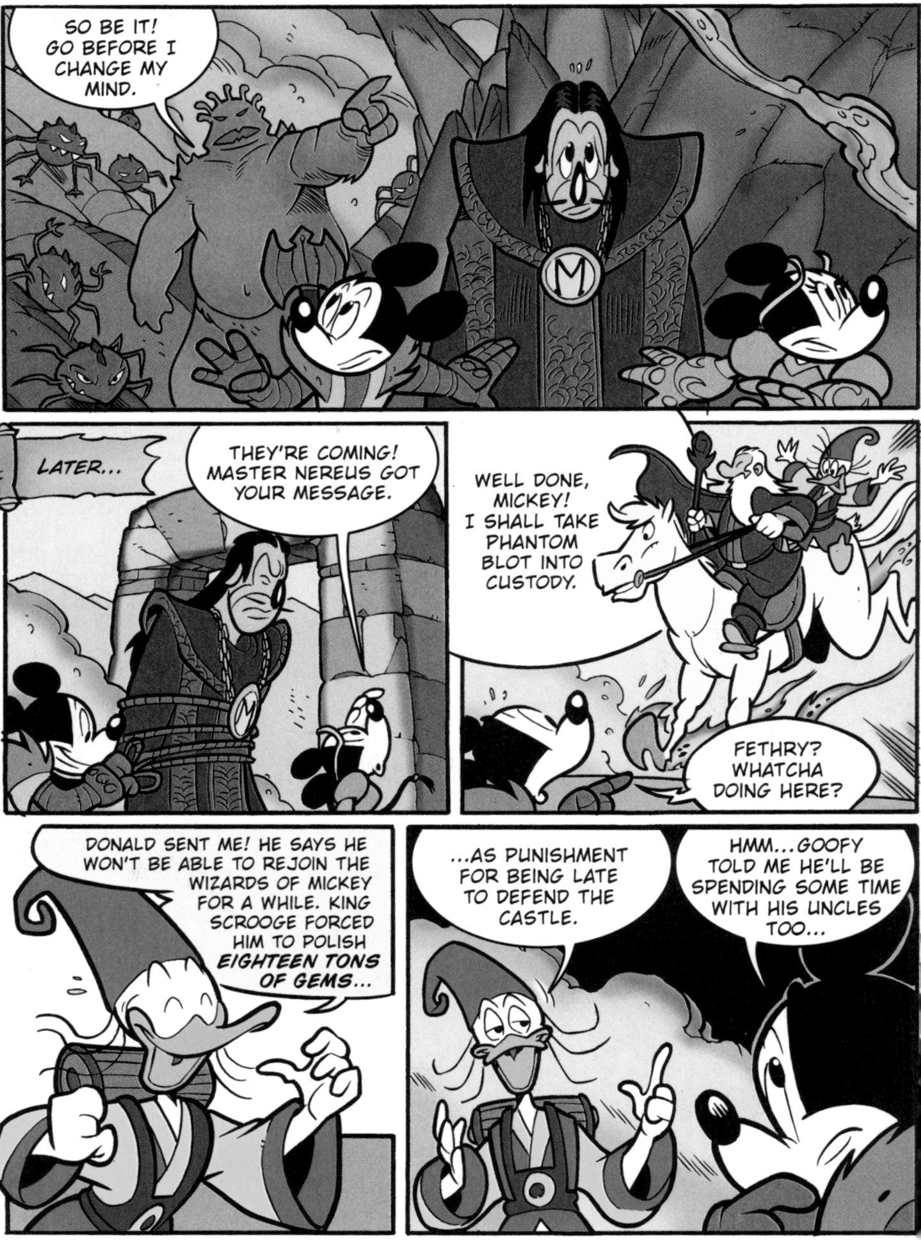

SO BE IT! GO BEFORE I CHANGE MY MIND.
LATER...
THEY'RE COMING! MASTER NEREUS GOT YOUR MESSAGE.
WELL DONE, MICKEY! I SHALL TAKE PHANTOM BLOT INTO CUSTODY.
FETHRY? WHATCHA DOING HERE?
DONALD SENT ME! HE SAYS HE WON'T BE ABLE TO REJOIN THE WIZARDS OF MICKEY FOR A WHILE. KING SCROOGE FORCED HIM TO POLISH EIGHTEEN TONS OF GEMS...
...AS PUNISHMENT FOR BEING LATE TO DEFEND THE CASTLE.
HMM...GOOFY TOLD ME HE'LL BE SPENDING SOME TIME WITH HIS UNCLES TOO...

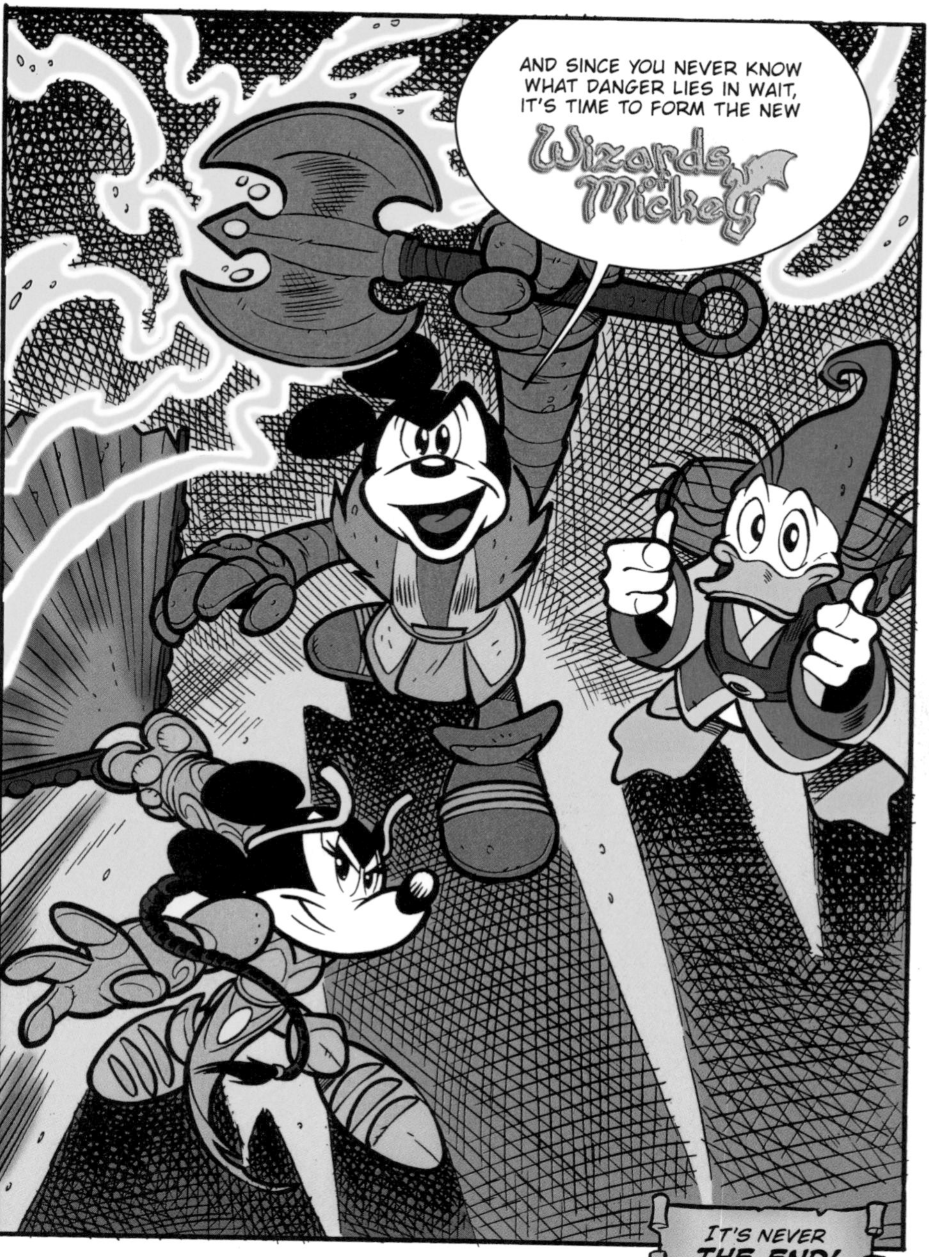
AND SINCE YOU NEVER KNOW WHAT DANGER LIES IN WAIT, IT'S TIME TO FORM THE NEW
Wizards of Mickey
IT'S NEVER THE END!

Wizards of Mickey

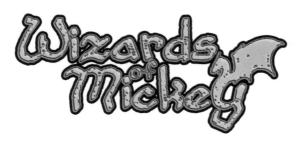

SEE YOU IN VOLUME 4!

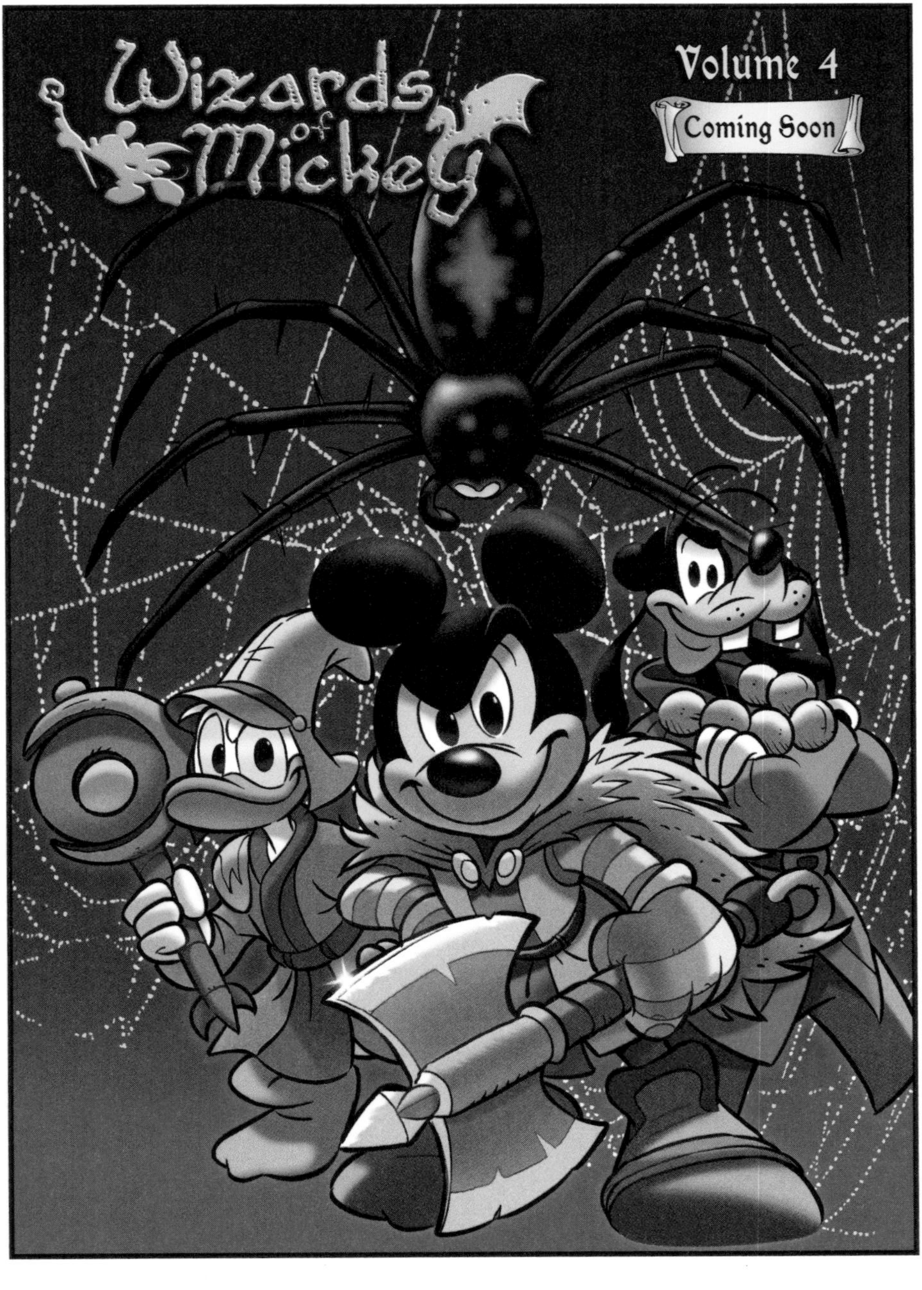
Wizards of Mickey
Volume 4
Coming Soon

Wizards of Mickey

Bonus Content

From the pages of *Topolino*, a world famous Italian comic anthology featuring works from Disney, *Wizards of Mickey* stands out as one of the most iconic Disney comics.

It is our pleasure to share with you here some of the magazine artwork from those original issues on the following pages.

Enjoy!

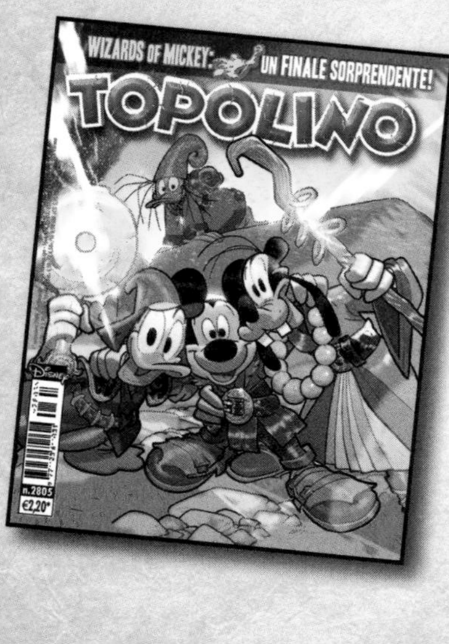
WIZARDS OF MICKEY:
UN FINALE SORPRENDENTE!
TOPOLINO
n.2805
€2,20*

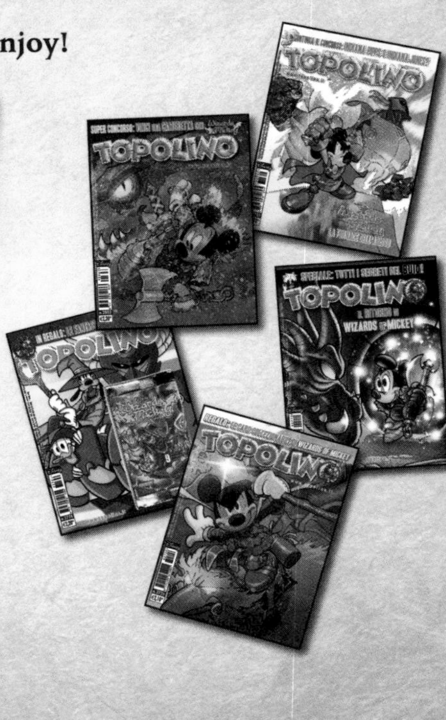
TOPOLINO
SUPER CONCORSO:
TOPOLINO
TOPOLINO
WIZARDS OF MICKEY
TOPOLINO
TOPOLINO
WIZARDS OF MICKEY

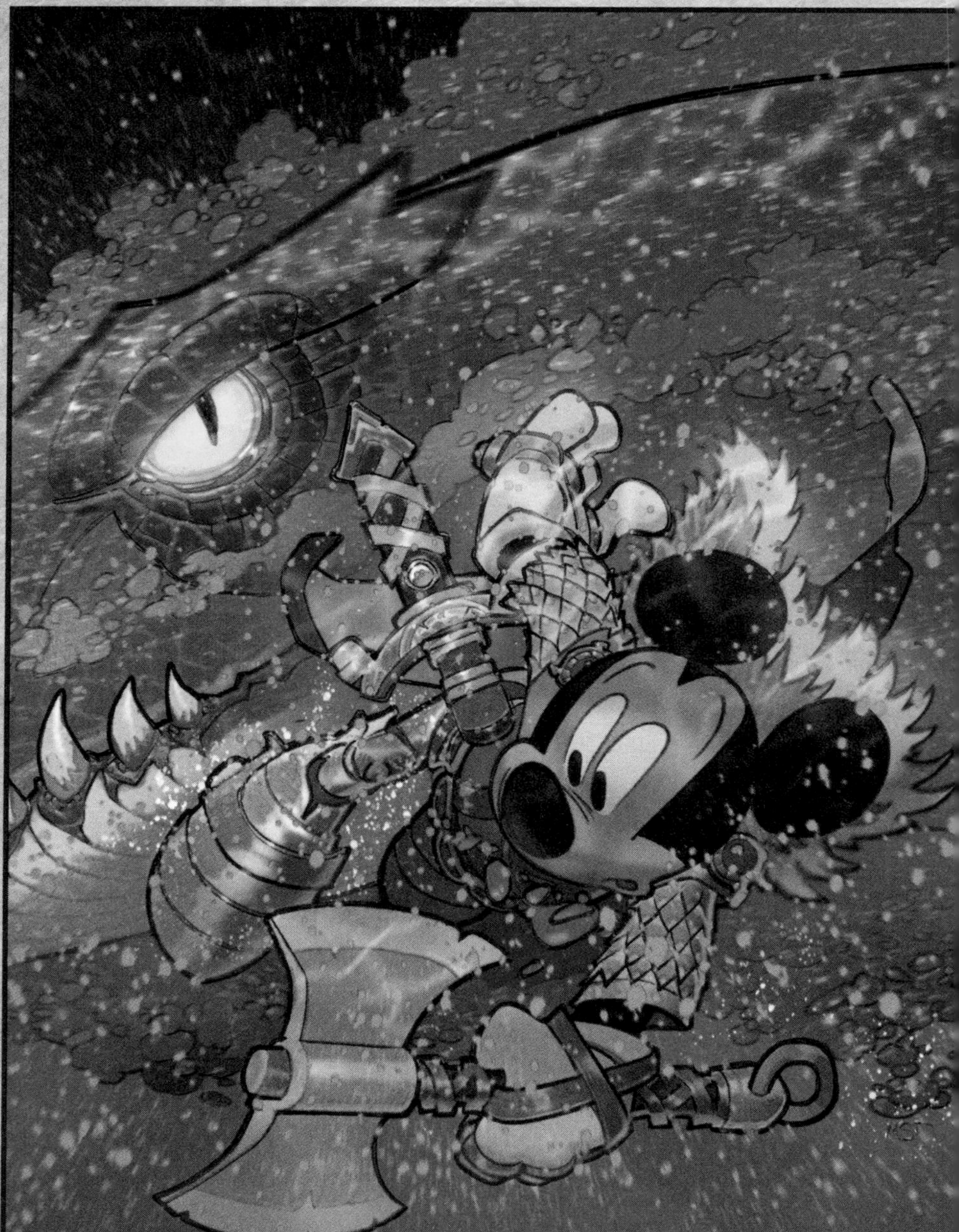

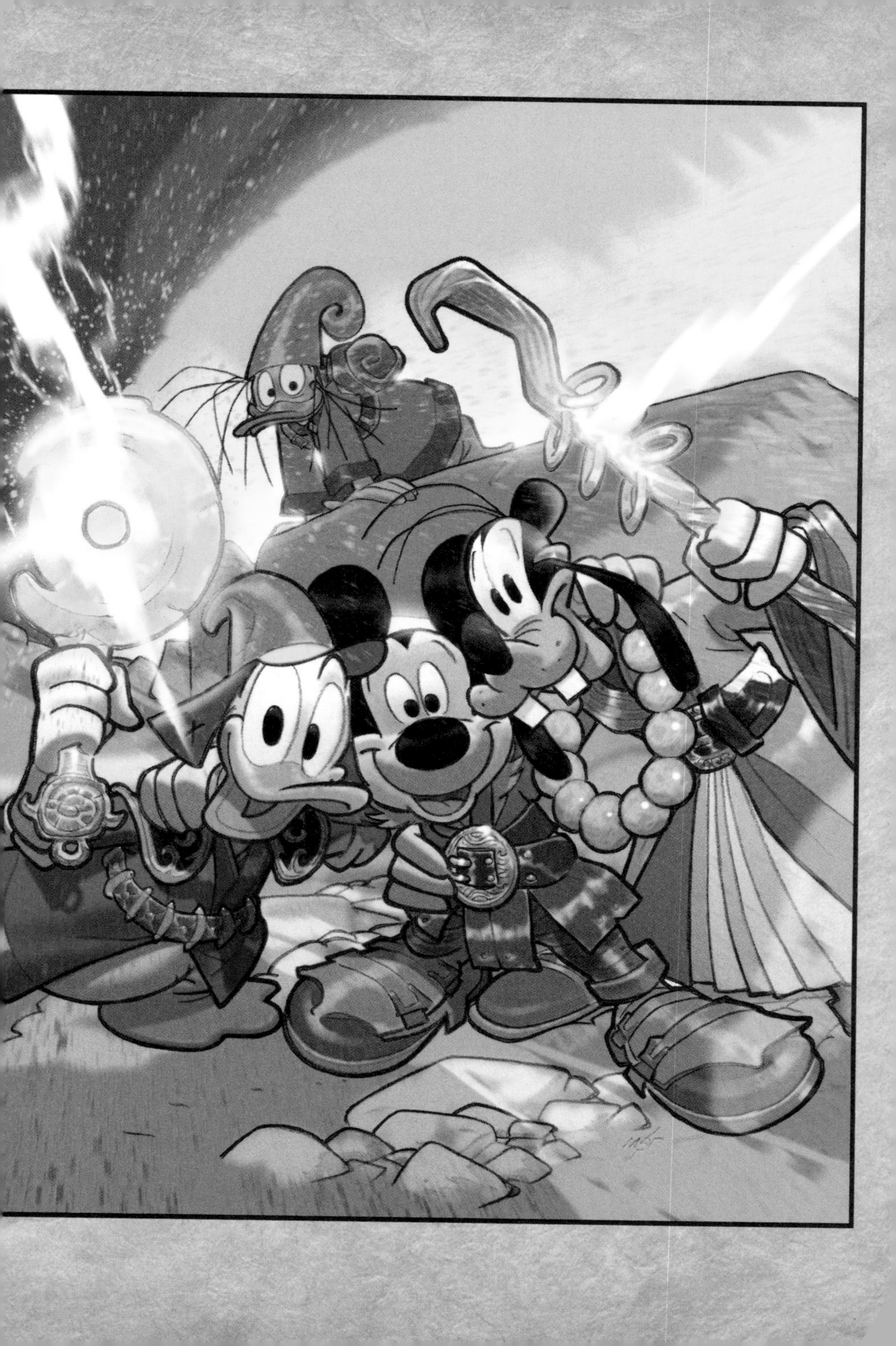

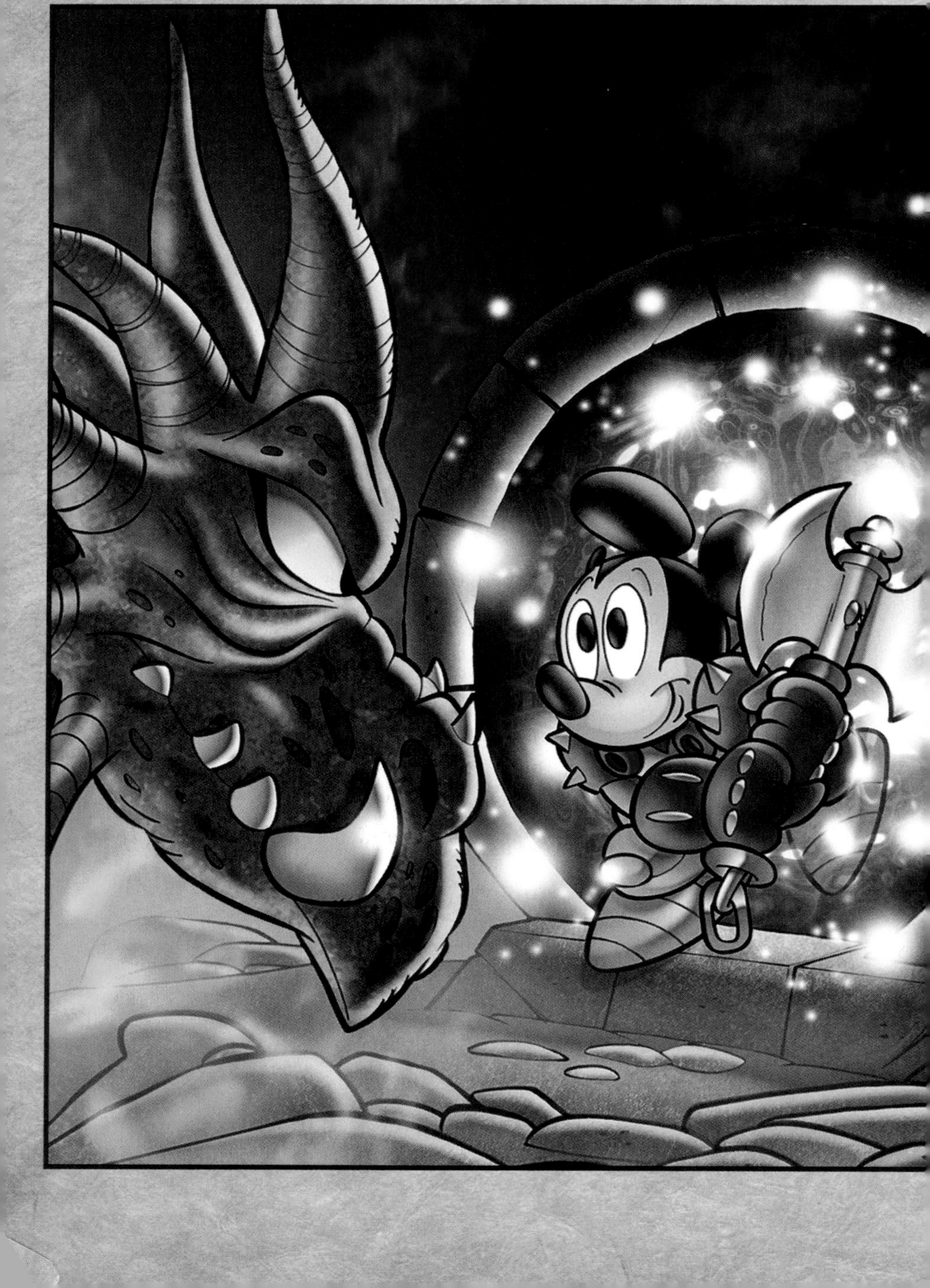

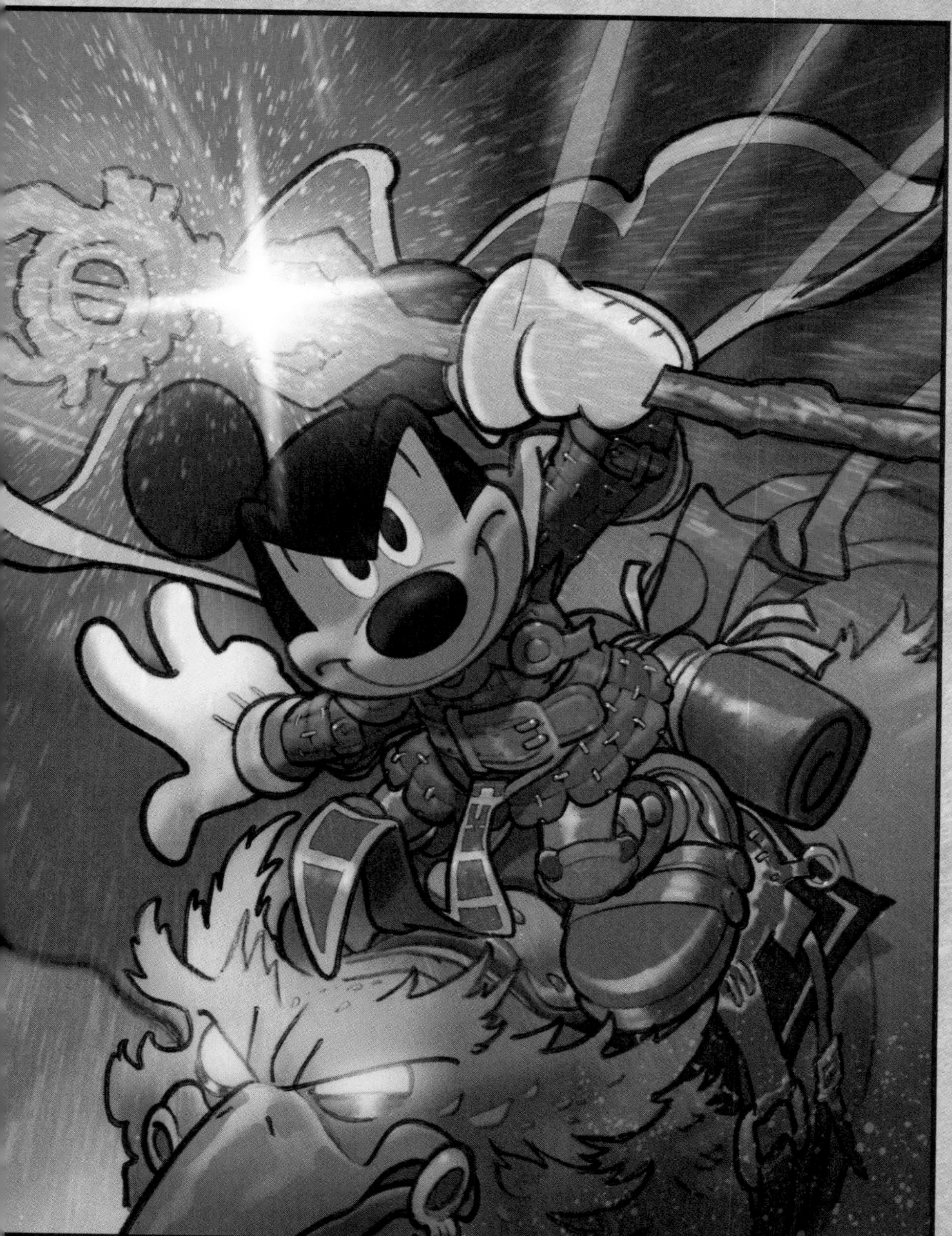

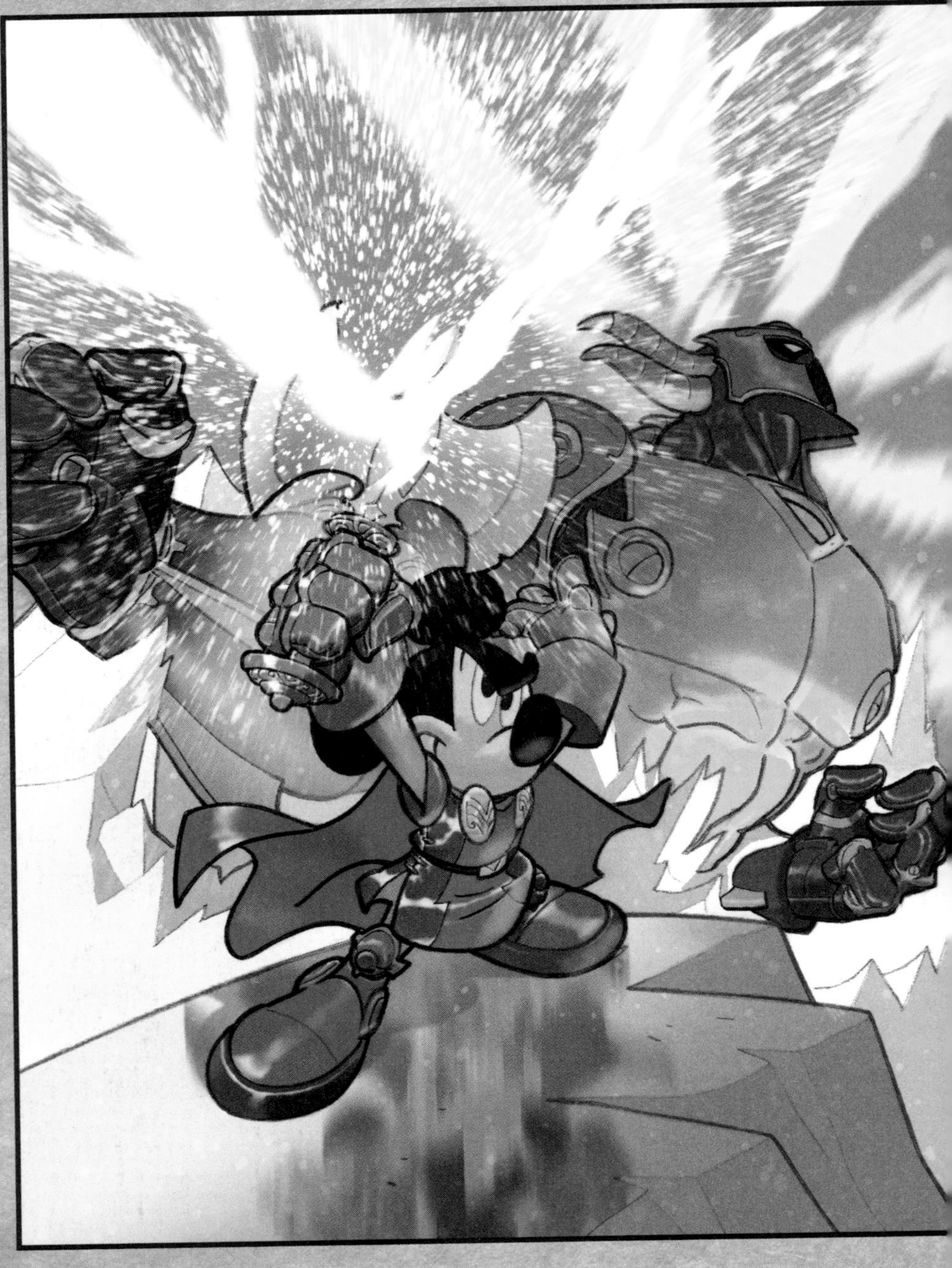

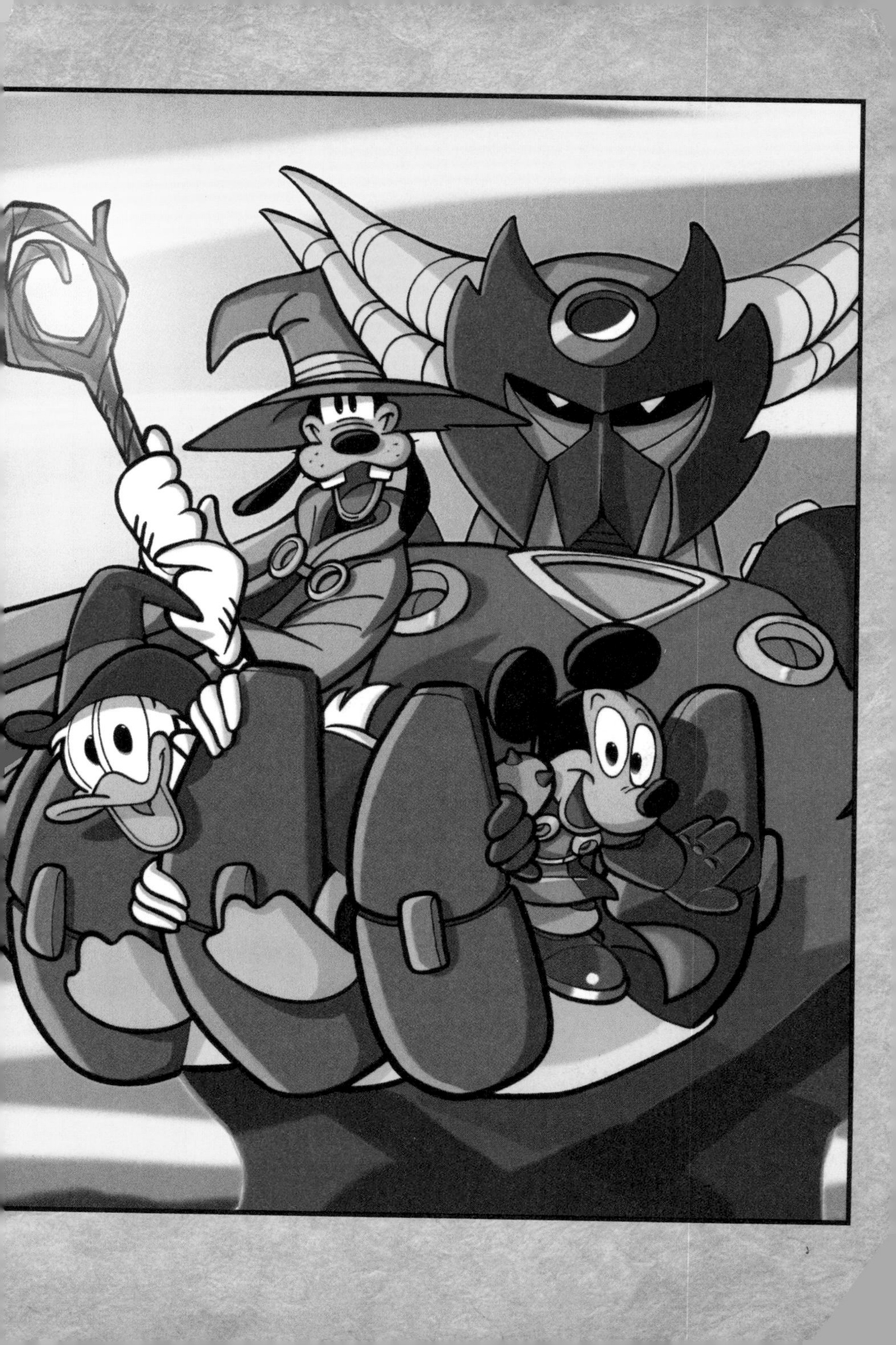

Wizards of Mickey

3

Wizards of Mickey, Vol. 3
© Disney Enterprises, Inc.

English translation © 2021 by Disney Enterprises, Inc.

JY
150 West 30th Street, 19th Floor
New York, NY 10001

Visit us at jyforkids.com
facebook.com/jyforkids
twitter.com/jyforkids
jyforkids.tumblr.com
instagram.com/jyforkids

First JY Edition: June 2021

JY is an imprint of Yen Press, LLC.
The JY name and logo are trademarks of Yen Press, LLC.

The publisher is not responsible for websites (or their content) that are not owned by the publisher.

Library of Congress Control Number: 2020944890

ISBNs: 978-1-9753-2317-2 (paperback)
978-1-9753-2318-9 (ebook)

10 9 8 7 6 5 4 3 2 1

LSC-C

Printed in the United States of America

Cover Art by Roberto Vian
with concept by Fabio Pochet
and colors by Massimo Rocca

Translation by Linda Ghio and
Stephanie Dagg at Editing Zone
Lettering by Katie Blakeslee

THE ANCIENT EVIL

THE NEVER-ENDING WAR
Story by Stefano Ambrosio
Art by Alessandro Pastrovicchio

THE MYSTERIOUS SLEEPER
Story by Stefano Ambrosio
Art by Lorenzo Pastrovicchio

THE TITANS OF ICE
Story by Stefano Ambrosio
Art by Lorenzo Pastrovicchio

THE FURNACE OF THE ABYSS
Story by Stefano Ambrosio
Art by Lorenzo Pastrovicchio

THE DAWN OF A NEW WORLD
Story by Stefano Ambrosio
Art by Lorenzo Pastrovicchio

THE NEW WORLD

THE LORD OF THE SEAS
Story by Stefano Ambrosio
Art by Lorenzo Pastrovicchio

THE CRYPT OF ONE HUNDRED LIONS
Story by Stefano Ambrosio
Art by Lorenzo Pastrovicchio

THE SIEGE OF SHADOWS
Story by Stefano Ambrosio
Art by Lorenzo Pastrovicchio

THE KINGDOM BELOW (Part One)
Story by Stefano Ambrosio
Art by Lorenzo Pastrovicchio

THE KINGDOM BELOW (Part Two)
Story by Stefano Ambrosio
Art by Lorenzo Pastrovicchio